A CROWN OF FEATHERS NOVEL

WINGS OF SHADOW

NICKI PAU PRETO

MARGARET K. McELDERRY BOOKS

New York London Toronto Sydney New Delhi

MARGARET K. McELDERRY BOOKS
An imprint of Simon & Schuster Children's Publishing Division
1230 Avenue of the Americas, New York, New York 10020

MARGARET K. McELDERRY BOOKS is a trademark of Simon & Schuster, Inc.
For information about special discounts for bulk purchases, please contact Simon & Schuster Special Sales at 1-866-506-1949 or business@simonandschuster.com.
The Simon & Schuster Speakers Bureau can bring authors to your live event. For more information or to book an event, contact the Simon & Schuster Speakers Bureau at 1-866-248-3049 or visit our website at www.simonspeakers.com.
Also available in a Margaret K. McElderry Books hardcover edition
Interior design by Mike Rosamilia
The text for this book was set in Adobe Garamond Pro.
Manufactured in the United States of America
First Margaret K. McElderry Books paperback edition July 2022
2 4 6 8 10 9 7 5 3 1
The Library of Congress has cataloged the hardcover edition as follows:
Library of Congress Cataloging-in-Publication Data
Names: Pau Preto, Nicki, author.
Title: Wings of shadow / Nicki Pau Preto.
Description: First edition. | New York : Margaret K. McElderry Books, [2021] | Series: Crown of feathers ; 3 |
Summary: "Veronyka has been revealed as the heir to the empire, but to protect her people, she'll have to face the most devastating enemy she could imagine: her own sister"—Provided by publisher.
Identifiers: LCCN 2020044678 (print) | LCCN 2020044679 (ebook) | ISBN 9781534466029 (hardcover) | ISBN 9781534466036 (pbk) | ISBN 9781534466043 (ebook)
Subjects: CYAC: Sisters—Fiction. | Princesses—Fiction. | Magic—Fiction. | Phoenix (Mythical bird)—Fiction. | Human-animal relationships—Fiction. | Fantasy.
Classification: LCC PZ7.1.P384 Wi 2021 (print) | LCC PZ7.1.P384 (ebook) | DDC [Fic]—dc23
LC record available at https://lccn.loc.gov/2020044678
LC ebook record available at https://lccn.loc.gov/2020044679

Praise for CROWN OF FEATHERS

"Absolutely unforgettable. It draws you in with the first flaming feather and doesn't let go. This is an instant favorite."

—KENDARE BLAKE, #1 *New York Times* bestselling author
of the Three Dark Crowns series

"A fierce and incendiary tale of warrior women, sisterhood, and the choices that define us, all set in a soaring new world that readers will fall in love with. I couldn't put it down."

—LISA MAXWELL, *New York Times* bestselling author
of the Last Magician series

"A beautifully told story about justice, sisterhood, and warrior women. This richly woven world had me turning pages well into the night. Nicki Pau Preto is one to watch!"

—SHEA ERNSHAW, *New York Times* bestselling author of *The Wicked Deep*

"The unique and imaginative world of the Phoenix Riders had my rapt attention from the first sentence. Nicki Pau Preto is a bright new talent, and I can't wait to read more!"

—MORGAN RHODES, *New York Times* bestselling author
of the Falling Kingdoms series

"A feast of magic, action, and romance. An immersive, deeply satisfying fantasy that will stay with you long after the story is finished. Nicki Pau Preto is an author to watch!"

—ELLY BLAKE, *New York Times* bestselling author of *Frostblood*

"This is a new twist on fantasy favorites, and Pau Preto's first novel is as ambitious as it is lyrical."

—*Booklist*

"An action-packed adventure that will leave fans of epic fantasies eager to find out more."

—*SLJ*

"The well-paced plot is chock-full of shocking revelations, betrayals, and moments of empowerment in the face of adversity that give this novel an epic scope and set up the beginning of a promising book series."

—*BCCB*

ALSO BY NICKI PAU PRETO

Crown of Feathers
Heart of Flames

TO JASON:

ఌ

brother, hero, father, friend

Gold won't make you rich, and wings won't make you fly;
power won't make you strong, and a crown won't make you queen.

—*Words attributed to Nefyra, the First Rider Queen, circa 1000 BE*

WINGS OF
SHADOW

For as long as there have been Ashfires,
there have been phoenixes.

- CHAPTER I -
VERONYKA

VERONYKA STUMBLED THROUGH THE darkness, her hands outstretched.

She couldn't see, couldn't hear anything beyond the sound of her booted feet slapping against the damp stone and the echo of her breath reverberating around her.

Left, right, left again.

Veronyka trusted the directions, followed them in a rush, even as everything inside her fought against rising panic. There was nothing to ground her, no way to know if she was close or far or completely and utterly lost.

She gritted her teeth. She was going the wrong way; surely she was—it had been too long since that right turn. She should have reached the end by now. She was just getting more and more lost, wasting more and more time.

Easy now.

Veronyka took a deep breath, but she'd never much cared for the dark. It brought her back to her childhood, when she'd been left alone for days—first by her *maiora*, and eventually by Val. She'd been older by then, but she'd still hated the solitude. The loneliness. The helpless waiting.

She felt it now, that isolation, that powerlessness, and the darkness that seemed to go on and on . . . until Veronyka walked straight into a roughly hewn wall, moving so recklessly fast that her hands weren't able to brace her against the impact. She smacked her nose with enough force to make her eyes water and her face tingle with pain.

She cursed, disoriented—then cursed again. She'd forgotten the additional left turn.

Swiping at her face to check for blood, Veronyka continued on, frustrated now. She tried to double back, seeking the missed turn—and her boot met with open air.

She knew a single moment of terror as her stomach lurched, her body tensing for the fall, when all her forward momentum came to a sudden, jerking halt.

Her ears ringing, Veronyka took several shuddering gasps before she understood—and heard Xephyra crooning softly behind her, the sound slightly muffled since her beak was clenched tightly over the back of Veronyka's shirt.

Thank you, she thought dazedly as Xephyra carefully drew her back.

With both feet on solid ground, Veronyka tugged off the blindfold she'd been wearing.

They were somewhere inside the underground passages of the Eyrie. Before her was a staircase that she'd have fallen down headfirst if not for Xephyra, and just behind was the left turn she'd missed—and the way out. A wash of torchlight colored the dark hall, and an uneven gait announced the arrival of Morra.

Veronyka groaned. She'd been *right there*, so close she could practically taste it, but had once again lost her head.

She and Morra had been practicing shadow magic together for weeks now, working hard to sharpen and extend an ability that Veronyka had spent her whole life fighting against.

Recently, they'd attempted to mimic some of the Phoenix Rider training exercises, working on range and communication. It had actually been Veronyka's idea to try wearing a blindfold while Morra spoke instructions into her mind, and she was now very much regretting that decision.

She'd thought they'd do it outside, somewhere in the stronghold or on the open field outside the village walls. She'd happily wear the blindfold *on* the walls—and risk a much farther drop—if it meant getting out of these oppressive tunnels. But there were virtually innumerable routes down here, and it allowed Veronyka and Morra to practice whenever they could squeeze it in—like now, before the sun had risen and Morra had to head to the kitchens and Veronyka to her other responsibilities.

Morra also seemed to think that cutting Veronyka off from other people and animals provided an additional level of difficulty—those things could work as distractions, true, but they could also spark her magic and increase her potency.

Down in the dark, Veronyka was very much alone with her bonds. It should be easy . . . and yet it wasn't. She should have *sensed* Xephyra's nearness—should have smelled the change in the air and heard the sounds of the Eyrie in the open passage behind Morra. But she hadn't.

How's your beak? Xephyra asked.

Veronyka touched her nose again, but there was still no blood, and even the pain had receded to a dull ache.

"You're still doing it," Morra said, leaning with both arms crossed over the top of her crutch. "As soon as things get hairy, you close up and block me out." Xephyra croaked, and Morra nodded. "You're also combining your shadow and animal magic again, so when you block me out, you block her out too. Xephyra was close enough for you to touch, but you didn't feel her. You were too preoccupied with being frustrated and lost."

Veronyka blew out a breath, hands on her hips as she stared down the shadowy staircase. "I know—I'm sorry. It's . . ."

"A defense mechanism."

Veronyka looked at the woman. Her voice went strange lately when they skirted around the issue of Val. Or rather, Avalkyra Ashfire. Morra had been a loyal supporter of the Feather-Crowned Queen during the Blood War, after all, and never spoke ill of her—no matter what she'd heard since about Veronyka's kidnapping and Tristan's capture, or the seventeen years of rumors and horror stories before that.

Despite her mixed feelings, *she'd* been the one to offer to help Veronyka. While Morra had always been a source of wisdom when it came to shadow magic, Veronyka hadn't known until very recently that she actually used to study it.

"I was something of a scholar," Morra confessed one evening inside the kitchens. "I was studying to become a High Priestess of Axura, specializing in magic and phoenix history—that was until I was conscripted to become a Phoenix Rider during the Blood War. Afterward, that wasn't the sort of thing one advertised in the Golden Empire. I got used to hiding it, just like my shadow magic."

She pushed hard—harder than she ever had during their infrequent conversations about magic before—and Veronyka could only hope it was because the woman believed in her and wanted her well equipped for the challenges that lay ahead. Challenges like Avalkyra Ashfire.

"It's not so much a defense mechanism," Veronyka explained, trying to find the words. "More a force of habit."

Because while keeping people out of her mind was indeed a method of defense, it was also the only thing she'd ever learned about shadow magic before now. The only lesson Val had ever bothered to teach her. Veronyka had never been able to risk showing her sister she was frustrated, scared, or confused, so it had been second nature to hide those things. What was it Val used to say? Old habits were like phoenixes, rising again and again.

As for combining her magic . . . it hadn't been that long since she'd learned from Morra that she shouldn't, and it was hard to untangle the two in her mind. She tried again now. Two magics, two rivers—both strong and freely flowing.

"You'll need to break that habit if you want to master your magic," Morra said sternly. "To ensure your connections are as strong as they can possibly be."

Veronyka looked away. That was the whole problem, wasn't it?

Yes, she wanted her bond with *Xephyra* to be strong and stable, and she even wanted the same for her bond with Tristan—which Morra did not know about. Veronyka wanted no barriers between herself and those she loved, no more fear or hesitation or self-defense.

But her bond with Val? She knew now that she could defeat Val inside her own mind—she had done so in Ferro—but that didn't make her any more eager to have Val there. In fact, while she didn't consciously block Val, she also didn't allow herself to really think about her either. Avoidance, she supposed, was another kind of defense, another type of wall.

Since she'd embraced her shadow magic, Veronyka had been adjusting to the sensation of allowing humans in and out of her mind the way she allowed animals. She had to teach herself to let the drifting thoughts and feelings of others pass through her mind just like the random noise of everyday life passed through her ears. Soon those distractions faded into the background, easy to ignore, and she was no longer taken by surprise or bowled over from sudden emotions bursting into her otherwise silent mind. It was like trying to hear a whisper in a crowd versus an empty room. Now she feared the quiet more than the noise, because it was in moments of solitude that she remembered her bonds. That she remembered their silence.

If her mind was a room, her bonds were hallways connecting her to other rooms. Because Xephyra was physically close to her, the hallway between them was little more than an archway, her phoenix's mind open and available, her thoughts side by side with Veronyka's own. The other two passages were capped with doors. For most of her life, Veronyka had first subconsciously—then deliberately—kept such doors closed, but now they were wide open.

Not that it mattered. Both Tristan's and Val's bonds were dark and silent. But while Tristan's bond was new and fragile, like a hallway made of fresh plaster and smooth, unmarred stone, Val's was ancient, immovable, and oppressive. The walls were wide and strong, built of massive blocks of stone. It was a place Veronyka did not want to be, and she suspected the feeling was mutual.

Neither she nor Val wanted to remember their connection just now . . .

not after Val's betrayal and Veronyka's rejection. Not after their volatile relationship had finally come to a head. If it were up to Veronyka, she would destroy the bond entirely and leave Val behind—a part of her past she needed to move on from, even if she could never truly forget it. But whatever her head and heart desired, it seemed her magic would never let her sever their connection entirely.

Val had tried to *kill* her. What further lines could they cross? What more could they do to each other? Veronyka did not want to know, even as she feared she would learn the answer sooner rather than later.

For now it seemed that no amount of anger or betrayal could dissolve their years of closeness, their love and hate and complicated, intertwined past.

A bond was forever.

It could survive death, after all, so why not *near* death?

If Veronyka had learned anything recently, it was that it was better to see the attack coming than to ignore the possibility of an approach altogether. She could no longer hide from or avoid Val . . . at least not with her magic.

Veronyka closed her eyes and examined the open door to Val inside her mind . . . then tore it off its hinges. Whatever happened from here on out, Veronyka would be ready.

She had things to do, and she would *do them*, even with a magical bond to her murderous sister-aunt. Val had taught her more than self-defense; she had taught her to be ruthless in the pursuit of what she wanted.

With Val's door gone—and then Tristan's too, for good measure—Veronyka's mind was truly open for the first time in her life. Welcoming, inviting . . . *daring* her bondmates to come in. Was that fear she felt thrumming inside her chest, or anticipation? Veronyka had this magic, this power, so she would use it.

She would save Tristan.

She would save Pyra and the Phoenix Riders from the Golden Empire—then she'd save the empire, too.

But first, Axura help her, she would make it through this exercise.

Morra helps you, her bondmate corrected, confused. Sometimes Xephyra took turns of phrase a bit too literally.

Veronyka smiled, turning to Morra. "Let's go again."

If Veronyka had thought going from Nyk to Veronyka was hard, going from Veronyka the poor orphan girl to Veronyka *Ashfire*, heir to the throne, was utterly isolating. The others had no idea how to act around her—with a few exceptions, like Kade and Sparrow—and most avoided her altogether.

It had all started a few days after their return from the empire, as their lives at the Eyrie slowly returned to some semblance of normal. With Rolan's forces no longer in Pyra—thanks to Veronyka and Val—and the border quiet once again, they had pulled the majority of their forces back to the Eyrie and settled on frequent patrols rather than permanent postings, while Fallon remained at Prosperity, running the majority of the surveillance.

Never before had Veronyka wanted so desperately to prove herself, or to suffer the blows of every slipup and failure. She wanted to *feel* it, to punish herself physically when her constant mental chastisement became insufficient.

She had made a grave error following Val that day, risking everything and allowing herself to give in to her own darkest tendencies. Her actions haunted her—foolish enough on their own, but even worse when taken in the context of who she was and what she was *supposed* to be. Her behavior had not been that of a leader of any sort, never mind a queen, and she couldn't move on from that mistake until she got Tristan back, safe and unharmed. Only then could she breathe properly again. Only then could she *try* to forgive herself and look ahead, to her future.

Until that time, however, Veronyka deserved to hurt, to feel her rage, anguish, and regret against her skin and muscle and bone as acutely as she felt it against her mind, heart, and soul.

But as Veronyka arrived in the training yard day after day, looking for a worthy opponent to spar with, the others refused to fight her.

It was partly due to uneven numbers. They weren't practicing as a single patrol, but with whatever other Riders were currently stationed at the Eyrie as well as some of the older apprentices who were ready for combat training. No matter how many turned up, Veronyka invariably found herself standing alone with all the others paired off. Kade partnered her whenever he could, but he was a beginner in many respects and was at a different stage in his training. Every time she asked someone else to join her in the ring, they insisted they already had a partner or were about to do archery or some other individual task.

But today, after her exhausting morning with Morra, Veronyka finally lost her patience. She wasn't yet ready to *order* someone to spar with her, but it was a near thing.

"Latham," she barked the moment he and the others walked into the training yard. It had rained all through the night, the overcast sky looming iron gray over the stronghold. Her breath fogged the air.

He hardly met her eye, whether out of deference for her newfound Ashfire glory or the usual dislike, Veronyka didn't care. "You've been itching for a chance to knock me on my ass—let's have at it."

"I don't—that's not—I already promised Anders," he sputtered, jerking a thumb in Anders's direction. Anders gave her a hesitant smile.

Veronyka looked around at them all. "I need to get him back," she said softly, forcing them to lean in closer to hear. "And to do that, I need your help. I need to be stronger—better. Please."

"It's just that, things have changed," Ronyn explained, looking uncomfortable. "You're the heir to the—"

"I am your *temporary* patrol leader and a fellow Phoenix Rider," Veronyka corrected. "And considering the fact that the empire is currently attempting to hunt down and destroy us, it's a toss-up over whether they'd put a crown on my head or cut it off." Ronyn snorted in response, and the others seemed to relax slightly. "As far as the empire is concerned, I am a rebel and a traitor—the same as all of you. There may come a time when you'll have to use your fancy manners around me," she said, trying to make light of the situation—though the idea made her stomach squirm, "but now is not it."

They glanced at one another, but no one spoke. Veronyka sighed, looking at the practice staff in her hand. "Sorry, Anders," she said, and when his smile faltered in confusion, Veronyka swung the staff around and knocked him in the shins.

It wasn't *that* hard—and he was wearing padded practice armor—but apparently, it was hard enough for him to cry out in surprise and drop to his knees.

Veronyka turned to Latham, whose mouth was hanging open in surprise. Ronyn and Lysandro wore matching expressions.

"Anders will need a minute. Why don't we have a go until he's recovered?"

Latham, it seemed, had no response to that, so he took up a practice spear and met Veronyka in the ring.

They began stiffly, but soon eased into the rhythm of attack and deflect, forward and back, the damp sand sliding beneath Veronyka's feet and sweat dotting her brow.

When at last Latham took her down with a neat sweep of the staff, Anders was standing beside the ring, arms crossed over his chest and a cool, competitive glint in his eye.

"My turn," he said, twirling a spear in his hands and taking up Latham's place across from her. This time his smile was wide and true—and edged with the promise of pain to come. Latham stepped aside, chest heaving as he drank from a waterskin, and Ronyn and Lysandro paused to watch the grudge match take place.

"Go for the shins," Latham advised. Anders laughed, and Veronyka couldn't help but grin.

Every night when Veronyka inevitably ran out of things to worry about and tasks to occupy her restless mind and body, she wound up atop Azurec's Eyrie's highest point—the temple roof with its golden phoenix statue.

It might be more distracting to return to the noisy barracks or stay late at the bustling dining hall, but Veronyka found it hard to be around most people these days. Maybe it was the Ashfire thing—the members of her patrol weren't the only ones who saw her differently now. Or maybe she'd been the one to put the walls up, like Morra suggested, protecting and secluding herself. Regardless, she didn't have the energy for laughter or gossip, her single-minded desire to free Tristan and fix the mess she'd made of things like a barrier between herself and the world.

While Veronyka would sit in silence, Xephyra liked to puff out her chest and mimic the golden statue's stoic manner and wide, outstretched wings, but she could never stand still long enough to give the pose any real weight. Sometimes Rex would do it too, just to prove how much better he was at being quiet and dignified—and Xephyra would nudge and nip at him until he was forced to give it up and snap back at her.

Rex left her to it tonight and was instead perched off to the side, staring into the distance.

From up here, they could see the stronghold and the village, the Eyrie and the grassy field beyond the gate. Sometimes Veronyka stretched her eyes—or Xephyra's through mirroring—ever wider, imagining she could see Tristan down in the valley below, or Val, wherever she was. Sometimes she even sought Alexiya, who had left weeks ago in search of her long-lost brother—Veronyka's long-lost father—and who had yet to return.

For all her searching, Veronyka saw nothing. She *felt* nothing too, and that was worst of all.

The closest she ever got was late at night, when she assumed Tristan was sleeping. With Rex by her side, Veronyka could manage the *feeling* of him—his heartbeat in her ears, his breath expanding and contracting in her chest—but nothing more.

Maybe that would change after today. She'd finally dropped the last barriers she had in place, opening her bonds wide. All of them.

Maybe tonight would be the night she got through.

A scrape of footsteps sounded behind Veronyka.

Kade emerged from the ladder at the back of the building, clambering over the pedestal that held the phoenix statue and crouching to sit down next to Veronyka. He didn't speak much—he didn't seem to feel the need to, the way others did—his quiet presence a soothing, undemanding comfort at the end of each day.

Though Rex remained distant, Xephyra cocked her head at Kade, who smiled and ran a hand down her beak. A second later another, smaller female phoenix fluttered to the roof—Kade's new bondmate, Jinx. She was a beautiful thing, elegant and long-winged, suggesting much growth still to come—which was good given Kade's height and weight. She stretched her neck and let out a soft, warbling cry before inching closer to Xephyra, her movements slow and deferential. Xephyra rather enjoyed the display, lifting her beak haughtily—but Veronyka knew what was coming. Jinx waited until she was right next to Xephyra, head still bowed respectfully, before she spread her wings wide in a sudden burst of feathers. Xephyra squawked and fell back, giving Jinx what she really wanted—not the respect of an older phoenix, but the best perch on the temple.

Xephyra relished the challenge, leaping forward to reclaim her spot at once, and the two were soon sharing the spot—with the occasional playful bite and jostle. Rex tossed them both a bored look. He was the largest of the three and would take the position himself if the two didn't quit making such a fuss. Xephyra snapped at him, and Jinx chirruped brightly, unfazed. She was clearly a bit of a rascal, bold and daring, and an interesting counterpart to Kade, who always seemed so serious.

Veronyka glanced at Kade now; he was grinning. She hadn't understood things at first, baffled that Sev had given him his only precious phoenix egg, the prize he had nearly died to deliver—his reward, his *salvation*, when all this was through. But then she'd seen the look in Kade's eyes as he'd described their time together and it had all made sense.

Veronyka and Kade had both left people they loved behind.

Thinking of Tristan made Veronyka turn her eyes south, and Kade copied her.

Tristan and Sev were there, alone in an empire of enemies.

"Any message for him?" Veronyka asked abruptly, but Kade understood.

Once she'd realized what Sev meant to him, Veronyka had explained more fully to Kade how she knew where Sev was, as well as the decision he'd come to that night. She hadn't just *seen* him with Tristan; she'd felt him there, felt his fear and the bravery and courage buried beneath. Kade was Pyraean and had heard enough rumors about shadow magic to act *surprised* but not shocked. He'd also worked closely with Ilithya Shadowheart—Veronyka's adopted grandmother—who had told him that the magic was real.

"And you believed her?" Veronyka had asked, stunned at his simple explanation.

He'd shrugged. "After all the impossible things she'd told me that turned out to be true—Phoenix Riders still existed, Avalkyra Ashfire lived—believing in shadow magic was fairly easy."

They'd traded more stories after that, tales of Ilithya Shadowheart, of Tristan and Sev. . . . It was painful, of course, but it also made them feel closer.

And every night when Veronyka tried to reach Tristan through their bond, she offered to try to send Sev a message too. Every time she failed, but still she tried.

"The same," Kade said in response to her question. It was a good message, after all, and not so very different from what she wanted to say to Tristan.

When all this is over, you and I will be standing together on the other side of it.

Maybe tonight it would happen. Veronyka's heart was open: her mind and her magic reaching for a connection.

Maybe tonight it would work.

For as long as there have been phoenixes,
there has been me.

- CHAPTER 2 -
AVALKYRA

SHE WAS A CHILD *again. Which child? A princess in silks, or a street rat in rags?*

And there was a sister with her.

Which sister?

Dirt floor. Dirty fingernails. And a belly aching from hunger.

She was Val, then, and this child was Veronyka.

Her magic felt muted, dull—until Veronyka looked at her with wide, adoring eyes, and her sister's magic surged up to meet her.

"Guard your mind," she snapped, and Veronyka's gaze faltered. The hopeful trust, the wary affection, all of it evaporated in an instant. But something lingered, warm as sunbaked terra-cotta tiles, gentle as a spring breeze. Stupid girl. Foolish girl. As if Avalkyra didn't have enough to worry about without adding Veronyka's magical ineptitude to the list.

It was late. The old woman should have been back by now. They had nothing to eat, no wood for a fire, no oil for the lantern.

Veronyka's worry was palpable now, her stomach aching worse than Avalkyra's.

You are projecting, Val said, not wanting to use magic—fearing the ease with which she could enter and exit the girl's mind, sensing it might be the start of something more—but needing to scare Veronyka into submission. There was nothing like words whispered into the mind to strike fear into a person's heart. To make them question themselves.

"I'm sorry," Veronyka mumbled, which only made Avalkyra hiss in impatience.

"I don't want your weak apologies. I want your control. I want your strength."

"I—" Veronyka began, but footsteps sounded outside the door. Avalkyra slapped her hand over Veronyka's mouth—they did not technically live here— but then the doorknob turned and Ilithya stood before them.

"Maiora!" Veronyka cried, pulling away from Avalkyra's iron grip and flying into Ilithya's arms. She hadn't even noticed the tension in the old woman's face . . . or the knife in Avalkyra's other hand.

Because she didn't have to.

Avalkyra stood, watching Veronyka and Ilithya embrace. Such simple, uncomplicated affection. Such willful ignorance.

Veronyka turned away from her adopted grandmother, but her gaze held none of its previous adoration. Her eyes were narrowed. Thoughtful.

"I noticed," she said.

Avalkyra reared back. The voice coming out of Veronyka's mouth wasn't that of a girl of seven or eight, as she was in this memory, but of a young woman. Of Veronyka now.

"You noticed what?" Avalkyra found herself asking. Her voice, too, had changed—before, she'd been watching the scene play out, but now she was controlling it.

Veronyka stepped away from Ilithya, and the old woman—as well as the world around them—shifted and blurred like fog, obscuring all but the two of them.

Avalkyra blinked, and Veronyka was grown. Avalkyra raised a hand to her own face and felt scars.

"I noticed the knife—I felt the tension," Veronyka said, her voice echoing slightly. She looked different, even from the last time Avalkyra had seen her in the real world. Her hair was longer, with several new braids, including one capped with her own signet ring, the other with Pheronia's pendant.

"You did?" Avalkyra repeated skeptically.

"I did. But I trusted you." She paused, shaking her head slightly and look-

ing around in confusion. "What are we doing here? What's happening, Val? I thought I was dreaming. . . . Did you come here for me?"

Avalkyra's lip curled at the arrogance. "Not everything is about you. As far as I can tell, you're the one who came here for me."

She also glanced around the strange, misty place they occupied. Their connection had started as a shared dream. The sleeping consciousness tended to drift beyond the boundaries of the mind, allowing shadowmages to pick up on the dreams of those around them—or those they were bonded to. But then it had changed. Now it was a regular shadow magic connection but within that dreaming framework. A conversation between their minds while their bodies slept.

The connection had been seamless, a startling realization given the physical distance between them.

They'd not conversed like this before.

"I wasn't looking for you," Veronyka said, crossing her arms. "I was looking for . . ." She sighed. "It doesn't matter. I don't want anything to do with you."

Avalkyra found herself smiling. There was nothing more familiar—and more comforting—than Veronyka's impotent anger. "But why not, Nyka?"

Veronyka's hands dropped to her sides. "You tried to kill me."

Avalkyra flashed back to Ferro, to the sky and the wind and the cold air that had crept into the place where Veronyka's hand had been right after Avalkyra had released it.

She shrugged. "You survived, didn't you? Clearly, I didn't try very hard."

Veronyka opened her mouth, gaping like a fish, before she released a soft growl and lurched away. "I'm done. I want out of here." She reached her hands into the mist, seeking walls or doors or some avenue for escape. Avalkyra felt the pull like a hook behind her navel.

This shared space they occupied was neither her mind nor Veronyka's, but rather inside the bond itself, and so in order to come and go, they both had to breach the distance or break the contact. Veronyka was pulling back now, but Avalkyra did not do the same.

"We are bonded," Avalkyra said. "You cannot simply walk away from me." Much as Veronyka might want to. Much as Avalkyra herself might sometimes want her to.

Veronyka whirled back, ready to retort. Then she paused, expression turning thoughtful. "It was happening here, wasn't it?" she asked, staring at the space between them as if she could still see the scene from their past. "The start of the bond?"

Avalkyra nodded. "I should have put a stop to it."

"Why didn't you?"

The question felt accusatory, and Avalkyra scowled. If she had known and understood what was happening, of course she would have put a stop to it. A human bond? What could be more perilous? As if loving Pheronia hadn't been enough to fracture an empire and topple a dynasty, but a magical manifestation of the same weakness?

Yes, she would have snuffed it out at once if she had known.

Had she known?

"I could have helped you," Veronyka continued, frustration bleeding into her words. "I could have shared the burden—if you'd let me. If you'd trusted me in turn."

Avalkyra snorted. "Trusted you? When your every thought and feeling was there for the taking? When your heart was as open and exposed as the rib cage of a corpse on a battlefield?"

"You made me that way—can't you see that? You made my magic weak by refusing to teach me. All I learned from you was fear and failure. You never showed me how to succeed."

That was definitely an accusation. Avalkyra's lip curled, and she stepped forward, into Veronyka's personal space. They were close enough to touch. Or they would have been, if they weren't miles apart. "I'll show you what success looks like."

Now it was her turn to pull back. Veronyka resisted her for a moment, eyes dark with something like regret, before she closed them and disappeared entirely.

Avalkyra thought she had forgotten how to sleep.

How to surrender herself to it. How to be free from her body, her mind . . . if only for a few hours.

She certainly thought she had forgotten how to dream.

Leave it to Veronyka to slice her open like a piece of fruit. No, Veronyka was more like an insect, a parasite, worming her way in slowly over time. But Avalkyra would not let her insides turn mushy and sweet, overripe with rot. She would not let Veronyka occupy space inside her mind, tainting her present with thoughts of her past.

She would not fall into that trap again.

Loving them is weakness.

She had spoken the words to Veronyka dozens of times, a warning against the girl's sentimental attachments. But now the words were a warning for herself. She had loved, and she had lost. Burned and bled because of it.

Loving them is weakness, and Avalkyra had no room left for weakness.

She had no room left for anything but the hatred in her heart, pure as poison. No room left for anything but vengeance.

Veronyka had betrayed Avalkyra, like her mother before her. She had chosen made-up loyalty and petty friendships over family, over blood—over a thousand-year legacy. She had taken everything from Avalkyra and stolen it for herself.

What, then, could Avalkyra do, other than take it all back?

Not for herself, of course. She no longer wanted it. All this time she'd yearned to remake the past, to reclaim what was lost. But now?

She would not seize the throne—she would topple it.

She would not rule the empire—she would obliterate it.

And Veronyka would be there; Avalkyra would make sure of it. Not as a sister or a fellow queen, but as an enemy to defeat. A target for her arrows, a symbol and figurehead of the world that had rejected her.

They would fight this war as it should have been fought seventeen years ago—both of them in the sky, on wings, with all the world watching. There would be no silent arrows in the night, no secret heirs and reborn queens.

There would be ash, and fire, and death.

Veronyka was strong, but Avalkyra was stronger.

The next time they met, things would be different. *She* would be different. There would be no looking backward. Only forward, into the future. A future of her own making.

A future where only one of them would be left standing.

Wingbeats sounded above, distant but discernible. Little else moved here besides the creaking, howling wind.

It was too dark to see, but Avalkyra knew who and what approached. She knew the darkness better than the light.

After all, it was in her darkest moment that she had unwittingly given that phoenix egg everything she had—every hatred, every fear, every bloody, blinding ambition—and tossed it into the utter emptiness that was once the Everlasting Flame.

And it was in her darkest moment that she had been given exactly what she needed. Not a glittering phoenix born of fire, but a strix born of shadows and night. A fitting partner at last.

After seventeen years, Avalkyra had a bondmate again.

Not just *any* bondmate, either. She had hatched a strix, and she would be the first-ever Strix Rider. She was living history. She was legend.

And with her new bond came power.

Such *power*.

She reveled in it, the way it grew with each passing day. She had forgotten what it was like to be powerful. Not the assumed power of a name or a legacy, and not the internal power of knowledge, or memory, or frothing, foaming rage.

No, this was true power, *magical* power, pure and simple.

Her shadow magic surged with every breath, every moment she and her bondmate spent together. It was overwhelming. Intoxicating.

Dangerous.

But not for her.

No. This power was dangerous for everyone else.

The wingbeats grew louder, and Avalkyra got to her feet. She had fallen asleep on a bench beside a dried-up old fountain in the central square of the ruins of Aura, the carved phoenix whose beak once spouted cool, clean water now cracked and crumbling.

The stony basin did collect rain, however, and Avalkyra caught a glimpse of herself in the reflection of the ink-black puddle.

She raised a hand to the rough skin of her face, to the tight scar tissue and the strange numbness of scorched nerves. To the eye that she'd nearly lost, which now remained partially closed and sensitive to light.

Sidra had helped her clean and tend the wounds, to smear them with salves and wrap them with linen. She had flown to villages to beg, borrow, and steal whatever herbs and tinctures she could, forcing them down Avalkyra's throat when she tried to lash out in pain.

In truth, Sidra had relished the opportunity to be of real use. She was threatened by Avalkyra's new bondmate, who had taken Sidra's place at her queen's side. Now she was a step farther, a spot lower, but no matter how her value and usefulness had decreased, Sidra was still a vessel for Avalkyra's will. So even when her own body rebelled, her mind and her magic knew she needed strength. Needed to heal and avoid infection. Needed to *survive*. And so she used Sidra for all she was worth.

After weeks of treatment, the scars were as good as they would ever be, mottled and tight, but Avalkyra could still hold a knife and aim a bow, and that was all that mattered. She would wear her wounds as a badge of honor, a symbol of her survival. If the world did not like them, they could look away.

Nearer, nearer, her bondmate drew—invisible until she wasn't, dropping out of the night like a scrap of darkness made solid. Like a sky without stars, inky and unfathomable.

Took you long enough, Avalkyra said by way of greeting, annoyed even as the sight of her bondmate and the surge of magic she brought was like her first deep breath of air in nearly two decades.

Those large ebony eyes fell on Avalkyra: *It takes as long as it takes.*

Avalkyra couldn't help but smirk. Her bondmate was precocious, and speaking exceedingly well for her age. Her attitude, on the other hand, was less welcome. Was it the futile rebellion of a youth on the cusp of adulthood? Or Avalkyra's own disregard for authority coming back to bite her?

Whatever it was, the strix would not be easily cowed.

The thought was both a challenge and a relief.

She needed a true partner, after all . . . not an equal, but an ally and an asset—a mount that could keep up with her. Someone strong and capable and made in her own image.

Avalkyra had spent days in convalescence, watching this new stranger just as the creature watched her, both wary of each other despite the magic that bound them.

Avalkyra did not easily trust, and she was no fit mother for a soft, new-made thing.

Luckily, her bondmate was neither.

Sharp as broken glass and ancient as the night, the strix didn't love Avalkyra—she *required* her—and that kind of relationship suited them both. Their bond came of likeness and necessity. Her mount hungered for something more than food. She craved *life*—not to revel in it, but to claim and destroy it.

Avalkyra knew the feeling, of course. She had given it to her.

When she had named her phoenix, Nyx, she had been young and idealistic. The name meant "victory," plain and simple.

But there was nothing plain and simple about the victory Avalkyra envisioned now. This victory had already come at great cost, and there would be more to pay, she knew. It would be a last, final, dark victory.

And then she had it. Onyx.

Onbra meant "dark" or "shadow" in Pyraean, and *Nyx* meant "victory." Together, she had the perfect name.

Standing before Avalkyra now, Onyx dropped her burden at her bondmate's feet and straightened.

Dead things. Always dead things. Avalkyra sent her for plants and animals, food and firewood—and every time she returned with dried-out husks and brittle bones. Nothing living.

Avalkyra sighed. She would starve at this rate. She would have already if not for Sidra.

Onyx lifted her head abruptly, and a sound reached Avalkyra's ears. Distant and echoing . . . More wingbeats? It must be Sidra, though Avalkyra had not sent for her.

The woman did not live here in Aura, but she always came when called—it was the nature of the bind, and Sidra's own subservient personality.

Avalkyra continued to listen, but the sound was gone.

Had it been Sidra? Somehow, Avalkyra doubted it. Neither she nor her phoenix could bear to be around Onyx for long. It seemed that the same thing that happened to plants and animals happened to all living things.

But it did not happen to Avalkyra. Maybe like called to like, and she did not have enough life left in her to drain.

Maybe the bond protected her.

Or maybe the bond took what it needed to grow strong, but Avalkyra didn't notice because it made *her* strong in turn.

That was the thing with bonds: You had to give in order to receive. Not just respect and affection—whatever Veronyka might believe—but *power*.

A mage gave magical power to their bondmate, and so too did they give power in turn.

This was why Avalkyra's magic was stronger than it had been since her last life. A bonded mage was always stronger than a solitary mage, but the connection came with risks.

Veronyka was proof of that.

Binds, being one-way, were safer, but they were also limited. More than she had truly realized until she'd hatched Onyx. Binds gave nothing but obedience, and worse, like a leech, they sucked energy and effort—they depleted her and her magic.

Onyx had given Avalkyra more power than she'd had in her entire second lifetime, but even that remarkable surge would not be enough. Not for what Avalkyra had in mind. Not for total, utter destruction. Not for vengeance that would shake the world and shatter its bones.

For that she would need more. They were only two, after all, and she was up against an empire.

She turned in the direction of the Everlasting Flame and the hundreds of eggs that littered the ground around it.

Yes, Avalkyra needed more of this power, and she knew exactly where to get it.

Day 9, Fifth Moon, 175 AE

I have a task for you.

You do not know me, but I know you. It is my business to know things.

I am a fan of your research, and Olanna Flamesong spoke most highly of you.

Has the war ended for you, like it has so many others . . . or are you still willing to fight for the Ashfire cause?

Meet me on Temple Street, tenth bell, tomorrow.

Come alone.

—S

But I did not come into this world alone.

- CHAPTER 3 -
TRISTAN

TRISTAN JERKED AWAKE, HEART hammering and sweat coating his skin.

It took a moment for him to remember where he was. It always took a moment these days. First there was the dull ache in his chest where Rex should be—not gone, exactly, but numbed almost beyond feeling.

When he pushed past that ache, he felt the ache of his failure. He'd flown into the empire to *rescue Veronyka*, not to wind up captured himself. He'd convinced his father, risked everyone's lives . . . and he'd just given Rolan one more bargaining chip to use against the Phoenix Riders. At least Veronyka was safe.

Veronyka. Her ache was the most painful ache of all. Every night he dreamed of her—but they were not comforting dreams. They were dark and lonely and echoing, her voice so faint he could barely hear it, her presence like a ghost haunting his mind. And last night's dream . . . He thought Val might have been there too, which was enough to send a shudder down his spine.

He pressed a hand to the breast pocket of his tunic, withdrawing half of a broken obsidian arrowhead. It was one of his only personal possessions, a keepsake he happened to have on him the day Rolan captured him. It reminded him of Veronyka, who had the other half, and as he rubbed his thumb across the smooth, shining surface, his anxiety eased.

Tristan sat up, the last and least of his aches—the physical ones—rolling over him in waves. His back was stiff from the thin pallet on its cold metal frame. His sweaty skin covered in chills from the damp, stale air. And the darkness . . . Tristan blinked, his cell materializing more solidly around him with every heart-pounding breath.

Three stone walls and the fourth made of bars. Barred window. Two guards outside his cell day and night.

As he came back to himself, Tristan realized that he hadn't awoken on his own—distantly a latch clanged shut, reverberating through the space, followed by the scrape of boots on rough-hewn steps.

Tristan glanced to the window—it was full dark out. There wasn't usually a guard change until dawn.

The footsteps finally stopped, and one of the guards outside Tristan's cell spoke. "Where's Mal?"

"Puking his guts out."

Tristan scrambled to his feet. He knew that voice.

Sev. It had been weeks since Tristan was taken as Lord Rolan's prisoner, weeks since Sev had gripped his arm and told him without speaking that they were in this together.

Weeks since Tristan had seen Sev at all.

Lord Rolan had been quick to relocate his household and his prisoner from Ferro—Tristan's old home and a place Commander Cassian knew better than Rolan himself—back to Rolan's ancestral home in Stel. Tristan hadn't even been certain that Sev had come with them.

"He had the fish at dinner," Sev continued, his voice bland and unassuming. There was a pause. "Wait . . . you didn't have the fish too, did you?"

The response was a low, gurgling growl that had most certainly come from somebody's stomach. "I did," the guard answered, voice slightly choked.

Tristan's groggy mind woke up. Mal and Ian were usually on the night shift. Mal had clearly run off to use the bathroom facilities, and Sev had taken his place. But it sounded like Ian wouldn't be far behind. There was another rumbling sound, followed by a gag.

"Go on," Sev said amiably. "I'll stay until the shift change. If anyone asks, I'll cover for you."

There was no reply, just a muttered curse and the sound of frantic, stumbling footsteps receding up the distant staircase.

A second later, Sev appeared at the barred wall of his cell.

He looked different from Tristan's memories of him, where he was dressed as a raider with an arrow protruding from his shoulder, or armored and dirty, fresh from a battlefield with sweat-soaked hair hanging in his eyes. Now he was clean, in a brand-new soldier's uniform, his hair cut close in the military style. It made Tristan's hand fly up to his own hair, which had been shorn as well. Since the Blood War it was empire tradition to cut off the hair of Phoenix Rider prisoners to remove any trace of their previous position. Tristan didn't wear any braids or feathers, but now it would be a long time before he could.

"It's all right," Sev said, as Tristan's focus shifted down the hall from where Sev had come. "We're alone. For now."

Tristan nodded, but Sev's gaze was roving, sizing him up.

"How are they treating you? Is the food okay?"

"It's better than the guards', apparently."

"Oh, they eat just fine," Sev said, waving away his words. "The fish wasn't the problem—I was."

Tristan gaped. "You"—he lowered his voice—"*poisoned* them?"

"Barely," Sev said with a crooked shrug. "Just enough to make them run to the toilet, not enough to kill them. I needed to talk to you, but I didn't need to leave a body trail. Not yet, anyway."

"So that means . . . ," Tristan began, his mind still bleary with sleep.

"No word—no plans," Sev said, his voice tinged with frustration. Tristan had come to stand directly in front of him, so they were just inches apart. Still, it was difficult to see Sev's expression in the darkness. "It's my fault. They're waiting on information. We can't make a move with Rolan here, surrounded by what's left of his army and his private household guard. We also can't afford to *try* and have Phoenix Riders spotted in the sky in Stel, when it could mean word getting back to the council and affecting their decision."

Tristan's heart was heavy in his chest. *No word—no plans.* "When *is* the Grand Council meeting?"

"I don't know," Sev said, looking away. Tristan could see a muscle in his jaw jump. "But Rolan's still here, which means it hasn't happened yet. With any luck, we'll get some kind of warning before he heads to the capital. When he's in Aura Nova, taking the majority of his soldiers with him, we'll make our move."

"But—what about the meeting? We can't split our forces even further. The commander needs to argue our case."

"Not according to his terms with Rolan. If Rolan knows your father has betrayed him before we've gotten you to safety—"

"So what?" Tristan said, his own frustration coming through. He didn't particularly like his father's mad plan to attend the council meeting with the intention of assassinating select members in order to delay the vote and strengthen their future alliances, but it was the only plan they had. If his father *didn't* go against his deal with Rolan, that might mean he intended to deliver on what he'd promised . . . including delivering Veronyka *to* Rolan as his bride. Tristan's stomach clenched painfully. His father wouldn't do that.

He wouldn't.

"So what?" Sev repeated incredulously. "You're the commander's son. You're valuable."

His tone made Tristan pause. He supposed for someone like Sev, the idea that anyone would want to rescue him would be a miracle, something he'd likely spent his whole life wishing for. And here Tristan was, taking it for granted.

"We're valuable," Tristan argued. "Whatever happens, you're coming with me."

"I'm not sure what kind of use I am beyond these walls. . . ."

"I'm sure," Tristan said staunchly. "You saved all our lives. We're in this together, and we're getting out of it together."

Sev didn't say anything, but Tristan thought maybe he stood a little straighter after that. "Well," Sev said eventually, "speaking of that—we've got work to do." He glanced over his shoulder, down the passage toward the stairs. Then his gaze flicked upward to the window in Tristan's cell. Already soft gray light was filling the space, meaning that dawn wasn't far off.

"We do?" Tristan asked, moving even closer and gripping the cool metal bars. He was desperate for something to do, anything to occupy his mind and make him feel useful and not like a total failure.

Some way to make it up to Veronyka and his father. To prove that he still had what it took to be a leader, not just a liability.

"Even if Rolan makes things easy for us and leaves with plenty of warning and the majority of his forces, you're still in an underground cell, watched day and night, surrounded by a full household guard inside a walled compound in Stel. They're gonna need some help."

"Help," Tristan repeated faintly, the task sounding insurmountable when Sev put it like that.

Sev nodded. "I've been doing what I can to memorize the guard schedules and the layout of the estate. Once I have a proper floor plan, we can start looking for weak points in the defenses, or possible routes for escape. The problem is this dungeon."

"What do you mean?" Tristan asked.

"It's strange," Sev began, tone thoughtful. "In a lot of ways, this house is similar to the estate in Ferro. Same rough layout, and a lot of the same features—courtyards, wide hallways, and open-air colonnades . . ."

"It was trendy for a time to mimic Ferronese architecture in Stel. A way to get in King Damian's good graces." Tristan smiled slightly at the injustice Rolan must have felt, hating Damian and Ferro and their rocky history with his ancestor Rol and yet living in a house inspired by their culture. "Although . . ." Tristan paused, leaning forward as much as he could to peer around the darkened hallway outside his door. "The Ferronese never built dungeons. Historically, our prisoners were kept in towers." Like *he* had been, before they'd come here. Like Veronyka had been.

Sev frowned. "It must be a newer renovation. This entire wing looks different from the rest of the house."

"If there was a renovation, there will likely be a record of it somewhere in the library. Including floor plans and technical drawings."

Sev perked up. "I'll check first thing tomorrow."

"How will you come back? You can't keep poisoning the fish."

Sev hesitated. Tristan had the feeling he didn't know how he'd come back but didn't want to admit it. "I'll figure it out," Sev said finally. "But you've given me a good lead. If I can find the fastest way out of here and the closest exits . . . we'll have a shot."

I had a sister, once. . . .

- CHAPTER 4 -
SEV

SEV WAS IN HIGH spirits when he left the dungeon at the guard shift change.

It had been a frustrating few weeks. When Rolan decided to leave the governor's estate in Ferro and make for his family home in Stel, Sev had scrambled—lying, sneaking, and eventually begging—to get transferred along with the others, and it had been a near thing. But even that success was short-lived. After casing the Ferronese estate for days with Kade, learning all the building's secrets, Sev would have to start all over again in Stel. And this time, he didn't have Kade with him.

After they'd parted, Sev hadn't slept until he'd gotten a reply to his letter to the commander. In it, he had vowed to stay by Tristan's side and keep him safe. He had also sent a letter for Kade—and a gift. His very own phoenix egg. Sev might have promised Kade a reunion, but that didn't mean he could deliver on it. But the egg, at least, he *could* deliver on. It was important to Sev to know that whatever might happen to him, Kade would have a life when all this was done. He would have a place to belong. It was the least Sev could do.

Even still, the commander's reply did not address Sev's note to Kade, nor his gift—it simply thanked him for the information, promised Kade,

Riella, and the others had returned to the Eyrie safely . . . and that they eagerly awaited his next report.

Sev was eager to give it. But after detailing the transfer to Stel, he'd had nothing further to report. It was like Tristan said; in Ferro, he'd been held in a tower, and it was easy enough for Sev to keep an eye on things and know that Tristan was okay. But as soon as they'd arrived in Stel, after a two-day march, Tristan had been hauled down into the dungeon, and Sev hadn't seen him since.

There was no way to wander past the entrance to the dungeons discreetly—they were housed in the renovated wing of the estate that was heavily guarded but otherwise unoccupied. So unless Sev got assigned to prison detail, he had no reason to go near the place. And Sev had tried. He had requested a new position, offered to trade or cover double shifts, but Lord Rolan had only his most senior soldiers guarding the exiled governor's son, and kept their schedules secret. Sev had had to watch the building day and night, forgoing sleep and meals, marking when people came and went, and putting together a rough schedule in his head.

Finally, he'd had enough information to do something, and so he'd *lightly* poisoned the midnight watch guards' meals. It was easier than the day guards, who ate in the soldiers' mess. The night watch was on a nocturnal schedule and so ate separately from the others. All Sev had to do was distract the kitchen servant with a series of stupid questions—he was embarrassingly good at this, asking about kettles and colanders until the girl clearly couldn't tell if Sev was trying to flirt with her or had never been inside a kitchen before—and sprinkle some dried oleander onto the dinner trays when her eyes were rolled. It might not have been as dramatic and poignant as the bloodred Phoenix Flowers Trix had so favored, but it was easier to get in Stel, and it was still effective.

Then Sev had simply made sure he was nearby when the first of the guards—the unfortunate Mal—came hurtling up the stairs to use the bathroom facilities. Sev offered to cover for him, and the man nodded vigorously before slamming the door and throwing up with a violent retch.

Sev felt bad about it . . . but not bad enough. He might not enjoy spy work, but that didn't mean he wasn't good at it. He'd done worse things, after all, and could deal with the comparatively moderate guilt of giving a couple of hardened empire soldiers diarrhea.

Sev would do what he had to do for as long as he had to do it, but it did not define who he was. He was a spy *for now*, and knowing it was temporary—a means to an end and not the end itself—made things easier.

The soldiers would recover, and in the meantime, Sev had taken advantage of the opportunity to talk to Tristan.

It was the first time Sev had gotten a good look at the commander's son since his imprisonment.

Tristan looked acutely out of place inside the dank, musty cell—his dirty, unevenly cut hair and lack of sleep failing to diminish him as he stood there, tall and broad-shouldered, his Rider leathers torn and sweaty but impressive nonetheless. He looked unbendable and intimidating and very like his father, and yet, after speaking to him, Sev realized he wasn't much like the commander at all. Yes, their looks were similar, their presence palpable—but Tristan wore his emotions plain on his face, his wariness and hesitation, his fear and vulnerability there for anyone to see. It had been there the night Sev had shown up at the Eyrie bringing news of impending death and destruction to the people under Tristan's care, and it had been there when Rolan had taken Tristan as hostage and Sev had shown him he was not alone.

It was a strange mix. It made Sev want to help him, but it also made Sev recognize quite plainly that Tristan was more than capable of helping himself. There was a rawness in him, an honesty that everything inside Sev rebelled against, and yet he admired it too. It seemed to speak of a different kind of life than the one Sev had led—even though Sev knew that the commander would be no easy father. Tristan had probably paid for his forthrightness and would have had to cultivate other forms of protection. But it was very easy to see him commanding forces and leading with confidence.

And Sev would get him there.

He would be the hand that tipped the poison, the keen eyes in the darkness. He would use every dirty trick he had—every self-preserving skill he'd ever honed—if it meant helping the Phoenix Riders. If it meant helping Kade.

There was still more work to do, but all in all, Sev was quite pleased with himself and the night's events.

So pleased, in fact, that he didn't see the newly minted Captain Yara dogging his steps until she wrapped iron fingers around his arm and yanked him into a darkened chamber.

An empty bathroom.

Gods, this is how it ends, Sev thought, looking around in panic. Teyke was getting him back for the diarrhea thing. Or maybe it was Axura, righting the scales of justice. That was far more likely. Sev rather thought Teyke would *enjoy* a good shit joke.

"Captain," Sev began in his best slow, nonthreatening voice. "What can I—"

"Enough with the dimwit act," Yara barked, turning from Sev to throw the latch and lock them inside. The only source of illumination was a small window where milky dawn light filtered into the room. Water dripped from a rusted hand pump used for quick washing, the sound echoing in the tiled space.

Sev stared at it, slotting the pieces of his story into place as Yara checked every corner of the room to make sure there were no servants or occupants or other eavesdroppers. At last she faced Sev again.

"Captain Yara, I'm not sure—"

"I told you to cut it out. I know where you were, just now, and I know where Mal and Ian were as well—not on duty, but making rather a mess of the bathroom on the first floor."

"The fish—" Sev tried again, but Yara held up a hand, silencing him. Sev's stomach convulsed painfully. He may not have eaten the fish, but it suddenly felt like he had.

"Do you know what it reminds me of?" she asked, almost conversationally. Sev shook his head. "It reminds me of Pyra. Of the Vesperaean caves. The sounds. The smells. It reminds me of that old woman Thya."

"W-who?" Sev managed meekly.

"You aren't nearly so vicious," Yara continued appraisingly, "or maybe you just aren't as good at your work, but it's clear you *are* doing the same work. I saw you two together more than once. But while she was caught red-handed—literally—you were not. No, you remained in Lord Rolan's service . . . and tragedy followed you. At least as far as the empire was concerned. First the caves and the failed attack on Azurec's Eyrie—I do not recall seeing you during the battle, incidentally—and then you returned to Pyra with the illustrious Captain Dill a few short months later, and once again, things went badly for Lord Rolan's troops."

Sev swallowed so thickly he felt the sides of his dry throat stick together.

"Several failed attempts at war with unarmed villagers"—her nostrils flared—"then the governor's forces were ambushed by Phoenix Riders. Over two-thirds of our number wiped out in a single battle. A battle you *were* present at, this time. And yet, remarkably, you returned safely. Luck, maybe? Coincidence? I cannot possibly attribute it to your fighting skills— I've seen you in the practice ring."

He was in for it now. She was circling him like a hawk, ready to pick him apart. Forget fighting skills—could Sev catch her off guard and bash her over the head with that bucket, then lock her inside the bathroom? No, if he wanted to be able to stick around and help Tristan . . . he'd have to kill her.

His heart hammered in his chest, fear and adrenaline spiking his veins, but he didn't move.

"The old woman is dead, but if her work is now your work . . ." Yara trailed off, her tone musing again as she took a single step closer. She actually smiled, twisting the burn scars along her jaw and neck. "Make no mistake—while I have no love for the Phoenix Riders, I like Lord Rolan even less."

Sev's thundering pulse stuttered, and he couldn't help the questioning look he knew must be on his face. The disbelief. What was she saying?

"I am no Rider, and I am no animage," she said in answer to Sev's skeptical expression, stepping even closer, forcing Sev to lean back slightly. "But I *am* Pyraean. And Rolan's plans? To march a thousand soldiers into Pyra *again* . . . I will not stand for it."

She finished on a deadly whisper. Sev's ears were ringing.

"That botched attempt on Azurec's Eyrie was one thing—stupid, careless, and ineffective—but his soldiers roaming freely along the border? This Grand Council vote?" she said, eyes fierce. "This will be the end of Pyra. They'll march in force and leave nothing, no one, behind. My family"—she paused—"what's *left* of my family, they're just now starting to rebuild, seventeen years later. I won't see Pyra burn to the ground or watch it slowly fall apart from raiders and bandits. Tell me what you need, and we will help you."

Yara's face was utterly serious, and she was smart, capable—in a position of power. Sev couldn't ask for a better ally.

"Wait—*we?*" he repeated.

Before Yara could answer, there was a soft knock on the door. She moved to open it, and Sev tried to put the scattered pieces of his mind back together.

It was a wasted effort.

When the door opened, Hestia—the resident healer at the governor's estate in Ferro—walked into the room, and Sev's brain broke all over again.

Hestia gave Sev an appraising sort of look. "All right, Sevro?"

He shrugged half-heartedly. It was a mistake.

The healer sighed heavily. "I see you haven't been tending your wound. Stiff as a statue—you can barely lift your arm. I told you to apply the salve every night, did I not?"

Sev opened his mouth, but no words came out.

"No matter. We can resume your treatment for the time being. We'll be meeting regularly from here on out?" she asked, turning to Yara, who nodded.

"H-how are you here?" Sev finally spluttered out—the least important of all the questions crowding his mind. At least he'd managed to speak.

Hestia shrugged. "Governor Rolan has been suffering from terrible indigestion these past weeks, and apparently only my tinctures can cure his digestive upset. They also *cause it*, of course, but he doesn't know that." She smiled blandly at Sev; she and Ilithya would have gotten along.

"But why?" he asked faintly. Hestia risked more than her position by tampering with Rolan's medications and helping Sev. She risked her life.

Hestia's expression turned dark. "To have Cassian's own son locked up in a cell beneath my feet . . . I brought that boy into this world, just as I helped the healer who delivered Cassian. Rolan has gone too far. The last thing this empire needs is another war."

Sev believed her sincerity and her love for Cassian and Tristan—she had served them for decades. He turned his attention to Yara. She stared steadily back at him.

Could he truly trust her? Yara already knew he was up to no good. If she wanted to turn him in, she could do so now. Her word would be enough.

Their involvement complicated matters, but Sev recognized that he alone wasn't enough anymore. He needed an inside look into Lord Rolan's plans and better access to Tristan—both of which Yara could offer him. And when it came time to free him, Yara would know every soldier's schedule and whereabouts—and be able to change them if needed. Furthermore, Hestia's knowledge of potions and herbs far outstripped Sev's own. They would both be invaluable allies.

"Tell us what you need," Yara said again, and Sev made up his mind.

"I need time alone in the dungeons with Tristan—every night, if we can manage it."

Yara nodded brusquely. "I will add you to the prison guard roster and adjust the schedule. Anything else?"

"I'm sure there will be, but for now? I need access to Lord Rolan's library."

- CHAPTER 5 -
ELLIOT

"ELLIOT!" SNAPPED RIELLA, WHIRLING on him for the second—or was it the third?—time that day.

He'd stomped on her foot. Again.

In his defense, she was marching all over the place like a chicken with its head cut off. She was helping Ersken tend one of the young phoenixes who had gotten into it with another, larger phoenix, squabbling over food, and the result was a slash across his face. There would be no lasting damage, but it had been a near thing: The cut ran diagonally across his forehead and cheek, dangerously close to his eye.

The phoenix that had wounded him was appropriately chagrined, crooning morosely and exiling herself to a corner of the courtyard at the bottom of the Eyrie, away from the others.

Elliot was helping Riella carry some healing supplies, but as he passed, he caught sight of Sparrow with hands on hips, chastising the guilty party in blunt, but not unkind, tones.

It made him smirk—and had distracted him just long enough that he'd walked directly into Riella's back, catching her heel with his boot.

"*Elliot,*" Riella said again, her tone tight with frayed patience. She snatched the box of supplies from him. "Don't you have somewhere you need to be? Patrols to fly? Errands for Beryk? *Something?*"

Elliot had been filling in on Tristan's patrol when he could, though he often shared the responsibilities with Doriyan, another Master Rider without a patrol. He was the newest member of their flock, aside from the apprentices, and had joined them after the events in Ferro with Avalkyra Ashfire and Lord Rolan. Doriyan's father, who was elderly and sick, remained under the healer's care—and had been a large part of Doriyan's decision to join them in the first place.

Since Elliot also worked as Beryk's assistant, he usually remained at the Eyrie whenever possible. He didn't mind—it meant staying close to Riella—but apparently *she* did.

"Excuse me, are you dismissing your big brother?" he asked indignantly.

Her face lit up. "Yes, that's exactly what I'm doing. Goodbye."

Elliot grabbed her arm before she could dart away. He stared down at her with his brows raised, mostly entertained, but also a bit uncomfortable with Riella's alarming maturity and independence. Where was the girl who used to follow *him* everywhere?

"I have the afternoon off, and I promised you we could go flying on Jax."

Riella expelled a great, long-suffering breath. "We can go riding anytime. But Maddox is hurt *now*." She pointed over her shoulder, where Ersken was feeding the phoenix candied ginger and pitted dates in an attempt to distract him for treatment.

Ever since they'd arrived at the Eyrie, Riella had been determined to be involved. In fact, her reaction to her trauma had been the exact opposite of Elliot's. When things went bad for him—by his own actions, of course, but still—Elliot had spent weeks shrinking back and distancing himself from people. Riella, on the other hand, was all the more determined to put herself in the thick of things.

Sparrow had been the one to shake Elliot out of his self-imposed exile and malaise, but it seemed that Riella needed no such push. She had taken to the Eyrie at once, and the first thing she did was find her way to the animals. Healing was her particular interest, so she was learning from Ersken and Jana how to make splints and bind wounds. She'd even taught Elliot—practicing on him and then having him practice on her—but a chance to treat a phoenix was a rare opportunity.

"Fine!" Elliot said, releasing her with a dramatic wave of his hands. In truth, he was proud of her. It felt as though he'd left behind a naive, innocent child, and now she was all grown up. "I guess I'll fly *alone*, then. Jax will be disappointed."

Jax was perched atop the gallery nearby. He tilted his head and chirruped.

"Oh yes, he looks quite devastated." Riella was clearly about to roll her eyes—they were halfway there—when something over Elliot's shoulder grabbed her attention. She beamed. "But I know just the thing! You can take Sparrow instead."

The girl in question had been walking past, her homemade spear in hand. A familiar raven was perched on her shoulder, tangled in her hair, while the rest of the occupants of the Eyrie—phoenixes and apprentices alike—skirted around her in an apparent attempt to avoid her notice. Today wasn't the only day she'd given a phoenix or their bondmate a stern talking-to.

She came to a stop next to them, her brow furrowed.

"You'd like to go for a fly, wouldn't you, Sparrow?" Riella asked brightly. While Riella had a knack for healing, Sparrow was talented at drawing all manner of animals to her side—especially the lost or wounded—and the two girls had become co-conspirators and fast friends.

"Me?" repeated Sparrow, her hands stilling on her spear, which she often twisted and twirled as she moved.

"Of course," Riella said eagerly. She shoved the box of supplies back into Elliot's chest with force, practically knocking the wind out of him, before sidling up to Sparrow. She touched the back of Sparrow's hand at first, a simple, relaxed gesture that told him Riella had done this before. Then she moved her arm around Sparrow's shoulders and squeezed.

Sparrow smiled, the expression soft and transformative on her face. She was usually a bit wild-looking, rough-edged and sharp-tongued, but now she looked . . . Well, the word that came to mind was *pretty*, but that didn't feel right. Sparrow was a lot of things: intelligent and opinionated, curious and compassionate—a force of nature. Calling her pretty was like calling the dawn sun pretty. Accurate, he supposed, but insufficient.

Riella tossed Elliot an appraising sort of look, as if she could read his thoughts, and heat crept up his neck. Sparrow was barely a year younger than Elliot's sixteen, but it made him feel strange to notice these kinds of things. Awkward.

Not nearly as awkward, however, as it had been when he'd learned Sparrow's age in the first place.

He'd been combing the Eyrie a couple of weeks back, looking for Riella, and had eventually found her sitting with Sparrow in his old haunt—the grassy field outside the village—wiling away one of the last truly hot days of autumn. Since he was no longer grounded, Elliot's time wandering the field himself while Jax flew above was gone, which meant he hadn't spent much time with Sparrow.

A stab of guilt pierced his stomach whenever he thought about it—about her—but he had more responsibilities now than ever: as a Rider, as Beryk's assistant, and as a brother. He'd only just gotten Riella back, and after being held prisoner by Lord Rolan for nearly a year, she deserved his whole focus. The commander had informed their father of her safety, but he was apparently being watched closely by his superiors at the Office for Border Control and couldn't risk a visit or even a decent reply to their letters.

It was all on Elliot, and he'd failed Riella once already, miserably, and he wouldn't ever let that happen again.

As they sat together for the first time in weeks, Sparrow mentioned she still spent most evenings wandering outside. For a wild moment, Elliot had flattered himself that she might be waiting for *him*—but then she'd explained that she'd made friends with an old, solitary phoenix the day after Riella's return, and had been hoping the creature would come back ever since.

It had been good to see her again, to hear her laugh that snorting laugh and sit among the tall grasses while all manner of animals jumped and crawled and ambled around them.

Then Riella had asked something about Sparrow's birthday, and it hit Elliot square in the chest when she'd admitted she didn't actually know the date . . . or her age.

Riella had been determined to do the math.

"Okay, how long have you been, uh, traveling?" she'd asked carefully. Elliot smiled at his sister's needless tact—Sparrow wasn't the easily offended sort.

Sparrow screwed up her face in thought at the question, hands slipping idly over Carrot the cat's mangy ginger fur. "Left the temple the same year as the Great Flood," she said. "I remember the bridge got knocked clean out, and the Narrows streets were ankle-deep with river water."

"That was . . . what, nine—no, ten—years ago, now?" Riella asked, turning to Elliot, who was busy trying to wrap his brain around the fact that Sparrow had been alone and wandering for *ten years*.

He nodded numbly. "We were still living with Great-Aunt Emilia in Stelarbor." In a fancy manor house, with full bellies and a roof over their heads.

"And they only take acolytes at age five," Riella mused. "How much time did you spend in the temple?"

Sparrow shrugged—or maybe it was a shudder. "Not long . . . Was dropped off at the end of the summer and was gone before the next spring."

"So you're about fifteen, then," Riella said excitedly. "The same as me!"

"You're only fourteen," Elliot pointed out.

"And a *quarter*," she corrected, stung.

Sparrow nodded somewhat indifferently. "Could be—I've had these for a while now," she murmured, pressing her hands to her breasts.

Elliot's mouth had fallen open, then he'd jerked his gaze away so fast he cricked his neck. Riella, meanwhile, let out a peal of laughter and dragged

Sparrow's hands away. Elliot's face had burned hotter than a phoenix in a fire dive, but Sparrow only shrugged and smiled her more familiar goofy—but no less affecting—smile.

He hadn't spent any time with her since.

"Jax has been talking about you nonstop," Riella continued, making Sparrow grin more widely. "So it's only fair you do him the honor. What do you say, Elly?"

Elliot hated that nickname. Sparrow's face faltered somewhat, unease flickering across her features. Even if she didn't spend her nights waiting for him, Elliot had wondered if Sparrow noticed his absence in her life—but of course she had. There was a reason the two of them had wandered the field outside the village in the first place. They were lonely.

While Sparrow looked unsure, Riella's expression was pointed, her brows raised. There was clearly only one answer he could give, according to her.

"Sure," he said, darting a glance at Sparrow. She seemed surprised; then a flush of pleasure crawled up her cheeks.

"Perfect!" Riella trilled, yanking the box of supplies from Elliot's hands once again and stalking off toward Ersken without a backward glance.

"Uh," Elliot began, but he was saved from coming up with anything to say to fill the silence when Jax soared down from the gallery to land next to them, his saddle jangling as he shook out his wings in excitement.

As Jax moved closer, Sparrow's raven squawked and puffed out his feathers in the face of the newcomer, and Jax let out a piercing shriek in response. The raven settled down at once.

"Serves you right, with ideas above your station," Sparrow said matter-of-factly to her raven, and Elliot felt the strange tension between them dissipate at once. He grinned.

"Will he join us?" he asked, running a hand along Jax's flank and quickly checking the straps and buckles. A fluttering sensation rose in him, and he felt like a green apprentice again—afraid and excited in equal measure when he was about to fly. Elliot had spent months grounded, and though it had been weeks since he'd been allowed to ride again, he still reveled in his ability to mount up and take to the sky.

"Not sure he likes to get his feathers ruffled . . . ," Sparrow said idly, and the raven croaked with indignation. "Well, then, make nice," she said in response, and the raven turned a baleful look at Jax. "Go on," Sparrow prompted, and then, with something that sounded very much like one of Riella's exasperated sighs, the raven hopped down Sparrow's arm and waited.

Sparrow lifted him, and Jax lowered his head curiously. The raven tilted his head this way and that, seeming to take the measure of Jax. The phoenix emitted a questioning croak, then the raven hopped onto his head, strutting around and poking his beak in among Jax's feathers.

"Ravens," Sparrow commented sagely. "All mouth and no manners."

Elliot chuckled. "Are you ready?"

Sparrow's smile slipped.

"Don't worry," Elliot said. "You just have to hang on to me. Jax will do the rest." She nodded, but her face was tight. Elliot reached for her—then hesitated. "Can I . . . ? Is it okay if I lift you?"

"Oh," she said, features flickering with even more uncertainty. "Right. Yes."

She held her arms out from her sides, waiting, and next to them, Jax lowered himself to the ground.

Elliot took her spear and leaned it against the wall before stepping in close, hands hovering over Sparrow's middle. Touching her this way felt too familiar, too intimate, but there was nothing else for it. "Here I go . . . ," he said, feeling like an idiot. Then he gripped her sides and lifted her into the saddle.

She sat sideways at first, but once Elliot released her, she felt around and lifted a leg across Jax's back, getting herself situated. The raven squawked and pecked, fussing, while Elliot guided her feet—bare, why were they always bare?—into the stirrups.

Climbing up in front of her was a bit of a challenge, especially without the stirrups for footholds, but he managed, settling slowly back into the saddle. The raven had fluttered over to Sparrow and perched himself in her hair again, but she still sat rigidly, her hands fisted and held out to her sides, as if unsure of where to grip.

Elliot's nerves were back again, but when he saw the uncertain look on her face, he forgot them at once. They weren't awkward acquaintances—they were friends—and Elliot wanted her to enjoy her first phoenix ride, especially since it was with him.

"Here," he said, reaching back to take both her hands in his and drawing them around his middle. The movement forced Sparrow to press against him—he felt the sharp point of her chin and the rapid-fire beat of her heart against his back. Her hands were still fisted, so he tugged gently on her fingers until they splayed against his stomach. His muscles clenched in response. "Hang on tight," he said.

Jax got to his feet and spread his wings wide. There was a gust of wind and a lurch, and suddenly they were ascending, climbing into the sky in a rolling rhythm that matched every pump of Jax's wings.

Sparrow gasped and dug her fingers into Elliot's stomach, and he felt her turn her face into his back, as if seeking something solid and reassuring. He couldn't imagine the jarring sensation of flight without his sight to ground him, but they'd left the Eyrie behind now, and as Jax leveled out, the ride became smoother.

Sparrow's iron grip loosened somewhat, and Elliot felt her draw back. Her hands trembled against him for a moment, then released. He twisted around as she flung her arms out wide, mimicking Jax's soaring wings.

He wished she could see it the way he did—the vast blue sky, the way the world faded away below, as if time and space and distance no longer mattered. But he also knew she saw it in other ways—ways that were lost to him. The scent of the cool autumn air, the sound of the wind, the taste of sunlight.

He felt the rumble against his back before he heard her wild laughter, whipped away on a gust of air and taking his own along with it.

Axura was my mother, the sun in the sky,
and my father was the earth below.
The rock from which I was born.

- CHAPTER 6 -
AVALKYRA

IT WAS DIFFICULT TO tell how much time had passed.

Daylight didn't quite reach them here, with the rising smoke of the Everlasting Flame to obscure it, but it was dark as night when a scraping sound punctuated the silence, followed by a resounding *crack*.

Onyx cocked her head and leaned over the edge of the pit, but Avalkyra shoved her aside, boots crunching on broken shells, to see for herself.

A phoenix required fire and bones to hatch, a tribute of life and death, but strixes needed neither. As far as Avalkyra understood, the less they got, the more likely they were to be born—they were made of aching hunger and desperate emptiness. They were voids made solid, absence given presence. They were made of nothing, and what was more *nothing* than the smoking remains of the Everlasting Flame? It had hosted a thousand births and deaths, created a queendom and a country—it had taken and given and taken again, until suddenly it stopped. Suddenly all that history, all that culture, disappeared in a snap.

This vacuous pit was all that remained—a perfect symbol of what happened when the taking went on too long . . . when there was nothing left to give.

Avalkyra understood that feeling. She had only her own nothingness—her own empty soul and hungry heart—to offer, and that's what she'd clung to as she'd placed the egg into the swirling mist.

Now she squinted into the gloom until a shape materialized in the haze.

It was a bird. Ink-black and agitated, scrambling over eggshells as it stumbled forward. The creature had none of Onyx's immediate grace and gravitas, and when the strix finally looked at Avalkyra, she understood why.

There was nothing between them. No bond—not even a hint of connection or awareness.

Avalkyra looked at Onyx, who lifted a single, midnight wing in a shrug. Her feathers were filling out now, but they alternated between a smoky, soft-edged luster and a spiky, pointed silhouette. It seemed to reflect her mood—even now, the color darkened, the lines hardening as she croaked at the hatchling, shoving it with her beak.

Disappointed, Avalkyra thought back to the night Onyx was born. She had been at her lowest, her angriest . . . her most vulnerable. Before then she'd spent a lifetime unable to lure a phoenix out of its shell. Clearly, she had lacked something those firebirds needed. She'd always assumed it had to do with her failing animal magic—which had become diluted in this second life—or her much stronger shadow magic. But perhaps it was more about vulnerability . . . an open, willing unguardedness that Avalkyra did not know how to replicate.

Veronyka could probably nurture a thousand bonds with a bleeding heart such as hers, but that was not Avalkyra. That was not how she did things. She didn't *ask* for respect or try to *earn* what she desired. She demanded it.

She stared down at the hatchling. The strix was alert and seeking—hungry, of course, and Avalkyra was the only living thing for miles.

"You can try," she said coldly, crouching down to look into its beetle-black eyes. It did, at first—a strange scraping, scratching feeling coming over her as the hatchling attempted to feed, to suckle on Avalkyra's life force like a newborn babe at its mother's breast.

Onyx bristled. Avalkyra sensed the possessiveness there, the territorial nature of her bondmate rising up in the face of this interloper.

But she would not give so easily. She gave to Onyx only because she received something in return.

Taking hold of that reaching tendril, that wisp of magic, Avalkyra followed it to its source. She could bind the strix, here and now, but such a hold would weaken her magic even as it strengthened her numbers. It wasn't good enough.

Avalkyra's primary experience with binds was with humans, whose natures were predisposed to want to serve her—or at least they had been, when she was a princess and then the Feather-Crowned Queen. Her one and only experience trying to bind a magical creature had worked, for a time—she touched her scarred face, her anger rising—but she had eventually lost all control. The cost had been too great, sapping her magic and her energy, and that ancient phoenix had turned on her with vicious contempt. Would Avalkyra run herself ragged trying to keep the strix in line, only to have it turn on her as well?

She couldn't risk it—the magical draining or the violent revolt. Now that she'd tasted strength, she couldn't bear the thought of returning to weakness.

She needed *more* strength if she was to bring the world to its knees. She needed to *be* more.

And she *was*, she told herself. She was a bonded Rider again, and her mount was a strix, the first born in a millennium.

The first born . . . Avalkyra cocked her head consideringly.

There was power in being the first. Age, experience—and yes, strength. Those that come after owed their allegiance to those that came before. The first child of a queen inherited the throne, and the first hatched phoenix had inherited the sky . . . *mundi apex phoenix.* The world's first phoenix.

That was the literal translation, but it was more than just words. According to the history books, being "apex phoenix" had conferred extra abilities on Ignix, including power over the other phoenixes. A magical or social hierarchy that forced them to obey her. With Queen Nefyra as her bondmate, that ability was doubled, for she held similar power over the humans who served her.

Ignix was the only apex ever recorded because even though she'd eventually disappeared from human knowledge, she'd never officially *died*. She'd simply faded away, along with the idea of the apex.

Avalkyra thought of the solitary phoenix she'd binded. It had been large and old . . . older than any of the other Phoenix Rider mounts she'd seen. It had also bucked her control before *breathing fire*. A sure candidate for apex, if indeed there was one.

She also recalled those distant wingbeats she'd heard the day before. This was where they had met, Avalkyra and the old phoenix. . . . Was it so strange to think she might return?

For a moment, Avalkyra was certain she felt eyes on her.

Had her once-bindmate come to pay her a visit? To finish what she'd started?

Or had she come to watch and wait?

Avalkyra shook her head and refocused.

Onyx, she barked, drawing her bondmate's attention.

If the world's first phoenix received special powers, surely the world's first *strix* got the same? As it was, Avalkyra felt no different beyond the regular increase in magic a bondmate provided. But the power of the apex came not from a single bond. . . . It came from a flock. Not just being a part of one, but leading it. *Ruling* it.

Make it bow to me, Avalkyra said, gesturing to the hatchling as it pecked its way across the ground. *To us.*

How? Onyx cocked her head.

Demand it.

Avalkyra felt the press of magic behind the command as Onyx turned to the new strix, felt the hatchling's resistance break under the force. It bent. It bowed.

And then something changed. Another bond. A secondary bond,

funneling through Onyx to Avalkyra. And with it came power. It wasn't much, but with each new hatchling, with each show of subservience, her power would grow.

She was no longer a Phoenix Rider, and she wasn't just a Strix Rider either.

She was *apexaeris*—an Apex Rider, and this was only the beginning.

Queen Nefyra has borne many titles in her lifetime.

First, she was a tribal leader, ruling her people on Pyrmont's highest reaches.

Next, she was the world's first animage, first shadow-mage, and first *phoenixaeris*.

Nefyra, Rider of Ignix, soon became known as Nefyra Ashfire, the First Rider Queen.

She would become a wife, a lover, and a mother. A warrior. A *winner*.

But one title that receives little attention is that of *apexaeris*.

Nefyra was the world's first Phoenix Rider, yes, but she was also the world's first and only Apex Rider.

Being bonded to Ignix, the world's first phoenix (or *mundi apex phoenix* in ancient Pyraean), came with certain social and magical abilities. This status helped Nefyra to gain much of the power and notoriety—and yes, titles—that she accumulated in her lifetime, yet the term has all but disappeared from most biographies and historical accounts of her life.

It seems that, much like Ignix herself, that particular title has been lost to time.

—*Queen Nefyra: A Retrospective*, the Morian Archives, 100 AE

My mother was fire and light, warmth and life.
And so I was what she made me.

- CHAPTER 7 -
VERONYKA

VERONYKA WAS FALLING.

Her stomach clenched and her breath caught as she hurtled through the sky. Helplessness turned her body to lead, her vision to tears, and all she could hear was the roaring of the wind as the earth rushed toward her.

But then Xephyra was there, the ground was there, and all was still. All was safe.

No, that was wrong.

As if on cue, Val appeared across the grassy field, with Ignix standing between them.

Veronyka was dreaming again, dreaming of Ferro and the moment her own sister had dropped her to her death. She knew what happened next and had no desire to relive it.

"Val," she said, breaking from the memory and stepping into that smoky, incorporeal place.

Val didn't answer, and resisted Veronyka's attempt to stop the dream sequence. The image shifted in and out of focus for Veronyka, and words she had spoken weeks ago echoed in her mind, even as her body resisted speaking them.

"Val, enough . . . Val, leave her."

And then Val's eventual reply—spoken to Ignix, not to Veronyka. "You will obey me, or you will suffer my wrath."

Despite her efforts to end the vision, to leave the dream, Veronyka couldn't help but watch as the phoenix lifted her beak and spouted a torrent of flames into the sky.

When she turned away, Val was watching her. In a snap, the vision disappeared, and the world around them turned into a wall of gray, swirling and churning like they were trapped within a coil of smoke.

"I have never seen a phoenix do that before," Val said slowly, idly, though her eyes shone with intensity. "Have you?"

"That's no ordinary phoenix," Veronyka said, gesturing to the place where Ignix had been.

"What kind of phoenix is she?"

"She doesn't belong to you anymore, if that's what you mean," Veronyka said. Val must have conjured this dream to drill her on purpose, though how she'd done that, Veronyka had no idea. "I broke your bind. Her life is her own again."

"Whose life?"

What was this about? Was Val actually curious to know the identity of the phoenix she had so brutally commanded—the one that had thrown her from her back and scarred her for life?

Veronyka didn't intend to answer, but she recalled what Val had said to her ages ago about the breeding enclosure inside the Eyrie, and couldn't resist throwing it back in her face. "I don't know how you dared, when Ignix herself might be among them."

Much to Veronyka's dismay, Val grinned. "I knew it."

Veronyka pulled back, but as had happened the first time, Val clung to their connection. "Let me go."

"You sent her here, didn't you?"

"Sent her where?" Veronyka asked.

"To spy on me—you sent her. Tell me the truth," Val demanded, taking a step forward.

"I didn't send her anywhere!"

Another step. "Then where is she?"

Veronyka would rather bite off her tongue than admit she didn't know. "Somewhere you can't touch her," she snarled.

"We'll see about that."

ლ ლ ლ

She wrenched herself backward so hard, she hurled herself into wakefulness with enough force that she rolled over, directly into a warm, feathered body.

Xephyra. And next to her, Rex.

Veronyka had fallen asleep outside again, and while her breath puffed into the air, her skin was coated with sweat. The phoenixes were still asleep, but she sensed them stir enough to shift closer to her.

She ran a hand down Xephyra's feathers but did not wake her. Veronyka had not slept well lately—did she ever sleep well?—and one of the worst effects was the way it also ruined her bondmate's sleep.

She got to her feet and slipped inside Tristan's rooms, where she had been staying since taking over his patrol, and splashed cold water from the basin onto her face. She had tried to reach for him again last night—and again, she'd found herself in a vision with Val instead. Ever since she'd dropped her last mental barriers, she had been plagued by shadow magic dreams.

There were the usual ones—wisps of feelings and memories from the people sleeping nearby, or those she had spent time with that day. She knew, for example, that Latham had his eye on one of Morra's kitchen maids, while *she* spent most nights dreaming about one of the village girls who worked with Jana in the stables. Anders flirted with both girls, but it seemed he did so only to get a reaction out of Latham, and Veronyka didn't bother trying to unravel those tangled threads.

There were also the not-so-usual ones—the dreams she'd not had since Val slept by her side. Dreams from the past. Worse, they were stronger than ever before. Was this, too, an effect of Veronyka finally lowering her barriers, or was it something else?

Besides the increased ease and clarity, these dreams were also different in that the visions weren't from Val's point of view, as they had always been. They actually weren't Val's memories at all. They were *Veronyka's*.

And yet Val was always in them—both visually, in the dream, but also magically. They had these dreams *together*, even spoke to one another during them, but Veronyka couldn't figure out if she was the one making it happen or if it was the other way around. Val insisted Veronyka was the one to initiate their first connection, but tonight's dream felt intentional. There was purpose in their contact, in Val's actions and line of questioning. This memory had been the moment Val lost Veronyka, her political pawn and bargaining chip, as well as the plans she had built around her.

She had also lost her bindmate and had been wounded terribly in the process. Veronyka couldn't fathom what Val's next move would be, but there was no way she would let Veronyka or Ignix off with what they had done to her. No, Val would make them pay. The question was when. And how.

The fact that she thought Veronyka had sent Ignix to spy on her showed that she believed their personal conflict was far from over.

Veronyka wasn't surprised that Val would fixate on Ignix after her perceived betrayal, but she was somewhat unnerved by the fact that Ignix had seemed rather fixated on Val too. Veronyka hadn't forgotten Ignix's dire warning after she'd removed Val's bind.

Prepare yourself. Forget your human foes. The true battle will be fought not on the earth, but in the sky.

And then, most chilling of all . . . *Avalkyra lives, and she is hungry. Like the devourer before her, she can do naught but consume. The light will not have her, so she will turn to the darkness instead.*

What did it mean? Clearly, Ignix believed Val was turning dark, but she had only just met Val. Veronyka had known her for years, and the truth was, Val had always been dark. How much darker could she truly go? Even if she managed to actually hatch and bond to a phoenix, she was still only one person—two, if you counted Sidra—and it seemed like a distraction and a waste of time to think about her when there was so much going on with the empire.

Veronyka had to be careful. It was one thing to stop hiding and quite another to let curiosity get the better of her. Still, she *would* have asked Ignix more, if she could. She might have even sent the phoenix spying, as Val had accused, if she'd had the opportunity. Unfortunately, after making her foreboding proclamation, Ignix had disappeared. Even Sparrow had no idea where she'd gone or what she was doing.

For now, if she wanted to know what Val was up to, all Veronyka had was their shadow magic connection, and even that was dangerous and unpredictable. During the day, their bond was quiet, though Veronyka had to admit it was not the calm of peace. Rather, it felt like the calm before a storm, charged and ominous. And at night? Val was the same as always: threatening and enigmatic, familiar and strange.

Too much interest in Val was unsafe, Veronyka knew, but avoidance wasn't an option either. She had tried that, blocking out Val, alienating Tristan, and hiding her own identity, and it had all blown up in her face. She couldn't run away from who and what she was, because there was always someone nipping at her heels. If Veronyka didn't claim what she did not want, someone else would . . . someone worse.

It seemed a poor reason to do anything, but what other choice did she have? All she could do was trust herself, work on what she could control, and try to be ready for whatever she couldn't.

You're up, came a voice inside Veronyka's mind, startling her so badly that she knocked over the water pitcher. The pewter rattled loudly against the stone floor, and Veronyka pressed a hand to her chest.

But it wasn't Val; it was Morra.

Xephyra squawked in surprise at the noise, and Rex turned a heavy-lidded stare at Veronyka through the open door. His head had been wedged underneath Xephyra's wing, leaving his feather crest askew, like bedhead.

Sorry, she mouthed at him, picking up the pitcher and quietly returning it to the ledge.

She hesitated before replying to Morra, who would want to practice shadow magic—which was what Veronyka *should* be doing. It went hand in hand with trusting herself and working on what she could control. But the stakes were higher than ever, and there was a steep learning curve. Whether it was magic or politics, there was little room for error.

Especially since the stronger she made her magic, the more easily—and frequently—she'd be able to connect with Val . . . whether she willed it or not.

But if she got good enough, she might be able to reach Tristan, and that was worth the risk.

Yes, I'm up, she said to Morra, tugging on her clothes for the day. *Ready when you are.*

They had a Rider Council meeting that night. Veronyka, Cassian, and Beryk gathered two or three times a week, with Fallon and Darius attending sporadically, since they were posted at Prosperity. The sessions were usually brief, meant to address scheduling, training, and other mundane details of running the Eyrie, but there was also the issue of preparing for war—if in fact war came. This was a difficult thing to plan for, but the commander was organized and efficient, stockpiling weapons and ammunition, repairing and commissioning armor, and keeping a close watch on the happenings in the province and beyond. He had contacts all over the empire and in Pyra, too, and would share whatever news or gossip he gleaned.

He also shared whatever word he received from Sev. This was the stuff Veronyka was most desperate for, and though he hid it better, she knew the commander was just as anxious as she was every time a scroll arrived from their soldier-spy.

So far there hadn't been much to report besides Lord Rolan's—and therefore Sev's and Tristan's—relocation to Stel, but even though Sev's weekly assurances that they were both alive and well gave Veronyka a swelling wave of relief, the short-lived feeling was always followed by another week of intense frustration and impatience.

At least she was being included. Veronyka had spent most of her time here fighting for her voice to be heard and to know the full truth of what was happening—and that wasn't counting a lifetime of being underestimated and excluded by Val. Tristan, too, had struggled against his father for years, and it was strange to think that this was truly becoming *their* fight, *their* war. It no longer belonged to Cassian and Val and the older generation alone.

The excitement of being included, however, did wane over time. Much of the information shared was dull and filled with seemingly useless details, but it reminded Veronyka of her *maiora*, with her lockbox of scrap paper and scribbled notes. This kind of work required patience, the big picture revealing itself over time, and it wasn't immediately evident what would become important in the long run.

"It appears the Rushlean farmers are at it again," the commander said with a sigh, staring down at an unrolled piece of paper. Beryk extended a hand for it, and Cassian passed it over. "This time they attacked a shipment of supplies heading to the refugees rather than the refugees themselves. So I suppose that's something."

The farmers from Rushlea were unhappy with the Phoenix Riders—for drawing the empire soldiers into Pyra in the first place, which resulted in Rushlea being attacked and its fields burned, and for the further damages incurred when the Riders chased the soldiers off. By the time the Riders had established a refugee camp on the outskirts of their village, tensions were high. They'd officially boiled over on the anniversary of the end of the Blood War—Veronyka's own birthday—and resulted in a scuffle with Tristan's patrol.

Veronyka had thought that would be the end of it, but even after the Phoenix Riders left Rushlea, the farmers had continued to harass the refugees, blaming them—as well as the Riders—for a shortage of supplies for the coming winter and their general dissatisfaction with the current political climate. Their numbers had swelled since that run-in weeks ago, and they had begun to attack travelers on the roads, stealing shipments of supplies, and generally acting more like lawless brigands than simple farming folk.

"We'll have to send a patrol," Beryk said, scratching his stubbled chin.

"Do you think this has anything to do with the uptick in raiding that Fallon reported?" Veronyka asked.

"Unlikely," the commander said. "There is always an increase in such criminal activity as the colder months approach, when game is scarce and travel less frequent. They want to strike now, before the heaviest rains hit and the river floods the road."

Veronyka searched the stack of correspondence until she found Fallon's most recent letter. "But what he describes . . . They aren't just assaulting travelers and traders along the road. There have been several attacks by large, organized groups, and they're targeting villages."

Houses on the outskirts of Vayle had been robbed and ransacked the previous week, and Petratec's fishing boats had been stolen or sunk.

"I agree that they are behaving with more focused desperation than we're used to, but they still appear to be random attacks."

"They're not random . . . ," Veronyka said, thinking aloud. "What do Vayle and Petratec have in common? Us." They'd had frequent dealings with both villages, and Rushlea had been a source of trouble and unrest for weeks now. All three were places the Phoenix Riders were known to have ties.

The commander pursed his lips. She sensed that he wanted to dismiss her concerns—either to reinforce the aura of calm and control he loved to cultivate or to reestablish his position in charge. She saw when he remembered who she was, the flicker of frustration behind his eyes. Like he'd forgotten he had to remain a politician even here, with his own subordinates—that he had to toe the line and play the part, hoping that part wouldn't be snatched away from him at any moment.

"What do you think we should do?" Veronyka asked quickly, turning her comments into a question—deferring to his experience and expertise. It was a small thing, a tiny redirection of the conversation, but she saw his acknowledgment of it.

He wasn't the only one reestablishing boundaries and behaviors.

Veronyka, too, was learning how to be a leader—to make people feel trusted and reassured without lying to them. To ask important questions without undermining, to show her concern without causing panic. It was, frankly, exhausting, and she admired Commander Cassian for how well he pulled it off, even if they did disagree on occasion. Then again, he'd been born into this role, expecting to lead one day, and in turn, expecting others to follow him. Veronyka, meanwhile, was in a constant state of playing catch-up.

"I think Beryk's right—we'll need to send a patrol. Once we're on the ground, we'll have a better chance at determining whether these are normal, isolated incidents or part of a greater concern."

Veronyka smiled, impressed. Gracious. Diplomatic. And still in control. He'd nailed it.

"Why don't you check it out?" he finished, turning to Veronyka.

Her smile faltered, panic seizing her throat. "B-but Tristan—the Grand Council—"

"Nothing will happen without you. As soon as I hear anything that we can move on, I'll send you a pigeon."

"A Rider," Veronyka countered. A phoenix was faster than any pigeon.

He hesitated for a fraction of a second, then nodded. "A Rider, then."

After Veronyka told the rest of her patrol of their mission and they readied for an early-morning departure, she returned to the commander's study. She meant to ask if they had any supplies to deliver, but he wasn't there—probably in the dining hall for a late dinner.

She wandered into his library, intending to wait for him, but found herself perusing the shelves instead. Dozens of books on kings and queens . . . but nothing about *how* to rule. No one to show her the way.

Maybe that was for the best. She'd had Val, after all . . . and it was safe to say that her advice should be taken with a grain of salt. Val's own mother died in childbirth, and Lania, Pheronia's mother, was another poor example. Maybe finding her own path *was* the only way.

Could Veronyka do it? Could she be a queen?

Or could she fight hard enough and live long enough to ensure that Val never did? Could she be a barrier, an obstacle, but never actually take the mantle for herself?

"Veronyka," came a voice from the doorway, making her jump. It was the commander, returned from his evening meal. "Are you here to resume our lessons?"

Several times a week, Veronyka and the commander holed up in his library to study history, politics, and statecraft. It had started by accident, with Veronyka wandering the shelves—much like she was now—somewhat at a loss, clutching at books and aimlessly seeking answers. He had first made recommendations, then provided supplementary reading, and before long, was sitting with her, discussing all manner of subjects relating to the empire, the Phoenix Riders, and their place within it.

It was no more than part of a well-rounded upper-class education, but they both knew these subjects had the potential to have a far greater bearing on her life in the future. A future that was coming both too quickly and not quickly enough.

They had studied the previous night, however, and rarely did back-to-back sessions.

Veronyka shook her head. "No. I just wanted to ask if you needed any supplies delivered tomorrow."

He nodded. "I believe Beryk is handling it."

"Okay," Veronyka said, but she didn't move. There was nothing else to do for the day, which meant it was time for sleep. And Veronyka didn't want to face the quiet of the stronghold or the noise inside her mind. She didn't want to face the lack of Tristan and the presence of Val.

The commander leaned against the doorframe. His eyes were very like Tristan's in color and shape, but always colder and more distant. Now they raked over her with a sharper, more focused attention than she was used to. "How are you feeling?"

"What do you mean?" she asked warily. Despite their frequent conversations and their lessons, they never discussed how Veronyka *felt* about any of it.

"Besides the brewing war with the empire and the threat posed by your resurrected sister-aunt, there's the looming Grand Council meeting, the deal with Lord Rolan that promises you as his bride in exchange for my son—a person you care deeply for—oh, and that's not considering the fact of your identity and how it will shape your present and your future. What I mean is, I imagine you're feeling a bit, uh . . . overwhelmed."

Veronyka blew out her cheeks. "How can you tell?"

He smiled gently. "You're gripping that book like it holds the answers to all the questions in the universe. But it doesn't, I can promise you."

Veronyka looked down in surprise. She did indeed have a clawlike grip on one of his Ashfire history books. She gave a shaky laugh and released the leather-bound volume. The truth was, most days Veronyka felt like she was hanging on by a thread. She was trying to do everything right, to work as hard as she could, but sometimes she felt like she had nothing left to give.

"I am a bit tired."

He barked out a laugh. "A bit?"

Veronyka smiled, then scrubbed at her face. It had been days since she'd had some decent sleep—and only complete and utter exhaustion did the trick. If things didn't change, if she didn't save Tristan soon . . . She didn't know how much longer she could stand it.

The commander cleared his throat. Veronyka looked up at him and realized she must look and sound truly pathetic, for he wore a soft, almost regretful expression when he spoke.

"For the record, I think you're handling things remarkably well."

That struck a chord inside Veronyka—getting his approval was important to her. Not just as her commander, but as his son's father.

"Tristan would have thrown a fit by now," he said then, his tone lighter. "He would have raged at me, to be sure, and broken something too."

Veronyka's lips twitched. "The raging, maybe . . . but I'm not sure he'd break anything."

"No," the commander agreed. "He doesn't pull those kinds of stunts anymore. Not since you."

She swallowed thickly, blinking away sudden prickling moisture in her eyes. It sounded like praise, though she wasn't sure exactly why. Tristan was wonderful on his own. It had nothing to do with her.

"He's become a man all of a sudden, and you've been a good influence on him. He's been lucky to have you."

An edge of unease crept into her heart at his words. He made it sound like past tense, like something that was already over. Like their time together couldn't last—and she thought she knew why. She was an Ashfire, heir to the throne, and with that came certain . . . expectations.

Hadn't they already addressed this?

Almost as soon as they'd returned to the Eyrie, Veronyka had made it plain that she wouldn't marry Rolan—and Commander Cassian had completely agreed. He had called it a poor political move to hitch her wagon to a man making a violent bid for the throne when it was hers by right anyway. Plus, they intended to rescue Tristan and betray their agreement long before the question of following through on their promises would even matter.

Since she'd more or less gotten the answer she'd wanted out of him, she hadn't bothered to argue that it wasn't the "political move" that made her refuse with such venom. She didn't want to marry *anyone* as a political move. Once she came forward and revealed herself—which she would very likely need to do, in order to get the council under control—there would be other suitors. She didn't flatter herself that they'd line up for her because she was some rare beauty. . . . They'd line up because of the title, the power, and the position that was at stake.

Did Cassian assume she'd feel obligated to make some other match, even if it wasn't Rolan?

No. Her mother had resisted it, and she would too. Of course, her mother had also died in a war she'd been unable to stop.

There had to be another way to secure peace. Tristan was the only person she wanted. They were magically bound, and so were their phoenixes. Plus, he had cared for her before he'd known who she was. In fact, that statement was true on multiple fronts. He'd liked her as Nyk the stable boy, as Veronyka the poor apprentice, and even now, as the Ashfire heir.

"He'll always have me," Veronyka said. She would not be a pawn in the moves and machinations of others.

"Then he is truly lucky indeed," the commander said quietly. He turned to go, but Veronyka stopped him.

"Commander?" He waited as Veronyka searched for the words. "Do you think it's possible . . . ? Could the empire survive without a king or queen?"

She was impressed by his self-control. The question was so obviously personal and hugely relevant to them all, but he didn't fix her with a panicked stare or immediately try to talk her down. He took his time considering her question, as if this were up for a philosophical debate and not Veronyka asking for advice.

"Yes," he said, surprising her. "Though it's not as simple as that. The throne would always be a lure to those who seek power."

"Of course," Veronyka said softly, though she didn't truly understand that desire. Power wasn't something she'd ever wanted—at least, not on such a scale. She'd wanted the power to protect herself and others . . . and she supposed that's exactly what the throne was, if in the right hands. But in the wrong hands, it was an excuse for more fighting, and the reason for more war. "I know it can't be Val," she said quickly. Better Veronyka than her, despite her reservations. "But if we make it through this war, if she's no longer a threat"—Veronyka tried not to think what that might actually mean—"could the Ashfires just . . . fade away?"

"Maybe," he conceded, his voice strangely melancholy. Not the raw, personal sadness of true grief or loss, but something closer to regret. "Though there would be hurdles. If we manage to neutralize Rolan and his cohorts, the council would be on more even footing. But it would always be an uphill battle, even for simple things like opening the borders to Pyra and reestablishing basic animage rights."

"I see," Veronyka said, wilting slightly.

"I understand your reticence," he said kindly. "I myself have thought long and hard about how the empire might function without such an institution. It was thanks to a bad queen that the empire was torn apart in the first place." Veronyka nodded, the whole thing feeling impossible and insurmountable. "But a good queen?" He smiled, dimples flashing so he looked more like his son than ever before. "She might be able to piece it back together again."

*But my mother had a sister, and she was darkness and
shadow, cold and hunger. She knew my father too,
and had children of her own.*

- CHAPTER 8 -
TRISTAN

WHEN TRISTAN SENT SEV in search of the governor's library and
household records, he'd expected the task to take several days—if it happened at all—and that it might be even longer until he spoke to Sev again
and learned what he had discovered.

What he *hadn't* expected was to see Sev the very next night *with* the
builder's plans in hand and *without* Tristan's usual guard in place. It was the
overnight shift, and Mal and Ian were nowhere in sight.

Tristan stood, peering out into the empty hallway. "Did you . . . ?" he
began, his throat a bit rough from another day of no talking. He swallowed
and tried again. "Did you kill them after all?"

Sev smiled, and it was a somewhat chilling sight—until he spoke. "Mal
and Ian are safe in their beds—and breathing."

"But how?"

Sev gave a familiar, crooked shrug. "I have friends in high places."

"How high?" Tristan asked dubiously. "Does Rolan know you're here?"

"No, he does not," Sev said with a firm shake of his head. "Actually, I
thought he'd be visiting you himself from time to time, considering who
your father is. . . ."

Tristan snorted. "And their past."

He gave Sev a quick rundown on the background of his father and Rolan's relationship, in case it helped Sev to better understand Rolan and figure out his next moves. But as Tristan spoke, all he could think about was how petty and incompetent the man was. He was more than happy to make Tristan and Veronyka—and Pyra and the empire, for that matter—suffer for not only the supposed sins of their parents, but the sins of their distant ancestors as well. It was absurd. Worse was the way he handled his business. He just barked out orders and let other people handle his dirty work—like imprisoning a thirteen-year-old girl just to have leverage over her father, or letting Val capture and coerce Veronyka into a betrothal. Thus far, Tristan had received similar treatment—locked away, out of sight, while Rolan busied himself with his more *legitimate* political maneuvers.

Sev whistled softly. "He definitely hasn't forgotten about you, that's for sure. I guess he's just got more pressing things on his mind."

"Like forcing Veronyka into marrying him and overthrowing the empire?" Tristan asked, his tone scathing.

"Exactly," Sev said, but then his gaze turned appraising, and Tristan suspected he saw more than Tristan wanted him to. "We won't let that happen," he added quietly.

Tristan was surprised at the emotion rising up his throat. He knew the deal with Rolan—the one that promised him Veronyka and Phoenix Rider support in his bid for the throne in exchange for Tristan and the freedom of animages in Rolan's new empire—was one the commander had had to make. He also knew, thanks to Sev, that they intended to try to free Tristan before such a deal could be acted upon. *But* . . . no one had said to Tristan outright that Veronyka *would not have to go through with it*. No one had promised it would not happen. Tristan knew Sev spoke for himself, not the commander, but it meant something to hear the words anyway.

Because there was no guarantee that things would go the way they wanted them to, and when push came to shove, his father might have to choose. The wishes of his son and the girl he loved over the good of every

Phoenix Rider under his command? Could he walk away from the promise and the power of an Ashfire bride?

Tristan couldn't voice all those fears, so instead he simply said, "We might fail."

"We might," Sev conceded. "But, I mean . . . she's an *Ashfire*," he said, sounding half-shocked, half-reverent. Tristan understood that feeling intimately. "I'm pretty sure she's going to do what she wants. And marrying Rolan isn't it."

Tristan actually smiled. Sev was probably right. Veronyka wasn't afraid of his father the way *he* was. She wasn't afraid of anything.

Sev lifted the rolled-up papers he held in his hand. "Once we get you out of here, he'll no longer have you as a hostage. She'll have no reason to even pretend."

Tristan nodded again—kept nodding over and over, staring unseeing at the document Sev handed him, the weight on his heart refusing to lift.

"If it meant protecting people . . ." Tristan thought of the battlefield they'd flown over on the way to Ferro, the devastation Veronyka and Avalkyra had wrought in order to save the animages held captive by Lord Rolan's soldiers. Tristan wasn't sure what Veronyka would and wouldn't do anymore, but he thought that saving innocent people's lives would be reason enough for her to risk almost anything.

When he didn't finish his thought, Sev nodded down at the piece of paper in Tristan's hand. As he unrolled it, Sev disappeared down the hall, his return heralded by a growing glow of lantern light.

Tristan laid the paper out on the cold stone floor, kneeling next to it and using the metal cup and plate from his dinner tray to hold the curling corners in place.

Sev put the lantern on the ground next to him as he sat, while Tristan leaned back on his heels and took in the floor plan. It showed the entire eastern wing of Rolan's estate, divided into three floors, including the dungeon.

"The renovations match the layout and exact dimensions of the upper floors," Sev began, indicating the top two schematics. "They're accurate down to the number of floor tiles used per room. But the basement . . ." He trailed off, frowning. "It doesn't match. This hallway," he continued, leaning back to indicate where he now sat. "It should extend beyond this cell, past *two more cells*, before wrapping around the north side of the building and leading to an additional exit. But as you can see . . ."

Tristan followed Sev's gaze, but he already knew what was there—the hallway ended right after his cell bars with a blank gray wall. No windows or doorways. Nothing but the same rough-hewn stone that surrounded him on all sides except for the barred opening between him and freedom.

"I don't know what's back there or why he walled it off, because the door on these plans doesn't exist on the outside, either, as far as I can tell. Obviously Rolan made more renovations after this, or else changed the initial plans and forgot to update the records. . . ."

"Maybe," Tristan said, frowning first at the wall and then down at the plans. "Or maybe he did it on purpose."

"Did what on purpose?" Sev asked. "Not update the records?"

"Or never created any to begin with. Stel used to be made up of at least thirteen different kingdoms, and they were always warring with each other. Assassinations and subterfuges happened practically every other day. The kings became increasingly paranoid and secretive—about their plans, their alliances. . . ."

"And their home renovations?"

Tristan smiled. "In a word, yes. King Hal actually built an entire decoy castle where a decoy king sat on the throne, and I think it was King Orl who had his home built like a labyrinth and then had the architect killed after it was complete so no one would know the way through but him."

Sev looked bewildered, but he recovered quickly enough. "So you're saying that Rolan did this on purpose so that someone like me wouldn't be able to discover the layout and free his precious prisoners?"

"It's more likely than the alternative. Even if they did make additional renovations, this layout doesn't make sense. Whatever weird setup he might have wanted down here, there should always be two exits in a belowground structure."

"In case of collapse?" Sev asked.

"During construction, for sure. But also . . . in case of fire."

Tristan had, unsurprisingly, become well versed in fire safety over the years.

Ever since the time he'd nearly set his father's study ablaze, Tristan had begun to wonder what he would have done if that servant *hadn't* rushed in and stamped out the burning rug. There had been large windows, an obvious choice for escape—or so he'd thought, until he'd learned that oxygen fed a fire, and throwing open the shutters would likely have sealed his fate even more quickly than the ancient, flammable rug could have done on its own. But the thickly woven curtains beside the windows? They could have stifled the fire, *if* he had the guts to approach the growing, licking, consuming flames.

The easiest option would have been to move his frozen feet and run for the door, but what if the exit had been blocked? Tristan started paying more attention to his surroundings after that. Every time he entered a room, he noted all the windows and doors, monitored crowded spaces, and picked out clear paths. When his tutors taught him about art and architecture, Tristan paid particular attention to building codes and floor plans.

When he and his father moved in with his cousin Lysandro's family, they were forced to live in the basement so they could hide in case soldiers came. That development led Tristan into a rather panicky redesign of the belowground chambers, locating a secondary door and ensuring their boxes of possessions were well out of the way in case they needed to make a hasty exit—because of the soldiers, he'd assured his father, who still did not know of Tristan's terrible fear of fire, and never would if Tristan had his way.

Sev sighed. "Unless I can find a way behind that wall or discover some concealed doorway, these plans are all we have. And they're not much use if they're wrong."

Tristan's instinct was to fight his way out, but not every problem could be solved with anger and physicality. He tried to channel his father instead, the man who had a plan for everything, who used his wits and his cunning to make other people do what he wanted them to do. The man whose endless patience made Tristan want to break something, but who could also strategize and outmaneuver the best of them.

"Tell me about this high-placed friend of yours."

Tristan had been extremely impressed to learn that Sev's ally was one of Rolan's own captains—and the person in charge of the prison wing itself.

Rather than focusing on sneaking around or understanding Rolan's bizarre dungeon layout, they turned their attention to the floors above. They couldn't act without coordinating with their Phoenix Rider associates, but they could sort out when the best time of day to escape was, which soldiers would need to be taken out or discreetly relocated, and how long Tristan's absence could go unnoticed.

They couldn't control everything—Captain Yara had authority only over the prison wing and not the entire estate—but they could still work whatever advantages her position gave them. She also had access to information that Sev would have to beg, borrow, and steal to attain.

"Our best chance would be at nighttime, during my shift, obviously," Sev said. It was the following night, and he was seated on the floor outside Tristan's cell again, a lantern next to him and another roll of paper—this time the guard positions and schedule—laid out in front of Tristan on the opposite side.

Tristan nodded. "The phoenixes will be invisible in the dark, and the ideal place for a pickup would be the roof, but we'd have to get there first."

"Getting you up to the roof unseen might be harder than getting you out the front door," Sev said, leaning back and stretching out his legs. "We'd pass more soldiers that way, at any rate."

Tristan opened his mouth to reply when the scuffing sound of boots on stone told him they had an unexpected visitor. He snatched at the papers and lunged to stuff them under the corner of his mattress while

Sev lurched to his feet, accidentally kicking over the lantern.

It rolled onto its side and into the wall that was proving the bane of their existence. The stone was obviously not flammable, but Tristan's heart clenched so tightly it was like a fist had reached into his chest and squeezed.

"Teyke's *cat*," Sev cursed, leaping for the lantern and hastily uprighting it. The flames left a smear of soot against the stone, but otherwise there was no damage. No cause for fear or alarm.

Tell that to the sweat dripping down Tristan's back. Tell that to the pulse hammering in his veins.

"Felix," Tristan muttered, his mind disassociating from his body.

"What?" Sev hissed.

"Teyke's cat is called Felix." It was a fact, a truth—something to cling to when his thoughts barreled out of control. "It means lucky."

Sev looked at him like he'd gone mad, but before he could reply, their visitor appeared.

"No need to stand on ceremony," said a woman in her forties with scars across her face and neck. *Burn* scars. Tristan swallowed.

"Captain Yara," Sev said, voice faint with relief. So this was his friend in a high place. The person who was helping get Tristan out of this cell. Her cool gaze flicked over him before returning to Sev.

"I've got updates, soldier," she said. "Lord Rolan is about to be on the move."

"Tell me," Sev said eagerly.

"*I* didn't hear anything. Lord Rolan had a meeting with his advisers yesterday, but I was not a part of it," she said stiffly, and Tristan frowned at that. As a captain, she should be apprised of the governor's plans and preparations, especially if she was to be involved in organizing protections and escorts. Rolan was obviously a secretive man, but Tristan couldn't help but wonder if he knew or suspected he had a spy in his midst.

"Then how did you . . . ?" Sev began, but he trailed off, grinning. "I knew she'd be of use."

"Who?" Tristan asked, but then more footsteps heralded the arrival of another visitor. She was older than Yara, gray hair drawn back from her face in a tight bun, but her posture was straight and her eyes sharp.

She turned to Tristan, and he was hit by a shock of recognition. Distant memories from his childhood reared up as the woman approached the bars.

"It's amazing what a man will talk about when he thinks there are only servants afoot," the woman said, speaking to the others. Then her full attention settled on Tristan. She smiled. "Goodness, you've grown. You're the spitting image of him."

"M-my father?" Tristan asked uncertainly.

She shook her head, gaze wistful. "Lucian, your grandfather. It's a shame you never knew him."

Then Tristan remembered—this woman had been a healer at the governor's estate in Ferro back when Tristan's family still lived there. They had left that house when he was young, but she and some of the other servants had traveled with them to one of his family's other properties in the wake of the war. That was when his mother was still alive. They'd eventually had to leave that home as well after his mother's death and his father's exile, and that time, none of their servants could go with them.

Still, he remembered her, a calming figure pressing a cool cloth to his feverish forehead or bandaging his scraped knees.

"Hestia," he croaked, and she beamed. He was a bit overwhelmed at what she was doing, working against her current employer for the benefit of her former. Then he remembered that Hestia's sons had died in the last war. Of course she did not want another conflict.

"What did you overhear?" Sev asked, bringing the conversation back to the topic at hand.

Hestia turned. "Lord Rolan is departing in five days. And he isn't the only one." She nodded at Tristan. "Rolan is traveling to Qorlland City to try his hand at recruiting some of the southern lords and ladies to his side. After that, he'll no doubt make for Aura Nova, as he mentioned no immediate plans of returning to the estate. When he departs for the south, his highly valuable prisoner will head north to an old fortress in the Spine."

Tristan's heart sank—they'd been having a hard enough time finding a way out of some rich lord's house. How on earth would they get him out of a fortified stronghold?

Sev saw his expression and stepped forward into the lantern light. He was smiling. "You're thinking about it the wrong way," he said, as if he could read Tristan's thoughts. "We don't need to get you out of the castle—we have to make sure you never arrive."

"An ambush," Tristan said, voice hushed even though his heart was galloping in his chest. "There's no better place for a Phoenix Rider to attack than in open space. It's perfect."

"We'll have to find out the exact route they plan to take so that we can coordinate with your . . . other associates," Yara said.

Tristan guessed that her burns hadn't happened in a house fire. He wondered why she was helping him at all.

"And I'll need to get on escort duty," Sev added, and Yara nodded her agreement. "In the meantime, I've got a letter to send."

Good King Orl—or Orl the Odious, as he was later dubbed by his sister and heir—ruled over the kingdom of Qorlland from his seat of power, the infamous labyrinthine castle of Orlmoat.

When construction commenced, it was initially met with much excitement and interest in the kingdom. Qorlland had recently expanded their territory by conquering the nearby kingdom of Tulland, which made its wealth along the river. The castle, built on the once-border between the kingdoms, was seen as a unifying gesture. Indeed, King Orl hired Tulland workers to build the structure, Tulland watermen to design the moat and fill it with flesh-eating fish, and he even hired his brother-in-law, a Tulland architect who had recently married his younger sister, Ilona, to engineer the labyrinth that would be its primary feature.

All was well during the ten-year construction, and King Orl celebrated its completion with a grand feast for all who had had a hand in building it.

And come morning, every one of them was dead.

Perhaps unsurprisingly, his sister, Ilona, did not take kindly to having her husband murdered, and likewise, the Tullanese people within Qorlland began to rebel. King Orl now needed his over-the-top safety measures more than ever, retreating deeper and deeper inside Orlmoat until it was said he rarely left the labyrinth's center and insisted on being holed up there alone with mountains of food and wine.

While the cause of his death is unclear, some sources suggesting asphyxiation or heart attack, what *is* clear is that the only living person who knew the way through the labyrinth was his sister, who eventually found his body some days—or possibly weeks—later. She had been busy taking his kingdom from him while he lived in isolation, and so the revelation of the dead king's body was a simple formality in ensuring her ascension to the throne.

It is said she fed his corpse to the flesh-eating fish in his very own moat and gave the families of the dead his bones—as well as whatever golden rings, jeweled earrings, and other extravagant ornamentation remained on his person—as recompense.

—"The Curious Case of Stellan Architecture: Decoys, Death, and Dismemberment," from *Stellan Art and Culture*, by Olbek, High Priest of Mori, published 129 AE

We were the first of our kind: apexes each.
Opposites, echoes, and evenly matched.

- CHAPTER 9 -

VERONYKA

VERONYKA AND THE REST of Tristan's patrol stayed in Rushlea for several days.

Since they were a Rider short, Doriyan accompanied them—not only was he without a patrol of his own, but he was from Rushlea, and so knew the town and the people better than any of them. It also helped to have someone with a bit of age and experience on hand, since the oldest person on Tristan's patrol was Ronyn at nineteen.

Veronyka was glad to have him. He'd done dozens of similar missions in his lifetime, and considering that their last encounter with the farmers had involved threats and assault, it was clear they needed all the help they could get.

Still, he let Veronyka take the lead.

"What would you like us to do?" he'd asked as they'd landed outside the village proper, temporarily taking the role of her second-in-command. He looked much better than he had when Veronyka had first met him—no longer wild-eyed with matted hair and a scraggly beard, but calm and clean-shaven.

Despite those improvements, something of the manic agitation she recalled resurfaced whenever they were together, and Veronyka had to admit she felt some of the same unease. He had been there the night she was born, had helped Ilithya Shadowheart spirit her away from her own father. Veronyka knew he wasn't truly to blame, that he'd been following orders—both magical and otherwise—and it had been wartime. He was hardly the only person to do something he regretted.

He'd also been told to hunt down and kill her father, which he had *not* done. That counted for something in Veronyka's books, even if it didn't count for much with her aunt. Alexiya had grilled him before departing to search for her brother—Veronyka's father—and had made it plain that she saw Doriyan as Avalkyra Ashfire's bootlicker and no more.

Veronyka knew it was more complicated than that. Her shadow magic allowed her to feel his remorse, his heartbreak—his own self-disgust. And his dreams? They were some of the worst she'd ever endured.

Besides, he was trying, which was more than Veronyka could say for the other surviving member of Avalkyra Ashfire's patrol. Sidra hadn't been seen since she'd swooped in to scoop up a savagely burnt Val and fly her to safety, but it was clear that while Doriyan regretted and was attempting to atone for what he had done, Sidra felt no such need. She was the true bootlicker, and Veronyka suspected wherever she was and whatever she was doing, it was on Val's orders.

Veronyka had considered how to approach things on the flight over and found herself thinking back to their time in Vayle after the empire's attacks had left the village damaged and the bridge destroyed.

"I'll call a town meeting to field questions and complaints," she said, remembering how Tristan had handled things. "Hopefully, we'll get a fuller picture of what's been happening and let the villagers know they're being heard. In the meantime, the rest of you will distribute the supplies we've brought and help in any way you can—repairs, cleanup, whatever they need." Doriyan nodded and moved to join the others, but Veronyka called after him. "I'd like you to join me."

Lysandro's gaze flickered—he was their unofficial clerk and correspondent, managing the messenger pigeons, sending letters, and taking notes at meetings. He had also accompanied Tristan in Vayle when he'd done the very same thing Veronyka was doing now.

However, she wanted a read on the people in the room more than she wanted a detailed record of what they said. She needed to know if they were afraid, angry, or resentful, and Doriyan was familiar with them. She had to nip any discontent in the bud and win them over—to the Phoenix Rider cause, yes, but also to her own. They didn't know who she was, but someday they might. And if Veronyka claimed the throne, she'd need Pyra's support.

She was proving herself everywhere she went, with every action and word. It was a daunting thing to think about until she considered how she'd already done it before.

When she'd first met Tristan, he had actively disliked her—and she'd won him over, had she not? It wasn't about tricks or deceptions. It was about showing them who she was and what she stood for. She had to prove that she was different from Avalkyra Ashfire—the renegade queen hell-bent on war—to everyone else, and also to herself.

"Lysandro," she added, before he could turn away. "I need you to pay attention to everything people are saying *outside* the meeting. There will be those who think the meeting is useless and want nothing to do with us. They'll be hardest to please—and potential allies of the farmers." He seemed surprised to be singled out but listened carefully to her orders. "I'd like a brief summary later—just the major points."

He nodded, chin high, any sense of being looked over or forgotten evaporating. Not only had she asked him to do something important, but she was trusting him to sift through what he found to give her what *he* deemed valuable. While Ronyn was oldest, Lysandro was youngest on the patrol. He was nearly as desperate to prove himself as Veronyka.

Like he had with her patrol, Doriyan followed her lead with the villagers, speaking up only when he had information to offer or insight that might help Veronyka better understand the situation. The meeting had been long and exhausting—and so well attended they'd had to hold a second one the following day.

It became clear fairly quickly that it wasn't only the farmers who were unhappy—or who were causing trouble for the villagers. Without proper government or military, the Pilgrimage Road was always dangerous to travel, whether alone or with wagons filled with wares. There was no one to protect civilians, and no laws to be upheld in the first place. But as Fallon had reported, coordinated attacks were happening all across Pyra, not just on the road. Supplies, winter stores—even livestock—were being stolen, and anyone who dared object was met with anger and violence.

"They call themselves the Unnamed," one of the villagers explained on the second day of their town-wide meetings. "They carved it into my fence post."

"I thought it was the Un*tamed*?" said another.

"Suppose it could be either," the first villager said dryly. "Their penmanship left something to be desired."

"It's the Unnamed," said Doriyan.

Veronyka turned. "You've heard of them before?"

"Rumors," he said with a shrug. "Ran into a handful of raider types months ago outside Petratec. Claimed to be 'nameless' when I asked who they were and 'homeless' when I asked where they were from."

"Close enough," Veronyka muttered. If they'd taken a name—or, she supposed, the deliberate lack of one—then it seemed they had indeed banded together in a larger sense.

"It's hard to know if they are related, but the Unnamed were an organized resistance to Ashfire rule in Pyra centuries ago," he continued. "Some said they were the remnants of the Lowland civilization, rallying together for another attempt to seize control. All they managed to do was attack travelers and make the poor *poorer*, and eventually their revolt was put down. Still, judging by the reports coming in . . . this behavior is much the same."

"Is that what they want, then? To rule Pyra? Or to take rule from us, the Phoenix Riders?"

"I suspect their interest is in a *lack* of rule," Doriyan clarified. "They might pretend at high ideals—and certainly some of their supporters could actually hold to them—but they are, at the end of the day, criminals robbing civilians. What they want is the ability to continue to do so without obstruction."

"So they don't want us here, but they don't want the empire here either," Veronyka said, and Doriyan inclined his head.

The farmers who'd accosted Tristan's patrol roughly two months back had had legitimate complaints, and she could hardly blame them for their anti–Phoenix Rider and anti-empire stance. The problem was that they were taking out their frustration on the innocent people of Pyra. Perhaps the Unnamed had more grievances against the province as a whole than the small faction of farmers, but until they turned up somewhere and made accusations—or demands—Veronyka would be unlikely to know.

What she did know was that while the Unnamed didn't want war with the empire, they didn't want peace, either. They didn't want to open their borders and welcome an influx of travelers and trade—and the soldiers that would come with them. They wanted their independence, and Commander Cassian's flock was just another government to them, his Riders just another kind of soldier leaving fire and death everywhere they went.

And they weren't wrong.

Veronyka realized that even her wildest dreams—no war, peace with the empire, and freedom for animages and Phoenix Riders alike—weren't perfect. Whatever the farmers wanted to believe, Pyra couldn't stand on its own. It needed to be unified with the empire again. It needed the infrastructure, the trade, and yes, the soldiers to enforce laws and make the roads safe. Only then could it truly thrive again, but with Pyra itself divided, there was no one solution to make everyone happy.

Veronyka hoped they could talk sense into the farmers' faction, but she didn't know how to convince them—her first problem being that they were nowhere to be found.

As for the road and the villages under threat, there wasn't much the Riders could do. They didn't have the numbers to post permanent patrols, and Veronyka feared that might exacerbate the problem anyway.

It was sunset when Veronyka and Doriyan emerged from their final meeting with the villagers. They joined the rest of her patrol—finishing their cleanup tasks for the day—before returning to camp.

They'd set up in the same place they had camped together in the summer . . . except this time, Tristan wasn't here.

An ache started building in Veronyka's chest. This was the place where she'd abandoned him, and it had ultimately led to his imprisonment. And before that, it had led to hers and Xephyra's.

She'd made so many mistakes—grave, terrible mistakes—and it was hard not to hate herself for them. To lose all confidence. How could she hope to be a queen, to rule over and protect an entire empire, when she couldn't even keep herself and her dearest loved ones safe?

She thought of Val, of the fact that every time Veronyka tried to embrace her power, her identity, it always meant facing her sister again. In the world and even in her dreams.

It's okay, Xephyra said.

Veronyka was sitting on the ground, pulling up fistfuls of grass and dirt under the same tree where she and Tristan had shared their first kiss. Xephyra loomed over her, visible in the twilight through the now-bare branches of the gnarled tree. The rest of her patrol were down the slope, seated around the fire.

Veronyka shook her head. *It's not okay. I hurt him. I hurt you—both of you,* she added, nodding at Rex, who stood just behind. The commander had allowed Veronyka to bring him, after she'd argued that patrol members— whether human or phoenix—should stay together as much as possible. For unity and flight patterns. For magic and morale.

For any and every reason she could think of, because she couldn't bear the idea of leaving him behind.

Xephyra huffed, tossing Rex an exasperated look before facing down her bondmate once again. *Not the boss.*

Veronyka sighed. She regretted teaching Xephyra that word. It had started when she'd called Xephyra "bossy" for ordering around some of the younger phoenixes; then it had devolved into a long conversation about semantics. Rex had eventually flown away out of boredom.

No, Veronyka conceded. *Not the boss. But I am your bondmate. I have your trust, and I shouldn't have made such a mistake.*

Xephyra shook her head, but it was Rex who spoke.

Not how trust works. Trust not . . . He struggled for the word, but it was Xephyra who found it.

Conditional, she said proudly. Veronyka realized her phoenix was fast becoming a know-it-all.

Rex nodded fervently. *Tried to help people. Made mistake. Rex still trust. Tristan still trust.*

Those words twisted in Veronyka's stomach like a knife. Trust was a wonderful gift and a terrible burden. She had given Val her trust over and over again. . . . Was it *her* fault for bestowing it, or Val's for betraying it?

She recalled their first dream-conversation and what she'd said to Val: *I could have helped you . . . if you'd let me. If you'd trusted me in turn.*

But Val had never trusted her. She'd accepted Veronyka's vulnerability but refused to offer any of her own. *That* was the difference.

Veronyka gave as well as received—and so did Xephyra, and Tristan, and Rex. All she could do was try to be worthy.

Come on, you two, she said, getting to her feet. *Let's go for a fly.*

Sometimes it felt almost selfish or indulgent soaring through the air with *two* phoenixes, the stars glittering above and the world rolling out below. But even though it always made Veronyka feel better, she knew it made Rex and Xephyra feel better too.

Lately she was able to feel Rex's emotions almost as easily as Xephyra's, and the satisfaction that surged through him during their flight told her that she gave him something he was sorely missing.

Veronyka wasn't Tristan, but a part of him remained inside her, thanks to their bond, and Rex liked to be near her because of it. And, of course, she liked to be near him for the same reason. Tristan's presence felt stronger when they were together, as if their combined fragments were like puzzle pieces—once united, they were a more complete version of the whole.

And of course Xephyra was also a part of that, the four of them magically entangled in ways Veronyka was still struggling to understand, though she knew the term.

Mated pair.

Or, at least, that was where they were heading.

She sensed Rex and Xephyra sometimes, reaching for each other magically and physically—an echo or amplification of her own feelings for Tristan— and made sure to give them time alone. She was always there, of course, but she could withdraw. It wasn't the same as putting up blocks or barriers. . . . It was more like respectful boundaries.

But for tonight what they needed was to be together.

Veronyka let them dictate their speed and style, and they chose an easy pace with leisurely pumps of their wings, riding air currents and soaring smoothly across the sky. After riding a while in Xephyra's saddle, Veronyka walked across her bondmate's outstretched wing until she stepped onto Rex's wing instead, then settled onto Tristan's saddle.

Xephyra didn't mind, taking the opportunity to shake out her wings and roll lazily through the air without concern for her Rider. Veronyka usually split her time between them, but tonight she had something specific in mind.

It was late . . . late enough that wherever Tristan was, he was probably asleep. It was as good a time as any to try to connect with him, but she'd never tried it while riding Rex. Surely the magic that bound phoenix and Rider was most potent, most powerful, during flight? Maybe Veronyka could latch on to that, on to the piece of Tristan inside her that responded to Rex, and vice versa.

She shared her thoughts with Rex, and he settled his flight into a steady rhythm, opening himself to her and his bondmate.

Veronyka relaxed her mind and body, closing her eyes and running her hands absently along Rex's feathers. She breathed in and out, in and out, and then there was a second set of lungs, a second heartbeat.

Tristan? she whispered softly, not wanting to break the spell.

In and out. In and out.

There was something there, distant, but growing stronger.

Her breath hitched—she was losing it.

She clenched her eyes and stilled her body, trying to ground herself in the moment, in the connection.

She was on Rex's back, the wind in her hair, feathers under her fingertips.

Feathers, smooth to the touch. Silken to the touch. Icy to the touch . . . Veronyka reared back, but too late. Coldness had settled over her, and she knew that the heartbeat she'd felt, the breaths she'd shared, did not belong to Tristan at all.

This isn't a good time, Nyka, Val said distractedly. *I'm hunting.*

Veronyka bit back a curse. Despite her frustration, the words unsettled her. *Hunting who?* she asked warily.

Your little spy, of course.

This again? Did Val really think she'd sent Ignix after her? *I'm not spying on you! I don't care what you do.*

Val grinned; Veronyka could feel it as if her own lips were pulling back from her teeth. *I've heard you say this kind of thing before, Veronyka. You always come looking for me eventually.*

Veronyka thought of her disastrous mistake to follow Val to Ferro. *Not this time,* she said.

I guess we'll find out, won't we? Val's tone was dark and detached in a way that made unease coil in Veronyka's stomach. *We may see each other sooner than you think.*

Sooner than I want, Veronyka snapped back, but Val was already gone.

Veronyka shook her head. She had vowed to let go of Val, to embrace her power and leave the burden of her past behind, but it wasn't that simple. Val wasn't just her past; she was her present and, quite possibly, an obstacle to her future.

Xephyra nudged questioningly at Veronyka's mind: She could feel Val through their bond, but she couldn't fully follow their conversation. Val wasn't open enough for that.

Everything's okay, Veronyka said. Xephyra feared Val was close in the physical sense, which she wasn't.

Was she?

Veronyka cast her senses and her magic wide—but she felt nothing at all.

Destined to fight as our mothers fought.
Destined to destroy each other.

- CHAPTER 10 -

AVALKYRA

AVALKYRA DIRECTED ONYX DOWN for a hasty landing.

They had been flying for hours, and despite Onyx's impressive size—growing larger and more powerful by the day—she was young and building up her stamina. The sun had still been up when Avalkyra had heard those cursed wingbeats again, and she and Onyx had been unsuccessfully chasing them ever since.

It had been a shocking but gratifying revelation that the phoenix she had binded all those weeks ago was Ignix herself, at least according to Veronyka, and it only made sense that she was the creature haunting these ruins. The two of them had unfinished business.

But now, thanks to Veronyka's lack of control, they had lost their quarry entirely.

Avalkyra waited impatiently as Onyx had a quick rest; then they returned to the city square.

They'd taken up residence inside the same soaring temple Avalkyra had occupied during her previous stay in the ruins of Aura, a monstrosity of a building lined with carved marble pillars that rose to a ceiling so high, no light ever touched it.

Avalkyra had thought it a strange place upon first discovery, because it had no windows at all. Most Pyraean architecture featured open-air oculi and wide windows and archways meant specifically for ease of access for phoenixes.

Then it had hit her—this was a temple to Nox. It was evident, now that she was looking, in the Dark Days carvings and the choice of gleaming black marble for columns and accents. The lack of light was essential, the building meant as a house for the goddess of night.

And a fitting place for Avalkyra to take residence as well.

As they entered, ghostly echoes filled the silence, their every movement reflected and amplified. The scrape of a boot, the flap of a wing.

And likewise, movements from above trickled down to them below. Distorted and unsettling. Ominous.

Thrilling.

She closed her eyes and listened, letting the sounds wash over her, but as she tried to envision her future—the actions against which these sounds would play like music—what she saw behind her closed lids was what she'd seen moments ago through Veronyka's eyes . . . hills and valleys, trees and rocks, rolling out below her. She had been flying, too, but where?

Avalkyra growled and opened her eyes. Veronyka's magic was as wild as it had ever been, intruding upon her thoughts and reminding her forcibly, repeatedly, that they were bound in ways beyond her power or control.

If anything, it was getting worse now that Veronyka wasn't so afraid of her own magic, though her ineptitude remained the same.

Unless . . . what if it wasn't ineptitude at all? What if Veronyka had *deliberately* tried to butt into Avalkyra's mind tonight, at the exact moment she'd been trying to seek out her spy? Avalkyra had assumed her distant, winged visitor was Ignix, but could it be Veronyka herself? No, surely Avalkyra would sense her nearness. Surely she would *know*.

She closed her eyes again, seeking the images from Veronyka's mind on purpose now. The landscape could be almost anywhere in Pyra, but it wasn't rocky and barren enough to be anywhere near Aura at Pyrmont's peak. But some instinct told Avalkyra that Veronyka was not on a simple patrol route or taking a leisurely flight around the Eyrie.

She clenched her jaw and dug deeper, paid closer attention to what she'd glimpsed. It was hard to mirror over such a vast distance, and Avalkyra had managed it for only a heartbeat or two. . . . *There.* That thrust of rock—that copse of trees. Avalkyra knew them, had flown over them a hundred times on her way to one of her underground bases. Veronyka was somewhere near Rushlea. Had she sent the spy ahead while she waited farther down the mountain? Was she planning something even now? A move against Avalkyra?

Sidra, she said, sending her magic wide. She wasn't far—Sidra never went far.

Yes, my queen?

Go to Rushlea. Learn what Veronyka is doing there, and who else is with her.

As you wish, she said at once, glad for a chance to serve, to prove her usefulness—to do anything that took her away from what Avalkyra was doing at the top of Pyrmont. Despite her enthusiasm, Sidra's distaste for Veronyka shone through her obedience. Her jealousy was tiresome, but it afforded Avalkyra more control over her than would otherwise be possible.

Do not touch or engage with her, Avalkyra added. She wanted Veronyka all to herself.

She had barely vacated Sidra's mind when another familiar awareness washed over her, one she associated with fire and failure. With rage.

It looked like her quarry had found *her* instead.

She whirled on the spot, blinking into the dark. The world outside her lair was visible through the arched door, silver with moonlight and dotted with stars, bright and clear compared to the black interior.

That was until a winged shadow descended from the sky, obscuring the view.

But she was no true shadow—she was a creature of light and life.

"Ignix," Avalkyra breathed, fists clenched at her sides.

Avalkyra, Ignix returned, inclining her head. She took in the temple surroundings, but her gaze was not idle. It was focused. Determined. Avalkyra prodded at her mind, but the weakness she'd found there that had allowed her to place a bind was gone, her mental defenses strong and sturdy once more. It seemed she would not be caught unawares again. *Daughter of Ashfires, why do you skulk in the shadows?*

What I do is no concern of yours, Avalkyra shot back, the scars across her face and arm tingling in remembered pain.

Onyx was close by, but out of the phoenix's sight behind a pillar. No doubt Ignix felt the strix's presence and would notice her at any moment, but Avalkyra wanted her near enough to mount when that happened. If they were to fight, she wanted to be in the saddle. She wanted to participate. To make the phoenix bleed.

And I do not skulk in the shadows, she said as Onyx stepped into view. *I am* the shadows.

Ignix's gaze snapped to Onyx, and Avalkyra felt her shock and revulsion, and somewhere underneath that, her fear.

Oh, how Avalkyra loved the sensation of it . . . the way it filled her up like oxygen.

She grinned and reached beyond Onyx, high into the rafters. She found them there, her shadows. Her future. Then she called them forth.

Whatever music she'd heard before, the echoing space exploded with it now—a screeching, flapping, scraping assault on the senses. A waterfall. An avalanche.

Ignix squawked in alarm, rearing back, but not before fixing Avalkyra with a last, piercing look. *Daughter of Ashfires . . . you are well and truly lost.*

Then she burst into flame.

Avalkyra was ashamed of the way she staggered back, stumbling behind Onyx, seeking some measure of shelter. Of protection.

But Ignix wasn't attacking her again. She was directing the flames not at Avalkyra's tender flesh, but at the ground, the archway—the building itself.

The stone billowed smoke, cracking under the heat, while the blaze licked and crawled, melting the centuries-old masonry. The fire rose up in a sudden, roaring wall of light, blocking any chance of pursuit as the phoenix tore off into the night.

Blocking the only way out.

The strixes swooped and scattered away from the burst of light, and Avalkyra stared at the flames so hard her eyes watered, her jaw ached, and her scars burned. *I do not fear you,* she said over and over in her mind—a litany, a prayer.

Distantly, somewhere outside, a creaking, groaning sound filled the silent night. There was a pause—a weighted breath—then a crash that shook the ground beneath Avalkyra's feet. She stumbled into Onyx, gripping her feathers hard enough to tear them out by the root.

Another crash, another rolling rumble that vibrated through the floor and caused dust and debris to rain down from above. Squawks and rustling echoed all around.

Enough, Avalkyra gritted out, leaping into Onyx's saddle. The strix was both unnerved and entranced by the flames. She wanted to taste them. To touch them.

She wanted to stamp them out.

The rest were the same, utterly transfixed by the sight but wary, too. Uncertain.

Through, Avalkyra barked, leaning low in the saddle. Onyx hesitated, but Avalkyra did not leave room for debate. *THROUGH THEM NOW!*

Onyx took a running, stumbling start, but after several pumps of her wings, they were in the air and on the other side.

Avalkyra gasped for breath, her clothes scorched and smoking. The scent was enough to turn her stomach, but she fought the heaving spasms down. She searched the ruins for Ignix, but saw only what she had done.

The archways that lined the Everlasting Flame had been knocked down one after the other, their massive blocks of stone landing inside the gaping pit, burying it. There had been thirteen archways, each dedicated to one of the First Riders and their mounts. There should have been fourteen, of course, but Ignix had never died. Barely a wisp rose from the once-smoking surface; all that remained of the Everlasting Flame was a pile of rocks. Still, silent—but not empty. Not vacuous and hungry. Just a ruin like everything else.

A buzzing filled Avalkyra's ears. No more strixes would be hatched there. No more soldiers for her army. Her future snuffed out in an instant by the same cursed firebird that had nearly killed her once before.

Avalkyra scanned the sky, fury boiling in her belly, replacing the bile.

There, a disappearing dot among the stars, moving ever farther away.

Ignix.

To me, Avalkyra ordered. Onyx opened her beak and shrieked, summoning them. All of them. She was Apex Master, and they belonged to her.

They were not the army she'd intended, but they were army enough for this.

They burst forth from the temple, fearless in the wake of Onyx's command, even though some of them caught fire and fell to the ground. The others leapt upon them, whether to devour their fallen brethren or to smother the flames, Avalkyra didn't know. Didn't care.

Onyx took to the sky, following Ignix like a beacon, a signal—their north star.

Behind them, the air filled with wingbeats, their flight the music Avalkyra had craved.

It was the sound of death and fury.

It was the sound of vengeance.

Was it always going to come down to this? Sister
against sister? Daughter against daughter?
Darkness against light?

- CHAPTER II -
SPARROW

SPARROW HAD GONE RIDING with Elliot every day since their first flight together.

He always asked Riella first—even though she always said no—but Sparrow understood. Riella was his sister, more important to him than anyone. Sparrow was just glad she was his second choice. Better than being no choice at all.

Tonight she and Riella were outside the village when Elliot found them. Riella noted his approach as she combed through the matted fur of a fox that had wandered across Sparrow's path seeking help. As Riella dug out the stubborn burs caught in his tail, Sparrow crooned and conversed, keeping the chatty fellow calm. They were surrounded by a ragtag group of critters, including Fine Fellow, her raven friend, and Carrot the cat.

Elliot sat next to them, crunching the grass underfoot and setting up a gust of air that smelled sweet and damp with yesterday's rain. Before he could open his mouth, Riella put him to work.

Sparrow liked Riella very much.

"Hold this," she ordered. Judging by the fox's annoyance and the lash and flick of fur, Sparrow guessed she was handing him the creature's tail. "I said hold it, Elly."

Elliot made an impatient noise in his throat at the nickname, though he didn't tell Riella not to use it.

Sparrow smiled, telling the fox to give the poor boy a break, before extending her senses wide. There was an uneasiness on the air, a kind of pressure that she had trouble placing or understanding. Maybe more rain was coming. Maybe something else.

Once the fox was tended—leaping out of their laps and darting after the other animals gamboling in the grass—Riella again denied Elliot's offer of a flight. Jax hopped forward at once, eagerly nudging Sparrow instead.

"Oh, all right, you great, needy creature," she said, grinning indulgently. Jax, meanwhile, shook himself like an overexcited puppy, his buckles and loops jangling loudly.

Riella laughed, the clatter of glass and ceramic telling Sparrow she was bent over and packing up her supplies.

"There's Kade," she announced happily, her voice moving as she straightened.

"Is *he* the one you're spending your time with when me and Sparrow are flying?" Elliot asked shrewdly. Suspiciously.

"So what if he is?" Riella retorted, as footsteps approached.

Kade greeted them while Sparrow turned to Jax. Excitement tightened her stomach as she rested her hands on the phoenix's flank. She was familiar with the process now, and lifted her bare foot for the stirrup—then froze. She cocked her head, listening hard. The animals all around had stilled, their senses piqued, and Fine Fellow—or Fife, as she'd taken to calling him—croaked.

"What's wrong?" Elliot asked, but before he could say more, a desperate, ragged shriek tore through the night.

A phoenix descended out of the dark sky, bringing with it enough roiling heat and frantic fear to knock Sparrow off her feet. Instead she stumbled into Jax, who squawked and curled himself protectively around her and the others.

This wasn't just any phoenix. Sparrow recognized her dark mind and ancient aura at once.

This was Ignix.

She is coming, the phoenix boomed into Sparrow's mind. The way Elliot and Riella gasped, Sparrow guessed she had spoken into their minds too.

"Who's coming?" Sparrow asked, attempting to extricate herself from Jax's bristling feathers while Fife dug his claws into her shoulder. "It's okay," she added to Jax, who didn't yet understand that Ignix wasn't a threat. "She's a friend."

"*This* is your friend?" Elliot asked. Jax remained on high alert, continuing to use his body as a barrier. "The solitary phoenix you've been waiting for every night?"

There is no time for this, Ignix snapped. *Young one, move aside.*

Sparrow felt Jax quail, his entire body shaking with tension, but he didn't back down.

I could force you, Ignix added softly, and the words sent a tremor of unease through Sparrow.

"It's okay, Jax," she said soothingly. "This is Ignix. She's a friend, and she won't hurt us. Elliot, tell him."

"Ignix . . . ," Elliot said faintly, incredulity in his voice. He shifted and murmured something; then Jax stood aside.

"What's happened?" Sparrow asked, slipping out from Jax's protection and reaching a hand for Ignix.

"Sparrow, be careful!" Elliot hissed, but Sparrow knew she was safe. Ignix was emitting powerful heat waves, stomping and rustling her feathers in obvious agitation, but that anger wasn't for them.

She is coming, she said again.

"*Who* is coming?" Sparrow pressed.

Avalkyra Ashfire. And she does not come alone.

"Are we under attack?" Elliot demanded.

You will be. Where is the other? Where is Veronyka?

"She's . . . she's not here," Kade said somewhat breathlessly. "She left with her patrol a couple of days ago. She's in Rushlea."

Then it is worse than I feared. I tried to stop her, to buy time . . . There was another gust of warmth, as if Ignix were tossing her head, and a hand—Elliot's?—closed protectively around Sparrow's arm, pulling her backward. *You are too outnumbered. The hatchlings, the young ones . . . we must get them to safety.*

"Why is she coming?" Sparrow asked, as Kade cursed and Riella muttered something to the animals that were scattered all around. "What does she want?"

Everything, I think, Ignix answered bleakly, her impatient movements finally going still. *But me most of all. I should not have come here. I thought I had more time. . . .*

"But *how* is she coming?" Sparrow asked. "Does she have a bondmate?"

She has many.

Many bondmates? Before Sparrow could ask, something prickled at the edges of her awareness. She extended her magic, but it was her ears that caught it first.

Rustling. Distant, but growing louder with every moment. It was the kind of sound that made a chill slip down her spine.

Whatever was coming, they were winged . . . but they were not phoenixes.

"The alarm," Elliot said, releasing Sparrow and turning away. "The beacon."

"I will go," Kade said, his fading footsteps echoing in the silence.

"Get onto Jax," Elliot said.

Sparrow didn't know who he meant until Riella spoke.

"Wait, Elly, what about Sparrow?"

Second choice. Sparrow had known where she stood, but Riella's question hit her like a blow to her chest all the same. Elliot had forgotten her.

"Can't you take her?" he asked, and it took a second to realize he meant Ignix. The sound of the approaching attack was louder now, and Sparrow wondered if the others could see what was coming. She wanted to prod Ignix again, to understand what they were facing, but there wasn't time.

"She doesn't even have a saddle," Riella protested, the creak of leather and metal fastenings telling Sparrow she was already on Jax's back.

No, Ignix said forcefully. *I must stay here and head them off.*

A flash of sensation came from the phoenix then—memory or imagination, Sparrow wasn't sure, but terror radiated from her, and the feeling of razor talons and sharp beaks scraped over Sparrow's skin. She shuddered.

"But we can't all fit on my saddle," Elliot argued frantically. "We just need to get Sparrow to—"

"I don't need nobody to get me nowhere," Sparrow snapped. Danger was coming, and all they could do was argue about who was stuck with her. "They need help!" She flung an arm in what she hoped was the direction of the village and stronghold. "And we're wasting time."

Then she turned on her heel and, with Fife's help, marched toward the village gate. She realized with a pang that she'd left her spear in the grass, but she refused to turn back.

She thought that Ignix might chase her, or that Elliot might shout after her.

But neither did.

Before she could feel too sorry for herself, a tide of cold swept over her, as sudden and shocking as if she'd fallen headlong into the River Aurys.

Fife squawked uneasily, and Sparrow staggered to a stop, whirling around. The animals that had followed her continued to flee toward the village, but Jax and Ignix remained rooted to the earth.

Jax crooned softly, but it was Ignix who spoke.

She is here.

Life is a cycle, after all. So it began, so too shall it end.

- CHAPTER 12 -

AVALKYRA

AVALKYRA WATCHED THEM FLEE from her, scattering like leaves in the wind. She was still several minutes away, but Onyx's vision helped her see far in the darkness.

Two phoenixes—one of them Ignix herself—made for the supposed protection of the village and the stronghold beyond.

As if such structures could defend against the likes of her. As if such obstacles could bar her passage.

Avalkyra was here for blood, and nothing would stop her.

By the time she'd reached the rocky bluff upon which Azurec's Eyrie perched, bells were ringing and torches moved to and fro across the stronghold's walls. She and Onyx had beaten the others here, but it wouldn't be long until they caught up.

Just long enough for Avalkyra to make an entrance.

She soared over the village, the people below running for cover, and landed in the middle of the courtyard *just* as the beacon flared to life.

Well, that was one way to get everyone's attention.

The flame burned so brightly that she was about to throw up an arm to shield her eyes—but she stopped herself at the last second. She'd rather scorch her eyeballs clean off than show such weakness.

Everyone in the vicinity had flinched at the sudden snap and hiss of the statue flaring to life, then whirled to see Avalkyra—mounted on Onyx—drop silently from the sky.

She sat tall in the saddle as, after a breath of hesitation, every guard on the wall scrambled to withdraw their weapons and point them directly at her. It was the middle of the night, but Ignix had gotten here first and had clearly raised the alarm.

Everyone halted in their tracks to stare at her, openmouthed with shock, before scurrying out of the line of fire.

Everyone except Commander Cassian, who remained standing alone before her.

"Avalkyra," he said, lifting a hand to the guards that lined the walls and the additional forces that spilled out from their barracks, halting their defense. He swallowed, his throat bobbing as he redirected his attention to her and the creature she sat astride. "Who, and what, is this?"

Avalkyra smiled. "Oh, I think you know, Cassian," she said, leaving off his official title just as he had left off hers. "We studied the history together, after all." He had been a few years older than her, but they'd still come through the same Phoenix Rider training.

"Living history, it seems," he said, mostly to himself, but the words carried across the silent courtyard, the only other sound the crackling of the beacon's flames and the whistling of the wind. "What do you want? She's not here."

He must mean Veronyka. "I know better than you where she is," she snapped, annoyed that he thought to tell her the whereabouts of her own bondmate. "I know her every breath and heartbeat."

Cassian's eyes flickered, as if Avalkyra had exposed herself in some way. As if her words were revealing.

"I am here for Ignix," she said, getting the conversation back on track. "She has taken more than flesh and blood from me." Her voice quivered as she spoke—not with fear or any softer emotion. It shook with rage. "She has taken my new base of operations, *ruined it*, and so I will take hers."

That seemed to startle him. "This is not—"

"I hereby challenge you for custody of Azurec's Eyrie, a place that should by all rights be mine to begin with. And I demand Ignix, the world's first phoenix, be your champion."

"You are in no position to make demands or threats."

"Aren't I?" she asked softly, savoring the words. "Shoot me down and you will unleash them. Even now, they are fighting my control."

"What do you mean?" he said flatly, tightly.

And then the sounds came. They'd probably missed them amid the chaos of their defensive preparations. But now all was quiet, and the music could not be missed.

Avalkyra smiled, lifting her head to listen as, high above, pulsing wing-beats filled the air like ragged heartbeats. The strixes were nearly impossible to see in the darkness—just shifting, ghostly shapes that blotted out the stars. But they were here at last, ready and waiting.

Cassian and everyone else within earshot looked up, fear stark in their eyes. The air grew colder, and the beacon guttered as if in a sudden, strong wind.

"They are dying to make your acquaintance."

With a last, wary look at the sky above and then a second, longer look at Onyx, Cassian clenched his hands into fists. He'd no doubt figured out who and what "they" were.

"I don't know where Ignix is," he lied. Was he really trying to save the ancient bird? Or did he think to take up the challenge himself? But he didn't know—hadn't yet figured it out.

She wasn't simply bonded to a strix—she was bonded to the *apex* strix. And the wingbeats above didn't belong to a simple flock; they belonged to the beginnings of a horde.

She had incubated them, hatched them, then with Onyx's apex status, forced them to bow to her. That deference created a kind of bond, feeding into Onyx's magic and, in turn, feeding into Avalkyra's.

Her power was twentyfold, each individual strix bonded to her and at her command. A single bondmate had made Avalkyra powerful, but a group bond made her nearly unstoppable—or it would have, if Ignix had not ruined her chances for more. It took a hundred birds to turn a flock into a horde, and Avalkyra would have gotten there if Ignix had not destroyed what she had started to build.

Cassian glanced behind him, where Riders could be seen perched on buildings and in the archway that led down into the Eyrie. Was the phoenix there? Were these others trying to protect her too?

There was one way to find out.

Onyx was fairly trembling with restraint beneath her, and the strixes above? They hummed with violence and possibility. With hunger. And Avalkyra wanted to see what they could do.

A bubble seemed to pop—a held breath released—and all at once they descended.

Two dozen black-winged strixes, trailing smoke and shadow, detached themselves from the darkness like scraps of the night brought to life.

Cries of confusion and panic echoed all around, bouncing off the stone walls and causing her flock to shriek and toss their heads in response. The raw voices, the pounding hearts . . . Her strixes lived for this, hungered for it, and Avalkyra intended for them to get their fill.

Ignix did not get to come after her, doling out punishment like a vengeful goddess come down to earth, then fly away without resistance or repercussion.

Only Avalkyra was allowed to do that. And she would. Ignix would pay for what she had done, for the wounds she had inflicted and the scars she'd left behind. She was one of many who owed Avalkyra recompense—but Avalkyra had to start somewhere.

The strixes dove this way and that, their flapping wings filling the air with a sound so vast and endless that it felt solid, as if the Eyrie itself had been walled in. They chased anything alive, their claws tearing and beaks snapping, and Avalkyra let them. Everywhere the shadowbirds touched blackened and turned lifeless—stone crumbled, wood turned to charcoal, and living things became dried-out husks. Animals, driven mad by fear, cried out and ran in fruitless circles, her strixes sucking them dry and tossing their bodies aside. The humans were no better, screaming and running and dropping like flies.

Cassian ducked and ran for cover as several crossbow bolts whizzed past, his guards finally unleashed, and Avalkyra drew her strixes closer to her, wrapping them about her like a cloak. They were precious, valuable to her and to her plans, but nothing was more valuable to Avalkyra than herself. So she used her magic to drag them in front of the line of fire—turning her cloak into a shield—feeling the impact of steel-tipped bolts as they pierced their feathered bodies, but knowing it was a worthy price.

The carnage would draw out Ignix. The carnage would leave a mark and send a message . . . to Veronyka, the would-be usurper queen, and the empire beyond.

Avalkyra Ashfire had returned.

Phoenix Riders entered the fray now, but while some attempted to attack Avalkyra inside her swirling protections, the majority were focused on getting their unmounted comrades to safety. Animals and civilians streamed around the edges of the courtyard, into buildings and under wagons, seeking shelter.

Avalkyra quickly grew bored of this not-fight. She wasn't here for them.

Where are you? she crooned, reaching beyond her flock for Ignix, but there was no reply.

Seeking a louder kind of message, Avalkyra turned her attention to the burning beacon atop the temple, the phoenix statue spitting and crackling and hissing down upon them all. So righteous. So false.

Avalkyra and her flock pounced on it, scraping and clawing and smothering the flame. The light flickered and dimmed, reshaping the scene before her from glowing spectacle to smoky devastation.

Avalkyra urged her strixes on as their talons peeled back curls of gold leaf to reveal the dull iron beneath. Pyraean statues were often made of solid gold—at least those from the Era of Queens, anyway—but this statue doubled as a brazier, and gold could not withstand such high heat. Like much of the empire in recent years, it was a fallacy, a lie painted over the darker, uglier truth.

Once the majority of the gold was gone and the statue stood stark and unlit, Onyx sank her talons into the carved phoenix's outstretched wings and pulled, the statue groaning in protest before it fell off the pedestal with a resounding clang, landing on its side atop the temple's roof.

At last Ignix heard their summons.

Emerging from the depths of the Eyrie and rising above the chaos in the foreground, she was massive and impressive with her deep red and purple plumage, long tail feathers, and vast wingspan. She shrieked as she rose into the sky, silhouetted against the darkness and covered in rippling, blue-white flames. With one last, echoing pump of her wings, she landed upon the phoenix plinth that extended over the chasm below and stood, waiting.

Your challenge, she roared, her voice echoing inside the minds of everyone around. *I accept it.*

Avalkyra grinned. "For control of the Eyrie," she said. "And for vengeance."

You must honor the traditional terms, Ignix pressed, *and cease your assault on those under my care—in victory or defeat, they will remain unharmed henceforth.*

Avalkyra's lip curled. Her flock had barely gotten a taste, a few scattered bodies and sobbing wounded, but she reminded herself why she was here.

With victory, they would flee, tails between their legs, carrying stories down the mountainside to Veronyka and the empire. Her legend would grow, her dark shadow stretching before her.

And, of course, there would be no defeat.

"Agreed," she said, and Onyx dove from the temple roof.

They whipped over the crowd with single-minded intent, bursting through the stone archway just as Avalkyra drew her spear. The pair of them barreled into the phoenix before she could react, and together they went tumbling over the edge, plummeting as strix and phoenix screeched at each other.

Wind buffeted Avalkyra as they fell, and she focused on staying in the saddle as the world whipped and spun and cartwheeled past.

Slow down, she ordered Onyx, who snapped one last time at Ignix before flinging her wings wide to halt their rapid descent. Her claws remained sunk deep into Ignix's chest, forcing the phoenix to land hard on her back, with Avalkyra and Onyx on top of her. The impact was enough to jostle Avalkyra's bones and send up a shower of sparks that singed Onyx's feathers.

Ignix croaked feebly before she began to thrash.

Her neck, Avalkyra ordered calmly, despite the rapid-fire beat of her heart. As Onyx lifted a clawed foot and pressed it directly onto Ignix's throat, Avalkyra lifted her spear and leveled it at the phoenix's large black eye, which was fixed on her.

"Did you really think you could disobey my commands and scorch my flesh, tear down my home and set yourself against me, and *not* be made to pay?" Avalkyra asked idly.

Anger boiled in her veins, fizzing and crackling against her skin, while her ears filled with a distant buzzing sound. It took her a moment to realize the noise wasn't her own rage consuming her, but the Eyrie's occupants filling the tiers above like an audience inside an amphitheater or spectators at the solstice festival games. As Ignix had so recently reminded them, traditional terms dictated that allies for either champion were not allowed to fight each other during or after the challenge, nor to interfere with the challenge itself.

The ruins of Aura are not your home, daughter of Ashfires, Ignix said, her voice weak in Avalkyra's mind. *That is Axura's domain, and there is no more fire in you.*

"There's more fire in me than in a thousand phoenixes," Avalkyra snarled.

Once, perhaps, Ignix said simply. *Now, you are the ashes, the dregs. . . . You're what's left.*

"That's right," Avalkyra said tightly, adjusting her spear so the obsidian point gleamed in the nearby torchlight. "I am the darkness between the stars, the shadow that looms larger than the light—I am Nox reborn and the Dark Days come again."

Her words reverberated off the soaring walls and caused silence in their wake, like a bell recently struck.

"There is a new apex in the world," she continued, as Onyx increased the pressure on Ignix's throat. "And she belongs to me."

Heat began to billow out from the phoenix, her chest glowing brightly from within. Avalkyra lowered her spear, preparing for a torrent of flame to come rushing out her throat, but just as quickly as the fire came, it faltered. Ignix drooped, all the tension leaving her.

Smiling grimly, Avalkyra raised her spear—then out of nowhere, Ignix exploded upward in a burst of fire and sparks. It didn't fill her chest or come spewing out from her beak as it had in Ferro, but it took Avalkyra and Onyx by surprise all the same. They flew backward, Avalkyra flailing to keep her seat, and Ignix darted toward the gallery.

Onyx didn't let her get there. Instead she clamped her beak onto the phoenix's gleaming tail feathers, causing Ignix to shriek in pain and come crashing back down. She whirled, snapping at them, but Onyx surged out of reach. Avalkyra took the chance to strike with her spear, landing a glancing blow across the phoenix's chest. Steaming blood spurted from the wound, but it was too shallow to do much damage.

Still, it slowed her down, making her retreat sluggish and giving Onyx time to leap atop her and rake her talons into the phoenix's exposed back. The crowd around them gasped and shouted, the phoenixes screeching their fury while the strixes crowed gleefully with avid, almost sick fascination. Every time Avalkyra drew blood or Onyx tore out feathers, their delight surged.

Their attention fed Avalkyra's adrenaline and fueled her magic. *This* was what it meant to be part of an apex pair, to reap the benefits of dozens of bonds and the power therein. She was dominating, diminishing Ignix, the world's first phoenix—the very creature that had used this ability against the strixes centuries ago. As if their collective memory led back to the dawn of time, the strixes responded to it. Reveled in it. The tables had been turned.

Avalkyra breathed deeply, their reverence like healing fumes or soothing incense. Like smoke after a blaze—both caustic and cleansing.

Despite being apex herself—somehow still bonded to her dead Rider all these centuries later—Ignix's magic was weak, her power limited. It seemed that despite her position, she'd not demanded the loyalty of the phoenixes around her, as was her due. Perhaps she'd been gone for too long and her status was in question with this young flock.

Perhaps there were others they'd rather bow to. . . . No matter. Avalkyra could destroy Ignix, here and now, and the knowledge made her feel potent. Invincible.

The phoenix's scarlet feathers were streaked with dirt and patches of gray from contact with Onyx, and her entire body seemed wilted. Steam rose from several slash wounds dealt by Avalkyra, but they were just playing with her at this point. There was a reason the Phoenix Riders were able to defeat the strixes during the Dark Days, and it was because together, human and animal were stronger than either was alone. Ignix had no bondmate—at least, not one living—and that made her weaker. She was apex, but her flock was not sworn to her.

Despite knowing she was outmatched, Ignix continued to resist, making another desperate dive for the gallery. Avalkyra thought she was fleeing, but then she realized the tactical advantage such close quarters would provide. They might allow Ignix to regain some measure of control, which meant they had to get to her first.

People were lined up along the walkway, watching with dread, but as Onyx gave chase and Ignix barreled toward them, everyone in their path fled—all save a few poor fools who simply ducked or cowered against the wall. A lone girl actually tumbled back into the passage where Ignix was clearly attempting to flee, which put her directly in harm's way.

The phoenix made it into the tunnel mouth just as Onyx extended her talons. They met with stone, missing Ignix by inches, but the force of Onyx's claws cut through the massive blocks like butter. The solid rock cracked and crumbled beneath her vicious swipes, shadows pooling and leeching into the masonry, reducing it to rubble and burying Ignix underneath.

In seconds the whole archway had collapsed, releasing a cloud of debris and an earsplitting, thundering crash, before abrupt silence.

Avalkyra sensed Ignix no longer.

Frustrated, Onyx swiped once or twice at the mess before coming to a landing atop the wreckage and shrieking. A chorus of strix replies broke out in response, and again the power in Avalkyra's breast swelled. With a nudge, Onyx flew into the open, soaring in wide circles. All around, the strixes halted in their celebration to lower their heads as Avalkyra and Onyx passed.

Apex. Queen. Like Nefyra before her, but reshaped under Avalkyra's will.

She breathed deep, relishing their attention and their submission. Even with a force as small as this, Avalkyra could terrorize the world. But she wanted more. And Ignix had taken that from her.

Perhaps she would not honor the challenge's terms after all. Perhaps they should suffer for harboring the phoenix and trying to deny Avalkyra her prize.

She spotted Cassian among the crowds, his gaze intent. Watching, waiting for what she would do next.

"My queen," came a voice from the gallery, scant feet away. Avalkyra squinted into the darkness, but soon a figure stepped out of the shadows and into the nearest torchlight. It was a woman, her steps irregular as she leaned on a wooden crutch to support a missing leg. She looked Pyraean, and her hair was braided—a female Phoenix Rider? She was old enough to have fought in the Blood War, but Avalkyra didn't know her. Then she noticed the ink-dyed feathers in her hair. *She* might have survived, but her bondmate had not.

Still, she had called Avalkyra queen.

"I offer you my service," the woman said, dropping laboriously to her good knee. Murmurs broke out around them, and Cassian's expression tightened.

"And why should I want your service, *wing widow*?" Avalkyra asked, using a rather insulting term for a Rider who'd lost their mount.

The woman seemed unfazed. "Because I offer it not only on behalf of myself: Morra, Rider of Aneaxi, but also on behalf of my master, Ilithya Shadowheart."

To her surprise, Avalkyra knew *both* those names. While Ilithya was her spymaster and pretend grandmother, the name Morra was familiar as one of Ilithya's alleged informants.

"And what is the manner," Avalkyra asked, glancing up at the restless crowd, "of the service you offer? I have no need for a cook." She reeked of cinnamon and cooking oil, not to mention her flour-dusted apron. "Or a one-legged once-warrior."

What about a shadowmage who studied bond magic, phoenixes . . . and strixes?

Avalkyra tried not to let her shock at being spoken to inside her mind show. *I didn't know strixes were studied in empire classrooms.*

They weren't, Morra offered with a small smile. *But they were in the right empire temples.*

Avalkyra was intrigued, despite herself. She wasn't necessarily inclined to take this woman's words at face value—shadowmage or no—but Ilithya chose her allies carefully, and Avalkyra was in need of exactly the kind of thing Morra might be able to give.

There was one way to find out.

What do you know about hatching strixes?

Morra glanced at Onyx. "She is apex?" she asked. Avalkyra nodded. "Then she will do it for you."

Relief rushed through Avalkyra, powerful as the River Aurys, but almost immediately suspicion reared up to take its place. Above, the restlessness of the crowd intensified as they waited in fear for what would come next. The strixes grew fidgety as well, awaiting her orders. Avalkyra had to make a decision.

"Why are you offering yourself to me? There are others who might benefit from your expertise. . . ."

"When last we spoke, Ilithya demanded from me a simple promise," she said. "That I would do whatever I could to see you on the throne."

Avalkyra straightened in her saddle. The throne might no longer be the lure it once was, but the sentiment was the same. And Ilithya was right about one thing. . . . She could use a servant such as this.

"The Eyrie is mine," Avalkyra announced, her words rising above her in the soaring space. With the prospect of expanding her flock restored, Avalkyra wanted to rid herself of them and their distraction. She wasn't here to decimate their pitiable ranks; she had her sights set on bigger targets, and she wanted to meet them at full strength—both hers and theirs.

And she wanted Veronyka to be there when she did.

In the meantime, she had an army to build. They said any flock larger than a hundred was considered a horde, and Avalkyra intended to have one.

"You will leave at once," she continued, "or suffer my wrath."

The crowd scrambled to flee, and though Avalkyra held her flock in check, she did allow them to chase and snap at those who took too long or tried to fight back. She wanted these people to know they lived and died by her hand and her will alone. All the while, Morra remained on her knees beside her, the first of Veronyka's supporters to turn.

Avalkyra suspected she would not be the last.

Distantly, a bell tolled, signaling evacuation.

Everything was falling into place. The next time she and the Phoenix Riders met, things would go very differently. There would be no escape, no surrender . . . and no survivors.

History has a way of repeating itself . . .
even without intention or instruction.

- CHAPTER 13 -
ELLIOT

ELLIOT STARED AT THE collapsed tunnel.

He kept replaying it all, over and over in his head.

After Ignix had flown away, Elliot snatched Sparrow's abandoned spear off the ground before climbing into the saddle.

"Don't," he'd said to Riella, who was glowering at him. *Yes*, it had all been poorly done. He should have insisted Sparrow ride Jax too, even if his poor phoenix buckled under the strain or Elliot had to run after them on foot. He should have found a better way.

Riella didn't heed his request. She reproached him the entire flight over the stronghold—preparing for an attack—and into the Eyrie.

"I know!" he'd finally said as Jax had landed in the chaos. "I'm going to fix it," he'd promised. "I'm going to find her."

But he'd barely gotten Riella off the saddle when the challenge had begun.

There was a Rider mounted on one of the black shadowbirds, and she was locked in a fierce battle with Ignix. The sounds of their shrieking fight—beaks snapping and talons flashing—echoed all around.

People watched, shocked and terrified, but Elliot had only one thought: If Ignix was fighting, where was Sparrow?

He dragged Riella over to Kade as soon as he'd spotted him. "Stay together."

"Where are you going?" Riella asked as Kade took her hand.

"To find Sparrow."

Stay here, he told Jax, who was perched on the balcony, watching the challenge with tense focus.

Elliot hadn't been looking long before a scream had cut through the tumult.

He'd looked for Riella at first, *again*, but of course she'd been safe with Kade.

It was Sparrow who needed him—Sparrow whom he'd failed.

He'd spotted her then, the source of that scream.

Ignix had been flying hard toward one of the tunnel entrances, apparently attempting to take cover or establish a better position. The mounted Rider, who was clearly winning the battle, hot on her heels.

A collision had been imminent, only, there were people in the way.

People like Sparrow.

And while the others ducked and ran, Sparrow remained rooted to the spot, her face a mask of fear.

Elliot's heart had twisted like a knife in his chest.

He didn't remember deciding to run, but he had, knowing that Sparrow was too far away—that even if he reached her, he'd be too late.

"Sparrow!" he'd screamed, and her face had turned to his, lit as it always was when she recognized his approach: with brilliant, aching light.

But as her head turned, she lost her footing and stumbled—backward, *into* the tunnel. Into Ignix's searing flight path.

Elliot had caught a single, momentary glimpse of Sparrow's face—eyes wide with terror and his name on her lips—before Ignix crashed into her, the Rider just behind.

The tunnel collapsed, an avalanche of stone crashing down.

In seconds the rest of the structure had given way, rocks tumbling in an earsplitting roar, exploding toward him as he ran along the gallery.

"Sparrow!" Elliot cried again, the name torn from his throat, his eyes streaming and his lungs coated with dust. Despite his frantic efforts, the slide of debris had been stronger than a current, knocking him back, tearing his clothes and skin and leaving aching welts and bruises.

Now he stood, staring at the place she had been moments—*seconds*—before.

He was barely aware of the distant sound of bells, or the way the noise around him changed. No longer dark and triumphant, but panicked and frenetic. Booted feet, phoenix shrieks, and voices calling out to one another.

Beryk materialized in front of him. He was bleeding freely from a cut on his face and looked as if he could barely stand up. "What are you doing, lad? It's time to evacuate."

"You don't understand—she's inside. I have to—"

"There's no time," he said distractedly, waving and shouting to anyone he could see. "Evacuate! Take only what you need!"

But Elliot didn't have what he needed.

Beryk pulled him by the shoulder, dragging him away from the tunnel before hurrying elsewhere. Elliot tried to turn around again, but then Riella was there, tugging on his arm. Her face was streaked with tears.

He felt like he was in some kind of daze. Jax was trying to get to him, to push his way through the chaos, but there was a swell of people and phoenixes blocking his path. The black birds circled above like carrion crows, and Elliot wondered how long they had before they started attacking again.

"Can you take her?" he asked Kade, whose bondmate stood just behind them. "Can she carry two?"

"No, Elly, I won't leave you!" Riella objected, but Elliot ignored her.

Kade hesitated. "She can carry us long enough to get out of here. After that . . ."

"I'll find you," Elliot promised, squeezing Riella's hand as Kade hoisted her onto his saddle. "Kade," he said, just as they were ready to go. "That's my sister."

It was an obvious fact, but Kade seemed to understand what he meant.

That she was precious to him, and Elliot was trusting her to his care. Kade nodded gravely, and then they were off in a gust of wings.

"Elliot!" came Beryk's voice again, this time from his saddle. He and several of the other mounted Riders were flying in low circles around the courtyard, keeping everyone on task. The evacuation protocol told them to regroup at Prosperity outpost, but not everyone here could fly. They'd be scattered and divided after this.

"Onto your saddle and into the air," Beryk ordered. "Now!"

Elliot nodded, climbing numbly into his saddle as soon as Jax arrived. Only then did Beryk move on. The air was cold as they took to the night sky, and though Elliot closed his eyes, all he saw behind his lids was Sparrow's look of fear as she'd called his name—begging for a rescue that wouldn't come—before the deluge of stone buried her alive.

The world began with Ashfire queens. . . .
Perhaps they will also be its destruction.

CHAPTER 14

VERONYKA

VERONYKA HAD NOT SLEPT well the night before. She hadn't had any shadow magic dreams, exactly, but only because she hadn't fallen into a deep enough sleep to actually make such a connection. But her restless night was plagued with the *feeling* of Val, with surges of magic and anger, of failure and triumph. It was an emotional tumult, interrupted with snippets from other minds, though they, too, seemed to be fraught with tension and upheaval.

She kept lurching awake, expecting to see . . . what? Val looming over her? Some trouble nearer at hand? Maybe it was those damnable farmers and their mob of Unnamed making Veronyka fear a raid at any moment.

She eventually gave it up for a lost cause and climbed from her bedroll, only to see Doriyan across their camp, sitting outside his tent in the pre-dawn mist.

"Trouble sleeping?" he asked, as Veronyka made her way over, rubbing warmth into her cold arms. Xephyra and Rex had kept out the worst of the chill as they'd huddled outside her tent, but she missed the days when it was warm enough—and dry enough—to sleep outside with them. As it was, the air was damp and heavy from an earlier rain, her tent beaded with drops of moisture and the grass slick underfoot.

Veronyka tried to shake the uneasy feeling inside her—and the temptation to reach out to Val again, like she'd inadvertently done the night before. She feared what might happen if she gave in, but she felt the overwhelming need to do *something*.

"Where do you think they are?" she asked, instead of answering Doriyan's question. "The farmers . . . the, uh, Unnamed?"

He gave her a significant look.

"You don't think . . . the mine?" she asked, surprised she hadn't thought of it already.

"That would be my first guess," he said, scrubbing a hand over his now neatly trimmed beard. He looked much younger than he had when they'd met—new clothes, tamed hair, and a few square meals had done a lot to improve his appearance, though his eyes still held that haunted look. "But Pyra is vast and wild, and filled with places to hide. Run-down inns and rest stops, whole villages abandoned and overgrown. I can think of at least five places near Rushlea alone."

"Good," Veronyka said. "We'll start with the mine and go from there."

She left word with Lysandro, who was on watch, and they set out.

Much to Veronyka's disappointment, the mine was utterly empty when they arrived, with no sign that any people or goods had been hiding there.

Though it was empty, being in the mine made Val feel incredibly close all of a sudden. Maybe it was the lingering connection from their conversation the night before, or the relentless tension of her dreams. Whatever it was, Veronyka was eager to leave it behind.

Doriyan took them to the outskirts of town next, where once-thriving farms stood barren and untilled, where uninhabited houses and barns creaked in the wind, their windows dark. From the sky, Veronyka could see swaths of scorched earth, still healing after the Phoenix Riders last clashed with the empire here, as well as trees and bits of equipment standing blackened and burnt.

Rex and Xephyra—who both insisted on coming—crooned at the sight, and Veronyka felt a pang in her breast at the destruction. This was what war did. Yes, people died, but so did the land, the animals. . . . The world itself had bled for this seemingly unending conflict. She understood the anger of the Rushlean farmers and their Unnamed allies, but it just proved to her that peace with the empire was the only way to stop this.

They moved on to the river after that, where grand inns and bustling markets had once thrived, their empty shells now providing ideal hideouts for criminals and stolen goods.

But as Veronyka and Doriyan combed through building after building, they found no sign that the structures were in use by the farmers, the Unnamed—or anyone at all.

Frustrated, Veronyka stalked out of the run-down stables outside an inn, shielding her eyes from the early-morning sun. They were due to return to the Eyrie later today, and she'd been hoping to have some kind of answers. Instead, she'd be back to waiting and wondering when the Grand Council would meet, if Tristan was okay, and what Val was up to.

Xephyra—who was perched atop the stables—squawked to announce a visitor.

No, multiple visitors. Lysandro, Ronyn, Anders, and Latham appeared, and with them flew Loran, Latham's younger brother and Phoenix Rider apprentice. They were all grim-faced, but Loran looked white as fresh-spun cotton.

"What is it?" Veronyka demanded as they landed before her. "What's happened?"

"There's been an attack. We lost the Eyrie."

"*What?* An attack? By whom?" she asked frantically, though her stomach sank as if she already knew the answer.

"It was her," Loran said with a trembling voice. "The dead queen. The resurrected queen. That's what everyone's saying. She landed in the courtyard riding this big black creature—like a phoenix, but darker, and colder, and . . ."

Veronyka was shaking her head. Did he mean . . . ? Could it possibly be . . . ?

"Commander Cassian called them strixes," Latham put in, hand gripping his brother's shoulder hard.

The word caused a chip of ice to lodge itself in Veronyka's breastbone. Xephyra shuddered. "Strixes?" she repeated in a hushed voice. "Plural?"

"She rode one, but there were others. We don't know how many—it was too dark."

Veronyka pulled on her hair in agitation. *Strixes,* she thought wildly. *Avalkyra Ashfire has hatched strixes.*

"Why was she there? What did she want?" asked Doriyan, glancing sidelong at Veronyka. *Had* Val gone there for her? But when they'd spoken the night before, she said she was hunting a spy. . . .

"She was asking for Ignix," Loran said uncertainly. Most did not know that she had survived all this time, though Veronyka had told the commander and a few others.

"But Ignix isn't at the Eyrie," Veronyka said uncertainly. Or at least she hadn't been when Veronyka left it.

"The phoenix—Ignix—came first, trying to warn us. But it was too late. Avalkyra swooped in and challenged her for the Eyrie, and Ignix accepted," Loran continued. "We couldn't help her or interfere after that. Next thing I knew, we were evacuating."

Silence descended, and everyone stared at Veronyka, expecting some sort of reaction. This was her once-sister, after all, and her rival for the throne. Surely this was a moment for a rousing speech—for words of comfort or assurance.

But Veronyka had nothing. All she could think about was last night, her strange talk with Val and how she'd been restless and unable to sleep. How something awful had been looming over her.

And she'd *ignored* it.

"What happened to Ignix?" If they'd evacuated, that meant she'd *lost* the challenge. . . .

"Buried in a rockslide," Loran replied shakily. "She wasn't the only one."

Desolation swept over Veronyka. Ignix, the one living creature that might be able to help them take on the strixes—who had defeated them before—was lost.

She had warned them about this, hadn't she? She had warned Veronyka . . . but Veronyka had not understood. And now it was too late.

"We have to go there," she said, calling Xephyra. Her mind was racing, skipping ahead, *leaping* over logic and strategy and avoiding the dozens of questions she should be asking in favor of one: how. *How?* How had Val done this? How had Veronyka not seen it?

"We're to report to Prosperity," Latham said, taking over from his brother, whose eyes were wet with unshed tears. "*All* of us."

Veronyka gritted her teeth. The Eyrie was only a couple of hours away. It was *right there*. Val was *right there*.

She reached for Xephyra's saddle, but her bondmate—who had fluttered down before her—turned aside, taking the saddle out of reach.

"Xephyra," Veronyka said, taking a step forward—but once again, Xephyra angled herself away from Veronyka's outstretched hand and brought her head down on a level with her instead.

She didn't say anything, but she didn't need to. Veronyka was doing it again—being drawn into Val's machinations no matter how hard she tried to resist them. She was about to make another foolish mistake, to go running after Val as if she'd been beckoned.

But Veronyka couldn't act like that anymore. She was a leader—maybe one day a *queen*. And Tristan was waiting for her. If she followed Val, if she screwed this up again . . . The thought of leaving the Eyrie in Val's hands made her stomach clench, but lashing out and retaliating without thinking? That's what Val would do.

Veronyka had to be better.

She took a moment to regain her composure. She was grateful for her bondmate's intervention, grateful that Xephyra had kept a clear head. She turned to the others. "Camp?"

"Already broken down and repacked," answered Ronyn. He gestured to their phoenixes, whose saddles were heavily loaded.

"The villagers?" she asked.

"They've been informed," Lysandro said. "The commander sent a letter, and they know to expect additional refugees in the coming day."

"Are they in a panic?"

"Not yet. The letter didn't get into specifics, I don't think."

Like the fact that the Phoenix Riders had been attacked by a flock of mythical creatures? And that the villagers might very well be next?

"They'll get the details soon enough," Latham said, hand still gripping his brother's shoulder. "Once the refugees arrive and they hear the stories."

All of them looked uneasy, but none so much as Loran. He had seen it firsthand. Doriyan, too, looked troubled, but his distant gaze told her he was trying to imagine what had happened, the same as her.

Though leaving the villagers felt wrong—not to mention the unfinished search for the Unnamed—Veronyka knew that Val didn't care about Pyra. She never had.

She had eyes for the Phoenix Riders and for the empire. Leaving might be the best thing they could do for them.

"To Prosperity, then."

Nefyra . . . How I wish you were here.
How I am glad that you are not.

- CHAPTER 15 -

SEV

DAYS HAD PASSED SINCE Sev informed the Phoenix Riders of Lord Rolan's plans, but no response came.

He continued to meet with Tristan, considering every aspect of his impending relocation in excruciating detail—would he travel in a wagon or a carriage, hands bound together or to the bench he sat on? Would he ride alone or with a guard? Two? Three? And what of the route the soldiers would take, and how many troops would march alongside?

Since Captain Yara was assigned to the prison specifically, she was only involved in the very earliest stages of Tristan's departure, things like the time he was meant to be removed from his cell and into whose custody he would be released. She had absolutely no information on the governor's movements. Despite her higher rank, she was also one of the only women among Rolan's soldiers—and the only woman in a position of power—which meant that her presence rarely went unnoticed. There would be no effortless eavesdropping for her, and she was hardly the sort to charm or cajole information out of anyone. She was more likely to beat it out of them, but that would, alas, be slightly suspicious behavior.

Hestia was more discreet, but her interaction with Rolan was limited, and they couldn't count on her to hear anything of note. Yara had at least managed to get Sev assigned to prisoner escort duty. She'd had to butt her head in for that—claiming she had no use for so many prison guards when their only prisoner was being taken elsewhere—but as a lowly foot soldier, Sev wouldn't learn the details of his assignment until they became relevant. As in, the day the assignment took place.

So they guessed and they plotted, they made contingency plans and contingency plans *for* their contingency plans, and all the while Sev knew that if they didn't hear back from the Riders before Tristan was marched out the door, their chance of freeing him might be lost forever.

He knew that Tristan knew it too. Still, both tried to remain positive, to say "when" they heard back from the Riders, not "if."

But as Sev arrived for his second-to-last shift before Tristan was due to leave, they shared a look, and he knew they had to stop kidding themselves and seize their chance before it was too late.

"We can't wait any longer," Sev said, and Tristan nodded, though his expression was pained—and not just because his escape was in jeopardy. Whatever no reply from the Phoenix Riders meant, it couldn't be good.

"When?" Tristan asked, getting to his feet.

Sev considered. "Tomorrow night, as soon as my shift starts. We'll take one of the wagons meant for the following morning. They'll be lined up outside and ready to go."

"But where would we go? Once they notice I've gone, they'll give chase."

"Let me worry about that," Sev said, because he didn't have an answer. They'd have to take the wagon as fast and as far as they could, then ditch it or send the horses off in the opposite direction. After that? Maybe they'd try Aura Nova. Sev doubted Rolan would look for them there, and it was the place Sev knew best. The easiest way to disappear wasn't in the middle of nowhere. . . . It was in the middle of a crowd.

They would need provisions, a change of clothes, and some gold if they could find it. With any luck, Yara would remain behind and be involved in the pursuit for the missing prisoner. They could tell her where they *weren't* going and hope their combined efforts kept the soldiers off their trail.

They spent most of the night considering the best ways to get Tristan out of the dungeons, and Sev returned to the barracks with his mind buzzing. He fell into an uneasy sleep, lurching awake often, dreaming of the *scratch, scratch, scratch* of a messenger pigeon that never came.

He finally awoke in the early afternoon, still adjusting to his nocturnal schedule, though he was glad to have the extra time. He was alone in the barracks, so he opened the nearest window and stretched his magical awareness to the best of his ability, but there was no sign of the messenger pigeon. Then again, he could hardly sense the squirrels chittering in the nearby trees, so that didn't mean much.

He sighed, missing Kade acutely in that moment. Kade's animal magic was well honed and impressive, but it wasn't just that. Sev always missed Kade most when he was alone, right before sleep each night and when he first opened his eyes each day. Sometimes, when his mind was hazy and his body heavy with sleep, Sev could almost *feel* him—the scent of his skin, warm to the touch, and the deep rumble of his voice. He would luxuriate in those moments, chasing the sensations, reshaping his memories into fantasies that had Kade with him, here and now, under the blankets and under his hands. . . . But then a distant cough or a creaking bed would remind Sev that he wasn't actually alone—he was inside the soldiers' barracks surrounded by enemies. He'd remember that he didn't want Kade there at all, had lied to Kade to keep him from this place, and the fantasy would shatter.

Sev closed the window now, his heart sinking. Though there were plenty of reasons why a messenger pigeon might have gone astray, he couldn't shake the feeling that something was badly wrong. He had hoped Kade would find safety and security among the Phoenix Riders, but perhaps there was nowhere for such a thing to be had.

He stopped by Yara's office to relay the new plans and beg what help he could get, then wandered the stables and front drive, watching as wagons— one elegant and meant for quick but comfortable travel, the other well worn and barred, clearly meant for prisoner transfer—were serviced and prepared for the journeys ahead. It was barely past midday, and Sev was surprised to see these duties being taken care of already. Rolan must be eager to set out, or have meetings that required a prompt departure the following morning.

Whatever the reason, these early preparations meant Tristan and Sev would need only to hitch the horses to a wagon and they'd be ready to go.

Before going back inside, Sev stared long and hard at Rolan's carriage, imagining breaking a wheel or loosening a few screws. After the events in Ferro, he had vowed to remove the man from the equation, but that was before he'd spoken to the commander and learned of his new bargain with the governor. Though Tristan was his main focus now, Sev couldn't help but feel his business with Rolan was incomplete. He'd have to settle with the satisfaction that Hestia was making his daily life miserable and he was stealing Rolan's prized bargaining chip for his kingly aspirations.

It would have to be enough.

Sev had just returned from ransacking the laundry when the double doors of the barracks banged open behind him and ten soldiers marched down the rows of beds.

His stomach dropped to the floor, and his hands went slack—releasing the bundle of clothes, though this was clearly not about the stolen socks and undergarments.

They'd found him out. Someone had seen him. Yara had told.

Sev's mind raced, but they didn't seize him by the arms or drag him to his execution; instead, they stood there, waiting, as if Sev was supposed to know what was happening. Yara materialized before him, her expression unreadable as she jerked her chin, meaning for Sev to follow her. He did, wondering when she had betrayed him and why it should surprise him in the first place.

But as they made their way out of the barracks, across the lawns and toward the prison building, Yara sidled up to him.

"This is not my doing."

It was little comfort—what was *this* anyway? Sev didn't look at her, but he sensed her tension. He wanted to believe her, though he supposed it didn't matter now. He was being taken to a cell, so whatever it was they suspected him of doing, he'd already been deemed guilty.

Sev was calmer than he expected to be until he thought of Kade. His heart clenched with the regret of broken promises, with the knowledge that he'd never see, touch, or talk to Kade again. That his fantasies of being together again would remain just that.

He was directed down the stairs, but when the soldiers unlocked Tristan's cell, confusion spiked in his veins.

When they shoved Sev inside that same cell, the confusion grew.

Tristan had lurched to his feet when the surge of soldiers descended the stairs and now stood in the far corner of the cell, his own bewilderment plain on his face.

A tiny, minuscule ray of hope sliced through Sev's panic when they didn't slam the cell door behind him, but even that flicker of optimism was short-lived. The soldiers kept staring between them: At Sev, then Tristan, then Sev again, and unease replaced whatever good feeling had tried to manifest inside him just moments before.

"What is this?" Sev finally asked. "What's happening?"

"Close enough," the nearest soldier said, turning to Yara.

"It's rather unconvincing, if you ask me," she said stiffly, gaze boring into Sev's.

The soldier who'd first spoken shrugged. "Good thing nobody is." Sev found himself bristling on Yara's behalf—she was the man's superior, and yet he spoke to her like she was just any other soldier. "Lord Rolan told us to use whatever prison guard was closest to his height and build."

"Height, maybe. Build, certainly not," Yara said unflatteringly, and Sev's indignation for her evaporated in the face of his own, though his heart was still racing. Why did they need Sev to be close to Tristan's height and build . . . ?

"It's the face," said another soldier, waving vaguely. "Smooth-cheeked and all. Same hair more or less. He's the closest in age, and they've both got a northern look."

Most of the household soldiers were Stellan-born—fair-haired and pale-skinned—but Tristan and Sev had mixed Ferronese and Pyraean ancestry. And at eighteen years old, Sev was the youngest of the prison guards.

"Nobody's gonna get a good look anyway," he finished. "Not until it's too late."

And suddenly Sev understood. He would be Tristan's decoy.

"Go on," the first soldier ordered. "Swap."

As the soldier waved his hand impatiently and Tristan began to peel off his Rider leathers, Sev realized Tristan wasn't going anywhere.

But he was.

Even if the Riders had received his letter, the information would be all wrong. Tristan would be here, Sev would be there . . . and their chance at escape was all but obliterated.

Day 15, Fifth Moon, 175 AE

S,

I have thought about your offer.
I accept.
We will see an Ashfire queen on the Golden
Empire's throne once more.
Tell me what you need; I am at your disposal.

—M

*How I am glad that you do not have to watch them
kill each other, these Ashfire queens.
These daughters of your daughters.*

CHAPTER 16

VERONYKA

VERONYKA FLEW TO PROSPERITY in a daze.

Her brain kept trying to do what it had started to do in Rushlea—leapfrog past all sense of duty and composure and rush headlong into emotion. Into rage.

How dare she? How dare Val *attack* the very people she had once led? And how dare she do so behind Veronyka's back?

She kept going over their recent conversations—if they could even be called that—trying to understand what she'd missed, wondering if she could have foreseen this. Fearing that she had somehow inadvertently given Val exactly what she'd needed to carry it out.

Her instinct to block her mind, to pull in on her shadow magic, reared up.

No, Veronyka chastised herself, letting the walls she'd just subconsciously rebuilt crumble. That was the path to *ignorance*. It was painful to feel vulnerable and exposed, but it was better than the alternative.

When they arrived at Prosperity in the afternoon, it was a mess of Riders and animals, stronghold guards and servants, though most of the evacuees had been forced to relocate to other places—the refugee camp in Rushlea, or to Petratec or Vayle or wherever they might have friends and family who could take them in. Prosperity was not large enough to house them all, and they were probably safer away from the Phoenix Riders anyway.

Suddenly all their careful training and preparation had ground to a halt. Would they be ready to face the empire if it came to war, or had the war already begun? They had enemies on all sides, it seemed, and Veronyka's head spun with frustration and futility.

And anger.

So much anger.

It started when she saw with her own eyes the injured and dying, the slashes from razor-sharp talons creating wounds that looked more like frostbite than anything else—blackened, deadened flesh with jagged edges. The phoenixes fared better and healed quicker than their human counterparts, but their hearts held a different kind of sickness. A bone-deep, centuries-old fear that the humans couldn't possibly feel or understand. Two of the Riders in Commander Cassian's patrol were dead—shot down by Val—but others were wounded, including Beryk. They had come through this attack, but it was not without cost.

"How did this happen?" Veronyka asked as soon as she'd entered the commander's makeshift meeting room.

He had summoned the Rider Council to his new, hastily assembled office the moment she'd arrived. The room was in chaos, with crates stacked haphazardly against the walls and papers sprawled out across the large central table.

"As I was just explaining to Fallon and Darius," the commander said, gesturing to the only other participants in the meeting—Beryk was being treated by the healer in the infirmary—"I am not entirely sure. Ignix arrived seemingly out of nowhere, telling us to prepare for an attack. Avalkyra was upon us before we could do more than raise the alarm. Even our scouts never saw her coming, not until it was too late."

Veronyka perched on the edge of her chair. "What I don't understand is why she bothered to challenge Ignix at all, when we were so outnumbered in the first place. She didn't need to even the odds. They were in her favor to begin with."

"She made it plain she was interested in Ignix from the jump. She knew you were not there," the commander added, speaking to Veronyka. His words felt accusatory, though she didn't think they were—just her own guilty conscience making her cheeks heat. "And so I think she issued the challenge to ensure she got a chance at Ignix herself, without interference or the opportunity for escape."

Val must have wanted a chance to get back at Ignix for what she'd done in Ferro, but it still seemed sudden. There was something they'd missed, though she didn't know what. Had Ignix been spying on her after all? "But how did she lose? Ignix has defeated Avalkyra before." And Val no longer had control of her mind, thanks to Veronyka. "She's older and more powerful. That means something, doesn't it?"

"It does," the commander replied wearily. "Being the first—or apex—confers upon the bearer a social and magical power. It is a tier that only one can reach. Or rather, one per species."

"One per species . . . ," Veronyka repeated, foreboding creeping into the words.

The commander nodded. "Ignix is the apex phoenix, but Avalkyra's strix is the first of her kind hatched since the Dark Days and is, therefore, the apex strix. It would be a relatively meaningless attribute if Avalkyra had not hatched so many more. It is the flock that gives an apex their power. Clearly, Avalkyra had no qualms demanding their subservience to her and her bondmate. Ignix, on the other hand, never asked for our loyalty, which might be why she was not strong enough to defeat her strix counterpart. Only an apex can overpower another apex."

Veronyka recalled learning something about the term "apex" when she was young, but since the word was only ever attributed to Ignix, it had been ancient history as far as she was concerned. She had never thought of it as relevant to the present, and neither had she ever considered the idea of a *strix* apex. Even if she had, she'd never have fathomed *Val* bonding to it.

Before this conversation, she'd assumed binds were at play, but not even Val could control so many. This was something else entirely. Something they were not prepared for.

And now Ignix was gone too.

The rest of the meeting was about immediate, pressing concerns—food and housing, patrol schedules and supplies. Veronyka tuned out and wasn't much use.

Her shock was fading, and her rage was back.

She was on her way outside when she bumped into Ersken, who was moving gingerly down the stairs from the infirmary, his midsection wrapped in thick bandages.

"Has there been any news of them?" he asked when he saw Veronyka.

"Who?" she asked.

"Xat—Ignix, rather," he said, and Veronyka recalled the months he'd spent caring for Ignix inside the breeding enclosure. Though he hadn't known her true identity, he had spent more time with her than most.

"No," Veronyka said with a sad shake of her head. "Wait—*them*? Who else?"

Ersken sniffed loudly, his eyes rimmed with tears. "It wasn't just her that got caught in the cave-in," he said, his voice pained, "but the little bird as well. Sparrow. Wrong place, wrong time."

Sparrow. Veronyka's heart throbbed painfully, temporarily robbing her of breath. Was there any chance the pair of them had survived? She might have hoped that a phoenix could handle such injuries, but Sparrow?

Ersken swayed slightly, and Veronyka helped him down the remaining steps, dragging over a chair from a nearby room for him to rest. What he needed was a cane or a crutch, something to—

"Morra," Veronyka said, throat tight around the word. "Where is Morra?"

Ersken lifted his face to answer, then shook his head. Veronyka made a choked noise, and he hastened to say, "Not dead, but . . ." He frowned. "She knelt and offered her services to Avalkyra."

Now Veronyka was shaking *her* head. "No." She wouldn't—she *couldn't*.

Morra had been ambivalent about Val since her identity was revealed, but . . . she'd *helped* Veronyka. Truly helped her—with her magic, of course, but with other things too. She wouldn't just turn her back on Veronyka and Tristan and the others.

She wouldn't.

"It was hard to hear," Ersken was saying, his tone regretful. "But those who were closest claim she promised to do whatever she could to see Avalkyra on a throne once more."

Veronyka swallowed thickly.

Morra was a shadowmage, and the only way Val could have hatched and bonded to a strix was through shadow magic. Her animal magic was too weak to hatch a phoenix, but her shadow magic was sharpened to a razor's edge. With someone like Morra on her side . . . someone with ancient, obscure knowledge and shadow magic of her own? Who knew what Val would be capable of.

Why hadn't the commander told Veronyka? Was he trying to protect her, or keep news of Morra's betrayal from spreading?

Unease tightened Veronyka's stomach. Even besides her magical knowledge, Morra knew a great many things about the goings-on at the Eyrie, and she knew quite a lot about Veronyka, too, including her struggles with shadow magic and her training regimen. Her affection for Tristan and his capture in Ferro.

Veronyka was certain Morra did not mean the Phoenix Riders or the people of Pyra harm, but Val most certainly did, and Morra had *chosen* to kneel to her. To offer herself.

And Val had probably accepted her service with a smile. Anger pulsed like a second heartbeat inside Veronyka's chest. Rage . . . rage . . . *rage*.

She wanted to scream—at the Unnamed for drawing her away from the Eyrie, at the commander for leaving some of their people behind, even if they'd apparently chosen it.

But most of all, she wanted to scream at Val.

Veronyka wanted answers, and thanks to Morra, her shadow magic was stronger than ever before. She would go to her sister and demand them.

Leaving Ersken behind, she stormed out of the tower into the darkening twilight. The world was awash in shades of violet and magenta, as magnificent as Xephyra's feathers, but Veronyka saw no beauty in it.

"Val," she said harshly, stalking through the shadows behind the stables. The compound had quieted somewhat, though the tension in the people and animals hung in the air, dense and suffocating.

She squeezed her eyes shut and steadied her breathing, gathering her magic with every inhale and opening herself wider with every exhale.

Val, she said again, throwing everything she had behind it. The world swayed around her, and a wave of dizziness sent Veronyka leaning against the back wall of the stables. But the touch of cool stone against her palm pulled her back to herself, so she jerked away and stumbled forward, blinking once, twice. . . .

Hello, xe *Nyka,* Val said, amused. *I knew you'd come looking for me.*

You're a coward, Veronyka spat. She got the impression Val was seated somewhere, quite at her leisure, though there was an edge of anticipation in her rigid posture. As if she'd been waiting for this. *And I'm not here for you—I'm here for answers.*

Do not call me coward in one breath, then ask for answers in the next.

There's no other word for it, Veronyka said, her chest heaving. *You watched and waited until I was gone, until the middle of the night, when—*

I watched? Val shot back, annoyance bleeding through her outward calm. *I was minding my own business while that decrepit old phoenix spied on me. Then she had the audacity to attack me and mine. And so I paid her back in kind.*

Ignix attacked you? Veronyka asked skeptically. Then again, if Ignix had seen what Val was doing, maybe she'd thought she could stop it. Prevent it from spreading. Veronyka would have tried to do the same.

She tried to take something from me, and so I took something from her.

Veronyka saw through the lie as easily as she saw through glass. *From me, you mean,* she said, surprised at the emotion in her voice. *The Eyrie wasn't Ignix's. The Eyrie was mine. It was important to me, and so were the people in it. And you took it.*

Val shrugged, then got to her feet, striding purposefully away. Veronyka's consciousness followed, sensing her movements and catching flashes of her surroundings—the cobblestones of the courtyard rolling out beneath her feet, filthy and scattered with debris and splattered with a dark liquid that was surely blood. There was a distant, irregular thumping sound—Morra?—but then Veronyka realized Val was holding a spear and using it like a walking stick. Like Sparrow.

Admit it! Veronyka snapped. *Admit that you did it to get at me. To hurt me.*

Veronyka was staring at the back of Val's head, willing the connection to remain strong, and reached for her shoulder. For what, she didn't know. To force Val to face her? To shake her? Though she swore she could feel the warmth of Val's skin, her hand passed through.

Val whirled around anyway, and suddenly her appearance was crystal clear: wild cap of jagged red hair, splotchy scars, and an obsidian-tipped spear in her hand.

I did it because I could, she said fiercely. *I did it because every inch of this country, this empire, belongs to me, and I take what's mine.*

They stood before each other—Veronyka could see the courtyard all around her and wondered vaguely if Val could see her at Prosperity. There was a gust of wind from above, stirring Val's hair and slipping across Veronyka's skin. But she knew, somehow, that the trees and grass outside the stables were undisturbed.

They were together but not: joined in this moment but worlds apart. Their connection had never been so strong.

A shadow passed over them, and then a creature out of legend dropped behind Val like a curtain. It loomed above her, around her, obliterating their hazy surroundings and casting Val into a startling silhouette against its utter darkness.

It was a monster, a thing out of nightmares. Its presence stole Veronyka's breath as if sucking the very life from her.

It shrieked, and the sound rent Veronyka's heart, causing a frigid rush of cold to flood her chest.

I am not merely a Strix Rider, the first and only of my kind, Val announced, pride and pleasure in every syllable. *I am* apexaeris. *Do you remember your ancient Pyraean?*

Apex Rider, Veronyka translated.

Apex Master, Val corrected with a smile.

Veronyka was afraid. Truly afraid. Of the strix, yes, but also of the Val who could hatch such a thing. How far Avalkyra Ashfire had fallen . . . How truly dark and devastating she had become. What a complete and utter tragedy.

Don't, Val snapped, and Veronyka struggled to draw herself back to the moment.

Don't what?

Don't look at me with your soft eyes and your bleeding heart. I am not the sister you knew. I am not the queen that never reigned. I am something else now, xe *Nyka, and you'd best stay out of my way.*

I can't, Veronyka said, stepping forward. Strange to speak like this, seemingly face-to-face, but without moving her lips.

Val's grip on her spear tightened, but she let Veronyka close the distance between them. The anger in Veronyka's heart sparked anew, blazing against the cold that had enveloped her, burning away her fear and her compassion. *You've come for the ones I love. You attacked the Eyrie and you attacked the Phoenix Riders, which means you attacked me.*

Val sneered. *Trust me, you'll know when I've attacked you.*

Is that what you want? Veronyka asked, taking another step closer. She was scant inches from Val now, close enough to touch—if this were real. *You want to attack me, Val? Then do it. Leave the others out of it and do it.*

All in due time, Nyka, she said, turning aside.

I knew it, Veronyka said, frustrated and angry and desperate to do something. *You're afraid to face me. Afraid to lose. That's why you took Morra, hoping for an edge.*

She reached out again, and this time, her hand snagged against the fabric of Val's tunic before sliding through. If she concentrated, maybe . . .

I have been through fire and death. I fear nothing, Val snarled, pulling away. *And I did not take your precious shadowmage. She offered herself on bended knee. She couldn't wait to betray you.*

Veronyka was breathing heavily now. She ignored the comments about Morra, knowing she'd struck a nerve. *Oh, you fear,* she said, feeling her lips curl into a smile. *You fear life. You fear love. You fear yourself, and you fear me most of all.*

Val bared her teeth and turned, bringing her spear down in an angry, slashing motion.

Sudden pain bloomed across Veronyka's chest in a fiery line from her collarbone to her stomach. The obsidian point had sliced neatly through her tunic in a sick parody of the last time she and Val had come into conflict at the Eyrie, when Val had cut open Veronyka's shirt to reveal her lies to Tristan. Except this time, the weapon cut through fabric and flesh, and for a moment, Veronyka could only stare down at herself. It took a breath for the blood to start, and then it was gushing, vivid red and entirely real. She staggered back, stunned, and as her eyes met Val's, they too were wide with shock.

Veronyka clutched at her chest, her fingertips coming away warm and wet, and then she fell backward, out of the vision of the stronghold's courtyard and directly into someone's arms.

The Prosperity stables exploded around her, spreading like an ink stain—starry sky, damp grass, and barren trees, and the soft murmuring of animals inside.

She struggled against the grip, confused, until she recognized Doriyan's gruff voice. Someone was shouting her name, and above her was Xephyra, wild-eyed and panicked.

Veronyka looked down at the bloody gash across her chest, inflicted by Val . . . who was miles of mountain and magic away.

"This . . . is not good," she managed, before she lost consciousness.

*They bear your name and your blood—and your magic,
too. That is, perhaps, the most terrifying part of all.*

- CHAPTER 17 -
VERONYKA

"PUT HER DOWN THERE. No, *there*. And get me some light."

That voice. Veronyka knew that voice.

"No need," came a reply. That was Doriyan. He had caught her and still held her now, though he was lowering her onto a hard surface.

Soft orange light pressed against Veronyka's eyelids, bringing with it another familiar presence. Xephyra. Yes, Xephyra had been there too.

Veronyka tried to lurch upright, but hot, stinging pain lanced across her stomach.

"Easy," came that voice again, and Veronyka blinked against Xephyra's fierce glow until she found Alexiya bent over her.

"*Tiya* Alexiya," she exclaimed—or tried, but the words came out slurred.

"Blood loss," Alexiya murmured, ignoring Veronyka as she fussed with something out of sight. Veronyka's eyelids were drooping again. "Get her something to eat. And drink. Something strong."

Footsteps crunched against straw. They were inside the stables, Veronyka thought, as she stared up at sloping wooden beams and sensed the presence of animals all around her. Her favorite horse, Wind, was here—safe and unharmed. He snorted loudly to reassure her.

Veronyka turned her attention back to her aunt. "Did you find him?" she asked.

Alexiya paused, but she knew who Veronyka meant. Her father. "No," she said softly.

Veronyka knew she should feel disappointment, but right now she couldn't muster it.

There was a loud, tearing sound—the flash of a knife and a tug at her shirt. Alexiya was cutting away the ruined fabric to expose Veronyka's chest. Xephyra continued to loom anxiously overhead and was giving her a rundown of what was happening.

Scrub, she said to Veronyka, right before a cold, wet cloth pressed against her chest. She couldn't help but hiss at the stinging.

"I know," Alexiya said soothingly, but she continued to swipe at the wound. The cold water actually felt good, so Veronyka gritted her teeth to stop from flinching.

Footsteps returned.

"Oh—uh, should I—"

"Some privacy please, Doriyan," Alexiya snapped. Oh right, Veronyka's chest was bared. She wanted to tell her aunt she didn't really care—the man had seen her as a baby, had he not?—but the burning pain was becoming distracting and bringing her out of her state of shock and more firmly into reality.

What in the dark realms had just happened?

Val had attacked her, nearly killed her, *through* a shadow magic link.

It would have terrified Veronyka if she hadn't seen and felt the surprise in Val's own reaction. Val hadn't meant to do this . . . hadn't known it was possible either.

That provided some measure of relief, but even still, the possibilities were alarming. Was this the result of Val's apex bond? It made sense that her shadow magic would be more powerful than ever before, and Veronyka had started embracing her own abilities for the first time.

It was a recipe for disaster. If tonight was a sign of things to come, of the kind of power Val now wielded, Veronyka doubted any of them would survive it.

With no small amount of trepidation, Veronyka sought out their bond. It was strangely, utterly quiet, as if her ears needed to pop. There was nothing but the most distant, echoing sense of Val. In fact, what she felt was the *absence* of Val, the ringing silence after a violent noise.

It was as if she had no bond at all.

The abrupt swing from one extreme to the other made Veronyka dizzy, but the muted bond seemed to promise at least one thing: She was safe for now.

Sting, Xephyra warned as Alexiya started rubbing some kind of antiseptic into the cut, muttering that it would "probably be okay without stitches," and then wrapped a thick length of bandage across Veronyka's chest to hold the smaller bandages in place. This, too, was reminiscent of months before when Veronyka had been Nyk and had bound her breasts.

"Here," Alexiya said, putting a hand under Veronyka's back. "Can you sit?"

Veronyka struggled to haul herself upright without engaging the muscles of her abdomen, but then another set of hands pressed against her back, helping leverage her. Doriyan.

Alexiya pushed his hands aside as soon as Veronyka was seated, then held out a tunic from her travel pack for Veronyka to shrug into, her old shirt nothing more than bloody scraps.

Doriyan stepped back, his gaze averted, and once Veronyka was clothed again, he held out a flask of wine and a bundle of cheese and apples.

Alexiya snatched them from him, so it was up to Veronyka to turn stiffly. "Thank you."

He seemed gratified by her words, though he eyed Alexiya warily. She didn't speak until she'd sliced an apple for Veronyka, adding several pieces of cheese as well, and then handed over the wine.

"Just a sip," she said. "It should help with the pain. For now. I'd bring you to the healer, but she's quite overwhelmed at the moment, and besides . . . I'm not entirely sure what I should tell her." She paused, chewing her thumbnail as Veronyka took another drink. The wine was heavily sweetened, and definitely taking the edge off the burning sensation radiating from her chest. "What *was* that? I thought, for a second . . . Doriyan told me he'd seen you by the stables, and then we rounded the corner, and . . ."

"I saw *her*," Doriyan said, voice rough.

"You did?" Veronyka asked.

"Who?" Alexiya demanded. Doriyan let Veronyka decide how she wanted to answer.

"Val—Avalkyra," she said, and Alexiya sucked in a breath.

"She's here?" she said, reaching for her knife, which lay on the table.

"No," Veronyka and Doriyan said together. He inclined his head, deferring to her again. "It was . . . We have shadow magic, Avalkyra and me," she said hesitantly. "You've heard of it?"

Alexiya nodded, frowning between them. "Do you have it too?" she asked Doriyan, taking an unconscious step back.

"He doesn't have it, but Avalkyra used it on him. It's how she managed her patrol. She used it to control, coerce, and communicate."

"You were doing a lot more than communicating," Alexiya said doubtfully. "She's at the Eyrie and yet somehow she nearly gutted you *here*. How is that possible?"

"Her range extended over vast distances before," Doriyan said softly. "And now she's bonded to the apex strix? It does not seem so difficult to imagine she can do this, too."

"It's okay," Veronyka found herself saying, gripping her aunt's arm. "I can handle it. I can handle her."

Maybe saying it aloud would make it true. That dull, ringing silence between them remained, which would have to be good enough for now.

Hurried footsteps sounded from outside the stables, and Alexiya adjusted the neckline of Veronyka's borrowed shirt, hiding the bandages. Veronyka flashed her a grateful look, knowing that both she and Doriyan would keep this a secret for as long as Veronyka wanted it to be one.

Doriyan poked his head out, then waved in a messenger who was clearly looking for Veronyka. It was one of the clerks Cassian used to take notes during meetings and help manage his paperwork.

"Master Veronyka," he said—Veronyka was still unused to being addressed in such a way. How much worse would it be, when people bowed and curtsied and called her queen? "The commander has called an emergency meeting. He has received word from the empire spy."

Sev. *Tristan.*

Veronyka leapt to her feet, heedless of the pain. Before she could run out the door, she whirled around. "Thank you," she said, hastily kissing Alexiya's cheek and squeezing Doriyan's arm. "Will you come?"

"I'm not sure we were invited," Alexiya said with a pointed look at the messenger.

"I'm inviting you," Veronyka insisted. She was too impatient to wait, so she left them to make up their own minds and hurried from the stables.

"What news?" she asked as she strode back into the commander's office, the clerk trailing behind. Fallon and Darius were back again, and Beryk remained at the infirmary.

The commander had been leaning over the desk, but he straightened at Veronyka's arrival. "A messenger pigeon was intercepted by Darius on his most recent sweep," he explained, lifting a piece of paper from the pile in front of him.

"Looking for you," Veronyka said to the commander, before staring avidly at the letter. The messenger pigeons were trained to find Commander Cassian, to sense his magical presence. It must have flown to the Eyrie after they had already fled, then wandered the province, seeking him. . . . How much time had they lost?

Veronyka rounded the desk to read over the commander's shoulder. This was fairly difficult given his height, so he handed the letter over.

Her eyes flew down the page. "Lord Rolan is traveling . . . relocating

Tristan—*tomorrow*? We have to go at once. Even if we fly straight there, it'll take at least ten hours to get to Stel."

"Veronyka," the commander began. "I—"

"I know what you'll say," Veronyka said, her voice tight. "I know we have a responsibility, that we don't have anybody to spare—that there couldn't be a worse time."

"Actually," he cut in, scrubbing a hand through the uncharacteristic stubble across his chin. He was usually impeccably groomed. "According to our patrols, all is quiet at the Eyrie, and the evacuees are settling in at Rushlea and the surrounding villages. There may not be a better time."

Veronyka's heart leapt, and the commander smiled. "What next?" she asked.

"We will have to split our forces. With Lord Rolan traveling south and Tristan being transferred north, we can't be in two places at once."

Which also meant *Veronyka* couldn't be in two places.

Capturing Lord Rolan and making him pay for what he'd done would not only give her great pleasure, it would put a stop to the Grand Council vote and buy them a reprieve they desperately needed. The commander had told her his original plans for the Grand Council meeting—plans that involved the mysterious poison dart that Tristan had shown her in Rushlea during their last visit—and she'd honestly been shocked. The idea that he would assassinate Rolan's co-conspirators and willingly putting himself at the mercy of the rest, no matter their old alliances or future promises, was far beyond his usual poise and calculation.

But the commander had made those arrangements *before* he'd known that Veronyka was Pheronia's daughter, that Avalkyra Ashfire lived, and that she flew at the head of an army of strixes from legend. His plans would no longer work.

No, everything would come down to Veronyka and Val, one way or another. Either here in Pyra or there in the capital.

Veronyka would have to face Val and the throne, but she did not have to do it alone. Tristan had taught her that, made her see that she could lean

NICKI PAU PRETO

on him, that they made each other better. So if Veronyka was to win this war, she wanted him by her side.

Lord Rolan and the Grand Council were important, but to Veronyka, Tristan was *more* important.

"I want to go to Tristan," she said, surprising no one—the commander least of all.

"I suspect his entire patrol will feel the same way, but that leaves no one to tackle Lord Rolan's convoy."

There was a knock at the door, and Alexiya and Doriyan appeared. Veronyka waved them in eagerly.

"Alexiya," said the commander in surprise. "I didn't know you'd returned."

"Only just," she said, sidling in with Doriyan behind.

Veronyka smiled. "Alexiya and Doriyan can go. I believe Ximn is one of the fastest phoenixes in the flock and that Doriyan has decades of experience tailing targets?" Both nodded. "They can track Lord Rolan, and the five of us will head off Tristan's convoy."

"Six," the commander corrected. Veronyka frowned, and he crooked her a grin. "I'm coming with you."

You would tell me to help them, I know.
You would tell me to show them the way.

CHAPTER 18

AVALKYRA

AVALKYRA STARED FOR A very long time at the place where Veronyka had been.

Then she stared at the obsidian spearpoint, tipped in blood. *Veronyka's* blood.

Avalkyra's breath came hard and fast. First there had been that incredible surge of power as they'd connected—as they had made *physical* contact—and now its sudden, gaping absence as they'd both pulled back.

No doubt Veronyka had torn herself away out of fear and pain, but Avalkyra had withdrawn her magic out of shock more than anything else.

Shock and awe.

She had breached a geographical distance spanning *miles* using only the power of her shadow magic.

Was this what the apex bond had given her? She and Veronyka had been bonded for years and had connected over long range many times . . . but this kind of connection was entirely new.

Her heart raced, but as she sought the bond in her mind—eager to poke and prod these new, expansive boundaries—she found the connection silent as a crypt. She pushed harder, reached deeper . . . and still nothing.

Avalkyra looked around. The stronghold was a mess of rubble, broken barrels, and scattered bits of glass and straw. Everything was gray, as if the strixes sucked not just the life but the very color from the world. The bloody spear was the brightest thing to be seen—even Avalkyra's hair was duller and less vibrant than before.

Morra stood several feet away, gaping wide-eyed at Avalkyra. Besides her flock, the shadowmage was the only other living thing in the courtyard.

"You saw?" Avalkyra demanded.

"Yes," Morra whispered. Her gaze landed not on Avalkyra or her spear, but on the drops of fresh blood spattered on the cobblestones.

"You studied bond magic. What just happened?"

She spoke the words as a challenge—a test. The woman had claimed to have all the knowledge Avalkyra required, including how to hatch more strixes with only her bondmate, but just because she said it didn't make it so. Avalkyra was no laywoman herself, but in all her years, in *both* her lives . . . she had never encountered anything like this.

"Is she alive?" Morra asked hoarsely.

Avalkyra narrowed her eyes. "Yes."

She spoke sharply enough that the woman's attention finally shifted from the bloodstains. She seemed to remember where she was and to whom she was speaking. "You know this? How?"

"I know because the wound was shallow. And"—she cleared her throat—"I felt it." Not as a wound to her own body, but rather, like an echo or a reverberation. The ghost of the cut but not the cut itself.

"You are bonded to her," Morra said. It was not a question.

Avalkyra lifted her chin. There was no point in hiding it. "Yes. Though . . ." Morra watched her closely, and though Avalkyra was about to ask what the sudden silence between them could mean, she found herself unwilling to admit she was unable to reach Veronyka. "We've never connected like this before."

Morra nodded, her lips pursed—as if she sensed that Avalkyra was withholding something. "Well, you are now *apexaeris*; therefore, your magic is more powerful than ever before, across all your additional bonds. Entering the liminal space of a connection and breaching those boundaries is exceedingly rare, though not unheard of. There are fragmented tales and secondhand accounts of Nefyra doing something similar with Callysta."

"Stabbing her?" Avalkyra asked dubiously. They'd been lovers, after all, not warring sisters.

A flicker of a smile crossed the woman's face. "No, my queen. But they passed items between each other—letters, flowers . . . ammunition." A frown creased her brow. "There was even a rather obscure story of Nefyra rescuing Callysta from a terrible fall, somehow pulling her onto Ignix's saddle, even though they were on opposite sides of the battlefield. . . ."

Scholars. Avalkyra was not interested in a history lesson. "You're saying it's because of the apex bond that this is possible? Because it's made my magic more powerful?"

"Yes."

"Could this boundary be crossed with anyone?"

Morra shook her head. "The accounts tell of Nefyra and Callysta alone. I believe it happens through a bond, not a temporary link."

Well, *that* was disappointing. Avalkyra considered all Morra had said, and an unsettling thought occurred to her. "Could Callysta reach Nefyra as well?"

"No," Morra said with a firm shake of the head. But before Avalkyra could bask in her relief, she added, "But Callysta was not a shadowmage. If the bonded pair *both* had shadow magic . . ."

She trailed off, letting the implication speak for itself. Callysta could not reach Nefyra, but Veronyka could reach Avalkyra.

She glowered.

"This troubles you, my queen?"

"I've just sliced Veronyka from neck to navel—I'm not much interested in her being able to return the favor," she drawled, trying to mask her alarm. Their bond was silent. Veronyka was nowhere to be found. But the moment that changed, Avalkyra would have to be on her guard.

"How is your bond now?" Morra asked, her tone determinedly light.

"It is . . . quiet."

"Quiet," Morra repeated, glancing away. "What happened tonight—a true, powerful connection that trespasses time and space—can be achieved only if both parties are open and willing."

"Which means?" Avalkyra pressed.

"It won't happen again unless you *both* want it to. If you do not wish to be reached, you won't be. There's no need to fear her."

Avalkyra heard Veronyka's words from that very night replaying over and over inside her mind. *You're afraid to face me. Afraid to lose . . . You fear life. You fear love. You fear yourself, and you fear me most of all.*

"You know nothing of my fears, shadowmage," Avalkyra spat, taking a sudden, violent step forward. She gripped the front of Morra's tunic. "That *child* you think I fear bled for me this very night, and she will bleed again before this war is through."

Morra bowed her head, and only once her gaze was averted did Avalkyra release her, breathing hard through her nose as she tried to calm herself.

Veronyka could not reach her until Avalkyra allowed it. That was a comfort, even if the sudden, jarring silence wasn't. Avalkyra had always kept her enemies close—her chief opponent in the Blood War had been her sister—but never more so than with Veronyka. If something was truly wrong with their bond . . . She considered telling Morra after all, but it felt like weakness to admit she couldn't find Veronyka in her own mind, the place where she had always been master. Worse, the woman seemed too suspiciously interested in it—and in Veronyka's well-being as a whole. Like her master Ilithya before her. Better to keep this part of her magic under wraps for now and be glad that Veronyka would not be able to retaliate.

They would come to blows again at some point—it was inevitable—but not yet.

Since the day they were born, they'd been like two runaway carts heading in the same direction on a long, twisting road. . . . It was only a matter of time before they collided. They'd bumped and jostled several times already, like the time Avalkyra had been forced to drop Veronyka from phoenix-back in order to save herself. What was true then was still true now: If it could only be one of them, it would be Avalkyra.

But not like this. Not the secret, silent death of an assassin. No, when they clashed for the final time, it would be spectacular. It *had* to be. Otherwise, what was the point of any of this?

Perhaps the bond magic was part of the reason Avalkyra enjoyed getting a rise out of Veronyka. It was so easy to provoke her, and her anger was like a newborn pup, clumsy and guileless.

Or at least it had been. Veronyka had grown. She was different now, and her anger had teeth.

But on some level Avalkyra knew that no matter what happened between them, they were in this together. No matter what she did, Veronyka would be there.

"Enough talk of Veronyka. Tell me about—"

A shudder of expectation went through her flock, and Avalkyra sought Onyx, perched atop the stronghold walls. *What is it?*

The strix lifted her head as if scenting the air. *Fireborn.*

That was her way of saying "phoenix." It was not, however, an impending attack. When Avalkyra extended her magic, she sensed a familiar bind drawing near.

Perfect.

As Sidra approached, every strix in the vicinity turned its head to watch. Their desire for her phoenix was palpable, a gnawing ache in Avalkyra's own belly.

Despite their hunger, they looked to Onyx—and by extension, Avalkyra—for guidance. Sidra was not a part of the flock, but she was not an enemy, either, and was to be left alone.

The command issued forward, rippling effortlessly through the group, and they did not waver. Using shadow magic in this way was easier than breathing, easier than anything she'd ever managed in a human or even phoenix mind.

It was thanks to Onyx, she knew. She who controlled the apex controlled the flock.

Well done, she told her bondmate. She knew better than to give too much praise, but too little had its own ill effects. She thought of Veronyka, of the bondmate who had rebelled and rejected her, and knew she must do things differently this time around.

Sidra landed before her, clearly on edge, though Onyx and the rest of the flock did not trouble her. Even still, as soon as she dismounted, her phoenix took to the air frantically—all grace abandoned—and made for an empty rooftop with all the speed she could muster. She looked shrunken, or maybe it was just the way her feathers wilted, her crest drooping, in the presence of so many shadowbirds.

"My queen," Sidra said, kneeling. She, too, looked pale and weak—even with the time away from Avalkyra's flock. "You have taken the Eyrie."

"Very observant," Avalkyra said sarcastically, indicating with an impatient wave that Sidra should stand. The woman noticed Morra then, but when Avalkyra didn't dismiss her, Sidra spoke again.

"It looks different," she muttered. The wind howled through the open stronghold doors, rattling on their broken hinges, and the scent of blood and decay permeated the air. With nothing alive left to eat, the strixes feasted on the buildings instead, gnawing on the edges of wooden beams and blocks of stone. Never satisfied.

They had come here before, around twenty years ago. The Pyraean governor Adara Strongwing had invited Avalkyra to some religious ceremony, attempting to force her eldest son on her, looking to make a match. He was a bold, conceited boy—but sheltered—and so Avalkyra and her patrol had lured him and his friends away from the celebrations into a series of escalating dares. How fast could his phoenix dive? How many times could he spin? Avalkyra and Nyx had beaten him in every possible challenge, and the boy had become more and more reckless in his attempts to salvage his pride.

He and his phoenix eventually crashed, and she and Sidra had helped him return—crying, with a broken arm and bloody nose—to the festivities.

Needless to say, his parents never tried to foist him on Avalkyra again. She didn't know what they'd expected. If you carelessly dangled a piece of meat above a fire, you couldn't act shocked when it got burnt. He'd died in the Blood War, along with his parents and his younger sister. Last of the Strongwings, gone the way of so many other of the First Rider families.

Avalkyra sighed. Those bloodlines were old, but they had become watered down and weak. Better to be done with them. Better a fresh start.

"That's because it *is* different," she drawled. *What news?* she said pointedly, drawing Sidra's attention back to her. She had sent the woman to Rushlea to learn what Veronyka had been doing there the night of Avalkyra's attack.

"There is an insurgent military movement operating inside Pyra," Sidra said hurriedly. "It appears the Phoenix Riders were addressing the concern in Rushlea, where they last struck. The insurgents call themselves the Unnamed."

Avalkyra knew that term—it came from history, though the idea that these people served the same order was doubtful. She had been so certain Veronyka was spying on her, but the knowledge that she was simply trying to save the world, one backward village at a time, made even more sense.

"And what do the Unnamed want?" she asked, hands clasped behind her back as she strolled the cobblestones. Sidra fell into step next to her.

"They hate the empire, of course, but they hate the Phoenix Riders as well. Their numbers are difficult to gauge, and many of them are mere farmers and herders, but I'd estimate there are at least one hundred and fifty. They are scattered and disorganized, but they are passionate. They do not want peace. I think they could easily be rallied to your cause."

That could come in handy. "Then rally them. Set up a meeting with their leaders."

"Yes, my queen."

Avalkyra considered. She turned to Morra, who had remained stationary as the two Riders walked together. At a look from Avalkyra, the woman hastened to her side.

"You said Onyx can do it for me." She nodded at her bondmate, who fluttered down from the wall. She brought a living, breathing cold with her, enough to make the women on either side of Avalkyra shiver. "Expand my flock."

"Yes," Morra said, flinching back slightly from the creature, though she couldn't seem to take her eyes off her. "I must confess . . . I'm curious to know how you hatched any at all."

Avalkyra's expression was smug as she recalled her discovery of a new use for the Everlasting Flame—but her smile slipped when she remembered how Ignix had thwarted her so soon after. "I used the Everlasting Flame," she said shortly. "Or rather, what was left of it. It was little more than a smoking ruin. Now, thanks to Ignix, it's not even that."

"I see," Morra said, obviously trying to piece together the events that led to her attack on the Eyrie.

"What does Onyx need?" Avalkyra pressed.

Morra pulled her attention away from the strix to look up at her. "You and your bond magic," she said. "And, of course, eggs. I assume you found more in the ruins of Aura?"

"More than you can imagine," Avalkyra said with relish.

"Well, then," Morra said, her voice all business, though her breath was uneasy and her forehead was dotted with sweat. Onyx's presence was clearly affecting her. "I suggest you bring them here—all of them, before you get started. Once it begins, I doubt you'll want to stop."

Avalkyra turned to her bondmate. *Return to the ruins. Take half the flock with you and bring back as many eggs as you can carry.*

Without a word, Onyx took to the sky, trailing strixes on either side.

"I have work still to do here and in the valley," Avalkyra said aloud, continuing her slow circuit of the courtyard.

Her confidence that Rolan could actually execute his ambitious plan to send the empire's forces into Pyra was waning. It must all come to a head if her victory was to be as awe-inspiring as she envisioned. "We must guarantee the empire will march."

"The Grand Council meeting," Sidra said. It should be happening any day now, if Rolan intended to march before winter set in and made campaigning difficult. "Surely we can tip the scales in your favor?"

"Rolan intends to prove the Phoenix Riders are a danger to the empire," Avalkyra mused, staring at her spearpoint once again. The blood was slowly drying now, turning darker and blending in with the obsidian tip. Sidra followed her line of sight, a question at the front of her mind, though she dared not ask it. "So, *prove it*, won't you?"

The woman's eyes sparked. "Yes, my queen."

But I think, perhaps, I have forgotten my path.
I think, perhaps, I am lost.

- CHAPTER 19 -
ELLIOT

ELLIOT SPENT MOST OF his time at Prosperity pacing.

First, he paced outside the infirmary, waiting for Riella to be checked over.

Then he paced outside the commander's office while the Rider Council had their second meeting of the day, alternating between trying to find the courage to enter and remaining as quiet as possible so as to hear what they were saying. He'd startled and stumbled aside when Alexiya and Doriyan turned up, but as soon as they disappeared inside, he was at the keyhole again. They were talking about a rescue mission for Tristan, and as much as Elliot would love to help, he had a rescue mission of his own in mind. He held Sparrow's spear—unable, for some reason, to part with it—staring down at its rough grain and knotted wood, smooth in the places where her hands constantly touched.

He stopped dead and squeezed his eyes shut. He'd been hoping to appeal to Veronyka—Sparrow was important to her too—but after missing his chance when she'd initially arrived, and now waiting seemingly endlessly for this meeting to be done, his patience was at its end.

He turned on his heel with a determined tread. There was someone else he could talk to, someone in a position of authority who wasn't in the Rider Council meeting.

Elliot poked his head through the door of the infirmary, where rows of occupied cots sat in darkness, with one or two bathed in pools of candlelight, their occupants still awake or being treated. Elliot scanned the faces until he recognized Beryk beneath the heavy bandage. He'd been slashed by one of the shadowbirds across his face and shoulder, the cuts patched up but slow to stop bleeding, according to what he'd overheard from others who'd taken similar wounds.

"Master Beryk, sir?" Elliot said quietly, stepping into the room. It was large and long, spanning the length of the building. The healer and her assistants were at the far end, and the people on either side of Beryk seemed to be sleeping.

"*Master* Beryk, is it?" he asked dryly. "You must have done something stupid." He paused. "Or you want something."

Elliot grimaced. It was true that he tended to stand upon formality when he was nervous—or guilty. Beryk's expression was patient, though, showing there was no resentment in his words.

"It's the latter, sir," Elliot said, sitting gingerly on the side of Beryk's bed. "Though I suppose it has the potential to turn into the former."

"Out with it, then."

"That cave-in at the Eyrie . . . with Ignix?" He swallowed, pulling up the image that he'd been trying so desperately to forget—Sparrow's terrified face, calling his name, and the rubble cascading all around her.

"Yes?" he said, voice subdued.

"One of the—well, I guess she was a servant?" He felt the absurd urge to laugh. "To be honest, I don't exactly know what her job was, but she helped Ersken, and Jana . . . and everyone." *And me.* "She got trapped along with Ignix, buried inside that tunnel. . . ."

Beryk looked sad, sorry—regretful. And maybe a little bit defeated.

"We have to go back for her," Elliot pressed. "For both of them. Don't we?"

Beryk sank into his pillows, looking impossibly exhausted all of a sudden. "The thing is, we don't have anybody to spare at the—"

"I'll go," Elliot said in a rush. "I'll go alone. I don't need anybody else to help. I—"

"Elliot," Beryk cut in softly, his dark eyes kind. "We can't spare you, either. I'll need your help once things get settled. It's been a hard day, and there are many who are missing or unaccounted for. No doubt word will trickle in soon enough about the girl. Have faith."

"But, Master Beryk, I can't just sit here and do nothing. It's my fault, you see. We got separated, and she was all alone, and . . ." Elliot was babbling now, and Beryk just listened, waiting until he had the chance to say no again.

"I think you should get some sleep, lad. We all need rest. Things will look better in the morning."

Deflated, Elliot wandered out into the hallway—and bumped directly into Veronyka.

"Sorry," he said, but though she grimaced at the contact, she shook her head to dismiss his concerns.

"It's nothing," she said, before her attention latched on to the spear in his hand. "I was on my way to speak to Beryk, and . . . Is that Sparrow's?"

Guilt gnawed at him. "Yes," he said bleakly.

The look she gave him was an appraising one, arms crossed over her chest. He had met both Sparrow and Veronyka in Vayle months back under less-than-ideal circumstances. He'd been upset about his sister, anxious about betraying the Riders, and come to think of it, he'd accused the pair of them of stealing.

He and Veronyka hadn't had much to do with each other until recently, when he helped out with Tristan's—or rather, *her* patrol. And now, apparently, she was an Ashfire and heir to the throne. No wonder he quailed under her assessing gaze.

"You care about her," she said, more statement than question. "You care about Sparrow."

How did those simple words make him feel completely and utterly exposed? He nodded, jaw working. "I was there," he said thickly. "I saw the tunnel collapse on her."

"If she survived," Veronyka said carefully, "she'll be trapped."

"I want to help her," Elliot said, contemplating his boots, "but I don't know how."

"Those tunnels are all interconnected, many of them hidden or unknown. There's more than one exit—more than one way through."

Elliot seized upon her words like a drowning man clinging to a life raft. "There is?"

Veronyka nodded fervently. "Which tunnel was it?"

"The one on the south side. With the entrance next to Ersken's office." Part of why Elliot had been so distraught was because he'd thought that tunnel led only to the upper levels inside the Eyrie. But if what Veronyka said was true, and there were ways in and out he didn't know about . . . Veronyka shifted, and that's when Elliot noticed a loaded satchel over her shoulder—apparently she was off again. To rescue Tristan. To save someone she cared about.

Maybe this was his chance to do the same.

She dug out a scrap of paper and smoothed it against the wall, scribbling across the page with a charcoal stub. What she'd drawn looked like a spider's web, or the roots of a particularly old and gnarled tree.

"I've been making my way through them recently, for practice," she muttered as she started adding labels. Practicing what, Elliot had no idea, but he watched hungrily as the image took shape. "I found more than a couple that no one uses."

At last she finished. It was a mess, but it was also his best shot.

"This is the main passage everyone knows about—the one the villagers and servants would have used to evacuate," she said, indicating an exit to the shortest, straightest squiggly line. "These lead back inside the Eyrie, up into the storage rooms, bedrooms, and main halls." She traced her finger over several more passages. "But *this one*," she said significantly, following the longest of the tunnels, "leads deeper underground before coming out here, on the eastern side."

Elliot tried to picture the Eyrie as seen from above, on phoenix-back.

He imagined the tunnel led somewhere near the switchback stair and way station.

"There are a couple of others," she said, indicating them briefly, "but they were never properly excavated when we retook the Eyrie. I know they're there. I'm just not sure anybody could make it through. Then again, if anyone *could* get through, it would be her."

Yes, it would be. Sparrow was a survivor, and she had an ancient phoenix with her. Surely together they could find a way through whatever cave-ins or other dangers lurked there.

If they were alive.

They are. She is.

And Elliot would be there to help them on the other side.

Veronyka handed over the makeshift map, and Elliot clutched it tightly. His muscles tensed, ready to act—until he thought of Beryk, who had told him to forget it and get some sleep.

Beryk, who had done so much for him. Who would *need him*, once things got settled.

The hope and excitement that had surged up inside him withered in his chest. He looked down at the map, then back at Veronyka. "The thing is . . . Beryk told me there's no one to spare. That I'm needed here."

Veronyka tilted her head, considering as she repacked her satchel. "When *I* first met Beryk, he told me that I should forget about the Phoenix Riders, that they weren't recruiting and that I didn't fit the requirements even if they were." She shrugged, a smirk on her face. "I'm very glad I didn't listen to him."

Elliot huffed a weak laugh, but it wasn't that simple. It was all well and good for her—she was a lost Ashfire heir, and she hadn't already betrayed these people once before.

It was like the hostage situation with Riella all over again.

Would he worry and fret and weigh his every action against what others would think of him, or would he step up and do the right thing, boldly and unapologetically, no matter the cost?

Veronyka was watching him, so Elliot collected himself. "Thank you," he said, his voice stiff and formal again.

Was it because he was about to do something stupid . . . or was it because he wasn't?

After Veronyka squeezed his shoulder and departed, Elliot found himself inside the dining hall. It was currently filled with cots and pallets for people to get some sleep until proper bedrooms and sleeping quarters could be arranged.

Like in the infirmary, there were pools of light where people talked and unpacked, a low hum of conversation filling the space, but mostly the room was dark.

Riella was seated in the corner, leaning against the stone wall, and Kade crouched in front of her. They were talking softly, their heads bent together, before Kade hugged her and stood.

He didn't notice Elliot lurking just outside the doorway until he stepped into the shadowy hall.

"Oh, Elliot," he said. "Are you looking for Riella? She's—"

"I saw," Elliot replied. He looked up at Kade—yes, *up*—and tried to quell the embarrassment burning inside at what he was about to do. "Thank you for everything you've done for her."

Kade seemed taken aback by the words—perhaps because of the way Elliot was staring at him, as if steeling himself. Or because he sensed there was more to come. He nodded warily.

"Are you—what are your *intentions* with my sister?" Elliot asked.

"My what?" Kade repeated.

"I can see that you're close, and you've rescued her twice now." Kade continued looking at him in complete and utter confusion. *Ugh.* Elliot really wished he'd never started this conversation. "And she's young, so it would make sense if she started to—I don't know, idolize or develop *feelings* for you, and . . ."

Kade actually laughed. "You've *really* got the wrong idea."

Heat crept up Elliot's face—he didn't know if it was from the whole mess of this conversation or the fact that Kade was laughing at him. "It's not that I'd have a problem with—"

The mirth quickly left the other boy's features. "*I'd* have a problem with it. I'm nineteen, and she's, what, fourteen?"

"And a quarter," Elliot corrected meekly, though he was extremely relieved. Not just that there was apparently nothing happening between them, but also that Kade found the idea absurd.

"I don't care if she's fourteen and *three*-quarters," Kade replied stonily—and somewhat protectively, Elliot thought.

He blew out a breath. "Excellent," he said, smiling brightly. Now they could *both* keep an eye on her. "Well, if you change your mind in ten years or so, then we can talk."

"I won't," Kade muttered, shaking his head as he walked away.

Riella caught sight of Elliot and waved him over. "What was that about?" she asked, nodding toward the hall, though Kade was already gone.

"Just your big brother ensuring there was nothing *inappropriate* happening between the two of you."

"Me and Kade?" she repeated, cheeks red, likely from embarrassment. Then she broke out laughing too.

Now it was Elliot's turn to flush. "What?" he demanded. "You're growing up, and he's . . . I mean, I'm sure some find him . . ."

"Elly, you're an idiot," she said fondly. Elliot was still trying to work that out when Riella changed the subject. "Has there been any news?" she asked anxiously, patting the bedroll she was sitting on. Elliot squatted down next to her.

"Nothing. I asked Beryk if I could look for her, but he said they can't afford to lose me. But then . . ." He hesitated, reaching into his pocket and drawing out the rough map. "I ran into Veronyka. She showed me this network of tunnels under the Eyrie, with more than one exit I didn't know about. So maybe . . ." Riella nodded, eager, and Elliot continued. "Maybe she can find her way out."

Riella stared at him in complete and utter confusion—then out of nowhere, she whacked him on the head.

"Ouch—what—" he began, then lowered his voice. "What was *that* for?"

She rolled her eyes. "'Maybe she can find her way out'?" she repeated incredulously.

Elliot rubbed the spot on his head, which smarted. "Look, I asked Beryk—"

"Did *he* know about the tunnels?"

"I'm sure he does, but it was Veronyka who—"

"Exactly! She's the bloody queen!"

"Well, not yet—"

"If *she* told you about them, she obviously approves of the idea and wants you to go. Just because she didn't explicitly say it—"

"I can't betray Beryk again. I've been trying for months to make up for the mistakes I made. To prove that I'm trustworthy. I have duties, responsibilities . . ."

"And what about your responsibility to her?"

"I . . . ," Elliot began, struggling to explain himself in the face of her rapid-fire questions. "I can't just ditch one responsibility for another!" he exclaimed, and someone shushed him across the hall. He glowered before turning back to Riella. "It's not only Beryk or the Riders. . . . You're my sister! We're at war! I can't just leave you here alone, even if—" He froze, unsure he wanted to finish that sentence.

"Even if you want to?" Riella asked shrewdly.

"What I want is to stay here with you and to make sure you're okay. I'm not leaving you ever again." Elliot's voice had gone a bit ragged at the end. He thought he'd masked it, but Riella wasn't fooled. She took one of his hands—prying it off Sparrow's spear—and squeezed it.

"I don't need you to save me."

"But you *did*. . . . You did need me, and I wasn't there. I can't fail again. Not with you," he added, because of course he had failed again—he'd failed Sparrow. The person who had helped bring him back to life, the person who had shown him how to go on even after terrible sorrow and heartache.

The person he'd ignored for weeks in order to follow Riella around like a puppy dog. Why was he always failing at everything he did? He'd failed at being a brother, a Rider—and now a friend, too.

Riella tugged on his hand, drawing his attention back to her. "You never failed me. The world failed me, but not you. How can you possibly take the blame for what happened?"

"I'm your big brother. I should protect you."

Riella sighed exasperatedly. "You can't protect me from *life*, Elliot. Life is messy and complicated, and bad things *will* happen. You can't stop them. We're in the middle of a war, and we both have to do our best—by ourselves, by each other, and by the people who matter to us. So stop using me as an excuse to do things you know aren't right, things you don't even want to do in the first place. Stop using me to hide from the truth."

Elliot was speechless. Was that how she saw his behavior? He never meant to turn Riella into some scapegoat, and yet . . . she wasn't wrong. He had turned into a spy for Riella, had been careless and dismissive of his relationship with Sparrow in favor of bothering Riella, and when a threat had approached, he had chosen Riella over Sparrow, leaving her alone and unprotected in the middle of an attack. Even now, when he knew he should go after Sparrow, he was trying to convince himself he shouldn't . . . because of Riella.

He had just wanted to make up for what had happened to her, but maybe it had never been his burden to bear. Riella had matured in their time apart, and she didn't want or need her older brother following her around, reminding her of her past trauma or behaving like she was some task he had to complete or some wrong he had to right.

And while she might have needed him when she was in her cell, she did not need him when she was here, among friends. But Sparrow did.

"I know it's been hard for us being apart, and with Mom gone and Dad . . ." Elliot stiffened at the mention of their father, and Riella trailed off. Their father had *chosen* this separation, had agreed to cut deals and put his children in danger. He had let Lord Rolan's lackey into their house. "You can't be my everything, and I can't be yours, either. You don't have to choose between us," she finished gently.

Elliot nodded, trying to banish the thoughts that told him that here he was, failing again and burdening his little sister with his inadequacies. She was right. She was wise beyond her years, and more perceptive than him— and she was right.

"Now," Riella said, lifting Sparrow's spear and shoving it into his hand, her voice blunt once more. "Go get her."

*In the beginning, we blazed the trail together, Nefyra
and I. We were the light that all others followed.*

- CHAPTER 20 -
SEV

SEV NOW UNDERSTOOD WHY the carriages had been prepared so
early.

He was ushered out of Tristan's cell in the dead of night—during his
usual guard shift—before anyone in the household could become aware of
his absence. Rolan's carriage was already gone, indicating that Sev's role as a
decoy was only a small part of the man's subterfuge. He obviously suspected
informants and had fed false information to his own people, including the
departure time for himself and his "prisoner."

Sev would be riding in a barred carriage that was covered by a canvas
flap as if to disguise its purpose and make it look like a cargo wagon, not a
prisoner transport. Rolan *wanted* the Phoenix Riders to chase this convoy for
as long as possible, but he needed the transfer to appear genuine for that to
happen. He couldn't have a prison wagon rolling boldly across the countryside. It was too obvious. This way, it appeared as if Rolan was trying to hide
his tracks. Sev *was* visible through gaps along the sides and back, but not so
clearly as to be easily identifiable. To the Riders, this would appear as a ruse
on its own—just a cargo transfer, no more—disguising Rolan's *true* ruse, the
decoy prisoner Sev.

In fact, he wouldn't be surprised if half of the deception—including

Tristan's clothes and the sack they'd thrown over his head when leaving the prison—was for the benefit of the soldiers guarding the transfer and the inhabitants of the estate, not just the Phoenix Riders.

Sev had underestimated Rolan's paranoia, even if he was right to be concerned. This was a lot of hoop jumping to avoid a confrontation with the Phoenix Riders, which Rolan's forces greatly outnumbered even with all the soldiers he'd lost in Pyra. He was obviously more frightened of them than he'd let on and desperate for his plans to succeed. By keeping his games secret even from his own people, the switch could remain undetected for as long as possible.

Long enough to carry Sev north into the Spine, away from Tristan and the Stellan estate.

Away from Rolan.

Sev was about to become a rather useless spy. He tried not to panic, but there wasn't much else to do.

If the Riders *had* received his letter, they were about to waste their time rescuing *him*. Meanwhile, Tristan was still in a cell, Sev's co-conspirators were out of his reach, and they were in worse shape now than when they'd started.

And if they hadn't . . . Sev would be in some ancient Stellan stronghold. He'd have to find his way back to the estate somehow, back to Tristan's—or Rolan's—side. Otherwise, what good was he?

Trix's words from months ago nagged at the back of his mind.

Be useful, boy, and you'll never want for a position in this world.

But Sev was useful no longer, and that did not sit well at all.

Soon gray dawn light began filtering into the carriage, striping the bars across the floor at Sev's feet and leaking in through the canvas flaps.

They had been rumbling across the countryside for hours already, making slow, tedious progress through the endlessly flat Shadow Plains. The land had only just started to rise, breaking up the monotonous landscape Sev managed to glimpse through the gaps of canvas.

He had told the Riders that their best point of attack would be *before* they reached the base of the Spine. Phoenix Riders preferred to attack in open spaces, and Sev feared a trap or ambush if they waited until the tightly winding mountain road. It would make for easy pickings if they wanted to perch and loose arrows, but Sev couldn't guarantee there weren't reinforcements hidden in those hills.

But as the ground rose on either side of the road, Sev knew beyond a doubt that he had failed. The Riders weren't coming, and if they were, it was too late.

Suddenly voices cut through Sev's dire thoughts, the soldiers next to the wagon speaking in low, urgent tones.

Could it be?

Sev edged along the bench, taking hold of the canvas and pulling it aside ever so slightly.

He couldn't see anything, but the voices around him shifted from low conversation to shouted orders and galloping hooves as they closed their ranks and rearranged themselves for defense. At last he heard the words he'd both longed for and dreaded—Phoenix Riders.

Sev's breath hitched. It felt like rescue, but this rescue wasn't meant for him. The Riders were going to fight and burn and peel back the canvas only to find Sev, not Tristan.

Panic set in. Sev could actually see the phoenixes now, distant specks growing nearer and nearer with each pump of their powerful wings. What could he do? Throw himself out the side of the wagon and risk getting trampled? Try to rock the wagon enough that it toppled over? Not only would that probably see him badly wounded—either from the fall or the retaliation from an irate soldier—but that might hurt the horses as well.

The horses.

Sev had never been much of an animage. He'd been too young when he lived with his parents on the farm to really hone his gift, and then he'd spent the next fourteen or so years hiding it and pretending it didn't exist. He had no real range and definitely no subtlety.

Luckily, for this to work, he needed neither.

"Teyke help me—and Felix, too," he muttered.

There were horses all around—the two that pulled the carriage, and at least a dozen with riders on either side of him. Sev couldn't begin to try to control them, but he was certain he could spook them.

With everything he had, Sev pushed his magic outward in a sudden burst.

The response was instantaneous. The wagon halted abruptly, rocking back and forth as the horses pulling it bucked and reared, while shouts from left and right told Sev that soldiers had been thrown from their saddles or currently hung on for dear life. Whinnies and snorts, the stomp and skitter of hooves, and still Sev pushed, refusing to relent, even as he felt guilt for the poor, startled creatures.

As the wagon tipped dangerously to either side, Sev flung himself forward and pulled at the canvas flap again. He could see the Phoenix Riders more clearly now, and from the voices of the soldiers nearby, their presence was being blamed for the horses' reactions.

Sev knew that was a boon, that discovery as an animage would definitely complicate his life, but all he could do was stare at the Riders drawing steadily nearer.

Veronyka was at the front, her beautiful phoenix trailing flames and bending the air around her with heat waves.

Sev thought of that moment in the tower weeks back when Veronyka had inexplicably spoken into his mind, begging for help. He hadn't understood it then, and he didn't understand it now, but it was his best chance.

So Sev begged now, sent his thoughts skyward to her, knowing it was a fool's errand but trying all the same, because what *was* Sev's life if not a long series of ridiculous failed efforts by a fool?

He's not here! Sev thought frantically. *Veronyka! Please hear me! He's not here—Tristan's not here. He's still at the estate!*

But as the Phoenix Riders flew ever nearer, with no sign of slowing or stopping, despair settled in. He had failed, had lost his chance, he—

Sev, came a voice inside his head—Veronyka's voice. She'd heard him!

He'd reached and reached, and somehow she'd heard him. *Thank you.*

Stunned, Sev watched as the Riders drew level with the wagon—then flew *past* it, continuing to soar high and fast and *away* from him, heading south. Toward Rolan's estate. Toward Tristan and their true goal.

Sev sagged back into his seat, the rocking motion of the carriage stilling as the soldiers calmed the horses. A head poked in to check on him, frowning, before disappearing again.

He sighed, allowing himself to feel a single moment of triumph. Then melancholy seeped into his heart, his bones.

Sev had achieved his goal, had warned the Riders off and avoided a senseless battle—but the victory was bittersweet.

He was now faced with the undeniable truth that he had finally become what he'd most feared . . . useless. A spy with no one to spy on.

And while he hadn't guaranteed Tristan's freedom, he *had* all but assured that he would not get his own.

Teyke has long been considered the god of tricksters and a symbol of luck in the empire, but his origins are difficult to trace.

In Ferro, cats were considered lucky, so some equated the god with the animal, insisting the two were one and the same. Perhaps thanks to Pyraean influence, it was later believed that the god was human-formed and had a cat companion. Given that animal magic was most prominent in Pyra during that time (circa 300 BE), it makes sense that their society would view their relationship that way.

Interestingly, Teyke's role as the trickster seems to contradict the recorded stories of his deeds during that time. The most complete—if not the most well known—stories are the aptly named *Scrolls of Luck*, discovered in Orro at one of the only temples dedicated to the god that was ever built and which no longer stands.

The tales of Teyke in the *Scrolls of Luck* first introduce the name of the god's cat—called Felix—and depict the feline with his famed gold-green eyes luring Teyke himself into a trap, suggesting that it was Felix, not Teyke, who was the true trickster.

Felix tricks Teyke no less than five times within the scrolls, but by the final tale, the two set a trap for Anyanke, the goddess of fate—who, of course, sees the deception coming. She punishes the two by tangling them in a spider's web, but thanks to Felix's claws—and Teyke's cleverness—they are able to escape. Their initial failure didn't stop the two from forming a legendary partnership, and according to myth and legend, the pair has been getting into—and out of—mischief together ever since.

—*Myths and Legends of the Golden Empire and Beyond*, a compilation of stories and accounts, the Morian Archives, 101 AE

We were magnificent. We shone brightly,
burned fiercely. We ruled the world and
banished the darkness.

- CHAPTER 21 -
VERONYKA

"WHAT'S WRONG?"

It was the commander, shouting from Veronyka's right-hand side as he twisted in Maximian's saddle, staring at the wagon and the convoy they'd left behind.

"Tristan's not there," Veronyka said shortly.

When they'd first had the wagon in their sights, she'd worried her bond to Tristan was weakened beyond recognition, that she'd lost the ability to sense him at all. Or worse, that Val's attack might have caused her magic to close up and block him out. The wound on her chest was a stinging reminder of her own vulnerability, which was greater than she'd ever even imagined, but the last thing she wanted was to lose touch with Tristan—especially now, when she needed every advantage to rescue him.

She wished she could talk to Morra about it all, about what had happened with Val and other ways to protect herself. But she couldn't. A pang of regret pierced her chest, but she pushed it down.

Xephyra nudged their bond, reminding her, and Veronyka sought out Rex. He opened himself to her, revealing that he couldn't sense Tristan either.

At least Veronyka's magic wasn't to blame, but that only increased her fear. If neither of them could sense Tristan, did that mean he was gravely hurt? Wounded and unconscious, or . . . or—the next word was so abhorrent to her mind that she couldn't even think it. No, Tristan was not *that*. He was fine, and she would save him. She had to.

As she'd scrambled for what to do next, the horses below began to buck and kick, causing such a ruckus she couldn't help but reach out to them. Surely the phoenixes' distant presence wasn't enough to make the horses lose their composure—especially not warhorses, who were trained to withstand all manner of noise and violence.

But if it wasn't the phoenixes causing them to behave so bizarrely, then what was?

By the time Veronyka contacted the animals, she knew they'd been riled up, not by their surroundings or the coming phoenixes—but by an animage.

A familiar animage. His presence in their minds was already receding, but Veronyka recognized his touch because she'd been in his mind before.

She turned in the saddle to find Kade, flying behind her. Veronyka had insisted he come with them, claiming his position in Rolan's household might give them important insight during the rescue—but really, she'd brought him because of Sev. He caught her eye, a frown on his face, then looked down at the convoy below.

Veronyka squinted at the wagon, subconsciously mirroring with Xephyra—willing her eyes to be able to see through canvas walls, though, of course, they could not. But then a rattle of the carriage, a ripple of wind—and the fabric opened to reveal Sev's face, shadowed by cell bars but unmistakable all the same.

Without direct eye contact, connecting with him was difficult, but now that Veronyka knew it was him, she sought other means.

Withdrawing from Xephyra's mind, Veronyka reached again for the horses, chasing the tendril of Sev's connection with them, just as she had once gone through Wind to connect with Tristan's mind.

The contact was fleeting; it was brief—but it was enough.

Sev had been shouting mental warnings out into the ether, calling her name, and while his words were garbled in his mind, his rampant thoughts painted a more complete picture. He was here in Tristan's place—a decoy meant to lure them away from their true target—while Tristan remained inside Rolan's estate, locked away and out of reach.

Not if Veronyka could help it.

They left the convoy behind and diverted their flight south, but Veronyka had no idea where to land or how to get inside Rolan's estate without turning it into a full-blown attack. Their only option was to wait for nightfall and approach under cover of darkness.

They were a party of six again; Veronyka had asked Kade to follow Sev's convoy at a safe distance and see what he could discover about the stronghold in the Spine. If he could get Sev out, he should—otherwise, he was to meet at their rendezvous point, where they would discuss next steps.

The patrol made temporary camp among what little natural cover they could find in the flat terrain, but neither Veronyka nor Rex could sit still. Even the commander seemed on edge, though he and Maximian maintained their usual dignified decorum.

Something must have gone wrong for Lord Rolan to fabricate a false prisoner transfer. Had Sev's cover been blown? Surely if it had, Rolan would have killed or imprisoned him rather than used him in Tristan's place. Either way, Rolan must have known he had an informant in his midst—or suspected that Veronyka and Cassian would not make good on their alliance.

As Veronyka paced, she cast an uneasy look at the commander. If Tristan's journey had been a ruse, had Rolan's travel been a ruse as well? And if so . . . where was he?

When at last darkness descended, Veronyka took point with Rex and the commander on either side, and Tristan's patrol fanned out behind them. A full-scale battle with Rolan's soldiers was a fight they might not win, especially if the Riders drew their notice *before* locating Tristan and getting him to safety. They had to be careful.

Though the commander didn't fully understand why Veronyka would be any use in locating Tristan, he did believe that Rex would be, and he knew that Veronyka and Xephyra were closest with the phoenix. It was the same way she'd explained what had happened earlier when she called an abrupt halt to the rescue mission. Rex was bonded to Tristan and had known he was not in that wagon. Veronyka was simply acting as the translator.

Or so she told them.

As they flew nearer to the estate, the building growing larger and larger below, Veronyka cast her magic as widely as she could. It had been so long since she'd truly sensed Tristan, she feared she no longer knew what it felt like.

But then, like a spark catching on dry tinder, the warmth of him flickered suddenly against her skin. Her heart clenched, and Xephyra jerked toward the feeling, their flight matching Rex's abrupt turn as they soared toward the eastern wing of the compound.

Veronyka's magic surged forward in a rush, seeking Tristan with inevitable force, bursting through their connection like floodwaters across a desert plain.

Somewhere in the dark, Tristan lurched to his feet.

But the world has changed.
The Ashfires reign supreme no longer.

- CHAPTER 22 -
TRISTAN

VERONYKA.

Tristan practically fell out of his bed and ran to the tiny window in his cell, but it was nighttime, and there was nothing to see. Still, his heart raced because though he didn't understand the ties that bound them, he could feel her presence in his mind.

He recalled their goodbyes in Ferro. The way she had filled his head and his heart and whispered into his very soul.

Veronyka? he tried, uncertain.

I'm here, came the soft reply. *We're here.*

Tristan's forehead fell against the bars, his breaths coming fast and shallow. There were a thousand things he wanted to say, apologies and promises and wild declarations. He settled on the only words he could coherently string together.

I missed you.

He felt her smile. It was like summer sun.

Rex burst into his mind then, fiery and strong-willed and impatient. Tristan closed his eyes to drink up the feeling, the loneliness of the past few weeks burning away, nothing but a distant, terrible memory in the face of the warmth spreading through his body. The silence of the bond had been one of the worst parts of their separation, but suddenly Tristan felt whole again.

Where are you? he asked, tossing a wary glance over his shoulder. One of his guards had turned at his abrupt leap from bed, but his gaze was disinterested as he watched Tristan stare out the window. Relaxing his posture and quelling his brimming excitement, Tristan leaned against the wall. After a few moments, the guard looked away again.

Tristan attempted to mirror with Rex, to figure out what was happening. He caught glimpses of the night sky, of the exterior of Rolan's estate . . . of Veronyka. She was beside Rex—they had landed just beyond the walls of the compound, hidden within a cluster of trees. They would be concealed until the guards completed their next circuit, and Tristan wished desperately that Sev were with him, for surely he knew their routes.

Perhaps sensing Tristan's presence in Rex's mind, Veronyka stepped in front of the phoenix and drew his head down so they were on eye level. Tristan's insides quivered at the intimacy of their eye contact, close but once removed, filtered as it was through Rex—strange and difficult to understand.

How do we get in? Veronyka asked him, speaking slowly. She was in *his* mind now, not Rex's, having somehow used his link to his bondmate to make the connection more easily. Tristan shook his head, not bothering with trying to understand the magic, only grateful that Veronyka was willing to use it after months of doing everything she could to block it.

Tristan didn't know if it would work, but he pictured the floor plans Sev had brought him, trying to show Veronyka the layout of the prison wing, the markings that indicated where soldiers were stationed and where *he* was, underground and under guard. He went over the conversations he'd had with Sev, how they might create distractions and draw soldiers in various directions, but whatever the strategy, there was only one door into the prison. Even if they managed to get in, getting out again would be another matter entirely.

Clinging to the images Tristan had shown her, Veronyka diverted his attention to the prison floor plan. There was a question in her mind even without words.

It's all blocked, Tristan explained, marveling at how quickly she had pieced it all together. How effortless it was to communicate like this—at least for him. He just wanted to relish her presence for a moment, to enjoy the feeling of knowing she and Rex were nearby, but time was not on their side.

Tristan showed her the wall next to his cell, how it didn't align with the floor plan. Rolan had filled it in and blocked it off.

But even as he tried to explain it, Tristan noticed something near the guard's boot—a crack in the texture of the walled-in hallway. And underneath it . . .

"Wood," Tristan said aloud. Both the guards turned to look at him this time. "Kill for a drink," he added hastily, clearing his throat. "Would kill for some ale or wine or . . . something."

One of the guards snorted. "You and me both."

Tristan gave him a crooked smile. Once they had both looked away again, Tristan stretched his arms and yawned, then lowered himself to the ground on the pretense of stretching his legs next, getting as near to the bars—and the guard on the other side of it—as he dared, squinting at the place on the wall. Sev had knocked over a lantern several days back, and there was a dark scorch mark where the flames had licked up the side of what they both thought was a stone surface. Somehow, either by contact with the lantern itself or perhaps by some random booted toe or heel, the "stone" finish had cracked, revealing white edges underneath.

This wasn't a stone wall, but a wooden one finished in plaster and then painted to *look* like stone.

Tristan's head spun.

If this wall was wood covered in plaster, did that mean the door beyond it—the one that led outside—was the same?

What door?

Tristan jumped, forgetting that he wasn't alone in his mind. Veronyka had clearly been trying to follow along, but confusion was plain in the feelings that filtered through to him.

Rather than trying to explain his theory, Tristan guided her to where the door *should* be based on the floor plans he had seen. According to Sev's notes, there were no guards posted nearby. Just those on the walls, those who walked the perimeter in sweeps, and those stationed at the other entrances and along the corridors.

If you can find a way to sneak inside the walls—

Done, she said shortly, cutting him off. He wanted to ask how, but of course she knew that, and showed him an image of Rex soaring way up into the sky only to drop a stone with a clatter below, drawing the nearest guard's gaze for Veronyka to slip behind him.

Tristan's heart warmed at the way they worked so seamlessly together, but he felt a pang of something like jealousy too—he should be out there with them.

Show me, Veronyka prodded, and Tristan focused his attention on leading her to where the door was supposed to be located.

It wasn't like mirroring, exactly, but Tristan got flashes of images and pulses of sensation. He knew Veronyka had gotten a scrape as she pushed through some bushes that had been planted to conceal the hidden entrance, though he couldn't truly feel it, and he saw her hands sprawled across the seemingly solid stone. The flash of a knife, the crumble of plaster. Triumph blazed.

You're right, she told him, and he watched her working the blade into the seam of the still-existent door. *I can get through in a hurry if we're not worried about noise. But we are, aren't we?*

Yes, they were. Even if they managed to get through that door and inside the prison, the only way to get to Tristan was to break down the wall directly in front of him. Not only would the guards know they were coming, but they'd raise the alarm too.

Then again . . . maybe raising the alarm was exactly what they needed.

There was a rope pull next to the stairwell, which led up through the ceiling and into the captain's room.

Yara's room.

The problem was, Tristan didn't know if Yara was still on his side—if she ever had been. Sev had trusted her, and Tristan had trusted Sev. But then their plans went to pieces, and Rolan obviously suspected or even knew for certain that he had an informant in his midst, given his complicated travel arrangements and decoy tactics.

Someone may have betrayed them, and that someone could easily have been Yara.

Tristan supposed he was about to find out one way or the other.

He didn't want Veronyka to draw attention to the exterior entrance—it would be their escape route—but once she was inside . . . *Get in as quietly as you can. I'll guide you down the hallway until you come up against another wall. Then wait.*

I don't have an ax, Veronyka replied. *I won't be able to get through a wall with a dagger.*

Tristan hesitated. *Bring Xephyra.*

Veronyka knew what he was suggesting. Even without a magical connection to his mind, she would understand what he meant—fire—and what such a strategy would cost him.

But she didn't question him, didn't doubt his resolve. He loved her for it.

The minutes dragged on as Tristan waited, his attention divided between the world outside and the world within.

First Veronyka had to tell the others their plan—Tristan's patrol, he thought, and was that his *father?*—then she returned to chip and hack away at the plaster until she could wrench open the exterior door. It was loud, the hinges groaning and squeaking, but there was nothing to be done for it. If a guard came running, the others would have to take him out from their places beyond the estate's walls. Tristan sensed Rex among them, angry to be left behind, but they couldn't fit the whole flock in the narrow hallway, and if anyone was going to ignite, it had to be Xephyra. Veronyka's bond would protect her from the flames.

She was inside the building now, and Tristan's pulse raced, matching her own as she stumbled through the darkness. Xephyra came in after her, emitting a soft glow that allowed Veronyka to pick her way through the passage littered with garbage and debris.

And Tristan was with her. He had no way of knowing for certain, but he assumed the old structure behind the false wall matched the original floor plan Sev had found and pictured it in his mind as he guided her. *Straight. Straight. Now right at the junction. Just a bit farther . . .*

Here, she answered back, and Tristan's heart leapt as he stared at the wall from the opposite side. He hadn't been this close to her in weeks, and now all that separated them was that wood-and-plaster barrier.

He glanced at the guards, completely unaware that an intruder was mere feet away from them.

Now make some noise, he said.

Veronyka studied the wall from the other side—he saw flickers of it through her eyes—the beams of wood that made up the frame and the slats that filled it in. He sensed her shrug, then kick out hard, the flat sole of her boot connecting with the wooden wall with an echoing *bang*.

The guards whirled around in alarm.

Again, Tristan advised, and Veronyka aimed her kick at a crossbeam. A crack appeared in the plaster finish, visible from Tristan's side.

The guards frowned—even they didn't know the wall was false—and backed away warily.

"The bell," the nearer of the two said, and the other hastened to pull the rope.

Now Tristan would learn the truth.

He took it as a good sign that Yara flew down the stairs not long afterward—and she came alone. She asked the guards to report, but as they spoke, her gaze darted to Tristan. He nodded. There was no turning back now.

With sudden, smooth precision, Yara drew the sword from her belt and clubbed the nearest guard in the temple with the pommel. He crumpled, and when the second guard turned and opened his mouth to cry out, Yara silenced him with a kick to the stomach and then another blow with the sword to his head.

She hadn't even broken a sweat. "We don't have much time," she said. "There were others in the room when the alarm was sounded. They will expect me to return shortly."

Ready, Tristan relayed to Veronyka, and almost at once he felt the air shift and become strangely oxygenless while the temperature rose.

"Barricade the door," he told Yara, who had sensed the heat as well and swallowed thickly—the first sign of any emotion at all on her face. Tristan noted her burn scars again and realized there couldn't be two worse people to be trapped down here with a blazing phoenix.

Still, she nodded and clambered over the bodies of her fallen soldiers to make for the stairs.

"And stay back," Tristan added, following his own advice and retreating to the farthest corner of his cell. He tipped his flimsy bed onto its side and crouched behind it.

His eyes began to water as smoke filled the underground cell, the tiny window not nearly enough ventilation for the fire that was brewing beyond the wall. Tristan's breath turned ragged, fear and anticipation filling his lungs. He dared to look beyond the upturned cot and saw the center of the wall blacken and shrink, a dark halo of destruction steadily spreading outward until, with an almighty *boom*, the wall exploded in a shower of plaster and wood.

Sparks rained down on him, and Tristan raised his arms over his head to protect his face. He coughed and squinted through the smoke, discerning a gaping hole in the once-wall.

And Veronyka standing silhouetted in the ring of flames.

*The darkness has returned. The strixes rise
again from the summit of Pyrmont.*

CHAPTER 23

VERONYKA

THE SPACE BEFORE VERONYKA was filled with clouds of ash and debris, the scent of burning thick in the air. Bars materialized out of the haze to her left, while in front of her was a stairwell. A steady, rhythmic thumping distinguished itself while the ringing in her ears from Xephyra's fiery explosion faded, and in front of Veronyka a figure rose to her feet, detaching herself from the shadows.

A soldier.

Veronyka reached for her dagger, but as she did, she noted two other soldiers—unconscious or worse—on the ground before her. She hesitated.

"That's Captain Yara. She's a friend," came Tristan's hoarse voice from within the cell, and Veronyka's eyes snapped to him at once. It was still hard to see clearly, whatever moonlight that filtered through the tiny window serving only to make the smoke thicker and more obscuring.

"The keys," Veronyka said, looking to Yara again. The woman fumbled at her belt, the jingle of a key ring cutting through the echoing bangs that continued to reverberate down the stairs.

"The door is barricaded," Yara explained, bending over the lock. As she fitted the key, she glanced warily over her shoulder at Xephyra, who stood behind the ruined wall, doing her best to rein in her fire. "It won't hold for much longer."

Veronyka nodded, turning to the cell door. Tristan stood on the other side, and they stared at each other, his face shadowed and hard to discern, but she felt his gaze like heat on her skin. After a loud *clang*, the lock opened and the door swung wide, and then there were no more obstacles between them. Veronyka leapt into his arms, heedless of her wounded chest, so forcefully that he staggered back into the wall behind him. She dug her fingers through his hair—cropped close to the scalp—and wrapped her legs around his waist, while he folded his arms across her back, caging her in.

Her mouth was on his, the kiss deep and desperate. Though the familiar taste and smell and feel of him was an aching relief, she didn't fail to notice the tremble in his muscles or how thin he'd gotten.

I'm sorry I'm sorry I'm sorry, she said through their bond, but Tristan only drew back slightly, pushing her hair from her face and fixing her with a stare so intense it made her gut clench. He shook his head—he didn't want her apologies, refused to accept them—then kissed her back slowly, tenderly, cherishing every touch of lips and tongues.

"Ahem," came a dry voice from behind them, and Veronyka pulled back, remembering that they were not alone. Tristan's eyes opened lazily, groggily, as if from deepest sleep. He stared at her as if he had in fact woken up from a dream and couldn't be certain if this was real, before his attention lifted over her shoulder.

He stiffened, arms still locked behind her, before gently lowering Veronyka to her feet. He kept a hand on her lower back as if he couldn't bear to break the contact entirely.

The commander stood on the other side of the cell. Through their connection, Veronyka knew that Tristan thought she'd come inside the estate alone. She might have done it, too, if the commander hadn't insisted.

"You need a lookout," he'd replied shortly when Veronyka had explained her plan. Again she'd had to give the credit to Rex. Tristan had told *his phoenix* where to get in and how, not Veronyka. There had been something slightly skeptical in the commander's eyes, but he'd trusted her, which felt like more than she'd have gotten a few weeks ago.

The realization caused suspicion to bloom in her mind. Was it because of her Ashfire lineage that he suddenly listened to her opinion and allowed her to contribute? Did he feel like he didn't have a choice?

She supposed it didn't matter. He'd given her the lead but followed at a safe distance behind, knowing Xephyra would need to ignite.

And now here he stood. Tristan's expression was wary at first, but then shifted into something soft and vulnerable. He'd been in trouble, and his father had come.

Veronyka stepped aside, giving the commander room to stride forward. He gripped Tristan's shoulders, surveying him at arm's length, before nodding at what he saw and pulling his son in for a tight embrace. Tristan leaned into the hug, resting his head on his father's shoulder, showing a rare moment of weakness.

Their reunion was broken up by a particularly loud *thump* on the barricaded door, and they pulled apart. Soon the whole estate would come down on them.

The commander shifted from father to leader in the time it took to turn around.

"How many?" He directed the question to Yara, and his tone and demeanor seemed to put the soldier at ease. Fire and phoenixes were unfamiliar and perhaps unwanted territory, but reporting to a commander was something she would be more comfortable with.

"Fifty posted at regular intervals around the estate's walls. Only ten positioned on the prison level, plus these two"—she gestured to the unconscious soldiers on the ground—"and two at the top of the stairs. The others walk regular patrols of the first floor of the building—windows, doors, and other checkpoints. There are more soldiers on the upper stories, but they won't leave their posts unless an additional alarm is sounded."

"Do any of them know of the concealed door we entered through?" the commander asked.

Yara shook her head. "No, sir."

"We have to get out of here and into the sky before that second alarm sounds."

"Agreed," Veronyka said. "Let's move."

"Captain Yara—we could use your continued support, unless you'd rather come with us?" the commander asked.

She shook her head, looking almost ill at the thought. Veronyka suspected those burn scars had not come from a house fire. "I will stay here. Now go, quickly. You don't have much time."

She glanced down at the soldiers at her feet, expression grim, and a sense of foreboding settled over Veronyka. There was only one way to make sure those soldiers didn't tell the truth of how they became unconscious . . . and that was to make sure they never woke up. It would be easy enough to blame the attack on the Phoenix Riders and to claim Yara had been hurt herself.

"One more thing, if you wouldn't mind," Yara said before they turned to go. She was looking at Veronyka.

"Oh, right," Veronyka said, withdrawing her dagger. Yara had to *look* like she'd been attacked, to avoid suspicion.

"The forehead, I think," Yara said, bracing herself.

Veronyka gripped the dagger in her hand, carefully lining up her shot.

Tristan hesitated on the threshold of his cell, but only for a fraction of a second. "Thank you," he said, before moving into the passage after the commander.

Yara nodded, then glanced to Veronyka. She was ready. Veronyka hit her with the butt of the handle, hard enough to split the skin and cause Yara to stagger backward, but not enough to knock her unconscious or cause any lasting damage.

Yara blinked, touching her fingertips to the blood dripping down her head. She nodded her approval. "I'll deal with them"—she jerked her chin toward the soldiers on the ground—"then I'll have to 'help' with the barricade. I'll try to muck it up as much as possible." A ghost of a smile flickered across her lips. "You probably have less than five minutes."

"Thank you, Yara," Veronyka echoed, before sheathing her dagger.

"Take care of Pyra," Yara said. "That's all the thanks I need."

"I will," Veronyka promised, then followed the others back into the passage.

As they approached the end of the hallway, Veronyka edged around Xephyra to peer out the partially opened door. Soldiers could be seen atop the estate's perimeter wall, pointing toward the prison complex, where no doubt smoke was still issuing from Tristan's tiny cell window.

It was night, which gave them pockets of darkness to pass through, but there were enough lanterns to make that a risky proposition until they were in the sky.

"We could use a diversion," she muttered. "Something to draw their attention away from the ground level of the estate."

"Rex," Tristan said, and she felt as he reached for his bondmate, directing the phoenix toward the estate's roof. He brought Maximian with him, and together they alighted upon the steepled roof and burst into flame.

Veronyka drew back from Tristan's mind in time to see the firelight flickering upon the ground before them, the soldiers along the wall craning their necks skyward to stare.

It was now or never.

"Call them down," Veronyka urged, but then a loud bang and echoing voices burst out behind them, followed by the clamor of boots on stairs. The time Yara had bought them was over, and the barricade was no more.

The commander withdrew a short sword from his belt. Veronyka had never seen him carry such a weapon—in fact, she'd never seen him fight. He trained exclusively with his own patrol, and never when any other Riders were in the training yard. "I'll hold them off."

Tristan opened his mouth to argue, but Veronyka put a hand on his arm. Rex would arrive at any moment, and they needed to get Tristan into the saddle as quickly as possible. She didn't want to point out the obvious and wound his pride, but he was not in the best condition to fight.

Behind them, a soldier crawled through the hole in the wood-and-plaster wall Xephyra's fire had burned, but the commander was on him before he could even straighten up. He ran the soldier through in a neat thrust before dodging an attack from another. Their bodies helped to partially block the passage, bottlenecking their pursuers, but surely one of them would have a crossbow in hand before long.

Xephyra croaked, drawing Veronyka's attention. Rex and Maximian were circling above, but they were unable to approach because of some soldiers on the second story gallery.

Then a volley of arrows came out of nowhere, peppering the soldiers along the wall and those perched on the gallery overhead.

It was Tristan's patrol. A surge of happiness bubbled up inside him at the sight.

"Now!" Veronyka cried, tugging Tristan's arm while he shouted for the commander.

They burst out of the bushes, Xephyra in the lead, and before them landed Rex and Maximian. Arrows continued to fall from the sky, protecting them as they climbed into their saddles, the commander last to clear the cover of the building.

They took to the air in a gust of wind, soaring away from the compound and the deluge of arrows into the safety of the sky.

I have a new Shadow Sister, and she has
bonded to an Ashfire.

- CHAPTER 24 -
SEV

AFTER THE PHOENIX RIDERS had flown over his convoy, Sev wondered what would happen next—to him, of course, but also to the prisoner
transport mission.

They didn't stop their progress or turn around, and it appeared they
intended to go through with the ruse, which made sense, he supposed.
Rolan was also traveling, so it stood to reason that the Phoenix Riders might
seek the governor out first. The soldiers didn't know that Sev had tipped
them off—he could hardly believe it himself—or that the Phoenix Riders
were unlikely to come back. The soldiers had orders, and they followed
them down to the letter, including continuing to treat Sev as the decoy
prisoner, hauling him out of the carriage when they finally arrived in the
fortress in the Spine and dragging him up a narrow staircase to be stored in
a tower.

It was basically like putting him on a silver platter.

They obviously *wanted* to draw the Phoenix Riders out; otherwise
they'd have put him underground, the same as Tristan had been. Instead,
their goal was to make the fortress an easy place to approach. They had
only a handful of soldiers openly guarding the perimeter, with the majority
of their forces inside the stronghold walls. Despite their outward lack of

defenses, Sev suspected they'd be ready to spring into action with volleys of crossbow bolts and waves of snagging metal nets the instant the alarm was raised.

The irony, of course, was that Sev himself had been charged with raising it. They had some lookouts in the surrounding hills, but with darkness falling, their ability to spot a Phoenix Rider approach was severely limited. They were relying on Sev to notify the soldiers posted outside his door should Phoenix Riders descend from the sky, though if such a rescue were to happen, Sev intended to do no such thing.

But it wouldn't.

The Phoenix Riders would be forced to choose, and between himself and Tristan? Well, it was no choice at all. They would get what they came for—one of their own, the commander's son—and then focus on Lord Rolan and the Grand Council meeting. They could be halfway to Aura Nova by now, or busy chasing down Rolan's carriage to prevent his attendance.

They wouldn't be chasing after *Sev*.

He was nothing to them, really. A useful tool that was useful no more. It would be foolish to waste time and resources, maybe even lives, to save someone like him. Someone with nothing to contribute beyond dirty tricks and a weak conscience, and even those petty offerings were moot now that he was locked away in a tower like a princess in a fairy tale. But unlike in the stories, nobody was coming for Sev.

Instead, he would sit here for the night—perhaps several nights—until he and the other soldiers received new orders. Should he try to escape before then, with or without the Phoenix Riders?

He choked out a laugh and slumped against one of the cold stone walls, sliding until he hit the floor. As if it hadn't crossed his mind a dozen times already. As if he didn't know it was impossible. He was at the top of a *tower*, at least thirty feet from the ground. Without a battalion of Phoenix Riders soaring to his rescue, the tower might as well be a hundred feet from the ground, for all the difference it made. He couldn't jump it, couldn't climb it with his bad shoulder. And even if he could, where would he go without supplies?

At least he had friends somewhere out there—some place he might *want* to go. He had Kade. If Sev *could* escape, he would make his way north, through Stel, then Ferro, then across the border into Pyra . . . all as a deserter in the empire's military. He laughed again. It was a hollow sound.

He was in the exact same position he'd been before all of this started: trying—and failing—to find a way out on his own.

He shook his head and rolled out his bad shoulder. He was missing Hestia's peppermint salve, which numbed the pain and helped him sleep.

He was missing a lot more than that, truth be told.

The missing went deep; it stretched all the way back to Kade, to Trix, and farther still, to his mother and father. The missing was like poison in his bloodstream, spreading, contaminating his entire being with every beat of his heart.

He even found himself missing things he could barely remember— things like home, like family—and longing for other things that weren't his to have in the first place. Somewhere to belong, people to care about and who cared about him in return.

He closed his eyes.

One night of self-pity, he told himself sternly. *Just one.*

He had known it would come to this. He had known the risks. And he was alive, which was a small miracle in and of itself . . . but the goal of staying alive whatever the cost was becoming less and less appealing to him. The price was too high, and the payoff too little. It was amazing to think he'd spent most of his life determined to be alone and alive, and now he was both and yet he'd never been more miserable.

A light scratching sound interrupted Sev's thoughts. He thought it was coming from the door opposite him, but then he heard a soft coo, and his breath caught.

He lurched forward, going for the window next to the door. It was tall and narrow—more a slit than anything else—and found a small gray pigeon picking its way along the short ledge.

A familiar pigeon.

His heart soared, lodging inside his throat, practically choking him with joy and causing his vision to swim with unshed tears.

Sev patted down his pockets, then spotted his abandoned dinner tray near the door. He found some crumbs and held them in his palm, and once the pigeon was ferreting around inside his hand, Sev reached for the scroll attached to its leg.

His fingers trembled so badly he could hardly remove it, causing the pigeon to flap its wings in reproach. Finally, he had the letter loose, dusting off the remaining crumbs on his hand and leaving the poor bird to peck in peace as he unfurled the message and read.

It was written by Kade! Sev would know his careful writing anywhere.

Sev, I am here. Can you squeeze out the southeast window?

Sev's pulse fluttered wildly. Kade was here. Kade had come for him.

He looked up at the narrow strip of night sky visible out the southeast window. Were the Riders here as well, perched on the roof?

Hands still shaking, Sev put down the letter and walked to the window in question and peered outside. The tower wasn't like the one at the abandoned Phoenix Rider outpost where Rolan had housed Veronyka. It was shorter and squatter, built on square foundations rather than circular ones. It was one of four, each on a corner of the square keep. Sev's tower was on the southeast corner, and the southeast window looked down upon rolling lawns with several soldiers strolling the perimeter. They faced *away* from the tower, not toward it, and when Sev craned his neck to look up, he saw no sign of phoenixes, heard no ruffling feathers.

Even if they weren't here yet, as soon as a Rider tried to fly in, the soldiers would see them.

Sev looked down again. Maybe they didn't intend to fly.

Heavy shadows draped along the sloping ground, turning everything but the starry sky and patches of silvery grass into inky blackness. The walls that extended from the tower on either side were impossible to see, thanks to the tower's square design.

Sev was in a blind spot.

He considered the vertical aperture, tilting his shoulders and contemplating his ribs and hip bones. He *should* be able to fit through, though what he'd do once he managed that was something else entirely.

Sev grabbed the note and flipped it over, patting his pockets for something to write with. He paused when his palm came against a smooth, hard thing in the breast pocket of Tristan's tunic. He peeled back the leather overcoat to find a broken obsidian arrowhead. It looked a hundred years old—a keepsake, not a weapon—but it had an edge. With no better options, Sev scraped it across the pad of his thumb until a smear of bright red blood welled up.

"Sorry, Tristan," he muttered, wetting the tip with his makeshift ink and scribbling a hasty "Yes" across the back of the letter.

He blew on the paper until it dried, then tied it to the pigeon's leg. He waited until the nearest soldiers' backs were turned before tossing it unceremoniously out into the sky. He watched until it disappeared into the night.

Then he paced, sucking his stinging thumb and trying to keep it together.

A reply came almost an hour later.

This time the fresh note had only two words.

Look down.

Sev ran across the tower and poked his head out. It was hard to see in the darkness, but a second later, he had to duck back as the end of a rope flew up from the shadows below.

Recovering from his surprise, Sev threw his hand out just in time, snatching the rope and pulling it inside. Understanding Kade's plan, he turned on the spot, looking for a likely anchor, and found nothing but the door handle. It would have to do.

Sev tied it as tightly as possible, hoping that none of the soldiers below would notice the rope until morning—or until they checked in on him, whichever came first.

Tugging the rope to check the knot, Sev returned to the window and looked down. It seemed much higher all of a sudden, making his breath grow thin and his vision tunnel. He'd have to go feetfirst if he had any chance of keeping his balance, then lower himself down as quickly as he dared.

With a soft whistle, Sev summoned the pigeon to perch on his shoulder, then climbed onto the window ledge. It was located low on the wall, likely to make it easier for archers to pick off enemies below, and so Sev didn't have to work too hard to get himself halfway through. He had to turn onto his side, but even that went okay until he reached his hips. This was the moment his body would shift, when his shoulders—one of which was very weak—would have to bear almost the entirety of his weight. He lowered as slowly as he could, legs dangling, until his elbows touched the wall on either side of the window. His shoulder was already complaining, and Sev knew once he lost that leverage and reached for the rope, it would be much, much worse.

He took a deep breath, extending one arm, then the other.

His shoulder's complaints went from grumbles to all-out yells, and Sev had to clench his jaw to stop from crying out. He practically fell when his body cleared the lip of the window, the edge scraping against his stomach sharp enough to break skin if it weren't for his Rider leathers. The pigeon squawked and took flight—Sev couldn't blame it.

Despite the cold, he began to sweat, his legs kicking and flailing until he managed to get the rope between his feet and knees, taking some of the weight off his arms—but not nearly enough.

Kade is the better climber, he thought wildly, remembering their rooftop adventures in Ferro—though, of course, Kade wasn't trapped in a tower. *Also, his shoulders never would have fit through that window.*

Sev gritted his teeth and continued to shimmy down the rope, his hands raw and aching and all his muscles straining. He tried to let himself slide, but the lack of control was terrifying, and bringing himself to a stop caused his hands to burn painfully against the rough rope.

Just when Sev thought things couldn't get worse, a snapping sound echoed down to him, and he felt the rope twist and spin, as if the threads were slowly unraveling.

He looked up in confusion—then he remembered the sharp window ledge. All his weight bore down on the rope, pressing it against that jagged edge . . . slowly slicing his only lifeline right out from underneath him.

He *was* sliding now, sacrificing his hands to make his escape faster. He dared to look down, and spotted Kade staring up at him, his face shrouded in darkness.

Another snap—this time Sev felt more than heard it. Then, in the blink of an eye, all the tension left the rope, and he was falling.

His feet hit the ground first, the impact rattling Sev's bones. Pain lanced from his ankles through his knees and then coalesced like a ball of agony in his back, where he wound up sprawled on the packed earth.

Kade was on him in an instant, a hand over his mouth to muffle his groans, while the other untangled Sev's hands from the rope. Kade bent his face over Sev's, likely looking for some indication of how badly he was hurt. It took Sev a moment for his mind to catch up with his body; his breath was coming ragged against Kade's palm, but once he blinked away the shock and the pain, he realized he hadn't fallen all that far—maybe a few feet. It was the surprise of the landing that hadn't allowed him to brace himself that did the worst damage, but as his heartbeat slowed and the pain receded, Sev bent his legs and rolled his ankles.

He was okay.

He nodded at Kade, who withdrew his hand. Kade's hair had grown out, a dark forelock dangling over his eyes, and he grinned as he stared down at Sev. Then he planted a quick kiss on Sev's lips before reaching for his hands and hauling him upright.

His hands. Sev pulled them back on instinct, and Kade released him with a grimace of apology. Sev looked down at them—they were bleeding across the soft skin of his palms and fingers, but he shook them out and focused.

They were a good fifty feet behind the circuit the perimeter soldiers were walking around the fortress, at the top of the sloping hill that led up to the tower, hidden in darkness. That was all well and good for right now, but they'd have to leave their relative safety at some point, which meant striding out into the moonlight and exposing themselves.

As Sev fretted about their escape, Kade hastily coiled the fallen rope and threw it over his shoulder. He stared thoughtfully at the frayed edge, cocking a curious look at Sev.

Sev shrugged easily, pretending it had happened as part of a genius scheme to hide their tracks from any soldiers patrolling the grounds and not a happy accident that could have killed him.

Kade smiled and took Sev's wrist, avoiding his damaged hands as he moved to the edge of the tower's shadow. They stood there for a few silent heartbeats—long enough for Sev to wonder why they were waiting in the first place—when a sudden racket of swishing leaves and snapping twigs burst from between the trees to the south.

A shout went up, and footsteps heralded the arrival of two of the perimeter guards, who moved in the direction of the noise. With attention focused in the other direction, Kade pulled him out of the safety of the shadows and into the moonlight. Sev held his breath, but it was a straight shot from the sloping lawns and into the forest. He could hardly see, but Kade tugged him along with purpose, and then Sev noticed the owl several trees ahead of them, flitting from branch to branch and clearly leading the way.

After long, silent moments in which Sev didn't dare speak, the ground started to slope away, and he thought he could hear running water. Kade slowed their pace now, as they were forced to climb steep ditches or scurry over jagged rocks. Still, he held Sev's wrist, and still, they didn't speak. The night felt too quiet, the steady pant of their breaths and the crunch of leaves beneath their feet the only sound. The distant shouts of the soldiers had faded into almost nothing, and Sev trusted Kade to lead the way.

They'd just reached a small clearing when a shadow descended from above. Sev fell back, trying to drag Kade with him, but Kade resisted his pull. A second later he realized why. The shadow was a phoenix.

Kade released Sev at last and walked toward the creature, who bowed its head.

Something *thunk*ed into place inside Sev's mind. This wasn't just *a* phoenix. . . . This was *Kade's* phoenix. This was the egg Sev had given him.

"Sev," Kade said, resting a hand on the phoenix's neck and turning to face him. "This is my bondmate, Jinx."

He wore a huge smile—Sev could see it in the moonlight—the widest smile Sev had ever seen him wear, pride radiating from him. For some reason, the sight made Sev feel sick.

This was everything he had orchestrated, all he could have wanted for Kade.

And yet . . . and yet.

In his mind, Kade and Jinx only happened if Kade and Sev didn't. It was supposed to be Kade's distant future, his insurance policy should all else fail. It wasn't supposed to be Kade's *now*.

The Phoenix Riders were in the middle of a war. Sev supposed he and Kade had been in the thick of things too, but now there would be no safety for him. No avoiding the battlefield.

And no matter how often Sev had thought that Kade would be a wonderful Phoenix Rider, that he'd fit perfectly among them, Sev had never held any delusions that *he* could do the same. His only value had been as a spy, as a soldier. He had made strides, had learned how to be useful and how to do what he could, when he could—but Sev was no proper animage, no fit Rider for a phoenix. How could such a creature ever choose an animage as weak as Sev?

He didn't belong with the Phoenix Riders, which meant he didn't belong with Kade.

And that was a tough realization to swallow.

The phoenix—who was female, with gorgeous purple accents and a long, elegant neck—leaned forward to peer around Kade, head tilted as she blinked at Sev with bright-eyed curiosity. Kade smiled indulgently at being shunted aside by his bondmate in favor of this new person she wanted to inspect, and all Sev needed to do was extend his hand and he could stroke her feathers and smooth, gleaming beak.

A tendril of magic brushed against his mind—*her* magic, reaching for him, inviting him in without fear or hesitation.

Sev's breaths came fast and shallow. She was beautiful and majestic and everything Kade deserved. Everything *he* didn't.

Doubt reared up, ugly and desperate, and he turned away sharply, the move abrupt enough that Jinx croaked and straightened. Her magic receded.

"You came alone?" he asked, pretending to look around the clearing.

When Sev chanced a look back at Kade, he was frowning. "Not alone," he answered, patting his phoenix's feathers again—this time to soothe rather than to greet.

Jinx continued to study Sev, but there was a wariness to her now that wasn't there before. Of course there was—she had sought him out, sensing his magic, and he had disappointed her.

Sev ducked his head, refusing to meet her gaze. Kade stepped in front of her, blocking Sev from view, and he sensed they were having a silent conversation. There was a rustle of wings, and then she soared off.

"Sev," Kade began, once the phoenix was gone, but Sev hastened to speak over him.

"You shouldn't have risked it," he said. If he made the conversation about this, about something *reasonable*, he could avoid saying something he'd regret. "I'm not worth that."

Kade closed the distance between them. "You're worth everything."

"Not . . . ," Sev began, swallowing down the choking, miserable feeling inside him. "Not your position with the Riders. I'm sure you're needed elsewhere."

"I'm needed *here*. I didn't sneak off. She—Veronyka—she *told* me to come for you. Did you think they were just going to leave you here after everything you've done for them?"

A bubble of happiness swelled inside Sev. He quickly stamped it out, afraid to get his hopes up. "But now that my cover is blown . . . I won't be able to do much else."

Kade gave him a funny look. "So what? I'd be here regardless. You're one of us. It doesn't matter if you never do another useful thing."

Sev doubted that very much, but he didn't say so. Kade would never understand. He'd always been useful—as a talented animage, as an ally to Trix, and now as a Phoenix Rider.

Kade continued to stare at him, then sighed. "Come on," he said, walking around Sev and toward a patch of particularly dark night—a cave mouth. Kade stooped to move aside some supplies—clearly, he'd found this place before, probably during the daylight. The opening was concealed by the heavy boughs of some ancient tree. The soldiers would have a hard time finding them unless they already knew this place was here.

"Don't worry," Kade said, watching as Sev looked around the low, cramped space. "Jinx will keep an eye out."

Sev nodded.

"Will you come here?" Kade asked, wariness in his voice. Sev hated it, but he didn't know how to settle back into their usual comfort. He didn't know how to forget this insurmountable barrier between them. Kade the Phoenix Rider. Sev the once-spy. Sev the once-soldier. Sev the no one.

Kade settled onto the ground with a pack next to him, and as Sev approached, the pungent scent of healing herbs hit his nose. He took a deep breath and slumped down next to Kade. Every muscle in his body hurt.

"Your hands," Kade said matter-of-factly, and Sev let him wipe away the dirt and grime, then rub in a tingling ointment. Then he wrapped clean linen across Sev's palms.

"Every day I thought of you," Kade blurted. His head was still bowed over Sev's hands, though his work was done. "Veronyka . . . she was trying to reach Tristan. To send him messages somehow. I asked her to send word to you as well. Did it work?"

"No," Sev said quietly, very much liking the idea of Kade thinking about him every day. He wished he could have received the messages, though. He thought of the way Veronyka had spoken into his mind in the tower in Ferro, the way he'd managed to convey to her that Tristan wasn't in the wagon on his way to the stronghold. It was somehow both impossible and entirely believable.

"Oh," Kade said. He sounded at a loss, and Sev didn't blame him. He gripped Kade's hands with his own stiff, bandaged ones, making Kade look up again.

"I thought of you every day too. When I saw Veronyka fly past the convoy . . . Everything I'd been doing was to get myself back to you. I thought I'd lost my chance to make good on my promise."

Kade's lips twisted into a smile. "I don't think we're at the end yet, but we're together."

Together. Even that word felt ruined for Sev, somehow. It was no longer just the two of them.

"Let's get some rest," Kade said, putting away the healing supplies and nodding toward the far side of the cave, where two bedrolls were already laid out. Side by side.

"Right," Sev said. He'd been exhausted a mere moment ago, but now adrenaline shot like lightning through his veins.

"I didn't think we should risk a fire," he explained, and Sev understood. The night was cold and damp, the short autumn season already giving way to the long, wet, rainy winter.

And without a fire . . . they'd need each other's body heat.

Sev lay stiffly on the bedroll nearest him, facing into the cave. Kade unearthed a blanket from his packs and settled down next to him. Sev couldn't see him, but he sensed every shift and movement and felt the blanket settle over him as Kade draped it along their legs.

Afterward, Kade's hand hovered in the air, visible in Sev's peripheral vision. Then it dropped, gently, onto Sev's hip. Sev's lungs froze, his entire body going rigid. They stayed like that for one breath, then two, but before Sev could think of what to do, a sigh escaped Kade's lips, his warm breath whispering through Sev's hair.

Kade's hand skimmed lower, along Sev's abdomen—Sev was quite certain he hadn't breathed in minutes—and then settled, splayed, on his stomach. Kade pulled, dragging Sev backward across the small distance that separated them until Sev was pressed flush against him—back against chest, legs against thighs. Even against his neck, he felt the brush of Kade's forehead, nose . . . mouth.

Sev squirmed, leaning back into the touch—suddenly completely wide-awake. Kade chuckled; it rumbled against Sev's back.

"Sleep," he murmured, the words hot against Sev's skin. "You need it—we both do."

With Kade draped over every inch of him, that was easier said than done, but Sev tried.

"I wanted to ask," Kade said after several minutes of silence. "Did you write that letter in blood?"

Letter? Sev's mind was already slipping into sleep, but then he remembered the note Kade had sent him in the tower and his own hastily improvised reply. "I'd hardly call it a letter."

Kade released a huff of laughter. "Blood, though? Very grim."

Sev shrugged, then lifted his bandaged hand to peer at the slice on his thumb, just barely visible in the moonlight. "What else was I going to use—my handy inkwell and goose-feather quill? It was *you*. . . . I had to reply."

Kade didn't answer; instead, he took hold of Sev's hand and pressed his lips against the tender skin of his thumb in a gentle kiss.

It burned more sharply than the cut, the sensation lingering long after Sev closed his eyes and drifted off to sleep.

Now there are two Apex Riders.
Two Ashfires. Two queens in the sky.

- CHAPTER 25 -
SPARROW

IT WAS QUIET.

Sparrow hated quiet, but this quiet was even worse than usual. Thick. Cold. Heavy, somehow.

It hadn't started that way. No. First it was louder than anything she'd ever heard, as if the world itself had cracked in two and swallowed her whole. There had been pain then, bumps and scrapes, and Sparrow thought she might have actually lost consciousness, because when she came back to herself, everything was still, muffled and close, the sound of her panting breath echoing strangely in her ears.

At least she was not alone.

Fine Fellow was nearby, scritching and scraping as he rooted around for worms and insects.

And *she* was here too—Ignix.

Sparrow had felt the phoenix's presence with her magic first, a distinctive, familiar awareness. Then she'd recognized her physical closeness, her wing arcing over Sparrow like a tent or a sloping roof. It muted the sound around her—the echoes gentler than those that reverberated from the rocks—and radiated warmth.

She could also hear Ignix's steady breathing, the rise and fall of her chest . . . a barely there noise, but amplified by the soft whisper of her feathers sliding against each other as her rib cage expanded and contracted. Ignix could sit incredibly still—stiller than any living thing Sparrow had ever heard—but she was *alive*, and things that were alive moved. Made sound. They filled out Sparrow's surroundings when her eyes could not, and truly, how better to understand the world as an animage than through the animals that lived in it? Sparrow didn't care for buildings and wagons and roads. She cared for living things, and they cared for her, too.

Well, *most* of them did anyway. People were harder.

The memory of Elliot's voice echoed in her head all of a sudden, tight with fear and dread—he had known what was coming, had seen what Sparrow could not. She thought back farther, to the moment outside the village when he'd forgotten her in favor of his sister. When he had tried to pawn her off on Ignix.

Yes . . . people were harder.

When Sparrow finally groaned and rolled over, coughing, Ignix sighed in relief.

You sleep like the dead. She was all around Sparrow, her wings encircling, wrapping—protecting—and was surely the reason Sparrow hadn't been crushed in whatever collapse or cave-in the monsters attacking the Eyrie had caused in the first place.

"Wasn't *sleeping*," Sparrow muttered, though she couldn't recall how she had wound up where she was, or how long she'd been lying there. Maybe she *had* fallen asleep.

The scent of blood was thick in her nostrils, but it wasn't the familiar, metallic tang of regular animal or people blood. It smelled like smoke and charcoal and was hot to the touch.

It was phoenix blood.

"You're bleeding," Sparrow informed Ignix, as if she didn't surely already know.

Mere flesh wounds, Ignix replied. *I will survive.*

"Does that mean . . . ? Did you lose?" Sparrow asked tentatively. It had all been very hard to follow. One second she was running toward the village, intent on helping Jana and the others get the animals to safety—the next, Ignix had scooped her up in one of her giant clawed feet and carried her through the air like an eagle with a twig for its nest.

Despite the confusion, Ignix had eventually explained exactly who was attacking them—strixes, of all things!—and Sparrow had heard the challenge and the acceptance from her place inside the Eyrie, right before the battle between Ignix and Avalkyra Ashfire began.

I lost, Ignix replied gravely. *I had hoped to lure her into the tight quarters of the tunnels—to regain the upper hand—but . . .*

But she'd run headlong into Sparrow, and the tunnel had collapsed on them.

I suppose I was just delaying the inevitable.

"What will happen now?" Sparrow asked, forgetting her own predicament in favor of worrying about her animal—and human—friends. "To the others? Are they . . . ?"

Avalkyra has honored the terms of the challenge. She has the Eyrie, but your friends do not belong to her. They are gone. Evacuated.

"Do you think those birds—those strixes—will chase them? Do you think they'll come after us in here?"

As far as their master is concerned, I am dead. She paused, and Sparrow had the sense she was reaching her magic, feeling out their surroundings. *We are safe from them, for now. But we will not remain safe here for long.*

"Right," Sparrow said, blowing out a shaky breath through her lips. "What do we do?"

We move.

And she did, turning in the tight, confined space—but in the tiniest, most careful of increments. Then she halted.

"What's the matter?" Sparrow asked.

Ignix didn't reply at first. *The passage is unstable. I fear the roof will collapse on you.*

Sparrow listened hard, listened to the shift of gravel and silt, the barely there grinding scrape of rocks. Was Ignix preventing a full-blown cave-in? That seemed impossible, no matter her age and strength.

"Only a little," she reasoned, and the phoenix expelled an irritated gust of air—it caused Sparrow's hair to fly across her face.

Or a lot. There is no way to know for sure.

Sparrow shrugged. "I can die now in a rockslide or I can die in a day or two from thirst or hunger. I'd rather take my chances with the rocks. I'll be fine, I know it."

Ignix sighed again, more heavily than before. *This will probably hurt,* she said, and Sparrow braced herself. The heat of Ignix's wings drew away from her as the phoenix got to her feet, scraping her talons against the stone.

As soon as she stood, clouds of dust settled on Sparrow's skin and inside her lungs. She began coughing instantly, and then a cascade of larger debris started to rain down on her. She tucked her head under her hands to protect herself—Fife leapt forward to scramble underneath her arms—but Ignix moved slowly, cautiously, and soon enough the cavern fell silent again.

"See?" Sparrow croaked. She needed water, her mouth was gritty and her throat raw, but the tunnel had not collapsed on her. Even better, the *air* was different now too—fresher, sweeter, and with the slightest bit of current.

She scrabbled onto her knees, ready to stand, when Fife squawked a warning, the sound echoing all around them. The ceiling was too low, or perhaps a broken bit of rock protruded above her, so Sparrow hunched as she ambled forward. She tilted her head toward that sense of movement— that clean, brand-new smell.

She followed it.

The passage to the south has collapsed. You cannot go that way, Ignix said, halting Sparrow in her tracks. *But there is another route we might take.*

Sparrow tilted her head, extended her senses. "That way?" she asked, pointing in the opposite direction of that fresh, flowing air.

Yes, Ignix said. *West first, then south again.*

"I know you can see in the dark and all, but your sniffer ain't as good as mine," Sparrow said primly, tapping herself on the nose. "I'm tellin' ya, we gotta go south."

It is blocked, Ignix insisted.

"There's a way through," Sparrow said, shaking her head. "I can smell it."

I will not wager the fate of the world on your sniffer, Ignix snapped, bristling. *I am the only one who can defeat her. I must get out of these cursed tunnels and quickly—I do not have time to play nursemaid.*

Sparrow's nostrils flared and her jaw clenched. "Nobody asked you to. I'm fine without you. Come on, Fife." Spinning on her heel, she headed south again, trusting her senses—and the raven's occasional croaks—to lead the way.

Ignix didn't follow. Instead, Sparrow discerned the soft clicking of talons on stone as she walked away, in the opposite direction.

"Phoenixes," Sparrow muttered, stomping forward.

The tunnel *was* caved in—barely fifty paces away—but Sparrow was not deterred. It wasn't just her nose that was guiding her now, but her ears as well.

"Help me," Sparrow said, and Fife left her shoulder to hop across the ground before her, picking a path over rubble and huge blocks of stone. She followed, scraping her knees and cutting open her palms. She lived for the outdoors, for the wind and the sun and the freedom that she could taste on that barely there whisper of bright, clean air that teased her with every labored step.

There was an opening at the top of the rock pile—Sparrow was certain of it. But it was tricky to reach. Fife cawed encouragingly, and as she followed the sound, her right hand found a gap in the stones. She pushed herself through with such enthusiasm that she fell headlong and tumbled down on the other side.

It hurt, a lot, nearly knocking the wind from her lungs—but when she finally drew in a breath, she released it again at once, laughter in her throat. The air here felt positively breezy in comparison to the cramped space on the other side of the opening, and Sparrow reveled in its crisp freshness.

She reached out, finding smooth walls against her hands—not jagged, broken stones—and Fife told her where to put her feet. She wished she had her spear, but realized with a pang that she had left it somewhere in the tall grasses outside the village.

They hadn't made it far before Fife crowed excitedly and took off in a gust of wingbeats. Sparrow frowned, still edging slowly after him.

"Bath?" she asked in confusion, trying to piece together the bird's frantic thoughts.

Then she heard a splash.

Sparrow stumbled forward, stubbing her toe painfully on something round and hard that thunked loudly—not the dull, flat sound of a rock, but the heavy, reverberating sound of a wooden cask or barrel. It was followed by a slosh and a splatter.

Sparrow stuck out trembling hands, her body catching up to the picture Fife had painted in her mind, and lowered them into the open barrel. Icy shock raced up her arms, followed by painful joy, and she wasted no time plunging her face into the water.

Fife squawked and splashed, and Sparrow drank greedily, stopping only once she'd had so much her belly felt waterlogged and her teeth ached from the cold.

Filthy, said a stuffy magical voice behind her, the word edged in distaste—but Sparrow only smiled as she turned. She and Fife had made such a racket with the water, she hadn't heard Ignix approach.

"I thought you were headin' west?" Sparrow asked smugly.

I thought I should check on you, Ignix said responsibly. Sparrow waited, then—*And . . . I encountered a dead end.*

Sparrow grinned more widely. "As you can see, we're fine."

Indeed. Ignix's voice sounded strained—distracted, even. Fife was still making a mess in the water barrel, the contents gurgling and sluicing onto the floor.

Despite Ignix's pretense at disgust, Sparrow knew the phoenix was as thirsty as she was. Once she and Fife were done, gasping and laughing and soaking wet, Ignix inched forward to delicately dip her beak. She made barely a sound—though she drank long and deep.

Sparrow investigated the area and found the barrel was outside a small storage room, filled with supplies, including sacks of grain, ceramic jars of preserves, and even bags of apples. She tried to orient herself, imagining where this place was in relation to the hallway they'd just left, but all the excitement was starting to catch up to her.

She ate an apple, leaving the core for Fife, and then climbed atop the bags of grain—which were cold and lumpy but positively feather-soft compared to the hard ground she'd been lying on since the cave-in. It became even more decadent when Ignix sidled in, slowly warming the place and causing the grain to smell toasty and fragrant, like Morra's kitchens in the morning.

"Looks like you shoulda trusted my sniffer after all," Sparrow said with a yawn.

Ignix huffed. *I would have found my way eventually.*

"Slowly," Sparrow corrected, smiling. "And you don't have time to waste."

No, I don't, Ignix replied.

Sparrow wanted to say more, but sleep pulled her under.

Another generation at war.

CHAPTER 26

TRISTAN

TRISTAN FELT EUPHORIC SOARING with Rex into the night sky.

As soon as he knew the danger had passed, he twisted around to see the estate and its many soldiers disappear into the darkness. Then he loosened his tight muscles, settling comfortably into the saddle and relishing the cool wind and rolling rhythm of flight.

Rex was focused on following the others to their chosen rendezvous point, but Tristan felt his pleasure at being reunited—the sense of rightness between them, the way they fit together.

Too skinny, Rex said abruptly. *Too light.*

It was rare for Rex to communicate verbally. He was hotheaded and emotional, the same as Tristan, and they understood each other perfectly well even without words. But Veronyka pushed Xephyra to be as verbal as possible, and Tristan couldn't help but wonder if this was another instance of things bleeding over between them. He glanced at Veronyka now, soaring just ahead of him. Their bond had saved him tonight—and it had saved her when she was imprisoned in that tower and Xephyra reached out to Rex.

Had Veronyka had a change of heart? Was she finally willing to use the magic that she had fought so hard against?

And if so, did that mean she was with him, even now?

She didn't look back or acknowledge that she might be inside his mind, so Tristan pushed the thought aside and stroked his bondmate's neck. *Not that skinny.*

Rex showed him a mental image of a twig. Tristan chuckled.

When at last they descended, it was on the northern shore of Seltlake. Most of the salt extraction from the lake happened on the southern shores near the salt flats, where an ancient, much larger body of water had slowly evaporated over time. Since it was the dead of night and they were on the barren edges of the Shadow Plains, they were safe to land and make camp.

No sooner had Tristan slid from his saddle than everyone was on him.

Rex was first, his all-business attitude gone as he ran his beak over Tristan's body, somehow managing to find—and painfully nudge—every bruise and aching muscle, leaping all over him like an excited puppy. Then he raked his beak through Tristan's short hair, as if confused about where the rest of it had gone.

At last Rex settled back on his haunches and released a huff of air. His gaze was still measuring, though his anxious energy had settled somewhat. *Stink.*

Tristan rolled his eyes. *Thanks, Rex.*

Veronyka was there next, and Tristan found himself extremely self-conscious—thanks in no small part to what Rex had just helpfully pointed out. Instead of squeezing her in another desperate hug, Tristan stood awkwardly, expecting her to give him a close inspection as well.

She didn't bump and jostle him like Rex—thank Miseriya's mercy—but her large eyes took in every inch of him.

"Are you okay?" she asked anxiously.

Tristan was about to give a dismissive response—it didn't matter; he was here now—but then he noticed a bandage poking out from the top of Veronyka's tunic. Now it was *his* turn to survey *her*, noting her stiff posture and recalling the somewhat labored way she'd moved inside the prison. He'd been so distracted by the sight of her, he'd just assumed it was nerves or other factors at work.

"Are *you?*" he asked, and her gaze skittered away.

"I'm fine," she said, then cleared her throat and fixed him with a rueful look. "I can't believe they cut your hair."

He smiled at that, running a hand over the short bristles. Before he could ask if she liked it, his patrol members surged forward.

Anders grinned widely at him but was quick to echo Rex's observations. "You look terrible," he said after a brief hug. He scrunched up his nose. "But you smell worse."

"He's been a prisoner for six weeks," Ronyn said, shoving Anders aside to clap Tristan on the shoulder. "What's your excuse?"

"Glad to have you back," Lysandro said, squeezing Tristan a bit too tightly.

"Thanks for keeping everything together while I was gone," Tristan said, ruffling his hair. Lysandro beamed proudly.

Latham stood before Tristan next. The others became conveniently distracted by starting a fire and setting up camp, leaving them alone. They hadn't properly spoken since their rather public argument in Rushlea, when Latham had accused him of being stubborn and reckless and called him out for how he ran their patrol and his preferential treatment of Veronyka.

Latham looked acutely uncomfortable. His hands were fisted at his sides, his features pinched. "Tristan, I—"

"It's fine, Latham," Tristan cut in, finding that his anger over their argument had long since faded. Latham had been upset about his bondmate, and after being attacked by the Rushlean farmers, tensions had been running high for all of them.

"It is?" he asked warily.

"We're good. You were right about a lot of that stuff. I'm still trying to figure it all out. How to lead, how to balance everything."

Latham nodded. "Still. I'm sorry for the way I acted. For what I said."

"You're allowed to disagree with me—and I hope you continue to do so. But *talk* to me, okay? I promise I'll listen. Don't wait until . . ."

"It's too late?" Latham asked, a crooked smile on his face.

"I was going to say until you want to punch me in the face, but sure—that works too."

Latham laughed, and they shook hands.

"Thank the gods!" Anders said from across the camp. "Our patrol is at peace once again."

Ronyn rolled his eyes.

While they started on food and boiled water for Tristan to wash with—he longed for a soak in the Eyrie's hot spring baths, but any hot water at all was a welcome sight—the commander summoned Tristan into his meeting tent.

Veronyka was already inside, and he took a seat beside her at the small table they'd set up.

For the first time he noticed the red armband across her biceps. His father had heeded his wishes and made Veronyka his official second-in-command, which meant *she* had been leading his patrol all this time. Reaching under the table, he took her hand.

His father relayed the events of the past few days, making any good feelings Tristan had at being free and reunited with his patrol quickly fade away.

"Hang on," he said sharply, lurching to his feet. "Avalkyra's taken the Eyrie? With strixes? *How?*" He shot that last word at Veronyka.

"We were at Rushlea," she said—she obviously meant her and Tristan's patrol. "I don't know where they came from or how she got them."

"None of us do," the commander said, indicating that Tristan should sit again. "But we do know that she's controlling them—she is bonded to the oldest and largest of the flock, the apex strix, and so wields that power over them. She won the Eyrie fair and square. She issued a challenge, and Ignix accepted it."

"I didn't know there was such a thing as a strix apex," Tristan muttered, retaking his seat. "How many strixes are there?"

"Two dozen at my best estimate."

Tristan nodded. "That's okay. That's a number we could beat."

"Perhaps," his father conceded, "if we weren't already spread so thin.

But this time she let us go. Next time I doubt that will be the case."

"I'm surprised she honored the rules of the challenge," Tristan muttered.

Veronyka shrugged, though Tristan knew she was anything but nonchalant. "Val got what she came for. She challenged Ignix and *won*. She took the Eyrie, and she took Morra, too."

"Wait, she took Morra?"

Veronyka shook her head. "Not exactly. Morra swore herself to Val," she corrected, her voice tremulous. "I just can't figure out why she'd want to serve someone who was trying to destroy the Phoenix Riders—she *was* a Phoenix Rider, and used to be a priestess of Axura."

"Not just Axura," the commander said. "Morra was a part of a very small, very exclusive Nox subsect within the Axuran Temple. The goddess of night used to be worshipped openly in Pyra, but by the time the empire was founded, they were no longer building temples in her name or sharing sermons about her glory. Hence, the subsect within Axura's own ministry. Their followers were interested in phoenixes and animal magic, but also shadow magic—a forbidden subject—and strixes, too."

Veronyka reared back. "She never told me that."

"She never told *me* that either, but I did some digging when I tracked her down several years back and asked her to come to Azurec's Eyrie with me. Their sect's beliefs were complicated and obscure, but I don't think she *worshipped* Nox or her dark legacy. She did study the goddess, though, study the magic, the history, and the lore. Of course, everything they learned was theoretical . . . until now. Perhaps she could not resist seeing the real thing up close. Perhaps there are other levels to this that we do not comprehend."

The commander didn't know about Veronyka's shadow magic, but he did know that Morra had been an important person to her. His tone had been surprisingly gentle throughout his explanation, and even now his expression was kind.

Tristan's, however, was not. "Why would you let her in if you knew she had this . . . interest in Nox and the strixes? If you knew she was lying?" He liked Morra, but he couldn't help feeling protective over Veronyka, who was the person who suffered most from this apparent betrayal.

The commander sighed. "She's a shadowmage, son—I don't doubt she lied about a great many things. But she was a Phoenix Rider and loyal to the cause. At the time, allies were few and far between, and the truth was, I needed someone with her skill set. I had no reason not to trust her, despite her scholarly pursuits. Your mother rode with her during the war and risked her life to get the woman to safety afterward. I trusted her judgment, if not my own."

Tristan scowled. He supposed none of them could have predicted this, but it grated all the same. Under the table, he squeezed Veronyka's hand. He should have been there, not sitting around in a cell. He could have helped.

"We cannot concern ourselves with the decisions of others, however inscrutable," the commander continued. "She is there, with Avalkyra, and we have Riders keeping constant surveillance. We will know if and when Avalkyra makes a move. For now, we have to turn our attention to the Grand Council."

Tristan edged forward in his chair. "What's happening?"

"So far, all we know is what we received in Sev's letter—that Rolan was traveling at the same time as you."

Sev. Tristan felt a spike of guilt, having completely forgotten about him with everything that had happened that night. "Where is Sev?"

"Probably in the stronghold in the Spine," the commander replied.

"But we sent Kade—a new apprentice—to check it out," Veronyka said. "With any luck, he and Sev will be able to sneak away sometime tonight. If not, Kade'll return in the morning with information, and we'll devise a rescue plan from there."

They sent an apprentice to rescue Sev from a castle? Tristan supposed they didn't exactly have an excess of manpower at the moment, and at least there was *someone* there to check things out and report back. It was better than nothing.

"And Rolan?" he asked, looking between them. He dearly hoped they hadn't sacrificed their chance at the governor in order to save him.

"Doriyan and Alexiya are in pursuit," Veronyka said, and Tristan wondered if she'd heard his thoughts, or if she could read the self-reproach on his face.

His head spun with all he'd missed out on. Alexiya had seemed to hold nothing but disdain for Doriyan when she'd described him to Veronyka and Tristan in her rooftop home in the Silverwood, and Doriyan himself had been so skittish, Tristan was surprised he'd agreed to join the flock in the first place.

"They should return before the night is out. They were to locate his carriage and report back—nothing more."

"But if my transfer was a ruse . . . ," Tristan began, and Veronyka nodded grimly.

"His might have been as well."

"So we still don't know the date of the Grand Council meeting? I thought you had contacts in the capital?"

"I do," the commander said, a bit defensively. "The council members have been extremely tight-lipped about the whole thing. We'd hoped Rolan's travel might indicate it was on the horizon, but if his movements have also been falsified . . ."

Voices sounded from outside the tent flap, and Anders poked his head in. "They're here," he said, and both the commander and Veronyka moved to follow him, Tristan a step behind.

Doriyan and Alexiya stood next to the fire, speaking in low murmurs until they saw Tristan and the others approach.

While Doriyan nodded to them, Alexiya stepped forward to hug Veronyka, keeping a soft, almost maternal hand on her shoulder. Tristan hadn't realized they'd gotten so close. The last time he'd seen them interact with each other, it had been a challenging sort of relationship, a battle of wills. Now they seemed closer than friends.

Like us, Rex said from his place with the other phoenixes across the fireside. Tristan reared back, oddly jealous at the thought.

Bonded?

Rex gave him a funny look, tilting his head. *Family.*

He darted a look at Veronyka, the question on his tongue—but of course, he didn't need to speak, not to her.

My father's sister, she explained. Then added, because obviously Tristan had a dozen more questions, *Later.*

"The carriage was headed south just as you said," Doriyan was explaining as Tristan drew his attention back to the public conversation. "We followed it past Qorlland City, and almost all the way to Stelarbor before we realized it wasn't him."

"It wasn't Rolan?" asked the commander.

Doriyan shook his head. "Another decoy." Apparently Tristan's patrol had filled him in on their side of things.

The commander cursed, stalking a few feet away and shoving an agitated hand through his hair.

"He stayed in the carriage for almost the entire journey," Alexiya explained to Tristan and Veronyka, though her voice was loud enough for the commander to hear if he felt like listening. "So I grew . . . impatient." She smiled somewhat viciously. "I sent a flock of doves inside the carriage. The thing shook and rattled for a good five minutes before the poor bastard finally called for a halt. He was running from the carriage before the wheels fully stopped, swarmed by birds and covered in cuts and scratches. I only got a brief glimpse of his face, but it was enough. Whoever he was, he wasn't Rolan."

"He could have been posing as one of his soldiers, couldn't he?" Tristan asked as his father returned to the group. "Riding a horse alongside the carriage?"

Alexiya shook her head. "We'd been watching them for hours, mirrored with our phoenixes. I'd already checked all their faces."

"But—where is he?" Tristan asked the group at large. Veronyka's eyes weren't on him or Alexiya but on the commander. He wasn't looking at her or at any of them—his gaze was turned to the east. To the capital city.

Tristan's heart clenched. "You don't think . . . ?"

"How long until dawn?" Veronyka asked, looking east as well. The sky was still dark—it couldn't be too far past midnight.

"It is unlike the council to meet before seven bells. Even on urgent matters. If we leave shortly, we can make it in time."

"In time for what? You can't mean to go through with . . . with your other plan," Tristan said, unsure how many others knew of his assassination plot or how much he should share.

The commander's gaze flickered, taking in Tristan's patrol. "Back inside the tent." Apparently, he'd decided such matters should be kept more private.

He signaled for Alexiya and Doriyan to join them, but while the commander reclaimed his chair, Tristan didn't sit. Neither did Veronyka, giving the newcomers a chance to rest.

"To answer your question—no, my previous plan will no longer work. It relied upon a certain amount of goodwill between myself and the council and the assumption that I'd not risk a chance at reclaiming my old position in the empire. However, given our arrangement with Rolan . . . the moment he laid eyes on me, he'd know that he'd lost his bargaining chip and that I'd betrayed him. Something he already suspects, given these decoy transfers. I won't be able to walk two steps through those doors without being accosted."

"You couldn't . . . but I could," Veronyka said.

Tristan stiffened, and everyone else turned to face her.

"He needs me if he's to have any claim over the throne—or at least, one that lasts longer than the time it takes for the army to reclaim the city. If I come forward, he'll have to corroborate my identity. He has to give me that power, if only so he has a chance at taking a slice of it for himself."

The commander was surveying her closely, and he looked impressed with what he saw. Veronyka's poise and confidence was a complete and total change from the last time she'd discussed her parentage and the responsibilities that lay before her. Tristan was proud of her, even if the reality of what she was offering to do made him feel slightly sick.

"I know it won't be as simple as that—taking the throne, or . . . whatever." She swallowed, showing the first signs of her unease at the prospect. "I'd have to be officially recognized as heir first, but maybe that would be enough for now? A distraction or a delay for the council?"

The commander was nodding thoughtfully. "Rolan will be forced to support your claim, perhaps even at the expense of his war plans against the Phoenix Riders. You are one of us, after all. . . ."

"Plus, it would officially take Avalkyra out of the line of succession," Doriyan added quietly.

"While I live, at any rate," Veronyka added as an afterthought. Tristan's heart clenched. "Maybe if we do this now, we'll get the time we need. Then, after, we can . . . figure out the rest."

The rest. As in, her ascension to queen of the empire.

"Is Rolan the only person with the evidence required to prove your identity?" Tristan asked.

Sev had told Tristan about the marriage contract and birth certificate he'd seen the lawmaker handling the day he was captured. Was that the same birth certificate Veronyka possessed?

She nodded. "Avalkyra burned everything else." She reached up into her hair, and Tristan noticed braids there for the first time. One of them was capped with the arrowhead he'd given her—his heart leapt at the sight, even though it reminded him with a pang that he'd lost his half—and the other two were tied off with golden objects that shimmered in the lantern light. "But I do have her signet ring and Pheronia's necklace."

"Not enough," the commander said, scrubbing his chin absently. "But if Rolan cooperates, it won't matter. He'll fight tooth and nail to get your identity verified and use the same allies he would turn against us to vote in your favor."

"She's still underage," Alexiya said. "Only just turned seventeen."

The commander waved her off. "She can't officially ascend, but she can still be named heir to the throne. It will give her certain rights, including calling votes—and canceling them."

"And after?" Tristan asked, working hard to keep his voice steady. "Rolan will want his Ashfire bride."

"I don't care *what* he wants," Veronyka said flatly.

Alexiya chuckled. "Spoken like a true Ashfire." The words were said with humor and affection, but Veronyka's expression faltered.

"We will worry about after, *after*," the commander said firmly. "For now he needs to think it will happen or our plans will fall to pieces."

"How long until we depart?" asked Alexiya.

"Eat and pack up as quickly as possible. The four of us will leave for Aura Nova at once."

Tristan blinked. "*Four?* I'm coming too."

"Son, you've been in a dank underground cell for six weeks. You need rest. You will remain behind with your patrol and await further instructions."

"Seriously?" Tristan said. "If you think I'd let her fly into that viper's nest without me, you're the one who needs rest."

He squared his shoulders, ready for a fight, and his father filled his lungs, preparing for the same—then, abruptly, he deflated. Sighing, he looked between Tristan and Veronyka. "Oh, very well."

Huh. *That* was a first. Was the commander finally starting to see things Tristan's way, or was he getting too old and tired to fight him on every point and issue?

Tristan grinned and followed Veronyka out of the tent.

Whatever it was, he'd take it.

This time, I fear we may not survive it.

- CHAPTER 27 -
SEV

SEV WOKE UP WARM and content, Kade's arm slung across his stomach and Kade's body pressed against his back.

It was still night, Sev thought, or maybe it was just the darkness of the cave—and his hesitance to open his eyes. He rolled over, nuzzling into the exposed skin of Kade's neck.

There was a sharp inhalation of breath, and Kade's body tensed. *"Sev,"* he murmured sleepily, relaxing somewhat, but the tension in his muscles soon returned, shifting from surprise to something edged in anticipation. The arm that had been hanging limp across Sev's middle moved, tightening against his back.

"Who else?" Sev said, lips moving against Kade's skin.

"No one . . ." Kade paused, swallowing audibly. His pulse was thrumming rapid-fire under his jaw. "No one else."

Sev liked that answer. He smiled, feeling the scratch of stubble against his lips as he moved, following the column of Kade's throat with openmouthed kisses, down to his collarbone.

The hand at his back twitched, pulling Sev close for a moment before gripping his shirt.

"We, uh," Kade said, somewhat breathlessly. "We should get moving. Before daybreak."

"Mm-hm," Sev hummed, unwilling to break contact with Kade's skin. He'd wormed his hands between them, and though his fingers were clumsy with bandages, he'd managed to start tugging at the laces of Kade's tunic. "In a few minutes. It's barely—"

He twisted, meaning to look around toward the cave mouth, but was stopped short by the rather alarming sight of two great big beetle-black eyes staring back at him.

He yelped and leapt to his feet, tripping as his legs tangled in the blanket and Jinx squawked in alarm.

Jinx. He'd forgotten. *How* had he forgotten?

She had been looming over them with her wings spread out, surrounding them in a cocoon of warmth. Now that he was out from under her protection, the air was cool enough to cloud in front of his face and set goose bumps rippling across his skin.

Kade lurched into a sitting position, looking dazed and disheveled, his eyelids heavy, while Sev remained where he stood, arms crossed and feet rooted to the cold stone floor.

"Jinx," Kade muttered, "what did you—get out of here," he said with mild exasperation, finally piecing things together. The phoenix cocked her head in innocent confusion before fluttering away, out the cave mouth. Kade ran a hand through his hair, laughing weakly, before his gaze settled on Sev. "Sorry," he said ruefully. "She's too curious for her own good—or for *my* own good, anyway."

He stopped talking, the sparkle in his eyes dimming when he saw that Sev wasn't laughing with him. "You could . . ." He gestured to the space next to him, the place Sev had so unceremoniously vacated, before darting a look toward the cave mouth. "We have some time until dawn, I think."

He looked uncertain, and the sight sent a pang through Sev's chest. He wanted to crawl back under the blanket. He wanted to pretend that Jinx didn't change everything . . . but she did. *They* were a pair now—Kade and Jinx—and Sev didn't fit within that framework . . . within that life.

The sooner they both accepted that, the easier things would be.

"I think you're right," Sev said, turning away. "That we should get moving, I mean. The soldiers will have noticed my absence by now." He didn't know that for certain, but they *would* discover it eventually, and the farther they were from here, the better.

Kade didn't say anything, forcing Sev to look at him again. He was frowning, and suddenly it felt like months ago when Sev was on Pyrmont, constantly earning Kade's grim looks and dark glares.

"Okay," Kade said at last, getting to his feet and tightening the undone laces of his tunic with halting movements. He left the cave without another word.

Sev knew he was probably looking for Jinx—so they could leave—but it felt prophetic, like seeing into the future. Kade was a Phoenix Rider now, and Jinx was his bondmate. . . . He would always choose her.

They were due to rendezvous with the other Phoenix Riders that morning, and the only way to make that happen was for Sev to *ride* Jinx with Kade. The prospect should have been exhilarating; generally, Sev had no qualms pressing himself against Kade and holding on tight, but he couldn't silence the voice in the back of his mind that called him a fraud. He was no proper animage and no Phoenix Rider. Surely Kade would notice how stiffly he sat in the saddle, how uneasy he made the phoenix feel?

Maybe it was for the best, then. The sooner Kade realized they no longer fit together, the better.

Right?

Except they *did* fit together. After Kade mounted up and reached for him, Sev slid neatly behind him on the saddle. But this wasn't what Phoenix Riders did—they didn't ride as pairs—and all Sev would be was extra weight, a burden to bear. No, for them to truly fit together, Sev would need a phoenix of his own, which was impossible. As his thoughts turned dark,

Jinx squawked and shuffled beneath him—further proof that was something that would never happen.

"She's excited," Kade said, soothing Jinx with a touch, making her as still and stoic as a cart horse. But Sev knew the truth: He didn't belong anywhere near a phoenix, and she knew it too.

Despite the awkwardness, Kade did his best, assuring Sev he would be safe, the flight would be relatively short—that no harm would come to him on Jinx's back. His every word radiated pride and pleasure in his bondmate, and Sev tried not to be jealous. Tried, and failed. Theirs was a connection Sev could never understand, a bond he could never compete with.

So while he should have been relishing their flight, watching the world reveal itself below as night receded and dawn approached, Sev pressed his forehead into the center of Kade's back, seeing nothing. He wondered bleakly if he should try to salvage his place in the empire—at least it would be familiar. At least as a spy-soldier he had something to offer. With Kade he would forever be lacking.

They arrived at the lakeside camp in the early morning, Kade signaling to the Rider on patrol before coming to a landing in the middle of a half circle of tents with a smoking cook fire at its center.

Kade dismounted first, reaching up to help Sev, who scrambled off rather gracelessly on his own. Kade dropped his outstretched hand, clearly hurt, but Sev didn't want to appear any more useless and pathetic than he already did.

Together they turned to face a group of young men close to their own age.

"This is Tristan's patrol," Kade said, voice stiff with formality—though it was obviously directed toward Sev and not the others. They hurried forward to shake his hand and greet him warmly, before turning their attention to Sev.

"So this is the spy," said one of the Riders, an icy blond who fixed Sev with a cool, measuring stare.

"I think you mean 'This is the ally who helped us free Tristan,'" supplied another of the Riders. He was tall and lanky with cool brown skin and grinned from overlarge ear to overlarge ear. "That's Latham, and I'm Anders," he said, holding out a hand.

"Sev—and did you say you managed to free Tristan? Where is he?"

"And Veronyka?" asked Kade, looking around.

"Both are in Aura Nova by now," said a thickset boy with a deep voice. "We're awaiting updates."

His name was Ronyn, and he shook Sev's hand and introduced himself just as the last member of their party—who had been on watch when they arrived—came in for a landing. While Ronyn had the look and accent of a Pyraean local like Kade, the other boy, Lysandro, had olive skin and soft brown hair that put Sev in mind of a shorter, skinnier—and yes, less attractive—version of Tristan.

"Doing what?" Sev asked the group at large. "Is it Lord Rolan? Or the Grand Council?"

"Both," said Anders grimly, clapping him on the back and steering him toward the fire, which Lysandro hastened to stoke as Latham mounted up and took over the watch. "Come on, we'll fill you in."

They ate breakfast as the others relayed the news of Rolan's decoy carriage and Commander Cassian's plan to fly overnight to Aura Nova and attempt to beat him to the Grand Council meeting, which they assumed would begin sometime this morning.

"Now we wait," said Ronyn, getting to his feet to take over the next patrol. He called over his phoenix, who was splashing with the others in the shallows of the lake nearby. Jinx had fluttered over to join them as soon as they'd arrived, and it felt surreal to see them behaving like any flock of birds having a bath. But the Shadow Plains were utterly deserted, and there was no one around for miles.

"You stay, Ronyn. I can go," offered Kade, while Anders and Lysandro began cleaning up the meal and talking about weapons training. "I need something to do."

Sev stared down at the empty bowl in his hands. The fire popped and guttered, and he lurched to his feet.

"I'll get firewood," he said, handing the bowl to Anders before walking off, toward the distant cluster of scrub brush that lined the shore of the lake.

Halfway there he realized he should have brought a bucket or a sling—something to carry the wood—not to mention a hatchet or a knife. His hands were still bandaged and tearing branches free was likely to be agony, but he couldn't stand the thought of sitting there while the others worked, having nothing to do and no skills to offer.

Scraping footsteps sounded behind him, and he turned to find Kade in pursuit . . . carrying both a hatchet and a canvas sack.

Sev expelled a breath through his nose and stopped next to the shrubbery.

"Forgetting something?" Kade asked, a tentative smile on his face. He nodded down at Sev's bandaged hands. "They won't be much use."

"Just like me," Sev muttered.

Kade frowned. "Are you . . . ? What's the matter?" he asked, dropping the bag and lodging the hatchet into the nearest branch, which was brittle and twisted with thorns. There had once been leaves on the plant, Sev thought, but they had long since died and blown away.

"I thought you were going to fly Ronyn's patrol?" Sev asked, avoiding the question as well as Kade's frowning amber eyes.

"He insisted on sticking to their schedule," he replied steadily. "Besides, I knew you'd need help."

"I'm not *completely* useless," Sev argued, scowling. He swallowed, looking down at his bandaged hands and then at the hatchet and sack. "Despite appearances."

Kade took a step forward. "No one thinks you're useless, Sev. Me least of all." The words were meant to be a comfort, but his tone was laced with frustration.

"Maybe not in general," Sev said, turning away from Kade to look back toward the camp, at the distant phoenixes and their Riders. "I'm a decent thief . . . good with a lock. But I am useless here—with them."

"You mean with me," Kade parsed.

Sev turned back to face him. "It's true. Don't deny it."

Kade crossed the distance between them and gripped Sev's biceps. "I can and I will. *We*," he said, gesturing to the Riders as well as himself, "wouldn't have been able to free Tristan. You made that possible."

"Veronyka—" Sev began, but Kade cut him off.

"—would have no idea where Tristan was without you. And while we're talking about Veronyka, who protected her from the soldiers that raided her cabin on Pyrmont? Who freed her phoenix from the cell in the Foothills while Veronyka herself was imprisoned? Who saved hundreds of innocent lives from Rolan's soldiers by figuring out the targets and sending word to the Riders so they could evacuate? Who saved every last one of the Phoenix Riders by warning the Eyrie of Belden's impending attack, as well as delivering a dozen phoenix eggs to help with their resurgence?"

"Trix, she—"

"Who saved *my* life, carrying me to safety when I had a spear through my side?" Kade continued, his voice ragged now. "And who gave me a brand-new life with the Riders when he could have easily taken it as his own? *You*, Sev. You. Do not call yourself useless again, especially not where I can hear it," he finished fiercely, releasing Sev at last, his chest rising and falling rapidly.

Sev's mouth—which had been hanging open—snapped shut. He struggled to reconcile his feelings of inadequacy in the face of Kade's sincere, overwhelming praise.

You'll see, he wanted to say. *I'm not good enough for you, for the Riders. Eventually you'll see.* But the smug part of him that wanted to be right wilted in the face of the desperate part of him that wanted to be wrong.

Kade's eyes, slightly wild as they roved Sev's face—searching, maybe, for a sign he'd gotten through—finally settled, but he hadn't found what he was looking for. His expression was weary, even defeated, but the spark of anger that made Kade who he was caught once more, and his gaze turned hard. Combative. He would rather keep arguing than win by forfeit.

"But none of that matters," he said, the words raw and tender—or maybe that was the way they felt as they grated against Sev's rapidly thinning skin. "It's about who you *are*, not what you can do. Until you see that, you'll always think you're wanting."

Sev heard the words, pressed them to his heart . . . but felt wanting all the same.

While resurrection in phoenixes is a common and well-accepted occurrence, resurrection of the human variety is hotly debated.

It is not the purpose of this paper to argue for or against its existence, but rather, to explore the repercussions of such an ability—if indeed it *were* possible.

We are well aware of the reciprocal nature of magic. A birthing pyre requires a tribute of fire and bones, of life, in order to awaken the phoenix. We also know that phoenix resurrection requires a similar payment.

But what *else* does resurrection require? For we give more to the pyre than mere blood and bones, do we not? We give of ourselves. That is how the bond is made. A connection is forged, and two lives are melded together.

Is the same true, then, of human resurrection? Except instead of forging a link with a bondmate who guides the revenant through, does this remade soul become bound to their past self?

Would they retain all their memories, preserved like an insect in amber... or would the events of their past life haunt them, like ghosts—indistinct and noncorporeal?

There is also the question of a resurrected individual's magic. Being born from death—even if it is their own—should, in theory, give the person shadow magic. If they were a shadowmage in their previous life, that ability has the potential to be even more powerful than before.

Going through such darkness might also make the magic of the living—animal magic—not only less desirable, but farther out of reach. Indeed, without a phoenix, animal magic might seem unworthy to a shadowmage, and surely that could result in its diminishment.

—"Human Resurrection," from *Essays on Magic*, by Morra, priestess of Axura, 166 AE

I know I must fight. I know it is my duty,
but . . . I am so very tired.

- CHAPTER 28 -
VERONYKA

VERONYKA'S HEART RACED THE entire flight to Aura Nova.

She hadn't been back to the Golden Empire's capital since she and Val had left it almost a year—had it been only a *year?*—ago. Then, she'd been an anonymous orphan girl traveling with her sister. Now? It felt like she was a new person going to a new place, and all the familiarity of it seemed to throw the differences in herself and her world into sharp contrast.

Veronyka *wasn't* an orphan—she had a father somewhere, though Alexiya couldn't find him.

Val *wasn't* her sister—she was a murderous queen, resurrected and reborn to reap bloody vengeance on the world, even if it took an army of mythical shadowbirds to do it.

Veronyka also wasn't anonymous, and her home wasn't the small one-room apartment she'd shared with her *maiora* and her sister in the Narrows. Her home was the Nest, where her mother once walked the grand halls and where dozens of Ashfires since Elysia the Peacemaker had lived their lives.

Or at least it would be, if she actually had to go through with this.

Veronyka had known that she would have to come forward and claim her identity at some point, but this was definitely sooner than she'd expected.

And despite her fears, she still clung to a small, fragile hope that even though she might become the empire's official heir, she might not actually have to become its queen.

She was still underage, after all, and they had no proof of her identity—plus, they were in the middle of wars on multiple fronts. This was a political move only, as temporary and ephemeral as her supposed betrothal to Lord Rolan. Words on the wind. Just one more move on a board in a game that was far from over.

Even so, it felt like everything was happening too fast. But perhaps that was for the best. It didn't give her time to dwell or reconsider. It didn't allow her to fixate on the fact that the Eyrie had been more of a home to her than any place before it—and surely any place that may or may not come after.

But Val had taken it from her. The least she could do was take this from Val in turn.

Except . . . did Val even want to be queen anymore? To live in the Nest, the place that had housed her rival sister and the council that lifted her up? Surely she did, if only to tear it down. And the last thing in the world she would want was for Veronyka to have it instead.

Dawn was stretching pearlescent fingers across the landscape by the time they arrived in the capital. In order to avoid being seen, they were forced to land on the sloping rooftop of an old bell tower where their phoenixes could hide among the long shadows while their Riders proceeded on foot.

Daxos had looped around for a better view of the courthouse, and when he landed, Doriyan wore a grim expression on his face.

"The council's flag is flying," he said. "They're in session."

"Already?" Tristan asked. He looked exhausted but also exhilarated, the flush in his cheeks and the sweat on his skin giving some needed color to his recently acquired pallor. "I thought you said they didn't convene this early in the day?"

"Rolan must have pushed them to meet at dawn," the commander said. "His little stunt with the carriage decoy proves he knows me better than I thought he did and expected us to betray him. No doubt he also expects us to arrive on his heels. Demanding a hasty vote is not outside the realm of possibility."

"So we've lost?" Tristan asked, looking at Veronyka. "There's no sense in Veronyka coming forward, then, is there? She won't be able to overturn the vote, will she?"

"We need to get closer," the commander said, apparently refusing to accept defeat. "Even if Rolan called a dawn vote, that does not mean the rest of the council members will be so obliging. Besides, these sessions take hours—we can still interrupt the meeting and potentially put a halt to the vote."

Though it was a risk, Alexiya and Doriyan remained saddled, intending to follow in the air. If they stuck to the right rooftops, they could act as lookouts and cover Veronyka, Tristan, and the commander should things go awry.

Xephyra and Rex were extremely put out to be left behind, but they couldn't very well soar into the palace compound on phoenix-back, which would be akin to a declaration of war. Veronyka made it a point to admire how calm and collected Maximian was being—how graciously he had accepted his bondmate's request to stay behind—and soon the younger phoenixes left off their sparks and stomps and remained sullenly still. They were just a few streets over from the courthouse, which meant they could come in a hurry.

"You will enter first," the commander was saying as they approached the high street, "but if it is amenable to you, I will do most of the talking."

Veronyka nodded, her palms sweaty. Tristan was looking between them, his brows raised as if surprised to hear his father defer to her or ask for her permission in any way.

Veronyka smiled at him but sighed inwardly. It was a good thing, to be listened to and respected, but it felt like only the beginning of the way things would change for her as soon as she stepped into that room and declared her identity. Would Tristan fall in line next, refusing to treat her like a normal person?

"It is a pity we didn't have the time to get you prepped and properly attired," the commander muttered, sounding almost nervous. He cast Veronyka an appraising glance. "You look very like a—"

"Phoenix Rider?" Tristan chimed in. They had pulled on hooded cloaks to obscure their telltale armor and Cassian's recognizable face—he was supposed to be exiled, after all—but Veronyka still wore braids in her hair and weapons strapped to her belt. "Because that's what she is. Ashfires have been Phoenix Riders since the beginning."

"Pheronia was not, and it is to her that we must prove Veronyka's relation. Not her aunt."

Veronyka's stomach tightened at that. She might be her mother's daughter, but she'd never met Pheronia Ashfire. All she had were visions through Val's eyes—and that was the heart of the issue. Veronyka had the touch of Val in every aspect of her life; everything she knew, everything she'd ever wanted had been affected by her sister. Her identity, her magic . . . Who was Veronyka without Val?

The fact that she couldn't answer that question made the prospect of taking the throne—of putting herself in a position of supreme power—all the more terrifying. Veronyka knew deep down all the ways they were different, but she knew all the ways they were similar, too. She couldn't help but feel like the world had given the Ashfires a second chance, and it was up to her to make sure they didn't repeat the mistakes of the past.

She only hoped she was strong enough to do so.

As the Nest came into view, Veronyka's heart skipped a beat. The highest turrets gleamed white in the early-morning sun—Genya's Tower, tallest of all—while the lower levels were draped in shadows. Though it was primarily an administrative building at this point, with meeting rooms and government offices, to her, it would always be the home of queens.

The Grand Council met in the courthouse, which was just outside the walled compound of the palace at the base of the Rock—the thrust of stone upon which the Nest perched—making it easily accessible to the public.

Everything looked quiet as they approached, but all the doors were shut—the council was definitely in session.

"This way," the commander said, leading them past the front entrance—which had guards posted—and toward the narrow alley between the walls of the Nest grounds and the courthouse. "We'll have an easier time getting in through a servants' door."

The building featured a large circular room that was dome-shaped and open to the sky in the center, while on the ground, it was surrounded on all sides by a double colonnade. The sturdy columns provided long, striping shadows for them to dart between.

And places for people to hide.

"I knew you couldn't leave well enough alone," came a cool voice from behind them.

Veronyka whirled, reaching for her knife—but a rough hand gripped her upper arm and yanked her hand away. She stomped hard on a foot, hearing a satisfying grunt, but more hands were soon upon her, and she struggled fruitlessly against their hold. A few short seconds later, the scuffling sounds coming from Tristan and the commander were also silenced.

Lord Rolan emerged from the shadow of the nearest pillar, striding toward the commander, who had no less than four soldiers—two on each arm—holding him back. A trickle of blood dripped down the side of his face, as if he'd been struck in the temple, though he appeared steady on his feet.

"Very good, Rolan. Are these the Grand Council's soldiers or some of your own?" the commander asked, sounding calm despite the circumstances.

"The two will be one and the same by the time I am through. I see you've brought me my future wife," he said, tossing a dismissive look at Veronyka before his gaze shifted to Tristan. "And liberated me of my prisoner—how thoughtful."

There were about twenty guards surrounding them, half holding their new captives and the rest flanking Rolan.

"How does it *feel*, Cassian, to know that you are too late?" Rolan asked smugly.

"This is not over yet."

Rolan affected an exaggerated, comical frown. "Why, of course it is! I already pleaded my case when the Grand Council convened *last night*," he said with obvious relish, "and the final vote is happening as we speak."

Veronyka's heart sank. Tristan was right—they'd lost before they'd even arrived.

As if on cue, a bell rang from inside the courthouse.

Despite what sounded to Veronyka as the echoing chime of their defeat, the commander straightened. The grim line of his mouth quirked slightly in the corners.

"Ah, yes, they are calling the members to order. And if my memory serves me," he said, head tilted to the side in thought, "the member who called the meeting and put forward the motion must be in attendance before they announce the results. And yet here you stand."

"I am not a schoolboy to be summoned at the whim of a bell," Rolan snapped, sounding just like the child he professed not to be. "I will arrive soon enough, and with *you* in my possession. Further—albeit unnecessary— proof of your treachery and intentions against the empire. Why, they might crown me right now."

"Don't count your phoenixes before they hatch," the commander said, not at all cowed by Rolan's words, though the other man's lip curled at the Phoenix Rider idiom. "And never leave the sky unguarded when you have Phoenix Riders in your midst."

Alexiya and Doriyan descended on silent wings, the only sound the creak and twang of bowstrings being drawn back and released. Alexiya took out both soldiers holding Veronyka—she staggered from their abrupt release of her arms—and Doriyan took out two of the soldiers holding the commander, leaving him to deal with the others as they tripped and stumbled away. Doriyan aimed his bow toward Tristan's captors next; they had already tried to flee but failed to outrun Doriyan's arrows as he sank one after the other into their retreating backs.

Veronyka and Tristan moved to each other, checking they were each okay before they faced the commander, who had neatly dispatched his last two guards.

Meanwhile, both Doriyan and Alexiya had leapt from their saddles. All of Rolan's protectors were on the ground, arrows protruding from their bodies, while Alexiya stood before Rolan with her next arrow aimed directly at the governor's head. She was barely three feet away from him and would not miss.

But they needed him alive. The vote was already under way, and even if holding him here would delay the announcement of the results, Veronyka doubted it would stop the vote altogether. No, in order to do that, she had to get inside immediately—*with* the proof Rolan had of her identity.

Rolan's eyes were round and frantic, seeking some ally, some way to get himself out of this. He licked his lips and shrugged, though it was a stiff movement, conveying none of the nonchalance he'd clearly hoped to embody. "No matter, Cassian. The council *will* vote in my favor. If you kill me here, you'll only prove your threat to the empire."

As he spoke, Doriyan was moving among the bodies, removing the phoenix-feather-fletched arrows with quick, efficient movements.

"I don't intend to *kill* you, Rolan," the commander said, standing with his hands clasped behind his back, quite at his ease. "I'm not a cold-blooded murderer."

"What, then?" Rolan's voice was petulant.

"Obviously, we don't want this war. You have a choice: Either you rescind all your allegations and brand yourself as the lying, scheming, over-reaching villain you are, *or* you walk in there with us, corroborate Verony-ka's claim to the throne, and call off the vote. If you follow through, perhaps we will consider your marriage proposal."

Rolan scoffed. "I have lost my bargaining chip," he said, gesturing at Tristan. "I'm not a fool, Cassian. You will use me to validate her identity, and then you'll sweep me aside."

"If you cooperate, I may allow you to keep your dignity and perhaps even your position on the council. We can chalk the whole thing up to a misunderstanding rather than a malicious move for the throne. You may not wind up king"—Rolan laughed harshly—"but you also may not wind up in a prison cell. Or in the ground."

Rolan made an ugly face, but he was clearly thinking over the commander's words. His gaze shifted to Veronyka, and then his lips twisted in an unpleasant smile. "No, Cassian, *you* are the one who has a choice to make. The war or the crown."

"Explain yourself," the commander said, and Veronyka noted that he did not look as cool as he had a few minutes ago.

"It's simple, really. I've lost my leverage in this situation, so I can't make any deals that rely upon your goodwill alone. That, as you have demonstrated"—he waved at Tristan again—"would be a mistake. Your choice is this: Come with me, now, and I will give you the proof you require to verify the girl's identity. In doing that, you will, of course, allow the vote to go through. The empire's armies will march on Pyra. This way, if you do not deliver on your word, I will be able to follow through on my original plan and take the throne by force. Your other option is to storm in there, attempt to claim her birthright and stop the vote . . . but I will *never* give you the evidence in my possession. I would rather burn the proof of Pheronia Ashfire's bastard child than bow before her."

Veronyka stiffened, shocked at his selfish ambition. He would doom an entire province rather than lose his chance at becoming king.

Could they do this without him? They had bits and pieces: Doriyan could testify, and they had Pheronia's necklace and Avalkyra's signet ring, but nothing that could identify her definitively. If Rolan refused to give them that proof, she might never be able to take the throne. That meant no way to keep Val from doing the same, and no power to halt or delay the vote. In fact, it meant no power at all—a thing they desperately needed. If the vote went through, the Phoenix Riders would be hunted into extinction once more, not to mention all the innocent people in Pyra—animage or not—who would get caught in the crosshairs.

"If we go with you . . . ," the commander began.

"No," Veronyka and Tristan said in unison. Tristan's eyes were flashing angrily, but he pressed his lips together and nodded at Veronyka to speak instead. "Commander, if there's still *any* chance of stopping the empire from marching on Pyra, we have to take it. We can't afford to fight two wars."

Rolan frowned at that—but, of course, he didn't know about Val's strix army.

"We already are," the commander said tersely. "The only way to take control of the situation is to claim your throne. It's an opportunity we cannot pass up."

"We'll find other proof—other ways," argued Tristan.

The servant entrance to the courthouse was a few columns away from them, and though the door was shut, a rumble of talk could be heard from within. How long had it been since the bell had sounded—and how long until people came looking for Rolan?

The commander turned to his son, ready with a retort, but Veronyka spoke over him. "I won't walk away and let them march on Pyra, not if I can stop it."

This was the thing Veronyka had been fearing since she'd told the commander who she truly was—the moment when she might have to question his power and authority. When she might have to overstep it.

He seemed to see it too. The anger on his face shifted, and he schooled his features into a reasonable expression. "If you go in there now, with no evidence and nothing to substantiate your claim, they could hold you for questioning for days—weeks, even. You are a Phoenix Rider, an animage. . . . You could be fined, imprisoned, and forced into bondage. And it won't change the results of the vote."

"I'll substantiate it," Rolan said, a spark of anticipation in his eyes as he watched their argument. "I'll supply everything you need—if you formally agree to the marriage. In writing. Today."

A spark of unease shot through Veronyka. In writing, today? In front of the entire Grand Council, too, she'd wager. How would she ever get out of a promise like that? Tristan's fists clenched, his head moving from side to side in a sort of numb, silent refusal.

Both of them were scrambling for a way out of this, but to both their surprise, it was the commander who whirled around in anger. "I will not make you king!" he bellowed, so forcefully that Veronyka and Tristan jumped, and Alexiya and Doriyan—who had been silent spectators—both darted a look toward the nearby doors, as if expecting a storm of soldiers to burst forward in response.

Veronyka had never seen the commander crack like this. Of all the people to resist the marriage so strongly, she would not have expected it to be him. But she knew this had very little to do with her or the romantic interests of his son, and much, much more to do with the past between these two men.

The commander was breathing heavily. "You know we can't agree to that, Rolan," he said through clenched teeth. "Not here and now. I have promised you a way out of your treasonous plans and the security of a position on the council. I have been more than fair."

"Fair?" Rolan snapped. "What was fair about your treatment of my sister? Or Pheronia's treatment of our betrothal agreement?"

"Tell me what's fair about making innocent people pay for a blow to your ego?" Veronyka demanded.

"*My* ego?" Rolan repeated, voice quivering with rage. "The slights against my family go back to the dawn of the empire, when King Rol was unjustly murdered, all thanks to the coward King Damian."

"You're starting a war, gambling thousands of lives, all for a two-hundred-year inferiority complex?" Tristan asked incredulously.

Rolan spluttered, his face red, but the commander stepped in, taking advantage of his speechlessness.

"For the last time, Rolan," he said, taking an angry step forward and pointing a finger at the man's chest. Veronyka feared they might actually come to blows, but the sudden move seemed to quell Rolan's anger. He was projecting a strange satisfaction—as if he enjoyed fighting with Commander Cassian, or maybe it was something . . . else.

Her head snapped up. Rolan's eyes were fixed on the commander, who was barely a foot away from him, but gleaming suddenly at his side was a knife that Rolan held in a white-knuckled grip.

Move! Veronyka shouted, saying the word not out loud, but through shadow magic. She didn't know why, only that it seemed the fastest in that instant between life and death. A word was a word, when spoken into the air between them. But a word spoken through magic could convey so much more. It could convey a thought, a feeling—a sense of danger and the direction it was coming from.

The commander's eyes rounded, and he reared back. Rolan lunged, blade flashing, and while Cassian had missed a direct blow, the blade sliced deep into his side, finding a gap in his leather armor.

He cried out as the metal bit into flesh, falling to one knee, and Rolan leapt toward his prone form. His eyes gleamed in savage triumph—Veronyka suspected he'd been trying to goad the commander into stepping close enough for him to make his move—and he now scrabbled to use the man as a shield, to get the situation back under his control.

Cassian wasn't defeated, however, and threw a vicious elbow into Rolan's gut. He doubled over and stumbled backward, only to lift his knife again—this time aiming directly for the commander's back.

The blade never made contact.

As his arm drew back, his face screwed up in rage, Alexiya loosed her arrow.

It landed in the middle of his chest, and Rolan collapsed to the ground.

Before any of them could speak, the commander toppled forward.

"Father!" Tristan shouted, diving to his knees to catch him. Rolan had managed to open a wound in the commander's side, just below his ribs, where no bones or muscle protected him. Blood pooled on the ground and drenched the commander's clothes, bleeding through both tunic and cloak.

Tristan's eyes were wild—his father wasn't responding, his face pale and chalky—and there was blood all over his hands.

Help me, he whispered in his mind, over and over again, and Veronyka didn't know if it was meant for her, or if it was a plea meant for the gods themselves.

Doriyan rushed forward, helping Tristan lower his father to the ground.

Alexiya stared at Veronyka. "I'm sorry," she whispered, looking between the commander's prone form and Rolan's body.

"No—you did the right thing," Veronyka said numbly. She thought maybe she was in shock. This man had tormented them for months, assaulted Pyra, aided Val—all for some distant dream of a crown on his head. Now he was dead, lying in a puddle of blood on the sidewalk.

What a waste of their time and energy. What a worthless distraction.

At least he hadn't gotten the chance to destroy the evidence of Veronyka's heritage or given the order to anyone else to do the same. Maybe they could still find it. Maybe they could salvage this.

"We have to get the commander to a healer," Doriyan was saying, and Alexiya went into her saddle for a medic pack.

Veronyka's mind was racing.

Tristan needed her, kneeling there on the ground. The commander needed her. The Phoenix Riders needed her.

Is this what it feels like to be queen? Needed by everyone and able to help no one?

She made her feet move. She reached out and gripped Tristan's shoulder hard.

"Get him on Daxos or Ximn," she heard herself say. Her voice sounded calm, and maybe that contrast was what made Tristan wrench his gaze from his father to look up at her. "We need to get him away from here as soon as possible. As for a healer . . . He won't be able to make it all the way to Prosperity."

"Hestia," Tristan said, his voice raw and ragged. "She travels with Rolan. She's probably in his house on Marble Row."

"I'll fly ahead to check," Doriyan offered. He had once again taken care of the body, dragging Rolan's corpse unceremoniously into the bushes like all the rest. Veronyka suspected it wasn't the death Rolan had had in mind for himself someday, living a long and luxurious life before being carried through the Aura Nova streets in a king's funeral procession with music playing and his subjects weeping as he passed.

"No," Veronyka said. Now all of them were staring at her. Why was her voice doing that awful, flat intonation? Was that fear or strength? "You're coming with me."

She turned, marching inexorably toward the servant door, Doriyan hastening to her side. She wanted to be there for Tristan and for his father, but she was no healer. This, however . . . This she could do. If she could delay the war, if she could stop the Grand Council vote, she could buy them the time they needed to regroup. They didn't have Rolan's evidence on them, but they knew it existed. They would find it.

A second bell rang as Doriyan swung the door wide, and Veronyka stepped into the courthouse.

They entered on the topmost level of a sunken room featuring rows of stone benches that descended to a judge on a podium at the center. Every head in the room swiveled to look at her—expecting Rolan, perhaps?

She'd taken barely two steps before guards, posted on either side of the door, reached for her and Doriyan.

"Who are you?" echoed a voice from below. The judge.

Be brave, she told herself.

She opened her mouth, but before she could utter a single syllable, a shriek tore through the silence. A *phoenix* shriek.

Above, perched in the open-air oculus, was Sidra of Stel mounted on Oxana. With a flap of her wings, the phoenix caught fire, eliciting cries and gasps from below.

"What is this?" the judge asked, looking between Veronyka and Sidra— as if this were a coordinated effort. As if they were allies. "How dare you interrupt a meeting of the Grand Council? Guards!"

All around the room, guards lifted their weapons and aimed them at Sidra. The hands holding Veronyka and Doriyan gripped tighter. No one attacked, however, waiting for the command.

Sidra paused, weighing their threat, and Veronyka suspected her position at the top of the dome put her out of the crossbows' range. Since she was shooting down, however . . . she had no such limitations, and an ideal vantage point besides.

Apparently coming to the same conclusion, Sidra drew her bow and nocked an arrow, aiming it at the judge.

"Sidra, no!" Veronyka cried out, stepping forward. She was going to ruin everything, to set their plans on fire when they were already torn to tattered shreds. The guard holding her shoulder pulled back roughly, while the judge flapped his hands at the archers all around, ensuring they didn't get him killed.

"I bring word," Sidra said into the silence, her voice carrying easily in the domed space. "Rolan of Stel is dead"—Veronyka's heart stopped; had Sidra seen their scuffle outside?—"and Avalkyra Ashfire lives. Ring your bells and rally your troops. The war has begun."

Then she lit her arrow and loosed it. The first hit the judge, who toppled from the platform, and then chaos broke loose. Flaming arrows fell like rain, landing in tables and chairs and bodies, while crossbow bolts flew ineffectually upward, unable to connect with the rapidly moving target as Oxana dove, trailing fire that set velvet banners and woven tapestries ablaze.

The council members made a mad scramble for the doors, but as they tried to run out, more soldiers were pouring in, blocking the exits.

Doriyan put a hand on Veronyka's shoulder, tugging her back the way they'd come. They'd been forgotten by the guards who'd stopped them and had a clear path to the door.

She took one last, regretful look at the burning Grand Council meeting, watching their hope at avoiding this war go up in flames.

*Before, we had each other. Nefyra was a different
kind of sister—one chosen, not made.*

- CHAPTER 29 -
TRISTAN

TRISTAN WAS DROWNING. HIS head was underwater, and his hands
were soaking wet.

But no. That wasn't the tide roaring in his ears but his own heartbeat.
And that wasn't water on his hands, it was blood. His father's blood.

Tristan might not be drowning, but he was definitely in a bubble.
Things were happening all around him, but he couldn't seem to hear or
understand. He thought he preferred it that way. There was something
urgent and terrible pressing on his chest, but the bubble kept it at bay.

Alexiya had directed him to put pressure on his father's wound, so that
was what he did. Simple, immediate tasks. That he could do. But anything
beyond that . . . His father, the commander, looked shockingly pale. His
eyelids twitched and fluttered, the only outward sign of life from his prone
figure—but Tristan latched on to it all the same.

Alexiya came in and out of his bubble; she had called Ximn to their
side, making room in the saddle for a body.

No, Tristan thought savagely. Not a body, a *person.* A living, breathing
person.

Alexiya knelt down next to Tristan to help lift his father. "What's
going on?" she asked someone—Tristan didn't know what she was talking

about or who she was talking to, but she wasn't looking at him.

"Sidra," came the flat response. Tristan knew that voice, felt it as if it came from inside him.

He turned to see Veronyka, drawn more by the sound of her than what she'd said. But as he met her eyes, the bubble around him burst. People were spilling out the doors to the courthouse in a rush of terrified shouts and thundering feet, and the smell of smoke was heavy on the air.

Wait—Sidra was *here*? That fierce shriek, those cries of fear . . . that was because of her? Sidra belonged to Val. Was Val here too? His hands clenched, and he realized he'd removed the pressure on his father's side.

"It's just Sidra for now," Veronyka said aloud, answering Tristan's unasked question. Alexiya cursed, and Doriyan began muttering under his breath. Distantly, Tristan heard wingbeats and wondered if the world was ready to fall apart right here, right now, with his father bleeding out on the cobblestones.

He bent over once again, reapplying pressure, and then Veronyka was next to him. "Maximian is here, Tristan. We have to lift him."

Max. So those weren't the wingbeats of impending death but of salvation.

His father's phoenix was soaring down for a landing, his movements rigid and edged in panic, while Rex and Xephyra fluttered down anxiously just behind him.

Maximian bent his head toward his unresponsive bondmate and nudged him frantically. Tristan placed a hand on Maximian's face. The large, dark eyes latched on to his and held, gaze steady even as his body twitched and shifted with fear and urgency. Tristan felt connected to his father's phoenix in a way he never had before—they were in this terrifying place together. Tristan dropped his hand, leaving a bloody print on the phoenix's great golden beak.

"Hold this," said Alexiya, handing Tristan a wad of bandages from Ximn's medic pack. Tristan pressed them against his father's side, while Alexiya wrapped a length around his middle to hold it in place.

The instant the bandage was tied, Doriyan took the commander under his arms. Tristan took his father's feet, and together they got him into his saddle, Alexiya reaching for the straps to tie him in place.

"Mount up," said Doriyan, nudging Tristan toward his bondmate. He was reluctant to leave his father, but soldiers had spotted them, and it occurred to Tristan that they would not know the difference between him and Sidra. This attack would be pinned on Phoenix Riders in general, and according to the empire, the war had officially begun.

As Tristan climbed onto Rex and Veronyka onto Xephyra, Doriyan withdrew his bow and quiver from Daxos.

"I'll cover you," he said over his shoulder.

Alexiya, already mounted on Ximn, opened her mouth to argue.

"Go," Doriyan insisted, his expression determined. Sidra had been his partner in crime, quite literally, as well as his closest friend before the war. He would cover their retreat, Tristan was certain, but what would he do after that?

Alexiya's expression was grim, but Veronyka nodded her approval at Doriyan and took control of the situation. "*Tiya* Alexiya," she said sharply, drawing her aunt's attention. "You know the way?" Alexiya turned away from Doriyan and nodded. "Then lead."

Rather than soaring as high as she could to get them out of the empire's crossbows' range, Alexiya flew low, weaving between buildings and narrow alleyways. The tight quarters protected them just the same, but it had the added benefit of not giving away their position. If they flew *over* the city, everyone in the capital would know they were here. As it was, they alarmed the citizens walking the streets or looking out their windows, but those were isolated occurrences.

Tristan didn't doubt the soldiers would be hot on their heels, but this strategy would buy them time.

Alexiya flew them to Rolan's Marble Row town house, where they landed in the courtyard, their presence concealed from the street and their pursuers by the building's ivy-covered walls.

Servants spilled outside as they landed, but Hestia soon pushed her way to the front. Her face paled at the sight that greeted her—the commander, slumped and unconscious in his saddle, covered in blood, while the yard filled with bristling phoenixes.

"All of you, inside at once," she said, her voice even and her tone authoritative. She was surely one of the most senior servants in his household, and no one dared to question her. She exchanged a look with her assistant. "My travel case," she said, and the girl hurried off into the house. Then she turned to someone who looked like a steward or butler. "Delay them." The woman nodded and departed.

"Guards?" Alexiya asked, shifting in her saddle and reaching for her bow.

Hestia moved about the courtyard, slamming the doors that led inside, as well as the shutters. "Osha will buy us a few moments."

She had just reached the last door when her assistant returned, hauling a sizable bag. Hestia took it from her and shooed the girl back inside.

"Where *is* the lord of the house?" Hestia asked idly, opening her bag and withdrawing clean bandages. Alexiya dragged over a wrought-iron chair from the gardens for the healer to perch on as she examined Cassian's wound.

"Dead," Veronyka said simply.

Hestia sighed. "Well, that simplifies things. Is this his handiwork?"

Alexiya nodded and gave her a brief rundown of what had happened. Tristan remained rooted to his seat, hands clenched painfully around his reins as he watched Hestia work.

He couldn't breathe.

When at last she drew back, her expression was grave. "I need to get him into emergency surgery. We don't have time to fly all the way to Pyra or even Ferro. I'd do it right here, right now, if I weren't afraid of being interrupted."

"We need to get out of here," Veronyka agreed. "Soldiers were on our trail the whole way here. They could find us at any moment."

Hestia enlisted Alexiya's help to wrap the fresh dressings around the commander's midsection as tightly as possible, creating a rigid support to keep the wound protected and the commander upright in the saddle.

"We could go to Arboria," Alexiya said hesitantly, once Hestia was done with her. "I haven't been able to locate my brother, but my mother is there."

Tristan was still thinking about the words "emergency surgery." He didn't care where they went, so long as Hestia had the time she needed.

Then he remembered that Alexiya's mother would be Veronyka's *grandmother*, and he darted an anxious look in her direction. He'd been so preoccupied with his father that he'd forgotten this had been a hard day for her, too. And it looked like it was about to get harder.

Veronyka nodded. "The river will slow down the soldiers should they try to follow us. Given how some Arborians feel about Phoenix Riders, they'll surely expect us to fly north once we cross the Godshand. It may prove to be the ideal place to lie low for a while."

It was a sound decision. Yes, she might want to meet her grandmother, but Tristan knew she was doing this for him, too. And for his father. Tristan met her eye, knowing he'd never be able to put his feelings into words—and relieved that for once he wouldn't need to.

She nodded, her large eyes glassy but clear, her heart open and aching for him.

"I should ride with Cassian," Hestia said, closing up her supply bag and standing. "I can monitor his breathing and his heart rate and ensure there aren't any sudden changes."

Tristan, Veronyka, and Alexiya looked at each other, uncertain. Surely it would be safer for her to ride with one of them, being that she was not only an inexperienced flyer but getting on in years as well.

"I am sturdier than I look," she said practically. "Just strap me in good and tight."

With a shrug, Alexiya helped the woman up into the saddle, while Veronyka leapt from Xephyra's back to grab Hestia's healer's bag, adding it to her own supplies. Tristan knew he was being quite useless, but he couldn't seem to make himself move. His gaze was fixed on his father's slumped form, and he was afraid that if he looked away, he'd miss something important . . . afraid that if he climbed out of his saddle, he'd crumple to the ground and be unable to stand again. Exhaustion was lead in his veins, weighing him down.

As Alexiya finished her work and mounted up, Veronyka moved to Maximian's side. "If something goes wrong," she said quietly, perhaps hoping Tristan couldn't hear, "pat Maximian's neck three times. He'll let me know, won't you?" She turned the question to Max, stroking his feathers to draw his attention. She got a melancholy croak in response.

This time, as soon as they rose into the sky, shouts and cries went up. Soldiers were crawling over every street within a two-mile radius, marching down Marble Row in small units, knocking on doors, while horse-mounted riders galloped through the main thoroughfares, sounding the alarm.

"*Vollancea*," Alexiya called over her shoulder. It was a spear flight pattern, which really just meant single file. Flying in arrowhead or triangle patterns worked well for attacking, but their goal now was to break through the enemy lines as quickly as possible, and flying in a row meant giving the soldiers on the ground fewer targets. It was also used as an escort flight pattern, keeping vulnerable targets—like the commander and Hestia—out of the attacker's line of sight.

Tristan was still in a daze, but Rex flew hard as they turned east, following Alexiya's breakneck pace and complex route.

The river came into view, the bustling docks filled with boats and sailors unloading their wares. There was always a heavy military presence there, where theft and smuggling were commonplace, but there were even more soldiers present with renegade Phoenix Riders on the loose.

Alexiya, it seemed, had expected this—she launched several carefully aimed arrows, which caused crates and boats to burst into flame, providing a perfect amount of distraction and chaos. Several return volleys made their way into the sky, but they had already flown out of range.

The river whipped by below them in a blue-gray blur, and then there was nothing but endless trees on the horizon. Tristan turned in the saddle, seeing soldiers try to commandeer merchant boats, but they'd never catch their flying quarry. And like Veronyka said, the Riders would be expected to turn their flight north once they'd evaded pursuit, so the odds of soldiers crossing the river at all were minimal.

They were safe.

For now.

Together, we were more.

CHAPTER 30

VERONYKA

IT WAS A RELATIVELY short flight across the Palm of the Godshand and into the dense forest of Arboria North. Even with Xephyra's superior eyesight, Veronyka would have had a difficult time navigating the towering wooden sentinels were it not for Alexiya leading the way. With the commander bleeding out in his saddle, hovering somewhere between the earth and the stars, they needed to travel with all haste.

It was lucky, too, that Veronyka had these grave concerns to keep her occupied. Between keeping her eyes on Alexiya's winding flight in front of her and Cassian's prone form at her side—not to mention her bowstring-taut attention on Tristan's mental state—she didn't have much brainpower left to think about what was to come. They were going to Alexiya's mother's house . . . which made it Veronyka's *grandmother's* house. The word "*maiora*" popped into her head, but of course, Alexiya's mother was Arborian, not Pyraean. Veronyka didn't even know the word for grandmother in their native tongue . . . or if this woman would want Veronyka to call her that in the first place. Perhaps she'd blame Veronyka and her mother for what had happened to her family—divided by the war and estranged ever since. And she wasn't wrong. The Ashfire legacy seemed to grow bleaker to Veronyka with each passing day. All she wanted was to do good in the world, but would anything she achieved even matter when it could never make up for what her own family had already done?

It would matter, she told herself firmly. She had to believe it was possible to change things, to make a new legacy.

Possible, Xephyra said definitively. *Like resurrection. To start over again.*

They were deep in the forest when they slowed their pace and Alexiya signaled for them to land—in fact, the trees were so tall and their growth so dense that it felt like twilight, though Veronyka knew it was closer to midday.

The trees that surrounded them were a good deal larger than those in the Silverwood, their roots turning the ground into rippling, undulating hills, while their trunks were easily as wide around as ten people with their hands linked together. Their color was different too, their bark a rich sandy brown, while the leaves were a bright, lush green—seemingly untouched by the coming winter.

The silence was dense, but there was the familiar wilderness chorus of chittering animals and buzzing insects, plus the sway and rush of leaves far above.

As Veronyka craned her neck, she couldn't see any signs of civilization, but when Alexiya dismounted, she strode purposefully toward a particular tree at the edge of the clearing.

That was when Veronyka noticed a set of stairs sticking directly out of the trunk and twisting around to lead up into the shadowy boughs where a small house sat among the leaves. With no connecting pathways or platforms in sight, she supposed this would be considered living in the "backcountry," isolated and away from neighbors. She glanced around at her fugitive, firebird-riding companions and was glad of it.

"Stay here," Alexiya advised, something like fear—or maybe dread—in her voice. "I'll call down to you when it's safe to fly him up. Oh, and Veronyka?" she added, lowering her voice so that Veronyka was forced to slide from the saddle and close the distance between them. "She will be shocked enough, seeing me, and she is not a young woman. I think it would be best, considering the circumstances . . ."

"We can wait for introductions," Veronyka agreed, secretly ashamed of the way the knot in her stomach loosened. For now, she could be Veronyka, just another Rider . . . not an heir or a queen or a long-lost granddaughter. It was a staggering relief.

Alexiya nodded and began her ascent.

Tristan remained in his saddle, staring at his father's prone form, chest heaving as if he'd just run a mile.

Veronyka sidled over and reached for his hand—he squeezed back tightly, refusing to let go. She ran her thumb along the back of his knuckles, sending soothing thoughts through the bond as they waited. Xephyra did much the same for Rex, preening his feathers and crooning softly.

The silence was broken by shouts and shattering glass. Veronyka caught only snippets of the conversation, but even without the words, she'd have had no trouble deciphering their tone.

"Twenty years—show your face—thought you were dead—*twenty years*—"

And then, in response, "Hands aren't broken—could've sent a letter—not a child anymore—"

A door slammed loudly, and then Alexiya shouted down to them from what appeared to be some kind of balcony.

"Mom's thrilled to have company," she said flatly. "Maximian, bring him up. Tristan, you come too—no doubt we'll need the extra hands."

"Extra hands?" came a sharp voice from behind Alexiya. "It'll be crowded enough as it—"

"And, Ximn, why don't you come as well?" Alexiya shouted over her mother, before turning on her heel and disappearing into the house. Ximn cocked her head but remained where she was.

Max took to the air, and Tristan released Veronyka's hand to do the same, leaving her behind without a backward glance. Veronyka's heart went with him, but eventually she withdrew.

"I guess we'll keep watch," she said with a sigh, and Xephyra crooned.

ల ల ల

Together they flew several short routes, familiarizing themselves with the area and determining likely approaches for soldiers on foot. They were deep in Arboria North, and since they had flown, their path would be impossible to track. As the day wore on and there was no sign of pursuit, Veronyka allowed herself to believe that they had made a clean escape.

Once back in the clearing, she turned her attention to the phoenixes. They milled around the forest floor, anxious and agitated, though Maximian was worst of all. He had tried to remain with his bondmate, but he was far too large, and surgery was careful, delicate work. After tossing his head and expelling gusts of sparks in angry bursts, he now remained rooted in place like one of the vast trees that surrounded them, keeping watch on the small house suspended above, where lamps now glowed from the windows.

She did what she could for him. After setting up food and water troughs and unsaddling each of the other phoenixes in turn, Veronyka came up beside him and gently patted his neck. Despite his rigid posture, his feathers twitched and trembled like leaves in a high wind.

Soon the others joined her. Xephyra was quite scared of Maximian in his disconsolate state, and Veronyka suspected Ximn and Rex felt similarly, but eventually they sidled up to him, offering their presence, their warmth, their support. He eventually calmed enough that Veronyka thought it was safe to remove his saddle, which was spattered with blood, and set to work cleaning and preparing it for his Rider. She couldn't bear to think of what would happen—to Maximian, to the Phoenix Riders, to Tristan—if the commander didn't survive this.

The others came in and out of the house in shifts—first Alexiya, stomping down angrily to "get away from that woman before I strangle her." Then "that woman" herself came out, nodding distractedly at Veronyka and muttering darkly as she drew water from a nearby well. There was a rather ingenious pulley system suspended above the water source, allowing her to fill three large buckets, load them onto a wooden platform, then tug twice on the rope. Someone above pulled the water up and out of sight.

On her next visit, Alexiya informed Veronyka that they'd be camping on the ground since her mother's house was too small and Cassian and Hestia would need what little room there was available. Proper dark was closing in around them now, and together they gathered wood and started a fire.

The one person Veronyka wanted to see who didn't leave the house—besides the healer and her patient—was Tristan. Rex was almost as anxious as Maximian, and Veronyka understood. She could feel the gut-wrenching terror funneling through their bond. She tried to soothe Tristan, to take the brunt of his fears and draw them from him like poison from a wound, but she didn't know if she succeeded. It seemed he didn't *want* to feel better, but rather, stoked and nurtured his anguish.

Guilt, she realized. He was doing his best to blame himself for this—if he hadn't gotten captured, if he had paid better attention to Rolan . . . but Veronyka had played such games with herself all her life. If she hadn't been young and weak, she could have protected her *maiora*. If she hadn't been so trusting, she could have prevented Xephyra's death.

If she hadn't let Val coerce her into abandoning her duties and attacking Rolan's army, Tristan would never have had to come rescue her in the first place. His guilt was her guilt too.

Xephyra nudged her then, a gentle butt of the head. Veronyka patted her absently, still dwelling on her failures, until her bondmate gave her a proper shove, practically knocking her over.

"Hey!" Veronyka cried out, annoyed. Xephyra bumped her once more for good measure.

Making things worse, she chided. Veronyka wanted to give her an angry retort, but Xephyra was right. She was supposed to be helping Tristan, lightening his load, not adding her own on top of it. Rex was positively drooping despite Xephyra's continued ministrations, and though Tristan wouldn't know it was coming from her, Veronyka's dour mood would only worsen his.

When at last he did come outside, it was because Hestia forced him to. Apparently there had been nothing for Tristan to do after his father was lifted onto a table and the surgery began, but still he had remained, forgoing meals and rest in favor of brooding darkly and pacing the small house.

He continued his restless movement at the foot of the stairs, and when Veronyka held out both water and bread, he only shook his head and continued his march.

So she took a seat across the fire from Alexiya, and they waited.

It was barely an hour later when Tristan stopped abruptly in his pacing, and Veronyka looked up to see Hestia descending the stairs. She didn't keep them in suspense.

"The surgery was a success," she said, and the tension in Tristan snapped like a twig. His knees buckled until he was sitting on a log near the fire, his head in his hands. "He is stable for now. I will monitor him throughout the night, but I believe the worst danger is over."

Alexiya handed the woman a cup of tea from a pot she'd recently brewed, and Veronyka rushed forward.

"Surely you need to rest? You've been working all day."

Hestia shook her head, blowing on the scalding tea. "I am quite used to burning the midnight oil. Agneta is watching him now, but I'll return shortly."

Veronyka realized with a jolt that that was her grandmother's name—she hadn't thought to ask. "After you've eaten?" she prompted, and Hestia smiled gratefully.

Veronyka busied herself with the food, moving stiffly after a day of flying and a still-healing wound of her own. As she handed the healer a piece of hot flatbread and cold cheese, Tristan watched her, lifting his head so his eyes reflected the firelight.

Before long Hestia left, patting Tristan gently on the shoulder as she passed. He got to his feet to follow her, and they shared quiet words outside the light of the fire. Veronyka thought he might have hugged her, but it was hard to see, and she didn't want to intrude with shadow magic. Alexiya stood as well, stretching and announcing she'd keep watch.

"You two sleep," she ordered sternly. "I'd rather sleep in the morning, when that one's awake," she muttered, jerking a thumb up to her mother's house.

With a flap of wings that caused the fire to stutter and spark, Alexiya and Ximn took flight, leaving Veronyka and Tristan truly alone for the first time since her birthday nearly two months ago.

Tristan turned to her, and the instant their eyes met, they were moving toward each other. This hug was gentler than their last—more a surrendering, an offer and a promise to hold each other up, rather than a frantic clash of bodies. Still, being close to him again brought about the usual stomach-squirming, heart-pounding feelings, no matter how exhausting and trying their day.

"I'm so sorry," Veronyka murmured into his neck, perched on her toes in order to get closer to him.

Tristan held her just a little bit tighter. "Thanks," he whispered.

When he drew back and looked down at her again, he was staring fixedly at her neck. Veronyka remembered that the edge of the bandage across her chest was visible. She would have to ask Hestia to change the dressings for her sometime soon. The wound felt itchy and hot, and she was certain she'd done more damage to it with the excitement of the past day.

"What happened?" Tristan asked.

"It was Val," she said, matching his quiet tone, though her voice wobbled slightly.

"But you weren't there," he said sharply, as if fearing he'd been lied to.

"No, I wasn't." Veronyka swallowed. "We've been . . . talking. At night—through dreams. Through magic. After the attack, I was so angry at her, I confronted her through our connection. I wanted to shake her, to *hurt* her, but then she whirled around, and *she* was the one . . ." Veronyka shook her head. "It was a spear, and she . . . I don't think she even realized what was happening—that it was even *possible*—but . . ." *She almost killed me.*

Tristan stared at her for a long time. Even his mind was silent. Eventually he nodded toward one of the tents Veronyka had set up. He was hesitant when he said, "Will you show me?"

Veronyka's eyes widened. The cut sliced her from abdomen to collarbone. In order to show him . . .

She felt herself nod, and Tristan took her hand, pulling her after him into the darkness of the tent. Rex and Xephyra were huddled together just outside it, while Maximian was perched on a branch above, keeping his silent vigil.

The tent muffled the sounds of the night, and as Veronyka took a seat on the already-laid-out bedrolls, Tristan ducked outside again. He was picking through their packs, searching for something, and returned with a kettle of hot water from the fire, a medic kit, and a lantern. He knelt to light it, then twisted to face her, uncertain, but the sight of the healing supplies made it easier for Veronyka to sit up and start pulling at the laces of her tunic.

Like the attack that gave her the wound in the first place, baring herself was an echo of the past. Tristan had seen her this way before—exposed— but that had been Val's doing. An involuntary reveal. This time Veronyka willingly bared herself to him.

Despite her newfound calm, her fingers fumbled at the strings as she went lower and lower. Then a hand covered hers, and she looked up from her struggle to see Tristan staring at her, his gaze warm and open. He knew what eye contact meant—what touching meant. He was exposing himself to her too.

And then it was simple, because they were bonded, and there was no one she'd rather be vulnerable with than him. No one she trusted more. He was a part of her, and her of him.

He helped her with the last few ties and carefully drew the cloth over her head. His touch was gentle but not lingering, and he hadn't yet looked down—as if steeling himself for the moment. He took her tunic and folded it with unnecessary care, then busied himself getting out fresh bandages and a washcloth. As he moved to pour the hot water into a basin, Veronyka crossed her arms over her chest. She did it unconsciously—the nights had grown cold—but Tristan noticed, and she sensed that he took it as a reproach. His shoulders tightened, and he kept his back to her as he soaked a towel, then wrung it out, steam rising from the surface of the bowl.

"You should remove the bandages, if you can, and I'll . . ."

Veronyka wanted to see his face again. Wanted him to know that it wasn't that she didn't want him here, but rather, that she wanted him here very much—too much—and that was a scary thing, the wanting.

She reached for his shoulder, pulling him until he turned to see her uncrossed arms, the wound and the bandages—and the bare skin on either side—revealed to him. His eyes were soft again, but something else stirred inside their darkened depths. Desire, anger, and fear warred within. She saw the struggle, felt it, knew it just as she knew her own.

"Help me?" she murmured, reaching for the lengths of linen that wrapped around her chest, holding the thicker bandages in place. He did, taking out a knife and cutting where the knots were too tight to unravel and gently peeling the last scraps of protection—of armor—away with them.

Now she was truly bare from the waist up, and the emotions inside him rose to the surface. He didn't say anything, but she felt his anguish as he trailed a featherlight touch across her skin.

She lay back, and he set to work.

She watched as he wiped at the tender skin, which was red and still bleeding in places. The wound stung, both from the open air and from the scrape of fabric, but she closed her eyes and focused on the quiet and the dark and the feeling of being alone with Tristan, one less barrier between them.

The healing salve burned worse than anything so far, and Veronyka hissed when his fingers touched her skin. He drew back at once, but she snatched his wrist.

"Just—be quick about it, will you?" she asked breathlessly, and he nodded with a small grin.

He cut clean strips of bandages and pressed them against her chest and stomach, cautious not to touch her anywhere he didn't need to. Veronyka was charmed by his gentlemanly restraint, but when he asked her to lean forward so he could tie the fabric behind her back, she deliberately pressed against him, her chest brushing his elbow.

He froze, then fumbled to tie the knot. They remained like that for a heartbeat; then he cleared his throat. "Done."

Their faces were inches apart, Tristan's breath stirring her hair. She took his hand and pressed it to her chest, against her wound and above her heart. "Thank you."

He smiled, then shifted as if he meant to take his hand back and put space between them. But Veronyka didn't want space. When he opened his mouth, she swallowed his words, pressing her lips to his and pulling him down on top of her.

He braced himself on his elbows, but Veronyka only arched underneath him, kissing harder and pulling him nearer. He drew back again—Veronyka made a frustrated noise of protest—but he was moving purposefully, determinedly, trailing kisses down her jaw and neck, and then lower.

His touch was almost reverent as it followed the trail of bandages down, across her abdomen to her hip bone. He looked up at her then, and the expression in his eyes was no longer careful or cautious. It was intense, raw, and potent—like a physical blow that sent her stomach swooping in response. The bond between them quivered and shook, rebuilding its strength after weeks apart.

And for once Veronyka didn't fight it; instead, she dragged Tristan's mouth up to hers and let the rush of feeling drown them both.

A single bond is one thing—perfect in its
balance and reciprocity—but the apex
bond, the group bond, is something else.

- CHAPTER 31 -
AVALKYRA

IT HAD BEEN THREE days since half of Avalkyra's flock—led by Onyx—
departed for Aura.

With only two claws apiece to carry them, the strixes were forced to
make multiple trips to get enough eggs to satisfy Avalkyra's ambitions. It
was less than efficient, but it gave her a chance to test her range, and it
gave the strixes a much-needed outlet for some of their pent-up energy and
aggression.

Avalkyra would have liked to get hatching as soon as the first eggs
arrived, but the shadowmage had advised against it. Better to do it all at
once, she said, so that Onyx could remain nearby during the hatching, and
form strong early bonds. And despite the power of the apex over the flock,
Aura was too far to send the flock without Onyx. They were likely to get
distracted or forget their purpose, so the apex had to remain with them to
keep them on task.

Every time she stared at the sky and awaited Onyx's return, Avalkyra
told herself they would begin hatching as soon as she got back . . . but then
the strixes would add their eggs to the pile growing in the center of the
courtyard, and she'd change her mind. Her impatience to get started warred
with her desire for an army large enough to blot out the sky, a true horde,

and so she'd tell Onyx *one more trip*, over and over, then watch hungrily as the pile grew larger still.

After days of this, Avalkyra decided she'd had enough. Onyx and the others were just delivering their final cargo, dropping their eggs onto the cobblestones before settling among the cracks and crenellations of the stronghold's walls, when Sidra turned up.

Avalkyra was annoyed by the interruption at first, until she remembered that Sidra would have news of the empire and the Phoenix Riders.

"My queen," Sidra said, dropping to her knee as soon as she'd dismounted. Once again, her phoenix hastened as far away from the strixes as possible, finding a village rooftop to perch on.

Sidra's eyes widened at the sight of the eggs, but Avalkyra redirected the woman's attention at once. "The Grand Council meeting?"

Sidra straightened, smiling proudly. "I arrived just in time. I killed the judge and a few others and set the chambers on fire. I told them you lived and that the war had begun. The council's out for Phoenix Rider blood."

Avalkyra nodded distractedly. Sidra, foolishly expecting praise, wilted slightly.

"Also," she added, "you should know that Lord Rolan is dead—shot by the Riders themselves outside the meeting—and the commander was gravely wounded. He might not survive."

"And Veronyka?" Avalkyra asked quietly, glancing over her shoulder at Morra, who was standing in the far corner of the courtyard. How strange to not know, to not be able to reach inside and confirm for herself where and how Veronyka was. She'd checked in on their bond daily and was becoming more and more convinced there was something truly wrong with it. Avoiding each other was one thing, but this? Veronyka had blocked her many times in the past, but the result was a closed door, locked and barred—not a door that Avalkyra couldn't even find.

As for Rolan or Cassian, Avalkyra didn't give a damn about either of them, but it was good to know her adversaries were scattered and dropping like flies. It was also not unexpected that Rolan should meet such a sudden and unremarkable end. Men who lived like pathetic cowards died like them too.

Sidra was surprised to be asked about Veronyka, but she quickly recovered. "She was there, but never had a chance to speak. She fled in the chaos, and . . ." Sidra paused, wary of rebuke. "I don't know where she went."

Veronyka could be any number of places, but with the border being watched and the commander badly hurt, Avalkyra would guess that she hadn't gone far. That was fine for now. It meant more time at the Eyrie, undisturbed. "What of the situation in Rushlea? The Unnamed?"

"I stopped there on my way back," Sidra replied, picking up steam again. "Their leaders are eager to meet with you. They are impatient, greedy, and want independent rule in Pyra most of all. Promise them that, and they will help you any way you see fit." Avalkyra considered that, preparing to turn away, when Sidra added, "Doriyan followed me from the capital." She blurted it, as if she'd had to muster the strength to speak the words.

"Doriyan, Rider of Daxos," Avalkyra murmured. She had wondered what became of him after she'd tied him up and left him for dead in the mine outside Rushlea. Veronyka or one of the others must have rescued him. "Where is he now?"

"I gave him the slip in the village," Sidra said, "but he was always a good tracker. No doubt he followed me here."

Avalkyra shrugged. The Phoenix Riders already had scouts watching the Eyrie, so what was one more? They were too distant to report anything of value and hadn't followed her strixes as they'd flown to Aura—she'd checked with Onyx. Since the strixes had been heading north, away from civilization, the Phoenix Riders hadn't attempted to stop them or engage. They didn't know what treasure Aura held, or that her flock had brought some of it back with them.

"Shall I deal with him?" Sidra asked, attempting to sound bold, to prove her ruthlessness. Sidra *was* ruthless, generally speaking, except when it came to Doriyan. Even now Avalkyra could sense her conflicted feelings. If she was Sidra's queen, Doriyan was Sidra's brother-in-arms. The closest thing to a friend she could ever find and a truer brother than her own family, who had disowned their animage daughter.

"Not yet," Avalkyra replied. With her bond to Veronyka silent and impenetrable, Doriyan might be Avalkyra's best hope of keeping tabs on her and the rest of the Phoenix Riders. "Leave him and the other scouts for now."

She turned her focus to Morra. It was time for the woman to earn her keep.

"Shadowmage," she said, waving her over and summoning Onyx as well.

The woman thumped across the cobblestones, gaze fixed on the heap of stonelike eggs that would easily quadruple Avalkyra's force. Sidra remained nearby, weathering the presence of the strixes for a chance to see her queen's ambitions come to life.

"Me and my apex bondmate," Avalkyra said, pointing at herself and Onyx. "Eggs." She pointed at the pile. "What comes next?"

Morra expelled a slow breath, as if steeling herself for a long-winded explanation. "As you may know, one of an apex's abilities is heartfire."

"Is that when they breathe fire?" Avalkyra asked, recalling the scene in Ferro again. The sweltering heat, the raw power against her skin . . . She wanted it for herself. Desperately.

"Yes," Morra said. "Heartfire is a formidable weapon, but it can also be used to incubate eggs. According to the myths, it is the very same fire that burned in the Everlasting Flame, a gift from Axura herself. What you've told me about hatching eggs in the *absence* of that fire, in the smoking ruin of the Everlasting Flame, supports the theory that there will be a corresponding strix ability."

They were operating on a *theory* alone? "And where did you learn this theory?"

"I was a priestess of Axura before the war. More specifically, a priestess within the Cult of Nox. We studied all manner of philosophies relating to strixes, shadow magic, and the goddess herself."

Ilithya certainly knew how to pick her allies and informants. Such cults had been banned well before Avalkyra was born the first time, and the library at the Nest had been purged of anything remotely related to its study or practice. After the Blood War, any mention of Nox and her children had been lost or destroyed, along with everything else.

"How do we make it, this heartfire?" she asked.

"In the temple, when we theorized the ability, we called it shadowfire—a bit inaccurate, perhaps, given that it would most certainly not be *fire*, but . . ."

Avalkyra looked at her bondmate, at the swirls of darkness that followed her everywhere, rippling off her feathers. Shadowfire, indeed.

"As apex, your bondmate would create the force—the shadowfire—but it's *your* magic that powers it. Well, yours and your benex."

"My what?"

"Just like an alpha has a beta—or a patrol leader has a second-in-command—an apex pair can only reach their full potential with the aid of a secondary bond, that of the benex pair. In your case, Veronyka and Xephyra."

Avalkyra swallowed uneasily, probing her mind again for any trace of the girl. She found none.

"What you say cannot be true," she argued. "Ignix used heartfire mere weeks ago in Ferro. Last I checked, Nefyra was dead. Callysta and Cirix were dead."

"You know what they say about bonds . . . ," Morra said with a shrug. "Even death is no match for them. Just because her mates are gone does not mean that Ignix has not kept the bonds alive. In fact, there is evidence to suggest that bonds can be carried within bloodlines, so the fact that Nefyra's descendants still live could potentially reinforce—"

"Fine," Avalkyra cut in, annoyed. Bonds survived death—she knew this—which meant that whatever was happening between her and Veronyka, they still had a bond. "How do we conjure it?"

"It is called heartfire for a reason," Morra explained as Avalkyra leapt onto Onyx's back. "The power coalesces in the breast before exploding up the throat."

Avalkyra nodded, sinking deep into her bond with Onyx. Together they reached into their joint well of magic—one that, in theory, connected to Veronyka's as well—drawing upward, pulling into Onyx's chest . . . but they came up with nothing.

There was a sudden, powerful kickback—a wave of exhaustion, dizziness, and fatigue rolling through her. She gasped, fighting to remain conscious. The feeling was not unlike what it had cost her to force the bind on Ignix, and so Avalkyra assumed it would be only a matter of time until she got it right.

She straightened in the saddle, gathering her strength. Then she dug deeper, pulled harder, beyond Onyx's level of comfort . . . and the next thing she knew, she was sprawled out on the ground, with two humans, her bondmate, and the rest of her flock staring down at her.

"Are you all right?" Sidra asked, offering a helping hand. Avalkyra refused it and struggled alone to her feet.

"Yes," she snapped, before rounding on the shadowmage. "Well? What happened?"

"I'm not sure," Morra said, looking away. Her gaze settled on Onyx, who also appeared dazed and disoriented. "It seems as though you tried to draw on your magic alone, and not on your benex as well. . . ."

Avalkyra flared her nostrils. Clearly, her bond to Veronyka was failing somehow, and it was preventing Avalkyra from siphoning magic from her.

It was preventing Avalkyra from moving forward with her plans.

"Maybe I was," she conceded. "Maybe I'm having trouble reaching Veronyka . . . since the spear attack."

"I see," Morra said, expression neutral. "Perhaps she is simply blocking you? I know she's done it before. . . ."

"Not like this. I can't feel her at all. . . ." She shook her head. "It's like she's disappeared."

It had been the singular constant in Avalkyra's tumultuous second life; through every trial and tribulation, every stumble and setback, one thing had remained: their bond.

Now it was gone.

"I can't say for certain," Morra began carefully, "but it sounds like a fracture."

"And what is that?"

"A broken or unstable bond. I'd guess your unexpected spear attack the other night caused you both to pull back so forcefully that you've caused a fracture in your connection. Such a thing can happen all at once or slowly over time, when bondmates drift apart or have too much physical or emotional distance. A bond requires a certain level of vulnerability, and after what's happened between you, it seems neither of you is willing to give it."

"And a fractured bond won't produce shadowfire?" Avalkyra demanded, cutting to the heart of the matter.

Morra shook her head. "I'm afraid not," she said. "But a bond is stronger than anything in this world and beyond it. It can be fixed. Reach out to her and repair your relationship."

Avalkyra had no interest in *repairing her relationship* with Veronyka. "There must be another way," she said through gritted teeth.

The woman deflated slightly, then cast an appraising look at Sidra. "A *second* human bondmate . . ."

"We are not bonded," Avalkyra said, outraged. "She is my *bind*mate—a servant, not a second. You have heard of a bind, haven't you, magical scholar?"

"A bind, of course. My mistake," Morra said, chastised. Sidra, meanwhile, projected nothing but sulky disappointment. "Then I'm afraid Veronyka is the only way."

Avalkyra snarled and stomped across the cobblestones. Veronyka, the bane of her existence, the thorn in her side, and the chain around her neck. And now, apparently, the person she needed most of all?

Was it any wonder, any surprise at all, that it would all come down to the two of them? That in order to achieve the height of her power, she would have to go, not around, but *through* the very person standing in her way? That they would have to do it *together*?

She refused to accept it, to give Veronyka that kind of sway over her.

"Without a human bondmate, without a benex, you will not be able to achieve shadowfire," Morra continued. She dropped her gaze, looking at the pile of eggs. "You will not be able to grow your horde."

Avalkyra curled her lip and called Onyx to her side. "Watch me."

All bowed before us. Now I begin to
understand the danger of this power.

CHAPTER 32

VERONYKA

VERONYKA OPENED HER EYES in the darkness of the tent. She was completely disoriented for a second, but then she rolled over into Tristan's warm body. He was already awake, watching her.

His contemplative expression turned into an embarrassed smile when he realized he'd been caught staring, but he didn't stop. She was covered in a blanket against the chill, but his eyes were on the bandage tied across her chest, and his face was . . . not troubled, exactly, but thoughtful.

"I suppose you think I'm a fool, allowing myself to get close to her over and over again," Veronyka said.

"I'm not sure *allowing* is the right word," he said with a frown. He reached out and gently traced a finger along the path of the wound, invisible under the bandages, though she got the sense he'd learned it by heart. "No, I don't think you're a fool. The people we love are always the ones best equipped to hurt us."

Veronyka knew that truth at a fundamental level, but she realized that Tristan knew it too. The commander wasn't Val, but Tristan put so much stock in his father's approval, reaching constantly for external validation he might never get. They disagreed deeply and often, and he understood Veronyka's struggle to define herself in the face of that conflict.

"Is there a chance it will happen again? Are you in danger—even now?"

Veronyka shook her head uncertainly. It was hard to explain. "There's something *wrong* with our bond, I think. . . . I can barely find her in my mind, and I can't feel her at all. . . ."

"Does that mean she's blocking you?"

"No, I—she's blocked me before, for the majority of my life, in fact. But ever since I learned we were bonded, I could feel her. Now it's almost like the bond is broken, like there's been a cave-in or something. The door is still there, but nothing's getting through. Even when I try to—"

"Maybe you shouldn't," he said hastily. "Maybe this break or whatever is your mind protecting itself."

Veronyka suspected that wasn't far off the mark. She hated to feel cut off—it was too similar to the way she'd blocked her magic before—but she couldn't deny the sensation of safety it gave her. Yes, the attack had caused a knee-jerk reaction, but they'd been heading in this direction for months. Bonds were built on trust, after all, and the goodwill between them was all but spent. It was no wonder their connection had fallen apart.

They lay in silence for a while. Veronyka never wanted to leave this tent, but daylight was creeping through the canvas, lightening the shadows, and she knew they'd have to face the real world again soon.

"So, speaking of shadow magic . . . I'm assuming this is okay now?" His hand moved from her bandage, sliding along the bare skin of her back instead.

"What, sleeping together?" Veronyka asked innocently.

"I wasn't referring to the *sleep*," Tristan said dryly. "You're not blocking your shadow magic anymore? Not worried about"—he waved his hand in the air—"eye contact . . . physical contact? I thought they were off-limits. I thought the bond between us was a bad thing."

Veronyka shook her head vehemently. "That's more nonsense Val fed me growing up. She wanted me weak, so she taught me wrong from the start. Held me back and made me afraid of my own power. I should have figured it out sooner—whatever Val believed, I should do the opposite."

Tristan chuckled at that. "It's not that I'm complaining," he said, dropping a kiss to her neck and lingering there, lips moving against her skin. "I just want you to be safe."

"Not hiding from it anymore is the best way. I'm actually learning my magic and not just suppressing it." She thought of Morra with a pang. "Well, at least I was. Morra was helping me, but now . . ." Veronyka pushed the hurt aside. If Morra had indeed betrayed her—betrayed them all—then, well, there was no point thinking about it. "I know more than I ever have, and the rest I'll have to learn along the way. If I'm going to possess this power, it's my responsibility to understand it. For my safety, of course, but also for others. I relied on ignorance before, but I can't any longer."

It reminded her of the throne. To hide from the power and responsibility inherent in her birthright was to be irresponsible. Like a sword in her hands or the magic in her veins, Veronyka must learn to wield that power with caution and care.

"Besides, my bond to her is one thing—but my bond to *you* is something else. It's a part of me, like my bond with Xephyra. I'd rather die than be without either."

A burst of joy welled up inside Tristan, and Veronyka was glad that she no longer had to pretend not to feel it. He squeezed her so tightly it hurt.

"I guess it's not all bad, then," he said, still smiling so wide his dimples showed. "What you did in that dungeon in Stel? That was pretty amazing."

"Speaking of that . . . ," Veronyka said, picking absently at a thread in the blanket. "Just because I've decided I'm okay with using my magic now doesn't mean *you* have to be okay with it. We can set boundaries that you're comfortable with—"

"I'm comfortable," he interrupted.

"And I'll always ask permission before—"

"You never have to ask with me."

He said it bluntly, he said it simply, and she felt the truth of it even as her heart clenched at the trust in it.

She rolled toward him and buried her face in his chest.

This was her burden to bear—this magic, this sister, this legacy in her blood. But it was nice, sometimes, to feel like she wasn't so very much alone.

When they exited the tent, Alexiya was sitting in front of the rekindled fire, cooking breakfast. She positively beamed at them.

"Sleep well?" she asked wickedly, eyebrows wagging, and Veronyka wanted to glower, but she couldn't quite manage it. Tristan looked appropriately flustered, though, which Veronyka enjoyed almost as much as Alexiya.

"Yes, thank you," he muttered, moving forward to fuss with the kettle.

"I sent updates to Prosperity and to Stel last night, as we discussed," Alexiya continued more seriously, standing and stretching. "I'll be meeting your patrol tonight and escorting them here, to ensure they arrive safely."

"Perfect," Tristan said. He glanced up at the treehouse.

"Hestia is sleeping," Alexiya said, nodding to one of the other tents, "but she said that your father is still stable and in a medically induced sleep. My mother watches him, and . . ." She trailed off, staring blankly over Veronyka's shoulder. Veronyka turned, following her gaze.

A man stood there. He looked wary, hands deep in his pockets. "Hi, Lexi."

Lexi. Veronyka had never heard that nickname before. When she turned back to her aunt, it was to see Alexiya's face had gone hard.

"Hello, Theryn."

The ground seemed to drop out beneath Veronyka.

Theryn. Her *father*? She thought Alexiya hadn't been able to find him, and now here he was out of nowhere?

"Mom contacted you, I presume? Of course she would know where you were. . . ."

Veronyka remained rooted to the spot but heard the man's footsteps as he drew nearer. Next to her, Tristan watched the scene with confusion.

"I came back home after the war. You did not. It's been seventeen years, Lexi. I must admit I'd given up hope."

Alexiya swallowed visibly; then her gaze finally left Theryn and darted to Veronyka. She drew back her shoulders. "This isn't about me."

"So I've heard." He glanced around the clearing, at Veronyka and Tristan and their phoenixes. "A strange visit indeed."

"I've been looking for you," Alexiya said, eyes flicking to Veronyka again.

"I didn't want to be found," Theryn explained.

"Not by me," Alexiya asked, though it sounded more like a statement.

"Not by anyone."

Veronyka could barely keep up. She thought *her* sibling relationship was tense, but this was possibly even more strained. She tried not to stare as they spoke, but it was nearly impossible. She kept hoping . . . What, exactly? That he would *know* her, recognize her as his? But his gaze passed over her with only the mildest interest and zero spark of recognition.

"Idiot," Alexiya said abruptly.

"Pardon me?" came Theryn's startled response.

"You're an idiot. Always have been. I'd like to tell you every which way, in detail, but now is not the time. When next you decide to go underground for nearly two decades, perhaps you should reconsider letting your little sister in on the details."

"I thought you were dead, Lexi. I—"

"You thought a lot of people were dead, didn't you? Most of them were, but not all. Not me, and not *her*."

Alexiya was beside Veronyka now, a hand on her shoulder. Her touch was heavy.

Theryn looked between them, clearly trying to work out who the "her" was in that statement. Then his eyes landed on Veronyka and stayed there. He'd already seen her, but he hadn't truly *looked*.

Now he did.

His eyes were brown—but light, like Tristan's, not near-black like hers—large and deep set. They were roving Veronyka's face, confusion pinching his forehead. His dark hair was messy and just long enough to curl around his ears and fall across his forehead. Veronyka could see all the ways he favored Alexiya, with their straight, elegant posture and smooth brown skin. He was surprisingly tall, given Veronyka's own height, and his shoulders were broad and thick. He still looked like a soldier, even all these years later. There was a rigidness to him, a sternness that made him look older than he was, and the lines between his brows said he spent more time frowning than laughing.

Veronyka wondered if that had always been the case, or if this was the result of all he'd lost.

"This is Veronyka," Alexiya said, the hardness in her voice receding. "Veronyka Ashfire."

He shook his head slowly, his mouth tight—doubtful—but his eyes . . . his eyes. They held Veronyka hostage, wide open and exposed. Never in her life had she so yearned to reach out with shadow magic, to know his thoughts, but she mastered the urge.

She wasn't sure she was ready for what she might find there.

A halting movement, and he closed the distance between them, hand outstretched. It brushed across her cheek—moving aside a piece of hair—and then his gaze landed on the necklace braided among the inky strands. Pheronia's necklace.

He seemed to sway on the spot, his attention snapping back to her, sharper now. He scanned her face, seeking, searching . . . Was Pheronia there somewhere? People said so. Would Theryn see it?

"Your daughter," Alexiya added gently.

A loud thump echoed through the clearing, and they both jerked apart.

Agneta was several feet away, standing on the stairs up to her house. She was staring at them, mouth hanging open, while a bucket—the source of the sudden noise—clattered down the last few steps to land on the ground.

"Mother, I—" Alexiya began, but Agneta ignored her as she hastened into the clearing, an alarming look of fury on her face.

"My own granddaughter outside my door, and I didn't know," she said, sounding equal parts weepy and raging as she pushed the others aside and enveloped Veronyka in a hug. She drew back, but only so she could survey

Veronyka closely. "Roots below and branches above, but you are skinny as a sapling—and sleeping out here on the ground like some wild thing! Upstairs at once. *All of you.*"

Her tone brooked no argument.

Veronyka looked helplessly at Tristan. He shrugged—this was family business, as far as he was concerned—and stayed out of it.

"Those two'll behave, mark my words," Agneta promised, nodding at her children as she wrapped an arm around Veronyka's shoulders to steer her. "Soth take me if they don't."

Then she made for the stairs, dragging Veronyka with her. Alexiya followed, and Theryn brought up the rear.

The house was small, the majority of it taken up by a kitchen and a living area, with doors off the main space that presumably led to bedrooms.

Alexiya and Theryn sat at opposite ends of the rectangular dining table, as if they couldn't get far enough from each other. Agneta gave them both severe looks, then ushered Veronyka to sit between them.

She bustled around, muttering and shaking her head. She rattled off questions but answered most of them before Veronyka got the chance.

"Do you like ginger and lemon? Of course you do—they're good for you." Then, "Are you hungry? No matter, I'll whip you up a small bite."

Her behavior seemed slightly manic—she chattered away, fussing and filling the silence—but when Veronyka saw the wide-eyed, tight-lipped look on Theryn's face, she thought maybe her grandmother's actions were very much on purpose. He was clearly in shock, and Veronyka tried to picture how she'd have behaved if Alexiya had dropped Theryn in front of her rather than telling her about his existence first. It was certainly a lot to take in.

After making Veronyka tea with honey, lemon, and ginger, then slicing fresh cheese and fruit, and putting out a bowl of nuts, Agneta finally sat.

She was directly across from Veronyka, staring intently. Veronyka had one bite, then two—followed by a sip of tea—but could see that this would not satisfy the woman. Despite not being the least bit hungry, Veronyka cleaned the plate, downed the tea, and reached for the bowl of nuts. Agneta beamed as she cleared away the plate and the cup, then yanked the bowl of nuts away and began shelling them herself.

Alexiya reached for some as well, but Agneta slapped her hand away, as if the nuts were for guests alone. Alexiya glowered sullenly, but her mother paid her no mind.

"Do you know what these would go great with?" Agneta asked, but once again, it was no question at all. She just leapt to her feet and bustled around the kitchen again, but this time she ordered Alexiya to help, leaving Veronyka and Theryn somewhat alone.

He still looked utterly shocked—maybe even panicked—and Veronyka felt a pang of compassion stab her chest. She had gained quite a bit of experience recently in dealing with startling revelations and understood a small fraction of what her father must be feeling. So, before she could overthink it, she reached across the table and squeezed his hand.

He met her eyes with a grateful, somewhat pathetic look on his face. Ashamed, maybe, that she had made the first move.

It was okay if he didn't know what to do and didn't have the right words. Veronyka didn't really have any either. This was a life-altering event—and not just his current life. Veronyka's existence reshaped his past, too, and the seventeen years since he'd thought he'd lost her. It wouldn't be easy to slot everything back into place. It wouldn't be easy to move forward.

When he squeezed her back, *hard*, Veronyka's throat grew tight. She nodded at him, blinking away the moisture in her eyes, and then turned her attention back to Agneta.

She was putting a large tray of some custard-looking dessert on the table, and though she scooped plates for Alexiya and Theryn, the portion she gave to Veronyka was the largest.

When she wasn't watching Veronyka eat, Agneta touched her—stroking her hair, rubbing her arm, and tugging at her clothes. Veronyka had never been so thoroughly fussed over in her entire life, and she rather enjoyed it.

After the plates were scraped clean, Agneta stood and cleared everything away once more.

As Veronyka looked up, her father and grandmother shared a significant look. "I think it's time, Theryn."

Alexiya—who'd been stealing a spoonful of dessert from the tray as her mother lifted it—froze.

"Time for what?"

The floor creaked, and then Theryn was standing next to Veronyka. He was the one to hold out his hand this time. "I'd like to show you something."

Veronyka took it.

They climbed back down the tree, Alexiya and Agneta behind them. Hestia took the chance to check on her patient, and after a hesitant glance at Veronyka—who waved him over—Tristan fell into step beside her.

Theryn led them deeper into the forest, over packed earth and knotted roots, between towering trees and hanging boughs. He released her hand to lift aside a swaying branch, but he reached back to help her underneath— never letting more than a breath of space open between them.

They eventually reached a ring of dense trees, their branches hanging almost to the ground and covered in great big leafy fronds. Through the greenery they went, finding a kind of valley on the other side with a massive tree in the center. It was so large that it seemed to draw the surrounding earth down with it, the humungous roots sticking out of the ground and in some places nearly as tall as Veronyka.

Theryn led them down the slope and around the rippling roots to the space directly in front of the tree, where a dark, yawning mouth opened. A door?

Glancing over his shoulder, he continued forward, *into* the great tree, its trunk probably thirty people wide at least. And inside . . . it had been hollowed out, carved to create a cavernous, soaring interior. As Veronyka's eyes adjusted, she saw signs of habitation—tables arranged around the edges of the space, shelves bearing supplies, and stairs like the ones that led up to her grandmother's house, but inside the tree rather than outside it. People were there too, emerging from what she could only assume were rooms above, carved into the branches and knots of the exterior tree. They watched the newcomers warily, ranging in age from small children to old folks.

Theryn looked back at her, smiling for the first time since they'd met as he watched Veronyka gape.

Because above it all, perched atop steps and shelves and every other available surface, were phoenixes.

Were we meant to spread our magic like rays of sunlight—touching all beneath us?

CHAPTER 33

SEV

NEWS DIDN'T ARRIVE UNTIL the morning after their arrival at Selt-lake.

Sev had spent the majority of the previous day at their camp sulking—with a kind of quiet dignity, he thought—as the Phoenix Riders flew patrols and trained together. While Kade was an apprentice and the others masters, they treated him with friendship and respect. Even the bitchy one, Latham. Kade was older than everyone but Ronyn, which helped, and from what Sev gathered by casual eavesdropping and the odd session of lipreading, Kade's closeness with Veronyka had clearly elevated his station at the Eyrie.

Sev knew Veronyka too—for just as long as Kade, if not so well—but he kept that information to himself. Which was, *yes* . . . sulking. Maybe he could have handled standing around bored or turning down offers to train in combat—he wasn't going to willingly embarrass himself if he could help it—if it weren't for Jinx.

She stared at him constantly. Phoenixes were curious by nature. Sev had figured that out soon enough. But while the others spared him little more than a cursory glance and a cocked, inquisitive head, Jinx stared at Sev avidly. When he actually drew near the phoenixes, they often squawked and shuffled away, as if his very presence were off-putting. He was clearly an anomaly—an animage who had no idea how to use his magic—but to Jinx, he was more. A puzzle.

I know, Sev had thought in resignation, watching her watch him from across the fireside during the evening meal. *You're trying to figure it out.* Trying to understand why her bondmate cared for Sev—when he wasn't busy scowling at him for what he'd called Sev's "stubborn bouts of relentless self-pity"—and how such a person could draw the notice of Kade in the first place.

I don't get it either.

When it came time to sleep, Sev helped Kade set up his two-person tent, but it was decidedly awkward. Sev warred within himself, knowing he should draw a line between them now, before things went too far, but also desperate to cling to whatever scraps of their relationship remained while he still could.

He was saved from having to decide because Kade had been inserted into their patrol rotation, and by the time he'd returned that night, Sev had been fast asleep. In fact, he didn't see Kade until he'd lurched out of the tent for breakfast, and that was when Lysandro returned early from his patrol with a messenger pigeon on his shoulder.

He was pale as he read the letter aloud over the damp, early-morning fire.

Rolan was dead. The Grand Council had been attacked by Avalkyra Ashfire's Phoenix Rider ally, guaranteeing war. And the commander was gravely wounded. In addition to the strix attack, which Kade had filled Sev in on the previous day, it was extremely hard to find a silver lining in their current situation. To imagine how they would make it through this.

Sev was also weirdly deflated about Lord Rolan's death. His actions had nearly gotten Sev, Kade, and half the other Phoenix Riders killed on numerous occasions, not to mention his imprisonment of Tristan and attempted marriage to Veronyka. He was finally out of the way, and yet, many of their problems remained.

"We're to fly to Arboria," Lysandro continued, frowning in apparent surprise, while Anders perked up.

"Where?" he asked, leaning to read over Lysandro's shoulder.

"It says to skirt south of Aura Nova; then Alexiya will meet us on the eastern shore of the Fingers, in Arboria South. She's going to lead us from there."

"Why, though?" asked Latham. "It's not much closer than Prosperity, and I can't imagine the empire is the safest place for us."

"I suspect they're watching the border closely," Ronyn said, "and we can't stay here. Better to be together."

The rest of that day was spent packing up and preparing, as they would fly through the night to hide their tracks and hopefully avoid detection. While the empire would no doubt be looking for them crossing into Pyra or flying near the border, it was very doubtful they would expect to find Phoenix Riders in Arboria. The region was covered with ready kindling and had a notorious dislike for all things firebird. Sev thought it was a clever place to regroup.

Though he had been avoiding both Kade *and* Jinx, when the time came to fly out, he was surprised and a little uneasy to learn he would be riding with Anders. Ronyn's phoenix was technically largest, but Ronyn was heavier even than Kade, and Anders was considered the better flyer.

Sev had flashed a confused—and if he was honest, slightly hurt—look at Kade, forgetting their argument in favor of this unexpected complication, but Kade seemed equally unhappy about it. Clearly, this wasn't his doing.

"Jinx is, what, barely two months old?" Anders explained, turning the words to Kade, who nodded stiffly. "She's already a good size for her age, but she's not used to flying so far or carrying such a heavy load. Kade's large enough," he added with a playful elbow to Kade's side. Kade remained stony and unsmiling, but Anders was unperturbed.

Despite his reassurances, when Sev approached Anders's mount, the phoenix balked. Sev's nerves were taut as a bowstring, and the phoenix could surely feel it.

It didn't help that Kade's dark expression followed his every movement as he mounted up and wrapped his arms around Anders's middle. Jinx squawked as if in reproach, and Anders's mount lifted his head imperiously, asserting his impressive status as a slightly older and slightly larger phoenix. Sev found their social dynamics interesting—or at least he would have, if he weren't so uneasy.

Flying during the day had been an overwhelming experience, a mix of fear, adrenaline, and visceral wonder at the world experienced from such a height, at such a speed, on such a beast. Of course, Sev had not let himself enjoy it, but he hadn't missed the fact that he was seeing the world as his parents had seen it—as Kade would continue to see it—and that had resulted in an influx of conflicting emotions.

But flying at night turned the experience into something personal and intimate—there was just the wind and the stars, with everything else fading away into peaceful oblivion. Anders was a friendly sort who made the journey less uncomfortable than it could have been, but Sev found himself desperately wishing he'd taken this nocturnal flight with Kade. As it was, he watched Kade fly alongside them, filled with awe and admiration. Kade looked utterly himself in the saddle on phoenix-back, and though Sev felt out of place in such a glorious scene, he was happy to be witness to it.

They paused briefly when they met with Alexiya—an older Rider and apparently Veronyka's aunt, though not on her royal Ashfire side—but they had to move on if they wanted to reach their destination before morning. Sev was meant to be pawned off on Latham next, but Kade stepped forward and insisted Jinx was up to the job in a tone Sev could only describe as both protective *and* possessive. He tried not to let his relief—and satisfaction—show. He couldn't let himself get used to being Kade's. He couldn't let himself need it.

Hazy sunlight was beginning to slice through the towering forest as they made their final descent. They landed in a clearing next to the largest tree Sev had ever seen in his life. It dwarfed even those soaring giants that surrounded it, and its roots dug so deep into the earth it had created a kind of sunken valley around its base.

And there, waiting to greet them, were more Phoenix Riders.

Veronyka was at the front, with Tristan standing just behind her. As she greeted Alexiya, he moved to speak to the members of his patrol. Kade landed near the back of the group, so the other conversations were too quiet for Sev to hear as he dismounted.

Kade got to his feet first, and Sev was surprised when he saw Veronyka there, hugging him tightly. Sev and Kade had spent only six or seven weeks apart, but apparently Kade and Veronyka had grown closer in those weeks than Sev had realized.

If he was caught off guard by their familiarity, he was completely shocked when Veronyka released Kade only to hug *him* next. His shock must have shown on his face, because Kade grinned broadly at him from over her shoulder.

"I'm so glad we got you out of there," Veronyka said, releasing him. "And thank you for everything you did. For us, for Tristan."

"Oh, it was nothing," Sev muttered, embarrassed—but immensely pleased—by her praise. First Kade, now her?

Tristan himself turned up then. It was strange to face each other without bars or the barrier of Sev's disguise between them. Sev extended his hand, but Tristan only gripped it long enough to pull him into a hug too. Once again Sev found himself somewhat flustered by the attention.

"Good to see you out of that dungeon," Tristan said, drawing back but keeping a hand on Sev's shoulder, fixing him with a rather dazzling smile. White teeth. Dimples. It was like getting punched in the stomach. In contrast, the grin on Kade's face slipped. "We need to get you out of these," Tristan mused, pulling on the neckline of Sev's shirt, and Kade's expression turned fractionally darker, a glower that Sev found himself surprisingly fond of all of a sudden. It made him feel elated and desperate in equal measure.

Distracted by his muddled thoughts, it took him a moment to understand Tristan's words. Then he remembered he still wore Tristan's dirty Rider gear from when they'd swapped clothes inside the dungeon. He suspected the clothes didn't suit him, and they were too big and in need of washing.

"I'll find him something," Kade interjected, a bit possessive again. It should have been funny—unnecessary, even—but no matter how much Sev wanted to be Kade's, he couldn't. Not for long anyway. Not without dragging Kade down. Not without making him choose.

Tristan didn't seem to notice Kade bristling next to him, or maybe he was distracted by Sev pressing a hand to his chest, pulling aside the padded leather armor. It was clear from both Tristan's and Kade's startled reactions that they thought Sev meant to get out of his clothes right then and there.

"Sev, what—" Kade began, but then Sev found what he was looking for. He withdrew the obsidian arrowhead and held it out. Tristan took an unconscious step forward.

"I thought I'd lost it . . . ," he murmured, taking it gingerly from Sev. He swiped a thumb across its smooth surface—Sev hoped he'd managed to clean away all traces of his blood—in a practiced gesture. Then he turned to Veronyka, whose expression went from puzzlement to warmth at the sight of it. That was when Sev noticed a matching piece, clearly the other half, dangling at the end of one of her braids.

Heat rushed to his face, as if he were witnessing something intensely personal and private.

"Thank you," Tristan said, words hushed, "for keeping it safe."

Sev cleared his throat. "Of course." It was the least he could do, really . . . and also, he realized, the last. He was suddenly, completely out of things to do or offer, out of anything worthwhile to give. Kade said it didn't matter, but Sev had a hard time believing it.

As Tristan tucked the arrowhead away, Veronyka stepped in to introduce him to Kade.

Sev looked between them all, believing for a single, precious heartbeat that he could exist here with them. That maybe he wasn't as out of place as he'd feared, that what he had to offer truly didn't matter.

The greetings over, Veronyka led them and the rest of Tristan's patrol members into the center of their camp, near the cook fire, which was set up in between several of the massive, twisting roots.

Sev couldn't take his eyes off the gigantic tree that soared up behind it. It looked ancient, and had a massive gaping mouth in the front, just visible in the gray light of the morning. Veronyka saw his attention and smirked.

There was a rustle and the scrape of footsteps; then out walked a group of around thirty or forty people. Above, in the gloom, the branches filled with phoenixes.

Sev's mouth dropped open, and he wasn't the only one.

Veronyka was looking around at them all, beaming. "I know you must be tired—" she began, but Anders cut her off.

"Not tired enough," he said, shaking his head, and a couple of the others laughed or nodded, jaws still slack.

She hesitated, waiting until a man stepped to the front of the group. He smiled tentatively at her before turning to the others. "My name is Theryn. Welcome to Haven."

Haven? Theryn gestured for Sev and the others to follow him as he walked a slow circuit around the back of the massive tree, where gardens sat in neat little rows—morning dew clinging to sprouting leaves—and picketed animals munched on grain. The majority of Haven's inhabitants had already dispersed to start their work for the day, pouring feed into troughs or pulling up roots, scrubbing clothes in great wooden buckets sloshing with water or hanging sodden, freshly laundered garments on lines to dry.

"I started Haven a little over seventeen years ago," Theryn said, surveying his small, gently buzzing community like a king taking stock of his vast, sprawling lands. "The empire doesn't know of its existence—nobody does. It's a safe place for anyone who needs it," Theryn finished. "For anyone on the wrong side of the empire."

Animages. That much was obvious, given the phoenixes still perched on the branches above, now mingling with the new arrivals. Sev spotted Jinx at once, drawn to her distinctive purple plumage and her now familiar, inquisitive chirrup, though there were other females as well. Veronyka's phoenix, for certain, and several others besides, but Jinx was youngest, her violet accents softer, subtler than the rest.

Their human bondmates were easy enough to pick out too, shifting and reacting to their phoenixes as if tethered by a string. Some were clearly veterans of the Blood War, with the haunted eyes and war scars to prove it, while others looked eager and untested, probably newly bonded when the war broke out and too young to fight.

By the looks on some of their faces, they were just as awed to discover these new-fangled Phoenix Riders as Veronyka and the others were to discover them.

But there weren't just Phoenix Riders. Among their ranks were rescues, runaways, escaped bondservants . . . people like Sev and Kade.

"Despite our seclusion and secrecy, we're always trying to grow, to seek out animages in dire circumstances—and Phoenix Riders too. There are dozens more in Arboria alone."

"There are *other* Phoenix Riders in Arboria?" Kade asked in disbelief. Sev had to agree. The fact there were any at all was extraordinary enough.

"You'd be surprised how many took refuge here. Arboria was neutral in the war, after all, and the trees provide superior coverage. Many prefer their solitude, but Erend joined us only last year. Whatever they choose, they know we're here, that we're an option, and that's a start."

Next, Theryn led them inside the giant tree. It was smooth and hollowed out, like the inside of a walnut, with a main living space in the center and stairs winding upward into the shadowy trunk and out of sight. People worked inside too, wrangling small children or weaving baskets, and everywhere were animals: cats and dogs, chipmunks and squirrels, all scratching and scampering and crawling over one another. There was a lively but peaceful feeling about the place, the kind of steady dependability that Sev had had precious little of in his life.

It was the idea of waking up and going to bed in the same place every day, of knowing the world would be the same in the morning.

It was safety.

Sev's heart surged with a kind of desperate, painful longing at the idea that *he* might have grown up in such a place. That Kade might have too. He glanced at Kade now, whose face was shining with wonder, and felt an entirely different kind of longing rise up.

After their tour, they sat around a large cook fire to have breakfast.

An older woman called Agneta fluttered around the fire, ladling great dollops of porridge into wooden bowls and making sure that Sev, Tristan, and some of their skinnier counterparts ate second helpings. Kade ate twice without prompting, and she beamed at him. The majority of Haven's occupants had eaten during their tour, leaving the newcomers to themselves.

After they finished eating, Tristan stood, announcing that he wanted a quick meeting with his Riders to share reports and get on the same page.

"We'll leave you to it, then," said Theryn, reaching for Agneta, who was busy gathering empty breakfast dishes. She allowed herself to be steered away, so all that remained were the members of Tristan's patrol, Kade, and Sev.

He wondered with a hot sense of shame if he would be ushered away next, or if he should take the hint and depart on his own, when Tristan reclaimed his seat next to him.

"You're not leaving, are you?" he asked Sev, who was hovering slightly over the log, uncertain.

"Oh, I . . ."

"It won't take long," Veronyka promised, from Tristan's other side. "And I want to make sure you're in the loop."

Sev wanted to ask *why*—he had nothing of value to offer—but he couldn't deny he was relieved to be included.

"So . . . how is he?" asked Lysandro, leaning forward in his seat. "The commander?"

"He's stable," Tristan said. "Hestia, the healer, performed emergency surgery last night."

"Hestia's here?" Sev blurted, a wave of relief crashing through him. "What about Yara?"

"Her cover is still intact, and she's on her way to Rolan's town house as we speak. Hestia received word this morning. All the captains were summoned to Aura Nova to await orders."

"Speaking of waiting . . . Are we to remain here while the commander heals?" asked Ronyn. "What about the Grand Council and the war?"

"They'll start by marshaling the provincial armies," Tristan replied. "Then they'll send them to the northern border to organize the attack."

"How long will that take?" Ronyn asked, voice tense.

"Weeks, if they await their full force. But they could muster a company large enough to take Pyra in mere days. It could have been even sooner had Lord Rolan not depleted Ferro's ranks with his recent ambitions. So I suppose we should thank him for that."

"Over my dead body." Kade scowled.

"Over his," Anders clarified. "Never mind the empire—what about the Shadow Queen?" he pressed.

"The who?" Tristan repeated.

"That's what the servants at Prosperity were calling her. Avalkyra Ashfire, the Shadow Queen."

Veronyka snorted. "She'll *love* that," she muttered darkly.

"What does she want?" Ronyn asked. "What is she after?"

Everyone looked to Veronyka. She opened her mouth—but hesitated before responding. "I . . . I don't know."

"Surely you must have some idea," Latham pressed.

"I know what she *did* want," Veronyka said. "She wanted to rewrite the past, to reclaim the throne, the crown, the titles and allegiances she saw as her due."

"But now?" Tristan prompted.

She looked up at him. "She knows she can't have them, and she'd rather destroy everything she once held dear than be denied. She is no longer a Phoenix Rider queen, beloved of her people and commander of flocks. Now she commands a different kind of army, one capable only of destruction."

"Then we should strike back at her right away," Anders said, looking around. "Shouldn't we?"

Kade grew tense next to Sev. Of the people here, he was the only one to have actually been present when the strix army attacked.

"We would likely take massive losses," Tristan said.

"Plus, we still have the empire to think about," added Latham.

"But the longer we wait, the more prepared she'll be," countered Anders.

"There has to be another way," Kade said. He didn't speak again until everyone's attention was on him. Kade was a man of few words, so when he spoke, people tended to listen. "A different way to defeat her, other than open warfare. Those creatures . . ." He trailed off. "Everywhere they landed, things died. The grass blackened and turned brittle like trees after a forest fire, only there was no smoke, no heat . . . just *nothing*, nothing at all. Wood became charcoal, and stone crumbled. Birds fell from the sky, lifeless, and the other animals that drew too near . . . There were heaps of them scattered across the cobblestones, dried-out husks as crisp and colorless as dead leaves."

A collective shudder ran through the group, and the bright morning felt suddenly cold and foreboding. Everyone looked scared and somber . . . everyone except Veronyka. Her eyes were bright, her expression determined.

"You're right. I'll find a way."

"It's not all on you," Tristan said, in a way that felt like a reminder.

"Isn't it?" Veronyka said, so softly Sev barely heard it, but everyone was looking at her.

"No, it isn't," Tristan said firmly.

She and Tristan shared a look, and whatever unspoken thing passed between them, Veronyka nodded, sitting taller. She glanced around at the others and expelled a breath.

"Of course not. *We'll* find a way."

There was a strange mix of softness and steel in her words—vulnerability and determination in equal measure. She had come a long way from the barefooted girl he had once met.

Despite the commander's injury and the impending war, Sev was feeling . . . not optimistic, exactly, but slightly more balanced and reassured as they broke apart to get some sleep. They were safe, at least for now, and it was good to be involved, even just as a spectator. Even if it couldn't last.

As they split up, though, one of the occupants of Haven stepped forward to direct Sev to the sleeping quarters inside the massive tree. He was confused for a moment, but then he realized it was because he wasn't a Rider. Veronyka must have told them before his arrival. The Riders slept in tents outside, and everyone else slept inside the tree.

Kade opened his mouth as if to object, but stalled out, uncertain. What could he say? Sev didn't want to be some . . . some *kept man* in Kade's tent. How embarrassing.

The truth was, he *didn't* belong with them. He wouldn't be going on patrols, wouldn't need to be roused in the middle of the night to take over a shift. . . . He wasn't a Phoenix Rider, which meant that he had no reason to sleep outside with them. No reason to sleep next to Kade.

"Thank you," he said to the woman.

Kade reared back in surprise, his eyes wide and maybe even hurt, but Sev pushed that aside and followed her.

No matter how much he tried to help or convince himself he belonged here, there would always be this barrier between him and Kade, a line that Sev would be unable to cross. Kade deserved a life in the sky, and Sev would do nothing but drag him down. And he couldn't do that, not to Kade.

And so, eventually, just as they had that night, Kade would go one way and Sev would have to go the other.

Were we meant to spread our magic
like fire—lighting, warming . . . consuming?

- CHAPTER 34 -
TRISTAN

THE COMMANDER AWOKE THE following evening.

Tristan had just returned from patrol, Anders taking his place as he came to a landing on the outskirts of Haven's central clearing. It was a relief to be outside again, back in the saddle and flying with Rex after so long inside Rolan's dungeon. He had also spent the morning training, and though he was rusty—and had the bumps and bruises to prove it—Tristan reveled at the chance to hold a spear and bow again. It felt good to hack and punch and knock down his patrol members, only to laugh and joke and help each other up.

Haven might have been well hidden, but he wanted to ensure they maintained regular training as well as surveillance of the area. He didn't relish the thought of any more surprises, and though he didn't know how long they'd be here, he wanted to be sharp if and when their next conflict came.

Not that he was in a rush to leave—not with war on their doorstep and Veronyka's aunt commanding an army of demons from myth and legend. It was nice to take a breather and to see that at least *some* of Veronyka's family wasn't hell-bent on tearing the world apart.

The four of them didn't get to spend that much time together, but when they did, the family dynamic shone through their simple interactions.

Agneta and Alexiya bickered constantly, but even as they argued and snapped at each other, Alexiya helped her mother cook and clean, and Agneta fussed over the state of her daughter's clothing and patched her leathers when Alexiya wasn't looking.

Theryn was clearly the strong, silent type, which turned his mother and sister's constant squabbling into a wash of welcome noise that banished any potential for awkwardness. He just smiled and shook his head or watched Veronyka—he was always watching Veronyka.

This slice of sanctuary had been built by him, and it was clear he'd had his seemingly dead daughter in mind when he'd created it. Alexiya—for all her bluntness—was warmer and more loving than Val could have ever been. And though Tristan hadn't known the grandmother who helped raise Veronyka, her father's mother fussed and fluttered about, doting on her and bringing out soft, tender smiles on Veronyka's face.

In fact, after Tristan unsaddled Rex and approached the fire for dinner, Veronyka was already seated, being stuffed full of food by Agneta.

She smiled ruefully at him but allowed herself to be forced into second and third helpings. Once spotted, Tristan was plied with more than he could possibly eat as well, the old woman tut-tutting at how thin he was.

"Who knew grandmas were such bullies?" muttered Sev—overfilled bowl in hand—who had apparently also drawn Agneta's special attention.

Tristan laughed, and had barely taken his seat when Alexiya strode up to them, her brother Theryn beside her. Well, beside wasn't the right word. She was walking as quickly as she could, and he was doing his best to keep up.

Tristan expected a message for Veronyka, but Alexiya's eyes were on him. "He's awake."

A breath whooshed from Tristan's lungs, and the constant pressing weight on his chest lifted. His father was awake, *alive* and awake, and the first thing Tristan did when he marched into the sickroom was yell at him.

Alexiya led him back to her mother's cottage, up the ladder, and into his room. Hestia was just leaving, a tray in hand, and the moment the door shut behind her, Tristan lost it.

"How dare you?" he demanded.

His anger, it seemed, was not a surprise to his father, though he did look a bit frailer than Tristan's rage was comfortable with. It was hard to scream at a man who was pale and drawn and somehow shrunken in his bedclothes, but Tristan did his best. It was what they were both used to, after all.

The commander did his best too, resuming his usual stiff-lipped disapproval and haughty scowl. "You'll have to be more specific," he drawled.

Tristan's fury increased, even though his father's voice was raspy and weak, but now that he knew his father wasn't going to die, all the anger he'd been feeling right up until the man was stabbed came rushing back.

"None of this should have happened," Tristan said hotly. He couldn't just stand there and stare at his father's exhausted eyes and sweaty brow, so he paced. "Not only were you willing to risk Pyra, but you let him get under your skin and inside your guard. There were better ways to handle that situation, and you know it."

"I agree," the commander replied mildly.

Tristan glowered. "Oh."

"I was trying to secure Veronyka's crown. It's more important than anything else. War is here, and the throne is empty. We cannot afford to have Avalkyra claim it instead."

"So you decide to sacrifice all of Pyra?"

"You exaggerate," the commander said with an impatient wave of the hand.

"And *you* ignored her wishes, as well as our own mandate. We're protectors. How could you advocate sacrificing thousands of lives on a bid for the throne?"

"Her wishes are not my command—yet," he said, though the words lacked heat. "I understand you have feelings for her and that she isn't just some Phoenix Rider—"

"Damn right she's not."

"But," he continued, "I am her commander. I am still more experienced in this game than either of you. However you view it, we are dealing

with forces bigger than Veronyka, than yourself—than the Phoenix Riders or even Pyra. Thousands, as you so put it. So, we must do what is best for the many, not the few. That is the whole point of this—of her heritage and her birthright. To make the empire safe for us and our kind." He scrubbed his face wearily. "You are thinking too small, convinced you can save everyone, when not everyone can be saved. You sound just like her."

"Like who, Veronyka?" Tristan asked in confusion.

A beat of silence. "No, not Veronyka. Your mother."

"My mother," Tristan repeated flatly, too stunned to say anything else.

"She . . . Her heart was in the right place," his father explained. "The same as yours. But she failed to see the phoenix for the feathers. Or rather, since we are in Arboria now, I suppose I should say the forest for the trees." Tristan continued to gape at him, not comprehending. His father sighed. "Your mother tried to save everyone too, and she paid for it with her own life. She couldn't see the big picture, the value in alliances and influence, and instead engaged in bold, heroic acts that got her *killed*."

Tristan clenched his hands into fists. "As far as I can tell, *your* strategy didn't work either—or did you *volunteer* to be exiled and stripped of your lands, titles, and *influence*?"

"This isn't about me. We don't just fight for the Phoenix Riders or for Pyra. We fight for the Golden Empire and the future of our world."

Afterward, Tristan found Veronyka waiting for him at the bottom of the winding stairs, Rex and Xephyra, both saddled, standing just behind her.

She gave him a tense, tentative look, and he didn't slow his pace or halt his momentum until his hands were in her hair and his mouth pressed to hers. He poured everything into the kiss, and when he finally drew back, she looked slightly dazed.

"Uh, want to go for a fly?" she asked, somewhat breathlessly, and Tristan released her.

"More than anything."

They didn't go far, but soared up into the canopy until they found a wide, sturdy branch to settle on. The phoenixes explored nearby, their curiosity at this new landscape limitless, leaving Tristan and Veronyka alone.

He settled himself in the crook of the branch where it met the main trunk, his back against the bark, and Veronyka settled between his legs, leaning her back against his chest. Despite how high up they were, the trees managed to obscure most of the stars, though slices of them could be glimpsed between their heavy boughs.

Tristan relayed some of the conversation with his father.

"And then he said I was trying to save everyone, like my mother."

Like it was a bad thing. It felt like an insult or an accusation, though Tristan couldn't figure out why. He also couldn't understand how they were ever supposed to work and lead together when they seemed to disagree on everything.

He glimpsed the edge of Veronyka's smile. "He and Olanna must have had some truly epic fights as well."

"What do you mean?"

"It's just, when I first arrived at the Eyrie, Morra told me a bit about her—about your family. I was, well . . . quite pissed at you, now I think on it." Tristan smiled ruefully while dropping a soft kiss onto her collarbone, at the very edge of her bandage. "When she told me the commander was your father, I didn't have a hard time seeing the connection. But," she added, as Tristan opened his mouth to object, "Morra insisted you were more like your mother."

She paused—it was obviously difficult for her to talk about Morra, and he couldn't blame her. It was hard to reconcile the person they had known with her actions now.

She cleared her throat and continued. "She said that the sooner you accepted that, the easier everything would be."

"I guess I always imagined my father and I fought because we were alike," he said. "I saw everything he did as a reflection of my own worst, most stubborn qualities. I assumed that when he looked at me, he saw the same."

"Maybe he saw something else. Someone he'd loved and lost."

Her voice was subdued, and Tristan realized she thought Val saw the same thing when she looked at her . . . not Veronyka, but Pheronia.

Wanting to lighten the mood, Tristan leaned his head back against the rough bark and stared up at a visible patch of stars.

"My nursemaid said their arguments used to shake the house—my mother and father—but that their laughter was louder. Old Ana said she could hear them from the gardens . . . when they fought *and* when they made up." Veronyka turned her head, smirking at the look of disgust on his face. He sighed. "I guess I never realized how much it mirrored myself and my father. Is it possible that all this time he's been arguing with *her*, not me?"

"No," Veronyka said seriously, "it's definitely been with you."

Despite everything, he laughed.

"Speaking of family . . . ," Veronyka said, making the humor dry up inside Tristan's throat. She shifted gingerly, thanks to her wound, turning in his arms so they were face-to-face. "Kade's right. We have to do whatever we can to stop Val."

Even with the possibility of the empire unleashing its full military might on their meager forces, it was the thought of a fight against Val that truly unsettled him. He had yet to see this strix force she commanded, but it wasn't even that otherworldly foe that he feared. It was Val herself, and the fact that her sights had always been set on Veronyka. Whatever she claimed to covet, Tristan knew she wouldn't rest until she had Veronyka either by her side or out of the picture entirely.

And the fact that she was a mere shadow magic bond away? That she had nearly gutted Veronyka without ever setting foot in her vicinity was more unsettling than anything that had happened so far. He wanted to protect Veronyka, but it was a fool's errand. She was the shadowmage, the one with the power and ability to stand against her, the one who understood Val best and could contest her in a bid to claim the empire's throne.

She was Val's equal—her better, Tristan believed with all his heart.

But it didn't mean he didn't fear for Veronyka, for what she might have to endure before all this was through.

What she might have to risk.

"I have a direct link to her mind. I can track her whereabouts, follow her every move, and figure out what she plans to do next."

"Can you, though?" he asked carefully. "I thought your bond was broken, that you couldn't sense her like you used to."

"I can't," she admitted reluctantly. "But maybe if I pushed, if I really reached . . ."

"Isn't that how she sliced you open the last time?" Tristan asked, his voice rising several octaves.

She blew out a breath and slumped into him. "It just feels . . . I hate to waste such an advantage. I know she wouldn't hesitate to use it against me if she could."

"Then maybe the fact that the bond is damaged is a gift. It puts you both on a more level playing field. If she can't reach you and you can't reach her, then neither of you can hurt the other."

Veronyka snorted. "Val can always find a way."

"To reach you or to hurt you?"

"Both," she said firmly. Tristan wished he could see her expression, but she was gazing off into the distance. "The thing is . . . I think she's lonely. I think she's always been lonely—even when my mother was alive. That's why I'm so important to her. I represent something she's never had."

"A friend?" Tristan offered sarcastically.

"Someone she can be herself with. Someone she can hate and love and fight, over and over, and know that I can take it. That I'll always be there."

It so closely mirrored Tristan's own thoughts about them that his chest constricted tightly. "I know if things get really bad, if the situation is dire, you'll have to try reaching out to her—but will you wait as long as possible?"

She frowned at him. "Wait for what? How much worse do we want things to get?"

Tristan scrambled for a reason. "For Fallon's next report. They've had lookouts posted outside the Eyrie since the attack, and he's sending us daily updates. We should have a clearer picture of what's happening soon—without the risk. Doriyan sent a letter too." Veronyka perked up at that. "He's been tailing Sidra. He followed her all the way to Rushlea and promises to send reports on her activity, as well as Val's. You might not even need to contact her."

"What is Sidra doing in Rushlea?" Veronyka wondered aloud. She made an impatient sound. "Don't you see? Whatever information we get, it'll be an incomplete picture if we don't know what Val plans to do *next*."

He sighed. "I know. It's just . . ." He scrubbed a hand through his hair. "I don't want you to rush into another confrontation with her. You're still bleeding from the last one. You're still recovering—we're *all* still recovering. . . ."

He trailed off, but the tension in Veronyka slipped away, replaced by something softer. "He'll be all right," she murmured. He knew she was referencing his father. "And so will I."

But she didn't push again. Understanding, either through his words or the emotions beneath them, that Tristan couldn't handle another close call at the moment.

Ever again, he thought darkly, but of course that was wishful thinking. The two most important people in his life had gotten sliced open in the last couple of days, and the war hadn't even really begun yet.

"But I'll wait for the report to come in before I take any more . . . risks."

"Good," Tristan said in relief. "Besides, being here isn't all bad, is it?"

She smiled. "No, it isn't."

"And she's not your only family," he added gently. "Remember that."

"I guess I could see what they're up to tonight . . . ," Veronyka said thoughtfully.

"Nope," Tristan said, moving his arms more tightly around her, while still being careful of her injury. "Tonight I want you all to myself."

They hadn't been alone with each other since their first night here, inside the tent, and Tristan couldn't stop thinking about it. He kept trying to find chances to sneak away together, but between training and patrols and helping out around Haven—plus their individual familial concerns—they hadn't found an opportunity. It had taken switching with Anders earlier to make sure they both had the night off.

Veronyka captured his mouth in a kiss. "We could sleep up here, you know," she murmured against his lips.

Tristan nodded eagerly. "That way I don't have to share you with anyone."

"Not even our tent."

He grinned. "You'll catch us if we fall, right?" he asked Rex and Xephyra, who were still somewhere nearby.

There was a squawk and a rustle—and then Rex's head poked out from behind a cluster of leaves. He had a large piece of wood in his beak, and before he could reply, Xephyra snapped at it, trying to take it for herself. They tussled for a moment before he lost his grip and the branch went careening over the edge.

"That was less than reassuring," Veronyka muttered, as the piece of wood snapped and cracked all the way down. Luckily, they were far enough from Haven they didn't have to worry about the branch landing on someone below.

Rex wilted at the loss of his prize, but Xephyra nipped at his feathers until he squawked and chased after her.

Veronyka laughed, and Tristan dipped his chin for another kiss, a smile on his face.

Day 3, Twelfth Moon, 179 AE

M,

Things are happening quickly now. I
thought I had more time. I thought we had
more time.

I may require your services sooner than I
expected. Be ready.

–S

To be apex is to wield loyalty as a weapon—to turn love into power. A dangerous thought.

- CHAPTER 35 -

AVALKYRA

ACCORDING TO MORRA, AVALKYRA could not create shadowfire— or grow her horde—without a benex, without Veronyka.

Morra was the authority, the magical scholar and priestess of Nox. The faithful servant of Ilithya Shadowheart.

And so Avalkyra had no choice but to disprove her, credentials be damned. She had been doing it all her life.

When there was no crown of gold and jewels, she had made one of feathers.

When there was no bondmate to be had, she had created a *bind*mate.

And when the phoenixes cast her aside, she had bonded with a strix instead.

She tried twice more that first night before crawling onto her bedroll, fury roiling in her belly and frustration itching like a thousand tiny hooks across her skin. She told herself she just needed a good night's sleep, that she would take what she needed from Veronyka like she always had. Surely the next day, it would happen. The next day, she would prove the woman wrong.

She'd slept nearly twenty-four hours, much to her surprise, but despite feeling truly rested for the first time in weeks, as soon as she climbed into the saddle and reached for her magic, she wound up on her back once more.

"This is your third attempt . . . ," Morra said, crouching down next to her on the cobblestones. The sky above was iron gray and bloated with the promise of rain, while nearer at hand, ink-black strixes perched upon the stronghold walls, silent spectators to her failure. "Perhaps it is time to accept—"

"I accept nothing," Avalkyra spat. Forget having shadowfire as a weapon . . . If she couldn't hatch these eggs, her plans would fall to pieces. She would be outnumbered against the Phoenix Riders alone, never mind the empire. This was her long-awaited return to power. Her rise, her glorious ascension. She could not—*would not*—fail.

"With no secondary bond to sustain you, you risk pushing yourself to the brink," Morra said. "Next time, you might not wake up. Now, if you reconcile . . ."

"Forget reconciliation," Sidra burst out, cutting off her reply. She had watched the proceedings with tense apprehension, but now joined the shadowmage at Avalkyra's side, bent on one knee. "I would be honored to become your benex. Choose me, my queen, and together—"

Avalkyra rolled her eyes and batted away Sidra's outstretched hand as she got to her feet. "A bond is not a gift to be bestowed upon the most deserving—or the most desperate." Sidra flinched as if slapped. "It is a meeting of equals. Equals in status, in magic . . . in blood. Are we equals in any way, Sidra of Stel?"

"No, my queen," she whispered, jaw clenched and head bowed.

"No," Avalkyra said. "Do not forget it. I do not need you or Veronyka or *anyone*. If that old phoenix could do it on her own, then so can I."

"She was not alone," Morra corrected softly, but Avalkyra ignored her.

She was not alone either, not truly. Their bond existed; it was simply damaged. If Ignix could reach across centuries—beyond death itself—Avalkyra could reach across a fractured bond.

She mounted up and took a deep breath, focusing on the pile of eggs. Beneath her, Onyx began to expand, her chest filling with smoke and magic, drawing the tendrils that usually trailed from her feathers inward, where it merged and expanded. Avalkyra felt the tug behind her own breastbone, and deeper, in the pit of her stomach.

More, Avalkyra ordered. This, they had done before. Onyx was combining her magic with Avalkyra's. This, she could do. But for shadowfire, she needed more—to dig deeper, into a secondary well she could not seem to touch.

More, she said again. Avalkyra dragged and Onyx pulled, tearing the magic from the bottom of her well, scraping it dry.

There was a surge of power—an exhilarating, euphoric burst—then she doubled over as a wave of fatigue rolled through her. Her magic flickered and popped in and out of existence, and in a panic, Avalkyra reached, taking magic from Onyx, from the other strixes in her flock—from anyone she could reach. It worked for a single, blissful moment before she was depleted all over again.

Avalkyra released her hold, blinking away the black dots crowding her vision. Her magic continued to crackle for several weighted heartbeats, and then it stabilized. But she would never forget that feeling for as long as she lived. If she delved too deep, tried to take too much . . . the kickback from that could probably kill her—or drain her completely. She shuddered.

"A fractured bond," she said grudgingly, sliding stiffly from her saddle. "How is it repaired?"

Morra seemed relieved when she replied. "The same way you establish one in the first place: openness, eye contact, and physical proximity."

Avalkyra sighed heavily, adjusting her riding gloves. "And then she will become my benex?"

"Well, no . . . not technically . . ."

Avalkyra whirled around. "Excuse me?"

The woman had been pitching this reconciliation from the start, under the pretense that it would solve all of Avalkyra's problems, but if Veronyka *still* wouldn't be her benex . . .

"Because of your bond, Veronyka is unwittingly a part of your apex flock—but she has not yet bowed to you, as these others have done." She waved a hand to encompass the strixes perched all around. "A benex must be willingly subservient to you. Considering your fracture, and the fact that you are on opposing sides of a war, I think it is safe to say that Veronyka is neither willing nor subservient."

In other words, she was a problem. A problem that could be solved only by reconciliation and restoration of the bond, as well as "willing" subjugation. Avalkyra was certain she could achieve both—given enough time and coercion, she could convince Veronyka of anything—but that would mean derailing her current plans.

It would take her where she wanted to go, if she let it, but it would also slow her down and buy her enemies time. It would even give Veronyka a chance to retaliate through the bond, as Avalkyra had initially feared.

Her gaze landed on the shadowmage. "You certainly kept that bit quiet."

"I meant no harm, my queen," Morra demurred. "I just assumed you understood the two went hand in hand—rebuilding the bond *and* forming some kind of alliance. Together, the two of you could—"

"Together," Avalkyra repeated flatly. She began to pace, working through the problem at hand. Poking at it. Finding loopholes. "In the wild, phoenixes bred and hatched their young, even without animages. The strixes should be able to do the same."

"In theory, yes," Morra said, her gaze downcast. "Unfortunately, no record or account was ever made, so even if there *was* a way, it has been lost to time."

"Look at me," Avalkyra said suddenly.

The shadowmage peered up through her lashes, her still head bowed. The image of a perfect servant.

Avalkyra knew better.

Morra had been very clever these past few days, donning the guise of deference or humility, but in actuality, using those behaviors in self-protection. These were not the habits of a loyal servant. . . . They were the habits of a liar.

A liar who was well versed in shadow magic.

Avalkyra moved quick as a flash, clamping her fingers hard on Morra's chin and wrenching her face up.

The action did what it was meant to, surprising the woman so much that her round, wide-eyed stare met Avalkyra's head-on, her defenses lowered, her mind open.

And Avalkyra saw the truth. Or at least, the truth that Morra was trying to hide.

No record or account *was* ever made of how strixes hatched eggs in the wild, but that didn't mean Morra and her fellow priestesses didn't have their guesses. Their theories and assumptions. It flashed before Avalkyra's eyes: fire and death and sacrifice—and taking, taking, taking, what strixes did best.

Nice try, shadowmage, she said into her mind, before releasing her with a rough shove.

"M-my queen," Morra sputtered, but Avalkyra turned away.

"Sidra, hold her," she barked, and her bindmate leapt to obey.

As the two scuffled, Avalkyra walked toward the pile of eggs and called Onyx to her side. What she'd seen in the shadowmage's mind was difficult to describe, so she showed her bondmate instead.

Do you understand? Avalkyra asked.

Onyx mulled the images over before turning her attention to the pile of eggs. Instead of replying, she nosed around until she found what she sought.

She lifted an egg in her beak, her movements careful and deliberate, then opened her mouth wide and swallowed it whole.

Avalkyra watched with eerie fascination, pressing a hand to her neck, her chest . . . following the egg's progress as if it were inside her own body, *feeling* as it slowly slid down Onyx's throat and came to rest low in her belly.

It was one thing to see this image in Morra's mind and quite another to feel it through her bondmate.

There was a surge of powerful magic. Onyx had consumed the life force contained within the egg, but the life force was fighting back.

Horror lurched up inside Avalkyra. This was beyond anything she could have ever dreamed up or imagined. This thing inside Onyx was not ready to give in. It was still alive, or struggling to be so, pulling and draining, making *Avalkyra* weak so it could be strong. This was worse than a bind, worse than trying to make shadowfire from nothing. . . . This was complete and utter vulnerability, a leech sucking her dry from the inside out.

Just as panic threatened to overtake her, the gut-wrenching feeling began to change. Onyx was fighting back—Avalkyra saw it in her eyes even as she felt it from within. They were both bent over now, Avalkyra with her hands against her stomach and Onyx with her back arched and her feathered crest standing up like spokes on a wheel.

Power flowed and ebbed and then flowed again. Strixes were made to *take*, and that's exactly what they did. Scratching and clawing for every inch. While phoenix mothers gave their lives to the birthing pyre, strix mothers *took* power from their young, and their young took back. They did not give. They were devourers through and through, and in that moment Avalkyra felt true kinship with them.

She did not give either.

Pheronia's words from a lifetime ago echoed in her mind. *You do not give, Avalkyra Ashfire. You take and take until there is nothing left. You have all of fire's hunger and none of its warmth.*

The struggle between Onyx and the egg reached a fever pitch. The convulsions in Avalkyra's stomach grew sharp and pointed, and the scraping sensation she'd associated with their devouring magic became too real, too visceral.

Was this what it meant to bear a child? Was this what Pheronia had gone through to carry Veronyka? In a flash, she saw how life might have been between them—Pheronia clutching her hand and pressing it to her belly, but her palm wasn't slicked with blood; it was sweat. It was tears. She smiled up at her sister, grimacing in fear and pain but endless joy, too. There was no arrow protruding from her chest—there was no fiery, bloody death crowding in. No, there was only life. And Avalkyra would see Veronyka enter this world; she would hold her in her arms, sense her magic, and know that she would be a powerful mage, a Phoenix Rider, and together Avalkyra and Pheronia would help her become the greatest Ashfire queen that ever lived. Together, all of them together—

Her gut twisted, wrenching her wide open—no, not her, but Onyx. Avalkyra cried out as her bondmate's stomach was split, and out came clawed feet and black feathers, a newly born strix, dripping black blood and shards of broken eggshell.

I'm dying—we're dying, Avalkyra thought wildly, on the ground now, writhing in pain. The hatchling staggered, its damp feathers gleaming like oil, and turned to face the mess it had made—the place from which it had come. Onyx was hunched, body tensed in agony . . . but she knew what to do. She cawed loudly, fiercely, and extended her magic in an oppressive wave. Avalkyra got to her feet and staggered to her bondmate's side, watching as the hatchling cowered, lowering its head and baring its neck to them both. Submitting to the apex pair.

A jolt of power went through them, the new bond taking root. The new creature joining the flock. Despite Avalkyra's exhaustion, she couldn't help but smile.

Onyx had lost several feathers in the fight, and Avalkyra stooped to pick one up. She twirled the feather in her hand, remembering a different time, when her Nyx had lost her very first feather. It had been a moment to celebrate, a rite of passage for the phoenix and a trophy for Avalkyra.

How do you feel? she asked her bondmate, whose ruined body was already healing and stitching itself together. Onyx shook out her feathers and extended her neck, much like a human might stretch after a period of physical exertion. The cobblestones were a mess beneath her feet, and it made a perfect kind of sense that *this* bloody horror show was the way strixes made new life. Nothing given, only taken.

The same, Onyx replied.

The same?

Hungry.

Avalkyra grinned. She felt breathless, exhilarated as she pointed at the stack of eggs. *Go on, then.*

Despite her excitement, she grimaced slightly at the idea of having to go through that over and over again. But nothing in life came easy. Avalkyra knew that, and the sacrifice would be worth it.

The other strixes had fluttered down, crowding curiously around Onyx and the hatchling. They gazed hungrily at the eggs and the bloody smears across the cobblestones.

Onyx shrieked, bringing them all to order, and Avalkyra watched as one of the older, larger strixes took up an egg, just as Onyx had, and swallowed it whole.

It wasn't long until Avalkyra realized she would feel this too—even if it was to a lesser degree than with Onyx—but she clenched her jaw and weathered the pain. Like calluses on a warrior's palms, the suffering would make her stronger.

Still, her legs buckled as the next hatching began, and she leaned against the stronghold's wall as she moved through the crowd.

Sidra and Morra had seen it all happen, ashen-faced as the strixes fluttered and snapped mere feet away. The shadowmage looked particularly ill, but Avalkyra suspected that had more to do with her betrayal than anything else.

With one problem solved, it was time to face another. Avalkyra didn't have a throne room or council chambers, but she needed somewhere to hold court. Somewhere to think.

Her gaze lit on the temple, where the toppled beacon sat. It would be as good a chair as any and give her an ideal vantage point for the hatching.

Bring her, she ordered Sidra, before climbing the ladder. Morra followed awkwardly, her crutch dangling from one hand, while Sidra brought up the rear, withdrawing a knife.

When she reached the summit, Avalkyra eyed the statue before sitting on the curved space where wing met neck. She lifted her head and rested her hands at her sides, regal as a queen on her throne, her strix feather still clutched tightly. Her breathing was steady, if a bit labored, her inhalations stuttering every time a strix swallowed an egg, every time a hatchling burst forward.

Even without a benex, Avalkyra had the ability to grow her flock and maintain her current position. It was a triumph, a victory, and yet . . . it did not give her shadowfire.

Perhaps it was a foolish thing to fixate on. A deadly thing. She didn't *need* it, and though she could imagine in gruesome detail the destruction such a weapon could wreak, the strixes were weapons all on their own. At least if Avalkyra could not have shadowfire, no one would.

Ignix was dead, after all.

Unless . . . "Shadowmage," she said, and though her voice was calm, the woman jumped as if she'd shouted. She was clearly waiting for punishment of some kind, but Avalkyra would get to that soon enough. "What happens when an apex dies?"

Morra swallowed, glancing at the knife Sidra held just below her throat. "The mantle will pass to the eldest in the flock."

Avalkyra was watching her closely, but the woman's mind was open and unguarded. She did not evade Avalkyra's shadow magic touch. She spoke the truth, and yet . . . there was a difference between lying outright and withholding information.

"Is that the *only* way an apex is made?"

Morra was uneasy. Avalkyra leaned forward, knowing she was getting somewhere.

"The position can be passed to a worthier candidate, much like a royal abdicating the throne. However, magical creatures do not bow down to the conventions of humanity—of kings and queens and ancient bloodlines. They bow down to power, and to those who command love and loyalty."

A splinter of doubt wedged into Avalkyra's chest, worming its way in deeper with every word the woman spoke, tearing her apart from within— or was that the hatching continuing to happen in the courtyard below?

Love and loyalty.

Avalkyra had what she wanted, but she also had a problem in the form of another Ashfire with strength and conviction and a flock at her disposal. With Ignix dead, the mantle of apex likely passed to Cassian's phoenix or another of the old guard. Would they hand the power over to Veronyka? Whatever Morra said about phoenixes not being interested in royalty and bloodlines, humans most certainly were. She was their chosen ruler, their Ashfire heir, and she had another human bondmate, Cassian's son, who would be all too happy to bow before her. To be *her* benex.

"Like Veronyka Ashfire?" Avalkyra asked.

"That's not—I only meant—"

"Cease with your falsehoods," Avalkyra bit out. "I know how they look at her—how *you* look at her."

Rage and frustration rose up Avalkyra's throat, choking her. There was one way to ensure Veronyka never reached her full potential, even if it meant that Avalkyra could also never reach hers. Shadowfire would be out of reach, but the world would be hers.

"I can't risk her becoming apex on her own and commanding a force to oppose mine." She nodded, as if the decision were simple. Easy. "I will have to kill her. Immediately."

Morra swayed on her feet, heedless of the knife at her throat, her grip on her crutch white-knuckled. She licked her lips, her eyes fluttering closed.

Avalkyra watched the display with fascination. The woman's affections were plain enough—she wasn't the first person to love Veronyka more than Avalkyra—but her loyalties remained uncertain. She had withheld information in an attempt to serve both Veronyka *and* Avalkyra, to reunite them, perhaps, but when that failed, what would she do? She had made a promise to Ilithya, and it was up to her now to follow through on it.

"If you do that, you'll never have shadowfire," Morra said, her voice surprisingly even. "But there might be a way to achieve both. A person cannot be benex in one flock *and* apex in another."

Avalkyra considered that. Getting close enough to kill Veronyka would require almost as much effort as it would to speak to her. With their bond fractured, attempting to kill her via a shadow magic link would be impossible.

If they stood before each other, could Avalkyra *force* Veronyka to become her benex? Could she come up with an ultimatum powerful enough to make her bend the knee?

If she could, she would gain shadowfire and remove the threat Veronyka posed in a single stroke, but it was even more than that.

She'd hated the idea that she needed Veronyka, had rejected it so strongly that she had failed to see the potential in it. Wouldn't it be sweeter to promise Veronyka salvation only to tear it away again? To chain Veronyka to her cause and force her to not only watch the destruction of the world she loved, but make her complicit in it? Surely that was better than a quick death—it would be a living defeat, like the one Avalkyra had lived for nearly two decades.

Of course, if she failed, she could use assassination as a fallback plan, but now her sights were set on something bigger.

"There is no shame in recognizing the value of a tool," Morra continued, still trying to spare Veronyka's life. "Of a weapon wielded in your service . . . to your ends. An archer requires a bow and arrow to become a true markswoman, but there is no question who is the master . . . and who gets the glory."

"And what am I to you, Morra, Rider of Aneaxi?" Avalkyra asked idly. "A weapon wielded in *your* service? To your ends? Or to Ilithya's?"

"My ends and Ilithya's ends are the same. I promised I would see you on the throne. I just thought, if I could keep you both alive . . . unite you, somehow . . ."

"You want *both* of us alive, do you?" Avalkyra said, amused. "And where do you think that will lead?"

She didn't reply—not a breath of air or twitch of muscle escaped her.

"Because as much as you might want to play both sides, I doubt Ilithya intended for you to pit us against one another."

"Not against, no," Morra said steadily. "She always hoped that you would one day rule together."

Avalkyra laughed; the sound rang off the stone walls, causing a burst of agitated rustling below. It had been *her* dream once. It had been her vision for the future. Now, the memory of her foolishness coated her tongue like ash.

"That will never happen. I will *use* her to gain shadowfire, and I will *use* her to destroy everything and everyone she loves. Then I will destroy her."

Morra's expression was bleak. "I made a promise."

"So you've said. *Anything* to see me on the throne."

"Not exactly," Morra said softly.

What did you say, shadowmage?

Morra lifted her chin. "Not exactly."

Avalkyra stood, bringing her full height to bear, looming over the woman. Sidra remained silent beside them, her knife trained on the shadowmage's throat.

"I promised Ilithya I would see you on the throne," Morra said, shoulders squared. "*With* Veronyka, or not at all."

Then she lunged, striking Sidra's stomach and dodging her swiping blade. Then she took hold of Sidra's arm and bent until her wrist gave out, dropping the knife into her outstretched hand.

The edge flashed silver-bright as it sliced toward Avalkyra, but rather than rear back, Avalkyra leaned forward, causing Morra's aim to falter. Her knife skittered across the side of Avalkyra's neck but avoided the fat artery she'd been aiming for. It was a stinging flesh wound—no more.

Sidra snarled, leaping into action, but Avalkyra already had it under control.

With one hand she gripped Morra by the throat, while the other scrabbled over Morra's flailing arm until she reached the wrist and squeezed, hard enough to snap the delicate bones. The knife fell to the roof of the temple with a clatter.

Morra gasped—or tried, but it came out as more of a gurgle. Avalkyra's fingers dug into her neck with bruising, choking force, and when the woman's bulging eyes stared up at her, Avalkyra stared back into them dispassionately.

With barely any effort at all, thanks to the pain Morra was in, Avalkyra broke into her mind, and saw it. Desperation and anger—and love. Love and loyalty and respect for Veronyka Ashfire, the would-be queen. And for Avalkyra? There was old love—stale love—and it had long since turned sour. That's all that remained: leftovers. Dregs.

It reminded her of Ignix. *You are the ashes, the dregs. . . . You're what's left.*

She also saw Ilithya's truth, the promise she had demanded from Morra. Avalkyra was fit to rule with Veronyka by her side—a calming, steadying force—or it would be the Blood War all over again. Avalkyra was fit to rule with Veronyka, or not at all.

Avalkyra was surprised at the tight, squeezing sensation in her chest. Ilithya meant nothing to her. She was a spy and a servant and a stand-in adult when Avalkyra was too young to operate in the world alone. Nothing more.

But Ilithya had been loyal, she'd thought, and had believed in her queen.

Apparently, the queen she believed in wasn't Avalkyra.

"Rest easy," she said, squeezing Morra's throat until panic flickered across her features. "Your promise does not matter. Your words and your life—meaningless. Ilithya is dead, and you are about to join her."

Then she shoved her off the edge of the temple.

To her credit, Morra didn't cry out or scream, but that was probably because of the damage to her throat. There was a sickening thump as she landed, sprawled in breathless pain, but she didn't die on impact.

The strixes were ready and waiting to pounce, frenzied at the smell of blood.

No, Avalkyra said, using her apex control on the full flock. They all snapped to a halt. *Leave her. Let her die . . . slowly.*

Sidra watched, her eyes wide. Then she dropped to her knees. "Forgive me, my queen."

"You were bested by a one-legged wing widow," Avalkyra said, smearing a hand across the stinging wound on her neck. "Forgive yourself."

"I will try, my queen," Sidra murmured, remaining on her knees.

Avalkyra wiped the blood on her pants and reclaimed her seat. Below, revolting crunching and tearing sounds filled the night, interspersed with moans and whimpers from the shadowmage. Next to her, Sidra reeked of self-recrimination.

Avalkyra blocked it all out and watched as her horde continued to grow, her mind working. Once again, the world conspired to keep Avalkyra from her goal—to doubt her ability to achieve it in the first place.

And so once again, she would prove them wrong.

Though none of the noble First Rider families can claim complete imperviousness to scandal, one of the lesser-known—but still socially detrimental—stories involves Cordelia Lightbringer, last scion of famed warrior and second-in-command Callysta Lightbringer.

With an older brother who died in his infancy from phoenix fever, Cordelia was the only surviving child of Arlo and Parthenia Lightbringer, of the non-royal* Lightbringer branch. Her parents intended her to marry into another noble family with good standing, perhaps a Strongwing or a Flamesong, but Cordelia had other ideas.

By all accounts an intelligent girl and a gifted animage, she allegedly spent more time in the stables than among polite company. She was known to go about dirty and barefooted, and there were even rumors she used to sleep *outside*, in the hayloft, like a common peasant.

It is perhaps not so shocking, then, that before her parents could make an official betrothal, she ran off with the stable boy. The next day, her favorite horse, cat, and dog—and a hundred gold pieces—also disappeared, never to be seen again.

—*A History of the First Riders*, the Morian Archives, 147 AE,

updated 171 AE

*The Lightbringers married into the royal Ashfire line through the union of the children of Nefyra and Callysta, and tracked their descendants all the way to the founding of the Golden Empire, despite taking the Ashfire name.

I could not leave such a power in her hands,
unchallenged. Unchecked.

- CHAPTER 36 -
SPARROW

SPARROW, IGNIX, AND FIFE stayed in the storage closet for a while.

Sparrow ate and drank and recovered her strength. She slept some more. She even *washed*. It seemed pointless, really, when they were just going to climb through the rubble all over again, but Ignix insisted.

After ensuring Sparrow was in good health, Ignix decided it was time to be off again.

As wonderful as this discovery had been, they were still trapped, still in danger. The water and apples wouldn't last forever, and Sparrow was eager to press on.

Unfortunately, Ignix had other plans in mind.

You will stay here, and I will go. Once free, I will send help.

"But that could take days!" Sparrow protested.

There is plenty here to sustain you. Do not fear.

Sparrow's lip curled. There was nothing wrong with fear, and the fact that Ignix warned against such an emotion was so very human. A dog would never tell Sparrow not to be afraid—fear was normal, natural. A defense mechanism. Fear had driven Sparrow out of that temple, away from those old priestesses who were cold and cruel and shrieked at her mice friends and chastised her for the bird droppings on her windowsill.

Fear was a good thing. It meant a person had something to lose. Something worth fighting for. But that wasn't the point.

"I ain't afraid," Sparrow argued. "You're treating me like deadweight, and I ain't that, either. I found the right passage. I could help you."

I do not need help.

"Everyone needs help! Didn't Veronyka break your mind free when Avalkyra put that curse on you?"

It was not a curse—

"And surely Nefyra, the First Rider Queen, helped you out once or twice? What about Callysta and Cirix? What about the millions of other people and animals you've met in the hundreds of years you've been alive? Huh?"

I've hardly met millions—

"What about Axura herself, your own mother, who made you first among phoenixes? Oldest and most powerful?"

Cease this incessant chatter. To be first is to be alone. That is the way of the apex.

Sparrow knew that was a Pyraean word, but she wasn't sure exactly what it meant. "If you say so," she said doubtfully. "Maybe your memory's getting bad in your old age."

Ignix huffed. *Watch your tongue,* she chided, but the words held no real anger. *My memory reaches farther back than you can fathom, young one. I have had companions, yes, and some who have shared my burden . . . but it was* always *my burden to share. Do you understand?*

Sparrow considered. "Is that why you fought her alone? Avalkyra?"

She challenged me. That is how challenges are fought.

"You could have refused her. Could have let the others fight with you instead."

Only an apex can defeat another apex.

"Okay, so *you* could have fought Avalkyra. What about the rest of the strixes? You didn't win during the Dark Days by fighting alone, did you? It was all of us against all of them."

Us? Ignix repeated, her tone grudgingly amused.

"Yup," Sparrow said, arms crossed. "Us. So, if you think you're fighting this war alone now, it's only because you choose to."

Ignix shifted her wings in a moment of seeming agitation, though her voice was calm when she spoke. *You are wiser than your years. And you know more about history than most.*

"I know more about *everything* than most," Sparrow said smugly. "I could recite *The Pyraean Epics* if I wanted. Volumes one *and* two."

As entertaining as that might be . . . A long-suffering sigh. *Do you promise to skip all that, if I allow you to come?*

"You drive a hard bargain," Sparrow said. Truthfully, she didn't know *The Pyraean Epics* by heart—but she did know a few stories. The priestesses had been fond of reading them aloud in the temple, but Sparrow hadn't been there long enough to memorize them all. "Agreed."

Come along, then.

Before they departed, Sparrow emptied a large jar of something pickled and slimy and filled it with water. She poured out a sack of grain and tied it across her shoulders like a satchel, filling it with the jar, handfuls of apples, plus anything else she could find that was edible. Fife perched on her shoulder, digging his claws into the rough burlap, ready for the next stage of their adventure.

"So, you don't like poetry?" Sparrow asked as they made their way down the corridor. "I'd've thought any phoenix would like *The Pyraean Epics.*"

The poetry is tolerable. The inaccuracies less so.

"What's inaccurate about them?"

Hours passed like that as they wandered through the oppressive silence, Ignix telling her how Xatara and Xolanthe weren't actually sisters—though their Riders were—and that Fire Blossom trees had grown on Pyrmont long before their infamous journey. She complained that many of the stories glossed over phoenix names in favor of their Rider counterparts, and insisted that the popular proverb "Fear is a luxury" originated from Roza Heartlight, one of the First Riders, not the dishonest bard who'd claimed it as his own.

Although the human scribes got that one wrong, Ignix insisted Nefyra's most famous words were remembered correctly.

"There is no bravery without fear," Sparrow recited. Everyone knew the phrase.

Indeed.

Despite finding the conversation fascinating, Sparrow grew weary of their adventure as time wore on. She was sick of the cold stone walls, sick of the way they reminded her sharply, painfully, of her months in the temple.

At least here she had some company—and company of the best sort, the animal sort.

Fife preened.

Not that she'd say no to having *some* people company, and that was a first in her life. She quite liked Ersken. He was good with the phoenixes and had been nice to Sparrow and Chirp. Veronyka had been her first human friend—she had said so herself—and Riella was her friend now too, Sparrow was pretty sure, even if Riella hadn't said it. And then there was Elliot. . . . Sparrow's eyes prickled. So much of her life spent alone and friendless, and now she had a whole flock of friends all at once. It was overwhelming.

And it was sad, too, because she was trapped here, and she missed them. Did they miss her?

They were all busy and important and off fighting wars. Veronyka was a princess. Ersken had to take care of the phoenixes, and Elliot had to protect Riella. No one was thinking about her.

That, at least, she was used to.

Despite Sparrow's superior sniffer leading the way, they came up against several cave-ins and blockages. Ignix used her fire to break through when she could, but some obstructions were too large to safely destroy—or in danger of causing larger structural damage—meaning they lost hours doubling back around to find a different way.

Sparrow had to take cover behind whatever protection she could find when Ignix used her flame, but the heat was intense, and her skin felt cooked and her throat raw.

Even still, she knew Ignix held back, and using such careful control was slow.

The water dwindled, the food disappeared, and Sparrow's hope faltered.

Ignix insisted they were on the right track when the passage started to lead lower, but it was a hard thing for Sparrow to force herself to go *toward* the deepest, dampest parts of the tunnel. To trust the phoenix's words when everything inside Sparrow told her to go higher, to seek air and the sounds of the world—but there were none to be found this deep underground, and Sparrow had no choice but to trust the ancient firebird.

Fife remained perched on her shoulder constantly now, and it was the only thing that helped Sparrow's trembling. She thought it was the cold at first, and while her feet ached with it and her fingertips felt clumsy and numb, it was that sense of being cut off from everything that made Sparrow shake. She hadn't thought there could be a real difference between one dank tunnel and another, but there was—she felt it in her weary bones and muffled senses, the stone around her pressing in on all sides.

The three of them slept huddled together, and though the shivers never stopped, Ignix's heat and Fife's steady heartbeat were a comfort all the same. When they pressed on again, Sparrow left her empty satchel and water jar behind.

Just when she thought she couldn't take another step, the muscles in her legs began to ache in a new, different way—the tunnel was sloping up, not down.

The journey became harder now, but Sparrow refused to give up. She slipped and skidded across dampened stone and dug her way through mud and muck—ever higher, ever nearer their goal.

The next cave-in they encountered, however, was large enough for Ignix to wilt beside her, and for Fife to croak morosely.

"What—what is it?" Sparrow gasped, straightening up.

It is a substantial cave-in. I may compromise the passage if I blast through it.

No . . . they couldn't have come all this way only to find the exit barred.

They *couldn't*. Tears threatened, tightening her throat and making her eyes sting.

"Will you try?" Sparrow choked out.

A pause. *Take cover,* Ignix warned, and Sparrow's knees buckled in desperate relief.

She hid behind a slight bend in the passage, but she felt the heat before she heard the shattering snap of surface fissures, followed by the lower crunch that vibrated through her feet. The tunnel shook, and bits of stone scattered across the ground.

"Ignix!" Sparrow shouted once the dust had settled. "Are you all right?"

Sparrow edged around the wall—and stopped short. Blissful, moving air brushed against her skin. It felt like the sun's rays on a warm day, like the misty spray from a waterfall. Soft as a whisper, but unmistakable.

The sounds had changed too, the echoes expanding, and there, distantly, were *other* sounds, sounds from the world outside.

"You did it," Sparrow said breathlessly, stumbling forward.

We did it, Ignix corrected gently.

Sparrow wrapped her arms around the phoenix's neck, hugging tightly, while Fife cawed in triumph, his cries bouncing around them like a chorus.

Abruptly, the sound changed.

"Watch out!" Sparrow shouted, trying to shove Ignix aside—but too late. There was a great, low rumble, followed by horrid scraping, renting sounds. Cracks. Booms.

Then pain.

Sharp, lancing pain through her arm, then nothing. Utter silence.

"Fife?" she choked out, trying to move, but she was buried in rubble and her arm was pinned down, stuck beneath a heavy chunk of rock. "Fife! Ignix?"

Here, child, came a low, groggy response, and Sparrow thought the phoenix might have been hit worst of all.

"Are you hurt? Fine Fellow, where is he?"

I am trapped. Your raven is fine indeed. Just shaken.

Sparrow's breath of relief turned into a sob. She was trapped. Ignix was trapped—and they were so close to freedom. Ignix's explosion must have damaged the tunnel, just as she'd thought it might.

You tried to save me, Ignix observed, an odd tenor to her voice.

"It's my fault," Sparrow moaned. "I asked. I *pushed* . . ."

Fife stirred then, claws scratching over stone as he righted himself and shook out his wings. He was a bit disoriented, but then he sidled over to Sparrow, running his beak through her hair, hopping lightly around her head, concerned.

"Is there a way through?" she asked him, forgetting the conversation with Ignix. Fife said there was a small gap that light was spilling through.

Light. Light meant air. Light meant outside.

"Go, Fife. Find help. Can you do that?" she rasped, her voice ragged with dust and raw with pain. "What do you think, Fine Fellow? Can you get us some help?"

She put as much magic into it as she could, but Sparrow understood animal limitations. What she was asking . . . Fife was loyal to her, but he was a wild thing, and the world beckoned. He could get lost or distracted, and she might never see him again.

Even he seemed to sense it. His horny little feet dug into her skin as he shuffled his weight, wings fluttering and anxious.

"Yes, you can," she encouraged him. "You can do it. Go now, quick, while you still have the light. Go on."

He nipped at her hair again, fluttered his wings . . . then left.

That was selfless of you. And kind.

"He'll be back," Sparrow said stubbornly, but Ignix did not respond.

Time passed in a haze of fear and pain, eventually so pervasive that Sparrow seemed to have left her body—left her mind—existing in a state of lifeless disconnect. She knew it was more than mere hours, though. Maybe more than days.

I could end it, you know.

Ignix hadn't spoken in a while. Sparrow had almost forgotten she was there.

End what? Sparrow replied, too exhausted to realize she was speaking inside her mind—but Ignix was open before her, and the magic thrummed between them.

This . . . agony. I could go to ash—we could go together. That is more than most get when they reach the end.

The words hurt Sparrow—first because they forced her to think, which meant reconnecting to her broken body, but also because they forced her to face truths that she did not want to face. The fact that this might be the end, whether Ignix offered it or not.

"I thought you said you were the only one who could defeat her!"

Right now I am. When I die, there will come another.

Anger sparked inside Sparrow. "But no one who's ever faced them before! Faced them and *won*. I said you didn't have to do it alone, not that you didn't have to do it at all! How dare you give up!" she demanded, the words coming out in a rush. "If I was as strong and powerful as you, I'd do anything to help my friends. So we're gonna help them, and they're gonna help you, and that's final."

Silence met her words.

You remind me of someone when you talk like that, Ignix mused calmly, while Sparrow huffed and puffed.

"Oh yeah? Who?"

Callysta Lightbringer.

"Callysta . . . Rider of Cirix?" Sparrow asked.

The very same. She was fierce and brave, but steady, too . . . a calming influence. When we were together—she and Nefyra, myself and my mate, Cirix—it felt as if anything were possible. . . . It has been a long time since I knew that kind of hope. Thank you.

"For what?"

For reminding me. The weight of the world is easier to bear with others by your side. I had forgotten.

"Been trying to tell you all along . . . ," Sparrow said, and Ignix snorted.

You have. Ignore my offer. I sought only to ease your pain.

"Worry about your own pain. I'm doing just fine," Sparrow insisted, though her voice was little more than a rasp. She swallowed thickly before she added, soft as a whisper, "Tell me about her."

Ashfires and their mounts tend toward anger and passion, but Lightbringers do as their name promises and bring light wherever they go. Callysta was blunt and unapologetic in her opinions, but I've never known anyone kinder. Animals loved her, and people loved her. And Cirix loved her too. He was a small, timid thing when he first hatched, but under Callysta's care, he flourished. He was blind in one eye. . . . Did you know that?

"No," Sparrow whispered, her heart clenching almost painfully at the idea.

A strix claw took his left eye, so he always flew on my right. Once they were gone—Callysta and Cirix—the world was darker for us both. And then Nefyra left . . . and it grew darker still. Ever since, I have been alone.

For Sparrow, the world was always dark . . . and she had spent most of her life alone too. At least until recently.

A wave of powerful longing rose up. She missed her friends, and not just the animal ones. She wiggled frantically, desperate to move. She wanted to *rage* against her circumstances, but pain shot dizzyingly up her arm, sudden and fierce, and she sagged back again. "I want to go *home.*"

Her voice broke on the word, bitter and painful in her mouth. Sparrow didn't have a home—she'd been forced to leave home when she was five. Her parents couldn't afford a child that wasn't able to work in the shop, so they gave her up. That was Sparrow's home—a place she was not wanted. A place where they did not care about her.

The temple hadn't been a home, and the same was true of all the other places she'd slept and squatted in over the years.

But the Eyrie had felt like a home. No one tried to give her up or push her away.

But no one came looking for her either.

And maybe that was the same thing.

Her mind wandered then, and she slipped into something like a dream.

A dream of wind in her hair, sun on her skin, and a precious, familiar voice calling her name . . .

I tried, Nefyra. But I was not the one meant to challenge her. I was not enough. Not without you.

- CHAPTER 37 -
ELLIOT

ELLIOT HAD BEEN SEARCHING for Sparrow for *four days*.

It had taken him the better part of the night after he'd spoken to Riella to gather what he'd need—food and clothes and medical supplies—and to pack up Jaxon without being seen. They'd set out just before dawn; he had tried to sleep, but it was no use, and by the time they'd cleared the northern patrols and left Prosperity behind, it was a bright and clear day, and he knew he wouldn't rest until he had the Eyrie in his sights.

As soon as he saw it, however, Jaxon grew tense and uneasy beneath him, and Elliot remembered that he had more than the landscape and labyrinthine tunnels to contend with. The strixes had control of the Eyrie now, and Elliot didn't delude himself that he'd stand a chance if they spotted him.

He also had to avoid the Phoenix Riders currently on patrol, as he was technically shirking his duty. A handful of Riders had set up temporary camp nearby so they could alternate shifts and keep watch on the Eyrie, but Elliot knew their routes and was able to avoid their notice.

He set up camp of his own inside the abandoned way station and got some sleep. The following morning, he began his search . . . and continued it well into the second, third, and fourth days.

The countryside was riddled with caves and crevasses that could easily be mistaken for tunnels, and Elliot had no choice but to search them all. Most of the tunnels he did find were blocked, wildly overgrown, or caved in. Elliot hacked and slashed, dug and scraped, and shouted Sparrow's name, but he couldn't get through. And if he couldn't get through this way, what hope was there that Sparrow could get through on the other side?

But Sparrow was with Ignix. Surely that meant they had a chance? Maybe they had already gotten out and were on their way to Prosperity.

Then again, Sparrow had made more than one mention of her life before the Eyrie, how she'd traveled and wandered and never stayed in one place too long. He'd thought she'd found a home with Ersken and the phoenixes, with Riella and the other animals, but maybe after Elliot had abandoned her and left her behind, she would decide to move on.

He shook his head. Sparrow wasn't like him—she'd never abandon the animals who had come to count on her, even if the people *she'd* come to count on had abandoned *her*.

That wasn't who she was.

It was part of why Elliot liked her. She was all the things that he was not, and yet she'd accepted him and his faults anyway.

But if Sparrow hadn't left, then it was up to Elliot to find her, and with no sign of her after four days of searching, his carefully controlled panic was creeping in.

His hands were shaking as he paced back and forth in front of Jax, struggling to keep calm and think clearly. Should he fly a full circuit of the area again? Should he try to get into the service tunnel? It led only into the stronghold and not the Eyrie proper, but maybe he could find a way to sneak around somehow? Or maybe he would have to fly in, with no cover, no reinforcements, and a flock of strixes ready to tear him apart.

Jax tossed his head uneasily, and Elliot knew he was right—what good would he be to Sparrow or anyone if he got himself killed?

Desperate for something to do, Elliot started putting together some food for himself and Jax when a rustle and a squawk drew his attention. He turned to find a crow perched on a nearby stone.

Typical. Trust a scavenger to turn up right when Elliot went for the food.

He tossed the bird some bread, mind still on what he should do next—when the crow squawked again. Elliot turned; the bird had fluttered closer to him, but he hadn't moved for the food.

"That's all I've got for you," Elliot said sternly. "No use turning your beak up at it."

The crow tilted its head and squawked again.

When Elliot turned back to Jax, it was to find his phoenix staring curiously at the bird. He let out a sharp croak—a questioning sound.

"What is it, Jax?" Elliot asked, distracted and struggling to parse his bondmate's thoughts. "You know this crow?"

Raven, Jax corrected.

Elliot's breath caught, and he whirled around, looking more closely. It *was* a raven, with a scar across his eye and chest. Elliot staggered forward, seeing more details—the rumpled feathers, the streaks of dust and grime.

"Fine Fellow?"

Another squawk, this one tinged with a mix of impatience and exasperation. *Finally*, he seemed to say, *this idiot gets it.*

"Where is she?" Elliot choked out. "Where is Sparrow?"

Elliot climbed into the saddle with Fine Fellow on his shoulder, and they flew back to the eastern tunnel, the one Veronyka had pointed out and Elliot had checked on his first day. It had been completely caved in, but before he could say so, Fine Fellow darted into a small, invisible-until-this-moment opening between the stones. An opening only *just* large enough for the bird to fly through.

Elliot reached with his magic, going with the raven as he fluttered deeper into the tunnel, revealing there was room past the cave-in. Some of the stones looked oddly melted and misshapen . . . as if they'd been burned. Ignix must have burst into flame in an attempt to blast their way through.

The raven drew his attention to a figure on the ground, crushed by rock . . . unmoving.

Sparrow.

Elliot's chest contracted painfully, before his brain could clarify—no, not crushed, but pinned, her arm stuck and her body partially covered in gravel and dirt. And Ignix, too, was stuck—and in worse shape than Sparrow. How was Elliot going to get them out?

Next to him, Jax puffed out his chest, as noble and brave as a hero's steed from an old folktale.

You're right, Elliot said, patting his bondmate's neck before jumping from the saddle. *We can do this.*

"Sparrow?" he called as he approached, climbing carefully over the heaps of rocks and debris, afraid to send any of the stones moving and cause more damage than was already done. "Sparrow, can you hear me?"

There was no response, but then Ignix reached for him, opening her mind, and he realized she meant to guide him. In a flash, he had a clearer picture of the cave-in than the raven could show, and a rough idea of how to carve his way through.

Elliot rooted around Jax's saddle for the tools he'd brought—an ax, a shovel, and a length of rope—and got to work.

It was slow going. Elliot had to first loosen the rocks carefully one at a time, ensuring he didn't cause heavier rocks above to slide down or fall in unexpected directions. Once he was certain of the angle and the stability of the pile, Jax used his massive claws to lift the stone and carry it away, while Elliot moved on to the next one. Some stones had to be split or chipped away at, and the larger ones had to be carefully tied off with rope and dragged away with powerful pumps of Jax's wings.

The fact that all the noise hadn't caused Sparrow to shout at him made Elliot's throat tight with worry, but he pushed on.

The sun was low in the sky when the last massive rock was pulled away, leaving a shifting, sliding cascade of smaller stones and pebbles. Elliot leapt into the mess, heedless of the shifting ground underfoot, knowing that they'd removed most of the load-bearing rocks and a further collapse was inevitable.

"Sparrow?" he said again, ducking under the low tunnel mouth and squinting into the darkness. Ignix was next to her, throwing off a faint glow that seemed to flicker and jump, her feathers drooping and one of her wings bent at an odd angle and crushed beneath another massive stone. It was a corner of this huge rock that had caught Sparrow's arm too, and Elliot realized with a rush of affection for the ancient bird that Ignix had tried to take the hit for Sparrow, and while she had managed to take the brunt of it, she hadn't been able to spare the girl entirely.

Elliot stared at the monumental slab, failure gutting him. There was no way they could move that rock, no matter how many hours they hacked and pulled and wrestled with it.

I can handle the stone, Ignix said into his mind. *You must handle the girl.*

"Handle the girl . . . ," Elliot repeated, trying to get his brain back on track. "How?"

He crouched down before Sparrow, who was curled in a ball around her trapped arm, Fine Fellow perched next to her. She seemed to be stirring now, but she was groggy and disoriented. Elliot's hand hovered over her, itching to touch her, to make sure she was okay, but afraid to startle her or cause any more pain.

Below, Ignix said, and Elliot stared down at his feet . . . which were standing in shifting gravel and soft sand. *Dig her out.*

Of course! Elliot didn't have to lift the rock, he had to lower Sparrow, digging around her until her arm was dislodged.

That was sure to hurt her. Elliot stared at her arm in Ignix's flickering glow, and while her forearm was indeed pinned, her fingers were visible, pale and pink and dirty, but not black-and-blue. Not crushed and bloody. She'd probably broken her arm, but it looked like a clean break—no torn skin or shattered, protruding bones.

"Sparrow?" he whispered, pitching his voice as gently as he could. Fine Fellow tried to help, running his beak through her hair. Sparrow blinked awake.

"You came back," she murmured. "I knew you would." Elliot's heart soared, until—"You're a Fine Fellow, ain't no mistake. I knew I named you right."

Elliot swallowed. "Sparrow?" Jax was moving behind him, lighting the way out, but there were other noises—more shifting shale and creaking rock. They didn't have time to waste.

Sparrow froze. "Elliot?" she said faintly, trying to lift her head, then crying out in pain as her arm caught.

"Shh," Elliot said, reaching out to touch her hair, to still her movement. "It's me. I'm here."

A weighted pause. "I knew I bumped my noggin," she said sadly, "and now I'm losing my marbles."

Elliot fought back a laugh. "You bumped more than your noggin," he said, shifting his position. "But you've still got your marbles. It's really me, and I'm going to get you out of here, but first I need to dig your arm loose. It's going to hurt."

Sparrow reached her good arm up to find where Elliot's hand was still pressed gently to her head. Her fingers found his—checking he was indeed real—before she took a deep, steadying breath.

"Well, go on, then."

"I'll go as carefully as I can," he said, asking Jax to come closer and help light the darkening tunnel. Then he sank his hands into the cool dirt, digging and shifting and clearing out space.

Sparrow opened her mouth several times, emitting a low hiss or a nearly silent gasp, and Elliot found himself murmuring assurances and praise.

"You're doing so good. Just a bit more, just a little longer . . ."

Hurry, came Ignix's urgent voice, and he became aware again of the passage around him, the echo of his own work and the distant rumble of some far-off shift. The strixes must have shaken the very foundations of the Eyrie with their attack. Either that or Ignix had been blasting her way through and caused more damage than she'd realized.

That burst of fear and adrenaline was all he needed. He shoved aside a last huge handful of gravel, finally making enough room for Sparrow to exclaim in triumph and pull, gasping and sobbing as her arm scraped against the rough stone. Elliot helped, and as soon as she was free, he was pressing the limb to her chest and putting his arm around her shoulders, guiding her over the uneven ground and toward the gap he and Jax had spent all day making.

Fine Fellow flew ahead, following Jax, while behind them, the sounds of moving stone grew louder. The tunnel was about to collapse again, but Ignix was still inside. She'd have to ignite, and quickly, if she wanted to free herself and get out.

"Ignix!" Sparrow said, stopping dead in her tracks, but Elliot dragged her forward even as he looked over his shoulder. The ancient phoenix was glowing brightly now, hot as an ember that had been burning for hours, her form blurring in rippling heat waves. She'd probably had to hold back all this time, but without Sparrow, she could give all her heat and strength.

There was a strange, vacuous feeling—as if the air in the tunnel was being sucked backward toward her—and then a sudden *boom* as the air shot outward again in a roaring explosion of fire and sparks.

Elliot was still clearing the cave mouth, and he shoved Sparrow in front of him as debris rained down around them. He took the worst of it, sharp pains peppering his back and neck and then something hit his head, and everything went dark.

Elliot came back to himself in pieces—damp grass underneath his body, aches and sharp pains radiating from his back and neck. He attempted to lift his hand to check for blood, when he realized there was another hand inside of his. Small and cold.

"Riella?" he said blearily, dazed, but then he opened his eyes to see the stars glittering overhead and Jax looming over him. It felt oddly familiar, especially with Sparrow's golden head coming into focus nearer at hand. She was on her knees next to him, her bad arm pressed to her chest and her other gently pulling her fingers out of his.

"No," she said, subdued. "Not her. Just me."

Suddenly he remembered—the tunnel, the *explosion*.

"Sparrow!" Elliot croaked, then snatched her fingers back and tugged her close, pulling her down against his chest in a shaking moment of happiness and relief. "You're okay," he muttered into her hair, breath hitching with the surge of emotion.

Sparrow made a startled sound as she flopped on top of him, halfway between a laugh and a sob, but then a sharp nip of pain lanced through his ear.

He jerked back to find that cursed raven next to his head. Sparrow sat upright. "Fife, stop that."

Elliot batted the bird away but didn't miss the grimace on Sparrow's face. He was every bit the idiot the raven thought he was.

"I hurt you," he said regretfully, struggling to sit up. His entire body felt like it had been pummeled, but one look at Sparrow and he knew his pain was nothing to what she had been through.

"Was already hurt—don't think you can take all the credit," she said, her voice reedy and thin. She was flushed, too, almost feverish, and her eyes were glassy and bright.

"Jax?" Elliot said sharply, looking around, but the phoenix was already there, legs bent to offer up his saddlebags—and a med kit.

Shelter, came Ignix's imperious voice in Elliot's mind. He spotted her a few feet away, a dull coat of dust across her usually gleaming feathers, her wing bent at an unnatural angle. Behind her, the entrance to the tunnel was reduced to a pile of smoking rubble.

Yes, they needed shelter—but with Ignix in that state, they wouldn't be able to fly back to the way station.

"There's a cave," Elliot said, craning his neck to scan the landscape and reorient himself. "Just down the slope and around that bit of stone."

Ignix set off at once, walking gingerly, her bad wing dangling by her side, and Elliot wished he had the benefit of Ersken's—or even Riella's—expertise.

"We need to get that arm set," he said to Sparrow, forcing confidence into his voice, even if he didn't feel it. "But I'm just going to wrap it in a sling for now until we find shelter."

She nodded, wobbling to her feet—and Elliot found his own head spinning as he stood, a dull ache forming at the base of his skull.

After hastily securing Sparrow's arm, he put away his supplies and turned to her once more.

"I'm going to lift you into Jax's saddle. Is that okay?"

She nodded, and Elliot took her around the waist—doing his best to avoid her arm—and hoisted her into the seat. She was distressingly light, and he made a mental note to get food going as soon as they were inside the cave.

"You're coming too?" she said uncertainly.

"I'll walk. I don't want to jostle your arm."

Sparrow wore a somewhat alarmed look. "I can't—I don't want—" she spluttered, her good arm patting the saddle, seeking somewhere to hold.

"Jax will fly slow. You won't—"

But Jax shot him an exasperated look at that point, craning his neck around to stare at Elliot and then, pointedly, at Sparrow. She was shaking, hand still fluttering across the straps and buckles, and Elliot realized that he was doing it again—that polite distance thing he did when he felt nervous or guilty, and right now he was feeling both. Guilty for abandoning Sparrow to this fate and nervous because she was important to him in a way he didn't fully understand. Distance was easier when you didn't know where you stood, and that had been Elliot's life at the Eyrie. At first because he was lying and betraying the people around him—guilt—and then because he'd been caught and exposed and so had assumed that his presence was unwanted or unwelcome—nerves.

But Sparrow had never given him that impression, not once. His chest ached at the realization that his life had changed recently because of it.

And now he was pulling away when what she needed was to have him close.

She'd never flown by herself; plus, she was badly hurt, half-starved, and had been trapped in a dank tunnel for days. Now was not the time to give her space.

Now was the time to reassure her that he'd never abandon her again.

He mounted up behind her, his arms caging her in on either side, ensuring there was no way she could fall or lose her balance. Her stiff, trembling body seemed to relax all at once, leaning into him, and he hung on tight as Jax lurched up and into the sky.

He soared low around the bend and toward one of the caves they'd checked earlier. It was relatively shallow but tucked into a recess of stone that should offer good protection while still keeping them safe from any potential cave-ins.

Ignix was already there, backed into the farthest corner, and after carefully helping Sparrow down from the saddle, Elliot got to work.

He splinted Sparrow first—she had a break in one of the bones of her forearm, so she still had mobility in the shoulder, which made things easier. Once it was wrapped tight and secured, he put the arm back into the sling and forced first some water, then bread into her good hand. He'd have to get a kettle going for the medicinal tea he had in his pack. Jax seized the chance to help, flying off with Fife on his saddle and returning with gigantic branches clutched in his beak—Fife with tiny twigs and leaves in his.

Ignix was trickier. She was irritable and impatient, and could tell quite plainly that Elliot was no expert. But she also recognized that her accelerated healing meant if she didn't get the bones set soon, she'd wind up with a crooked, unusable wing.

Once the fire was going, Elliot had to enlist Jax's assistance. Ignix's wingspan was vast, and the appendage appeared to be broken in two places. If Elliot was wary of the old phoenix, Jax was properly terrified, jumpy and twitchy and fluttering every time she squawked or snapped at him.

Get it together, Elliot ordered after twice losing hold of his bandages when Jax anxiously bumped his arm.

Elliot swore he felt something like amusement come from Ignix then, and he secretly suspected she was enjoying giving Jax a hard time.

When at last Elliot had secured the bones as best he could, he wrapped the wing tightly against her body and stepped back.

She sank low to the ground, looking small and forlorn and not the least bit terrifying, and Elliot expelled a sigh of relief. He gave her food and water, too, and she took it without complaint before closing her eyes and going to sleep.

Elliot put the kettle on, and while the water boiled, he unpacked all his camp supplies, setting up a bedroll for Sparrow with thick blankets and clothes piled underneath to soften the hard ground. She needed a wash—Elliot did too—but her eyes were drooping as she chewed her bread, hunched over against the cave wall, and he decided it could wait.

He made her drink a cup of the pungent tea, trying not to laugh as she coughed and spluttered and pulled ridiculous faces, and then he guided her over to her bed. Jax took up a position at the cave mouth to keep watch, and as the fire started to burn low, the night's cold seeped in.

Sparrow shivered under her blankets, and though Fine Fellow nuzzled in against her neck, it wasn't enough to banish the chill.

Elliot sighed, fighting an internal battle with propriety, uncertainty, and just plain common sense. He unrolled his bed several feet away from hers, paused, dragged it closer—and closer—then stopped again, annoyed at himself and not entirely sure why.

He straightened, then walked over to the cave entrance. Jax had been watching the sorry display and cocked his head as Elliot approached. "Go ahead, Jax," he said, for the phoenix was staring at Sparrow's small, shivering form with obvious concern. "I'll keep watch instead."

Jax was confused about his bizarre behavior—Elliot couldn't blame him—but fluttered obediently to Sparrow's side, hunching down low and emitting a soft, golden glow whose warmth Elliot could feel across the cave.

The tension in Sparrow unspooled; her shivers stopped, and before long her breath turned steady and rhythmic.

Elliot turned his back on them as he settled against the cave mouth, arms crossed and legs outstretched, staring up at the starry sky. He was relieved and restless in equal measure, but thought that for once in his life, he'd managed to do something right.

But there is another Ashfire. One who
could carry the weight . . . if I let her.
One who could challenge Avalkyra and win.

- CHAPTER 38 -
SEV

LIFE AT HAVEN FELT very much like Sev's time on his parents' farm, and though that had taken up such a small part of his life, it seemed some habits dug roots and refused to budge—like the stubborn weeds he wrenched from their vegetable gardens.

Kade and the other Riders were always busy with training and patrols, and so Sev found other ways to make himself useful. He fed the animals, collected chicken eggs, and found a veritable treasure trove of wild berries hidden in a thick patch of overgrown bushes and bramble that he helped clear away.

Though slightly rough around the edges, Haven was a well-run, self-sustaining place. Theryn was the undisputed leader, and surprisingly not an animage but a military man. Sev had wondered at his background, noting his rigid posture and the orderly way he governed his people, but while he might have guessed Theryn had once served in the army, he'd never have guessed his ties to Veronyka.

Learning the man's identity and the full truth of Veronyka's childhood definitely helped him understand how Haven had come to be.

"Wait—he thought they'd *both* died?" Sev asked Gus, one of the non–Phoenix Rider animages who lived at Haven. They were at the well, drawing up buckets of water.

"Mother and daughter," Gus confirmed grimly. He was a quiet man, not prone to gossip, but he was also the oldest member of Haven and had been there from the beginning, so he knew more than all the others. Sev found he opened up after a few hours of work, and today was no different.

"You'd think that'd make him hate everything to do with Phoenix Riders," Gus said thoughtfully, pausing after he hoisted a newly filled bucket to the ground. "But he knew his child had been an animage. This was his way of honoring her, I think."

Sev straightened and peered through the trees, toward Haven. It seemed to him that being around animages and Phoenix Riders would be a constant reminder, both of his pain and his position on the outside. But maybe it was better to remember, better to do *something* than to do nothing.

If an ex-soldier like Theryn could find his place among the Phoenix Riders, was there a chance Sev could too?

Footsteps echoed from the staircase that led up to Agneta's cottage, and Gus fumbled the second bucket, dropping it with a loud clatter. Sev smirked—he suspected Gus was sweet on Agneta, though he was worse than Sev when it came to keeping his cool or articulating his feelings.

"Not working him too hard, I hope?" Agneta asked once she'd reached the ground, gesturing to Sev. Hestia was with her.

Gus smiled and spluttered and shook his head, hands clasped behind his back like a schoolboy. "No, ma'am."

Agneta snorted.

"How is it, Sevro?" Hestia asked, nodding at his shoulder. His movements were still somewhat restricted, but it was mostly stiffness now, not pain—and he rolled the joint and rotated his arm in demonstration. She nodded. "I'll whip up a compress for later anyway, just in case."

It was completely unnecessary, but Sev had learned by now that it was Hestia's way of *doing something*, and Agneta's constant movement was much the same. The pair of them stared fondly at him, and Sev wondered at his ability to charm older women. It seemed each one he met wanted to pester and smother and overfeed him.

"Finish that and wash up," Agneta said, as she and Hestia headed for the path that led through to Haven. "I'll have a plate made for you by the time you're finished."

Though there were many others who could cook—and sometimes did—Agneta had appointed herself unofficial mother of Haven, taking every chance she could to fuss, particularly over Veronyka, though he received his fair share as well.

Gus stared wistfully at Agneta's retreating back.

"You could talk to her," Sev said, and Gus leapt as if he'd been scolded.

"About what?" he asked, bewildered.

"Maybe about the flowers you leave her every time you drop off vegetables from the garden?" Sev asked innocently, and Gus's face turned redder than a beet. Sev held up his hands. "Just a suggestion."

Sev had been carefully avoiding Kade ever since they'd arrived at Haven. That meant coming to mealtimes late or leaving early, and tonight was no exception. But despite Sev turning up a good hour after their usual dinnertime, Kade, Veronyka, and Tristan, plus several other Riders from the Eyrie and from Haven, were still seated by the cook fire. Most of the rest of Haven's occupants had already come and gone, and even Agneta remained only long enough to hand him a plate before disappearing into the darkness back to her house.

After choosing a spot across the flames from Kade, Sev picked at his food in silence, aware every moment of Kade's burning gaze on him.

Low conversation hummed around them. Things had seemed a bit tense at first between the Eyrie Riders and the Haven Riders—a certain wariness pervading their interactions, as if each side feared what the other thought of them. Veronyka and Tristan's Riders were fighting a war and were obviously worried about bringing danger to the small slice of safety the members of Haven had sought. Meanwhile, the Haven Riders probably worried the others judged them for hiding away or not being involved.

However, once they started speaking to one another, it was clear that they were all just extremely glad to find others like them, whatever the circumstances. Latham and Sarra had family connections through their parents in Aura Nova, and Jonny had seen Anders's parents perform with their acting troupe in Stelarbor. Ronyn and Gus talked for hours about Arborian farming, and Tristan and Lysandro had lived in the same border town in the Foothills as Erend and knew a lot of the same people.

Even Sev could talk easily with Rosalind, who had been a Phoenix Rider courier—something he had never heard of before. She used to fly messages all over Aura Nova and knew every neighborhood and corner of the city better than he did. She was short and slight—as was her phoenix, which made for good speed and agility—and had such a sharp eye for detail, she'd have caught Trix's interest at once. She'd pegged Sev's Narrows accent instantly and guessed that Kade had been a bondservant because of the tiniest of tan lines across the back of his neck where his chain had once lain.

Kade, on the other hand, was particularly interested in Ivan, who was big and brawny as well and who used to work Phoenix Rider construction. Ivan and his large, steady mount helped create bridges and buildings with other teams of phoenixes, who were able to lift huge beams of wood and heavy slabs of marble, creating structures like they had in ancient Pyra, which were impossible to achieve without flying builders. In fact, much of Aura Nova had fallen into disrepair since the Blood War, their grounded construction crews ill equipped to fix soaring archways or towering buildings.

Despite the lingering tension between him and Kade, Sev felt warm and content sitting in front of the crackling flames, the leafy canopy above and towering trees fading into the darkness on all sides. It was peaceful just listening as Anders laughed at a joke Jonny told and Veronyka leaned into Tristan, whispering in his ear. It all felt strangely . . . normal.

"To be honest, I never thought I'd get accepted in the first place," Rosalind was saying when Veronyka asked how she wound up a courier.

"Why not?" Sev asked.

"I was dirt poor, for starters," she said. "I could barely read and write. And I was never much of an animage."

"Really?" Veronyka said, leaning forward curiously.

Rosalind shrugged, but Sev found himself hanging on her every word. "Couldn't make our damned house cat do what I wanted, never mind an unfamiliar creature or wild animal."

"Cats are notoriously tricky," Tristan said fairly.

"So are phoenixes," added Veronyka, and everyone grinned.

"But I wanted to *fly*, so I applied. There's a test they give you," she said. "Or they used to, anyway." She cleared her throat. "They brought all the new applicants into the arena. First they made you walk past a group of full-grown phoenixes."

"To see how the applicants reacted?" Veronyka guessed.

"*That,*" Rosalind said with a smirk, "but also the firebirds themselves. The humans reacted fairly predictably—fear, excitement, or even indifference. But the *phoenixes* . . . They've got a sense for these kinds of things. They'll single out humans who interest them, who have active minds and open hearts."

Awareness prickled over Sev's skin, and he caught Kade staring at him from across the flames. His expression was confrontational, challenging.

Sev glowered. Just because Jinx stared at him didn't mean she'd "singled him out," and it *definitely* didn't mean he had an "active mind and an open heart."

It didn't mean anything.

"So what happened?" Veronyka pressed.

Rosalind flashed a smile. "One of them chased me. I ran away screaming—but I managed to navigate my way through the labyrinthine tunnels without getting lost, and that caught the attention of one of the courier masters. I passed the other tests, and they admitted me. Wasn't long until I'd hatched Xippolyta—Xip, for short."

A rustling sounded above; Xip herself, along with the rest of the phoenixes, perched in the shadowy branches.

Sev stared at his feet, hating the hope that Rosalind's story caused to bloom inside his chest.

It was so tempting to believe that it could happen for him, too. That he was special, that he could belong here with all of them, but he knew this slice of life was temporary—that it would be foolish to get comfortable here. Time was not on their side, and just because Rosalind had been given a chance didn't mean Sev ever would.

"So how did you come to be here, then?" Anders asked the group at large, though it was Jonny who replied. He was probably in his forties—as light and smiling as Anders was—and had been a fully trained Phoenix Rider when the war broke out.

"I knew Theryn from the Stellan Uprising," he explained. "I'd been injured in the fighting"—he lifted his arm to show a nasty scar from elbow to wrist—"and he was in the healer's tent more often than not, on guard duty with the princess." That must be Pheronia, Veronyka's mother. "So we got to talking, and then afterward I was stationed in Aura Nova, so we'd see each other every now and again. But then, well . . ." He swallowed, and the light seemed to leave his eyes as he continued. "We next saw each other during the Last Battle. Things were totally unraveled by then: friend or foe, enemy or ally . . . None of it seemed to matter when so many were dead. We left the capital together. He was already with Gus—he'd been a hostler in the capital and helped manage Theryn's horses—and so I traveled with them. I left for a few years to look for my family, but I found my way back. Even found Ivan along the way!"

Ivan chuckled, nodding.

"Every few months we send out scouts, looking for others," Jonny explained. "Hanging out in taverns and the like. Ivan was working on the docks in Estia."

The others shared their stories too: tales of being chased from their homes or hidden away by family members until various contacts or lucky encounters found them here.

"All tragedies, every one," Jonny said, "but it's Theo's story that keeps me up at night."

The woman in question was standing just outside the glow of the fire, unseen, until Jonny mentioned her name.

"Is *that* why you're last to wake every morning?" Theo said, causing many in the group to jump in surprise. "I thought it was laziness."

Her voice was flat, and Sev couldn't tell if she was joking or not, but Jonny seemed to take it in stride. "That too, Theo, that too—but you lurking in the shadows doesn't help much either."

"Sorry to remind you of my hardships. I'll lurk elsewhere."

She marched off, and everyone glanced around uneasily at one another. "Oh, don't worry about her," Jonny said with an airy wave of his hand. "All doom and gloom—not that I blame her."

The words were light, but Jonny's gaze was thoughtful—maybe even concerned—as it searched the darkness where Theo had disappeared.

"That's what happens when you lose your bondmate," said Rosalind quietly, and Sev frowned. He hadn't known that Theo was a Phoenix Rider. She was around thirty years old, tall and fair with wildly curling red hair and freckles. She was stoic and unsociable, and spent more time alone than with any of the animals. Sev hadn't even been sure she was an animage.

"Her phoenix died?" asked Veronyka.

No one answered, and a sense of foreboding filled the silence, giving it weight.

"I daresay that would be some kind of mercy compared to the truth," Gus muttered, and several heads bobbed their agreement.

"Theo's patrol was still in training when the war broke out. This was early on, mind you. Avalkyra had fled to Pyra, and there were rumors of rebellion and separation, but nothing official yet. Still, the Feather-Crowned Queen couldn't very well abscond in the night with young hatchlings and schoolchildren—or at least, that was how *she* put it," Jonny said, words disdainful. "And so, inevitably, people were left behind. The entire training ground was filled with young Phoenix Riders and their teachers, who were technically innocent of Avalkyra's machinations—but also prime suspects for any Phoenix Rider insurgency. Times were precarious, and as I understand it, they were held as *political prisoners*."

The way he said the words seemed to imply that it was an incorrect term.

"Hostages?" Tristan asked.

Jonny tilted his head. "In a way. The empire had it in their heads they could *convince* the captured Riders to fight for them. They tried all manner of things . . . torture, bribery, cruel tests and tricks, but of course there was no way to guarantee their loyalty, and even if the humans could be swayed . . ."

"Phoenixes won't willingly fight each other," said Veronyka.

"They can be provoked, of course, and Azurec knows they tried," Jonny said bleakly. "What it came down to was trust and control. Think if it were you—if they put you in your saddle and let you loose, would you follow orders . . . or escape? Rider and phoenix were only of use to the empire when they were together, but they were also their most dangerous and difficult to control that way too. It was a lost cause. Pity."

"Why a pity?" Sev asked, confused—but then realization dawned.

Jonny nodded grimly. "While they were experimenting, the Phoenix Riders were still of value to them. As soon as Pyra officially separated, everything went downhill. The war began in earnest between the empire and the Phoenix Riders, and those they held in captivity were now a liability. Since they couldn't be trusted or used to benefit the empire, the council's first order of business was to eliminate the threat."

Even though he'd been expecting it—had heard the stories—Sev's stomach clenched.

"Bloody slaughter," said Rosalind. "Apprentices and trainers, phoenixes and eggs—bonded, unhatched . . . didn't matter."

"But how could such a motion get voted through?" Veronyka demanded angrily. "They were children! Untested and half-trained. Innocent."

"I believe it was a wartime decree," Jonny said, glancing at Ivan, who nodded gravely. "It didn't require the full council's approval. Some nonsense rule that gives additional power to the general during military conflicts. The general is usually the king or queen, even if it's just a formality, so I don't think anyone realized the danger of such a law when there's no one on the throne. Pheronia had not officially been crowned, so it gave General Marcellan huge amounts of power . . . though I suspect Rast was pulling the strings even then."

"Rast . . . where have I heard that name before?" Tristan asked, brows knit together.

"It's General Rast now. Marcellan died in the war, but Rast was his protégé. Young, hungry for success, and ruthless. He came from nothing—born and bred in the Aura Nova slums—but he had grand ambitions. From what I've heard, he was behind the attempts to convert the Phoenix Riders as well."

"But I thought you said Theo's phoenix wasn't dead," Sev said, confused.

"They killed most—but not all. Rast was just getting started, you see. For all his brutality, he wasn't stupid, and was always looking for opportunities. The apprentices might have proven impossible to turn and utilize as weapons outside the empire, but that didn't mean they couldn't be wielded *within*. Just because Avalkyra was unwilling to negotiate for their lives didn't mean no one would."

Sev frowned. "I don't understand."

"Their families," Tristan said, straightening in his seat. "Who were their parents?"

Jonny pointed at him. "Good question. The training grounds were held on lockdown for months, and Rast did his homework. He handpicked those with significant ties . . . not to Avalkyra or the Phoenix Riders, but inside the empire itself. Remember, before the war broke out, it was common practice for animages of high social standing to join the Phoenix Riders. It was considered a worthy military posting, and Rast found he had quite a few highborn children in his midst. He convinced Marcellan to spare them."

"For what?" asked Sev dubiously.

"At first they were simple political hostages," Jonny said, poking at the fire. "It was an easy matter to guarantee their families' continued loyalty and support in exchange for their child's life. The massacres in the training grounds surely convinced them the general and his right-hand man were serious. That's how Rast was voted to replace Marcellan even though there were many more qualified commanders. He was only a captain then. He even got himself the old Pyraean governor's mansion on Marble Row—the Strongwings died in the Blood War, and of course Pyra was no longer a province of the empire—and other comforts besides."

"But that was seventeen years ago. They can't have been captives all this time?" Tristan said.

"No, not as such," Jonny said, his tone changing, his lips pursing as if he were only now reaching the most distasteful part of the story—which, Sev realized, was an appalling thought. "Most of this was swept under the rug. The massacre, the prisoners, and their attempts to convert them. All of it lumped together as part of the horror that was the Blood War, but us animages know that there was much more still to come. And General Rast was at the forefront. I doubt it was his specific idea, but he spearheaded the registry and the magetax and was responsible for enforcing it—quite violently—in the early days of its conception. They say in those first few months, he dragged in hundreds a week. Any guesses how he did it? I mean, for a non-mage, he had an uncanny ability to sniff out animages in hiding."

Sev's stomach flipped over. "The captives. He used animages to find other animages."

"*Still* uses," said Rosalind. "They work for the registry to this very day."

"Gods," muttered Veronyka, and she wasn't the only one. Curses and mutters broke out over the small group.

"They didn't do it willingly, of course, but with their phoenixes also in captivity . . . If they step a toe out of line, Rast will execute their bondmate. If their parents rescind their support—and annual monetary tributes—he'll kill their child."

"But why don't they come forward? Appeal to the council? If they're powerful, influential people in their own right, couldn't they undermine or supplant him?" Tristan asked, outraged.

"I'm sure some of them considered it. But the tide changed quickly after the war, and it suddenly became an awful liability to have a Phoenix Rider in the family. These once-apprentices were saved from scandal, trial, or imprisonment. Whatever blight might have been on their family name from being on the wrong side of the war was wiped away; in fact, most people don't even know that they'd ever trained to be Phoenix Riders. Better that than what General Rast could have done if they'd refused: tear down their whole families, brand them as Phoenix Rider sympathizers, rebels, and traitors, and probably accuse them of keeping phoenixes in the capital to boot. It would be his word against theirs, and in the current climate . . ."

"We're villains again," said Rosalind with a heavy sigh.

"We never stopped being villains," Ivan countered. "But now we are a *threat* again. I wouldn't put it past the council to act first and think later. These families and their wayward children are stuck."

"But what does this have to do with Theo?" asked Tristan. "How did she end up here, and where is her phoenix?"

"She and her best friend—a new trainee, but unbonded at the time of the war—tried to make an escape when things took a turn for the worse. Sneaking through storm drains or something. Theo made it out, but before she could reach back and help her friend and her phoenix through, they were caught. She ran, hoping to get help, but they chased her out of the city. Meanwhile, her friend claimed her name and her bondmate. That way Theo's phoenix wouldn't be executed."

"Why hasn't she tried to go to her family?" Tristan pressed.

Jonny shook his head. "She doesn't dare. She and her family were never particularly close. She thinks if she told them the truth, they'd stop paying."

"And then Rast would kill her phoenix," Veronyka whispered.

"And her friend too, I'd wager," said Jonny. "And so Theo stays here, alone, paying a different kind of price. The prisoners work for the registry, which has offices inside General Rast's own home. He had an addition built on—to keep a close eye on his work, he claimed, but he needed to keep a close eye on his prisoners instead. As for the phoenixes . . . nobody knows where they are for certain. Theo and I used to talk about rescues back in the day and even snooped around the arena once—but the drain she used to escape through was closed off, and we couldn't find any other way in. Besides, we have no idea if the phoenixes are still inside."

Sev looked around the fire at those who had bonded to a phoenix. They all seemed tense, uneasy in a way that reminded him of how it had felt when Kade had run off on Pyrmont with two soldiers in pursuit and Sev hadn't known if he was alive or dead. The not knowing was worse than knowing. . . . Even his parents' deaths, which had shattered his world beyond repair, had been sure and final. He had seen them die, which had given him some sense of closure. It had allowed him to move on, painful as it was.

Theo hadn't been given that chance.

Surely she knew her bondmate was alive, but that was probably all she knew—and the separation must be like an open wound that refused to heal. Never mind the friend who had risked everything to take her place . . . No doubt that debt weighed on her as well.

Quiet descended after that, everybody seemingly lost in their own thoughts. Veronyka stared intently into the fire, unseeing, while Tristan studied her, a frown on his face.

Meanwhile, Sev stared at Kade.

When Kade had been run through with a spear, Sev had felt the ground quake, as if the world were breaking apart beneath his feet. It had felt as if *he* had been gutted, and carrying Kade's limp body across the battlefield had been one of the hardest things he'd ever done. But no matter how shaken he had felt—no matter how broken his heart, how palpable his fear—it had been better to be there, to have Kade in his arms, than it would have been to be apart. To not know what had happened, or worse, to hear it secondhand from someone else hours or days later. People died and went missing all the time in war; people were lost without their loved ones ever knowing how or why.

But Sev could choose to *be there*. No matter how hard. No matter how devastating.

Sev could be there.

Even if it was temporary. Even if they were destined for different futures, certain to be pulled apart eventually . . . if what Kade wanted now was Sev by his side, Sev would be there for whatever time they had left.

Veronyka got abruptly to her feet, stalking off into the darkness, and Tristan followed her.

Not long after, Anders drew out his lyre, playing several quiet songs that threaded through the silence and cut the lingering tension.

Rosalind jumped in with a sweet, melodic voice that was ruined when Anders turned the performance into a duet, adding swear words whenever possible and causing Jonny to spit out his drink and Latham to double over with laughter.

Slowly the group started to disperse. When Kade got to his feet, Sev did as well.

It was difficult to see outside the pool of firelight, but Kade's silhouette became visible as Sev drew near. Reaching out, he grasped Kade's hand, hoping to catch him before he reached his tent.

The instant Sev's fingertips touched Kade's, however, Kade jerked back. He seemed startled as he faced Sev—had he not heard approaching footsteps?—but the emotion quickly turned to anger.

"What are you doing?" he demanded.

"I—can we talk?" Sev asked.

Kade's expression was barely visible in the gloom, but Sev could feel his gaze cutting through to his core.

He expected Kade to deny him, to balk—to unleash the pent-up frustration he emanated with every shallow breath he breathed. Instead, he marched away, not to his tent, which was clustered in a group with the others, but away from camp and into the darkness of the forest.

It reminded Sev of when they'd first met, talking treason with Trix as they walked among the trees.

Kade continued until Haven and the warm glow of the fire were lost from view. Sev's eyes adjusted enough so he could pick out Kade pacing between the trees.

"You've been avoiding me for days," he burst out, rounding on Sev. "Now, suddenly, you want to talk?"

"I . . . ," Sev said.

"I thought we were in this together," Kade said. The look of hurt he sent Sev's way was enough to knock the wind out of him.

"I'm *sorry*," Sev said, his voice catching on the word.

That show of emotion—or maybe the word itself—seemed to calm some of Kade's anger. He ran his hands through his hair. He laughed, though it was a hollow sound. "I can't believe after everything we've been through . . ." He trailed off, jaw working. He tried again. "How can *this*, the idea of being together, be the thing that breaks you? That breaks *us*?"

Us. That word had always held power for Sev. It had been the thing that made him truly commit to Trix and Kade and their cause. The lure of "us" and all it promised.

"What are you so afraid of?" Kade finished on a whisper.

Fear. Sev hated to admit that's what this was. He was afraid to want, afraid to get what he wanted and then lose it, as he was surely destined to do. To lose to death or war was one thing, but to lose because of his own shortcomings, his lack of anything to offer . . . That was something much worse.

"It's just," he began, swallowing around the lump in his throat, "even if everything goes right—even if we all somehow survive this—what's the best-case scenario? I'll never be one of you. I'll never be good enough."

"Good enough for *what*?" Kade demanded, angry again.

"For you!" Sev shouted. "For you and the Riders. I'll always be on the outside . . . but I don't care anymore."

Kade moved closer to him now, so close that Sev could trace the tense lines of his mouth and count every rapid-fire blink of his eyes, trying desperately to understand.

"I'd rather be there and on the outside than not at all," Sev finished.

Silence pulsed between them.

"You're wrong," Kade said, his body unlocking bit by bit, muscle by muscle. He tilted his head, considering.

"About what?" Sev asked, aware of every shift of movement, trying to gauge Kade's words. His actions.

"A lot of things," he said. Sev let out a huff of laughter, though Kade remained serious. "But you were never on the outside. Not with me."

And then they were kissing; Sev didn't know if he'd been the one to move or if it was Kade, but his back was scraping against the trunk behind him, and Kade's mouth was on his, and he didn't care. It had been weeks since they'd last kissed, since he'd last felt the slide of Kade's tongue and the drag of his lips, and maybe that was why he'd been able to convince himself he could leave this behind.

Kade, who saw all his flaws and fears and liked him anyway. Kade, who made Sev feel alive in a way he never had in all those years alone on the street. Alone, alone . . . always alone. He didn't want to be alone anymore.

But he wasn't. Kade was here, warm body and strong hands, and Sev knew he could never, *ever* give this up.

Some people are meant for power, for greatness.

- CHAPTER 39 -
VERONYKA

VERONYKA WANDERED AIMLESSLY THROUGH the trees.

She couldn't keep sitting there, doing nothing. Not when she was capable of doing something. She couldn't rectify the past, couldn't fix the wounds already inflicted . . . but she *could* stop more from happening. The problem was, not all scars came from battlefields.

Because even if they won this war—or stopped it altogether—the ills of the world wouldn't end there. Bad things happened before, during, and after war. It had been seventeen years since the Blood War, and still innocent people bled for the Ashfire queens.

Veronyka might want to convince herself she could temporarily take the position as heir, hold the throne like a placeholder until she was no longer needed . . . but she knew now that time would never come. Animages and Phoenix Riders, people inside the empire and beyond—they all deserved better. If *she* didn't give it to them, who would? When could she ever truly walk away from this?

She halted in her tracks, realizing for the first time that maybe she didn't want to. Maybe the crown wasn't just some burden to bear. Maybe it was a chance. She wanted to be a protector. . . . What better, greater way than that?

If it was up to her to claim her throne and the empire for herself, it was *also* up to her to stop Val, and Veronyka wasn't sure she knew how to handle one without damaging her chances at the other. There was war coming on two fronts, and no matter what direction Veronyka faced, the responsibility lay with her.

If she came forward now, underage and without any actual proof of her identity, she might succeed in delaying the empire's march, but she'd also be forced to spend days—weeks? months?—in Aura Nova searching for her birth certificate, winning over politicians, and establishing order.

That fight—the political fight—would take her away from the Phoenix Riders, and more importantly, it would take her away from Val. What damage might Val inflict in that time? She had already stolen the Eyrie away while Veronyka was distracted. Would she take all of Pyra? Would she claim it, or destroy it instead? Val had torn the world apart back when she *cared* about the pieces. Now Veronyka feared there was nothing she cared about at all.

Except, perhaps, for Veronyka herself.

Who would be able to stop Val if not her? But if Veronyka focused on Val alone, the empire would march unchecked into Pyra. They could wreak enough damage on their own, without Val's interference.

But while the commander was better equipped to deal with the empire and the political machinations required to get her onto the throne, there was no one better suited than Veronyka to take down Val.

She wasn't the best fighter or flyer—she and Xephyra were young and green compared to some of the other Phoenix Riders—but she was the only one with shadow magic and the only one who was bonded to Val. Only *she* could discover Val's plans. Only *she* could wield the same dark magic that controlled Val's shadowy flock.

Veronyka had to find a way to use this to her advantage.

To use *Val* to her advantage. But *how*?

Gravel crunched behind her, drawing Veronyka from her thoughts. She sensed Tristan before she heard his voice.

"Veronyka. Wait."

She halted midstep, registering her surroundings for the first time. She hadn't stormed back to camp, where their tents were set up, but down the path toward her grandmother's house.

Tristan came to a stop next to her. "Are you okay?"

"It's been two days," she said by way of a response.

He understood at once. "According to Fallon's last report, she hasn't left the Eyrie. Until she does . . ."

"I hate this."

"I know. Waiting is—"

"It's not that." Veronyka crossed her arms over her chest, staring into the shadowy trees, unseeing. "It feels like before. Back when . . . I've always been afraid of her." She darted a self-conscious look at him, but his expression was warm and understanding. "Even before I knew who she truly was and what she was capable of. I was afraid to step out of line, to do something wrong. . . ." She swallowed thickly, aching for the child she had been. "Sometimes, it felt like the shadow magic was a punishment. Another way for me to fail, another way for her to hurt me."

Tristan reached for her, intending to pull her into a hug, but Veronyka swiped at her eyes and shook her head. She didn't need or want comfort. "But now I see it all for what it really is—exactly what I need to defeat her. I'm not afraid anymore."

"Well, I am," he said flatly, and Veronyka couldn't help but chuckle. He seemed pleased by that, sliding a thumb across her cheek to capture a trailing tear, but the smile quirking his lips flattened out. "But I'm not asking you to wait because I doubt you. I know what *you're* capable of—but I guess that's the problem. I'm more afraid of what you'll do . . . what you think you'll *need* to do to save the rest of us from her."

Veronyka took a shaky breath. That was . . . Well, she didn't know what to say to that. She *would* do almost anything to stop Val. Where the line was, she wasn't quite sure, and she could understand how that might scare him.

She wouldn't want *him* risking his life for her, but she would do the same without a moment's hesitation. She looked guiltily up at him.

"Tristan . . ."

The soft thud of footsteps on wood echoed over to them, and Veronyka realized they were nearer to her grandmother's house than she'd thought.

"Lexi," came a sharp voice—Theryn's, pitched low, but still carrying in the quiet night. Another pair of footsteps joined the first, and Veronyka blinked upward, realizing that Theryn was chasing Alexiya down the stairs.

She could hardly see anything in the darkness, but two silhouettes were visible, illuminated by the soft light spilling out from the windows above.

"Stop calling me that—I'm not a kid anymore," Alexiya said crossly.

"Where are you going?" he asked. They had reached the ground now, though they were still a good fifty paces away from Veronyka and Tristan and had yet to notice they had an audience.

"Where do you think?"

"Let your commander deal with it. There's no need to go running off in the middle of the night. You know they'll want to jump on their saddles and take off. They're young. They're—"

"They're *warriors*, Theryn. They'll do what they have to do."

"They don't *have* to do anything!" he said in frustration—Veronyka had never heard him raise his voice before. "They're safe here. *She's* safe."

Alexiya stopped short. "We're in the middle of a war. There is no safety, not for someone like her."

Her. They were clearly talking about Veronyka.

"You could be safe here too. You all could."

"Don't pretend you care about *my* safety," Alexiya said scathingly. "In case you've forgotten, we were on opposite sides of the last war. You didn't care that I might die. You just cared that I might die for the wrong queen."

Ringing silence followed those words.

"You're wrong," Theryn said quietly. "I never gave a damn about Ash-fire queens. I loved a girl, Lexi, and she was carrying my child. Up until three days ago, I thought I had failed them both. Lost them forever." His voice broke on the words, raw emotion drenching every syllable. "But by some miracle, she's here, she's alive, and I cannot, *will not*, lose her again."

Alexiya sighed heavily. "You might not care that they're Ashfires, Theryn—but they *are*. She can't walk away from this."

"Yes, she can—"

"But I won't." Veronyka stepped out of the shadowy path and into the clearing where Alexiya and Theryn stood. She could just make out their faces in the dappled moonlight. She turned to her father. "You might not like it, but this is my war—my fight. There is no walking away. And even if there *was*, I wouldn't."

He looked at her for a long time. "You sound just like her," he announced at last, his tone half awe, half agony. "Just because you were born to that bloodline does not mean you have to make up for their mistakes. Or pay for them with your life."

"I have no intention of dying," she said reasonably, though a dull ache had begun to build behind her chest. It felt something like guilt.

"She didn't either," he said softly. "No one ever does."

"I am not her," Veronyka said, her voice wavering as she fought to keep her emotions in check. She had said this to Val before. Why was she always having to say it? "You can't undo the past. You can't bring her back."

He recoiled at that. "I'm not trying to bring her back," he said, shaking his head. "I'm asking *you* to stay."

Veronyka's throat tightened. She'd cherished these past days with her father and grandmother and aunt—this chance to be a family together— but she'd always known it was temporary. She'd assumed he'd known it too.

And though part of her was happy that he wanted her to stay, she also hated that he'd ask it of her in the first place. She fought against the sinking realization that he didn't actually know her at all.

"I can't," Veronyka said, the words coming out clipped. It didn't matter what news Alexiya bore or how urgently they had to leave—they *would* have to leave, one way or another. Veronyka had *just* found the strength to accept herself and who she was—with all the power and responsibility that came with it—and she couldn't allow her father's request to weaken her resolve. To make her doubt herself.

"You underestimate her," Tristan said, moving to stand next to Veronyka. "She doesn't fight because she thinks she has to." He looked down at her, fierce pride in his eyes. "She was fighting long before she was a Phoenix Rider, an Ashfire, or an heir to the throne. She fights because it's who she is, because she would never stand aside and let the people she loves come to harm."

Veronyka's chest swelled at his praise. Tristan knew her—better than anyone—and she was humbled at the vision of herself through his eyes. She straightened her spine, doing her best to be the person he thought she was.

She turned to her aunt. "What's happened?"

Alexiya sighed, staring down at a letter in her hands. "She's gone."

"Who?" Veronyka asked unnecessarily. Who else?

"Avalkyra. She's left the Eyrie."

But power over the many does not come without cost
for the few. Every defeat, every death . . . Nefyra
suffered for it. I suffered for it. Will she suffer too?

- CHAPTER 40 -
AVALKYRA

AVALKYRA AND SIDRA FLEW to Rushlea.

The Unnamed were spread all over Pyra, but several of their leaders were situated in the village, and Avalkyra intended to meet with them. She decided against bringing her flock, knowing they might cause more panic than good and that Onyx would be intimidating enough.

Besides, the entire point of this operation was to lure Veronyka into a face-to-face confrontation, and Avalkyra wanted to keep the size and scale of her horde a secret. At least for now. She was also certain that if she were surrounded by her strixes, Veronyka would insist on flying here in force, or not at all.

And that simply would not do.

Avalkyra had a bond to repair, and such a thing could be done only through touch, proximity, and eye contact. They were what made magic possible—what made *bonding* possible. There was no bond without extended time spent together. Emotionally, yes, but also physically. One could not develop a magical bond through letters and good intentions, after all. Even the apex group bond, which seemed to defy many of these rules, required Avalkyra's and Onyx's presence so the strixes could prostrate themselves and allow the connection to take hold.

With their bond fractured, Veronyka was a weak link or a loose thread, but if they reconnected and reopened their bond, there was a chance Veronyka could become so much more. If Avalkyra said the right words and made the right threats, she could have everything she'd ever wanted.

But if she failed . . . Veronyka could become apex herself and command a force of her own.

If she failed . . . she would have to get rid of Veronyka entirely.

"My queen, I do not wish to speak out of turn—"

"Then don't," Avalkyra said disinterestedly.

They had landed on the outskirts of town and were making their way to the agreed-upon meeting place—an old, dilapidated barn. Apparently, some of the villagers were actually helping the Unnamed hide in their basements and cellars; meanwhile, the Phoenix Riders kept sending aid and support in the face of their looting and attacks. There were apprentices stationed here even now. The village was divided, but Avalkyra would handle that. She would handle everything.

"Why bother?" Sidra blurted. Avalkyra paused, tilting her head to look at her. The bind was still in place, her loyalty unquestioned. But this outburst came from somewhere deep, some well of resolve and resistance Avalkyra hadn't known existed. She poked at it, peeling back the layers, but all she could find was fervent devotion and a powerful, though not unsurprising, hatred of Veronyka. Sidra's jealousy wasn't romance—she liked her women buxom and blond—but something closer to hero worship. Avalkyra was in her head, after all, and knew her adoration was purely platonic, but that didn't make it any less foolish.

With or without Veronyka, Sidra could never command Avalkyra's attention or affection.

"Speak plainly," Avalkyra ordered, and Sidra obeyed.

"You do not need a benex. You are powerful on your own and in control of the largest flock in the world. You need not lower yourself to reasoning with her. She is unworthy of your efforts. Would it not be better—easier—to kill her outright? I would do it gladly—"

"You will *not*," Avalkyra snapped. "She is mine to deal with. *Mine*. Do not speak unless spoken to, and do not presume to tell me where I should expend my efforts."

Sidra walked the remaining distance to the door in silence. It was a roiling, simmering silence, but she knew better than to speak.

Before they could knock, footsteps sounded from inside the building. The door creaked open, a beam of lantern light slicing through the darkness. The glow illuminated archers poised in the rafters above, their weapons trained on the newcomers.

Avalkyra had expected such a reception, which was why they'd dismounted around the bend and approached on foot.

"Two things," she said, before the man could speak or usher them inside. "Your lookouts will leave their weapons by the door or I will remove them by force."

The man glanced to Sidra, then back to Avalkyra. He nodded, waving to his people to lower their crossbows. He hesitated on the threshold. "That's one thing. What about the second?"

"There will be an additional member to our party."

At that, Onyx descended from the sky in a rush of wind, silent and terrifying. She landed in a crouch, crest tall and wing feathers spiked outward— like a predator ready to pounce.

The man cried out, staggering backward into the building, and Avalkyra followed in his wake.

Keep watch, she ordered Sidra, leaving room for Onyx to enter and slamming the door behind them.

Avalkyra strode into the center of the room, quite at her leisure, while Onyx followed more slowly. The strix had to crouch to fit under the doorframe, but when she straightened to her full and impressive height, her plumage gleaming in the flickering glow of the lanterns, the people inside gasped in fear. They backed against the walls, stumbling over benches and hay bales, giving Avalkyra and her bondmate the floor.

After sticking her beak into the corners and poking around the barn,

Onyx took to the rafters, scuttling like a beetle over a branch. The lookouts who had been poised there rushed to climb down, half falling to the ground and dropping their weapons by the door.

"Does anyone speak for you?" she demanded of the silent room.

Eventually, two people stepped forward—a man and a woman. "We represent the Rushlean faction of the Unnamed, but we have people all over Pyra."

Avalkyra nodded. "I hear you dislike the empire. I dislike the empire as well." She strode around the room, her boots crunching on straw, but otherwise all was silent. "I hear you dislike Phoenix Riders. . . . In that, we are also agreed."

"But you're one of 'em," someone interjected from the back of the crowd. The others parted to look at him, and he faltered, his gaze darting up to Onyx before he added, "Aren't you?"

"I *was* one of them . . . and they betrayed me. Scarred me"—she gestured to her face—"and left me for dead."

"So what? Just because we dislike these interlopers doesn't mean we can stop them," said the female leader, her arms crossed and her expression unimpressed. "The empire is mustering along the border as we speak. We nabbed one of their scouts—he's in the cellar. He says they're intending to march any day."

Avalkyra had suspected as much but hadn't had any new updates since Sidra was last in the capital. An empire scout could be very useful. . . . "And Phoenix Riders rule our skies, unapologetic and unchallenged."

"Not for long," Avalkyra said, her words hard. "I am master of a different kind of flock. I have a horde of strixes under my command. You are Pyraeans; you know your history. If phoenixes are Axura's so-called warriors of light, then we are Nox's servants instead. Whatever *they* stand for— empire rule, soldiers in your villages, and Riders patrolling your skies—then we are the opposite. I intend to use my considerable strength to stop both the empire and the Phoenix Riders . . . *violently*. I have no interest in peace treaties or alliances. I am interested in blood and redemption, and in a free and independent Pyra."

After all, there wouldn't *be* an empire once Avalkyra was done. She would tear it all down, brick by brick, monument by monument, until only the ashes remained.

You are the ashes, the dregs. . . . You're what's left.

They looked excited, eager, afraid. Like they wanted to cry her name or fall to their knees. Like they wanted to run and hide but didn't dare.

Avalkyra lifted her chin, surveying the group with her best imperious stare. "But first, I'll need your help."

Back outside, Sidra waited in the darkness, her shoulders pulled tight in an uneasy line.

What is it?

"Oxana senses something."

"An apprentice?" Avalkyra asked, lifting her head and extending her magic.

"No," Sidra whispered, just as a familiar ripple of awareness drew Avalkyra's attention to the forest. No, not an apprentice.

Onyx, she said, sending her bondmate after the sensation, though Avalkyra already knew what she would find.

There was a rustle of disturbed leaves and a crack and splinter of wood, then a muffled sound of pain. Onyx burst out of the trees, a human eavesdropper dangling from her beak.

"Doriyan, Rider of Daxos," Avalkyra said as Onyx landed before her. "I thought you were done sneaking and spying."

He had been following them since they'd left the Eyrie—just as Avalkyra had hoped he would. She had made sure that the Phoenix Rider scout saw her as well, so that both could corroborate that she was here, in Rushlea, and without her horde.

With nothing but a fractured bond between them, Avalkyra had to adjust her tactics and find new ways to get in touch with Veronyka.

Onyx stomped irritably, wanting to snap Doriyan's neck and tear his flesh, or simply sink her claws into his body and drain him dry—but

Avalkyra shook her head. She knew her bondmate was getting tired of always being held back and pushed down.

Soon, Avalkyra promised her. *Soon you will have your fill.*

With a snort, Onyx tossed the man to the ground like a rag doll, where he sprawled into the dirt. Then she claimed a perch up in the trees, alert and watchful. Doriyan's phoenix was no doubt somewhere nearby, as was Oxana, but Avalkyra reminded Onyx again that now was not the time. She bristled at the restraint, scraping her claws in the bark of the branch beneath her in long, savage swipes.

Even his brief contact with Onyx had put a sheen of sweat across Doriyan's skin, and his muscles trembled with the effort of getting to his knees. Sidra did not look much better.

"No farther," Avalkyra said softly, and he froze, huddled on all fours like the dog he was.

To her surprise, he didn't spare her a moment's glance. His focus was entirely on the woman next to her.

"Sidra," he said, voice pleading. "You don't have to do this anymore. You're a *Phoenix Rider.* You don't have to serve her—you don't have to serve *that.*" He flung a hand at Onyx. "I can see it's killing you. It's killing *her.*"

Avalkyra was confused for a second; then she realized he must be referring to Sidra's bondmate. It was true that Sidra looked worse for wear these days, and her phoenix was positively droopy whenever Avalkyra laid eyes on her. Doriyan had probably noted both when he'd followed Sidra from Aura Nova.

"I have a message for your new master," Avalkyra said.

He frowned. "I have no master."

"Don't you?" she asked with a smile. "That's what happens to all strays. Cast aside by one master, they go seeking another."

He lifted his chin. "I was never cast aside." He turned his gaze to Sidra. "I *left,*" he said entreatingly, as if to show her that she could do the same.

"That's right," Avalkyra jumped in. "You left *her.* Shows what your loyalty is worth."

Sidra's face faltered—she'd never thought about it that way before. Avalkyra grinned. She would now.

"If you're loyal to Veronyka," she continued, "then you'll deliver my message. Tell her that I wish to speak to her here, in Rushlea. Tell her to come alone. If she fails to heed my request, the village will pay the price."

"Why should I play your errand boy?" he asked, getting cautiously to his feet.

Avalkyra tilted her head, considered breaking into his mind. He had rejected her bind once before, but she had been bondless then. Hordeless. She was *apexaeris* now; she could crack him open like an egg if she wanted to, but she fought the urge. Veronyka would sense it and distrust his message at once.

"I plan to offer her terms, that's why." He looked surprised at that. She shrugged. "You are scattered and outnumbered, and the empire is about to march. You need any advantage or opportunity you can get. Do you really have a choice?"

He took a step back from them, then another.

Sidra reached for the bow and arrows slung across her back, but Avalkyra held her in place. Onyx, too, tensed on the branch above, ready to dive.

Leave him.

Doriyan paused, unnerved by her apparent restraint.

"Go on," Avalkyra encouraged, all benevolence and grace. She need not wrench a promise out of him. . . . She knew her message would be delivered whether Doriyan liked it or not. "Run back to your master like I know you will."

He hesitated a moment longer, then there was a gust of wind as his phoenix landed between them. Doriyan was still climbing into the saddle when the creature took off again.

Sidra watched him disappear into the sky.

He would rush to Veronyka's side to share whatever scraps of information he'd overheard inside the barn—nothing Avalkyra was worried about—and while he was at it, he'd have no choice but to tell her about Avalkyra's message.

Veronyka *would* come. Avalkyra might not hold the same sway over her she once had, but still, when she beckoned, Veronyka came—as long as there were innocents involved. Avalkyra had proved it time and again. And whatever Veronyka might want personally, the Phoenix Riders couldn't ignore this chance.

They would attempt to use the opportunity to plead their case, to beg for friendship, for mercy, for whatever might save them.

Little did they know, there *was* no saving them. What Avalkyra wanted and needed was their complete and utter destruction. She suspected even Veronyka knew that, and still . . . she tried.

"Come, Sidra," Avalkyra said, turning back toward the barn and, more specifically, its cellar. "I have a task for you, and you'll have to leave at once."

She followed, but not before glancing back over her shoulder. "What if he doesn't deliver the message?"

"He will," Avalkyra said smugly. "He still has hope."

Foolish hope. Avalkyra's favorite kind.

In the study of Axura and Nox, little attention is paid to the importance of balance.

Yes, Axura *must be* victorious, elsewise Nox would devour all—as is her nature—and shroud the world in night.

But Axura's victory did not bring us endless day, did it? No, we still require that darkness, for it reminds us of the importance of light. During the night, the moon thinks of the sun. And during the day, the sun remembers the moon.

Too much of either would lead to ruin, and so the two will battle each other for all eternity.

That is the balance.

—"The Importance of Balance," from *Essays on Magic*, by Morra, priestess of Axura, 166 AE

*To be apex is to shoulder the glory and the blame. To
be at fault. To be the first and last defense.*

- CHAPTER 41 -
TRISTAN

VERONYKA SHOOK TRISTAN AWAKE in the darkness.

"Rider Council meeting," she said urgently, tugging Tristan's hand. As
they exited their tent, dawn was little more than a gray haze in among the
towering trees.

He didn't think she'd managed a wink of sleep. She'd spent half the
night trying to connect with Val, and when that failed, she'd spent the rest
tossing and turning, fuming about it.

Tristan was secretly relieved. He knew it was cowardly and selfish, but
his own sleep had been brief and uneasy, broken up with half-formed nightmares of Val bursting out of thin air and stabbing Veronyka in the heart. He
wished the bond between them would dissolve entirely.

They rushed to Agneta's house, the rest of Haven still sleepy and silent,
and filed into the commander's room. He was sitting up in bed, Hestia next
to him, with Alexiya and Theryn in attendance as well. Tristan shut the
door and walked into the center of the room.

It was still hard to see his father like this, expression drawn in pain and
his usual leather armor or finely woven tunics replaced by some thread-
bare nightshirt someone had given him. His face had more color than the
last time Tristan had visited, however, and his bedside was surrounded by

papers and empty teacups. There was a window against the far wall, its shutters thrown wide to reveal Maximian perched comfortably on an outside branch.

"It seems both our enemies are on the move," the commander said as everyone stood around his bed. His voice was strong, even if his appearance was not. He reached for a letter on the top of his stack, wincing slightly. "As you all know, Avalkyra left the Eyrie yesterday, and according to my contact in Aura Nova, the empire is preparing to march as well."

"But their armies couldn't possibly have gathered that quickly," Tristan said, glancing to Theryn for confirmation. He was a soldier, after all—or had been—but it was the commander who spoke again.

"They will make do with the forces immediately available to them. Lord Rolan's death has achieved more than his fearmongering while he was alive ever did. They are frightened, and even those who do not truly believe we mean harm can't argue against the threat we pose. They know we are responsible for his death, and Sidra's attack on the Grand Council made us an easy scapegoat."

"How many?" Theryn asked, his expression grave.

The commander glanced down at the letter. "General Rast himself will be leading the attack and is taking whatever soldiers were on hand in the capital or within a day's march. Their best guess is five hundred, give or take."

Five hundred. It was a fraction of what the empire could muster if given more time, yet it was still too many. Rolan's soldiers had done plenty of damage over the past few months, and he'd never sent such a large number—and certainly not all together.

"That will just be the initial march. The rest of the army will continue to gather outside Aura Nova, and if we prove . . . *resistant*, well, the empire could send nearly two thousand before the week is out."

"Resistant. You mean, if we fight to defend our lands?" Alexiya asked heatedly.

"Or if Avalkyra does," Veronyka said. All heads turned in her direction. "Whatever we want, Avalkyra will not let them leave without a fight—even if it's one she can't win. She'll attack and antagonize and blame it on us, like she's done with Sidra. Which means the empire will just send more soldiers against us."

"Not to mention all the civilians caught in between," Tristan muttered. "Can't we tell the council? Explain to them that there are other forces at play here?"

The commander shook his head. "To them, she is one of us—whatever she rides. I'm afraid they see us all as the same thing: Mages. The council has voted, and it cannot be overturned. The general is the sole person who could negotiate a treaty now, and it would be a temporary measure. A wartime cease-fire. Only then could they call another Grand Council meeting and hold another vote."

Veronyka actually perked up. "So we'd just have to convince *him* instead of the whole council?"

"He is not a man to make peace or cut deals," Theryn warned.

There was a soft knocking on the door.

"Are you expecting someone else?" Tristan asked.

"Come in," his father called, rather than answering, and the door swung wide to reveal Doriyan silhouetted in the frame. He looked almost exactly as he had when they'd first met, his hair wild and his eyes wilder. "Doriyan arrived from Pyra barely thirty minutes ago. I wanted to get him fed before we—"

"Doriyan?" repeated Theryn, his voice unnervingly flat. He was staring fixedly at the new arrival, his face a mask of open hostility.

Standing next to her brother, Alexiya looked between them before realization dawned. It struck Tristan a moment later. Doriyan was there the day Pheronia died and Veronyka was whisked away.

Alexiya reached for her brother's arm, but she met with air as Theryn lunged for Doriyan, his hands closing around the man's throat and slamming him into the wall. The entire house shook, and Tristan wondered idly at the maximum capacity for these aerial treehouses as he darted across the room.

Theryn's teeth were bared, his arms corded with muscle as he attempted to choke the life out of Doriyan, who despite his bulging eyes and stumbling feet scrambling for purchase, did not fight back.

There was a shriek somewhere outside, and the commander shouted something. Beating wings and scraping talons on the roof above told Tristan that Daxos must have been perched nearby and, sensing Doriyan's distress, had rushed to his bondmate's defense. Maximian, also nearby, had likely intervened.

Tristan got his hands on Theryn's shoulders, while Alexiya gripped one arm and Veronyka the other. Veronyka was wide-eyed with shock, and Tristan too was surprised at the potency of Theryn's anger, the way it rolled off him in waves.

Together they pulled, allowing enough room for Doriyan to breathe around Theryn's fingers, though Veronyka's father continued to struggle.

Slowly he came back to himself, noticing the pressure on his arms and the surge of people around him. He released Doriyan's neck as if it were hot to the touch, his fingers splayed as he took a halting step backward. Tristan let him but remained close to his side, a hand on his shoulder in case he decided to make another move.

Theryn didn't resist it, but the look he tossed Doriyan was filled with molten anger so powerful that Veronyka swayed on her feet. She had been standing between the two men, and now bent to rest her hands on her knees.

Are you okay? Tristan asked, certain this had something to do with shadow magic—he himself felt a little woozy—but Veronyka was already straightening. She nodded.

Doriyan's expression was bleak. He remained against the wall, body slumped and chest heaving as he caught his breath.

"He was following orders," Alexiya said to her brother, before moving to check on Doriyan. "Like all of us."

"He watched me weep over a cold, dead baby that I believed was my own child," Theryn spat, his voice ragged. "And he did *nothing*."

"That's true," Veronyka said, moving into her father's eye line until he was forced to drag his burning gaze off Doriyan and look at her. The violence in his expression dimmed. "But afterward, he was ordered to hunt you down and kill you—*and he did nothing*."

Theryn was apparently startled into silence, and beneath Tristan's hand, the tension left his shoulders.

Veronyka turned to the commander and the room at large. "This is Avalkyra's doing," she said. "We have to stop her. *I* have to stop her. Doriyan, please—tell me you have something."

"I know where Avalkyra is," he said, his voice rough from the recent attack to his vocal cords. "And I know what she wants."

He was looking at Veronyka.

"No," Theryn whispered.

"What did she say?" Veronyka pressed, ignoring her father and moving closer to Doriyan, blocking Theryn from the conversation.

"She wants to speak to you in person—alone," Doriyan replied. "To discuss terms. She has joined forces with the Unnamed and taken control of Rushlea. If you don't meet her there, she will take it out on the villagers."

The Unnamed. Veronyka had already told him that the Rushlean farmers who had accosted them weeks back had allied with raiders and bandits and turned themselves into a full-fledged, homegrown militia—but their alliance with Val was new. And troubling.

"That is exactly the kind of stunt she used to pull with Pheronia," Theryn said pleadingly to the commander, his hands clenched into fists, and his hair askew. He looked like a man on the edge of a precipice, his patience fraying down to its last threads. "It will not save the villagers. It will do nothing but feed into Avalkyra's egomaniacal needs."

The commander pinched the bridge of his nose. "It is not just the villagers at risk. Some of our apprentices are there."

"What? Who?" Tristan demanded.

"I'm not exactly sure. The oldest recruits . . . They were sent several days ago to help with the usual supply runs and to make sure those fleeing the attack on the Eyrie were safe and settled."

"What if we went in full force?" Alexiya asked.

"The Unnamed," the commander said, turning to Doriyan. "How many are there?"

"Difficult to know for certain," Doriyan replied. "I've seen no more than forty or fifty at any one time, but I overheard some of their meeting with Avalkyra. I did not hear exact details, but I think they mean to ambush you. They could use the mine. Not only are there two entrances next to Rushlea, but it connects to tunnels all over Pyrmont. They could bring in forces from anywhere, and in any number."

"This is too dangerous," the commander said, shaking his head. "There's too much we don't know. We could be flying into a trap."

"Of course it's a trap!" Theryn burst out. "She's sending Doriyan to do her dirty work, just like before."

"Even if it is," Veronyka said steadily, "I want to go."

"Why would you risk it?" Hestia asked, speaking for the first time. "What could she possibly say to you?"

Veronyka's eyes sparked. "I don't care what she says, I care that she's there *without* her flock."

"That *is* what Fallon reported," the commander said thoughtfully. He looked at Doriyan.

"I followed her directly from the Eyrie," he confirmed. "Besides Sidra and Oxana, Avalkyra has only the strix she rides."

Tristan's heart started thumping in his chest, feeding off the spark of excitement coming from Veronyka.

"We may never get another shot at her this vulnerable," she said. "She left her best defenses behind so that I'd come, so that I'd feel like I was safe from her—but *she* isn't safe from *me*."

"What do you mean?" Alexiya asked, but Tristan thought he was following Veronyka's line of thought.

"The Grand Council might not be unified in their support of me, but they *would be* in their hatred of her," Veronyka continued. "Think about it. She wants me there to fight me or capture me or force me to do something I don't want to do. But what if we go there to capture *her* instead?"

"Then we offer her to the empire as a bargaining chip," Tristan said, and Veronyka nodded eagerly. "It might be the one move that could guarantee peace on both fronts."

"Surely General Rast could be convinced to call a temporary cease-fire if he was able to hand over the greatest war criminal in the empire's history?" Veronyka asked.

The commander leaned back against his pillows, blinking as though stunned—but Tristan recognized it as his thinking face. He was rifling through all the angles, all the possibilities.

"Meanwhile, we could reclaim the Eyrie and hunt down any remaining strixes," Tristan said carefully, taking up the thread. "They'd be leaderless. We'll be able to keep Pyra safe and have time to prepare for the next Grand Council meeting. They'll see that without Avalkyra and Rolan, there are no attacks. That we want peace."

The commander looked at Veronyka, his gaze measuring. "How?"

That almost sounded like submission. There was a level of respect between them that had grown in recent weeks, a give-and-take that Tristan was rather envious of. Veronyka deferred to him as commander of the Phoenix Riders, but that didn't mean she would step aside or follow orders like an obedient soldier anymore. Furthermore, he included her and listened to her opinions—and she did her best to *convince* him of them, not merely barking her plans out as a command, daring him to contradict her.

It was smooth and subtle, and if Tristan didn't know any better, he'd have thought they'd been working together for years.

"I would go with a small force—just our patrol," she said, indicating Tristan. She glanced apologetically at Alexiya and Doriyan. "She knows you both and would sense you more easily than the others, who are strangers to her."

"Sense us?" Alexiya repeated, brow furrowed. Veronyka gave her a significant look before turning her attention to the others.

"The reason we can't sneak up on her or fly with a large force is because Avalkyra is a shadowmage." She paused. "We both are."

Everyone in the room stared at her—Theryn and Hestia with confusion, Alexiya and Doriyan with grim understanding, and the commander with something like resignation. As if he couldn't expect things to get any worse or any weirder.

"That's how she was able to bond to a strix in the first place," Veronyka explained. "And it's how she's communicated with and controlled her patrol members in the past."

"She can control people?" the commander said, clearly uneasy. Despite his apparent shock, Tristan had to hand it to him—his father was taking it better than *he* had when he'd found out.

Veronyka nodded. "*Some* people. I doubt she ever managed it with you," she said with the ghost of a smile. "It involves a level of familiarity and openness to be effective."

"Her patrol, you said," he continued, glancing at Doriyan. His head was bowed, expression ashamed. "That makes a great deal of sense."

"She can also use the magic to communicate with people. As can I." She halted here, her eyes boring into the commander, as if willing him to understand something.

"To communicate . . . ," he repeated, his gaze growing distant. Thoughtful. "Outside the Grand Council chamber—Rolan's blade. I did not *see* it, but somehow . . . I knew it was there, knew it was coming."

"Because *I* saw it," Veronyka said.

Tristan whirled around to gape at her. She'd saved his father's life? Heedless of the others in the room, he crossed the distance between them and wrapped his arms around her.

"Thank you," he said, pressing his lips against her forehead. She seemed embarrassed—and maybe a little pleased—at his gratitude.

"That is remarkable," Hestia murmured as Tristan drew back.

"Indeed," the commander said, his eyes surprisingly soft as he looked at the pair of them. "You have my thanks as well."

Veronyka gave him a small smile, then cleared her throat. "As I was say-ing . . . she knows Alexiya and Doriyan and would be more likely to sense their presence, which would give us away."

Tristan's heart sank. He knew what would come next. "But Tristan," his father said, not missing a beat, "she knows him as well."

"Yes, she knows Tristan," Veronyka said carefully, looking between father and son. "Which is why he'll act as lookout in case she decides to call her flock after all."

Tristan opened his mouth to argue, then stared down at his feet. Lookout? *Trust me,* Veronyka said softly, speaking into Tristan's mind.

He relaxed his shoulders. *I do.*

"But . . . how do you intend to capture her?" asked Alexiya. "Even if you manage to sneak your patrol into the village, they'll need to focus on containing her reinforcements. It'll just be you against Avalkyra Ashfire mounted on a strix."

"Plus Sidra," added Doriyan. "I don't know what her role will be, but she's dangerous."

Veronyka frowned, her gaze growing distant as she considered. She didn't take offense at the implication that she couldn't defeat Val one-on-one, as Tristan probably would have done. She had learned from previous mistakes and would never take Val lightly.

What they needed was something Val wouldn't expect, a secret weapon, a . . . He had it.

Spotting his father's saddlebags and other possessions stacked against the wall, Tristan bent and rummaged until he found what he sought: an elegant walking stick.

He lifted it, triumphant. "She'll use this."

As everyone watched, Tristan unscrewed the finely carved phoenix-head handle, plucking out one of the darts contained within.

Veronyka's face lit with excitement as she stepped forward and took the projectile from Tristan's hand. "Hestia," she said, "can you give us a potent sleeping draft? Something that works instantaneously?"

She seemed taken aback by the question but nodded. "I have the necessary ingredients in my travel kit."

Everyone turned to the commander, hopeful.

Except for Theryn. "Don't tell me you're actually considering this," he said stonily.

"You *are* the heir to the throne, Veronyka," the commander said. "Your plan is worth considering, but I'm not sure we can risk you."

"You won't be able to pull it off without me," she said, arms crossed and chin jutting out. "She asked to see *me*. She'll probably shoot anyone else on sight."

"It's still too great a risk," Theryn said desperately.

"And what do you think, Tristan?"

Tristan jerked his head up, surprised to be asked his opinion. Had the commander sensed his frustration at playing such a small part in the plan? Was he trying to exploit it?

"I think it's better than sitting here, waiting. I think it's better than monitoring her movements but not acting on them. I'd follow Veronyka anywhere, and I think you know that."

The commander raised his chin. "Will you give us the room?" he asked, turning away from Tristan to address the others.

Doriyan made for the door at once, followed by Hestia, who murmured something about taking a look at his neck. Alexiya left next, keeping a wary eye on her brother—and her body between him and Doriyan. Theryn, however, glared at Cassian the whole way out. Veronyka took a step to follow them, but hesitated.

It's okay, Tristan reassured her, though he didn't feel terribly reassured himself. He suspected a fight was coming, and he honestly didn't feel up to yelling at his convalescent father again.

But he would if it meant supporting Veronyka. He would if it meant finishing this. Finishing *her*. He was sick and tired of the way Val held sway over so many lives, but he hated the way she loomed over Veronyka most of all.

"Son . . . ," the commander began as soon as Veronyka had left.

Tristan steeled his resolve and looked up, ready to go on the offensive. He was shocked into silence by the tears sparkling in his father's eyes.

"How am I to do it?"

"Do what?" Tristan managed, his throat suddenly tight.

"How am I to sit here and watch you go?"

Tristan dropped his head, searching for words. "It's a good plan," he whispered.

"She had a good plan too. Your mother. Sometimes it simply does not matter."

"We might fail," Tristan conceded. "But that doesn't mean we shouldn't try."

His father huffed out a sound that was almost a laugh but lacked humor. "It wasn't so long ago that *I* was champing at the bit to fight, to take action. Then, somewhere along the way, I decided I had too much to lose. Then I lost, and I thought I would feel less afraid after that . . . but now I cling more desperately to what's left."

Tristan considered that, thinking about the ways his father had shown his fear: slowing him down and pushing him aside, the countless moments of grudging concession and convoluted approval. The suggestion that Tristan should be steward, that he was not yet ready to lead. All out of fear.

He closed his eyes. "I need you to stop," he said, opening them again. His father's face was pinched, his hands clenched into fists in the bedding. "You're not keeping me safe. You're holding me back."

"I never meant to do it, you know."

"To hold me back?"

"To try to shape you in my image when you were so clearly born in your mother's. She died saving lives, and just because she didn't save them *all* doesn't mean what she did was foolish or wrong. You are a living, breathing part of her—and I am proud."

"Oh, I . . ." Tristan swallowed thickly. "Thank you."

They both avoided looking at each other, and when his father eventually spoke again, his voice was back to its usual, crisp tenor. "This plan—are you ready to risk your life on it? *Her* life?"

Tristan looked up, nodded.

The commander sighed. "So be it."

I am loath to burden her so. But my back is bent; my soul is weary. . . . There is no other way.

- CHAPTER 42 -
VERONYKA

VERONYKA DID HER BEST *not* to eavesdrop on the closed-door conversation between Tristan and his father. Despite the close quarters of her grandmother's house, the walls were thick and covered in tapestries and other textiles that dampened sound, but while their words were muffled, she still had her bond to Tristan.

She'd expected a steady stream of anger and frustration—arguing, it seemed, was their preferred mode of communication—but she sensed feelings closer to confusion and grief. She could have pushed to hear more, but it was one thing to overhear a loud voice through a closed door and quite another to deliberately spy on Tristan's mind.

When the door opened, Veronyka whirled around in surprise. They hadn't spoken long at all, and Tristan—who strode purposefully from the room, leaving his father behind—looked slightly out of sorts. He stood straight-backed and square-shouldered, as usual, but his eyes were red, and his mouth turned down at the corners.

He seemed lost for a moment, and then his gaze landed on her. The shaky tenor of their link as he struggled against his feelings strengthened and solidified. Determination flared between them.

He nodded. "Time to go."

A fire burst to life inside her, equal parts fear and anticipation. Val might have a few tricks up her sleeve, but Veronyka had some tricks of her own.

While Hestia had remained upstairs with Agneta and Cassian, Alexiya and Theryn—along with Doriyan, who stood off to the side—were waiting for them at the bottom of the stairs, accompanied by Tristan's patrol, Sev, and Kade.

They had all heard about the late-night news and the early-morning meeting by now and were eager for an update.

"Who's on patrol?" Tristan asked as he and Veronyka came to stand before their fellow Riders.

"It was supposed to be Alexiya," Anders said, "but Jonny covered for her."

"I didn't think it wise to leave just yet," she said, her narrowed gaze flicking between Theryn and Doriyan.

"Oh, relax," Theryn said, voice tired. "I'm not a rabid dog that needs muzzling."

Alexiya raised her brows. "All evidence to the contrary." She actually smiled a little. "I've never seen you like that before. . . . Need I remind you we had to *drag you* off of him?"

"No, you do not," Theryn muttered, darting an uncomfortable look at Veronyka.

It had been quite the shock to see him lunge at Doriyan, ready to choke the life from him then and there. He might have been silent and stoic, but there was clearly more happening beneath the surface. Even though she'd known he'd been a soldier, she had truly *seen* it in that moment. He'd been out for blood, and despite Alexiya's suggestion that it was out of character for him, it was clear to Veronyka that it wasn't the first time he'd attacked with the intent to truly harm. Even kill.

His rage had washed over her, through her, and it had been harrowing.

She'd seen flashes of his grief, old and new—losing Pheronia *and* her in a single, black night. Then reliving it over and over again in the years since. Doriyan had been a trigger, a reminder of that pain, and it had overwhelmed and overtaken him in a sudden, powerful rush.

Veronyka didn't know how she could leave him now, with that poison swirling inside him. But she also knew she couldn't stay.

Tristan got straight to the point. "The commander has approved a special mission," he announced to his patrol. "Prepare to depart as soon as possible."

They arrived at camp and packed up their supplies, Veronyka's mind racing. If things went well, they'd deal with Val *and* the empire in a single move. After that, they'd be hunting down strixes and planning for another meeting with the Grand Council.

Her heart fluttered at the possibility of avoiding open warfare even as her stomach sank at the realization that however things shook out—good or bad—she wouldn't have cause to return to Arboria or Haven anytime soon.

After insisting that Doriyan sleep and recover before joining them in Pyra, Tristan asked Alexiya to carry word to Prosperity.

"Tell Beryk about the empire's impending march and see if he can contact their leaders. We might be able to forestall them if we request an audience to discuss terms. They'll assume we mean to surrender—let them. I don't want to promise Avalkyra until I'm certain we can deliver her."

Alexiya was just about to mount up when Agneta approached her. Alexiya stiffened—clearly expecting a fight or rebuke—but Agneta only pulled her into a gruff hug. Alexiya relaxed into it for a breath before disentangling herself and climbing into the saddle. She nodded at Veronyka across the campsite, and then she was off.

Finished packing, Veronyka wandered over to Agneta, who stood with Theryn. He had a comforting arm around her shoulders.

"I have to go too," Veronyka said, her throat dry.

Agneta turned pleading eyes on Veronyka. "Do you?" she whispered, taking hold of Veronyka's hands. "You are so very young, the same as your parents were when this war started. And look what happened."

Veronyka felt as if she'd been fighting this war—against Val, against the past and the ramifications of it—her entire life. She was better prepared now than she had ever been, and the only way to stop this vicious cycle was to put an end to it once and for all.

To Veronyka's surprise, Theryn didn't use the opportunity to take up his mother's cause and argue against her leaving. Instead, he pried Agneta's hands from Veronyka's. "She has made her choice," he said.

Veronyka found herself swallowing around a lump in her throat. "This isn't about *choice*—about *choosing* a war or a throne or an empire. It's about what's right and what's wrong." Distantly Veronyka sensed other people watching them, but she didn't care. "They want to take our freedom from us. Not just Phoenix Riders, but all animages. I will do everything in my power to make sure that doesn't happen. I will make whatever sacrifice. I pray it doesn't come to bloodshed, but if it does, I will stand and fight."

"Then I've already lost you the same way I lost her."

Silence pressed in on Veronyka, masking everything but the beat of her heart and the sound of her breaths rattling in and out of her chest. "You haven't lost me."

"Maybe not yet—but I will." The words were jagged, scraping at Veronyka's heart. "Unless you stay here with us," he finished softly. "With me."

"Don't," Veronyka said harshly. Theryn's mouth snapped shut, his jaw working, while Agneta looked between them, expression frantic.

Veronyka turned away. Perhaps it was foolish to hope that he would really *see* her so soon after they'd met. That he'd understand her. That he'd support her and *help her* instead of dragging her down with overprotectiveness and guilt.

"Theryn," Agneta fluttered, taking Veronyka's hands again. "Stop her. You can't just—"

"Let her go, Mother."

Veronyka whirled back around. "Is that what you did when Pheronia continued to fight?"

"What?" he asked, blinking in confusion.

Veronyka lifted her chin. "Let her go?"

He seemed completely taken aback by that. "I never . . . I always . . ."

"Why was she alone that night?" Veronyka demanded. She didn't know where the words—or the anger—came from, but suddenly they were bubbling up and spilling out. "Where were you while my mother bled out in the arms of the woman who killed her?"

Theryn's face went slack, his eyes wide and unseeing. "I begged her to leave with me. To go into hiding. After months, she finally agreed. I wanted to leave before the fighting started, but I think she delayed on purpose. She kept sending me off—to ready the horses, to carry the trunks. I think . . ." He licked his lips. "I think she wanted to see her sister one last time."

"Maybe she wouldn't have sent you off," Veronyka said, her throat tight, "if you'd agreed to fight *with* her instead of against her."

To that he had no response. He wilted, no longer her long-lost father with kind eyes and strong shoulders, but an old, sad man. Defeated. Broken.

Veronyka sighed and turned to her grandmother again. "Thank you for giving me this."

"Giving you what, child?" Agneta asked, face pinched with worry and tears dampening her cheeks. She reached for Veronyka again, tugging at her tunic and smoothing her hair.

"Something like a home," Veronyka said, forcing a smile on her lips. "Something like a family."

Agneta's eyes welled up again, but she didn't break down. She sniffed loudly and straightened. "Mind you don't forget to eat dinner," she said, some of her usual stern brusqueness back in place. "There's plenty of food, so take what you need. Take extra."

Veronyka smiled genuinely then. "I promise I'll send word." She noticed that the clearing around them was filled with people now—Tristan and the rest of his patrol, Sev and Kade, as well as some of the inhabitants of Haven. "As soon as we're finished. With any luck . . . that'll be the end of it."

"Send a fast pigeon, won't you?" Agneta whispered.

Veronyka nodded before wrapping her arms around the woman in a tight hug. When she pulled away, she found Xephyra edging nearer, worry filtering through the bond. Veronyka wanted to bury her face in her bondmate's neck, but she fought the urge and leapt onto her back instead. Avoiding Theryn's heavy gaze, she settled in the saddle and waved at her grandmother. The rest of the Riders mounted up, and with Tristan in the lead, they took to the sky.

As they whipped through the forest, an ache started building in Veronyka's chest. It was part nostalgia for a life never lived and part longing for a future that might never come.

But as their flight turned north and they made their way back into Pyra, Veronyka's focus sharpened and her hesitance evaporated.

She didn't know if she was ready to face Val, but she was about to find out.

Like all power, magic on such a scale can achieve
wondrous and terrible things.

- CHAPTER 43 -
SPARROW

SPARROW AWOKE WITH CHIRP in her hair and a grizzly bear at her back.

No . . . not Chirp—her heart throbbed—but Fine Fellow. And not a grizzly bear but a person, someone sleeping nearby and snoring louder than a rockslide. Sparrow could say that with certainty, having very recently experienced the sound. Then the night came back to her, and she craned her neck, listening for the source of the echoing, rumbling noise.

Sparrow could sense Ignix near the back of the cave, while Jax was close enough to touch, and no doubt the reason she was so warm and comfortable.

So the snoring . . . it must be Elliot.

Fife croaked an irritated affirmation—she wasn't the only one who'd been wakened by the racket—and Sparrow slumped back against the soft blankets, a small, tentative smile settling on her face.

Elliot had come back for her. Sparrow's chest ached with the truth of it, strange and overwhelming. No one ever came back for her.

Another impossibly loud snort cut through the silence of the morning, and next to her, Jax expelled a sigh.

Sparrow smiled more widely, but apparently Fife did not find it amusing. A gust of wind rippled over her face, followed by a cry of pain and rustle of movement, as if Elliot had just been brought abruptly—and painfully—to wakefulness.

"Bloody raven," he mumbled, and she heard him swipe and swat helplessly at the air, because of course Fife was already back on Sparrow's other side, smug and self-important as usual.

A low warbling sound came from Jax—something that sounded very like laughter.

"You're just gonna let him treat me like that, are you?" Elliot asked, speaking to Jax, who chirruped and rustled his feathers. There was a pause, then—"I was? Did I wake . . . ? Uh, morning, Sparrow."

There was a scrape of boot on stone, and footsteps coming Sparrow's way. She felt nervous all of a sudden, and tried to sit upright again, though her balance was off, thanks to her arm. She managed it, but then her head swam with the movement. She thought she was about to topple over again, but then Elliot was there with a bracing hand on her shoulder.

"Maybe this will help," he said, pressing something long and smooth into her hands. *My spear.*

"I thought . . ." She swallowed, her throat tight. "I thought I lost it."

"Well, I found it," Elliot said, his tone light—but she thought he sounded pleased. Proud, even.

Sparrow clutched the stick against her chest, feeling foolish and embarrassed but also immensely happy. She had the sense Elliot was studying her closely. She did not like it. No doubt she looked even worse than she felt. Her arm ached something fierce, but she refused to acknowledge it or ask for more medicine. She also felt light-headed—luckily, it was her stomach that did the asking. It grumbled loudly, and Elliot laughed.

"Food," he said firmly. There was noise: sloshing water and the clatter of tin, a dull thumping that sounded like a wooden spoon, and the crinkle of waxed paper. Jax's talons scraped into the earth next to her, and she suspected he was going to help Elliot with the fire.

"Thanks, Jaxon," she said. "For keeping me warm."

He preened—satisfaction emanating from him—and Sparrow smiled. Jax was the most unguarded phoenix she'd ever met, and the easiest to read even when his mind wasn't open to her. Everything in his sounds and demeanor was earnest and warm. Elliot, on the other hand, was prickly as a porcupine.

Humans, she thought darkly, and Fine Fellow croaked his agreement.

Sparrow yawned so widely her jaw creaked, and she thought about lying down again but knew she needed to eat to get her strength up.

"Sorry," Elliot said, his voice moving as he finished what he was doing by the fire and sat down. "I was keeping watch and must have drifted off. I don't normally snore." Fife huffed skeptically, and Sparrow swore she could *hear* Elliot's grin. "That's enough out of you," he said with false sternness. "My ear's bleeding, you savage creature."

Fife snapped his beak several times and croaked again. "Fine Fellow says it's *his* ears that are bleeding, what with you snortin' like a pig and all."

There was a stunned silence, then a bark of laughter. Sparrow grinned stupidly.

"I have a feeling you embellished that a bit," Elliot said fondly. "Never known a raven to speak so eloquently."

"Fine Fellow says you haven't known enough ravens, then," Sparrow replied innocently. It was true she'd dressed it up a little—only phoenixes could speak with words like that, but if Sparrow got to know an animal well enough, she could easily put into words the sentiments they put into her mind.

"I guess not," Elliot conceded, laughter in his voice. "Shame, because I do love a smart-mouthed bird."

Jax and Fife squawked at the remark, but Sparrow found her cheeks heating. She was a bird too, was she not? Or at least named for one. And it wouldn't be the first time she'd been called smart-mouthed . . . but it would be the first time it felt like a compliment.

Elliot cleared his throat, and she wondered if he'd meant it that way too.

"Chirp . . . was he a sparrow?"

Sparrow was surprised by the question. "Yes."

"Is that where your name comes from?" There were sounds again, stirring and scraping—food being prepared.

She shrugged. "Sorta. Sparrows were always my favorite growing up—meaning no disrespect," she added to Fife, who accepted her apology with good grace. "I used to always have a flock of them with me wherever I went, so people started calling me Sparrow. But then once Chirp was born—I had his ma in my flock for a while—he became my special friend. They were city birds, my flock, but I was ready for the country. Chirp was the only one brave enough to come with me."

Sparrow didn't talk about her time in Aura Nova much. After the temple, after her parents had given her up. It made her feel raw. Exposed.

But then Elliot was moving again, and she sensed him crouch in front of her, his body blocking the heat of the fire. "Here," he murmured, plucking the spear from her hand and giving her a warm bowl. "It's on the ground next to you. And breakfast is hot, so make sure to eat slow."

Sparrow crooked the bowl against her chest using the hand in her sling, the warmth seeping through the fabric of her shirt, then slowly stirred its contents, breathing deep the scent of honey and toasted oats. She wanted to gobble it down, and her first mouthful was both scalding hot and far too large, so it was lucky Elliot was there to clap her on the back and hand her a cup of water.

"Slow," he said firmly, but not without kindness, and Sparrow sighed and settled in to wait.

"Maybe I should be Raven now," she said thoughtfully as Fife perched on her shoulder and helped himself to several beakfuls of her breakfast. "Since I'm keeping different company."

Elliot sucked in a breath of air to speak—then didn't. Sparrow fidgeted, wanting her spear again to spin and twirl to channel her restless energy.

"But then what happens when you become a Phoenix Rider?" he asked after a time, and Sparrow's lungs hitched in her chest. How did he know it was her dearest wish? A stupid, foolish wish, because she was poor and blind, and who would ever choose her?

"W-what do you mean?" she asked, still breathless.

She heard him shift—a shrug. "Well, we'd have to call you Phoenix, then, wouldn't we? Seems a bit confusing. I say you stick with Sparrow." He paused. "I like it."

Sparrow cheeks warmed. "I like it too," she agreed.

There were several moments of comfortable silence, then—

"Look," Elliot said, moving closer to her. "Sparrow, I want to say sorry. I never should have—"

Sparrow shook her head resolutely. "Don't."

He made an unhappy sound. "I didn't mean to choose Riella over you, or make it seem like I didn't care about your safety as much as hers. I was just . . . I couldn't let her down again, but then I let you down instead. And I hate it."

"She's your sister," Sparrow said reasonably. "And you're a good brother. I wish—" She halted.

"You wish what?" he asked. He was so close to her now, she could feel it when he breathed, the fabric of his clothes scraping against hers.

Sparrow tried to find the words. What did she wish? That she'd had an older brother like Elliot to care about and miss her? That she knew where her siblings were, that maybe *she'd* let *them* down too, even though her parents had been the ones to give her up? But wishing did no good. . . . Sparrow had learned that long ago. "You didn't let me down," she said finally.

"I left you behind," he said, like the words pained him to speak aloud. "I put you second."

Sparrow shrugged, but her throat was tight. "I don't mind, really, being second to her." It was better than not being on the list at all, though she decided not to say that part out loud.

"You're *not*," he said forcefully, angrily. "You are *not* second, not to me. You're—" He faltered, and Sparrow would have given anything to hear the rest of that sentence. He took a deep, calming breath. "I promise I won't ever make you feel that way again. I won't ever leave you behind. That is, I mean . . . unless you want me to. If you'd rather—"

"No, I wouldn't," Sparrow said quickly.

"Good," he said, sounding relieved. "You're stuck with me, then."

Sparrow beamed.

She slept most of the day, though Elliot woke her in the afternoon so she wouldn't wind up being awake all night. He'd brought her a change of clothes that must have belonged to Riella, as well as a bucket of warm water to wash with. Fife, determined to be of use, fluttered and fussed, but he only spilled the bucket and got tangled in her hair. Elliot wound up helping her into one of his tunics instead, the sleeves large enough for her splint to fit through.

Sparrow's face was scorching hot, but Fife assured her that Elliot was being a proper gentleman and looking the other way—and even nipped at his ears again when he half turned to see if she was decent.

Ignix was silent and watchful, surveying their interactions with mild interest. Or at least, that's how Sparrow perceived it.

"What're you lookin' at?" she demanded after Elliot took away the bathwater to dump outside the cave.

Mating rituals, Ignix said. Sparrow spluttered in outrage, but Elliot had returned by then, so she didn't dare reply. *At least,* the phoenix added, humor in her voice, *that is how it appears to me.*

"Then you're blinder than I am," Sparrow muttered.

Ignix huffed, the sound like laughter, and Sparrow fought off her own smile—as well as the growing bubble of hope inside her chest.

After checking Sparrow's injury—first, she noted, not second—Elliot unwrapped Ignix's bandages. She tested her wing, filling the cave with gusts of air.

"There's no pain?" Elliot asked. Ignix must have shaken her head or replied directly into his mind. "Then you're ready to fly."

Sparrow waited, breath held for what Ignix would do next. Would she leave them now? Take off to fight Avalkyra on her own, as she insisted she must, or would she let Sparrow and the others help her?

What of the chick? Ignix asked—and Sparrow was indignant to realize the phoenix meant *her*.

"Sparrow? She won't be using her arm anytime soon, but I think she should be able to manage the flight to Prosperity, once she's eaten."

I shall escort you, then, and ensure you arrive safely.

"You will?" Sparrow blurted, unable to disguise the surprise in her voice. "But what about Avalkyra? I thought you were the only one who could defeat her?"

Ignix shifted slightly. *That is what I thought too, for many years. Centuries, in fact. There were times when I might have stepped aside and shared the load, but I thought to do so was to be a coward. To hide from my responsibilities. And so, when Lyra the Defender needed to unify the entirety of the world's Phoenix Riders, I summoned them and led the charge. When Elysia the Peacemaker traveled down the mountainside, her queendom at her back, I called the ranks together, and I blazed the trail. They flew behind me, but never in front. Never beside. But perhaps . . . Perhaps I need not do it all alone.*

Sparrow's head was spinning. All these grand moments in Phoenix Rider history, made possible because of Ignix. And yet . . . "Why isn't your name mentioned in the history books? In *The Pyraean Epics*? Why does everyone think you just disappeared?"

Because I let them. The distance suited me, and with no one close to me . . .

"You couldn't get hurt," Sparrow offered gently. It was why she'd always kept moving, never staying in one place too long—never bothering with people friends. She was rejecting them before they could reject her, but Ignix had been practicing avoidance of a different sort, though the result was the same. Loneliness.

Avalkyra changed all that, Ignix said, her words harder now. *I thought I'd seen enough when she tore the empire in two and condemned the hatchlings to die in the Aura Nova training grounds, but she wasn't finished. She broke into my mind and took what little I had left. But then the other one, Veronyka . . . She gave it back. I will do all I can to help her. Avalkyra must be dealt with, and we will face that hurdle together. All of us.*

Sparrow grinned from ear to ear. It seemed the phoenix had taken her words about everyone needing help to heart, and Sparrow relished the idea that she'd made a difference.

"So what's been happening?" Sparrow asked Elliot as he prepared one last meal before they departed. She was itching to get back to her friends—the animals, of course, but also the humans. Riella and Ersken and Veronyka, too. Her friends, her flock.

"I have no idea," he admitted. "When I left, they were still scrambling to settle Prosperity, though Veronyka and the commander were heading south to rescue Tristan and deal with Lord Rolan."

Sparrow scowled at the name of the man who'd blackmailed Elliot and held Riella hostage.

"I've been looking for you ever since," he continued. "The Riders have been patrolling the area, but at a very safe distance. I think they just want to know if she leaves." There was a pause as he hefted a pot onto the fire, its contents sloshing and sizzling as they made contact with the flames. "It would be nice to know, well, *anything* else about what's going on in the Eyrie, but I don't know how we could without putting ourselves at risk."

"I think I do," Sparrow announced, turning to Ignix, who was standing at the mouth of the cave. "You can sense them, can't you?"

I can, Ignix agreed warily. *That is how I knew Avalkyra was up to something on Pyrmont's summit. . . . I could feel the darkness there.*

"Could you reach them from here? Find out what they're doing?"

Unease radiated from her. *I have been keeping my magic close in order to conceal our whereabouts, and to hide the fact that I survived in case it brought them down on us. To reach for them now could alert them to our presence.*

"But we're leaving anyway, right? This is our last chance to figure out more for Veronyka and the others," Sparrow said. "Besides, you're apex. You're special. No one else has the kinda range and power that you do."

You may cease with the flattery. I will do it.

Sparrow snorted. "Knew you were a vain old thing."

As Elliot doled out their meal, Sparrow found herself edging closer to

Ignix. Some desire or instinct told her to put a hand on her silken feathers—to offer what support she could. Ignix was rigid with focus, her mind as distant and unknowable as it had been the first time they'd met. But she unfurled like a flower at Sparrow's contact, and the trust that had developed between them felt as beautiful and delicate as a spring blossom.

But the contact brought more than those soft feelings. There was a flash of pain and a wash of cold—and someone reaching . . . reaching. Sparrow jerked away.

"What's happening?" Elliot asked, immediately at her side.

"Something . . . ," Sparrow muttered, trying to understand. "Something was reaching back."

Not something, but someone. Come, Ignix said, lurching to her feet and shaking out her wings. *We must fly to the Eyrie at once.*

It could bring all the world together, this magic . . .
and it could tear all the world apart.

- CHAPTER 44 -
VERONYKA

THE SUN WAS SETTING as they approached Rushlea, turning the River Aurys to a stream of molten gold—as its name indicated—and setting the rooftops of the village ablaze with brilliant light.

Everything looked so peaceful, Veronyka was tempted to be lulled into the easy contentment of soaring through the sky with Xephyra. But before the shimmering vision could truly take shape, she reminded herself that Val was in that village. There would be nothing peaceful about this night.

The patrol parted ways with Tristan just north of Vayle, but first they landed at Queen Malka's outpost to iron out the details of their plan.

Latham was, rightly so, concerned about his brother.

"Do you know *which* apprentices are there?" he asked before they'd even sat down.

"No," Veronyka said. "All the commander knew was that several of the older apprentices had been sent to Rushlea." She didn't say the rest—that besides Kade, who was in Arboria, Loran was the oldest Apprentice Rider in their flock. He *must* be there.

Latham didn't respond, but his jaw was clenched tight enough to make the muscles jump.

"Nothing's going to happen," she assured him, turning to the others.

"The mine has two entrances: Ronyn and Lysandro can watch the north, and Latham and Anders can watch the south. You should be able to bottleneck any Unnamed that are hiding inside and keep them there. Tristan will be on lookout at the Eyrie to ensure Avalkyra's flock stays put."

"But if they do leave . . . how will you warn us in time?" Anders asked, frowning.

Tristan glanced at Veronyka.

"I'll use shadow magic," she said bluntly. No time like the present to put all her cards on the table.

"Shadow magic," Ronyn repeated uncertainly. "I didn't think it was real."

"It's real and it's rare," Tristan said. "Veronyka has it . . . and Avalkyra has it too."

"But what does it do?" asked Latham, looking between them.

Veronyka lifted her chin at Tristan. He was probably better at explaining it than she was.

"She can talk to you inside your head," he explained. "Use words and images . . . and she can understand your thoughts in turn."

"That's . . . oh," Anders said, struggling for his usual nonchalance.

"It saved my life," Tristan said. "Veronyka knew I wasn't in that wagon headed to the Spine because she could connect with Sev, and he told her the truth. She rescued me from Rolan's dungeon because she could sense where I was and I could talk her through the underground passages."

Silence descended, and though it was tense—Veronyka could read minds, and that was enough to make anyone on edge—it was also tinged with something close to wonder. Maybe even respect. She was something *more* to them now, and as such, their confidence in her and this plan grew.

Tristan smiled proudly. He couldn't sense what she could, but Veronyka suspected he had said all he'd said hoping for such a result.

"Suffice it to say," he finished, "if the strixes mobilize, Veronyka will know as soon as I do."

As Tristan headed west and Veronyka and the others headed north, she felt the gap opening between them with every beat of Xephyra's wings.

Though her heart still ached with the memory of their weeks apart, she was desperately glad to have him nowhere near Val. If everything went wrong, at least he would be safe. For now.

Everything could *not* go wrong.

Still with me? he asked her—as he had done every few minutes since they'd parted. He was the only person she could reach at such a distance, the only person who could tell her if the strixes were coming to Rushlea.

He was an invaluable part of the plan, and she didn't want Val to know where he was or what he was doing.

Yes, Veronyka said, as she had done every time, *but we're close to town. We can't talk anymore.*

He understood. *I'll see you on the other side.*

Unless something bad happened, of course.

Tristan? she said softly, and she sensed his attention sharpen.

Yes?

I love you, she said.

Warmth blossomed in his chest, radiating from their bond. *I never get tired of hearing that,* he said. *Tell me again?*

I love you, she said, smiling.

He beamed. *I love you too.*

As Veronyka and the rest of the patrol neared the village perimeter, they split again. While the others made for the entrances to the mine, using the growing darkness as cover and taking up their positions, Veronyka sought out Val.

It was strange not to *know* where she was—not to sense her impatience or feel her presence. It should have been a relief, but it seemed only to amplify the tension growing inside her. Val could be anywhere, planning *anything*, and Veronyka would be none the wiser.

Luckily, she didn't have to look long.

Val became visible almost immediately, standing in the middle of the village square, watching Veronyka's approach.

Torches lined the streets, flickering in the evening breeze, but otherwise, the village was deserted. Veronyka sensed people, though—dozens of them, holed up inside the buildings that lined the road or pacing restlessly at the edges of town.

She saw no sign of a struggle as she came to land before Val; nor did she see any of the Unnamed roaming the streets or guarding entrances. Were they all inside the mine, then? Or were some of them in these very buildings, holding their occupants hostage? Sidra, too, was conspicuously absent.

Veronyka carefully dismounted, and since Val was without her bond-mate, she told Xephyra to take up a perch atop the nearby buildings.

Stay alert, she warned, and Xephyra croaked in response.

Then Veronyka was alone and unprotected in the middle of the street, save for a knife strapped to her belt and a quiver strapped to her back. Even her bow remained on Xephyra's saddle.

Val looked like some sort of gaunt specter in the waning twilight: Strands of her uneven red hair poked out from under a hood, blowing ragged in the breeze, and her skin was waxen and mottled with burns. Her clothes—and whatever weapons she might be carrying—were obscured by a long black cloak trailing across the ground.

"Hello, *xe* Nyka." Val smiled, wide and wolfish, her dark eyes reflecting the torchlight. And then she pulled down her hood.

She was wearing a crown.

But this circlet was not wrought of phoenix feathers shining bright as the dawn. No, these feathers were black as charcoal, and smears of inky blood trailed down her forehead, as if the quills had been torn from their host rather than cast off naturally.

The sight was so jarring that Veronyka took a step backward. Val looked like an entirely different person, distant and untouchable, but no matter how much Veronyka hated this version of her, she couldn't deny that Val was still beautiful, still awe-inspiring. Perhaps more so.

She looked impressive. Powerful. And yet . . . it also looked like armor, like a costume. Somehow ill fitting. Val had gotten thinner, Veronyka realized. There was something brittle about her now, something worn out. Like logs that had burned in the fire too long, like steel beaten too thin.

It made a chill slip down Veronyka's spine. This was the Avalkyra Ash-fire of Veronyka's wildest imaginings, the warrior she had spent the majority of her life idolizing—powerful, fierce, and yet twisted into a darker version of herself.

A nightmare version. All sharp angles and spiky intention, her very presence like barbs against Veronyka's skin.

"I see you received my message," Val said smugly, enjoying Veronyka's apparent speechlessness. "Once a lapdog, always a lapdog."

She must mean Doriyan. "I did, and I'm here," Veronyka said curtly. "Now tell me what you want."

Any reluctance to speak on her part was only liable to make Val talk more, and that was exactly what Veronyka needed. She glanced around surreptitiously—as if looking for danger—but in fact trying to catch a glimpse of the setting sun. The orb was flame-bright and sinking lower by the second, but Veronyka had to keep Val occupied until it fully disappeared.

Her patrol members had agreed that they would be in position by the time the sun dipped below the distant peaks of Pyrmont, and she didn't dare reach for them to check lest Val sense the magic. Their bond might be all but gone, but she was still a shadowmage, and sharply attuned to its use.

"What, no pleasantries for me?" Val asked, a theatrical pout on her face. "No dire warnings?" She took several steps closer but remained a good ten paces away. "It's as if you barely missed me at all."

Veronyka snorted at that, relieved that Val had taken up the chance to needle her a bit longer. "I wasn't a fan of your parting gift," she said, gesturing to the line Val's spear had cut down her middle. "Maybe some time apart is exactly what we needed."

The sun gilded the edges of the mountain with one last burst of golden light, then disappeared, leaving a blushing indigo sky in its wake. Veronyka shifted and rested a hand on her belt—the opposite side from her dagger. Val followed the movement but lost interest when she saw the weapon was still out of reach—of course, that was not the weapon Veronyka needed to get to. The commander's cane was strapped to her quiver, the butt of the weapon sitting flush against her back. A few inches away from her hand.

"Time apart," Val scoffed. "We are not sweethearts in a lover's quarrel. You and I are bound together—by blood and birth . . . and by magic. There is no denying that power or hiding from it."

"It hasn't been so powerful lately," Veronyka mused. "Our bond is weak, Val. Broken. Perhaps beyond repair."

Val's entire being sharpened at Veronyka's words. For whatever reason, she didn't like this problem with their bond . . . this malfunctioning connection. Veronyka could think of a thousand reasons why she might wish to repair it, ranging from finishing what she'd started with her spear to spying on the Phoenix Riders and figuring out their plans, but she wouldn't know for sure until Val wanted her to know.

"A bond cannot be so easily severed, *xe* Nyka. You should know that better than most."

She was talking about Xephyra. About death. If the bond survived that, perhaps there was no destroying it entirely.

"I thought I had already reached the height of my powers," Val continued, "but I was wrong. Only with you by my side can I do that."

It sounded like more of Val's typical nonsense—they were better together; they should rule side by side—but there was a glint in her eye that made the words sound more dangerous than ever before. The height of her powers . . . What did that mean? She clearly didn't mean political or physical power, but something magical. She was already bonded to the apex strix, with a flock at her disposal. How much more powerful could she get?

"But," she said with obvious relish, "we will not be able to rebuild what is broken between us if we cannot trust each other. . . ."

Footsteps echoed from behind her, and Veronyka turned carefully—never letting Val out of her sight. Her stomach dropped. Latham was being led into the street, a knife pressed to his throat. Beside him was his brother,

Loran. Latham must have abandoned his post and gone looking for him. Veronyka frowned. The people who held him and his brother captive . . . they were familiar.

Not angry Rushlean farmers, not raiders or bandits, but villagers—people who had attended her meeting here with Doriyan not ten days before.

The truth of it hit her square in the chest. Val didn't need lawless bandits to hold the villagers hostage. They were more than willing to play the part themselves. Latham was red-faced and frantic, but he stared at her with wide, pleading eyes. *Save my brother. Please, save my brother.*

Veronyka couldn't help the furious look of betrayal she sent the villagers' way, but she bit back her anger and refocused. This was Val's doing. She had likely threatened them, forcefully, into helping her. Even without her flock, Avalkyra Ashfire astride a strix would be enough to scare most people into obedience.

As Val ordered them to keep their knives on their captives, Veronyka threw caution to the wind and sought out Anders, whom Latham had left behind.

He was not alone, as she'd expected. No, he was surrounded outside the cave mouth, with a dozen villagers pointing pitchforks and makeshift spears at him. A quick hop over to Ronyn and Lysandro showed the same.

"I asked you to come alone, Veronyka," Val said, taking slow, measured steps toward her. "And you have not."

"You also told me the villagers would pay if I didn't turn up—clearly, they were never in danger."

Val stopped midstride. "Oh, yes they were—still are," she said softly, and Veronyka sensed the people holding Latham and Loran stiffen and stare at her in confusion. Fools to have trusted her. But then again, Veronyka was just as guilty. This was exactly how Val always got what she wanted—by constantly changing the game and bending the rules. By being more ruthless and cunning than Veronyka could ever hope to be.

Her fingers twitched at her side.

"What do you want?" she asked again, this time through clenched teeth. "Doriyan said you wanted to discuss terms."

Up on the rooftop, Xephyra shuffled nearer to Veronyka, anxious and on edge. Veronyka wondered where Val's strix was.

Val continued walking. She was close now, too close for Veronyka to be able to withdraw her weapon and get off a clean shot. And if she failed, she risked not only her own life, but Latham's and Loran's as well.

She considered moving backward, putting distance between them, but she also wanted Val to finally say what this was all about.

"I want peace between us, Veronyka. I want to forge a new, stronger connection."

Whatever Val said, this wasn't about *real* peace. This was about something else.

The height of my powers . . . a new, stronger connection.

Their bond was broken, and Val wanted to fix it. But why? To what end?

Val moved closer. One step, and another. Alarm bells sounded in Veronyka's head. Val would surely strike her, lash out and hurt her. Try to force her to do . . . something.

"We are sisters—in all the ways that count," Val continued, when Veronyka opened her mouth to argue. "Take my hand, embrace me as family, and I will spare them."

Val extended her arm.

The alarm bells inside reached a fever pitch, so loud and insistent that Veronyka turned her attention inward and realized the warning wasn't coming from her own mind at all, but from someone else's.

Tristan.

There's a reason power, like magic,
is not given to everyone.

- CHAPTER 45 -
TRISTAN

THE EYRIE WAS IN Tristan's sights before the sun set.

He spoke with the Rider who was patrolling the area, confirming there had been no new activity. Then he took up a stationary watch outside their former base.

If things went the way Tristan hoped, Veronyka would be done with her plan before the night was through, and they could resume regular patrols on the next shift. In fact, if things went *better* than he hoped, they might be retaking the Eyrie by this time tomorrow, the empire marching back where they belonged with Avalkyra as their prisoner.

The impulse to reach for Veronyka surged up then, but Tristan squashed it. He didn't want to distract her or flood the bond with useless worrying. He wouldn't contact her unless there was something she *needed* to know.

But when two phoenixes soared up out of the darkness near the way station and made straight for the Eyrie, Tristan's resolve was tested.

Were there other Riders out on patrol? But why on earth would they fly *into* the Eyrie, when there was a flock of strixes still inside? Or had Val somehow found *more* Phoenix Rider allies?

Whatever was happening, he had to check it out. If the strixes were attacked or provoked, they might go to Val on their own, or burst forth with aimless, destructive rage—like a kicked hornet's nest. But he wouldn't contact Veronyka before he knew exactly what was happening.

Adrenaline spiking in his veins, Tristan drew his bow and nocked an arrow.

Better not ignite just yet, he told Rex, who was fairly trembling beneath him with pent-up energy.

Tristan didn't want to draw attention to himself, especially if these Riders weren't friendly. But as Rex looped around and approached the village from the east, unease built inside him. Mirroring with his bondmate for a closer look, Tristan expected to see the infamous black shadowbirds around every corner—but the village was empty.

Perhaps they were simply cloistered in the Eyrie. The place was built for roosting, after all. But where had those Phoenix Riders gone?

As Rex soared past the empty village, Tristan caught movement inside the courtyard of the stronghold. Many of the buildings were damaged, with smashed windows, broken beams of wood, and crumbling stonework, just as Kade had described. It looked like an abandoned battlefield, which is exactly what it was.

As they drew nearer, Rex tensed, heat building beneath his wings while he scanned the sky, but Tristan's gaze was fixed on two figures on the cobblestones—one was small and pale-haired, while the other had long, dark braids and a leg that was amputated just below the knee. . . . *Morra.*

A third figure appeared then, rushing out of the gaping double doors that led into the dining hall, their arms laden.

Before Tristan could call out, Rex threw his wings wide, bringing them to such an abrupt halt that Tristan almost fell from the saddle.

He'd barely righted himself when another phoenix surged up before them, crying out a warning so loud it rang in his ears. She was truly massive, her feathers long and dark purple on the ends.

She was also familiar.

"Ignix!" a voice cried from below, echoing in the silent courtyard. The last time Tristan had seen this phoenix, she'd been carrying a captive

Veronyka into the sky before dropping her from a sickening height and then exploding in a violent rage that seared half Val's face off.

"It's okay!" another voice called out. Was that Elliot? It was, and after putting the armful of whatever he'd taken from the dining hall on the ground, he added, "He's a friend."

Rex, meanwhile, was spoiling for a fight—snapping his beak and tossing his head as they flew up and down in place, still blocked by Ignix.

Easy, Rex, Tristan muttered, not wanting to insult his bondmate's pride by suggesting that he wouldn't last five minutes against that ancient creature—but, well . . . he wouldn't last five minutes.

At last Ignix turned her back on them and joined the others, landing in the courtyard below. Rex released a puff of sparks, his head held high, then followed her.

As soon as they reached the ground, another phoenix swooped over. Jaxon, Elliot's bondmate. Tristan left Rex with him and hurried to the others.

The pale-haired person was Sparrow, and she was crouched over the prone figure of Morra. Tristan's stomach clenched with anger and fear, until he truly saw the state Morra was in—her body bruised and broken and clearly left for dead.

Elliot, meanwhile, was sprinkling herbs into a steaming cup. Tristan caught the scent, his nostrils stinging from the pungent brew, and Morra coughed. Ignix loomed over them all, watching closely.

Whatever she had done, Morra was suffering, so Tristan pushed aside his resentment and eased behind her, gently helping the woman sit. There was blood matted into the hair on the back of her head, red welts banding her neck, and her remaining leg was swollen and bent at an odd angle. Her skin was ashen and waxy beneath the scratches and smeared blood, and her movements were halting and frail.

Now that she was upright, Elliot held the cup carefully to Morra's lips. Her eyes opened, and she forced down a gulp.

"Disgusting," she muttered, and Tristan took that as a good sign.

"You should know," Sparrow said brightly. "You made it."

Morra chuckled at that, then began to cough. It was clear she was badly hurt, and she seemed weak beyond her injuries. Wilted.

"Where are they?" Tristan asked, not wanting to push but realizing with a pang that if the strixes weren't here, he or the other Riders on patrol must have missed something. He craned his neck to look around and saw that Rex had already done that, swooping back from a flight around the area. He shook his head, having found nothing.

"They left," Elliot said. "We were hiding out in a cave, getting ready to head back to Prosperity, when Morra reached us. Or reached Ignix, rather." He spoke a bit uncertainly, and Tristan understood the feeling—this world of ancient phoenixes and legendary shadow magic still felt slightly beyond his grasp too.

"How did no one see?" he asked.

"They went underground," said Elliot. "There are tunnels underneath the Eyrie. Some of them lead outside, but others connect to networks that lead all over Pyrmont."

Like the mine outside Rushlea?

"*Veronyka,*" Tristan muttered, moving to stand—but then Morra's hand shot out, gripping his arm with surprising force.

"Where is she?" she asked, her voice jagged as broken glass.

The others were staring anxiously. Even Ignix's attention was fixed on him.

"Why do you care?" Tristan asked, unable to help the censure in his voice. "You betrayed her. Betrayed all of us."

She didn't, came Ignix's voice in his head. *I have seen her mind. Everything she did, she did for Veronyka. To delay Avalkyra. To buy us time.*

Tristan looked down at Morra, gravely wounded. Proof of Avalkyra's wrath. Of the cost of Morra's actions.

"Forgive me," she said, a tear sliding down her cheek. "I tried to do right by her, by all of you. I fear I have failed."

Tristan nodded, but it wasn't *his* forgiveness she needed. Not really.

"Veronyka, she's . . ." He swallowed, sensing that there were larger problems than the strix army to worry about. "She's in Rushlea with Avalkyra. She is going to try to capture her."

"She's not alone, is she?" Morra asked, her hand on Tristan trembling.

"No . . . she's there with my patrol. I'm sure they can get away. I'm sure . . ."

That's when Tristan really noticed what had made such a mess of the courtyard. It wasn't just random rubble and debris. There were curved bits of broken rock, smeared in black filth, and in the center was a pile of smooth stones . . . No, not *stones*.

"She has grown her ranks," Morra said, following Tristan's line of sight. "I thought she had gone alone, but they followed soon after."

It couldn't be. . . . There were so many.

They had been prepared for an ambush, for a betrayal, but not of the winged variety. And even if they had, they'd have expected twenty-odd strixes, not however many dozens more had been hatched here.

Worse, their plan was to hold Val's reinforcements inside the mine, but strixes would not be so easily contained.

They'd be slaughtered.

I will go, came a voice booming into his mind. Ignix crouched, ready to leap into flight, but Tristan held out a hand.

"Wait!" Then he turned his attention inward. *Veronyka!* he shouted into the bond. Rex edged nearer, sensing his bondmate's distress, while Ignix's head whipped around to stare at him sharply.

Tristan had trouble telling if Veronyka heard him at the best of times, but right now, with his blood pounding in his ears, he could barely hear his own thoughts, never mind any of hers.

What are you doing? Ignix demanded, breaking his concentration.

He stared up at her, then around at the others. He supposed it wasn't much of a secret anymore. "We're bonded. I don't have shadow magic, but she does. I should be able to reach her."

A human bondmate . . . , Ignix mused, tilting her head consideringly.

Like Nefyra before her. She turned to Rex. *Support your Rider. Your magic amplifies his.*

Tristan had never seen Rex obey an order so quickly. The phoenix was pressed against his side in an instant, and his warm, solid presence bolstered Tristan's heart, if not his magic.

Veronyka? He tried again. *Are you there? Are you okay?*

"It's no good," he said, intending to stand again, but Morra held on.

"She must not touch her," she said urgently, chest heaving with the effort. "Do you understand? She must not let Avalkyra touch her, and she must not under *any* circumstances kneel."

"Is Avalkyra going to try to kill her?" Tristan asked. Veronyka would never willingly kneel to Val . . . unless she thought it would save lives. Unless there was no other option.

"You are not Veronyka's only human bondmate. Avalkyra intends to repair their fractured bond. Then she will chain them together more completely than ever before."

The benex to her apex, Ignix said solemnly. Morra nodded.

Chain them together? Tristan didn't know what any of it meant, but it didn't matter. Val wanting to hurt Veronyka was one thing, but her wanting to bind them more tightly together was something else entirely.

Veronyka! he tried frantically, again and again . . . but there was no response.

Day 22, Third Moon, 180 AE

M—

My situation grows precarious, and I must cease all contact. I have done all I can for them, I think. Now it is your turn.

Remember what I told you. Remember your promise.

Together.

They must rule together, or Avalkyra must not rule at all.

—S

*Even the strongest among us could be led astray, and
the weakest could be lost entirely.*

- CHAPTER 46 -
VERONYKA

VAL'S OUTSTRETCHED ARM WAS frozen in place, hovering in the air mere inches from Veronyka's own. Take it, and Val would spare them.

Veronyka wrenched her hand away.

Tristan was calling for her, throwing everything he had into their bond. The communication was frantic, confusing, but amid the din was the overwhelming feeling that *whatever* Val wanted, Veronyka should not give it. There was something else, too, some other important warning, but Veronyka couldn't discern it amid his panic.

The instant Veronyka pulled back, Val's nostrils flared, her lip curling in a dangerous snarl.

The next few seconds would make or break their chances. Make or break them all.

Veronyka reached behind her back and withdrew the commander's cane and the concealed blowpipe within. Val reared back, perhaps expecting a blow, but Veronyka wheeled the weapon around and aimed it at the villagers holding Latham and Loran instead. Two quick bursts of air, and the two of them staggered away from their captors, who crumpled to the ground.

Run! Veronyka shouted at them. She had no idea where their phoenixes were, but hoped they were unharmed and somewhere nearby. Xephyra was already diving down toward Veronyka, but then a black blur whipped out of nowhere, tackling Xephyra in midair and sending her careening off course.

Veronyka felt the hit like a blow to her own body, her breath whooshing from her lungs. But then Val was upon her. Veronyka raised the cane, intending to hit her with it as Val had originally feared, but the swing was blocked. Val held a dagger with both hands—something stolen from the Eyrie, Veronyka guessed—and she'd caught the cane in the cross guard. They both pushed hard, fighting for the upper hand, and Val seemed to recognize as they did that Veronyka wielded no ordinary wooden cane. The dagger scraped against the metal surface with a screech, and Val bared her teeth before using her leverage to twist their locked weapons and fling the tip of the cane toward the ground. Veronyka stumbled, but before she could raise it again, Val kicked hard against the side. The hollow metal cane bent in half, rendering it useless.

Val grinned up at Veronyka, and a hand shot out, closing around Veronyka's throat.

Their eyes met, and instantly there was a spark, a flicker—their bond repairing itself. Both of them froze, held hostage by the surge of magic—but then Veronyka lifted her foot and put her heel square in Val's stomach. She staggered back, releasing her hold, but it was too late. Their bond was stabilizing, growing stronger by the second, and Veronyka barely managed to draw in a ragged breath as she tried to stumble away. She hefted the bent cane and swiped for good measure, forcing Val to fall to her knees to avoid the contact.

It was the space Veronyka needed. Xephyra had managed to disengage herself from Val's strix and was making her way toward Veronyka.

Veronyka didn't look back but ran to meet Xephyra. She leapt into the saddle, Xephyra's claws scraping through the dirt road before she took off again into the sky.

If Veronyka could get to the mine entrances, she might be able to rain down some arrows and clear a path for the others before—

A sound reached her then, a distant, brittle rustling—the kind of noise that set her teeth on edge and made a shudder crawl down her back. It felt like it came from within her own skull, incessant, no matter how hard she shook her head or covered her ears.

She whipped around in the saddle to see Val getting to her feet in the middle of the street, her strix next to her.

"You haven't properly met yet, have you?" Val called, laughter in her voice. "This is Onyx, my new bondmate. Together we are the apex pair. I am Avalkyra Ashfire, the Feather-Crowned Queen, and this"—she lifted her hands, and the strix beside her raised her head to the sky and released a shriek loud enough to rent the night and echo for miles around—"is the Black Horde."

A chorus replied, screeching and snapping, and the rustling grew louder and louder as it reverberated through the air and bounced off every rock, tree, and building. The sound was coming from the direction of the mine.

What was it that Doriyan had said? The mine was connected to tunnels all over Pyrmont. Some, maybe, that led directly to the Eyrie?

The rest of Tristan's warning came to her then, as if her brain had received the message and held it safe for when she had a moment to actually hear it.

They're coming. The strixes are coming.

Veronyka had barely made it halfway down the main street when they burst forth in the distance, rising over the trees like a swarm of bats. They dipped and swerved, their sharp beaks and sharper talons reflecting scraps of moonlight, while their feathers gleamed thick and dark as burnt oil.

There were so many. More than the estimated two dozen that had attacked the Eyrie. This was easily double, triple that amount. Val had called it a horde. . . . That meant there were at least a hundred of them.

How? When? *How?*

Xephyra swooped back around, while Veronyka sent her magic wide, seeking the rest of her patrol. The villagers had scattered in the face of the strixes, attacked indiscriminately by the creatures—alliance with their mistress be damned—and the Riders had used the opportunity to get into the air, but while the bulk of the strixes were heading toward Val and Onyx, small groups had broken off, unable to resist chasing down the errant Phoenix Riders. They wouldn't be able to hold them off forever. They wouldn't be able to escape.

None of them would make it out of here alive—not if Val didn't want them to.

Veronyka spotted the blowpipe, bent and broken on the ground below, and cursed savagely. The strixes were coming this way fast, and she had no way to get to Val from this distance—not without firing arrows, and that would be too risky. She might wind up killing her, denying the empire their prize—and killing a part of herself in the process. For all Val had done, for all she had yet to do . . . Veronyka didn't think she had it in her.

She fought against a wave of despair. Would Val hesitate? Would Val spare her? She shook her head. It didn't matter.

I am not her.

That realization brought clarity, and her mind kicked into action. The darts . . . she still had half a dozen in a pouch on her belt. Without the blowpipe, she'd have to get in close.

Very close.

Would it be enough to save them as well as their plan?

Veronyka closed her eyes and reached. Their bond was alive and well—but weak. Like a smoldering fire, it was seconds away from roaring into life or sputtering out entirely, so she did the only thing she *could* do.

She fanned the flames.

She extended herself with all her magic—knowing it was a risk, knowing it was dangerous—reaching through their quaking, newly re-formed bond until she found Val's mind. She felt a lifetime away, but she was there. Veronyka opened her eyes and gathered her strength.

She thought back to the night Val had sliced her open, how she'd followed Val across the stronghold's cobblestones, even though her body was behind the stables at Prosperity.

Relying on her physical senses at first, Veronyka stared hard at the place she wanted to be—*behind* Val, looking at the back of her head, just as she had before.

Her efforts left her feeling strangely disembodied—that was good; that meant she was living in the dream space, the shadow magic space. But she needed her *body* to make contact, not just her magic. She tried to remember the emotions from the last time, the reckless desire—the stubborn will.

She reached again, harder and with more determination, feeling the weight of her hand and the extension of her arm. The strands of Val's ragged hair slipped between her fingers, snagging against her skin—until an iron grip clamped down on her wrist.

Val spun around. Her face was alight with triumph, her teeth bared, but she didn't strike Veronyka with her dagger or throw her aside.

Instead she pulled, wrenching Veronyka forward. She felt her body lift from her saddle, felt the breath leave her lungs as she blinked out of existence. She had been pulled *inside* the bond—mind, body, and magic. There was a terrifying moment of complete and utter nothingness, and then she reappeared inside the physical world and slammed down hard onto the ground at Val's feet.

Veronyka gasped, dazed, her mind struggling to catch up with her body. Xephyra shrieked from high above and yards away, her saddle empty, while Veronyka lay prone on the dirt road. Shadow magic had done this. Shadow magic had teleported her across the space between them, disobeying the laws of time and space and putting her at Val's mercy.

Val bent over Veronyka, grabbing her wrist again and dragging her upright.

At this close proximity, Veronyka noticed a bright red slash across Val's throat—a cut barely starting to heal.

Val saw her attention and smiled. "Courtesy of Morra, Rider of Aneaxi." Veronyka's heart surged, until—"Right before I threw her to her death."

"Liar," Veronyka spat, trying to break free of her hold. She refused to believe Val's words, even though logic told her Val would not take an attempt on her life lightly.

Despite her fear and denial, a small bubble of hope grew inside Veronyka's chest. Did this mean Morra hadn't betrayed her after all?

"Why don't you let me show you?" Val asked, her other hand gripping Veronyka's chin and forcing her to look Val in the eye. Veronyka saw it—a flash of Morra falling from the temple roof—and then the floodgates opened. Their bond exploded back to life, blazing and more powerful than ever before.

The apex bond was far more potent than Veronyka had truly realized. Bond magic on such a scale was breathtaking. Every single strix, no matter how far or how wild, flew as if they were one being—one monstrous creature—sharing Val's will and determination and intent. It didn't make sense, it shouldn't be possible, but Veronyka felt it. She was bonded to Val, after all, and so she was a part of it too.

Val held her tightly, fingers digging into Veronyka's wrist and chin hard enough to bruise. She released a long, shuddering breath, then closed her eyes. She looked triumphant—exultant—and when her eyes fixed on Veronyka again, there was purpose blazing in their dark depths.

"You see, Veronyka? You are mine, as they are mine. Say it. Bow your head and bend your knee and *say it.*" Veronyka struggled, but Val refused to let go. "Become benex to my apex, and we will take over the world. We were never meant to oppose one another; we were meant to fight and rule and die together."

Veronyka had no idea what a benex was, but even still . . . what Val said might be true. They'd been born together, after all, and Veronyka might have shared her dream to fight and rule and die together . . . once.

But no longer.

Her free hand swung up from her belt, a poisoned dart gripped tight. Before Val even noticed the movement, she had plunged the pointed tip deep into the side of her neck.

Val jerked back, her hand flying up, but already the effects were slowing her movements, the poison slipping into her bloodstream. She stumbled—Veronyka had never seen her make such an ungraceful movement—and her eyes glazed.

"This . . . is not . . . over," she slurred, staggering against Onyx, who had rushed forward to catch her. *I am coming for you . . . for everyone.*

Then she fell to the ground.

The bond that had so recently blossomed back to life inside Veronyka faded to a distant, dull presence, leaving her head ringing and her body heavy with the sudden absence.

And that wasn't the only side effect.

All around her, the endless cacophony of shrieks and flapping wings faltered. As one the strixes reeled and fell from the sky—stunned, dazed, but not truly affected as Val was. They felt it through their bond, but not physically. Even Veronyka had to fight against the wave of exhaustion that rolled through her, but she had the benefit of being prepared for it.

Onyx, who would feel it stronger than the others, managed to crouch defensively over Val's prone form—a barrier between Veronyka and her prize.

Veronyka hesitated, hand on the hilt of her dagger. If she could just drag Val *with* her, if she could manage that one thing . . . But even as she thought it, the other strixes started scrambling to their feet, staggering woozily and haphazardly flapping their wings.

It wouldn't be long before they recovered, and even if she managed to bypass Val's bondmate, she'd never get away. The strixes were too many, and if she had Val in her possession, they would chase her.

But if Veronyka and the others left now, *without* Val, they might make it out of this alive.

Farther down the street she saw Latham and Loran scrambling onto their phoenixes, and with a sweep of her magic, she found the other members of the patrol taking this chance to shake their pursuers.

As if to make the decision for her, Onyx shrieked, drawing several more unsteady strixes to her side, shoring up her bondmate's defenses.

Veronyka's chance at getting Val was gone. She turned on her heel and ran for Xephyra.

"Retreat!" she yelled as she climbed into the saddle, as if the Phoenix Riders weren't already several steps ahead of her.

Xephyra soared through the sky, and regret pooled in Veronyka's stomach as she felt the last scraps of Val's consciousness slip away.

It was a relief, but she knew the reprieve would be short-lived.

Their plan had failed. Val would recover, soon, and make good on her promise.

But for one who is worthy, this power
could make all the difference.

- CHAPTER 47 -
VERONYKA

THEY HAD JUST CROSSED the river on their way back to Prosperity when they were hailed by a group of Phoenix Riders coming their way. Veronyka kept glancing over her shoulder, expecting the strixes hot on their tail, but they did not follow.

As they met the oncoming Riders, Veronyka recognized her aunt at the fore. She must have rallied a patrol in the hope of helping them.

Veronyka was thankful they had not made it in time. They might have tried to fight then—seeing the strixes' momentary daze as opportunity—but even with that brief advantage, the Phoenix Riders were too outnumbered.

It was a miracle they had gotten away unscathed.

Or had they?

As they met with the secondary force and came to a stop along the river, Veronyka realized that they had not made a clean escape after all.

The Riders who landed ahead of her, including the members of Tristan's patrol and the apprentices who had been in Rushlea when it was taken, were clustering around Anders, blocking him from view.

Veronyka sent a wary tendril of magic toward him and found intense, alarming pain on the other end.

She darted a glance at Latham, who flew just ahead of her, and the pain seemed to double. He had abandoned Anders in order to find his brother, and that decision had not come without consequence.

As they landed, Latham dismounted and pushed through the crowd to get to Anders. Veronyka followed close behind.

He was slumped in his saddle, those around arguing over whether they should help him down or strap him in tighter while his phoenix emitted soft, frantic croaks.

"It's okay," Veronyka murmured to the creature. She ran a hand along his feathers, which were splattered with streaks of inky black blood and dotted with bits of ash, but he seemed unharmed.

Anders, however, had an ugly wound in his shoulder, where three distinctive gashes sliced through fabric, flesh, and muscle. It looked like one of the strixes had raked him as it flew by or tried to tear him from his saddle.

He was hunched over, bleeding profusely, while Darius—who had come with the reinforcements—used a wad of fabric in an attempt to stanch the flow.

"Anders!" Latham shouted, trying to get close enough to see his face. "Anders, talk to me."

"Someone check his head . . . ," Anders muttered, still bent over his saddle. Latham looked around in alarm—the words were slurred and made little sense. But then Anders managed to raise his face enough to meet Latham's eye. "People usually . . . only tell me to shut up."

"You're an idiot," Latham choked out, not without affection. Anders smiled in gratification, though the expression quickly shifted into a grimace. Veronyka felt a severe pang of guilt, and while she had plenty of her own to contend with, that particular burst came directly from Latham.

"Veronyka."

Alexiya sidled over to her, worry written across her usually stoic features. They pushed through the crowd, allowing the others to tend to Anders, so they could speak in private. Xephyra followed them, anxious to be near Veronyka after everything that had happened.

"We—I—it didn't work. I managed to hit her with a dart, but I couldn't take her with me. She had her strixes with her after all, and there are more . . . many more than the first attack."

"Are they pursuing?" Alexiya asked, turning her attention north.

Veronyka shook her head. "I don't think so. I think they'll wait for Avalkyra to recover."

"How long?"

"Around twenty-four hours, roughly. At least, that's what Hestia said."

Alexiya took her shoulders and gave them a gentle squeeze. "It's okay. It was worth trying. We'll . . ." She paused, looking around at their small party. "We'll figure out our next move at Prosperity."

"I need to send word to Haven. I promised."

Alexiya nodded. "I'll handle it."

"Tell them—" Veronyka started, then stopped. Their backs were against the wall, and they needed all the help they could get. "Ask them if they'll fight with us. Not for me or for the throne, but for each other. Only together can we make it through."

Alexiya nodded.

"Use a fast pigeon," Veronyka added. "Agneta will be worried. And we don't have much time."

"I'll use the fastest pigeon I can find," she promised.

As Darius finished securing the fabric to Anders's shoulder, ordering the others to strap him in tighter so he could be taken to Prosperity for a proper healer, Veronyka turned her attention inward.

Tristan? she tried tentatively.

Veronyka! came the quick reply, laced with heavy relief.

I'm sorry, she said hurriedly. *I never meant to keep you waiting. It didn't work, but I'll explain everything at Prosperity.*

It was well past midnight when they arrived, but the entire outpost was up and waiting for them. Veronyka left it to Alexiya to share the basics with those who asked, and Ronyn and Lysandro filled in what details they could. Latham followed Anders all the way to the infirmary, his brother trailing behind, but Veronyka had eyes only for Tristan.

He was craning his neck, seeking her out, and when the crowd finally parted for them, he scooped Veronyka up in a hug so tight, it lifted her off her feet. Somewhere behind them, Rex tackled Xephyra. Theirs was a much less elegant reunion, all talons and feathers, but the sentiment was the same.

"Are you okay?" he asked. Veronyka nodded into the crook of his neck. He put her down, sharp eyes raking over her body, looking for damage.

"I'm fine," Veronyka insisted.

He looked like he wanted to press, then shook his head. "I know you are. You always are." His smile faltered, and his eyes turned somber. He jerked his chin over his shoulder. "You need to come. Quick."

He led her around the building, across the outpost grounds to a clearing surrounded by heavy-boughed weeping willow trees. It was bathed in silvery moonlight, and there at the center were a cluster of people and two phoenixes.

Veronyka's heart jolted—that was Ignix, and next to her was Sparrow. Elliot was there too, his bondmate beside him, and they all turned at Veronyka's approach, revealing a prone figure between them.

"Morra?" Veronyka whispered, rushing forward and dropping to her knees. Morra was lying in the grass, several blankets underneath and piled up around her.

It was hard to see in the darkness, but then a soft, golden glow filled the space. The phoenixes Ignix and Jaxon—plus Rex and Xephyra, who had followed them through the trees—were each emitting waves of warmth and gentle, buttery light.

"It's me," Morra said, reaching for her hand. She was thin and trembling, with blood-soaked bandages visible on her arms and dark bruising around her neck.

Val. Veronyka clenched her teeth. "She needs to see a healer," she said angrily.

"There's no point," Morra said matter-of-factly. Her voice was rough, but her tone brooked no argument. "No point."

Veronyka's throat was tight. No point? Did that mean . . . ? *Yes,* Morra said simply, her eyes fixed on Veronyka. "Forgive me, child," she said aloud. "I thought it was the only way—the best way—so I went with her. Ilithya always hoped, dreamed of a world with you together. . . ."

Ilithya—Veronyka's *maiora*? "What do you mean?"

"Ilithya reached out to me, once. She knew my work—do you believe that? Avalkyra Ashfire's own spymaster knew about me. This was after the war, of course. I had long since stopped my studies and was working in a cookhouse. But Ilithya found me. Our acquaintance was brief, but life changing. She told me of Avalkyra, how she had resurrected, and asked me all manner of questions about how such a life could change a person. She feared her, I think. Ilithya feared her queen." She paused, catching her breath. "Yes, we spoke often about Avalkyra, but very little about you."

Veronyka's heart lurched painfully at her words, but Morra shook her head vigorously, as if sensing her thoughts.

"She was protective of you. I think she knew, even then, that you were the key to everything. She made me promise. Promise that I would see our queen restored to the throne but only—*only*," she added forcefully, "if *you* were with her. She did not tell me your name—she was concerned for your safety, even then—only that I would know you when I met you. I'm ashamed to say I didn't, not until it was too late."

She paused, coughing, and Veronyka made soothing noises. "It's okay," she said, because she didn't know what else *to* say. "It's okay."

"I did my best to stall her," Morra said on a sigh, "to slow her down, but it was no use. She was coming for blood—coming for you—so I tried to take some blood of my own."

Veronyka recalled the fresh cut on Val's throat. *So close.*

"But I fear I gave more than I took," Morra continued. "She broke into my mind, figured out how to hatch more of them—but I *told her* about the benex bond. Despite that, I have given more to you." She nodded vigorously. "I gave her knowledge, yes, but I have given you pieces of myself— my love and my loyalty. And that is what Ilithya gave you too."

"But she kept me a secret," Veronyka whispered. She didn't know why she said it, but it hurt, somehow, to hear that Ilithya had kept the very person who was meant to help her in the dark about Veronyka's existence.

"Not just any secret," Morra said fiercely, "but a secret *weapon*. A hidden gem. She spoke often of Avalkyra, her virtues and her flaws, but you? You, she cherished and held close to her heart. I think secretly, deep down, she did not want you to rule. Avalkyra was twice-living proof of what the pursuit of the throne could do to a person. But deeper still, she knew you were the only person for the job. Love and loyalty," she repeated, reaching a trembling hand to swipe at a tear on Veronyka's face. "*That* is all you need and something you have earned every day of your life. And it is something Avalkyra will never understand."

"You have my love and loyalty too," Veronyka said thickly.

Morra smiled. "Thank you."

Xephyra crooned, and it filled the air like music.

"What now?" Veronyka whispered. "What can I do?"

Morra shifted to better see her. "For me?" she said. "Nothing. I am happy here, with the stars above and a halo of phoenix fire to keep me warm. I am filled with such cold. . . ." She trailed off, and Elliot knelt and held out a cup. After she drank laboriously, she continued. "Did Avalkyra get her hands on you?"

It seemed a silly question, but Veronyka knew it wasn't. Knew that Val had wanted, *needed* something from her, something that she couldn't get while their bond was broken and unstable. "Yes, she did. Our bond . . . ," she began, trying to explain how it had grown weak, but Morra's expression said she already knew about it. "It rebuilt itself. Stronger than before. And then she asked me to kneel to her, to become the benex to her apex."

"Did you?" Morra asked urgently. "Give her your allegiance?"

"Of course not," Veronyka said, indignant.

Morra smiled softly. "Of course not."

"But what does it mean, Morra?"

"The apex pair is the highest-ranking bondmates in a flock. They are often oldest and strongest—though that is not always the case." She spoke easier now—likely thanks to whatever Elliot had given her. "It is a social position, but it comes with increased magical power. A group bond forms, allowing the apex pair ease of connection and control over the flock, but only with a benex can she reach the height of her powers."

The height of her powers . . . Val had expressed that desire to Veronyka mere hours ago. "But what *is* a benex?"

"A *secondary* bonded pair, linked to the apex pair. It's like a magical second-in-command, sworn to serve the apex."

So *that's* why Val had wanted to fix their bond. Why she'd demanded that Veronyka prostrate herself. "And if I *had* bowed to her, she'd be even more powerful?"

"Yes, but it is more than that. If you had become benex in her flock, you could not become apex of your own."

Veronyka frowned, looking up at Ignix. "But I'm not—Xephyra and I, we're not oldest or strongest. . . ." But even as she argued, Veronyka recalled that Morra had said that wasn't always the case.

"Her paranoia is possibly even more powerful than her ambition," Morra said quietly. "But in this case, I do not think her fears are unfounded. Regardless, I believe she will try again, and ask more forcefully when she does."

Veronyka expelled a heavy breath. It was a lot to take in—Val's endless schemes and Veronyka's potential to help or hinder them. Yet at the same time, it was nothing new. Veronyka had not asked for this, but Val would punish her for it all the same.

"She doesn't scare me," Veronyka said firmly.

"She should. But fear is not the only motivator at her disposal. . . ."

Veronyka knew the truth of that. Val had taken her love and affection for the people in her life and used it against her, threatening Xephyra and Tristan and everything she cared about. Val would promise their safety if she knelt. . . . She would promise all manner of things to get what she wanted.

Then she would destroy it all anyway.

She'd start with the empire. It would be brutal and bloody—and it might even seem like a boon, given the fact that the empire was ready to march on them. But once those foes were vanquished, where would she turn her attention? And what kind of world would be on the other side of it? An empire where daughters paid for the sins of their mothers? Where vengeance was doled out brutally and without mercy? And after all those countless innocent lives were taken—their families broken, their livelihoods ruined—would Val be the one to pick up the pieces? What did she know about peace? The empire would be demolished, its people beaten down, and hatred for Val and the Ashfires, for all animages and winged magical creatures, would be at a new high. Tensions would boil over, and they would fight this same war over and over and over again, which might just be what Val truly wanted.

They didn't need more bloodshed. They needed to unite, not fracture even further.

It would take a skilled leader to bring these forces together for the greater good. Could Veronyka be that leader? Would it mean being queen *and* apex? And however things looked on the other side, would she be strong enough to repair and rebuild and *remake* the world?

"What do I do?" Veronyka asked desperately. "How can we stop her, when she's already so powerful?"

Morra smiled widely. "It's simple. You're powerful too. Whether you choose to become apex or not."

Was it her choice? She glanced at Ignix again, who watched the scene with somber but otherwise inscrutable eyes. If Veronyka decided she wanted such a position, what would she have to do to get it?

"And you, Veronyka, are *my* Ashfire queen," Morra continued. "Whether you make that choice or not."

She started coughing then, a dry, rasping sound that plainly came from deep inside.

Veronyka squeezed her hand and looked up at the others, who each wore subdued expressions.

She wanted to fight, to bring the healer here—to do something—but it was clear that what Morra wanted was peace.

Her eyes fluttered, her breath rattled, and she reached out her other hand. Veronyka didn't know what for, until Ignix bowed her head and pressed her beak into Morra's open palm.

"The world's first phoenix. You did me a great honor carrying me here, Old One—gave me a funeral parade the likes of myself could never have hoped for. And a last chance to see the world that way . . . from on high."

Veronyka's vision sparkled, and when Morra's hand dropped, she did not move again. The hand Veronyka held was slack too, and she laid it gently down.

Sparrow was staring off into the middle distance, uncertain, but then Elliot bent and whispered to her, and her face crumpled. Veronyka noticed for the first time that Sparrow wore a sling on her arm and was quite bruised and banged up herself.

"Thank you," Veronyka said as she stood, addressing their small group. Tristan's hand was on her back, rubbing slow circles, though she didn't recall when he'd put it there. It felt as if it had been there all along. "For bringing her back, for taking care of her. For taking care of each other."

Elliot nodded, glancing down at Sparrow, who was stroking her raven's shining feathers.

"It makes it easier, somehow."

Veronyka didn't know exactly what she was trying to say. Sometimes she felt as if she carried the whole world upon her shoulders—and never had she felt more bent with the effort than she did at this moment, with Morra's words still ringing in her ears.

Despair opened like a chasm beneath her feet, threatening to pull her under, but Veronyka could not let it.

She turned to Ignix, the world's first phoenix, just as Morra had said. Surely she would know something of value for the battle ahead. Surely she was the missing piece to Veronyka's rapidly crumbling plans.

Come on, then, Ignix said, as if she'd heard Veronyka's thoughts. She flew away without another word.

Tristan pulled Veronyka gently around, his expression inquisitive as he ducked his head, trying to catch her eye. He opened himself to her, offering all he had to give.

Will you—can you . . . ? She struggled to speak the words, even in her mind, as she stared down at Morra.

I'll take care of it, he promised. *I'll take care of her.*

And she knew he would.

Ignix had left the clearing and had flown to Prosperity's second tower—all that remained of the ancient, original structure. Veronyka was both desperate to talk to the phoenix and afraid of what she might say.

As Tristan spoke quietly to the others, Xephyra fluttered over. She nudged Veronyka in the chest, and it was a surprise when Rex was there too, doing the same. Tristan glanced over his shoulder, a soft, tender look on his face to see his bondmate comforting Veronyka, before he turned back to the task at hand.

Their shared presence bolstered Veronyka, a mix of life and love and magic that brought her back to herself. The stars twinkled, the trees rustled, and all manner of creatures croaked and trilled and chittered away.

Veronyka patted Rex fondly before climbing into Xephyra's saddle. They soared the short distance to the tower, Xephyra dropping her on the building's sloping roof before departing again.

"I'm glad you're alive," Veronyka said, sitting on the ledge next to the phoenix. She was different from the last time Veronyka had seen her, raging at Val and predicting their coming doom. She seemed oddly at peace. "And Sparrow, too."

Ignix followed Veronyka's gaze as she looked toward the clearing where they'd left the others behind.

She is a good chick.

There was affection in her voice that Veronyka had not heard before. Her lips tugged up at the corners before grief and fear dragged them down again.

"I've been wondering," Veronyka began, picking at a groove in the stone beneath her. "Did you accept Avalkyra's challenge at the Eyrie because you were the only one who could defeat her? Apex against apex?"

Yes and no. It is true that only another apex can match her, but that apex was never me. I was weaker than her even then, and now? I wouldn't stand a chance.

"But you're the world's first phoenix, over a thousand years old," Veronyka said, somewhat desperately. "How could anyone be better than you?"

They both knew that when she said "anyone," she really meant herself.

My bondmates are ashes on the wind, and this flock does not know me. I am little more than a ghost to them.

"Not a ghost—a living legend. No one could challenge you."

Perhaps not, she conceded. *But there is someone I could bow down to instead.*

"Why me?" Veronyka said, barely above a whisper.

I think you know why, Ignix said gently. *You are the ideal choice to replace me. Your flock admires and supports you, and your human bondmate would make the perfect benex. Plus, you are bonded to her, which means you know our foe better than any other. Better than I, certainly. It must be you.*

Veronyka swallowed, trying to gather her courage.

I know it is a burden, Ignix said. *I have borne it many long years. But you are not alone. Those you love will help carry the load.*

"I wish they wouldn't," Veronyka said. "I wish I could take all the danger and make it my own."

Ignix turned an understanding gaze on her. *That is the mistake Avalkyra makes—the mistake I myself have made—and it is the surest way to fail. Together, as Axura intended. We were never meant to be alone.*

That was the heart of magic, wasn't it? Togetherness. With every new facet learned and ability discovered, Veronyka saw that it was all about connection, about lifelong ties and the strength that came from them. It was hands held in the dark. It was the stars against the black of night—one alone was not enough, but together the sky was alive with glittering light. And what was apex magic if not the epitome of that truth?

Her bond to Xephyra made Veronyka strong and brave. Her bond to Tristan made her life richer, her expression and understanding of love deeper. Even her bond to Val had changed her irrevocably and taught her what could happen if she let herself succumb to great sorrow and loss.

What might dozens give her? And more to the point, what might she give to them in turn?

"How did you manage it alone for a thousand years?" Veronyka asked in awe.

I wasn't alone for as long as that. Closer to eight hundred years, in fact.

"Does that mean . . . ? Did Nefyra really rule as queen of Pyra for two hundred years?"

Ignix inclined her head. *Axura had chosen her—had chosen us—to defeat the strixes, and so, the goddess gifted her with long life to match mine, so that we might finish what we started and see the battle through to its end. Nefyra's life was tied to the war. Once it was finished . . . so was she. Then I was truly alone. The pain was . . . Well, it changed me. I couldn't bear the thought of losing another, so I tried to protect myself, to wear my apex status as a shield. But while it may have safeguarded my heart—and kept the burden of the apex from falling on the shoulders of any other—it also isolated me.*

Veronyka couldn't fathom such loneliness, but she also understood the impulse to protect others. To carry the responsibility alone.

I failed to see that connections are what give such a power purpose. And so I forged none and saw only the duty. The obligation. I forgot what it was to share the load. I forgot what it was to have companions and comrades.

Veronyka saw Val in Ignix's words and recognized what might have allowed Val to break into the phoenix's mind in the first place. A life without connection was a cold and lonely one, and it was clearly something the two had in common. Val saw her love for Pheronia as a fatal flaw and the one great mistake of her past. She was determined to learn from it, to love nothing and no one. In some ways it made her stronger—it certainly gave her less to lose—but like Ignix said, her power lacked purpose. What would she do with it if she succeeded and there was no one left to hate and nothing left to destroy? She'd become an empty shell, much like Ignix had been.

Veronyka expelled a slow breath. Just like the throne, she knew the apex power was a gift and a curse, a boon and a burden—and that it was better to seize it for herself than to let Val wield it unchallenged.

"How do we do it? Become the apex pair? Do we have to challenge you?"

Ignix's eyes crinkled, almost like a smile. *You need not battle me, daughter of Ashfires. What you seek will be freely given—from me and from your flock. Phoenixes admire bravery and heart, love and self-sacrifice, and you have given them that in spades. They are already more yours than mine.*

The words made Veronyka's cheeks hot. Such praise coming from anyone would be overwhelming, but coming from apex Ignix, Nefyra's own bondmate?

"But if there's no true challenge . . . how do I get them to accept Xephyra as apex? To bow before us?"

Ignix twitched her wing. *Nefyra had only to ask.*

A question answered was better than one that was never asked at all. Like magic as a whole, it could be forced and demanded—or it could be requested and bestowed, and it had never been in Veronyka to take.

Not that she relished the idea of standing before the Phoenix Riders and asking them to bow to her. Asking them to give her power over them.

"What did Avalkyra and Morra mean when they said the height of apex powers? There's something more than the group bond, isn't there? Something to do with a benex?"

There is. It is called heartfire.

The word conjured the image of Ignix on the outskirts of Ferro, enraged as she spouted a fountain of flame from her beak. "I saw you use it before, didn't I?"

Ignix nodded gravely.

"Is that what Avalkyra wanted? To be able to make heartfire?"

Indeed. Only an apex-benex bond can achieve it.

"But how did you?"

The bond survives death, Ignix said simply. *And I have been bonded to Nefyra for a long time. Also, the Ashfire bloodline has kept the connection alive and strong. The Lightbringer line survives too, I think.*

"Callysta was Nefyra's benex?" Veronyka asked, momentarily transported into the world of history and legend that she'd adored so much as a child . . . and which often felt a bit too real recently. "And the Lightbringer bloodline is still intact?"

Ignix fixed Veronyka with an amused look as she was bombarded with questions. *Yes, she was—and yes, I believe it is. I sense Nefyra in you, just as I sense Callysta in her.*

"Who?" Veronyka whispered, though somehow, she already knew.

The little bird, of course. Sparrow.

A soft smile spread across Veronyka's face. "Does she know?"

I do not think so. Yours is not the only bloodline that lost some of its daughters along the way.

"Tell me about heartfire. Is that how you destroyed the strixes?"

It is a powerful weapon. It can destroy, create, and unmake. It is Axura's own flame, hotter than the sun. Strixes can survive a brush with phoenix fire, just as a phoenix can survive contact with a strix's shadows. But touch them with a single spark of heartfire and their entire body will burst into flame.

A shiver went down Veronyka's spine. She understood why Val would covet that power so fiercely, even if she would never want it for herself. It was too much power, too much responsibility. And yet . . . it would be the fastest way to end the fighting. It could save lives—the lives of her friends and family—even if using it would make Veronyka's stomach turn.

Val had hatched more than a hundred strixes, which meant Veronyka would have to *kill* more than a hundred strixes. For all their wrongness, their dark intent and soul-sucking power, they were animals. They were living, breathing beings with minds of their own, however foreign to her. And they were only back in this world because Val had summoned them.

Veronyka hated to condemn them to death for the will of their master.

"Was it hard?" Veronyka asked. "To kill so many?"

Yes, but none were as hard as the last. She was my Shadow Twin.

"Your what?" Veronyka thought she might have heard the term before. . . . For some reason, it made her think of Val.

My False Sister—the apex strix. We were both first of our kind, born together . . . and destined to kill each other. Only with her death was our mission complete and the world safe.

Veronyka's heart went cold. Ignix's words were about the past, but they felt prophetic. Much as she wanted to hide from the truth in them—in all she had heard tonight—she knew she couldn't.

Being apex *would* be a burden. It would put lives in her hands and give her the kind of power and control she had never wanted. But if that power was given freely and not taken or forced, if that power was *earned* and not bestowed by birth and blood . . . it could be wielded with care and in defense of those she loved.

Maybe it wasn't what she wanted for herself.

But if she and Val were destined to clash, Veronyka *must* win.

She would bear the burden because she wouldn't wish it upon another.

She would be their sword, their shield, their light in the darkness.

It was not the same as being a queen . . . but it was not so different, either.

The Everlasting Flame burned for nearly a thousand years.

Some said it was a clock, counting down until the fall of the queendom.

Others claimed it was a beacon, lighting the way home.

But the Everlasting Flame was not just any fire. It was *Axura's* fire, blazing not from wing nor feather—but from heart and soul.

—*Myths and Legends of the Golden Empire and Beyond*, a compilation of stories and accounts, the Morian Archives, 101 AE

And so I will give it to her. I will keep fighting the
same war I fought centuries ago.

- CHAPTER 48 -
TRISTAN

TRISTAN WAS ALL OUT of sorts when he arrived at the Rider Council meeting. He hadn't seen Veronyka since she disappeared to talk to Ignix, and he'd been busy ensuring that Morra's body was carefully preserved until they could have a funeral pyre. Tristan insisted on carrying her himself—he'd promised Veronyka he'd see to it, hadn't he?—and only once she was laid down in a quiet room, a blanket pulled over her body, did he attend to the rest of his duties.

He should have spoken to Elliot, gotten a full report on what had happened in their time apart or sought out his patrol members. As it was, he managed only to look in on Anders—unconscious, with Latham by his side—before making his way to the commander's rooms.

Veronyka arrived not long after him.

She kept her head down, murmuring apologies before standing next to Tristan.

She wasn't okay; she hadn't been since their run-in with Val, and Morra's death—and whatever that ancient phoenix had said to her since—wasn't helping.

Everything rested on her: Val and her strix army, the empire and its vacant throne. Worst of all, their plan had not worked, and though Tristan didn't fully understand the magic at play here, he knew that things were going to get worse before they got better.

Despite all that, when he caught her eye, her gaze was steady and her jaw set. She was shaken, not broken. It was one of the things he loved most about her. . . . No matter how many times she was knocked down, Veronyka *always* stood back up.

Tristan returned his attention to the group, which included Fallon, Darius, Beryk, Alexiya, Tristan, and Veronyka. Beryk was still heavily bandaged from the strix attack at the Eyrie, but it was good to see him on his feet again.

The table before them was spread with maps and letters, with carved obsidian markers indicating empire troops and Avalkyra's army.

They hadn't done more than catch up on the day's events before Veronyka arrived.

Once they were settled again, Beryk's tired gaze fell on Tristan. "I received a letter from your father."

"My father?" His heart squeezed—had his condition worsened? Was he going to call them back to Haven?

"He sent explicit instructions for how we are to proceed," Beryk continued. He noted the wary expression on Tristan's face, and his lips turned up at the corners before he looked down to relay the letter's contents. "He apologizes for disregarding the order of command, but considering his present condition, has requested that you replace him as commander for the interim and gives you his full support."

"You?" Tristan repeated. "You who?"

Beryk smirked. "*You* you." He cleared his throat and read aloud, "'Tristan is fully apprised of the situation here and in Pyra, and provided he consults with Veronyka, would be best suited to lead the Phoenix Riders for the foreseeable future.'"

Tristan realized his mouth was hanging open. He snapped it shut, trying to find the right words. He was confused, elated—confused again—but also uncomfortable. His father's second-in-command was meant to take the lead if and when the commander himself was unable to perform his duties.

"Beryk, I . . ."

"It's clear to me," Beryk said, speaking over Tristan's attempts at a response, "that the commander—excuse me, former commander—has the right of it. I am not in much better shape than he is, truth be told, and I do not wish to contest his decree or claim my position in the order of command. Times are changing, and the war we fight today is vastly different from the war I fought seventeen years ago. We're all in over our heads, and I seek only this: to be helpful. So, Commander Tristan, tell me how to help you, and I will do everything in my power to do so."

Tristan looked around the table, expecting surprise or even outrage. But Fallon only watched the proceedings with mild interest, while Darius appeared wholly focused on the grim picture the map with its markers painted before them. Alexiya examined her fingernails.

Had his father truly given his blessing? He looked at Veronyka, who, despite her tense posture and troubled eyes, smiled at him.

"Thank you, Beryk," he said at last. "I welcome any insight you have to offer—and that goes for everyone at the table. I'll need all your help if we're to make it through this. Now, tell me about the empire."

"They have agreed to meet with us," Fallon said, sliding his chair forward as he stared down at the map. "But their supplementary forces remain in place across the border. One false move, and they will send their full power against us."

"Should we be focused on them with the bloody Black Horde on the loose?" Alexiya asked.

"I don't think we can afford to ignore them," Tristan said. "If we don't stop them, they'll haul in any known animages for questioning, not to mention those they discover that are unregistered—whether they live outside the empire's control or not. They won't miss the opportunity to swell their coffers with taxation on anybody who breathes near an animal, never mind communicates with one."

"We sent out messengers to alert the villages of the coming danger,"

Fallon said. "If the soldiers march, they'll light the beacons. At least the people will be prepared."

"My primary concern is this meeting," Beryk said. "Without Avalkyra to use as a good-faith bargaining chip, what can we truly offer them?"

"Is there any hope of making a second attempt?" asked Darius, directing this question at Veronyka.

She shook her head. "We won't be able to get that close to her again. Next time we see her, she'll be swarmed by strixes."

"Which will be when, exactly?" asked Fallon.

"Sometime tomorrow evening."

"Then we're doomed," Darius said hollowly. "If their numbers are greater than they were when they attacked the Eyrie, then we don't stand a chance. We're hemmed in on two sides."

"Not necessarily," Tristan said. "Surely the empire is expecting us to surrender—that's what this is all about. They want to intimidate us. Think about it. . . . They're mustering the entire army but are marching with only a fraction. They're impatient and not actually anticipating a fight, so let's give them what they expect and meet to discuss terms. Then we'll convince them of the true threat and form an alliance instead."

Everyone gaped at him.

"Why bother convincing them, when we have the heir to the throne on our side?" Fallon asked. "She could order them to fight for us, could she not?"

"It isn't that simple," Tristan said, glancing at Veronyka. "She has no proof of her identity—at least, nothing the council will accept. Even if she did, they'd need to authenticate it, have meetings and contracts drawn up. It won't help us tomorrow."

Beryk sighed heavily. "I'm still not sure how we can possibly persuade them that a resurrected queen and an army out of myth is their true enemy, and not the enemy standing directly in front of them." He scrubbed his chin thoughtfully. "Perhaps it is better to avoid a direct confrontation and keep out of sight. Old habits die hard."

"All we need to do is delay them," said Veronyka. "The empire will see the truth soon enough. She's coming for us, for them . . . for everyone. They'd be fools not to ally with us. We're their best chance at survival."

With the clock ticking down, they dispersed to get some sleep and prepare for what the next day would bring.

Tristan was completely exhausted, but even still, he knew Veronyka was worse. She had expended mental and emotional energy today that he couldn't fathom, and when she inadvertently leaned into him in the hallway, it was second nature to put his arm around her and at least physically help carry the load.

His father had a room to himself near the top of the tower, and so Tristan began to lead them there, trying not to think too hard about the fact that it wasn't actually his father's room but the *commander's* room. Veronyka halted at the base of the stairs.

"I . . . Can we go outside?" she asked, her gaze distant. Tristan knew, somehow, that she wanted to see Xephyra. He nodded, redirecting them down the opposite end of the hallway.

They rounded a corner, and Latham stood before them. His face was flushed, as if he'd been running, and he came to a halt at the sight of them.

"Latham. How's Anders?" Tristan asked.

"He won't be able to fly tomorrow," Latham said roughly, and Tristan's hackles rose. He knew Latham and Anders were close—and that Anders had been badly hurt during their failed mission today—but if Latham dared to attack or blame Veronyka for that . . . They had made up recently, and Tristan was tired, but not too tired to put his fist into Latham's jaw if need be. Then he could have a bed next to Anders, and Tristan and Veronyka could get some much-needed sleep.

"He could have been killed," Latham said. His tone was still ragged, but though Tristan was expecting him to shout at Veronyka, she didn't look at all wary of him. In fact, her face was soft with the kind of tenderness she usually reserved for animals—and for him.

"But he wasn't," she said gently.

"He *could have been*. He told me it was okay. He told me to go look for my brother, and—"

"You found him," Veronyka said, still using that quiet, delicate tone. "You saved Loran."

"No, *you* saved Loran," Latham said. He was close to shouting, but it was clear now that his anger was directed at himself. "You saved me, too. You had a clear shot at her, but instead . . ." His voice hitched, and his face crumpled.

"I don't regret it," Veronyka said at once. "I need you. Both of you. We'll find another way."

"I thought—when they had the knife to his throat . . ." He swallowed, and Tristan could tell he wanted to turn aside, to hide his emotion, but he refused to look away from Veronyka. Tristan hadn't yet heard the details from the attack earlier, but he was suddenly very eager to get the full story. "And then you told us to run. Not with words, I don't think, but . . ." Latham shook his head. "I heard your voice—felt your magic—before I understood the warning. Before I was safe, I *knew* I was safe." He released a huff of laughter. "I'm not making sense."

"You are," Tristan said. He'd had the same experience in Rolan's dungeons, when Veronyka used her magic to find him.

"I guess I just—I wanted to say—" Latham moved haltingly, then took Veronyka's hand and squeezed it. "Thank you," he whispered.

He released her and turned back toward the infirmary, leaving Tristan and Veronyka to continue down the hall, alone once more.

Outside, they walked through the crisp, starry night, the moon fat and silver and veiled by wisps of clouds, giving the world an icy tint.

They found Xephyra and Rex atop the stables, sleeping in a heap of feathers so intertwined it was impossible to tell one from the other. There were proper roosts in the tower, but maybe Veronyka had called the phoenixes down before they arrived. Or maybe Xephyra had sensed that Veronyka needed something, needed her, and so had come down to wait herself.

The sight of her and Rex together always warmed something inside Tristan. It filled him with a sense of rightness and felt in many ways like the physical representation of his bond to Veronyka—the proof of it.

The closeness of his bondmate along with the soft, sleepy presence of the horses and other animals in the stables—even stubborn, taciturn Wind—eased the tension that had been tightening Tristan's shoulders. One look at Veronyka and he understood that this had been on purpose. She felt it too.

Xephyra fluttered down to them, and Veronyka and Tristan clambered onto her saddleless back. They hadn't ridden together like this since the empire attacked the Eyrie. It was a brief flight up to the roof—barely a blink and they were there—but Tristan savored it, running a hand softly along Xephyra's flank, Veronyka riding in front of him as they leaned forward and held on tight.

The roof sloped down toward the ground, and so it was a natural thing to first sit and then lean back, lying flat as they stared up at the sky. Rex and Xephyra settled on either side of them, their wings loose at their sides, creating a kind of barrier between them and the buffeting gusts of wind.

Despite the bubble of warmth, Veronyka shivered. Tristan wrapped an arm around her shoulders and pulled her in close, so her head rested in the crook between his shoulder and chest. She sighed against him.

Tristan glanced at her, then waited.

When she eventually spoke, the words were tentative. *I need to ask something of you. . . .*

"It's yours," he said at once. "Whatever you need, it's yours."

She craned her neck to look up at him, her large eyes black in the darkness. "Ignix wants to make us apex," she explained, gaze flicking to Xephyra. "So we're strong enough to oppose her."

Tristan nodded. "That makes sense. You're the best of us."

Veronyka turned her face into his chest, hiding it from view, though he caught a glimpse of her shy smile. "You're embarrassing me," she mumbled into his tunic.

He laughed. "Good."

"But it's not just us. It's you, too. Having a human bond—a benex, it's called—makes the apex pair stronger."

"How?"

"It gives us heartfire. I saw Ignix use it, once. It's like breathing fire, but its more potent than even regular phoenix flame."

Tristan understood her hesitation. Ignix wanted Veronyka to mow down their opponents. Even if they were strixes, he knew that would not be easy for her. The fact that it was Val riding one of them made it all the more complicated. And what if the empire decided they'd rather fight than ally? It had the potential to be a bloodbath.

"Callysta was Nefyra's benex," she added quietly. Tristan rather liked the idea of joining such famous ranks of warriors, and Callysta and Nefyra had always been his favorites.

He nudged her until she looked up at him again. "I know you'll do the right thing, whatever it is. So if and when you need something from me, from us"—he looked up at Rex, who nodded in agreement—"you take it, okay?"

Her eyes shone, reflecting the starlight. He hoped she felt his faith in her. To be tied to Val made Veronyka wary and on edge, but being tied to Veronyka made Tristan feel invincible.

"Okay," she said, nodding her pointy chin into his chest before settling back down again.

"Okay," he repeated, holding her tightly.

Even with their close proximity and their phoenix barricade, the temperature was dropping, and she began to shiver again.

With fingers stiff from cold, Tristan unlaced his padded vest, turning on his side and inviting her into the warmth held between the leather and his cotton tunic. The frigid air crawled in with her as she shifted closer, and his abdomen clenched as her icy hands slipped past another layer, up his shirt to the bare skin underneath. He wanted to cry out in protest, but the way she breathed and pressed herself against him, tucked under his chin, quickly distracted him from his discomfort. He wrapped his arms around her back, enclosing her in the open folds of his coat and drawing her close, while Rex and Xephyra edged nearer, blocking out the wind and the stars and everything except for them.

The war that, it turns out, we did not win at all.

- CHAPTER 49 -
SEV

THINGS WERE TENSE AT Haven for the entirety of the day and half of the night, which most people did not sleep through. Doriyan napped for a few hours but was gone again well before the sun rose.

Sev and Kade remained by the cook fire—which burned bright all night—talking little and jumping at every rustle and creak from above as they awaited a messenger pigeon from Veronyka.

He tried not to think about what the letter might say when it arrived. He tried not to think at all.

It was early morning when a shout echoed from the direction of Agneta's cottage.

It was Agneta herself, and she rushed through the pathway to Haven, brandishing a letter for her son, who had been sitting in stoic silence across the fire. He leapt to his feet and snatched it from her grip.

Sev stood too, as did Kade and many others. Everyone held their breath, waiting, as Theryn's eyes roved the paper.

"Everyone is alive . . . but they have failed. Avalkyra's strix army has grown in size—estimated at more than a hundred—and that is not including the villagers and raiders who now support her. The empire, too, intends to march tomorrow. Or rather, today. They will be in Pyra by nightfall."

"So it's war, then," said Jonny softly.

"They are so few . . . ," murmured Rosalind. "The Phoenix Riders. They don't stand a chance."

"She has asked us to fight—Veronyka," Theryn continued, eyes still on the letter. He cleared his throat and read aloud. "She says: 'Not for me or for the throne, but for each other. Only together can we make it through.'"

He looked around at the faces of each and every person who'd gathered— but his gaze lingered on the Phoenix Riders, young and old.

"I will go," Theryn said, nodding fervently. "I must. I won't force any of you to follow me, but this is something I have to do. Something I should have done a long time ago."

"We're not much help," Jonny said in his easy way, rubbing a hand across his chin—though his eyes gleamed.

"Barely a dozen," said Rosalind, turning on the spot to survey the crowd. "And that's if all of us come."

"I will go alone if I must," Theryn said.

"That won't do at all," said Jonny, shaking his head. "I'm with you, old friend. Where you go, I go."

"Me too," said Rosalind.

"And me," added Ivan. Others came forward, nodding and giving their assent.

"We *could* use more, though," Jonny said thoughtfully, staring around at their small group. "*Any* more, really."

Theryn's eyes narrowed. "What are you thinking?"

Jonny shrugged. "We have until nightfall? I suggest we send Riders across Arboria, north and south. Surely we could scrounge up a few more."

Theryn nodded. "You head east. Ros—north and south."

"North *and* south?" Jonny repeated.

"She's twice as fast as you," Theryn replied. Rosalind smiled smugly. "Besides, we've got plenty to do here. We'll need weapons, saddles. . . . By the time we're ready, we'll probably be flying directly into a fight." He glanced toward his mother's house, where the commander and his phoenix were. "Which means I'll need a ride."

Then he marched off, Veronyka's letter still clutched tightly in his hand.

The tense, uneasy bubble that had hung over Haven since the previous day popped, and suddenly the place was filled with noise and manic energy. Packing and preparing, prying open dusty crates of weapons and supplies and cleaning off old saddles and armor.

Even their relatively small numbers would swell the Phoenix Rider ranks and could make all the difference in the coming fight. They would lend their support and stand together.

Well, those who could fly, anyway.

Sev felt rooted to the spot, staring silently as the arrangements were under way, as those who could help, did.

And those who couldn't?

He had been waiting for this moment for days—weeks, even—and still he was not prepared. Kade would leave with the rest of the Haven Riders, mounted astride their fiery steeds, to join Veronyka and Tristan and all the others as they fought for themselves and each other.

They were heading into a battle, and none of them could afford to carry an extra rider, especially a dropout empire soldier like him. Sev guessed that Theryn would ride the commander's phoenix in his place, but there were no spare transports for Sev.

He would get left behind.

For years he'd been avoiding the fight, avoiding caring, and now that he'd finally committed and found something and someone—several someones—he wanted to fight for, he couldn't.

The irony was not lost on him.

His fears of being useless, of having nothing to offer, reared up again.

Sev slipped away in the commotion, but Kade eventually found him feeding the chickens. He needed to do something with his hands and to get away from the anticipatory excitement that had filled everyone around him.

The chickens squawked and fluttered at his feet—precious, idiot birds. Sev felt a perhaps unflattering kinship with them.

"They're planning to leave late afternoon," Kade told him. "They want to wait as long as possible for any reinforcements they might muster. Too bad Doriyan's already gone, or he might have carried word to Prosperity."

"They?" Sev repeated. "What about you?"

"I'm not going," Kade said simply.

"What?"

He clarified. "I'm not going . . . unless you come with me."

"I'll be nothing but deadweight. Jinx would fly slower with a second person, and if anything happens, you'll have to protect me—I can't let you take that risk."

"We promised we'd be together at the end of this, and that's looking like it might be sooner rather than later. I'm not going anywhere without you."

"Kade, I . . ." Sev swallowed around the bubble in his throat. "I can't let you turn your back on them. They're your friends, your equals—they're important to you."

"*You* are important to me," Kade said stubbornly. "And in what way are we not equals?"

Sev gave him an exasperated look. "In every way imaginable—but let's start with the fact that you're a Phoenix Rider."

"I was only able to become a Phoenix Rider because you *gave me* your phoenix egg," Kade said desperately. "It could have been you—*should* have been."

Sev shook his head. "I'm a terrible animage. . . . That was never in the cards for me."

"You're only terrible—" Kade stopped abruptly, realizing he'd conceded at least partly to Sev's argument. He pinched the bridge of his nose. "You've never used your magic, never even tried to learn or develop your ability. Inexperience does not equal ineptitude."

"Jinx hates me. All the phoenixes do."

"*You* hate Jinx," Kade said. "She's as enamored of you as I am."

Heat crept its way up Sev's neck, and he was forced to blink and look away so he didn't lose it in front of Kade.

"*Why* do you hate her?" Kade asked softly. "I thought you'd be happy to meet her, that you *wanted* this for me."

"I did—I *do*," Sev stammered, wanting to squash that rough, wavering edge to Kade's voice. He expelled a breath and met Kade's eyes. "It's just . . . I wanted to give you somewhere to belong, but I didn't realize I was giving you a place to belong where I couldn't."

"Do you think belonging has to do with ability or skill or *usefulness*?"

Sev shrugged—he supposed he did, to a certain degree. It was his usefulness that had brought him and Trix together, and therefore, him and Kade. It was also his usefulness that had allowed him to continue to serve the Phoenix Riders ever since.

Kade fixed him with a knowing look, as if he could read his thoughts. "Belonging is not about give-and-take, like some transaction. When I look at you, I don't see a list of useful attributes. I see your clever eyes and your warm smile. I see the pain you've been through and how you've come out stronger. When you freed Riella, you didn't do it so she could give you something in return. When you gave me my egg, it wasn't so that you could benefit. That's not what belonging is, or friendship. Or love." The word lit up Sev's insides like a firefly trapped in a jar, but Kade just kept going. "You did those things because you're good and generous, and you've always been that, whatever else you've been doing. As a soldier, a spy . . . you've always been that. You've always been *you*, and that is more than enough."

"Well, that's . . . I . . ." Sev didn't know what to say. Kade had the ability to tear him down and build him up in the same breath. He felt raw and exposed, but somehow better for it. As if all his fears and doubts, which he had once worn like an ill-fitting cloak, had been stripped away.

"I know Ilithya put that idea into your head," Kade continued, "and I hate her for it. I suppose I didn't help either, judging you the way I did when we first met." Kade took him by the arms and squeezed. "But you don't need to be *useful* in order to have the right to exist. To have a place. You are a part of this because you care about this. You belong because we want you with us."

Sev squeezed his eyes shut, then let his head fall back so he could stare up at the leafy canopy above. When he lowered his face, tears had pooled in his lower eyelids, there for Kade to see.

Sev released a shuddering breath. "I was jealous," he said abruptly. Kade frowned. "Of Jinx. She loves you, and you love her, and . . ." He swallowed. "Is it ridiculous or pathetic to be jealous of a phoenix? Or is it both?"

Kade didn't humor Sev with a laugh or a smile. Brows low and gaze intent, he drew Sev into a slow, deliberate, deep kiss. Sev felt like he was dying, like he was living—like his heart would burst from his chest.

"Come with me," Kade said, drawing back just enough to speak, so the words whispered across Sev's lips. "We'll find a way. They're going to need all the help they can get."

Sev pressed his forehead against Kade's. "But even if I'm enough—"

"You are," Kade interjected.

"Right, I am enough—actually, I believe you said I was *more* than enough?" Sev asked, leaning back.

Kade rolled his eyes, but he was smiling. "Too much, at the moment."

"But I want to do something more. Even if I don't *need* to prove anything or earn my place . . . I can't shake this feeling like there's more I could be doing than being a passenger on Jinx's back."

He scanned the faces of the people moving about, searching for some inspiration, when he spotted Theo at the edges of the crowd. She looked exactly how Sev felt—frantic, frustrated, and desperate to do something.

But what good could they be without phoenixes? What other task could they set themselves?

Kade followed Sev's line of sight. "Jonny's story . . ."

"Was brutal," Sev said, thinking of those people, held against their will for seventeen years, weaponized against their own kind—and that was *after* they'd been tortured and threatened and forced to watch their fellow apprentices and phoenixes slaughtered.

"It was," Kade agreed. He hesitated, and Sev shifted his focus back to their conversation. "It made me think of Ilithya."

"What about her?"

"The phoenix eggs we brought into Pyra?" He waited for Sev's nod of recognition, as if he could ever forget them. "Most of them were stolen from an underground cache in Aura Nova. I went with her. The eggs were hidden beneath the abandoned training arena."

"How did you get in? It's supposed to be all boarded up and inaccessible." The training grounds in Aura Nova were built partially into the base of the Rock, then extending beyond, taking up several city blocks. It had been closed the entire time Sev had lived in the capital, and guards were posted at the entrances day and night. He doubted even a thief as enterprising as Trix could have gotten in past so much security, and according to Jonny, the drain Theo had escaped through had been blocked since her escape.

"The main entrances, yes—but the arena was also accessible through *underground* entrances. There are all sorts of passages inside the Rock—for servants, spies, and message runners. It's a Pyraean thing. Most lead to the Nest, the courthouse, and other government buildings, but they also connected to the training grounds. And every governor's house has access. We got in through a passage from Lord Rolan's town house. That's why she got herself transferred into Rolan's service in the first place." Kade straightened, a thoughtful expression settling over his brow. "I wonder if there are more than just eggs down there. . . ."

"The arena *is* extremely well guarded for a supposedly abandoned building," Sev said, thinking out loud. "And didn't General Rast bargain for the Pyraean governor's house specifically? He could have had any Marble Row mansion, so why that house?"

"Ego?" Kade said, though his tone was doubtful.

"Could be," Sev conceded, "but I think he had something else in mind."

"You don't think . . . ," Kade said, glancing at Theo again.

"Didn't Jonny say Rast built the registry headquarters in his own house as well?" Sev asked. He scrubbed a hand absently through his hair and started to pace. "He's clearly the kind of man who has to maintain control. They've lived with him for seventeen years, doing his dirty work. I bet he rarely lets those prisoners out of his sight. Except today."

"Today . . . ," Kade repeated. Then his eyes lit up. "The march into Pyra—he's leading it."

"Exactly. They'll still be heavily guarded and monitored. The general's house probably has as much security as the Nest. But despite his desire to keep all his shady dealings under his own roof, he obviously couldn't do the same with the phoenixes. They'd set his house on fire, for starters, and would be too conspicuous. But living in a governor's house would give him direct access to those underground tunnels."

Where else would you keep a creature that could fly and burst into flame? Somewhere they couldn't escape, somewhere that wouldn't burn.

While Sev continued to stalk back and forth with restless energy, Kade had gone still. "When we went down there, into the arena . . . ," he began, speaking slowly, as if carefully dredging up the memories, "there were guards. Posted *inside*. I thought it strange, especially since they weren't actually guarding the eggs we found. But maybe they were guarding something else." He finished with a wide-eyed stare, turning to Sev in shock.

"We need to get into those tunnels," Sev said, excitement kicking against his ribs—until he remembered his blown cover. If he were still a soldier in Lord Rolan's employ, he might've been able to get himself into the governor's house in Aura Nova. But Sev had run away, and he doubted he could think of a story that could excuse deserting his post more than a week ago and being absent ever since.

But there was *another* soldier in Rolan's employ who might help them. . . .

"Yara," Sev said hoarsely.

"What about her?" Kade asked, trying to follow Sev's train of thought.

"Yara could let us inside Rolan's town house."

"And then we'll take the passages to the arena?" Kade asked.

"First we'll go to the general's house," Sev said. "Think about it. We could save the phoenixes *and* their Riders. We'll enter the house through the tunnels, and once we get them underground with us, you'll lead us toward the arena. The closer we get . . ."

"They'll be able to sense their bondmates," Kade filled in. "All that stone probably makes it impossible now."

He was quiet after that—likely running through the possibilities, just as Sev had. But this was Sev's wheelhouse. This was who he was and what he had to offer. Himself.

The preparations for the Haven Riders' departure were still under way, so for this rescue mission, Sev and Kade were on their own.

Well, not entirely. With any luck, they'd have Yara. As soon as they arrived in Aura Nova, they'd send a runner to Lord Rolan's house, asking Yara to meet them at a dockside location in the Narrows. If she turned up, they could figure out the next part of their plan together, but there was someone else Sev needed to rope into their scheme *before* they left Haven.

Theo was alone when they found her, as usual. She listened to the plan, growing stiller and stiller with every word Sev spoke, until Sev wasn't sure if the words angered her, thrilled her—or if she'd fallen asleep.

"Why?" she said gruffly. Again her voice was flat, like Sev remembered from the campfire, and her expression was equally difficult to read.

"Why? Because it's wrong, for a start, and the Phoenix Riders need all the help they can get. Besides, the general will lead the march into Pyra— there couldn't be a better time."

Theo shook her head. "But why *you*? You're not a Phoenix Rider."

"I know that," Sev said, only a little defensively. "I'm nothing, okay, but—"

"You're not *nothing*," said Kade sharply, and Theo's gaze darted between them. She seemed to put something together, and her suspicion cleared.

"I'm tired of *doing* nothing, then," Sev corrected hurriedly. "I want to fight, and this is the best way I know how. Sneaking and stealing."

Theo was quiet for several moments. "The entrances to the training arena are barricaded and heavily guarded. If your friend doesn't come through—"

"She will," Sev said firmly—more firmly than he felt.

Theo was silent for a while, and Sev worried he'd lost her. Then—"We'll need a boat," she said, and Sev's heart leapt. Theo looked more alive than Sev had ever seen her before, cheeks flushed and eyes bright. "And a crate."

I try to remember the beginning.
I struggle to envision the end.

- CHAPTER 50 -
VERONYKA

THAT NIGHT, VERONYKA DREAMED. Despite the poison flooding her veins, Val dreamed with her.

It was an incoherent blur—vivid, but confusing. Veronyka saw and felt and tasted Val's bitterness, her anger. It tore at them both, like claws, sinking deep and leaving scars.

There were flashes of sounds and sights: Aura and the smoking ruin of the Everlasting Flame, buried in rubble; the Eyrie's cobblestones, smeared with black feathers and blood. Doriyan and Sidra, strixes and phoenixes—and Veronyka. Of course Veronyka. Ignix appeared next, telling Veronyka it had to be her, and then Morra's face, calling Veronyka her queen.

Rage rippled through the air . . . rage that was not Veronyka's.

Suddenly a scene coalesced: Val was huddled somewhere in the dark, surrounded by endless rustling and chittering. She looked more like a captive than a queen, and Veronyka had the desperate urge to rescue her—to save her from the shadows.

Nearer she drew, Val's eyes closed but fluttering, as if she was struggling to open them. Veronyka needed light, needed fire and warmth—and Val needed it too, didn't she? She looked so small and fragile, Veronyka feared she would catch a chill, but light would wake her, and Veronyka feared that possibility most of all.

The darkness was alive, though, pressing in on her. Making it hard to breathe. A little light wouldn't hurt, would it? A little light . . . She reached inside, into her heart, drawing the light forward. But it didn't stop there; it spread, turning into blazing fire, crawling across her arms and legs, filling the darkness.

The creatures in the shadows screamed, and Val's eyes snapped open.

Veronyka awoke on the stable roof, her back aching and her toes numb. Her face and hands were warm, though, tight in the circle of Tristan's arms, and she inhaled the scent of his skin with every sleepy breath.

But something was shifting, disrupting her sleep as it squirmed between them, tiny paws digging into her stomach. She looked down in confusion.

There was a mangy, three-legged orange cat wedged between her and Tristan—and that wasn't all. There were squirrels, chipmunks, raccoons, and a dozen varieties of birds, pressed up tightly against them on all sides.

The night had been frigid, and Prosperity was not large enough to accommodate the same number of animals as the Eyrie. Evidently, the lure of two animages—and two hot-as-summer phoenixes—was more than these animals could resist. Besides, Sparrow, with whom these animals likely usually spent their nights, had slept in the infirmary, and Veronyka suspected the healer would have turned these critters away.

Veronyka sat up, the cold racing into all the places that had been warm mere seconds ago, while Tristan rolled onto his back, throwing an arm over his eyes—and dislodging a dog that had nestled in close to his neck. How had *that* fellow gotten up here?

Wouldn't stop whining, Xephyra informed Veronyka, sounding distinctly grumpy. *So I lifted him up.* She and Rex had been nudged and jostled aside to make room for what was clearly every animal from the Eyrie and several newcomers as well.

The dog yipped, and Tristan lurched upright. "What the—"

"Veronyka?" came a voice from somewhere below.

Alexiya smiled when Veronyka's head popped into view—and it stretched wider when Tristan sat up after her, the laces of his jacket undone.

The small glimmer of mirth faded, though, as she gestured for them to come down.

"What is it?" Veronyka called, fear banishing any embarrassment she might have felt at being caught sleeping on the roof with Tristan.

"It's the empire. They reached the bridge," Alexiya said.

It was their agreed-upon meeting spot, if not their agreed-upon time. "So they're early? That's okay. We'll just—"

She shook her head. "They reached it and didn't stop."

"Didn't stop," Veronyka echoed, still confused as she scrambled to her feet, gently moving aside animals as she reached for Xephyra. Then, finally, it sank in. "They don't intend to meet with us, do they?"

Alexiya sighed. "It doesn't look like it."

Veronyka considered this as she and Tristan rode their phoenixes down to the ground—Tristan, slightly bemused and half-asleep, clutching the whining dog to his chest.

Beryk had made no mention of handing over Val in their request for a meeting with the general, so Veronyka could only assume that he had never intended to speak with them in the first place. That did not bode well for the day to come—nor for their hopes of being allies when Val finally did make her move.

As it was, they'd be lucky if they could spare the majority of Pyra the devastation an army could wreak by sweeping through in search of so-called dangerous animages and their phoenixes. Never mind the fact that if the Phoenix Riders didn't stop them, the soldiers would just wind up marching blindly into Val's strixes. They didn't deserve that, whatever their empire had ordered, and they wouldn't stop Val—not now that she had such power and control. They would simply die, which meant *more* soldiers would come. More death.

No, they had to stop the soldiers' progress, but how?

They couldn't just show up wings blazing—that would send the wrong message, obviously, and weaken their chances of reaching some kind of agreement. But the meeting could go bad no matter how they arrived, so their flock had to be nearby and ready to act if that was the case. There was a balance they had to strike between showing strength and humility.

It was a harmony Veronyka had become newly acquainted with in recent weeks and a difficult equilibrium to achieve.

She and Tristan rushed back to the meeting room from the previous night, where the Rider Council reconvened once more.

"Who are we dealing with?" Tristan asked, and Beryk handed over the initial response they had received. It was signed by General Rast and witnessed by several commanders and captains, as well as a lawyer, a notary, and a member of the Office for Border Control.

"William of Stel," Veronyka said, pointing at the last name. "Is that . . . ?"

Tristan looked up, surprised, but it was Beryk who answered.

"Elliot's father," he said with a nod.

"I think we have our new bargaining chip," Veronyka said.

Beryk sent a horse-mounted rider ahead of them with a message announcing their coming and reminding the empire's leaders—*politely*—that they had agreed to meet with the Phoenix Riders and that they would be arriving shortly.

Their next steps were a little trickier.

While Elliot and Riella's presence *should* ensure they weren't shot down on sight, thanks to their father, Veronyka didn't like the idea of having a young, untrained girl on what could quickly devolve into a battlefield. But she couldn't deny that they needed any bit of leverage they could get. Besides, the siblings hadn't seen their father in two years. . . . Who knew if they'd get another chance?

When they called both Elliot and Riella to the meeting room, it appeared Elliot thought he was in some kind of trouble.

"Where's Riella?" Veronyka asked as he entered alone and closed the door behind him.

"It's not her fault," Elliot said, which made no sense to Veronyka—but apparently, he wasn't talking to her. His eyes were fixed on Beryk as he continued. "And it's not Sparrow's, either. It was all my idea, so if you want to punish someone, it should be me."

Beryk sighed. "We're on the brink of war, lad. Now is not the time to fret over such things."

Elliot shook his head. His body language was tense and bracing, his face downcast, though he held Beryk's gaze. "I disobeyed your orders and abandoned my duties. I had good reason—and I succeeded in rescuing Sparrow and Ignix—but that's no excuse."

Now Veronyka understood. "I gave him permission," she interjected before Beryk could reply, and Elliot shot her a surprised but grateful look. "I told him which passages to check, and—"

"Enough," Beryk said, holding up a hand to silence her. He gave her an apologetic look afterward, clearly unsure where he ranked when it came to her, but she could offer no real insight in that regard. He turned to Elliot. "You did the right thing, and I'm glad you disobeyed me." Elliot's mouth fell open, and Beryk smiled in mild exasperation. "You weren't grounded after the attack on the Eyrie for trying to help your sister or for disobeying my orders. You were punished because you acted foolishly and put all of us in danger. As far as I can tell, what you've done now is the exact opposite. You deserve to be commended, not rebuked."

"Thank you, sir," Elliot said, speaking to his feet. "For that, and for everything you've done for me since. If there's anything I can do . . ."

"Funny you mention it," Beryk said, tossing a smile at Veronyka. "There is."

Elliot was, at first, vehemently against the idea. After they summoned Riella, she helped to convince him.

"It would be good to see Dad again, wouldn't it?" she asked hopefully.

Elliot's mouth was a flat line. "Is Ignix coming?"

Veronyka's heart sped up. If she was to become apex, Ignix would have to be there to bow her head and show her allegiance. In front of everyone. "Yes."

"And Sparrow? I won't come unless she does."

If Riella's presence was a dangerous risk, Sparrow's was downright reck-less. "Sparrow has no reason to be there and would be safer—"

"The thing is," Elliot cut in, "I can't leave her again." He lowered his voice. "I made a promise, and I know it might not seem like that means anything to me given what I've done in the past"—he swallowed—"but I need it to mean something."

"Elliot, I . . ."

"And," he pressed doggedly, "I don't expect Ignix will agree to come without her either."

Veronyka sighed.

The truth was, nowhere was safe at the moment. Those who couldn't fight—the wounded like Anders, plus stable hands and kitchen helpers and everyone else who wasn't a bonded animage—were set to relocate to the nearest underground caverns along the *Sekveia*. There wouldn't be enough Riders left to properly guard Prosperity, plus many of its defensive advantages—like rounded towers and crenellated walls—were negated by the fact that their enemy could fly too. If Val *did* decide to send her strixes there, they'd find it abandoned and would hopefully move on. She couldn't very well check every tunnel and cavern across Pyrmont, and with scouts posted, their people would have a chance to flee.

And so Veronyka agreed with Elliot's request, and his face lit with intense relief. They both wanted Sparrow to be safe, and she was glad that Elliot had made it his personal mission since Veronyka herself had so many other things on her mind. The people in her life were starting to take care of each other, and it was a wonderful thing.

She had enough to worry about.

Despite their strange, shared dream the previous night, Val had been unreachable all day. It might be the poison still flooding her veins, or per-haps it was the apex magic making it easier for Val to protect herself. What-ever it was, Veronyka made sure to stay on high alert and kept her belt stocked with poison darts, just in case.

While the group that would attempt to negotiate with the empire consisted of Veronyka, Tristan, and Beryk, accompanied by Elliot, Riella, Ignix, and Sparrow, the rest of the Riders in their flock would remain nearby. There was no telling how the day would go, and they couldn't afford to be separated.

The other members of Tristan's patrol would station themselves to the north to keep a watch for Val, while Fallon's patrol held a perimeter to the west. Cassian's patrol, supplemented by Alexiya and Doriyan, who had arrived from Arboria, would position themselves to the east. If things went badly, Elliot would take Anders's place on Tristan's patrol, and Beryk would return to Cassian's. The apprentice Riders who were old enough to fight but had yet to graduate and join a patrol were currently helping with the evacuation of Prosperity, but they numbered only five, and Veronyka and the others were hesitant to involve them unless absolutely necessary. This wasn't like the attack on the Eyrie, when the choice was fight or die. Even if everyone else was killed, they could live in the caverns indefinitely and remain in hiding. Their orders were to protect the evacuees, and Veronyka took comfort in the idea that whatever happened, some Phoenix Riders would survive what was to come.

For a moment she thought of Haven, of Jonny and Rosalind and the rest. She thought of her father and grandmother.

Had they received Alexiya's letter? And if they had . . . would they come? She had hoped they might get word before they departed, and fought against a pang of disappointment when they didn't.

Veronyka could understand why they might not come. They had safety in their isolation. Once they left, there'd be no going back to that quiet, peaceful existence. If they didn't come, that meant more Phoenix Riders would survive this . . . even if it lessened the odds that Veronyka and those on either side of her would be among them.

Even if that survival was contingent upon hiding and living in secret.

She couldn't shake the memory of the way she'd parted with her father, the request he'd made and the accusation she'd thrown at him. He'd asked her to stay, and while remaining behind and out of the fight was never possible for Veronyka, she prayed he might decide to join her instead.

As they left Prosperity to meet the empire's march, Veronyka turned in the saddle and stared—she'd never seen so many Phoenix Riders together at once, flying off to battle. Saddles creaked, feathers rustled, and wingbeats filled the air.

Her senses buzzed with their collective presence, and she couldn't help thinking what it might be like to be their apex—their chosen leader. How much more formidable would they be if they were magically united in the face of all the danger that approached them? How many more of them would survive if Veronyka had the courage to claim that position and that power?

When they drew nearer the empire's location, Veronyka and the meeting party separated from the main force, leaving their reinforcements to take cover and await orders. Alexiya had already volunteered herself to be Veronyka's contact through shadow magic, and even that small showing of trust and faith bolstered Veronyka for what was to come. Through her aunt, they could respond to whatever the empire sent their way.

Though she'd heard the numbers and read the reports, it was still a shock to see the army unfold before them: line upon line of soldiers standing ten across along the road, the occasional wagon or wheeled catapult dispersed among them. They were five hundred strong, according to the commander, and this was only a fraction of their military. Veronyka's mouth went dry.

The soldiers had already passed Runnet, which was visible to the west, and the Riders' forward scouts claimed they'd left the village untouched. As a border town, it was frequented by empire citizens and considered sympathetic to the imperial cause. It was no place for animages in hiding or Phoenix Riders.

Instead, the soldiers had pushed on, coming to a halt before them in a portion of the road carved through sheer rock on one side and dense forest growth on the other. The trees obscured the view of the river, though Veronyka could hear it as they descended, the silence of the soldiers' camp taut as a bowstring.

She didn't like it. It was a terrible place to stop: They were essentially fish in a barrel in the tight quarters of the road, practically begging Val to descend upon them from the sky. But they didn't have the time or position to demand that the empire march onward or fall back.

Like the messenger they'd sent ahead, Veronyka's party bore a white flag, ensuring the empire understood this was a peace offering, not an attack. In the middle ground between the soldiers and the approaching Phoenix Riders, a tent was being erected. No doubt they would have paper and ink inside ready for the Phoenix Riders to sign their formal surrender.

They would be disappointed in that regard.

Veronyka's party landed in the open space before the tent, the Riders dismounting.

Veronyka had barely climbed down from Xephyra's saddle when she sensed something was amiss. Her head snapped in the direction of the forest, where barely a second later, twenty soldiers armed with loaded crossbows stepped out of the trees. Their weapons were pointed at the Riders and their mounts as they moved to encircle the newcomers.

It looked like the "negotiations" were off to a bad start.

Veronyka glanced at Tristan, whose face was a storm cloud, rage pouring off him in waves. Beryk looked resigned, his hands held up, and Elliot pushed Riella behind him, wedging her between him and his phoenix. Sparrow remained in the saddle, but Ignix was as still as a statue, her gaze alert.

Veronyka turned her attention back to the tent, where a man appeared in the open flap.

His face was in shadow, but surely this was General Rast. Apparently he did not intend to welcome their arrival, nor to heed the terms set forward by the white flag of peace.

Veronyka's breath quickened. They did not have time for this.

Anger burned low in her gut. They had come to warn the empire, to ally with them . . . to help.

And now?

They might have to fight their way out of here.

We fought because our mothers fought.
We were made in their image.

CHAPTER 51

VERONYKA

VERONYKA'S HANDS CLENCHED INTO fists at her sides, and next to her, Xephyra bristled, sparks dancing along her feathers. She fought the urge to lash out with words or actions and did her best to quell the same instinct in Xephyra.

Then she reached wide, skimming over the hundreds of minds nearby, human and animal, until she found Alexiya.

We have a problem. Prepare yourselves.

"Welcome," boomed the general as he strolled out into the late-afternoon sun. He was a large man with a heavy jaw, barrel chest, and thick, meaty hands. With his shoulder-length russet hair and wide-set eyes, he put Veronyka in mind of a prideful lion—but one that had gone slightly to seed. He had a smug self-importance about him that told her he had gotten overly comfortable in his position and his success. That it had been too long since he'd had to fight for every scrap.

Too long since he'd been challenged.

"*This* is how you welcome representatives bearing a flag of peace?" Tristan asked scathingly.

"This is how I welcome *threats*. I am General Rast, here on behalf of the Golden Empire. Inside this tent you will find the documents of your surrender already drawn up. You need only sign them, and this will be finished." He turned toward one of the soldiers. "Take their weapons."

"You will not," Veronyka snapped. Xephyra punctuated the response with a fierce shriek. The soldier who had moved to follow his general's orders halted midstep.

"You hardly need them, if you indeed come in peace."

"We *came* in peace," Tristan corrected. He gestured at the ranks of crossbowmen. "You have not greeted us in kind."

At that moment, another man stepped out of the tent, flanked by additional soldiers. While the surrounding figures were clearly captains or commanders—soldiers of rank and importance—the man in the middle was dressed as a nobleman, with soft leather boots and a fine velvet coat. Despite his attire, he looked pale and drawn, his eyes raking restlessly over their group.

"I told you to remain—" the general began, but then Riella surged forward.

"Dad!" she said, but Elliot gripped her hard and pulled her back between him and his bondmate. The crossbows on either side followed their every move.

So this was William of Stel. He looked too old to have children as young as Elliot and Riella, his face lined and his hair gray, but perhaps the trials of the last few months had aged him beyond his years. "These are my children, Rast," he choked out. He drew himself up and squared his shoulders, facing down the general. "Tell your soldiers to lower their weapons and let them through."

"Your children will be fine—well, your daughter, at any rate. As I understand, she is innocent in all this. As for your son . . ." He tilted his head, considering Elliot in his Phoenix Rider leathers. "First he must surrender, along with the rest of his kind."

Tristan's jaw clenched. "We did not come here to surrender."

"We came to propose an alliance," Veronyka said, before the general could get the wrong idea. "The coming war does not begin and end with us."

"I beg your pardon? I do believe the war started with *you*—your attacks on Ferro and Arboria North, not to mention the assault on the Grand Council meeting."

"The former attacks were orchestrated by a dirty empire politician and the latter by renegade Riders that have absolutely nothing to do with us and our flock."

"Ah, yes, the 'dirty empire politician' who was shot dead outside the Grand Council meeting—the same meeting that was attacked by a Phoenix Rider—and can no longer speak in his defense," General Rast replied, laughter in his voice. "A perfect scapegoat."

"He's not the only person who could speak to his guilt," Beryk rushed to say, looking to Elliot's father.

He nodded, chin held high. "As I have explained several times, Lord Rolan used blackmail and other forms of coercion to ensure I allowed his soldiers to move in and out of Pyra unchecked. He took my daughter as hostage, not to mention—"

"And as I explained to *you*, William, it is rather hard to prove your claims when you have no evidence."

"You have my word and the word of my daughter," William said, voice stiff in affront. He might have looked beat down and emotionally exhausted, but he had power within the empire and expected to be treated with more respect. But this was wartime, and apparently, the general's opinion mattered most—Veronyka could see it in the way the other commanders looked to him for his every comment and response. Her tentative hope that William's position and the presence of his children could help quickly deflated.

"Your animage sympathies are well documented, and it serves you and your family"—he nodded at Elliot—"to speak in favor of the Phoenix Riders. If you had notified someone of your alleged predicament *while* it was happening, we could have investigated. But as it stands . . ." He shrugged regretfully, though the gesture looked utterly insincere. "I have an empire to protect. However," he continued, turning back to the Riders, "if you were to surrender, I may be able to argue for lighter sentences, as well as—"

"Whether we surrender or not, a war *will* be fought here," Veronyka said, her patience evaporating. "We told you, those attacks did not come from us. We have a common enemy, and our chances improve if we face them together."

"A common enemy—these so-called *renegade Riders*?"

Tristan hesitated. "Not exactly."

This was the part of their negotiations Veronyka had feared—the point she'd been certain would lose them. But given how things had turned out . . . they couldn't lose what they didn't have.

"I'm sure you've heard the legends," she began carefully, "no matter how hard you've tried to erase them from the empire's memory. Sun and Moon. Axura and Nox. Phoenixes and strixes."

"Strixes?" scoffed the general. "Supposedly evil shadowbirds no one has seen or heard of in a millennium? Is this truly your strategy, using nonsense and superstition to win wars?"

"They *are* real," Veronyka said, her voice cold and cutting. Wind whipped through their gathered group, causing the tent to flutter and snap, and something in her demeanor actually caused the smile to slip from the general's face. "I have seen them."

"You," he said flatly, looking wholly unimpressed. "And who exactly are you?" From his perspective, she was just some Pyraean girl. He was wrong.

They had tried to come in peace, to come with facts and logic and reason. But for some people, that would never be enough. Like Val, who was hell-bent on destruction, so too were politicians like Lord Rolan—and generals like Rast—determined to *win*, as if the world, the empire, were some prize. As if the right to rule belonged to the victor, even when the game was rigged.

But for Veronyka, the empire wasn't the prize—peace was.

And if the crown wasn't the final payoff, then it became a means to an end: a way to keep people like General Rast in line and a way to keep people like Val from destroying them all.

When Veronyka looked at it like that, it was positively easy to say what came next.

"I am Veronyka Ashfire, daughter of Pheronia Ashfire and heir to the Golden Empire."

She said it loudly, the words reaching the leaders in front of the tent, the soldiers who stood in a semicircle around them, and even farther, to those who stood behind the tent, out of range for most of their conversation, but not for this.

Tristan's head jerked in her direction. Her coming forward wasn't part of the plan—at least not right here, right now, after failed negotiations in the middle of what was about to become a battleground.

But this wasn't like the Grand Council meeting. Veronyka wasn't afraid as she had been then. She wasn't looking to be crowned, or for Rast and the others to bow to her. Instead, she was looking to sow doubt. She was also hoping to buy them some time.

As they spoke, Alexiya and the rest of their flock were drawing near. If the general wanted to play dirty, *they* could play dirty too. They certainly didn't have the numbers to take on the entire five-hundred-strong force that stood before them—at least not without major casualties—but they might just be able to turn the tables and force the general into signing some papers of their own. If they could take him into custody, they should be able to gain control of the situation.

Besides, Veronyka was tired of hiding, tired of pretending she was anything other than who she truly was.

General Rast smiled mockingly. "If you intend to make some half-baked bid for the throne, I suggest you bring your false claim before the Grand Council. I'd be happy to escort you there—as a prisoner."

Tristan took an angry step forward, and the shift and creak of crossbows followed him. "Don't make idle threats, General. You won't be taking any prisoners today. You have no authority here."

The general opened his mouth to retort, but Veronyka held up her hand. His eyes bugged at the gesture, and he looked ready to erupt, but the others soon heard what Veronyka had.

Hoofbeats.

A crossbowman behind Veronyka called out, "One of the scouts has returned."

"It's about time," the general muttered, waving for the scout to be let through. Clearly, the empire had sent riders ahead to ensure they weren't marching into an ambush, and with the Phoenix Riders' attention pulled in multiple directions, they hadn't been watching the road as closely as they used to.

The rider looked weary and travel-worn, the horse's head drooping and the rider's clothes dusty and ragged, but the saddle bore the empire military's crest. The late-afternoon sun was warm against Veronyka's skin, yet the rider was wrapped head to toe, from thick leather boots and gloves to a heavy head scarf obscuring their face.

No.

"Well?" the general barked, staring expectantly at the rider, who had moved through the Phoenix Rider ranks and had come to a halt several feet in front of the tent. "You're a full day late. What news?"

It was no surprise at all to Veronyka when Avalkyra Ashfire pulled down her scarf and lowered her hood.

Red hair. Scarred face. And a strix-feather crown.

The older members of their party gasped, while the younger looked around in confusion. Avalkyra was the same, but different—thirty-five years of age and yet barely a day over seventeen. Murmurs broke out. Whispers. And fear—the place was suddenly ripe with it.

Val had always loved to make an entrance.

How had Veronyka missed her approach? Now that Val was standing before her, it was easy to sense her through their bond. Maybe Veronyka had been too distracted by what was happening. Despite her confident entrance, Val looked like someone who'd been poisoned the day before. Onyx must have flown her south while she was still unconscious . . . perhaps on Sidra's orders. And where *was* Sidra? Veronyka hadn't seen her in Rushlea, but that didn't mean she wasn't somewhere nearby.

Val flashed her teeth in a predatory grin before calmly dismounting. She moved aside her ragged robe as if it were the finest silks and strode forward.

"Who are you?" General Rast demanded. He gestured to the soldiers on either side of them, and they all angled their weapons toward Val.

"This is your last chance," Val said, speaking directly to Veronyka. She ignored the general entirely.

Veronyka's brain was still playing catch-up. Val had obviously come here masquerading as a scout so that she could get close enough to speak. If she'd flown in on her strix, she'd have been shot down before she got within hailing distance.

But now she stood open and undefended in a crowd of enemies, without so much as a whisper of concern in her mind or on her face.

Morra had been right; Val had not given up and was intent on forcing her into the position of benex, no matter the risk.

"Bow to me, and I'll spare them." She gestured to Tristan and the other Phoenix Riders, who were still under crossbow guard. One pulled trigger, and Veronyka would lose someone she cared about. Val spoke slowly, clearly, so everyone could hear. "I'll do your dirty work and take care of the soldiers. You won't have to beg them for mercy or watch your people die. You won't have to get blood on your hands."

"Now, listen here," the general interjected angrily. He had been watching them with wide, startled eyes but had evidently had enough. Val's gaze flicked in his direction, annoyed. "I don't know who you are, but I have you surrounded and outnumbered."

Despite his words to the contrary, Rast was old enough to have seen Avalkyra Ashfire during the Blood War. He could deny it all he wanted, but he knew exactly who he was looking at.

Still, Val saw fit to help him along. "I am Avalkyra Ashfire, the Feather-Crowned Queen and Apex Master of the Black Horde."

She flung an arm to the north, where, far off in the distance, a haze of black shadows materialized. They were almost lost in the darkening sky, a cloud of winged terrors, their distant shrieks just barely distinguishable from the rustling leaves of the nearby trees.

"This is preposterous!" the general spluttered. He waved at his archers. "What are you waiting for? Shoot her!"

They lifted their weapons, wood creaking in their tightened grips, bowstrings taut—all but one. The last soldier on the right turned her crossbow in the opposite direction and pointed it at the general instead.

Veronyka looked closely for the first time and recognized with a jolt Sidra's familiar hardened face and cropped hair.

The other archers kept their weapons fixed on Val, but the general blanched. He was utterly exposed, with no hope of cover. All Sidra needed to do was shift her finger a fraction of an inch, and he was done for.

"Don't shoot!" he shouted angrily, though Veronyka didn't know if he was pleading with Val and Sidra or speaking to his own soldiers. Regardless, nobody moved.

"Drop the weapons," Val said idly, picking a piece of lint from her cloak.

"Do it," the general barked, and two dozen crossbows fell into the dirt. Veronyka's impression of him—already low to begin with—plummeted. He was putting his own life above his duty and his purpose here. His soldiers could easily take out Val and Sidra, as well as all the Phoenix Riders here, and the only cost would be his own life. He might even survive if Sidra didn't land a kill shot. Doubtful, but he didn't know her pedigree.

Despite her curled lip, Veronyka was glad for his cowardice. It meant she and her fellow Riders still had a chance of making it out of this situation alive.

"What do you want?" he asked as the ring of soldiers held up their hands.

Val smiled. "I want nothing from you, General. You are here to bear witness, to watch in fear and failure as I tear you and your pitiful army apart."

Sidra's crossbow creaked ominously, and the general's entire body flinched—but no arrow loosed. His gaze darted from Sidra to Val, then up to the Black Horde as it spread like an ink stain across the sky, drawing ever nearer.

"Veronyka," Val said, taking a casual step forward, though her voice was urgent. "Lower your head, bend your knee, and save your people."

They stood before each other, Ashfire to Ashfire, with empire soldiers and Phoenix Riders on both sides.

That was where Val got it wrong—where she had always gotten it wrong.

Her people weren't just the Phoenix Riders. She was heir to the throne, a queen by blood and birthright—but also by choice. She wanted that position now, so she could use it for the greater good. She didn't want to save a select few. She wanted to save everyone—animages *and* non-mages, Riders *and* soldiers. All were *her people*.

"No."

Val's expression flickered. "Careful, *xe* Nyka. I will not ask again."

"Good," Veronyka said, her voice carrying in the calm before the storm. "I will never bow before you. *Never.* Not with a knife at my throat or a boot on my neck. Not with a thousand strixes could you make me serve you and your war. I won't fight for you or for a crown. If I fight for anything, I fight for peace."

Val's mouth opened, ready with another retort, when Ignix moved into her line of sight. She'd taken only a single step, but Val had been too pre-occupied with Veronyka and the general to pay attention to the Phoenix Riders around her. And, of course, Ignix didn't usually have a Rider at all.

"*You,*" Val said, her face contorted in a mask of twisted fury. Her gaze darted between Ignix and Veronyka, her eyes slightly wild. "I see you've chosen my sister, just like everyone else." She shrugged, determinedly nonchalant. "No matter. I defeated you once, and I will defeat you again. You're a pathetic excuse for an apex. I don't fear you."

No, you do not fear me, Ignix said calmly. *But you fear her.* She inclined her head toward Veronyka. *And I will not be apex for long.*

Val sneered, her attention shifting to Veronyka once more. "If it's a fight you want, you'll get it."

It was Veronyka's turn to smile, though it was a sad, weary thing. "I've never wanted a fight, Val. . . . That's what I've been trying to tell you all along."

Then you will lose.

Val moved to retake her horse, her movements jerky. Sidra, meanwhile, kept her crossbow fixed on the general, even as she took several steps toward the forest. The distance was no match for the weapon, so everyone remained frozen.

Val rode off through the ranks of unarmed soldiers without a backward glance. As soon as her master was out of sight, Sidra turned and ran into the cover of the trees. The soldiers scrabbled for their dropped weapons, loosing a few bolts into their trunks, but it was too late.

All they could do was stand and stare at the coming darkness.

We fought because we were
different—it seemed simple then.

- CHAPTER 52 -
SEV

IN ORDER TO GET to Aura Nova undetected, Sev, Kade, and Theo needed to hire a boat. They decided their best chance was to head to the busy docks on the eastern shore of the Palm, the wide bay that separated Arboria North from Aura Nova.

Sev rode with Kade on Jinx, and Theo convinced Jonny to give her a ride. Jonny didn't pry into what they were doing, but apparently Theo asking for a favor was extraordinary enough that the man agreed without question. He was flying east anyway, attempting to recruit any Riders-in-hiding to their cause.

As Sev rode in Jinx's saddle, he thought about what Kade had said . . . that Jinx didn't hate him at all, that it was Sev who hated Jinx. Guilt gnawed at him. Despite his lack of skill, he was still an animage, and she must have heard or sensed his feelings. Sev thought that if he wanted to, he could reach out to her—that she would open her mind for him as she had done before, when they'd first met. That trust was overwhelming, and it was a shock to realize that he *wanted* to do it, but fear tightened his gut and made him a coward.

She's just as enamored of you as I am.

Sev thought of all the times he'd seen her watching him, blinking those curious eyes. In that cave in the Spine, on their first flight together and when they'd camped in Stel . . . plus a dozen other times besides. Did she care for Sev because *Kade* cared for him? Surely that was it. Why else would a phoenix be interested in him?

He did his best to cast aside the self-deprecating thought and remember Kade's words. *You've always been* you, *and that is more than enough.*

More than enough for Kade, anyway. The thought made Sev's insides feel light as a feather, buoyed with hope. If he was more than enough for someone like Kade, could he be enough for a phoenix someday too?

When they arrived at the docks, Jinx balked at the storage crate Theo had found for her, poked with tiny air holes and small enough that she'd have to crouch, but it was necessary in order to bring her with them undetected. Sev thought they were asking for trouble—especially since the interior was packed with extremely flammable straw—but Theo assured them this was how they transferred live animals across the channel. Besides, it would be easier to convince city officials they were transporting a harmless animal like a calf or a goat than pretending what they hauled was some inanimate cargo. Sev knew she was right, that lies that stuck closer to the truth usually succeeded above those that pushed the boundaries too far.

Still, he found himself as anxious as Jinx as she scrambled inside the crate, eyes darting wildly and feathers standing on end.

Kade remained nearby, murmuring soothing words of encouragement and adjusting the straw bed beneath her. Sev distinctly heard the phrase "not *that* bad," and when Jinx's head swiveled in her bondmate's direction, she let out a huff of air that caused bits of straw to fly up into Kade's face.

Sev hastily turned his laugh into a cough, and Kade's look of mild chagrin transformed into a smile when he saw Sev's obvious amusement.

Once they had Jinx safely stowed away, it was easy enough to purchase a crossing on a barge that was setting out for the day. They were on the docks of the Narrows before the sun reached its peak in the sky, and Theo proved herself a well-practiced liar, arguing with the dock official in her bored, inflectionless voice and gesturing irritably at the cargo she had to get to her client in a hurry. Kade played the obedient bondservant—he'd even kept his tags and put them on again to complete the ruse—and Sev and Theo wore soldier uniforms. Sev had reclaimed his from Tristan, and Theo borrowed one from Theryn. They looked no different from the dozens of other servants being escorted about their duties by bored-looking household guards.

As Theo continued to argue, Sev asked why Kade still had the tags. He shrugged and ran a finger along them in a gesture very similar to the one Sev had seen Tristan use on that broken arrowhead.

Once cleared, they flagged down a runner and paid double to ensure their message made it to Yara as quickly as possible. Then they went to the dockside alehouse where Sev had told her to meet them and waited. Since bondservants weren't generally given leisure time to drink and gamble, Kade stayed outside with Jinx's crate.

Sev's nerves had been buzzing ever since he set foot on the Aura Novan docks. He hadn't been here since before he'd become a soldier—nearly a year. He had gone straight from the city watch station house to the enlistment office and from there to the training barracks. So much had changed since the last time he'd been here, and Sev was confronted with a whirlwind of emotions: Nostalgia for favorite haunts and familiarity at the sights and sounds of the city, but there was also an uneasy tension, a fear that he might wind up back here—alone and afraid, hiding what he was—even after everything he'd been through.

Despite his worries, Sev couldn't deny a certain amount of anticipation as well. These were *his* streets; this was *his* battleground—the place he'd had to fight to survive a thousand times over.

So what was once more?

Theo ordered them both drinks so they'd blend in, but strained silence enveloped them as they stared out the grimy windows, waiting . . . and waiting. The sun moved across the sky, the patrons shuffled out and new ones took up their abandoned stools, and still, nothing. Theo ordered more drinks, and Sev slipped out to check on Kade and Jinx.

What if the letter never made it? What if it wound up in the wrong hands instead? It had been relatively vague, but what if, even now, soldiers were headed this way to capture and question them?

When Sev sidled back into the alehouse and found Theo speaking to an unfamiliar soldier, his stomach dropped—until the soldier turned, and Yara's face peeked out from behind a thick hood and a high collar.

Relief swept through his body, and he hurried forward.

"Not here," said Yara, as Sev opened his mouth to speak. She nodded toward a back exit, and they filed outside into the dingy alley that Kade had been hiding in.

Once the door swung shut behind them, Sev explained what he had in mind.

"Will you help us?"

"I'd not have come here if I weren't going to help," she said, her voice as flat as Theo's.

"Can you get us into Lord Rolan's town house?" she asked her.

"*You* won't be a problem," she said to Theo, "but him"—she nodded at Sev—"and *him*?" she added, indicating Kade. "They're both runaways from the governor's service."

"But with Rolan dead," Sev said reasonably, "what are the odds any of his city staff know about it?"

Yara tilted her head, considering. "The household has been in disarray since his death . . . and most of the soldiers he traveled with have already been reassigned. It's just his usual staff in residence."

Sev beamed. "They won't even remember me. Most of my time in Aura Nova was spent in training. And Kade—"

"They will remember me," Kade cut in. "I spent months here with Ilithya."

Sev sighed. "I think we need a bigger crate."

Luckily, regular shipments of Lord Rolan's various possessions had been coming and going sporadically ever since the governor's death, items from his offices inside the Nest arriving one day, only to be repackaged and shipped to his family's ancestral home in Stel the next. He was no longer the governor of Ferro, and soon even the town house and its occupants would be emptied and redistributed or assigned a new master.

Most things had been arriving hastily packed and unmarked, and the steward was apparently in a right state, refusing to go through it all and instead having it wheeled into storage until further instructions were sent.

And so, when Yara returned that afternoon with a couple of empire soldiers and a large crate in tow, they were directed to the service entrance without a second glance.

As soon as they were alone, Sev wrenched open the lid.

Kade scowled out at him, bits of straw sticking to his sweaty skin. Jinx was behind him, looking equally ruffled—but Sev got the impression that now that Kade was with her, she was having fun. She chirruped brightly at the sight of him.

Sev was oddly flustered by the gesture, the way she seemed to light up when she saw him. "How're you doing?" he asked Kade, as Yara handed him a water canteen.

"I've been better," he said dryly, before taking a long drink.

Jinx gave him a look that called to mind Kade's earlier assurance that the arrangement was "not that bad." Sev had the urge to smile again.

"You're going to have to stay in there for most of the day," he said apologetically, glancing over his shoulder at the sound of voices and footsteps in the hall beyond. "We'll be back in to check on you and bring food."

Kade nodded, handing Yara the empty flask.

She reached out, but Theo stopped her. "You better keep it."

Kade frowned. "For what?"

Theo shrugged. "That water's gotta go somewhere."

Kade opened his mouth, then shut it, pulling a slightly mortified expression before taking the empty container back for future use.

"I'm sorry," Sev whispered, planting a hasty kiss on his cheek. That seemed to mollify Kade, and his expression was equal parts baleful and resigned as they shut him in once more. Behind him, Jinx chirruped again.

Sev turned to the others. "Now what?"

Yara led them to the small captain's office that was currently occupied by her alone. She shut the door, and they considered how they might get into the general's house to find out where the captives were being held.

"His house is well guarded—there'll be no sneaking in, and we can't just burst out of the hidden passage in the middle of the day."

"We need to get word to Emma and the others so they know to be ready for us." Emma, Sev assumed, was Theo's friend.

"Even if we do, we'll probably need to wait for nightfall," Sev said with a frown. "Otherwise, the house will be bustling with servants, and we'll be seen."

"Where is the tunnel entrance?" asked Yara.

"According to Kade, it's in the basement," Sev answered.

"All the governors' houses were built at the same time, and they follow very similar floor plans," said Theo. "It's safe to assume it's the same inside the general's house."

"I don't suppose we can send a pigeon with a letter for Emma?" Sev asked, getting to his feet to pace. "Or a messenger?"

"Too risky. We don't know if the mail is filtered or how closely they're watched. With General Rast gone, he might have added security measures."

Sev heaved a sigh. "Then there's only one way. Through the front door."

It was surprisingly simple. They had Theo change out of her soldier uniform and into regular street clothes. Then she strolled up to the front door—not of the general's main house, but the attached building that served as the offices for the registry.

Her business? She knew the name and location of an animage in hiding.

"Will they recognize you?" Sev asked as Theo straightened her tunic and finger-combed her tangled hair.

"Maybe not at first . . . except Emma. I think *she* would." Her voice was filled with a raw, aching hope that made Sev unable to stop himself from thinking of Kade.

He cleared his throat. "Ask for her, then. Though I suppose she's going by Theo now. Ask for Theo—the registry enforcers are well known in the city, so it wouldn't be unusual for an informant to know them by name—and when we cause the diversion, slip her the letter."

Theo had already written it, explaining everything that was happening, in case their meeting was supervised. As for the diversion, Sev and Yara planned to watch from the street and throw rocks at the window of their front meeting room. Yara had been inside the office several times on business with Lord Rolan, so she knew the layout.

"Get out of there as quickly as you can. We'll be waiting."

Theo was displaying nerves for the first time that day, her hand trembling as she took the letter and folded it into her pocket. Having seen her lie through her teeth, smuggle a phoenix, and impersonate an empire soldier for half the day, Sev knew it had nothing to do with the upcoming deception and everything to do with seeing Emma and the other prisoners again. Facing the life she had escaped and all the guilt attached to that.

It was midafternoon when they arrived at the general's house. Sev and Yara waited outside, watching as Theo knocked and was admitted into the registry building. They were positioned so that they had a view through the window and could see Theo sit in front of a desk with a woman facing her on the other side. Was it Emma? Sev hoped so. He didn't want to leave anything to chance, and the others might not recognize Theo or could be suspicious of the letter.

They edged closer and closer, waiting until Theo craned her neck, glancing their way.

Sev already had a stone in his hand, and after aiming carefully, lobbed it over the wrought-iron fence and dense shrubbery that separated them. It landed true, colliding loudly with the wooden shutter. He ducked, peering up through the branches in time to see a guard poke his head out the window.

They waited until he returned his attention inside the room, where Theo was nodding her goodbyes. They fled to the street and waited for her.

"Well?" Sev prompted, as soon as she was in earshot.

She looked clammy and pale, but nodded. "I gave it to her."

"Now we wait."

It took longer than Sev wanted for Rolan's household to settle down for the night, though he knew they needed to wait equally long for the general's to do the same.

Impatient, Sev wandered the house as innocently as he could and spent some time inside Lord Rolan's study. There he found a locked box set into the wall behind a painting and let his curiosity get the better of him.

Afterward, he asked Yara for her fastest pigeon and sent what he'd found to Commander Cassian at Haven.

As soon as the servants and attendants retired after dinner, they got Kade and Jinx out of their crate and waited together with Theo inside the storage room until even the steward withdrew to her private rooms and the guards on the evening shift took up their positions at the front and back of the house.

Sev was aware that every moment slipping away was a moment Veronyka and the others were outnumbered. He wanted to rush into the tunnel, burst into the general's house, and make a run for the arena, but it would all be for nothing if they got caught before they'd even found the phoenixes.

Perhaps sensing his agitation, Kade took his hand. Sev was reminded of the time on Pyrmont when he'd run away without thinking, stealing a llama—and weeks of Kade's hard work in the process. That llama had been killed for Sev's foolishness, and he had jeopardized Trix's plans. He squeezed Kade's fingers and expelled a slow, steadying breath. He was different now. Better.

Yara popped her head into the room, and all three of them stood.

She nodded. It was time.

They were in the underground tunnels in minutes. Kade's familiarity with the hidden latch and tightly winding staircase made the entire thing quick and silent. Getting Jinx inside was marginally harder—the phoenix clearly loathed the idea of entering another dark, cramped space, and Sev couldn't blame her—but she followed Kade anyway, and Sev admired her bravery. He reached without thinking, stroking the trembling feathers of her neck and making soft, soothing noises.

Kade whirled around, but then the door shut behind them, plunging their company into darkness. Jinx began to glow, providing much-needed light, and Kade's confused gaze landed on Sev's hand. He frowned, uncomprehending, and looked up into Sev's face.

Sev had the bizarre urge to snatch his hand away—but he didn't.

She's as enamored of you as I am.

Kade's expression softened as he looked between them, and he seemed reluctant to turn his back on them when it was time to move.

They'd studied several maps in Yara's office to figure out the rough direction of the general's house, and did their best to maintain that course, even as the tunnels twisted right and left and right again.

Finally they located the correct passage, and followed it to the hidden entrance.

They had already decided that Yara and Theo would enter the house, while Sev, Kade, and Jinx waited below in the darkness. Sev paced back and forth while Kade fiddled unnecessarily with Jinx's saddle.

It didn't take long.

The hostages filed out, tense and wary, each clutching a bundle in their arms—likely all their worldly possessions. Despite appearing like lost children at first, their eyes burned with intensity not unlike what Sev had seen in Theo's expression when Sev promised her a chance at freeing her friend and her bondmate.

While they appeared fit and strong and healthy, there was a guardedness about them—a hard, haunted look that made a chill run down Sev's spine.

That was until their gazes settled on Jinx.

They approached her with an eagerness that made Sev wary at first. There was a fearful desperation, a *hunger* in them, and he had the urge to step in front of Jinx, to *protect* her, which was ridiculous—she was a firebird, and more than capable of taking care of herself.

His muscles tensed anyway, and so did Kade's next to him, but Jinx gave them both a quelling glance. Then she lowered her head for the captives to run their hands over her feathers, to stroke and whisper to her. Some of them were crying all of a sudden, while the others clenched their hands into fists after they touched her, their expressions edged in self-recrimination and guilt.

They were Phoenix Riders, but they had spent as much—even more—of their lives being forced to hunt down and punish their own kind. Those two parts of their identities couldn't be easy to reconcile, and Sev felt a wave of understanding wash through him. He knew what it was like to deny himself and his people, and to serve the wrong side. And he'd had far less cause than they had. They were doing it to keep their precious bondmates alive. Sev had been doing it only for himself.

The tension in his body melted away, and instead he reached out a hand to introduce himself. They seemed startled at first, but Sev smiled, his expression earnest, and they each returned his handshake.

"I'm Sev—animage and former empire soldier. This is Kade, Phoenix Rider and former bondservant. And this fine lady is Jinx." She bowed her head gracefully, and the group smiled and nodded at her. "This is Yara— she's a captain in the military and gleefully betraying her superiors as we speak." Nothing about Yara was gleeful, but she nodded tersely at them all, and the introductions seemed to be lightening the mood. "And I think you all know Theo?"

She was just returning to the tunnel after closing the hidden door behind her. She seemed surprised to have everyone staring at her and crossed her arms tightly over her chest.

"You're all grown up, Theodora," said Clara, her voice kind.

"How are Theresa and Thomas?" asked Joshua, who looked like the oldest of the group. "And your parents?"

"They're fine, from what I hear. Thomas has a daughter, and another on the way. I haven't seen them since . . ." She trailed off. That's when she noticed Emma, standing off to the side, staring at her. She held a piece of paper in her hands—the letter Theo had given to her before?

Forgetting the others, Theo strode purposely toward her, though her steps faltered as she drew near. Theo stared at her, searching for words, then dropped down to her knees.

She took Emma's hand. "You *shouldn't* have," she said thickly, speaking to her palm rather than to her face.

"*You* would've," Emma countered, her own voice wobbling. "And I would again."

Theo looked up at her, eyes wide with anguish—then she wrapped her arms around Emma's middle, forehead pressed against her stomach. It was as if Theo couldn't bear to look at Emma, or to have Emma look at her.

Emma bent over, murmuring quietly into Theo's hair, urging her to stand, and Sev looked away.

More than a few sniffles cut through the silence, but when Theo got to her feet, the atmosphere in the group changed.

"Come on, then," Sev said, taking the lead with Kade beside him and Jinx lighting the way. Yara brought up the rear.

The others continued to stare at the phoenix, walking close enough to touch her feathers or chase one of her trailing sparks before fading back into the group. However they reacted, they seemed to take strength from her—to walk away with straighter shoulders and clearer eyes.

It seemed to Sev they were coming back to themselves, as if waking from a dream—or he supposed, a nightmare—and were steeling themselves for what was to come.

"Sometimes," Kade whispered, watching Clara gaze at his bondmate with awe in her eyes, "I can't believe she's mine."

Sev tilted his head to consider Kade. "I know the feeling."

Kade flashed him a wide, startled smile, and Sev returned it.

Since Theo's note explained the gist of their plan, they walked mostly in silence through the underground tunnels, Kade pausing at every junction to make sure they were heading in the right direction.

"Why now?" Emma asked abruptly, speaking to Theo. "How did this happen?"

"The war provided a unique opportunity," Theo said grimly. "But the tunnel idea was thanks to Sev and Kade."

Sev saw an opportunity. "Actually, we're here on Veronyka's orders," he lied. "Veronyka Ashfire. She's leading the Phoenix Riders now, fighting against Avalkyra and the empire."

Tension fell over the group. He wondered what they'd heard about the resurrected queen, the woman who had left them to their fate more than seventeen years ago. Either way, he wanted to differentiate Veronyka from her as much as possible.

"She heard your story from one of the Haven Riders and asked us to intervene," Sev continued. Kade and Theo were staring at him now, and he hoped they didn't give him away.

"So we can fight for her?" asked Joshua, his voice tight.

Sev shook his head. "So you can fight *with* her. You're Phoenix Riders, which means you're a part of her flock. She'll fight and die to defend you, whether you choose to fight with her or not."

The group fell into a thoughtful silence, and Sev flashed Kade a grin. Whatever happened once they freed the phoenixes, he wanted these people to know that Veronyka was not Avalkyra. She brought people together; she didn't tear them apart.

After a time, Sev noticed a member of the group walking off to the side, alone. While the others seemed to grow livelier with every step, whispering excitedly to one another or staring ahead with intense focus, he did not. He seemed listless, like a boat drifting out to sea.

Theo noticed him too, and Emma whispered, "Aron's phoenix went to ash. I think . . ." She lowered her voice even further. "I think Aron had given up, and so his phoenix did too. That was after his brother, Adam . . . They were twins, you see, and Rast liked to pit them against each other. I only need one, he'd say, over and over. And then Adam finally snapped, turning against Rast, and . . ."

Sev looked at Aron again and realized that he alone had not approached Jinx . . . had not even looked at her.

They reached a juncture in the tunnel that had a narrow offshoot with stairs leading straight up. It went into another, secondary passage that led to the street. Yara checked the tunnel quickly and nodded that it was safe.

Theo stopped and took Emma's hand. "Go up there and get word to your family. I . . . I didn't dare tell them you were alive in case I was wrong."

"I'll go too," said Aron. He looked miserable, but also somewhat relieved, as if he would rather face his family and the empire's politicians than the empty cell where his bondmate had once been. "My parents . . . They need to know about Adam. About everything."

"Tell them to contact all our families," said Theo. "Now that you're free, *they're* free to act against him. He might have thought himself clever to get them under his thumb, but he didn't consider the other side of that coin—how unwise it would be to piss them off."

Aron nodded and marched off alone, into the darkness of the passage outside Jinx's light, leaving the others to call out their goodbyes.

Emma, meanwhile, was hugging Theo tightly. "Don't do anything stupid," she whispered.

Theo had her usual gruff expression in place, though it seemed false and put-upon. "You know I always do."

"I'm not kidding."

Theo swallowed, glancing at Sev and the others. "I won't. I promise."

"Does anyone else want to go?" Sev asked as Emma followed Aron into the dark. "There will likely be danger ahead—here, and once we get outside. You'll probably have to fight."

They looked at each other, and it was a moment before anyone spoke.

"I have been waiting seventeen years to be able to fight," said Dane, the youngest of the group, his voice eager and energetic. "If there is danger, if there is fighting—I am ready for it."

Nods and murmurs of agreement followed his proclamation. Even Jinx stood tall and proud, chest puffed out.

Sev wondered if their tune might change once they were reunited with their bondmates. It didn't matter. They deserved their freedom, whatever they chose to do afterward, and it was their best chance at helping Veronyka and the others.

He had to try.

But if one focuses on the differences alone, it is only a
matter of time before sister fights sister.
Before your victory becomes her loss.

- CHAPTER 53 -
VERONYKA

HEART RACING AND BLOOD thundering in her ears, Veronyka strode to the general and withdrew her dagger. She held it out between them—not close enough to touch him, but the threat was plain.

Everyone's attention flickered between her and the immediate threat she posed, and then higher, farther, to the looming threat on the horizon. With every flap of the strixes' ink-black wings came an unnatural, trailing darkness—like shadows that had become untethered from their solid forms, able to ripple like flags in the wind or hang heavy and oppressive as the thickest fog.

Then you will lose.

"Well?" Veronyka snapped, drawing everyone's attention back to her. Some of the crossbowmen pointed their weapons at her uncertainly, awaiting the general's orders, while others remained frozen in surprise.

Veronyka realized for the first time that the rest of the Phoenix Riders had arrived and were perched atop the nearby trees and soaring stone outcrops, their bows raised. Alexiya was among them, her jaw clenched and the muscles of her neck corded with tension. They'd obviously been there for some time, watching the showdown between Veronyka, Val, and General Rast but unable to do something lest one stray arrow cause crossbow bolts to go flying and lives to be lost.

Even as their eyes met, Alexiya nodded toward Val's retreating form, asking if they should pursue—but the situation here was still precarious. Their presence leveled the playing field.

The general glanced up at them, then waved at his archers, telling them to stand down.

Veronyka lowered her blade. Behind her she sensed the other grounded Riders mounting up and preparing for battle, but she remained on her feet. "What will it be, General?"

He ran a large hand through his hair. "That . . . How did she—what—"

Veronyka was pleased to see genuine fear in his expression. *Not so legendary after all, are they?*

This was the moment. If the sight of the Black Horde didn't convince him that their alliance was not only preferable, but *necessary*, nothing would.

"Are we enemies or allies?" Veronyka pressed.

The general licked his lips, gaze darting from her to the Phoenix Riders and then beyond, to the strixes. As soon as he looked away, Veronyka knew.

"This is not our fight. I will not see the empire weakened and left defenseless." He turned to the commanders behind him. "Order a retreat at once."

They hesitated before complying, glancing at one another. They had seen Val, heard her words—and Veronyka's claim of her own parentage. They were clearly conflicted, but their allegiance was to General Rast and the empire, not to the Phoenix Rider rebels. So despite their obvious reluctance to do so, they complied, shouting orders to the nearest soldiers. The army began to reconfigure and march in the opposite direction, away from the coming attack. Fleeing while they still could—though even if Veronyka and the Phoenix Riders managed to hold the strixes for a time, they would not be able to hold them forever.

As the empire moved out, the rest of Veronyka's flock landed on the ground and watched the approaching horde with restless fear and agitation. Their anxiety fluttered inside her chest, and their tension made her muscles taut. Their blood *pounded, pounded, pounded* inside her own veins, thundering in her ears.

She could fight this, or she could use it.

Understanding her intention, Xephyra sidled over. Veronyka leapt into the saddle, and as they turned to face the other Riders, Ignix let out an ear-piercing shriek, calling them to attention.

"Listen, all of you," Veronyka said into the silence. "The truth is, we need each other if we're to win this war. We need to work together. That horde . . . Some of you have seen them before. Some of you haven't, but it doesn't matter. What you need to know is this: They have grown in number and strength, and Avalkyra has grown with them. She is not just a resurrected queen, a shadowmage, or Ashfire heir. . . . She is bonded to their apex, and she uses that power to control their every move."

Unease filled the group.

"I thought Ignix was apex," said Darius, giving the ancient phoenix a dubious look.

"She is first among phoenixes," Veronyka explained, "but each species has their own apex. Their own leader. And with Ignix's permission, I would like to be yours."

Murmurs broke out. Ignix had moved close to Veronyka, and many looked between them in confusion.

You have it, Ignix said, and everyone in the vicinity jumped. She had spoken into all their minds, and with their attention fully focused on her, Ignix turned to Veronyka and bowed her head.

Everyone stared.

Go on, Ignix nudged, speaking to Veronyka alone.

"The apex is usually oldest and strongest among the ranks, but another can be chosen." Veronyka swallowed, her mouth dry. "When the flock gives their loyalty, a group bond develops, a connection that allows them to fight and fly as one under the guidance of the apex pair. Ignix has been the apex phoenix since the Dark Days, but Avalkyra is a different kind of foe. She is my foster sister, my blood aunt, and the greatest threat to our existence since Nox herself. I don't have all the answers, but I know *her,* and I know we can defeat her. Together."

She stopped, looking at each and every person in turn. Looking at their phoenixes. The tension in the group shifted, changed, moving from anxiety to consideration.

"I am not her," Veronyka said loudly. She had said it over and over again—to Val, to others, and to herself. In this moment, she truly believed it. "I will *not* take control from you. I will *not* rob you of your will. I swear it."

Silence descended.

"I guess what I'm saying is," Veronyka finished, "let me lead you. Let me guide your hands. Trust me, if you can."

"I can," said Tristan immediately, voice carrying in the quiet. Then, seated in his saddle, he dipped his head in a bow. Rex did the same, bending so low that his beak touched the dirt.

"So can I," said Latham, surprising Veronyka with his sudden, powerful support. He too dropped his head, his phoenix following suit.

"Of course," said Alexiya, making Veronyka's throat tight as she and Ximn bowed in unison.

One by one they gave their assent, first with words and then with actions, until only Doriyan remained seated upright.

Veronyka could imagine that handing magical control to another Ashfire would be difficult for him, but when at last he agreed, she knew his words to be sincere. She felt it. "I can, and I will." And then he bowed as well.

Veronyka took their allegiance, their trust, as the gift that it was.

And in her acceptance—both of their loyalty and her worthiness of it—power shot through her like an arrow. It reminded her of how she'd felt the first time she'd looked into Xephyra's eyes, but while that bond had been light and joyful, this bond was heavy and powerful. She understood what Ignix had said about the burden of the apex status. All these lives were in her hands.

She breathed deeply, her heart expanding inside her chest, filling her with fire. With hope. Conversely, next to her, Ignix seemed to sag in relief, freed from a weight she'd carried for far too long.

Her flock lifted their heads and opened their hearts to her. She felt their bonds strengthening and solidifying, and they felt it too. They looked at her and at one another, and Veronyka realized that not only did the apex status bring them closer to her—it brought them closer to each other. She was the web that connected them, the threads that bound them, but their strength and power came not from her, but from their togetherness.

"Apexaeris," said Beryk, his voice loud and carrying as he turned to Veronyka. "What are your orders?"

Veronyka smiled so hard her face hurt. Then she blinked away the moisture gathering in her eyes and released a shuddering breath. She had asked for their trust, and now she had to earn it.

This is shadow magic, she said. The words rang out between them, a group conversation rather than an individual one. She had never been able to speak into multiple minds before.

Some of them jolted in their saddles as they had when Ignix spoke to them, while others, like Tristan's patrol, had a better idea of what to expect, though they still appeared rattled.

It's how I'll speak to you when we separate, and it's how you can speak to me. Just reach for me like you would your bondmate, and I'll hear you.

She looked to Elliot, who had put Riella in his phoenix's saddle but remained standing. His father was by his side, uncertain where to go in the chaos, but clearly preferring to be near his children. Ignix was next to them with Sparrow on her back.

"Get them out of here," Veronyka said, indicating the non-warriors William, Riella, and Sparrow. "Drop them beyond the ridge; they should be able to find shelter until this is over." The strixes wouldn't be interested in them—not with Val at the helm. They'd be interested in phoenixes and soldiers and little else.

Elliot was pale and wide-eyed, realizing he had more Riders than mounts and trying to find a solution.

Help him? Veronyka asked Ignix, who nodded. She fixed Elliot with her piercing gaze, and he sprang into action, helping his father up behind Riella and then climbing behind Sparrow on Ignix.

"We'll return as soon as we can," Elliot promised, as he and Ignix wheeled into the sky, heading west.

Veronyka turned back to the others. "We need to stop their forward progress," she said, switching to verbal communication as she spoke to the group. "Without Riders, they don't have long-range weapons of their own, so space is our friend. It will also counteract some of their abilities. Avoid their shadows as best you can—or any touch at all, in fact. Those talons do more than tear flesh. They seemed to kill it on contact. The less we have to engage with them directly, the better." She pointed at Fallon. "Your patrol will arrange themselves at our rear and loose arrows—as many and as fast as you can—to hold the line. Nothing gets past you."

"Got it," he said, gesturing to his Riders to ready their weapons and prepare extra artillery.

"Beryk," Veronyka continued, turning to the older man. "Split your patrol and guard the flanks. I know the strixes want to engage us, but we can't lose track of any of them and risk an attack on civilian settlements. Keep them *here*. The geography should do some of the work, and your Riders will do the rest." At last she looked to Tristan. "We're going to slice through and divide them into smaller groups, then send them left or right or into your back line," she said, glancing to Beryk and Fallon.

"We're only five without Elliot," Tristan said, gesturing to Latham, Ronyn, and Lysandro.

Veronyka considered. "They'll fly in a *trivol* pattern, and we'll have to ride as a pair."

A queenstrike, Tristan said in his mind. The modern patrol system was based on the ancient First Rider attack patterns: They had flown in two teams of six, with Queen Nefyra and her second-in-command, Callysta, flying as a separate pair. The apex-benex pair, Veronyka realized. The pattern was technically called a *duovol*. It was only a "queenstrike" when a queen led the charge.

The word sent a chill down her spine, but it wasn't an entirely unpleasant experience. She thought perhaps she liked it. He flashed her a wide grin.

"What about the soldiers?" Fallon asked as his patrol began to fan out across the width of the road, their mounts itching to take to the sky. He glanced toward the general, who was arguing fiercely with his commanders and demanding someone saddle his horse. The tent was partially taken down, the task abandoned in the face of the coming horde, and papers and packs were strewn everywhere. "Are we fighting them or protecting them?"

A shriek tore through the cacophony of shouts and rumbling, stomping feet. The strixes were nearly upon them.

"Forget them for now," Veronyka shouted, urging Xephyra up into the air. "And get into position."

Fallon's patrol flew into staggered ranks of three just behind Veronyka and the others, and together they raised their bows and nocked their arrows, preparing for the onslaught. Beryk zipped to the left and Alexiya to the right, each leading a *trivol* to sweep wide of the mass of birds winging their way, ready to hold the perimeter, though they didn't yet engage.

Veronyka's magic stayed with them, her bonds allowing her to feel their actions and decisions, but she didn't yet attempt to take hold. She'd have to feel it out as the battle developed.

Tristan's patrol remained just in front of Fallon's line of archers, poised and ready in the saddle, bobbing up and down in place.

The strixes were closing the distance between them with alarming speed, but as the Phoenix Riders moved into defensive positions, their pace came to a slow halt.

And then Veronyka saw her. She was barely visible through the constantly shifting wings, but Val was there in the middle of her horde, mounted on Onyx. Calm and cold—plotting, assessing.

Veronyka took a deep breath and surveyed the battle unfolding before them.

This was where they would make their stand. It was in Pyra, where the phoenixes and the strixes first met, so it seemed fitting to do it here again.

She only hoped that the warriors of light could claim victory once more.

Before fighting is all you know.

- CHAPTER 54 -
AVALKYRA

AVALKYRA HAD FELT THE moment Veronyka became apex.

She was no longer a potential benex, an ally in her horde.

She was an enemy within.

Avalkyra had known it would happen, of course. Had felt it in her bones. After hours of drifting between sleep and wakefulness, poison singing in her veins, she had dreamed that Ignix survived, that she had named Veronyka her worthy successor and bowed her head.

When she woke, Avalkyra had convinced herself it was only a dream—as if that statement could ever *really* be true for a shadowmage—and decided she would give Veronyka one last chance to save herself. One last chance to save her people. Even after her refusal in Rushlea, even after the *poisoning*, Avalkyra had graciously offered it.

But no, Veronyka *still* thought she could stop this war. Still thought she could save everyone and everything. That brazen, high-minded heroism had won her a flock of her own and had taken shadowfire out of reach for Avalkyra forever.

Her emotions spiked as she stared at her enemies ranged before her. Heartbreak, betrayal, disappointment . . . each flitting through her mind, then out again, barreling through her like a windstorm.

So much boiling rage and endless frustration.

Why, then, could she not stop smiling?

Now that she thought on it, this was what she'd always wanted. What she'd imagined ever since Pheronia had refused her letters and torn her treaty in two.

If they could not rule together, they would tear each other apart. That war had ended with a fizzle, not a bang, but the world had seen fit to give Avalkyra another chance.

Here she was again, sister against sister, except this time they would not fight in council chambers and war rooms, through treaties and letters and endless back-and-forth.

They would fight here and now, *on wings*, as was their birthright.

They would meet in battle not as mere sisters, but as divine powers—as forces of nature—and the world would shake and tremble before the clashing of goddesses in the sky once more.

They would fight with ash and fire, with smoke and shadow, and only one of them would be left standing.

Forgive me, Onia, she thought, recalling the promises she had made. *I cannot protect her from everything. I cannot protect her from myself.*

For two hundred years, Nefyra and I fought, hunting
Nox's children, chasing them to every corner of the world.

- CHAPTER 55 -

VERONYKA

NOW THAT SHE'D SEEN how Veronyka had set the field, it appeared that Val was preparing counter maneuvers.

Well, well, if it isn't Veronyka Ashfire, Apex Master of the Phoenix Riders, Val sneered. *You mean to contain me?* She sounded amused, though the humor was pointed. *You can try.*

Veronyka wrenched her mind away. Val would try to bait her, to distract and emotionally compromise her, and Veronyka could not allow it. Instead, she let Val's words pass in and out of her head, like so much useless white noise.

Then a wave of strixes broke free of the flock—rolling down the mountainside like an avalanche. Veronyka sensed the tremor in Tristan and Ronyn to her right and Latham and Lysandro to her left, the sudden fear, sharp as a blade.

Steady, she said, emanating all the calm she could muster as the strixes drew nearer and nearer—beaks and claws and vicious, inky eyes distinguishing themselves from the dark mass of feathers and wings and strange shadow smoke. *Steady.*

Veronyka turned in her saddle to find Fallon. His entire patrol had ignited, and the sight of those rippling, crackling flames kindled hope in

Veronyka's heart. She looked back around, at the coming darkness. *Now.*

"Loose!" Fallon cried, and a volley of arrows arched over Veronyka's head to descend before her, leaving perfect fiery crescents in the sky before landing home. The first line of strixes dropped, their terrible shrieks cutting through the night.

Veronyka's breath caught; she'd *felt* it. Through Val, she had a connection to these creatures, and their pain echoed in her mind, raw and terrible.

There were more coming up behind them, and Veronyka had no time to lament their fate, no time to think of another, better way. She closed her eyes and pushed the feelings down as far as they would go. Buried them deep, beneath all her other bonds, and locked them away inside her mental safe house. They were still there, still a part of her, but distant. Numbed.

Veronyka opened her eyes, and the next charge was upon them.

Another volley of arrows. Another flaming arc.

The strixes grew hesitant as they recognized the danger, but those that broke away from the charge—dipping and weaving or pulling back around—were either shot down by Beryk or Alexiya, who guarded their flanks, or sent careening into the main horde by Val's heavy magical touch. Slowly she got them back under control, and the charge slowed to a trickle, then stopped.

Veronyka clamped down on the feeling of triumph that rose all around her. This wasn't a victory—this wasn't anything. Val was testing them, seeing what they would do.

There was also no way she'd failed to notice that the empire's forces remained uninvolved.

Veronyka could feel the smile on Val's face as she sent the next barrage of strixes forward.

This time she sent *two* charges—the first followed the previously established route, making straight for the Phoenix Riders that floated in the air, but the second? It flew right behind the first, but fast and low, targeting the soldiers instead. Those at the rear heard the strixes' battle cries, and their carefully organized ranks bunched and stumbled together as they struggled to get away.

Fallon's archers were shooting arrows at will now, but they hesitated—unsure which line to target.

Focus on the first charge, Veronyka advised, before turning to Tristan.

With me, she said, and Rex flew up next to her and Xephyra. She turned to the rest of Tristan's patrol. *Await my order and have your bows ready.*

While they continued to fly in place just in front of Fallon's archers, Veronyka and Tristan moved into the foreground. Their patrol was now stacked, two in front, three behind, and Fallon's patrol several yards behind them.

The first charge was bearing down on them, but Veronyka waited until the last possible second before acting.

Drop! she shouted, and Rex and Xephyra tucked their wings and descended until their feet met the ground.

The strixes—and Val, their master—hadn't seen that coming, and so the second charge veered back up again, right into Ronyn, Latham, and Lysandro. Arrows loosed, and those that managed to dodge them wound up careening into the first charge. Squawks and shrieks assaulted Veronyka's ears, while fiery arrows zipped through the tumult, hitting home with dull thuds and crackling flames that engulfed their targets in seconds.

Again, Val withheld the rest of her forces, waiting until the last strix was shot down from the sky and Veronyka's forces reestablished their positions.

You handle plots and planning well, Nyka. Your mother would be proud. But how do you handle chaos?

And then she set them loose—or as loose as someone like Val could truly allow. She might pretend to welcome pandemonium, but she wouldn't have sought apex powers just so she could relinquish control. No, Val needed it, thrived upon it, and even if she didn't control her horde's every movement, she had made them, and their will was hers.

Veronyka noted that Val had not yet tried to break through their shadow magic connection and make physical contact, and she thought she had the poisoned darts to thank for that. Likewise, Veronyka couldn't risk trying to poison Val again and being wrenched from her saddle clean across the battlefield and thrown to her death, so she, too, avoided anything beyond conversation between them.

She watched as the black mass of wings disintegrated before her, strixes flying in all directions, and gripped Xephyra's reins so hard her joints ached. Now the real battle would begin.

Val had lost maybe a dozen strixes thus far, but the coming horde looked no less imposing. Not all those the Phoenix Riders had turned back or shot down were actually killed, and it was clear that Val was forcing them to fly even with torn wings and scorched flesh. Her cruelty grated at Veronyka's fraying nerves, their pain a dull throbbing in the back of her mind, but she had other things to worry about.

Though the strix numbers seemed endless, Veronyka knew they were closer to a hundred. That put their odds at around five to one. She looked behind again, at the fleeing soldiers, and wished things had turned out differently.

Ready? she asked, turning to the others. *Time to engage.*

Leaning low in the saddle, Veronyka held on tight as Xephyra pumped her wings, surging forward with all the strength and speed she had. Rex soared tightly behind, covering Xephyra's back just as Tristan—with an arrow nocked and ready—covered Veronyka's. Heat built underneath their wings, trailing behind them in crimson waves, but it was still ordinary phoenix fire. She had asked Ignix how to produce heartfire for the battle ahead, but the phoenix had said it couldn't be forced. She promised it would happen on its own and that she and Xephyra would know when it did.

Veronyka could only hope it happened sooner rather than later.

They shot through the coming charge, and Veronyka felt the phantom rip and tear of beaks and talons whipping past—Xephyra's speed too great to allow much contact, though her fire had managed to cause several of the strixes to shriek and cry out or turn aside, their feathers charred and smoking. Despite such close quarters, Xephyra appeared to be unharmed, the only side effect of their close brush with the strixes several streaks of soot-gray across her brilliant feathers, quickly burned away by her fire.

Again, Veronyka urged both Xephyra and Rex. She threw her magic wider, speaking to everyone, telling them to keep it up, to stick to the plan—praising and pushing in equal measure. Whenever there was a stray strix or a dangerous situation, she called out warnings and nudged people out of harm's way.

It should have been exhausting, and while it certainly split her focus and made it hard to concentrate, Veronyka's magic was as strong and as steady as it had ever been. It was relentless, flooding through her body, but it also made her feel oddly separate and detached from herself. She usually reached *inside* for magic, but being connected to so many bonds was like drawing water from an overflowing well—she had no need to reach within; she just let it bubble over into her open hands.

As they made another pass, Tristan fired several arrows to cover her back, ensuring none of the strixes got too close as they soared through the fiery hole Xephyra had punched through their ranks.

They looped back around in time to see Ronyn flying as point, with Latham and Lysandro on either side, cutting through much as they had, choosing to veer to the right and corral several of the shadowbirds toward Alexiya's awaiting bow. All of them met the coming darkness with a reckless bravery that made Veronyka's throat ache.

As long as they kept moving, as long as they stuck to their plan, they should be able to keep this up for as long as necessary to take the strixes down.

No sooner did she have the thought than a strange, incongruent bubble of excitement surged inside her. Not *her* excitement, but someone else's. She found Val across the battlefield, eyes glittering as she looked to the south, where Pyra rolled out before them.

Veronyka twisted in her saddle, staring down the sloping hillside.

The soldiers' retreat had halted, their procession bunching together thanks to a distant obstruction. Not strixes, but humans—a dark swath of them spreading across the road, blocking their retreat.

Veronyka's stomach dropped.

It looked like the Unnamed had decided to join the fray after all.

One of the more enigmatic mysteries of our world history is that of the Lowland civilization. We know little of their people or their society and can only postulate based on what has survived the ages or been absorbed into other cultures.

The Lowlanders occupied much of modern Pyra as well as Arboria North. While the disputed border territory remains unclear, tensions between the Lowlanders and the Queendom of Pyra eventually reached a fever pitch.

Despite being utterly wiped out by Queen Lyra's Red Horde, the Lowland civilization was a formidable enemy. It was from their designs that the empire developed their concept for modern catapults, and the metal nets favored during the Stellan Uprising also originate from early Lowland warfare tactics. The Lowlanders had been fighting—and winning—against the ancient Pyraeans for decades, and even though their civilization is considered extinct, there are some who suggest their people survive to this day.

Various freedom-fighting militias have risen up in Pyra over the centuries, the most popular being that of the Unnamed, who some trace all the way back to the now-lost Lowland civilization. Despite this claim, there seems to be little that unites them, save for their location and their desire to see a Pyra free from Phoenix Rider rule.

—*The Lowland Civilization*, the Morian Archives, 175 AE

I gave the strixes all the fire I had, all the fury. What might have happened if I'd given them something else?

- CHAPTER 56 -
TRISTAN

TRISTAN FOLLOWED VERONYKA'S LINE of sight and gaped. There was something happening on the road, past Runnet, near the bridge that crossed into the empire. Fighting.

Rex snapped his beak in agitation, and Tristan borrowed his eyesight for a better look. A ragtag group of warriors had descended upon the road, engaging with the retreating soldiers, who were evidently ill prepared for an assault coming from that direction. There weren't nearly as many attackers as there were soldiers—maybe a quarter of their number—but they'd had the element of surprise and were using the geography to box in and bottleneck their enemy.

This must be the Unnamed . . . but how had they gotten here? Perhaps they *had* used the tunnels after all, not to ambush Veronyka and the others but to make their way south undetected.

Things had been going fairly well thus far. The fighting was intense, their foe fearless—or at least reckless, which was down to Val, their leader. But Veronyka had been keeping everyone together, calling the fight, orchestrating their defense with a calm bravery that made his heart soar.

The truth was, they needed her, and she'd risen to the occasion magnificently.

But just like that, the fight had changed.

"Val's cutting off their retreat," Veronyka said, voice strangled.

She was right. The line of empire soldiers below them stretched along the road from the crumpled command tent all the way to the bridge, which the attacking Unnamed now held. While this approach served to keep the retreating soldiers in Pyra, it also served another, possibly more fatal function.

"Not just retreat," Tristan said faintly. "The bridge—they'll cut off retreat *and* any hope for reinforcements."

Because on the far shores hundreds more soldiers were ranged, huddled around tents and wagons and massive wheeled catapults. There they stood, ready and waiting in case the Phoenix Riders proved resistant to the empire's first efforts. In case Pyra required a full-scale invasion the likes of which hadn't been seen since the end of the Blood War. A threat the empire surely never expected they'd need to deliver on, and a thing Tristan would have very much wished to avoid, except that now it might be the difference between victory and defeat.

If the empire could be convinced to fight *with* the Phoenix Riders, they could make a truly formidable defense—and break the lines that separated them from their reinforcements.

But how to get them to such an alliance?

As the soldiers formed ranks and drew weapons, the Unnamed were also reorganizing their attack. Those that had been stationed on the bridge rushed to the northern side just as a flaming Phoenix Rider appeared in the sky.

Sidra, Veronyka said into his mind, her eyes narrowing. Of course. But what was she up to?

She kept diving across the bridge, swooping back and forth. Tristan thought she was simply trying to scare away the empire soldiers who had begun to crowd the far shore, until he saw one of the bridge's supports catch fire.

This was no scare tactic—it was a strategic attack. They meant to take down the bridge.

When the flames began licking across the beams and struts, the soldiers redirected their attacks, launching crossbow bolts into the air. The Unnamed did their best to cover Sidra, until she landed in the middle of the broad, wooden bridge for one final strike. Her phoenix burst into flame with enough power to send the nearby soldiers and Unnamed flying off their feet, setting the bridge fully ablaze and sending great beams of wood cracking and crumbling into the river below.

Tristan drew back from Rex's mirrored vision.

They were surrounded, hemmed in by the geography of the land and with Val's forces closing in on them from either side. The Phoenix Riders had more mobility than the soldiers below, but the message was clear: Val wouldn't let anyone escape this. Not the empire, not the Phoenix Riders. She wasn't trying to create a diversion so she could slip by—she could have done that already. This was exactly what she wanted: a brutal fight, a devastating blow to the world that had rejected her.

She didn't care about the empire or its citizens, and she clearly had no desire to rule.

She just wanted to make absolutely sure Veronyka didn't. That there would be nothing left *to* rule.

Though he was too far to hear it, Tristan swore his ears rang with the sound of wrenching wood and roaring flames. He thought of the distant shores, where soldiers stood in rank upon rank—armed and ready but with no way to cross.

Suddenly Tristan knew what he had to do.

"Let me go," he said to Veronyka. "To the bridge. It won't affect the apex-benex bond, will it?"

Her head snapped in his direction. Her initial distaste for the idea was plain on her face, but she shook her head slowly in answer to his question. "I don't think so."

"Good. It's not that I want to separate," he said, and then continued in his mind, because shouting the words to her didn't feel right. *It's that I want to help you.*

He hated the idea of leaving her here to face off with Val, but when had he ever been anything but a complication and a liability when it came to a matchup between them?

He would be of more use to Veronyka in the south. More use to all of them.

There was no retreating for the soldiers now. Not only could he provide backup, but he might just be able to unify these armies against Val. He could rally the soldiers and put together a proper attack plan. For the Phoenix Riders, and for Veronyka.

Please, he begged her. *If I can salvage the bridge, we'll have the reinforcements we need to end this.*

Veronyka turned in the saddle to see the fight raging all around them. They were really just treading water—surviving, enduring, but too outnumbered to actually win. The Riders fought desperately in the sky while the soldiers scrambled fruitlessly below, but if the empire joined the fight . . . if *hundreds more* swelled their ranks . . . Val didn't stand a chance.

He won't like it, Veronyka said, nodding down at the general, who was working his way through the mass of soldiers to the southern front.

He doesn't have to, Tristan thought in reply. *I don't need him.*

It would be nice to have the general's support behind him when he attempted to galvanize the empire's troops, but he and Rex would get to the border faster than the man—or any decree from him—could.

You can't go alone, Veronyka said. She looked around. *Take Doriyan with you. You can worry about the empire; he can handle Sidra.*

That was . . . valid. If Doriyan could keep Sidra occupied, it would buy Tristan time to corral the soldiers into helping him defend and rebuild the bridge. Even if they didn't want to fight for Pyra or the Phoenix Riders, they could surely be convinced to fight for their lives.

Will you be able to reach me? he asked hesitantly, as Veronyka used shadow magic to call Doriyan to their side.

She nodded.

The fear on her face made him move. Rex steadied his flight and extended his wings as Tristan stood in the saddle and walked across his outstretched arm until one foot left Rex's wing and the next landed on Xephyra's.

Veronyka stood to meet him, and they embraced fiercely, desperately, clinging to each other as the wind whipped their hair and the battle raged all around.

Veronyka pulled back only long enough to take him by the tunic and drag him down to kiss her.

Ever since the night of her birthday and their weeks apart, Tristan had loathed being separated from her. Refused it whenever possible. They were stronger and better when they were side by side, but that also meant trusting each other when they were apart.

Besides, like any bondmates—like any apex-benex pair—they were *always* together.

What might have happened to them?
And what might have happened to me?

- CHAPTER 57 -
VERONYKA

VERONYKA WATCHED TRISTAN STREAK away with Doriyan just behind him, trusting that they were doing the right thing—for others, if not for themselves.

Still, there was a leaden feeling in her gut as she turned her attention back to the fighting that surged and pulsed all around her. She'd been tucked safely behind Fallon's shakily held line, but the strixes were gaining ground. As his row of Phoenix Rider archers moved farther and farther back from its original starting point, the soldiers below were forced to scurry out of the way. Veronyka had the sense they were being corralled like livestock in a pen, with the strixes applying pressure from the north and any progress they tried to make south halted by the Unnamed at the opposite end of their march.

As it was, they were three armies clashing on two fronts, but Tristan was right: If they allied, they could combine their efforts into a single fighting force and overwhelm Val's attacks no matter what direction they came from.

Several commanders and captains were nearby, trying to create order in their general's absence. They had seen or heard of the attack to the south, and the mess to the north was unfolding before their very eyes. Many of them were fighting now, preferring to meet the threat head-on than continue to run and turn their backs on it.

Veronyka seized her chance.

She urged Xephyra to swoop down and land in their midst. They leapt back at the sight of her, mounted and looming above them, but she didn't have time to comfort them.

"Retreat is no longer an option. We must fight this common enemy together."

"General Rast . . . ," began one of them uncertainly, while their collective gazes shifted over her shoulder, where fiery phoenixes and swarms of strixes swooped and shrieked through the sky.

"Is gone," Veronyka said shortly. "You'll have to decide your own fate now. There is no escaping this. Fight or die."

One of the commanders stepped forward, wary but firm. "What do you need us to do?"

Veronyka watched from the sky as the soldiers formed ranks and the cavalry mounted up in attack lines. Behind them, wagons were unloaded and war machines unveiled.

After a quick count, Veronyka surmised they had about two hundred foot soldiers and fifty cavalry prepared to fight the northern attack, and beyond the murky middle of their lines, where dozens more bodies swirled and struggled to organize themselves in the chaos, Tristan likely had a similar amount. All told, it was a relatively small force, especially considering the additional empire troops trapped beyond the river.

But it was more than the Phoenix Riders had on their own. They might be the ideal match against the strixes, but they were too outnumbered.

After Veronyka spoke with the commanders and captains, they decided to set up several pinch points where Phoenix Riders could lure strixes toward awaiting catapults and nets.

The cavalry was harder to utilize. They were typically the more specialized and skilled of the empire's military, but their speed and strength were undermined by the tight quarters of the battlefield as well as the fact that their enemy could fly. Still, they provided a useful focal point and diversion, running similar attacks and sweeps on the ground as the Phoenix Riders were in the air, leading the strixes toward preset traps of empire weaponry or Phoenix Rider ambush.

Veronyka looked around, at the rough Pyraean landscape and the smooth Pilgrimage Road, filled to the brim with soldiers who were, for the first time in her life, friends and not enemies.

Despite the circumstances, joy swelled in her chest, but her brief flare of hope was fleeting. They fought hard, on the ground and in the air, but this was a battle for their lives.

Riders were chased off course, patrols were split, and attack plans failed.

People were hurt. Phoenixes were hurt. And Veronyka truly understood what it meant to be a leader in a war.

She had reassigned her patrol after Tristan left, flying with Latham at her back while Lysandro and Ronyn paired off. They continued to sweep and dive, attempting to stop the strixes' forward momentum, but their charges were no longer clean. Xephyra shrieked as a beak snapped at her wings, tearing out feathers, and Latham cried out as a talon raked his arm. Ronyn and Lysandro weren't faring much better.

Though Val had relinquished some measure of control, she was pushing the strixes hard. Rather than simply dodging aside when the Phoenix Riders shot through, as they had previously done, the strixes started to slip *past* them, making for the empty space the Phoenix Riders had left behind. Fallon's patrol—which continued to hold the rear—was soon bombarded, forcing Veronyka to tell Ronyn and Lysandro to abandon their sweeps and help retake the back line.

But Val would not be deterred and would gladly sacrifice dozens of strixes if it meant her victory. She forced them to fly with brutal speed and hold fast to their route, refusing to budge, causing collisions that rarely left both sides unscathed. It was in one such crash that Lysandro was thrown bodily from his saddle.

Veronyka had a single second to make her choice, and she did. She pulled hard on Ronyn's mind, redirecting him and his phoenix midflight into a terrifying dive. They caught Lysandro just before he hit the ground, but their rescue had left Lysandro's phoenix unprotected. No fewer than four strixes leapt onto the creature's exposed back, snapping and tearing. A volley of arrows from Fallon's patrol scared them off, but the phoenix was left smoking and lethargic. He half flapped, half fell into the trees, and though Ronyn pursued with Lysandro on the back of his saddle, Veronyka knew the moment the phoenix's life winked out.

Her throat closed, and hot tears slipped down her face. Lysandro's pain reached her, a second wave of grief, and it was all she could do to remain upright.

She had done this. Her decision had condemned that phoenix to die.

Her decision. Her fault.

She wasn't Val—she didn't need to control everything—and now she would not only have to see but feel members of her flock die without being able to stop it. Even if she controlled their each and every move, she was only human, and she couldn't protect them all.

Fallon went down next, his shoulder slashed in a wound similar to what had happened to Anders, blood pooling in his armor and dripping down his side, while his phoenix attempted to fend off the crowd of strixes enveloping them. Veronyka and Latham launched arrows, but it wasn't until Darius and his mount charged through, sending the strixes flying, that Fallon's phoenix was able to extricate himself and make a rushed landing.

Darius watched him go, wild-eyed, and Veronyka sensed his intention to abandon the fight and chase after him. She couldn't blame him, but he was needed here, and Fallon would be fine. . . .

There was a sudden, powerful tug on her magic. It came from Fallon, or maybe it came from his bondmate. In an instant, Veronyka understood.

The wound was *not* the same as the shoulder injury suffered by Anders. No, this wound was much, much worse.

Wait, Veronyka said, speaking to Darius. Anger sparked inside him, and he looked ready to object, until he followed Veronyka's sorrowful gaze.

Fallon was slumped in the saddle, motionless, as his phoenix landed below. The creature was making low, mournful sounds, craning his neck, trying to get his bondmate's attention, but Fallon didn't move.

The phoenix spread his wings and lifted his head to the sky, his anguished cry piercing the night before he burst into flames, burning away to ash and taking Fallon's body with him.

Veronyka bowed her head, swirling emotions buffeting her on all sides.

Darius, she said as soon as she could speak. The battle continued to rage, and Fallon was beyond their reach. *This is your patrol now.*

His face was a mask of shock, but at Veronyka's words he looked around; their back line was in tatters, and the soldiers on the ground were paying the price. The strixes swooped and dove without obstruction, dragging their claws through the crowds and soaring back up again with bodies clutched in their talons. There were still lives on the line, still people they could help.

Darius ran a hand through his hair and nodded. As he shouted orders and brought his patrol back to order, Veronyka tried to get a grip on her own. They were down to three, and the emotions of the fight were starting to weigh on her.

She struggled to regain control, but her mental safe house was no longer protecting her. Her mind was awash in pain.

Torn flesh. Broken bones.

Lives snuffed out.

It didn't matter if she was bonded to them or not—Veronyka was a shadowmage; she could feel every cry of agony and stab of grief, no matter who it came from.

This was the price she had to pay for this power, and she tried to remember why it was a good thing. Why she needed it.

But when Beryk went down, his bondmate pierced through by a strix-feather-fletched arrow, something inside her broke.

Several more arrows followed the first, riddling both Rider and mount as they fell from the sky. They crashed to the ground in an explosion that left scorch marks across the rocky earth and set the nearest strixes ablaze, their cries of anguish silenced by a volley of phoenix-fletched arrows.

Veronyka's sorrow was raw, exacerbated by those around her—the other Phoenix Riders mourning the loss of their most senior warrior and mentor. She felt their hope waver.

Emotion, hot and visceral, pooled in Veronyka's stomach, rising up her throat.

She intended to stifle it, to swallow it back down, but that's what she'd been doing all along, and suddenly it seemed like exactly the wrong thing to do. The reason she'd accepted this position, this burden, was because with it came a powerful tool.

Heartfire.

Veronyka owed Beryk and Fallon and everyone else more than what she was giving. She owed them all of her strength, and everything she had inside. She was their apex, their leader, and her flock needed her.

Yes, these deaths were breaking her, but rather than try to piece herself together again, she let herself crack wide open.

The spark ignited. Her fear had held her back, but now she let it go, and the heat inside her grew.

When a handful of strixes started tailing Alexiya, Xephyra followed hot on their heels, and Veronyka let the fire burn.

Ximn was flying as fast as Veronyka had ever seen her, dipping and rolling and looping around, desperate to shake her pursuers, but they persisted. Xephyra, too, was just barely keeping up.

Too slow, Nyka. Veronyka craned her neck to see Val watching from the middle of the battlefield, a vicious smile on her face. She had clearly targeted Veronyka's other aunt on purpose. Making it personal. Goading her. It had also been *Val's* arrows that had killed Beryk.

A pulse of anger, sharp and bright, ripped through Veronyka's body. It made her powerful, and the heat inside Xephyra's chest surged.

Val would regret provoking her.

Xephyra pumped her wings, staying close on the strixes' heels, but no matter her efforts, Veronyka could not alter their pursuit. She nocked an arrow and aimed her bow, but she couldn't risk shooting at them and hitting

Alexiya instead. Even if they managed to make heartfire, Alexiya would still be in the way.

They needed a new approach.

Tiya Alexiya, Veronyka said, as Xephyra slowed. *Bank hard just before the trees and loop back around. On my mark, dive.*

Alexiya did as told, though Veronyka sensed her panic. Any kind of turn would mean a reduction in speed and a chance for the strixes to trap or ambush her. What had happened to Fallon and Beryk was fresh in her mind, but Ximn was agile and quick, and Veronyka knew it was their best chance.

As Xephyra moved them into position, there was a feeling of anticipation fluttering between them. The heat in her chest had turned into swirling, pulsing energy—steadily building, drawing from deep within. From her heart. From her very soul.

Alexiya and Ximn slanted hard and swooped back around, flying straight for Veronyka and Xephyra and bringing the strixes with them.

Dive! Veronyka cried into her mind, and Ximn pointed her beak toward the ground, bringing them to a sharp, sudden drop.

Then it was just Veronyka and Xephyra facing the coming charge.

With a shriek that made her ears ring, Xephyra unleashed the power within.

Fire erupted from her beak in a blast that filled Veronyka's lungs with heat and set the strixes aflame in brilliant, crackling crimson light. They exploded in a burst of sparks and blackened feathers.

Alexiya lurched in the saddle, shocked by the explosion and trying to hang on as Ximn regained her balance.

Despite the blazing heat she and Xephyra had just unleashed, a wave of cold swept over Veronyka as she watched the strixes burn up and blow away like ashes on the wind.

She had felt their deaths, and while this was nothing new, she had been blocking it until now. Ignoring it. But in order to unleash the heartfire, she'd had to embrace her emotions. All of them.

It wasn't as painful as feeling members of her own flock die, but it wasn't painless, either. Did Val feel the phoenixes dying too? And if she did, would that sensation slow her down or spur her on?

As their eyes met across the battlefield, she knew it was the latter. She also knew Val hadn't missed her use of heartfire, and that the real fight had only just begun.

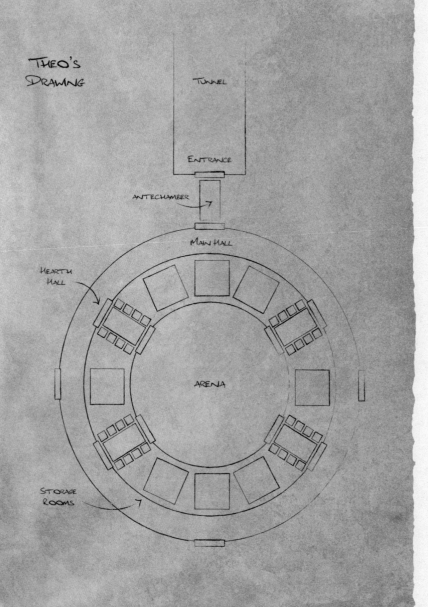

Perhaps I was meant to be here for this.
Not to light the way, but to pass the torch.

- CHAPTER 58 -
SEV

SEV WONDERED WHAT TIME it was outside the tunnel and what was happening in Pyra. From the tense expressions on Kade's and Yara's faces, he knew he wasn't the only one.

The rest were likely entirely fixated on their bondmates, and they frequently stopped to tilt their heads or mutter quietly before moving on—sensing, reaching for their phoenixes as the physical distance closed between them.

Using Jinx's eyesight to keep watch ahead, Kade called a halt to their progress, their panting breaths cutting through the silence as they ducked into an alcove.

Jinx's glow dimmed, and as Sev's eyes adjusted to the darkness, he saw a different flickering illumination up ahead. Torchlight. The end of the tunnel was capped with a set of double doors—one of four entrances leading into the circular arena from each cardinal direction. The torchlight was a good sign—clearly, soldiers were still posted, as they had been when Kade was here with Trix.

Back in Lord Rolan's house, Theo had done a rough sketch of what she remembered of the inside of the training arena, and according to her, beyond the double doors was a narrow hallway that acted as an antechamber before another set of doors that led into the arena proper. From there, a curving hallway led left and right, wrapping around the circular inner arena and leading to the three additional entrances, plus various other rooms and hallways.

They knew the phoenixes were nearby, but their bondmates were having a hard time figuring out exactly where.

"They're inside some kind of cell . . . ," said Dane.

"Made of stone, but barred in metal on one side," added Joshua.

"Why are there cells inside the Phoenix Rider training arena?" Sev asked.

"There aren't," said Theo, blinking as she drew back to herself. She turned to the others, face lit with understanding. "It's a hearth hall—the niches used for incubating eggs," she added for Sev, Kade, and Yara's benefit. "The general must have had them modified."

"That makes sense," Sev said, though the idea of it turned his stomach. They would have been designed to handle high heat, but they couldn't be large enough to comfortably hold full-grown phoenixes, let alone give them room to fly and move about. "Where are they?"

"There are four hearth halls, interspersed between the four entrances," answered Theo.

"She's close," whispered Clara, eyes blazing. "I can feel her."

"The soldiers are posted here, so it all adds up," Sev said, his heart kicking against his ribs in anticipation. "Do we know how many?"

Theo shook her head, a note of frustration in her voice. "It's hard to tell. They seem to see only two guards at a time." The others, probably trying to confer with their own bondmates, murmured their agreement.

"And there's two outside the door," Kade said. "Could that really be it?"

"I doubt it," said Yara. "There are surely other guards nearby, even if they aren't actively on duty. We should be careful and make as little noise as possible. With any luck, we can incapacitate them before they get a chance to raise the alarm."

Sev nodded, turning to Theo and Kade, who had taken up their weapons—Kade with his recurve bow and Theo with a dagger pilfered from Lord Rolan's armory. "Ready?"

Theo unhitched herself from the wall and strode purposefully forward. She was dressed as an empire soldier again, and it wasn't long until she was hailed by someone at the other end of the tunnel.

Jinx was perched out of sight, eyes fixed into the distance, and Kade was connected with her, watching, waiting, his bow ready.

The voices at the end of the tunnel grew louder; there was the sound of scuffling and someone cried out. Kade stepped around the corner of the wall and loosed an arrow into the darkness. There was an echoing whistle and a thump, and then a heartbeat later, the ringing of a blade unsheathed and a cry of pain quickly stifled.

Kade glanced at Jinx, then waved the others out of the alcove. "Let's go."

They ran the distance to the double doors, Sev and Kade leading the way, with Jinx soaring alongside them.

Theo was there, unharmed, and digging through the clothes on the limp bodies on the ground before a jingling sound reached their ears. Keys.

She held them up, frowning. Only two keys sat on the old metal ring.

The first set of double doors was already open—the two men had clearly made themselves comfortable in the small anteroom, with a table and chairs and assorted crates of supplies—so Sev shuffled down the hall to the second set of doors and slipped one of the keys into the lock. It fit—which was good news, Sev supposed, but it posed a different problem.

He glanced about the hall, checking the table's surface for containers and the walls for hooks.

They had two keys for two sets of doors, but they didn't have keys for the phoenix cells inside.

"Still have your picks?" Kade asked, sidling up next to him.

Sev grinned. "Since Ferro, I never leave home without them."

As the captives filed into the antechamber, he bent to retrieve his picks from his boot. He still had the same improvised picks he'd made from a saddle's belt buckle in Ferro, plus some proper picks he'd scrounged together during his time at Rolan's estate in Stel.

It was smart not to leave keys to the cells down here—surely the guards could feed the phoenixes through the bars—but Sev hoped that was as far as the general's caution went.

Their group was filled with mounting excitement, eager to press on, and Theo was just calling for them to hurry when a bell started clanging out of nowhere.

Sev whirled around to see one of the downed guards tugging on a rope pull, and though Yara stepped forward to silence him, it was too late—thundering boots echoed from somewhere directly overhead. That's when Sev noticed a stairwell next to the exterior doors that must lead to a barracks or guard room on the floor above.

"Inside!" Yara shouted.

It was a mad scramble through the second set of doors as Yara slammed the first set closed and threw down the latch.

It might slow the soldiers, but it wouldn't stop them—they would surely have keys of their own. Still, Sev didn't speak this thought aloud, and moved forward with the rest until Yara closed the next set of doors with a resounding bang.

There was a very good chance they were going to have to fight, and soon, and as Sev looked around at the captives' tense faces, he knew it would not be an easy battle. They needed to arm themselves, but they also needed to free the phoenixes as quickly as possible.

The hallway curved away in both directions, but the captives moved unconsciously to the right.

As they rushed down the corridor, passing doors that led into various offices and storage rooms, several of the prisoners cried out. Fear gripped Sev's heart, but he realized the sounds weren't of terror or despair. They were sounds of painful joy.

They'd reached a barred door set into the interior wall. The room inside was long, filled with shadowy niches, while on the opposite end of the room was a secondary door, also barred, leading into an expanse of darkness beyond. Sev closed his eyes, picturing Theo's drawing, and realized this room was more of a passage that led from the main hall, where they now stood, into the inner arena where the Riders would have once done their training.

A burst of sparks filled the air, followed by the rustling of feathers and scraping of talons. Muffled sounds of delight and desperation came from the group as they pushed forward to cling to the bars.

"Theo," Sev said sharply, drawing her tense gaze from the phoenix cells. "You said there might be supplies—saddles, weapons?"

"Yes," Theo said, shaking her head as if to clear it. "They destroyed whatever they could find, but there were a few emergency stashes tucked away in case of fire or attack. I doubt they found everything."

"Take them and find what you can as quickly as possible; then meet us on the far side of the hearth hall, inside the arena." He turned to Yara. "Once we get inside, we'll be vulnerable."

"I'll cover you," she said shortly. Distant shouts could be heard now, echoing down the curving hallway from the entrance they'd come through. It sounded as though the first set of doors had been breached.

As the prisoners continued reluctantly down the hall, toward the storage rooms, Yara glanced around. She found a table in a room next to them, old and dusty but made of thick planks of wood. Kade helped her haul it over and lay it on its side for cover, directly in front of the barred door where Sev stood.

She knelt behind it, facing the direction of the approaching soldiers, crossbow aimed and ready.

Sev bent to the lock.

It was too dark to see clearly, but then a soft golden haze fell over the lock—Jinx, sidling up next to him and lighting his work—and for some reason Sev's throat closed up. Everything was riding on him, and though he couldn't see the end of the road, thanks to Jinx, he could see the next step.

"Thank you," he murmured, and she crooned softly in response. Her dark eyes shone with keen intelligence and curiosity. She was helping him, yes, but she was also fascinated by his lock picks, her gaze fixed on the tools as he worked. Sev couldn't help it—he smirked. Kade had a type, it seemed.

The lock was difficult, even with Jinx's help, and his hands shook. Behind him, the soldiers' voices grew louder.

The mechanism clicked just as a loud *bang* echoed from the direction of the entrance. It sounded like the *second* set of doors had also been breached.

Sev released a shaky huff of air and wrenched the barred door to the hearth hall wide, shoving Kade and Jinx ahead of him.

Yara remained outside in the main hall, loosing crossbow bolts into the dark. Because of the rounded passage, she couldn't see the soldiers, but her arrows pinged and ricocheted, causing them to take cover and shuffle backward.

She had a good position, able to see as soon as any of them poked their heads around the bend, but she wouldn't be able to hold them forever.

"Come with us!" Sev shouted, but she waved him off and remained outside in the corridor. There would be no defending them from within that room—no way to get a clean shot off. And if the soldiers made it around the corner, they'd all be sitting ducks.

Turning his back on the danger, Sev took in the room before him with a moment of stunned silence. Each wall had a square niche of stone, charred and blackened from decades of fire and closed in by thick, roughly soldered bars that clearly did not belong. Perched within each of those somber lodgings, crouched among a smattering of crumbs and bits of straw, was a single phoenix. They were mostly full grown and far too large for their tiny cells, but they could all bear their Riders, which was some measure of relief. The cell directly next to him was empty—Sev thought of Aron with a pang—while he couldn't see into those at the end of the line.

"Quickly," Kade said, and Sev crouched in front of the first occupied cell. The phoenix inside retreated in fear, flinching at the noise, but Jinx crooned and soothed as Sev worked. Luckily, they were similar locks to those on the door he'd just opened, so each became progressively easier as he repeated the movements over and over again. The instant a lock clicked, Kade shoved him on to the next one, swinging open the grate to release the prisoner. Jinx was there to welcome and settle the creatures, the glowing light increasing with each phoenix they set loose—as well as the heat.

Sev slipped into a trancelike state, focusing on the task at hand and blocking everything else out.

"That one's empty," Kade said distractedly, as Sev was just finishing a lock.

Another one? he thought dazedly, lurching to his feet. He hadn't even looked inside. . . . Something made him pause, and he squinted into the shadowy recesses of the apparently unoccupied cell. Something shifted and caught the flickering light from the other phoenixes—excited and agitated and putting off sparks, no matter how much Kade tried to calm them—and then a small creature pecked its way forward, crawling out from under scraps of straw and old feathers.

It was definitely a phoenix, but a tiny little thing, his red and gold plumage coated in ash as if he were newly hatched.

Or newly reborn.

Sev looked at the top of the cell, where plaques with names had been affixed to keep track of which phoenix belonged to which bondmate. And above this pitiful creature was the name "Adam."

It was Aron's dead brother. So while Aron's despair had caused his own phoenix to give up hope and go to ash, when Adam himself died, his phoenix remained behind? How long had it been since Adam had died . . . and how many times had this phoenix resurrected himself?

Sev had finished unlocking the cell without realizing it, and reached inside tentatively. But the phoenix wobbled forward on tiny golden legs, and when Kade shouted for him, Sev scooped him up and tucked him into his front pocket.

Theo and the others had arrived inside the arena, peering in at them from the barred door on the opposite end of the hearth hall. The phoenixes squawked and fluttered excitedly, and it was growing hot enough that Sev's clothes clung to his skin and sweat dripped down his temples.

They were so close he could almost taste it, but Sev still had two more cells to go, and the sounds of Yara's defense behind them were growing louder. A glance backward told him Yara's makeshift barricade still held, the table's flat surface peppered with crossbow bolts, but the battle was drawing nearer.

Another lock clicked open. More shouting. And then the final cell swung wide.

Sev pushed through the crush of feathers for the barred door that led into the arena, the last barrier between these freed phoenixes and their bondmates . . . and his heart plummeted inside his chest.

The door *wasn't* a door at all. There was no handle, no latch—no lock. It was simply a wall of inch-thick metal bars, latticed together in a barrier Sev had no way of breaching.

His expression must have said it all, because Kade cursed, looking down at every inch of the bars, searching, while Theo did much the same on the other side.

Hope, like a flickering fire, died inside Sev's chest.

"The way we came in," Kade said, turning, but the words had barely left his mouth when a resounding crash filled the corridor. Yara's table toppled backward, sending her flying, and partially obstructing the barred door. Sev ran toward it, peering around the pocked and damaged wood.

Yara was already on her feet, fighting the two soldiers who had charged her. She dispatched them one by one, then glanced around at Sev, panting.

"Go," she gasped with finality.

"No!" Sev cried, rattling the bars, but the door was blocked by the table. There was no getting in or out that way. "Just drag that out of the way, and—"

A volley of arrows showered the ground and walls around them, forcing Yara to duck. When she stood again, she was wobbly, hands pressed to her stomach, where an arrow protruded from her side.

She looked down at it, then up at him. "Go," she said again, then wrenched the table up with all her might—not out of the way, as Sev had asked, but onto its shortest side, so it was tall enough to completely block the door between them. A last line of defense between them and the soldiers.

Between them and Yara.

Sev stared at the slab of wood until a series of thumps reverberated through the table—more arrows slamming into the wood in the exact place Yara had been moments before.

He swallowed. There was no going back. Only forward.

He returned to the opposite side of the hall, looking at the bars again, then around him, at the flock of phoenixes bristling and squawking and emitting puffs of sparks.

"Can they melt it?" he asked, speaking to Theo through the bars. She had been wrenching on the iron lattice with wild desperation, but now she stilled.

"A single phoenix? No. But all together . . ."

"Wait—what?" Kade asked sharply, looking between them. Theo was wearing a searching expression, her eyes raking over Sev with something like respect.

It was simple, really. Sev and Kade were trapped inside the hearth hall with ten phoenixes, separated from freedom—from their bondmates—by impossibly thick metal bars. There was only one way they were getting through.

"Tell them to ignite," Sev said more loudly, speaking to the others, who were crowded behind Theo.

"No!" Kade shouted, the word ripped from his throat. "You're not bonded. You won't be protected!"

"Do it," Sev said again, and Theo nodded grimly. She turned away, shouting instructions to the others.

"What, no, stop—you can't!" Kade said, screaming through the bars and then back at Sev, his eyes glittering. He followed Sev as he shuffled back, making room for the phoenixes to crowd forward. Kade's hands landed on

Sev's upper arms, clinging, pulling—begging. "You can't," he repeated in barely a whisper.

The noise behind the wooden barricade was growing louder, the soldiers using whatever weapons they had at their disposal to hack at the table, which Yara must have somehow wedged into place. They would break through soon, and the phoenixes were trapped, and *yes*, yes, Sev could.

All his life, he had prioritized survival above all else—a not-uncommon trait, but something he had put particular emphasis on every single day.

Survival had felt like the only way to repay his parents and make their sacrifice feel a bit less senseless. Then he'd met Trix and Kade and had taken the idea a step further—if he was to live when people like Trix died, then Sev would make his life count. It had been the driving force of his existence ever since. But what if . . . what if instead of doing everything in his power to survive, to make his life count, he'd found something worth dying for instead?

With Sev's *death*, he could ensure Kade and the rest of these Phoenix Riders were free—truly free—and maybe, just maybe, help Veronyka and the others win this war.

It seemed an easy trade, when he looked at it that way.

But tears were streaking down Kade's face, the room was growing blisteringly hot, and Sev knew his choice would not come without pain.

"You're only doing this because you think you don't matter—that you're worthless. But you *do* matter. To me, to us . . ."

Sev shook his head. "I believe that now, thanks to you. I know I'm worthy. You chose me, and I can think of no greater gift. But now I'm choosing you. My parents died for me, and I'll die for you. Gladly."

"You promised," Kade said, agony in his voice as he crowded Sev, tried to push him away from the growing heat and licking flames. The air was already hazy with heat, making it difficult for Sev to draw full breaths, though Kade seemed mostly unaffected, his bond magic at work.

"I promised we'd be together at the end—and we are. This is *my* end, and we're together. It's okay. I want this," Sev said, trying to reassure himself as much as Kade. He could smell burning now, and his skin felt tight and itchy with heat. They had foolishly slammed the empty cells closed again in order to make room to move about, and there was no time to unlock them again. But not even one of those stone niches could truly save him. Not from so much fire all at once. Not from temperatures hot enough to melt iron bars. "I want my last moments to be with you."

Kade's face crumpled, and he pressed Sev more firmly against a patch of wall in the farthest corner, caging him in—bringing Sev back to a time beside a waterfall on Pyrmont, when everything had changed between them. The stone behind him was as cool against Sev's back as it had been then, but the world around him was dry and hot, the nearest metal bars starting to glow.

The soldiers had cleared out, Sev thought—probably smelling the smoke and seeing the growing flames—because he couldn't hear crossbow bolts or hacking blows or anything at all, actually.

Maybe that was the roaring of the flames, drowning everything else out.

Maybe that was the soundlessness of death. The peace.

His eyes were fixed on Kade's, and there was the peace he truly sought, the place he wished he could remain forever. Then a pair of red and purple wings rose up behind Kade, *around* him, and Sev saw Jinx there, enfolding them both in her embrace. Protecting them, or trying to. But not even Jinx could block the heat and flames from so many other phoenixes. It was like being inside an oven. Oxygen was sparse in Sev's lungs, and the air rippled with heat.

"I never hated her," Sev found himself saying, but he wasn't sure Kade heard him or if he'd even spoken aloud. *I never hated you,* he said to Jinx, and she crooned. It filled him up like music, warming him in a way that had nothing to do with the fire rising up all around.

Or maybe it was something else.

Sev bowed his head, and there, pressing against his chest inside his pocket was the hatchling phoenix. He felt the creature's warm body, his heartbeat that skipped and jumped and then slowly matched rhythm with

Sev's own. Their eyes met—and held—and then the fire exploded around him in a sudden, violent burst. Kade crashed into him, Jinx's wings were buffeted aside, and the world around Sev blinked and wavered and slipped away.

I have protected them, Nefyra. I have
fought and burned as best I could.

- CHAPTER 59 -
VERONYKA

VERONYKA HAD VAL'S ATTENTION now—and it wasn't just hers.

The crowds below pointed and stared, and the Riders in the sky halted their progress, momentarily dumbfounded. They had seen her use heartfire, their expressions awed, and even the strixes had taken note, their black eyes following Veronyka's and Xephyra's every movement.

But it was Val's focus that cut through Veronyka like a knife.

Thus far she'd been enjoying the battle, flying left and right, taking down soldiers and targeting Phoenix Riders with reckless, joyful abandon.

In truth, Veronyka had never seen her look so alive.

This was what she truly wanted—not the so-called prize at the end of the game, but the game itself. The thrust and parry, the attack and counterattack. She had no patience for pretenders and posturing, but she valued a worthy opponent, and Veronyka had proven herself to be one on multiple occasions.

This was not the soft, delicate maneuvering of politics, which shifted in slow, steady tides. This was the blunt, powerful immediacy of war. Make a mistake and pay a price—instantly. Make the right move and see it play out in front of you.

Except this time, Val had made the wrong move.

She had deliberately targeted Alexiya, wanting to hurt Veronyka—to make her desperate—but clearly had not realized what that desperation would yield.

Heartfire. It's what she'd wanted from Veronyka in the first place, and it was the one thing she could not have without her.

They stared at each other for several weighted heartbeats; then Val hefted her spear—the same spear that had sliced Veronyka open?—and dove back into the fray. Her rage left Veronyka breathless as she targeted soldiers and Phoenix Riders alike with renewed, vicious vigor, trailing strixes the way the strixes themselves trailed shadows.

Despite Val's fury, she didn't actually go after Veronyka. It seemed she didn't want to give her the satisfaction, and instead deliberately focused her attention elsewhere, as if to say Veronyka didn't concern her—no matter what kind of magic she could do.

It allowed Veronyka to release a shuddering breath and notice for the first time another bondmate who was vying for her attention.

Veronyka! Are you okay? It was Tristan, frantic on the other side of their bond. He'd been calling her for a while now.

Yes, she said reassuringly. Then, remembering what had just happened— *That was heartfire. Did you feel it?*

I felt it, he said, his emotions a swirl of relief and tension. *Like a pull on our bond.*

Does it hurt? Do you feel weak?

She sensed him slowly shake his head. *Never felt stronger.*

For some reason, that answer made Veronyka's throat ache. Heartfire was right, natural—an extension of apex magic and her benex bond.

Why, then, did using it make her feel sick?

What's happening? she asked, needing a distraction as she and Xephyra continued to soar around the battlefield.

Doriyan's working on Sidra, and I'm working on the soldiers.

Do you think you can repair the bridge? she asked. As it stood, the battle was raging on fairly even footing—the outnumbered Phoenix Riders bolstered by the ground troops and their war machines, but reinforcements would be enough to turn the tide in their favor. Val wouldn't retreat. If they could make a proper stand here and now, they could finish this.

I'm going to damn well try, he said, and Veronyka couldn't help but smile.

As she refocused on the fighting around her, Veronyka's bonds flickered and surged, with bursts of life and death on both sides. Whatever Nefyra and Ignix had done, they had not had to endure this. . . . Being bonded to Val and her horde meant that there was no peace for Veronyka, no joy or victory to be had in destroying their enemy.

But was there ever *joy* in war? Maybe for someone like Val, but bond magic or not, Veronyka could never find happiness in this. It was a dark duty, just as Ignix had said, but it had to be done.

Spotting a pair of strixes at the edge of the battlefield, Veronyka nudged Xephyra to pursue. Now that they'd managed to conjure it, she felt the heartfire smoldering behind her breastbone, ready and waiting to be called forward.

The strixes were heading toward a regiment of soldiers. Xephyra flew fast and hard, gaining ground and bringing the strixes within range. Despite her fierce flight and expert maneuvering, Veronyka sensed Xephyra's uneasiness as well. They were one, after all, and the pain and suffering Veronyka felt? Xephyra felt it too.

They breathed together, stoking the heartfire that was building inside both their chests. Xephyra opened her beak, ready for release—and at the last moment, Veronyka nudged her to shoot the flames in *front* of the strixes, not directly at them. The spout of heartfire forced them to squawk and veer off course, scaring them away from the soldiers rather than killing them.

The soldiers looked around in confusion—their crossbows raised, prepared for an attack that did not come.

Veronyka cursed. Whose side was she on, if all she sought to do was keep everyone alive?

But she couldn't shake the terrible fear that she would lose something, some indefinable part of herself, if she gave in to this ability. If she gave in to reckless, unstoppable destruction. But what other choice did she have?

Laughter filled her mind. *Ah,* xe *Nyka,* Val said, terrible, patronizing fondness in her tone. *I knew you did not have it in you. You are not a fighter, not truly. Not a winner. You must be willing to do whatever it takes to succeed, and you are not.*

Veronyka refused to respond, but it seemed Val didn't need her to. She was cleaving through Veronyka's forces with ease, like an ax through wood. She decimated a regiment of cavalry with obvious relish, tearing through their ranks one moment before homing in on the war machines in the next. She lost half the strixes charging behind her to arrows and artillery, but continued to push and push until Onyx collided with the arm of a catapult and knocked the payload flying. The wood splintered and crumbled underneath her talons, while the remaining members of Val's charge set upon the soldiers who were working the weapon, causing them to flee in terror or drop by the dozens at Val's feet.

Veronyka was disgusted—at Val and at herself.

Xephyra wheeled around and darted into the throng. She was burning hotter than Veronyka had ever felt before, heat waves rippling and blue-white fire blooming across her feathers. But rather than scare their enemy off, the threat of heartfire seemed only to spurn the strixes on, the creatures driven wild by that spark of life they so desperately coveted. They bit and snapped at the trailing flames, hungry, devouring—mad with need and want that was sickening, that emanated from them like the very shadows that draped across their feathers. Was this their overwhelming desire bleeding from them, or Val's?

Veronyka twisted and loosed a volley of arrows to gain them some space. She hit one of the strix's wings, sending it veering off course, but the others dodged and weaved and continued their pursuit.

Xephyra tossed her head in anger and decided she'd had enough. With her wings thrown wide, she flipped around in midair, opening her beak to let loose a torrent of roaring flames. The burst of heartfire enveloped the remaining strixes, their screeches ringing in Veronyka's mind—not keening death wails, but cries of painful joy. Of release.

Veronyka stared, shock crashing through her in waves as she watched the shadowbirds fall back down to earth, their inky feathers flashing red and gold before burning up, into ash.

But not the ashes of destruction.

The ashes of rebirth.

But they did not need me. Not truly.
They have saved themselves.

- CHAPTER 60 -
SEV

SEV OPENED HIS EYES.

Everything was dark—but not the darkness of death or even sleep. It was smoky, the air thick and clogging his throat. His lungs hitched, and a ragged cough tore through his throat, but then the clouds of smoke billowed and dispersed as Jinx moved her wings. The room was still hazy, but Sev could see movement—the phoenixes scrambling through the wreckage of the melted metal grate and out into the arena where the others stood.

His ears were ringing, and as he blinked his stinging eyes, his gaze settled on Kade.

He had his arms wrapped around Sev, using his body as protection—his back as a barricade, his shoulders as a shield—and behind him was Jinx, adding her protections to his. If Kade was armor, Jinx was a fortress.

Just as Sev had fought for them, so too had they fought for him. They'd all chosen each other.

Kade was staring at him with unguarded shock, with raw, desperate wonder. He pulled back just enough to really *look* at Sev, before crushing him against his chest. Kade's whole body trembled, and he pressed his face against Sev's temple, breathing deeply—Sev felt wetness, either sweat or tears, and the warm press of Kade's mouth.

"I'm okay," Sev managed, and Kade let out a shuddering laugh that transformed into a sob halfway and gripped him tighter. "Careful," Sev murmured, looking down, and Kade followed his gaze to the tiny phoenix pressed against his chest. His *naked* chest. His pocket was gone, his *shirt* was gone, burned to little more than scraps of singed fabric, and somehow Sev was holding the tiny bird with both hands.

The phoenix only chirruped and blinked up at them both, expression mild and curious and not the least bit concerned.

"Axura above," Kade whispered, but Sev kept thinking about Teyke and his cat. About luck and timing and every odd twist and turn his life had taken to lead him here.

Distant coughs and groans echoed from somewhere behind them, and Sev realized the blaze that had somehow failed to kill him had managed to destroy the barricade Yara had built, and whatever damage had happened to the soldiers in the explosion, they were now stirring.

Gripping Sev's shoulders protectively, Kade steered him toward the opposite end of the room, where the remains of the metal bars still glowed hot and red like coals in a fire. Sev glanced over his shoulder, afraid to look but needing to know, and spotted Yara's prone form amid the wreckage, crossbow bolts in her chest.

His grip on the phoenix twitched and tightened, but the creature only nuzzled against him. Sev stroked the soft down, the knot of anger and guilt that tried to take root loosening. Sev had dragged her into this. . . . Her death was his fault.

But it wouldn't be in vain.

He stumbled over the melted wreckage of metal bars, emerging into a dark, cavernous space. There was sand underfoot and stone benches rising up into darkness all around. The roof above, where the arena would have opened to the sky, had been boarded up, the tiniest cracks of moonlight filtering in from above.

When he drew his attention back down, it was to realize that everyone was staring at him—human and phoenix alike. They were gaping, their own joyful reunions put on hold to gawk at him.

While he and Kade were both equally sweaty and smeared with soot, Kade had been wearing his fireproof Rider leathers, so his clothes remained mostly intact save for the smoking edges of his undertunic.

Sev, on the other hand, was more or less naked.

He just stared back at them, the tiny phoenix pressed to his chest, until Jinx moved in front of him, her wings raised to protect his modesty. She was fairly glowering at the onlookers—the phoenixes were the first to lower their heads and turn their attention aside—but it was nothing to the expression on Kade's face.

The disapproving, jealous tinge to his features almost made Sev want to laugh. They weren't ogling Sev's rather unimpressive physique—of that he was quite sure—but they were stunned nonetheless to find him alive, whole and unharmed. The heat had been intense enough to turn his clothing to ashes, to say nothing of what it had done to the metal bars, and yet, there wasn't a burn or a welt on him.

Sev was stunned too.

Kade turned his back on the others to reach inside Jinx's saddlebags, which were also treated with fireproof sap, though they were wilted, their metal fastenings melted together. As he struggled to find what he was looking for, Clara cleared her throat and tossed him a rolled-up blanket. Kade nodded his thanks and draped the fabric over Sev's shoulders.

Jinx lowered her wings, and Sev smiled at her. He realized that trying to resist her had been an impossible feat, when she was so clearly an extension of Kade—a piece of his heart. And a piece of Sev's, too.

The noise from beyond the phoenix cells had faded away, and Sev wondered if the soldiers there had decided to retreat—or if they were simply circling around or going for reinforcements.

The others were apparently thinking the same thing, remembering they were in the middle of an escape and hastily turning away to saddle their mounts and adjust their borrowed armor. Despite the tension, their touches were lingering, their words soft as they fussed and hugged their bondmates. Tears flowed freely, but they were tears of happiness.

Kade looked at Sev, his expression shifting from protective anger to wonder and confusion. He stared, uncomprehending, and then his attention slid to his bondmate.

"Jinx . . . ?" he said uncertainly. Sev tilted his head. Was that possible? Could a phoenix extend their protection like that? Did something of Kade's feelings for Sev get transferred to Jinx and then some of her bond to Sev?

But then the creature in his hands squirmed, trying to get comfortable— or perhaps draw his attention—and he wasn't so sure.

Theo stepped forward then, offering to take the phoenix so Sev could get dressed in the clothes the others cobbled together for him, but Sev clutched the hatchling tighter. He fought against a mad urge to yell, to snarl, and shook his head.

Over my dead body. "No," he said, fighting down the irrational anger. "No. He . . . he stays with me." Always. Forever.

Suddenly Sev knew, and by the way Kade's eyes narrowed—then widened—it seemed he knew too.

Bondmate.

There had been a moment in the cellblock, an instant of eye contact between them that had reverberated through Sev's heart—deeper, even, to his core—and it had happened *after* he had chosen to die. After Sev had finally accepted himself as worthy. That love, that sacrifice . . . Had the phoenix felt and connected to it?

This tiny creature, this newly made thing . . . he belonged to Sev, and Sev belonged to him. They had saved each other. They had *chosen* each other. Sev had saved him from his cage, and this phoenix had saved him from the fire.

It was lucky Sev had seen him, small and cowering in his darkened cell.

Kade inched closer to the pair of them, his movements slow—perhaps sensing Sev's panic at the prospect of being separated. Instead, Kade reached out tentatively, gently, to stroke a thumb down the phoenix's tiny spine. A corresponding shiver of pleasure slid down Sev's back.

The slightly hysterical dread pressing against his chest receded, and Sev looked up into Kade's warm amber eyes. And over his shoulder was Jinx, her gaze bright and curious, but wary, too. Hesitant.

"You," Sev swallowed, knowing that time was ticking on, that they had to get moving. He tried again. "You can hold him, if . . ."

The gratification, the fierce pride in Kade's expression made Sev's throat tight, but he only nodded and took the phoenix from Sev's hands so Sev could stumble into the proffered clothing.

Kade bent his face low, continuing to pet the phoenix with a careful touch, while Jinx cocked her head this way and that, making soft chirruping sounds. Sev had to stop to stare at them, at this small slice of life he'd never dared to dream for himself. That he'd never thought possible.

Not for him.

Emotion tightened his throat again, and his eyes prickled. Kade seemed to sense something was wrong, and stepped closer, holding Sev's phoenix— Sev's *bondmate*—out to him.

Sev shook his head, blinking away the tears, and lurched into Kade's arms instead. His phoenix was pressed between them again, and it felt perfectly right—or almost perfect, until Jinx enveloped them in her warm wings once more.

Now it was perfect.

Sev was overwhelmed. He took several steadying breaths, his forehead pressed against Kade's chest, and he felt Kade speak before he heard the words.

"What will you call him?" he asked.

Sev considered. "I think I'll name him after Teyke's cat, Felix."

Kade drew back, smiling down at him. "Because he's lucky?"

Sev shook his head. "No, because I am."

It was full dark by the time they found a way out of the arena, and Sev braced himself for the eventuality that leaving would be more complicated than getting in, but he was wrong. They didn't have to fight their way free or sneak down the quiet evening streets—even the soldiers that had been pursuing them from behind seemed to have disappeared or else been caught up in what was happening aboveground.

The Aura Nova streets weren't *quiet* at all. Instead, they were wild with panic, soldiers running to and fro, while civilians huddled in groups, whispering, or stared concernedly from doorways and open windows.

"What is it?" asked Sev, lurching out of the alley in which they'd been hiding and flagging down a civilian. "What's happened?"

"They say the war's happening, right on the banks of the Aurys! You can see it from the watchtowers. My brother's city watch—he saw it with his own eyes."

Sev craned his neck, glad they didn't need a watchtower to get a better look.

"They say it's not just Phoenix Riders," the man continued, gripping Sev's arm. "There are *monsters* coming outta the sky! Black-winged monsters! The gods are punishing us," he finished, his last words carrying through the streets. "The gods are punishing us all!"

Sev pulled his arm free. "You should get inside," he said. "Somewhere safe."

"The temple!" the man cried, eyes bright.

"Good idea," Sev muttered, mostly to himself. They weren't far from the gods' plaza, and the temple to Axura was the highest ground to be found that wasn't a watchtower.

Sev climbed onto Jinx, and together their group flew to the temple roof, doing their best to stay clear of the torchlight. Theo risked flying a bit higher for a better look and reappeared grim-faced and white-knuckled.

"That man was right—religious ravings aside. There's fighting happening on both sides of the river. Strixes, Phoenix Riders, and soldiers—but it looks like the Riders are fighting *with* the empire. There are other forces on the ground—they look like raiders, without proper uniforms—and they've destroyed the bridge."

Riders fighting with empire soldiers. That was an interesting development. "Nothing makes fast friends like a common enemy," Sev said.

"Strixes," muttered Clara, voice faint. "I did not think the world could get darker than it already was."

"Why destroy the bridge?" asked Dane. "If their enemy is winged . . ."

"To stop reinforcements," Sev said, trying to picture the battlefield in his mind. "There are hundreds of soldiers trapped on this side of the river. The strixes likely attacked from the north and had these raiders cut them off in the south. It traps the soldiers that are already inside Pyra, along with the Phoenix Riders, who won't abandon them there to die."

"They won't?" asked Joshua skeptically.

"Veronyka won't," Sev said firmly, glad he'd already laid the foundation for who she was and what she stood for.

"She is not Avalkyra," added Kade.

"What do we do?" asked Dane, his voice slightly panicked. "There are soldiers and city watch everywhere. Whatever's happening by the river, I doubt all of the empire will see us as friends."

But even as he spoke, civilians from the street below—currently piling into the temple of Axura to pray—spotted them, pointing and crying out.

Sev tensed at first, fearing they were about to be targeted by city watch, but then he actually heard what the crowds were saying. Apparently, word of the strixes had spread like wildfire through the city, and the people below weren't shouting in fear or anger. They were begging for help, for protection, thanking the goddess for heeding their prayers.

Just like that, Phoenix Riders were no longer the empire's enemies. Not with that dark threat from legend looming. Not with bells ringing and soldiers stomping and defenses being mounted.

Even with all those soldiers—and all those miles—between the border and Aura Nova, the people of the city knew that winged warriors could cross that distance in no time. That their high walls and ranks of soldiers would not keep them safe.

Only Phoenix Riders could do that.

Among the throngs below, Sev spotted lit candles and dusty old phoe-nix idols—clearly cherished relics that had been hidden for years. Waiting, it seemed, for the Phoenix Riders to return. Hoping.

And here they were, symbols of the goddess herself, perched atop her soaring temple. What else *could* they do but protect these people? Sev's chest tightened, and he felt like a child again, watching his parents soar off bravely into battle. Certain, in his heart, that good would prevail.

They were no saviors—they were the most ragged group of Phoenix Riders Sev had yet seen—but they were *something*, and they could help.

"What do we do?" Sev repeated, voice strong with conviction. "I know what I want to do. I want to help—in any way I can. But I understand if you want to get on your phoenix and fly far away from here. You deserve freedom and to have your lives back with no strings attached. I also under-stand if you don't know who you're fighting for. Avalkyra did you wrong, just as General Rast did—but that doesn't make Phoenix Riders evil, and it doesn't make the empire evil either."

Sev looked between them all, at their tense expressions and the way they stood side by side with each other and their bondmates.

"But," he continued, "I think if I were a Phoenix Rider, I'd fight for the Phoenix Riders I know, for those on either side of me." He looked at Kade and Jinx to his right and Theo and her bondmate to his left. "We have friends fighting, and they're up against something bigger than the empire, bigger than laws and borders and political affiliations. They're fighting for us, for animages, for *life*, and I want to help them. *We* can help them. Together. Tonight."

The feeling in the group was changing. The phoenixes stood taller, and their Riders lifted their chins. Below, voices continued to cry out for them, shouting and pleading.

"When all this is over, you can swear your loyalty to the Phoenix Rid-ers, to the empire, or to no one at all. You can be whoever you want to be. But right now, I hope you'll be with us."

Sev moved toward Jinx, surprised to find himself face-to-face with Kade. His eyes were bright, his expression fierce, and it made a tingling heat sweep across the back of Sev's neck. He thought maybe it was embarrassment—he'd never expected to make a rousing battle speech in a million years—but he found he didn't mind. Not if it made Kade look at him like that. It occurred to Sev how much easier it was to be brave when he wasn't always questioning himself. Maybe he was the hero Kade had accused him of being. . . . He'd just never truly believed it until now.

Kade's eyes remained glued on Sev as he stepped aside, helping him into the saddle before climbing up in front of him. Next to them, Sev sensed Theo doing the same.

Sev adjusted Felix in his front pocket, hands shaking with adrenaline. But when Felix nipped his finger and Sev looked up, he saw each and every one of the others mounted up as well. Waiting on him.

Kade twisted in the saddle, grinning, and then Jinx leapt into the air, leading the charge, the rest of the phoenixes shrieking excitedly and flapping their wings. Trails of sparks glittered behind them, and every street they soared over echoed with cheers and applause, with *hope*.

Fear was an iron fist in Sev's stomach, and he was unsure how helpful he could possibly be, a passenger on Jinx's back and with a new hatchling clutched to his chest. But as they swooped past the city walls—even soldiers cheering out as they whipped past, toward the fight—a nearby phoenix cry drew their attention, and Sev's mouth fell open.

Jonny and Rosalind were suddenly there, coming from the east with the entirety of Haven's Phoenix Rider force soaring behind them.

But it wasn't just them.

There were others, unfamiliar faces, grim and determined as they soared off to battle. Clearly, their recruitment efforts had not been in vain.

The commander's phoenix, Maximian, was in the lead, Theryn on his back—and looking more than a little queasy. The rest fanned out behind him like individual sparks of fire.

Sev's heart soared, and the others whooped and laughed, calling out greetings to one another. They seamlessly combined their forces, tucking in behind Maximian and making for the distant battle.

Sev gripped Kade more tightly; he had so much more to fight for all of a sudden, and so much more to lose.

But then he thought of his parents, fighting together—and dying together—and he realized that he had already made his choice. And it was a surprisingly soothing notion.

It was like he'd said to the others. Kade was a Phoenix Rider, and now Sev was a Phoenix Rider too—or he would be, once Felix was large enough. They were his to fight for, to protect, and wherever Kade and Jinx went, Sev and Felix would follow.

They remind me of us, when the world was young.
When we were young.

- CHAPTER 61 -
TRISTAN

TRISTAN SURVEYED THE BATTLE below.

It had taken some doing, but he and Doriyan had managed to convince the empire soldiers that they were friends, not enemies.

First, they'd had to take care of Sidra. Not only had she destroyed the bridge, but she'd made quick work of anybody daring to try to cross what remained of it: Bodies lay strewn along the shore or bobbing in the current, some of them as burnt as the bridge, others shot through with arrows.

"Can you keep her occupied?" Tristan had asked as he and Doriyan approached.

Without replying, Doriyan withdrew his bow. He nocked an arrow, touched it to Daxos's crackling feathers, and loosed.

Tristan supposed killing her outright would work too—but apparently that wasn't what Doriyan had in mind. Sidra turned before the arrow even left his fingertips, and Doriyan, for his part, looked wholly unsurprised as it whizzed past her head. His aim had been true, but Sidra had shifted ever so slightly to avoid it. She might have been stretching her neck or finding a more comfortable position in her saddle—and *not* narrowly dodging an attack that would have ended her life—for all the concern she showed.

The flaming arrow left a trail of smoke in the air, and Sidra touched the side of her face, as if feeling the residual heat. Then she leaned low in the saddle as her bondmate shot toward Doriyan. He fired another arrow, this one merely diverting Sidra's flight, before urging Daxos to dive. Sidra followed him tightly, his every dip and maneuver mimicked, like she knew what he was going to do before he did it. They looked like dancers flying a complicated choreography, and something about it made Tristan's chest tighten—they had been close once, and now they fought on opposite sides. But he supposed that was war. . . . It made a person choose.

With Sidra appropriately distracted, Tristan had turned his attention to winning over the empire soldiers. Luckily, the Unnamed provided a useful focal point. Several sweeps and a volley of arrows was all it took to show the soldiers where his loyalties stood and to get them on his side.

The bridge had mostly stopped burning by now, the wood charred and blackened, but the frame remained. They could rebuild it.

While the soldiers on the northern shore rallied together and kept the Unnamed busy, drawing them deeper into the fray and away from the bridge, Tristan crossed the river to the southern shore.

There was a good deal of disarray and no small amount of petty blustering between the border guards, who had their own internal pecking order, and the commanders and captains of the military. That wasn't to mention the squabbling between soldiers, who bristled at taking orders from officers from other provinces. The general was the one person who outranked them all and could bring order to the chaos, but Tristan had no idea where he was or if he intended to do so.

Their desire for information, however, outweighed their suspicion of Tristan as he approached—and after he shared what he could of the attack in Pyra and their need for reinforcements, everyone fell in line and listened to his plan. Despite the fact that they had mustered in order to attack the Phoenix Riders, everyone seemed to take it as a given that while Tristan and the others *might* be dangerous, the strixes *definitely* were and, along with the Unnamed, posed the more immediate threat. The shadowbirds were drawing closer and closer to the river, whole groups of them breaking through

Veronyka's back line, and Tristan knew it was only a matter of time before they reached the river.

Veronyka had trusted him to handle the bridge, and given the way the battle was progressing, he *had* to get the reinforcements through.

Though Veronyka had finally managed to create heartfire—it scorched his lungs and seared against his breastbone, vibrating like an irregular heartbeat—Tristan could feel more than just the magic funneling through. He could feel what it cost Veronyka to use such a devastating, violent force.

It was not in her nature to destroy.

But if he did this right, if he salvaged the bridge, Veronyka might not even need to use heartfire. If hundreds of soldiers came rushing into the battle, maybe Val would see sense and retreat. Or better yet, maybe they'd capture her, and avoid any more bloodshed altogether.

Tristan's strategy was simple: While the Unnamed were distracted with the fight on the northern shore, the soldiers to the south would attempt to rebuild the bridge with whatever they had on hand—which meant disassembling catapults and wagons for lumber. They didn't need a perfect structure, just one that would allow foot soldiers to cross.

Tristan soared overhead, giving both sides the benefit of his aerial view and launching arrows at the odd strix that broke through and reached the river, and to discourage any Unnamed who thought to fall back or defend the bridge. Crossbowmen lined the southern shore, providing cover each time soldiers dragged forward a plank of wood and launched it across the damaged structure to the remaining support beams, still solid underneath.

It was slow, it was imperfect—but it was working.

At least, until Sidra noticed. Then it was all Tristan and Doriyan could do to keep her occupied, diving and attacking and hurling arrows. She managed to get the attention of one of the Unnamed leaders, and soon they had organized themselves enough to split their numbers, half fighting the northern forces and the rest trying to undo the progress on the bridge.

Sidra fought with single-minded determination, and though Doriyan matched her in skill and style, it was clear he pulled his punches—he didn't actually *want* to hit her with an arrow. He didn't actually *want* to defeat her.

Bringing him might have been a mistake. The idea of killing a Phoenix Rider made Tristan's stomach roil—but he *would* do it if it meant ending this. He wasn't sure Doriyan could do the same. Not to this Phoenix Rider.

But he stuck with her, and managed to lure Sidra off again, giving Tristan a chance to pull back and survey the scene below.

The sun had long since set, and it was hard to distinguish friend from foe. Even in the sky, the strixes blended into the darkness, but night only made the phoenixes glow all the brighter, sparkling like falling stars.

"Uh, Phoenix Rider, sir?" called one of the captains from the southern shore.

"My name is Tristan," he answered reflexively, landing before him.

"Daniel," the man replied. It was a strange, utterly human moment amid the horror of battle, and Tristan was grateful for it.

If they had met under different circumstances, they'd have tried to kill each other. Now, thanks to Val, they were allies.

Daniel gestured toward the river, where massive planks of wood were piled near the water. "We could use your help with the larger ones, if you're able."

Rex puffed out his chest.

Considering the size of the beams and the span of the river, Rex *and* Daxos would have been ideal, but they did what they could on their own.

With archers covering them, Tristan and Rex soared low and took up one end of the heavy beam. Rex's claws dug deep, slowly dragging the wood across the river, while a handful of soldiers carried the back end. Tristan watched carefully, Rex glowing as brightly as he dared while holding ready kindling, and thanks to the illumination, Tristan was able to signal the exact moment when they should release. The plank landed with a dull, reverberating thump onto the still-standing supports.

One down, Tristan thought, as Rex shook out his wings and unclenched his claws.

They repeated the action with a second beam, and this time some soldiers from the empire side of the river rushed forward, allowing Rex to lower the log more slowly and giving them the chance to carefully line them up. It was still a bit too narrow for crossing, but Tristan thought a third might allow soldiers to walk single file.

They were halfway there with the third plank when a cacophony of shrieks drew Tristan's attention upward.

It wasn't a lonely strix or two but a pack of them, bearing down on him fast. He cursed.

Rex, let go! Tristan said frantically, and his bondmate released the heavy log with a splash, causing soldiers on either side to cry out and jump backward. Tristan whipped up his bow, but before he could nock an arrow, the strixes cried out and tumbled from the sky, peppered with crossbow bolts.

They landed along the banks of the Aurys, and the soldiers from both sides of the river pounced on them before they could take flight once more. The rest fell into the water and were swept away.

Glancing around, Tristan saw Daniel and the other crossbowmen that had saved him.

He blew out a breath and waved his thanks. "Cover me?" he asked, and Daniel nodded.

Rex dove down to reclaim the fallen log. It was difficult to get the submerged end out of the river—they were both soaked by the end, and Rex was actually steaming—but finally they managed to soar up again and drag the log into place.

The soldiers on both sides of the river cheered, but their victory was short-lived. The shouting soon changed, becoming angry and confused. Tristan turned in the saddle to see the soldiers to the north parting to allow a horse-mounted rider to pass through—though the rider didn't give them much of a choice. Anyone in the way was knocked aside, and soon General Rast's grim face became visible. Behind him, the battle raged, the strixes running amok, not just on the northern front but attacking everywhere, tearing the ranks apart.

"What are you doing?" the general bellowed, bringing the frothing horse up short. His narrow-eyed gaze roved the dismantled catapults, the muddy footprints and evidence of struggle all along the riverbank, and then at last, the damaged bridge with its temporary crossbeams in place.

The soldiers on the southern shore were in the middle of organizing themselves for a march, but their progress had halted. They couldn't hear what was happening on the northern banks, but they saw everyone's attention shifting to the general.

"What does it look like?" Tristan asked as Rex landed close enough to be able to talk but far enough to avoid appearing like a threat. "Rebuilding the bridge. We need to get reinforcements into Pyra as soon as possible."

With that, he turned his back on the man and waved across the shore. Soldiers rushed forward, marching single file over the narrow planks. Tristan would rather be in the air next to them, should the strixes return or one of the beams fail, but the general wasn't finished.

"We most certainly do not!" the general raged. "Pyra is no longer a part of the empire, and therefore we owe it no defense. I have ordered a retreat."

And with that he urged his horse forward, onto the makeshift bridge he'd just chastised his army for rebuilding. Several of his soldiers were already halfway across, and with a shouted "look out," they leapt for the shore or scrabbled to hang on to whatever handholds they could find as their general barreled through.

Tristan cursed as he and Rex followed the general to the southern shore. "Help them," he said to Rex, indicating the soldiers about to plunge into the icy river, before dismounting and facing off with the general.

Rast had dismounted as well, insisting he needed a fresh horse for the rest of the way to the capital—but Tristan waylaid him.

"This won't stop in Pyra." He pointed to the sky, to the strixes that continued to move steadily south. It was hard to tell if the Unnamed were still fighting, but they had done their job in delaying the reinforcements and condemning many of the northern forces to death—unless Tristan could make the general see. "Now is the time to stand and fight."

He shouted those last words, making sure that the soldiers ranged around them—and maybe even some on the far shore—could hear.

"I will determine *when* and *where* this army fights," the general snapped. "Now fall back! Make for the capital! Form ranks and *fall back*!"

The commanders who had been so efficiently following Tristan's lead stared at one another. Retreat was a common tactic, especially if the intention was to move to more defensible ground, but there was no better place to engage the strixes than right here. Aura Nova's walls wouldn't keep them out, and the city wouldn't be prepared for an attack—all their soldiers and war machines were here, ready and waiting to be used. Besides, outside the capital, there were no innocent civilians to get caught in the crossfire—no families and livelihoods at stake.

General Rast's eyes bulged slightly, his jaw working.

"Sir," said Daniel, moving to the front of the group to address the general. "I agree with Tristan that we are ideally placed and ready to engage now. If we retreat, they'll come at our backs, and—"

"You *agree* with the Phoenix Rider," the general cut in flatly.

There was a shriek somewhere above: Another strix had broken through the chaos and was making straight for them. Tristan took a halting step forward, but Rex insisted he could handle it. After dropping one of the soldiers he'd rescued onto the far bank, he burst into flame and collided into the strix in midair.

"Look at this!" Rast snarled, flinging a hand at the two legendary birds fighting in the sky. "He's one of them. They are our enemies! We came here to eradicate them, not chitchat about battle strategy."

But even as he said it, Rex flung the strix aside and the soldiers below shot the shadowbird full of arrows. It crashed to the ground, crushing several of the soldiers beneath as it scrambled and lashed out, but then they swarmed the creature and finished it off.

Together.

The general turned his back on the scene. He seemed to be considering what to do next, but any feeling of hope Tristan had died when Rast's cool gaze fell on him.

"As a matter of fact, I think a Phoenix Rider hostage would be a valuable asset. Take him prisoner."

Tristan gaped, his hand dropping to the hilt of his dagger. This wasn't—this *couldn't* be happening. He looked across the river, where Rex continued to fight *with* the soldiers, swooping and diving and forcing the strixes to fall back. Then he looked at the soldiers all around him. Didn't they see? He and Rex were fighting for *them*, for everyone. Would they really turn their backs on him?

Despite the tension that had descended over the group, no one moved.

Across the river, the soldiers seemed to sense that something wasn't right—that their strategy might be changing. They edged nearer the water, heedless of the cries of oncoming strixes, and started to climb on the rickety beams of wood. They were utterly vulnerable out over the river, but whatever confidence Tristan had instilled in them was quickly dwindling.

"Fine," General Rast snapped, drawing a sword from his belt. "I'll do it myself."

Tristan stepped backward and unsheathed his dagger—a less-than-ideal match against a sword, but it was all he had. His jaw clenched, with both annoyance and frustration. "You came here to fight, General. Why are you backing out now?"

"I came here to *win*," he spat. "I came here to accept your surrender. To prove a point and finish what I started. I did not sign up for *this*."

The soldiers surrounding them continued to watch, uncertain, but Tristan couldn't expect any of them to come to his defense.

"General, they're overwhelming the northern banks!" a soldier cried out. Heads swiveled in that direction, including Tristan's. Rex and many of the soldiers were being swarmed. Rex was barely visible in the melee, and Tristan felt a true pulse of fear. Here he was, dealing with stubborn pride and fragile egos, while his bondmate was fighting for his life.

With a curse, Tristan put away his dagger and reached for his bow instead, determined to help Rex, but the general wasn't finished with him. He lifted his sword, bringing the tip to Tristan's throat. One good thrust, and that would be it.

Tristan took a careful step back, but the rush of the river—and the ten-foot drop into it—was not far off. "General Rast, why don't we—" he began, but the man closed the distance between them, teeth bared, and Tristan knew he was out of time.

An earsplitting screech rent the air, and Tristan whirled around to see a massive phoenix come out of nowhere, ripping past and colliding hard with the general.

He went flying one way and his sword the other, but both wound up in the river. The firebird wheeled back up into the sky, and Tristan's heart soared when he recognized Maximian. He bore a Rider, but it wasn't his father—it was Veronyka's, holding on for dear life. Distantly, impossibly, a chorus of additional phoenixes took up the cry.

Tristan gaped, and he wasn't the only one. Every soldier on both sides of the river did as well, and even the strixes that had been surrounding Rex squawked and jumped, startled, into the sky.

There were twenty, maybe even *thirty* Phoenix Riders tearing toward them. They didn't slow or stop but crashed into the strixes with explosive vengeance, beaks snapping, talons flashing. A cheer went up from the soldiers—*empire soldiers* cheering and clapping at the arrival of Phoenix Riders.

Rex extricated himself with their help, rushing to Tristan's side. After they checked each other for injuries, Tristan hugged him tightly, then took a closer look at their rescuers.

Theryn had come with the Phoenix Riders from Haven. Tristan knew what his arrival would mean for Veronyka and waved his hands to get the man's attention.

"She's on the northern front!" he shouted.

Max came in for a landing, intending to stay here, so Theryn quickly dismounted and flagged down Jonny so he could climb onto his saddle instead. The reinforcements split, some following Theryn to help Veronyka and the rest staying behind with Tristan.

He frowned again at the group. Their numbers didn't make any sense—there were only a dozen phoenixes at Haven, so who were these others? Where had they come from? Theryn had mentioned other Riders hiding in Arboria. . . . Had they somehow recruited fighters to their cause?

And then he spotted Theo . . . riding a phoenix. *Her* phoenix, surely. It couldn't be, could it? The captured phoenixes from Aura Nova . . . Tristan's mouth hung open. Sev and Kade were among them too, with Sev riding in the saddle behind Kade. Had *they* done this?

As Daniel got the soldiers to form ranks and the phoenixes cleared a path over the bridge, giving room for line upon line of fighters to charge through, Tristan thought that maybe they weren't so outnumbered after all.

That maybe they could even win.

*I thought I was here to teach them, but they have
taught me instead, these bright young things.*

- CHAPTER 62 -
VERONYKA

SOMETHING WAS HAPPENING HERE, something Veronyka had only just begun to understand.

Phoenixes and strixes . . . they weren't separate species, hell-bent on destroying one another. They weren't even personifications of the goddesses Axura and Nox. They were like any living thing. . . . They gave back what was put in, only in their cases it was tenfold. Give them love and life and warmth, and they grew into phoenixes.

Give them hatred and hunger and cold, and they grew into strixes.

It had been in front of her all along—it was even in their creation myths. Born from the same rocks, the same eggs, but turning into either a phoenix or a strix, depending on who hatched them.

Veronyka had always seen their separate existences as an irrevocable sentence. A state of being that could not be changed.

But what if it could?

What had Ignix said about heartfire? *It can destroy, create, and unmake.*

Val had been living off cold hate for years, but once she had been bright as phoenix fire and able to bond to a creature of light, no matter her darkness. In fact, wasn't Nox herself once a phoenix? Until her endless hunger, her vast longing, consumed her?

People could change. They could be reborn. They could be unmade and remade all over again.

Xephyra was thrumming beneath her, alive with Veronyka's thoughts and the swirling possibilities of the heat coiling within her.

Val was still fighting with a vengeance, still determined not to concern herself with Veronyka quite yet, even though she'd just used heartfire again. One of the catapults launched a massive rock Val's way, annoying her enough to loop around and attack it, a trail of strixes following behind her.

The distraction bought Veronyka time to experiment.

Spotting a solitary strix, Veronyka urged Xephyra to chase it away from the battle, giving them a chance to attack with more deliberation. Again Veronyka's chest began to swell with building heat, the power coming from way down deep, making her feel both hollow and expansive—empty and explosive.

With a great, fiery burst, Xephyra hit the strix in the shoulder joint of its left wing—and something strange happened.

Typically the strixes burned up quickly, like paper, dissolving into nothing and blowing away on the wind. But this time there was that flash of red, a sheen of scarlet against the inky darkness of its plumage, and the creature pumped its wings once, twice—desperately—before at last being consumed by the blistering heat.

But there had been something, a flicker of possibility. . . . Veronyka thought back to when she'd seen Ignix breathe fire. She remembered the sight of her great rib cage swelling, glowing from within—the incandescent light spilling around her feathers, suffusing them with color and gilding them like the sun forcing its way through the clouds.

She also thought of the feeling she had when Xephyra built her fire . . . the way it seemed to coalesce behind Veronyka's breastbone, as if she were holding a firestorm inside her chest. Heartfire, indeed.

And then it clicked.

It was their hearts. Xephyra had to hit them in their hearts.

Ever since the strixes had arrived in her life, Veronyka had been confronted with nothing but death and destruction. But here was a chance at something else, bright and pure as the dawn, and she had to chase it.

Soaring back toward the battlefield, Xephyra bobbed and weaved, setting her sights on another solitary strix. It took nothing but a shriek to draw the creature toward them, and Veronyka saw now that the strixes didn't chase them so much as *hunt* them, like a starving wolf that's sighted its first deer in weeks. Frenzied with hunger and wild with panic—that was how the strixes flew, how they followed Xephyra and the rest of the phoenixes, their desperation only ratcheted up by the presence of their fellows, who were competition, not companions. This, too, was how Val felt about friends and so-called allies—that was why Sidra was her servant, not her equal or the benex to her apex. That was why she and Veronyka now faced each other as enemies, not sisters. Not family.

This time when Xephyra gained a lead and whipped around, her aim was careful and true—directly into the heart of the coming strix.

The creature seemed to freeze in midair, its wings outstretched, its head tilted upward in agony or ecstasy—Veronyka couldn't be sure. But Xephyra's heartfire didn't incinerate the strix or cause it to go crashing to the ground. Instead, the flames licked and spread—emanating from that burning heart—until they covered the bird but somehow didn't consume it. It almost looked like a phoenix as it pumped its flaming wings, a smoldering ember trying to catch fire. It picked up speed, the strix shrieking and flying and burning. Had they found a new, more painful way to kill the sorry creatures?

The strixes nearby actually halted their flight to watch, and so too did the Phoenix Riders and soldiers below. The entire battlefield ground to a halt as the burning strix continued to fly, struggling and veering almost drunkenly, but still aloft. Still alive.

Veronyka sensed something then, something beyond the pain and hunger she usually felt from them. It was the gentlest of whispers, and when she reached, she found she wasn't using shadow magic as she had to with the other strixes, but animal magic instead.

It was the barest flicker, like a guttering candle. Fighting, struggling against a strong wind.

But then Veronyka was there, soothing, comforting, welcoming this new creature into an old world. Into *her* world, into *her* flock. Another shriek and a great flap of flaming wings—crimson wings, feathers bright as blood and tipped in golden honey. The darkness was gone, burnt and cast away like ashes on the wind.

Triumph blazed inside Veronyka's lungs, searing her with every breath, and tears stung her eyes. The creature had been frightened and alone, but Veronyka had shown it the way. Had ushered it back to the light.

A chorus of phoenix song filled the night, causing the strixes to cower and flutter around frantically, while the firebirds soared and arced and expelled great gusts of flame. Sparks swirled and danced through the air, and suddenly the shadows didn't seem so dark.

Xephyra crowed in excitement, and Veronyka sought out their next target.

This was how she'd win this war. Not with death and violence, but with hope.

They'd barely moved when a silent presence loomed behind them. Veronyka whipped up her bow, only to find herself face-to-face with Ignix. She appeared angry and agitated, heat crackling in the air, but since Sparrow still rode in her saddle, she didn't ignite.

"What's wrong?" Veronyka asked, already reaching into her mind. She'd been preoccupied throughout the fight, but never more than in the past few minutes. Last she remembered, Elliot and Ignix had been flying away from the battle.

"We were ambushed as we tried to escape," Elliot explained, launching arrows in a defensive arc, giving them time to speak. "Jax got my father and sister to safety, but Ignix never had a chance to land."

"Are you okay, Sparrow?" Veronyka called out.

She jumped, her body rigid in the saddle. "Been better," she said. Her raven friend squawked, and she nodded. "Also been worse."

Veronyka smiled, despite everything, but Ignix tossed her head to bring the attention back to herself.

You know not what you do, she said, before turning her ancient gaze on Xephyra. *Only Axura's heartfire is truly limitless.*

"You said heartfire could make and unmake, that it could create. . . . That's what we're doing," Veronyka explained. "We don't have to kill them. We can set them free."

Ignix looked away. *I've never seen such a thing. . . . I fear it will come at a terrible price.*

"Then I'll pay it—*we'll* pay it," Veronyka said angrily, and Xephyra shrieked her agreement. "Don't you see we have to try? Instead of slaughtering dozens of strixes, we could make dozens of phoenixes! We could save the empire and everyone in it."

When you give them heartfire, you're also giving pieces of yourself. The cost—

"If I have to die, then so be it!" Veronyka shouted. "We will stop this. We will stop her."

Xephyra moved to go, but Ignix blocked them again.

There are worse things than death, she warned, the words hanging in the air.

Xephyra cried out a sudden warning, and Veronyka and Ignix looked around.

Avalkyra Ashfire was on the move and coming straight for them.

Go, Ignix said, moving in front of Xephyra—no longer to block, but to protect. *I will keep the so-called queen busy.*

"Alone?" Veronyka demanded.

Ignix cocked her head. *No, not alone,* she said, glancing over her shoulder at Sparrow. Elliot, too, soared next to them, bow drawn and ready to fight. *Together.*

Veronyka's nodded. *Thank you.*

Then Xephyra sprang into flight, tearing through the sky, determination humming through the bond. They would make this work—they had to.

They could save them all.

Veronyka looked over her shoulder as Ignix and Onyx prepared to clash in the sky.

Maybe they could even save Val.

They have taught me how to love and love and love,
even if it consumes you.

- CHAPTER 63 -

AVALKYRA

AVALKYRA HAD NEVER SEEN anything like it.

And she had seen many things.

She had seen life, and death, and that place in between.

She had seen the sky fall, the earth shake . . . the foundations of the empire crumble.

She had lost much. She had taken more.

Still, she had never seen anything like this.

A fire-breathing phoenix, spouting not the flames of destruction, but the flames of resurrection.

Veronyka was more than a queen, more than an Ashfire. . . . She was Axura herself, *making* phoenixes, creating them from nothing.

No, it was even more than that. She was taking the empty vessels of Avalkyra's horde and filling them up, up, up until the aching hunger and endless yearning were satisfied.

She was giving the darkness what it had sought all along. She was giving it light.

Avalkyra gritted her teeth and clenched her fists so tightly, the spear in her hands snapped clean in half. She chucked it away and refocused.

Just as she had felt her strixes dying, she could feel the moment of conversion when she lost a member of her horde. But because she was bonded to Veronyka, she could also feel when the new-made phoenix joined Veronyka's flock instead.

Veronyka was not just weakening Avalkyra's power—she was *stealing* it.

Rage scorched Avalkyra's chest and seared her lungs. Every breath burned with the fire of it. She had known that heartfire was a possibility—had even expected it, given Veronyka's bond to Cassian and Olanna's brat. But she had also known that Veronyka was soft, that she would hesitate and hold back. Avalkyra had counted on it.

But *this*? How much more could she be expected to take? How many more chances could she give?

Veronyka, like her mother before her, was the one obstacle Avalkyra could not overcome. She would take Avalkyra's strixes one by one, and then, if she had a backbone, she'd come for Avalkyra.

Unless Avalkyra came for her first—while she still had the power of the horde. While she was still bonded to an apex.

Onyx shot through the sky like an arrow, Veronyka in her sights, but then that cursed, ancient phoenix loomed up before them. Onyx squawked and brought them up short, trying to go around, but Ignix blocked their flight path.

"Out of my way, no-longer-apex," Avalkyra drawled. Ignix had a passenger on her back, some tiny little thing, and there was another Rider pair nearby. "I need to have a word with my niece."

I'm afraid I can't allow that, Ignix replied calmly, bobbing up and down before her.

"You don't *allow* me to do anything," Avalkyra snapped. "I am still Apex Master."

Ignix tilted her head thoughtfully. *For now.*

Avalkyra bared her teeth. She would shut this phoenix up once and for all.

Onyx shrieked and pumped her wings fast, no longer trying to avoid colliding with the phoenix, but rather aiming for it.

Onyx was fast, but Ignix was faster. She tucked her wings and rolled, dodging the impact by inches. Avalkyra cursed as Onyx banked hard and flew back around. Again they tried to crash into the foul firebird—and again, the creature rolled out of the way.

But for all her elegant acrobatics, Ignix's size made her slower. Onyx was gaining on her, and already Avalkyra could feel her talons tearing into the phoenix's flesh, her beak ripping out feathers. Tasting blood.

Her attack was thwarted *again*, this time by the other Phoenix Rider, who blocked their strike—not with avoidance tactics and tricky maneuvers but with artillery.

Avalkyra wobbled in the saddle as Onyx veered off course to avoid the arrows, and with a curse, Avalkyra grabbed her bow and launched a return volley. She didn't bother to aim, just loosed them in the other Rider's general direction, forcing them into a retreat. Then she reached for the nearest strixes and sent several after them for good measure before refocusing on her prize.

This time, when she and Onyx drew near, a damned *raven* dove in front of her face. Avalkyra swatted at it, but it wasn't alone. All manner of winged critters burst out of the night, circling her head like a cloud of midges. Pigeons and doves and sparrows, too, snapping and scraping and squawking in her ears.

Animages, Avalkyra thought bitterly, knowing that girl on Ignix's back was to blame.

Avalkyra reached tentatively, but her animal magic was all but dried up. She couldn't connect to a single one of them.

With a cry of frustration, she swatted and batted them aside. When that failed to deter them, she pushed Onyx into a vicious barrel roll. The abrupt dive lost the worst of them, but Avalkyra came up scratched and bloody.

She'd had enough. Avalkyra sought more strixes—as many as she could reach—and drew them to her. All of them.

It was time to finish this. She'd start with the world's first phoenix, and then she'd destroy the rest.

They have taught me how to give and give and give,
until there is nothing left.

- CHAPTER 64 -
VERONYKA

VERONYKA WAS ALIVE WITH their success, happiness reverberating through her magic and tingling in her veins.

With Val busy battling Ignix, Veronyka and Xephyra had to act quickly. The problem was, even with Val distracted, the strixes were wily, unruly creatures, and it was difficult getting them alone. Xephyra's strike needed to be exact. Otherwise the heartfire would simply burn them up like it had before.

But what remained of Veronyka's flock was scattered, busy working with the empire to reestablish a back line and chase down the strays that had made it south.

Veronyka knew she could rake them all back in with the apex bond, but she was hesitant to undo their hard work. What she needed was *more* Phoenix Riders, but she'd been wishing for that ever since this business with the empire started, and to no avail.

Then, as if in answer to her thoughts, a rise of awareness sent her attention south, where a swell of soldiers surged northward into the heart of the battle. Tristan's efforts to repair the bridge must have worked, freeing the reinforcements that had been trapped beyond the river.

And . . . there were *Phoenix Riders* with them. Glowing balls of fire near the bridge, and more of them soaring through the air toward Veronyka and the center of the fighting.

Her heart skipped a beat. It was the Haven Riders! Most she recognized—Rosalind and Ivan, Sarra and Erend—but there were others she'd never seen before. More Phoenix Riders soaring toward her than she could have ever imagined.

Jonny was also there, flying at the front, and he was not alone. . . .

Veronyka's eyes pricked with tears. Her father. Theryn sat behind Jonny in the saddle, here and ready to fight *with* her.

"You came," Veronyka said as soon as Jonny and Theryn were within earshot. Her father looked terrified but determined, his knuckles white where he clung desperately to Jonny's back.

"We're with you, no matter what," Theryn said gravely. "*I'm* with you."

Veronyka nodded, unable to speak.

"Tell us how to help," Jonny prompted, Rosalind and Ivan and the others waiting for orders.

Veronyka blew out a breath. "I need you to help me trap them—the strixes."

"Trap them . . . ," repeated Jonny uncertainly. "Shouldn't we be killing them instead?"

Veronyka couldn't help but smile. "Trust me. We need to separate them from the group so I can face them one at a time."

"Should be easy enough for Xip and me to bait them," said Rosalind.

"And we'll chase off the strays," said Jonny, indicating himself and the others.

"Theryn," Veronyka said, turning to her father. "Can you take control on the ground? The general abandoned his troops, and the commanders are doing the best they can, but we've got wounded phoenixes and their Riders, plus reinforcements rushing into the fight, and they won't know how to handle what's coming next." He looked confused. He wouldn't be for long.

"I need somewhere safe for the new phoenixes."

"New phoenixes . . . ," Theryn repeated blankly. Then he shrugged. "Okay."

Jonny dropped Theryn below, where he wasted no time getting in touch with the nearest soldiers and coordinating their efforts. There were already some healer tents being set up, but Theryn was directing them toward some rocky ground that would be more easily defensible. Groups of prisoners could also be seen, tied together under heavy guard as the reinforcements to the south tipped the ground battle in their favor.

The focus now was on containment, on using catapults and crossbows to turn the strixes away and back, while the phoenixes helped hold a wider perimeter.

With Jonny, Rosalind, and the rest of the Haven Riders at their side, Veronyka and Xephyra seized their chance.

Together they tracked and trapped the strixes, and one by one she liberated them, setting fire to their lifeless prisons, then reaching with mind and heart and magic to welcome them into the fold.

The Haven Riders stared in awe the first time, then redoubled their efforts, finally understanding what Veronyka was trying to do.

The new phoenixes emerged exultant—but also disoriented, flapping their wings and fluttering in erratic, confused circles. Veronyka tried to steer them away from the battle, down to the ground, where her father was waiting. He might not be an animage, but he'd been saving and protecting phoenixes for Veronyka's entire life. She trusted him to get the job done and knew the rest of the Phoenix Riders would help do the same.

As the strixes' numbers dwindled, she could feel them straining against Val, trying to buck her control. They yearned for Xephyra's heartfire, for the freedom they saw in the strixes that Veronyka and her bondmate lit up in heavenly light.

Despite Val's immense will, Veronyka's efforts were destabilizing Val's position as apex, and her hold was waning. Not only was Val's horde shrinking, minimizing her power, but the newly converted phoenixes were now part of Veronyka's flock, strengthening her instead.

Veronyka was certain Val had noticed, but she was still fighting Ignix across the battlefield, joined now by Latham and Ronyn and some of the others. Whether by Veronyka's unconscious will or their own observations, they'd seen what was at stake and had rushed to give Veronyka the time she needed.

Even with her increased power, the work was exhausting. But it was exhilarating too, banishing the tiredness, the fatigue, into the farthest reaches of Veronyka's mind.

She thought of Ignix's warning that heartfire was limited, that they only had so much to give—but what was that threat compared to this feeling? Every time she and Xephyra turned a strix, the Riders cheered, their phoenixes shrieked, and even the soldiers below clapped and stared, mesmerized by the sight before them.

The air was alight with shifting shadows and glowing firebirds, but Xephyra's heartfire was the brightest, most remarkable thing to grace the sky since Axura herself. It glowed like molten lava, shone like burnished gold—it was the sun itself brought down to earth.

Ignix and the rest of her Riders were fighting bravely, but Val would not be put off her purpose forever.

Veronyka had managed to transform most of the surviving strixes, but Val drew any that remained to her side, surrounding herself with what little barrier she could form as she struggled to break free.

It wouldn't be long until they faced each other.

Veronyka couldn't help the hope kindling inside her chest, mixing with the heartfire to create a palpable, almost painful ache.

If the strixes could be saved . . . why not Val?

It was a dangerous thought, powerful in its intensity. Veronyka would have to take Val out one way or another, so why not this way? Avalkyra Ashfire had been through worse, had survived worse, so maybe she could survive this.

Dangerous, foolish hope—but Veronyka held it close all the same.

As Val once again shook Ignix and wheeled around in search of Veronyka, she changed her strategy. Instead of bringing her few remaining strixes *with* her, Val sent her last protectors surging outward in an explosive burst, directly into the nearby Riders. They ducked and dispersed in surprise, buying her the space she needed to go straight for Veronyka.

Leave her, Veronyka ordered as her scattered flock attempted to gather themselves to chase her down once more.

Leave her to me.

In order for this to work, Xephyra needed to get a clear shot at Onyx's chest, but to do that, she'd have to let Val get close . . . *very* close.

And so they did.

Val gained on them quickly, flying tight on Xephyra's tail, gaining with every pump of Onyx's wings. There was no room for error now, no quarter given. The instant Xephyra let up, Onyx would be upon her. That could work, in theory, but if the heartfire didn't hit Onyx in the exact right spot, it would all be for nothing.

After maintaining their chase across half the battlefield, Val grew impatient and drew her bow. A second later she had an arrow nocked, and Veronyka was in her sights.

Veronyka did the only thing she could think of, which was to raise her own bow. She turned backward in the saddle, and Val's eyes widened to find Veronyka facing her, arrow ready.

But Veronyka didn't release it, and Val's shock faded.

"Always a bleeding heart," she called, the wind whipping through her hair and almost taking the words away with it, but Veronyka read them on her lips and sensed them through their bond.

Val's gaze slipped away, skipping over the growing ranks of phoenixes soaring erratically through the sky before settling back on Veronyka. "It should have been me."

Veronyka shook her head. *Maybe before.*

Val's face contorted. *Before what?*

Before you lost your way.

Val snorted dismissively, but Veronyka wasn't done.

You're nothing but a shadow now, a ghost of what you were.

You *are the shadow!* Val snapped, her disdainful mask fracturing for a moment, splintering to reveal the raw emotion underneath. *You were made for this, to serve as my benex! You were born in my shadow, have lived in my shadow, and will die in my shadow too.*

Val straightened her bow, and they remained like that, their mounts tearing through the sky, weapons trained on each other. Veronyka's arms trembled with the tension of holding the bow drawn, her focus switching between the black of Val's eyes and the black of the obsidian arrow aimed straight at her head.

Even if I die in shadow, Veronyka said solemnly, *at least I have lived in the light.*

Val's haunted expression pained Veronyka—she didn't know why. Maybe it was because for two lives Val had lied, cheated, and killed to reclaim what she'd lost—to become the person she had once been—but every step she'd taken had led her farther from her goal. Life had robbed Val of her humanity, and despite everything, Veronyka knew that Val missed it. That whatever she said to the contrary, Val ached with the loss of it.

"All this time," Veronyka said, voice choked, "you've wanted to rewrite the past. You can't. But you also don't have to relive it."

Val shook her head fiercely, teeth gritted and jaw set, but her eyes were wild. Unguarded. *You know nothing of light and shadow,* she said. *Or of life and death.*

Then her gaze narrowed, piercing Veronyka down to the bone. Her knuckles turned white, her bowstring drawn taut, and the arrow loosed.

It had been useless, Veronyka knew, her efforts to try to save Val. Maybe she'd been trying to save *herself* from the pain of this decision.

But it was already made.

If she loosed her arrow, she would be the same as Val, her own legacy marked by killing her sister, and she would become the thing she'd fought against.

No. Instead she would love and try to save Val until the very end. It wasn't that she *could not* kill Val. It was that she *would not*.

But that didn't mean Val could not—would not—kill her.

Veronyka released. Not the arrow, but the tension holding the bowstring taut. Time stuttered to a halt as Val's arrow shot toward her, steady and true. A death stroke. A clean shot.

She should not be surprised.

She should not be hurt.

But then the death shot wasn't a death shot at all, because Xephyra was dropping, wings clutched tight to her sides, so that the arrow zipped over Veronyka's head, missing her by a mere hair's breadth. And then Xephyra was spinning, and Veronyka was upside down, disoriented as Xephyra came to a halt—not in front of Onyx, but beneath.

And then she opened her beak and shrieked with all her might, hitting Onyx's exposed underside in a torrent of heartfire that made Veronyka's breath rattle in her lungs.

The heartfire was wrenched from her body, her mind, her soul, pouring forth in an exploding rush, surging into Onyx's chest. The strix shrieked, the sound ringing in Veronyka's ears, and then she was nearly jostled from the saddle as Onyx crashed into Xephyra, the pair of them careening to the ground, and taking Veronyka and Val with them.

Veronyka felt Onyx's talons digging into Xephyra's flesh, sensed Val's rage and fury as she clung to the saddle. She would not go down easy.

More! Veronyka cried, terror seizing her as Xephyra struggled, weakened by the use of the heartfire and the razor-sharp pain of Onyx's claws. *More!* she said again, the drag and pull like water sucked down a drain. *All of it. Everything.*

Give her everything.

We are all the same—I see that now.
Sun and moon and stars, we are all the same.

- CHAPTER 65 -
AVALKYRA

WHEN AVALKYRA FIRST MET Veronyka—truly met her, not touched a bloody hand to her heartbeat as it thumped within her mother's womb—it had been inside that dirt-floored apartment in the Narrows. Ilithya had wanted to name her something plain and common, but Avalkyra had insisted she be named for her mother. The Pyraean version of the name, not the absurd Stellan one.

And so had begun Avalkyra's foolish attachment to the girl.

She thought she'd learned a lesson. Surely someone who passes through fire and death should come back changed for the better? Like steel in a forge, beaten and hammered—like pottery in a kiln, baked and hardened. Avalkyra should have come out stronger.

But every time she looked at that girl, she thought she was looking at Pheronia before her, trusting and earnest, and whatever resolve she'd felt to guard herself, to pull back, would crack and crumble.

And so in willful ignorance—the very same thing she criticized Veronyka for—she had let the bond between them grow. She stood aside as it dug deep roots and stretched strong boughs, reaching, reaching for the sun. For life.

Had Avalkyra inadvertently fed and watered the very vines that would choke the life from her? Was this self-sabotage?

Or was it love?

That arrow . . . it was good that it had missed. Good that the battle should not be won so easily.

Pheronia's words, from a lifetime ago, sounded in her ears. *What will you do, where will you turn, when there is nothing left to take?*

The memory grated, for she still did not have an answer.

Even now, with her army falling apart around her, the wind slicing through her hair, her skin, and her fingers raw from the bowstring and the arrow that did not land . . . she didn't have an answer.

Onyx shrieked as their quarry dropped out of sight. Then they were locked together, and that blazing, blistering heat—that life-giving, war-ending flame—was coming for them.

Avalkyra felt the moment it made contact with Onyx's flesh—through her bondmate beneath her, but also through Veronyka. It was like being strung together, beads on a braid.

But there was violence there, for all the love that Veronyka poured into it.

Aching, aggressive love. Like being speared through the heart. Avalkyra was cut wide open, bleeding out.

Onyx shuddered, and distantly, Avalkyra realized they were falling, crashing into Veronyka and her phoenix and plummeting through the sky.

Another shudder, and then a screech, pulling deep within Avalkyra. Pulling on their bond. Asking, *begging* . . . for something.

Was this death? She thought she knew the feeling.

Was this life? Apparently she'd forgotten.

The warmth, the pain . . . Was it working? Was Veronyka saving her, bringing her back to life, just as she had done on the battlefield over seventeen years ago?

If she was . . . If she was, that would make this the end, wouldn't it? Nothing left to take, no more battles left to fight. The end of the road and the start of something new.

What would that world look like? And where would Avalkyra fit in it?

How *could* she fit in it, after everything she'd done?

The simple answer was that she couldn't. Veronyka would love her, fight *for* her instead of against her, but it wouldn't matter.

Avalkyra was a war criminal. She had killed queens and sisters and daughters and mothers.

She had torn the empire apart, had brought Pyra to its knees, had laughed and spat in the face of any who would dare to check or challenge her.

And she had lost. If this was the end, she had lost.

They would not let her walk free or fly through the sky. They would tear her down and lock her up. She would be powerless. She would be nothing. Not an apex, not a queen.

Once this was done—once the fighting was done . . . it would be all over. This life, this freedom . . . these moments between them.

All over.

Avalkyra screamed, Onyx shrieked, and the fire flickered and died.

And there was nothing but darkness, and disappointment . . . and silence.

But I am old now. So very old.
And I think this is the end.

- CHAPTER 66 -
TRISTAN

WITH THE BRIDGE HOLDING and the extra Phoenix Riders available to keep the strixes from harassing the troops, reinforcements crossed into Pyra in droves. It was satisfying to see the battle change in the distance, to see the chaos settle and the tide shift. These soldiers were fresh and inspired, not caught off guard by their supernatural foe, and they seemed bolstered by the presence of the additional Phoenix Riders too—something Tristan still struggled to believe.

Despite her side's obvious defeat, Sidra continued to fight Doriyan. The two were trading arrows and insults in the air over the river, and Doriyan had even waved off the reinforcements—determined, it seemed, to take her down on his own.

Maximian landed before Tristan, who had dismounted to allow Rex a chance to rest. After an awkward beat, Tristan stepped forward to press his hand to the great bird's shining beak. He was brought back to the last time he'd done so, his hand smeared with his father's blood, and was struck by how much had changed. Maximian's presence here felt like approval, like *recognition* from his father, and Tristan had a hard time putting into words what that meant.

"Thank you," he said—to Max or his father, he wasn't sure. Maximian didn't speak or even open his mind to Tristan, but he nodded in recognition of the words.

The ranks of soldiers were thinning out on the southern shore, and Tristan thought it might be time to rejoin the main battle to the north and leave the military to handle the crossing alone. He was about to call Rex over to get into the air when his bondmate let out an anguished shriek.

Danger!

Tristan's head whipped around; the general stood on the muddy shore not twenty paces away. He was soaked and covered in mud, but in his hand was a dry and perfectly functional crossbow, loaded and pointed at Tristan.

Oh, Tristan thought dumbly. His hands were empty, and even if they weren't, it was too late.

The general's finger clamped down, the bowstring twanged, and the air was sliced through with violent, deadly precision as the bolt rushed toward him.

But then there was a massive, feathered body between Tristan and the arrow—between him and death—and the air shuddered with the impact as Maximian took the shot meant for him.

The phoenix shrieked his pain, then stumbled, revealing the arrow protruding directly from his chest. Tristan lurched forward—to do what, he wasn't sure—but then the bolt began to catch fire and burn, and the flames didn't stop there. They tore across Maximian's chest and neck, spreading fast, pulsing, but Max wasn't about to explode in anger and rage. . . . He was about to burn up.

"No," Tristan whispered, eyes stinging. "No!"

The general was reloading his crossbow, but Tristan spared the man a single, vitriolic look before the recently arrived Phoenix Riders took charge. They had whirled in midair at the sound of Max's screech, and now that they saw their foe—the very man that had ruined their lives—they exploded into action.

General Rast fumbled to reload the weapon, seeing the others barreling down upon him, then dropped it and threw out his hands. "I saved you—I saved you all! You would be dead if it weren't for me."

Tristan watched as the phoenixes landed and their Riders leapt from their saddles, weapons drawn. They forced Rast to his knees, while their phoenixes crowded close, feathers bristling and crackling with flames.

Rast looked around wildly, tense and waiting for a blow that didn't come. "Just kill me already!" he barked.

"They don't take orders from you anymore," said Theo, stepping to the front of the group, her expression glacial.

With a wave of her hand, the others moved forward to bind their prisoner's hands and feet. General Rast would not have the easy way out. He would stand trial and be made to face—and pay for—his crimes.

Tristan, sick with anger and despair, turned back to Maximian, who was croaking feebly. After staggering and flapping his wings several times but unable to take to the air, he settled on his haunches. He stilled, patient and dignified as he'd always been, even as flames licked up his sides.

Rex arrived then, fluttering anxiously next to Tristan—trying to help, to support, but Tristan had eyes only for his father's dying bondmate.

"No, Max—no. It'll be okay. . . . It's going to be okay. . . ." But Maximian fixed him with his somber gaze, and they both knew Tristan lied.

The phoenix lifted his head to the sky as the last of the flames engulfed him. Tristan staggered back, but despite the terrifying wildness of it, he didn't shy away. He stayed there, kept his vigil, no matter how his eyes watered and his throat stung.

Maximian's shape was visible as a dark silhouette within the flames, blurry and indistinct, before it slowly disappeared, and there was nothing but fire.

Tristan knew that somewhere in Arboria, his father's heart was breaking—as it hadn't done since Tristan's mother was executed. *You're not alone*, Tristan thought, but he feared it would not be enough—that he had never been enough. *You're not alone.*

When he came back to himself, he was on his knees before a smoldering pile of ashes. It was like Maximian was never there at all, but he had been—or else Tristan wouldn't be.

"I'll stay with him," came a voice by his side, and Tristan looked into the eyes of Sarra, one of the older Riders from Haven. "I knew some of the Mercies, before. I know what to do."

In case he resurrects, Tristan reminded himself, getting painfully to his feet. His hands were streaked with soot, his knees burned through from how close he'd been to the flames. His face felt cold suddenly, in contrast to the heat of Max's dying inferno.

Then he became aware of Rex nudging him through the bond.

Tristan looked up, following Rex's urgent prodding, and mirrored in time to see Veronyka and Val come together in a violent clash of fire and shadow before plummeting to the ground.

Tristan felt the impact—not in his body, but somehow in his magic. He felt scraped out and raw, empty in a way that didn't make sense.

Sidra and Doriyan, who had been tussling nearby, also turned to stare at the commotion, but Doriyan was first to recover.

He lunged from his phoenix while Sidra was still distracted and knocked her out of her saddle, tackling her to the ground. They weren't very high up, but it was a far enough fall to knock the wind out of her upon impact. Daxos leapt onto Sidra's phoenix, not hurting but holding her, trying to keep her from rushing to her bondmate's side.

Doriyan, meanwhile, was restraining Sidra—who was gasping for air and cursing his name—and begging her to listen to him.

"Give it up!" he was shouting, rearing back as Sidra got an arm loose and threw a vicious elbow. He dodged it neatly before catching her wrist and pinning it to the ground. "The fight is over. You're one of us. *Be* one of us."

Sidra spat in his face, but he didn't relent.

"She doesn't care about you, Sidra! She's *using* you. It's just as before: She loves only the Ashfires. She loves their dusty names and their ancient legacy more than any living thing."

Sidra struggled once more—half-heartedly, it seemed to Tristan—before finally relenting. She slumped against the ground, her heaving chest the only movement.

Doriyan remained still, poised above her, before relaxing slightly.

Then Sidra's other arm broke free, and this time she held a knife. There was a flash of steel, then a spurt of blood as she slashed across Doriyan's exposed throat.

Tristan's muscles locked up in shock, but he was too far away to do anything but stare. The instant that metal met flesh, Daxos released Sidra's phoenix, and she scooped up her Rider before racing toward the battlefield without a backward glance.

Tristan lurched forward on shaky legs. Daxos crooned, low and warbling, and Rex bumped him out of the way, giving Tristan room to work.

There was so much blood, but Doriyan was wide-eyed and alert, scrabbling at his throat. Tristan tore a strip of cotton from his shirt to stanch the flow, and then someone was there. A soldier with a white sash across his chest—a healer.

Tristan had never been so happy to see an empire soldier. He allowed himself to be pushed aside, hands drenched in blood, while the healer reached into his medic bag and shouted for his assistants. They got Doriyan onto a stretcher and carried him to a distant tent marked with a white banner.

"Go with him," Tristan said to Daxos, hastily wiping at his trembling hands with the scrap of his shirt he still held. Rex stepped away, giving the phoenix room to shake out his wings. "Keep up his strength. Help him fight." *Help him live.*

Tristan had seen too much of death this night, and Veronyka and her sister had just fallen out of the sky.

Fast, Rex, Tristan thought desperately, leaping into his saddle. *Faster than you've ever flown before.*

I thought I'd be ready to say goodbye, to join the ranks
of warrior queens and festoon the evening sky.

- CHAPTER 67 -
VERONYKA

GIVE HER EVERYTHING.

The request echoed in Veronyka's mind, even as the world around her seemed to disappear.

The sense of spinning vertigo, the scent of fire, the wind and stars . . . all of it gone.

Next thing she knew, she was sprawled on the ground. She lurched to her feet, her surroundings muffled—distant, as if her ears needed to pop. As if she were underwater . . . cut off from everything and everyone.

No. The word lodged itself in her throat, unspoken.

Veronyka blinked, reached outside herself, beyond the darkness.

No.

She fell to her knees.

Ignix's words resurfaced in her mind. *I fear it will come at a terrible price.*

And Veronyka had paid—not with her life, but with something else.

There are worse things than death.

She had lost her magic. She had given everything. *Everything.* And she had lost.

Xephyra was gone.

Tristan was gone.

Val was gone.

The horde was gone, and Veronyka blinked dazedly, drunkenly at the phoenixes soaring overhead, at the soldiers crowding around.

But then there was a face swimming in front of her vision—a familiar, once-dear face. Now it was the face of her enemy. Veronyka got unsteadily to her feet once more, trying to muster fear—the will to fight, to live—but instead she just stared. The face was speaking, shouting as she staggered toward her.

Val.

She gestured behind her, where Onyx had turned into nothing more than a pile of ashes and scattered feathers, blowing away on the wind. They must have missed, Veronyka thought distractedly. They must have missed Onyx's heart. It was a miracle Val was mostly unhurt, though she moved with a limp and her body was smeared with blood and ash.

She was still yelling, and had taken hold of Veronyka's shoulders, shaking her roughly. Then, abruptly, she stopped. Her gaze bored into Veronyka, and Veronyka knew she came up with nothing. White noise.

"What have you done?" Val whispered, jerking away.

Veronyka's face crumpled.

Despair welled up so quickly and fiercely that she thought she might choke on it.

Death seemed sweeter, easier, than this living nightmare.

She thought she finally understood a fraction of the horror Val had woken up to seventeen years ago. She had still been a mage, of course, but she had lost her bondmate. Lost her sister. Lost her very life.

Veronyka pitied Avalkyra Ashfire.

But in this moment, she pitied herself more.

Next to them, Xephyra crooned low, shaking her head—lost, confused, alone.

Veronyka's heart ached—but it was just *her* heart. Xephyra wasn't there any longer . . . at least not in the way she had been. She was a separate entity now, almost a stranger as their eyes met and there was no spark of magic, no sensation like looking in a mirror at another part of her soul.

There was a commotion nearby heralding the arrival of a Phoenix Rider.

Tristan. Veronyka thought she might break at the sight of him, a sight that was somehow flat and two-dimensional. How foolish she had been, trying to block their bond, spitting in the face of such a precious gift.

He dismounted, ready to rush forward—but he stumbled to a halt, confused, as Rex let out an anguished cry. Tristan's face was screwed up as his eyes flickered from Rex to Xephyra and back to Veronyka. He held her gaze for several halting breaths, and then his mouth trembled. He understood, even if he didn't. He felt it, somehow, some way. He reached for Rex, gripping his feathers with painful force, but his bondmate didn't seem hurt by it. He only leaned into the touch.

Veronyka lifted her face to the sky, to the stars, to the phoenixes glowing like fiery lanterns strung across the heavens. The fighting had stopped, the last strixes had been shot down, and the soldiers were allies.

It was worth it, wasn't it? She'd said she would pay the price, and now she had.

There was peace, finally, peace for the others—even if there would be no peace for herself.

And that would be enough, she told herself. It would have to be enough.

But when she lowered her face, her cheeks were wet with tears, her vision crystalline and shimmering.

Out of nowhere, two hands landed on Veronyka's chest and shoved. She stumbled, blinking in surprise as she refocused on Val standing before her. All around, bodies tensed, but Veronyka's did not. She just stared at Val, flat-eyed and hollow.

"Don't you dare," Val ground out, shoving Veronyka again and again, forcing her to stagger backward. She looked angry, desolate—and were those tears on her face too?

Veronyka tried to drudge up some kind of resistance, but she couldn't. "I'm tired, Val."

"*You're* tired?" Val demanded, her voice shrill. She glared at Veronyka for several weighted moments, then reached into her belt. She withdrew a knife. The people watching raised their weapons, but before they could react, Val had thrown the blade down at Veronyka's feet.

From any other person, Veronyka might have thought it was surrender.

"This isn't over," Val said, before drawing another knife from her boot and crouching into a loose combat stance.

Veronyka didn't reach for the weapon.

"Don't just stand there," Val snarled. "Fight back! Fight me!"

"I won't," Veronyka said, and Val's grip on her knife turned her knuckles bone-white.

Veronyka had often thought that Val might hate her, but it was clear now that she hated this weakened, defeated Veronyka most of all.

"This isn't over. This isn't the end. Don't be like her! *Be better!*" Val actually sobbed, her voice closing up around the words. "You were always better."

Veronyka's heart clenched. "This *is* me being better, Val. I won't fight you. I won't kill you."

Val hesitated, a twitch of her face. "What if I don't give you a choice?"

Veronyka held her arms wide in invitation—and Val lunged. She tackled Veronyka, knocking her clean off her feet.

Her back hit the ground hard, Val on top of her.

"Don't," Veronyka gasped, the wind knocked from her lungs. Val was poised above, blade flashing, but she did not bring it down. *"Don't,"* Veronyka repeated, daring to take her eyes off Val to scan the soldiers and Riders who had encircled them, ready to intervene.

Tristan was there, and Alexiya and Theryn. Her father's eyes were dark and his grip sure as he leveled a crossbow at Val, the woman who had stolen his love, his daughter, his whole *world* from him. Veronyka shook her head, pleading, and with a look that seared her skin, he resisted.

Val shoved Veronyka to regain her attention, baring her teeth, her chest heaving. There was no sound but their panting silence. "We're not finished here," she gritted out. "This isn't over."

"It is for me," Veronyka said. "I won't fight you anymore. I *can't*." Her voice cracked on the word, and fresh tears streaked down the side of her face, into the dirt. "You're my sister, and I love you."

Val's grip on the knife shook. "Stop it," she hissed, closing her eyes. "Just stop it."

There was a rustle of movement and a gust of wind. The nearby soldiers and Riders shifted their attention—and their weapons—at the newcomer.

It was Sidra, leaping from her saddle with her bow already drawn, an arrow nocked and pointing at Veronyka.

"Just say the word, my queen, and I will do it."

Val cursed, getting to her feet and whirling around. "You think I need *you* to do my dirty work, Sidra of Stel? You *are* my dirty work," she snarled, unleashing all her anger and frustration. "I need nothing from you."

Sidra's weapon remained pointed at Veronyka, who got slowly, carefully to her feet, while Sidra's eyes were fixed on Val. "All I've ever done is serve you willingly."

Val laughed cruelly, viciously. "You served me because I bade you to, and you were too weak-willed to refuse me."

Sidra's stony expression faltered. She looked utterly lost. "I only want to stand by your side. To fill the place that she doesn't deserve to occupy," she said angrily. Desperately. The tension between them quivered, ready to break, but no one dared move to cause the snap. "Why do you choose her, when she disrespects you at every turn? Why *her*?"

"*We* are Ashfires. *You* are nothing."

Sidra's face hardened, and her gaze shifted onto Veronyka. Pure hatred burned there.

Val must have lost her hold on Sidra at some point during the battle, for her face flashed a single look of total disbelief when she realized what the woman was about to do.

Sidra released her bowstring, and the arrow flew, her aim true . . . and it would have landed home, right in Veronyka's heart—

If Val had not flung herself in between.

The arrow thumped into Val's chest, sending her body jolting backward into Veronyka, who tried to catch her as she fell.

Her sister.

Her aunt.

Her enemy.

Veronyka lowered her to the ground, dropping to her knees to survey the damage. Her strix-feather crown was askew, her clothing torn, and the shaft of the arrow—fletched in phoenix feathers—protruded from her chest.

Sidra gasped aloud, the only sound in the echoing silence, and didn't resist as soldiers apprehended her and took her weapon. She only stared unblinking at Val, her face a white mask of shock as she was dragged away.

Veronyka noted all this absently in her peripheral vision, her attention wholly on Val. She took Val's bloody hand in hers and squeezed.

Val's eyes were hazy as they settled on Veronyka.

"Val," Veronyka whispered, pressing Val's hand against her face, her fingers icy. Was that because of the arrow wound, or had she always been this cold?

Val closed her eyes slowly, agonizingly, and Veronyka stared hard, willing them to open again. They did, and a single tear slid a track down her face.

"Stay with me," Veronyka found herself saying—knowing it was no use, knowing that if she did, everything would be the same. That there was no other end for them than this.

It was why Val had wanted to keep fighting. . . . Even she had known what the end would bring. Them, apart from each other forever.

"Please," Val said, her voice softer, gentler than it had ever been before. "Let me go, Onia. . . ." Veronyka's heart bled, cut open by the realization that maybe she had only ever been a stand-in, an echo, a shadow of the sister Val had lost a lifetime ago. That it had never been about the two of them at all. But then she realized where Val was looking . . . not at *her*, but up at the stars. "Let me go."

"It's okay," Veronyka said, and Val's gaze shifted, latching on to her with sudden, fierce clarity.

"*Xe* Nyka . . . ," she murmured, sighing in something that sounded like relief. "Do you think she will forgive me?"

Veronyka nodded, her throat too tight to speak.

"And *you*?"

She nodded again, over and over, her vision swimming. Val watched her for this reaction, needing it.

Then she smiled and closed her eyes. A look of peace spread over her face, a look that Veronyka had never seen on her sister in life. The expression tore the last shreds of Veronyka's composure, and she sobbed as Val's hand went limp, dropping from her cheek, and the world was darker for it. Veronyka's world was darker. There were people all around her, people she loved, and yet . . . And yet.

She had never felt so alone.

I will die in a bed of ash and flame.

- CHAPTER 68 -
VERONYKA

COME, CHILD—THERE ISN'T much time.

Veronyka looked up to find Ignix's great head before her, eyes so dark she saw her face reflected in them.

"Time for what?" Veronyka asked, dazed. She realized Ignix was speaking to her now with shadow magic . . . because Veronyka no longer had magic of her own.

Her heart wrenched in pain, and her hand clenched—her fingers still clutching Val's limp, dead ones. Ignix's wings were curled around them, closing them in on all sides, providing momentary sanctuary from the world beyond.

Bravery.

Veronyka straightened, understanding dawning. "But . . . I'm afraid."

There is no bravery without fear.

They were strong words. *Nefyra's* words, spoken right before she'd walked into Axura's flames.

Though Veronyka no longer had her magic, she saw the truth when she stared into those ancient eyes. What Ignix was offering.

Heartfire is a powerful weapon. It can destroy, create, and unmake. It is Axura's own flame.

If Veronyka could unmake and remake the strixes, if she could pour magic into *them*, could Ignix pour magic into *her*?

"You're apex again," she said, and Ignix nodded. Without her magic, Veronyka could not wield the apex power, and their flock had bowed to her and Xephyra together. They did not recognize Xephyra's status without her. "But what about the price?"

I will pay it, Ignix said calmly. She took a deep, fortifying breath, her chest expanding between them. *It is time for a new beginning.*

Veronyka's throat tightened. "Will it hurt?" she asked.

Ignix tilted her head before leaning back and craning her neck toward the sky. *Whenever I asked Nefyra about her trial by fire, she said only this: It was worth it. Always, it was worth it.*

Veronyka looked down at Val again, bolstered by the words. She had lost Val. She had lost her bonds. Her magic. Nothing could hurt more than that.

"Will I be reborn? Like Val?"

Ignix shook her head. *You will get only what you have given—your magic. Hold on to your life, your reasons to remain, and I will handle the rest.*

Veronyka's mind worked slowly through all Ignix had said. Her reasons to remain flitted through her mind. She looked down at Val's body, then around, between the gaps in Ignix's feathers. She had Xephyra, her precious bondmate. She had Tristan and Rex, Alexiya and Theryn and Agneta, Sparrow and Elliot and Sev and Kade. She had the Phoenix Riders.

Veronyka was on her feet now, though she didn't remember standing. Ignix shook out her wings, breaking the temporary bubble that had enclosed them, and the world outside rushed in.

"Veronyka?" She turned to see Tristan there, expression grave.

She released Val's hand, reaching for his. It was warm and strong, and she pressed it to her cheek, over the dried blood print Val's hand had left there. She breathed deeply, memorizing his scent, and the feel of his skin against hers.

Then she let go.

There was heat behind her, building in steady waves against her back. It was comforting, like a warm embrace. She longed for it.

"Wait, what are you—" Tristan began, and behind him were Alexiya and Theryn, both looking wild-eyed and confused.

"Hold him, will you?" Veronyka asked Alexiya. She opened her mouth as if to argue, then closed it and nodded.

"Hold who?" demanded Theryn, moving closer, but Alexiya gripped his shoulder, halting him.

Ronyn and Latham were nearby, and when she looked at them, they rushed forward. Even without shadow magic, they sensed her summons and obeyed it. She smiled, then nodded at Tristan.

"Veronyka, what are you doing?" Tristan cried, reaching for her, but then Ronyn was there with a firm hold on one arm and Latham on the other.

Veronyka wanted to go to him, to give him comfort—but what she longed for most of all was the connection they'd shared that went beyond the physical realm. She ached with its absence, their bond a gaping wound inside her.

She didn't know what would happen now, but she knew she had to try.

"I love you," she said to him. His eyes were wide and brown and rimmed with tears.

She turned to Theryn and Alexiya. "I love you. Both of you."

A low, keening sound had begun to fill the silence, and Veronyka found Xephyra—so strange to have to *look* for her, to not sense where she was at every moment—pushing to the front of the group, Rex on her heels.

Veronyka reached for them both, ran her hands over their smooth beaks and satiny feathers.

"Sweet Flame," Veronyka murmured, taking Xephyra's head in hers. "Flame Sister." She kissed her on the beak. It was hard to find words, when their entire lives together, they hadn't needed any.

Xephyra crooned softly, nudging her chest.

Rex edged closer, and Veronyka kissed his beak as well. "If this goes wrong . . . take care of him, won't you?" she whispered. "Take care of each other."

Veronyka turned. Ignix was burning hotter and hotter, flames rippling across her body in carefully controlled waves. Someone was shouting, crying out and struggling—it was Sparrow, being held by Elliot—and Veronyka was glad there was someone to look out for her, too. Next to them were Sev and Kade, watching her with sad, solemn eyes.

But they were together—together and safe. All her people had someone to look after them.

Her gaze fell to the body on the ground. There had been no one to look after Val. That had been Veronyka's job, and she had failed. She had been unable to hold Val back from the flames of her own destruction, and the grief of it was like strix talons tearing her open and flaying her alive.

"Can she come with me?" she asked Ignix, whose chest was glowing now, pulsing a steady, thrumming beat. Heartfire.

It is a worthy pyre for a queen.

It was difficult, but Veronyka managed to lift her sister into her arms—she was thinner than Veronyka remembered, as if life were a tangible thing, a weight that could be stolen away—and stood.

Ignix spread her wings wide, fire roaring and snapping across her feathers, and it didn't scare Veronyka. It looked welcoming, like the arms of a loved one.

Xephyra shrieked, Tristan struggled and fought, calling her name, and Alexiya and Theryn held on to each other.

Veronyka's heart was full, despite it all. Her heart was full.

She stepped forward, into the flames, and Ignix wrapped her wings around them both in an explosion of light and life and love.

The world disappeared. There was nothing but fire.

Val became ashes in her hands—a star in the sky.

And she wasn't the only one.

સ૦ સ૦ સ૦

It did hurt, at first. The flames were hungry and they tore at her—not her flesh and bones, but her heart and soul. They wanted to consume the very essence of her, to pull her apart, and it was all Veronyka could do to keep herself together. If her will was less, her desire weaker, she might not have made it through.

But she did.

She fought them; she clung to her life and her reasons to remain, and she fought them.

Eventually the pain lessened, and the fires withdrew. Even Ignix faded away, becoming one with the distantly swirling flames. The blaze stretched and expanded, transforming into a cyclone, a tornado—a hurricane—and Veronyka was at its center. She was in the eye of the storm . . . but she was not alone.

Darkness descended, but only so that she could see the stars.

They were suspended around her, as beautiful and glittering as gemstones upon velvet. Achingly near, close enough to touch, but ethereal as smoke.

Veronyka understood that they were with her. *All of them* were with her.

Ilithya Shadowheart, her *maiora*.

Pheronia Ashfire, her mother.

And Avalkyra Ashfire—Val, her sister.

There were others, too. Morra and Beryk and Ashfires stretching back to the dawn of time.

They weren't just stars; they were constellations—tied to one another, to her, to the sun and moon and the sky above.

They smiled down on her, soft as starlight, fierce as the blazing sun.

She breathed deeply, feeling hope and love and *magic* ignite in her chest.

She would join them, one day.

But not today.

So it began, so too shall it end.

CHAPTER 69

TRISTAN

TRISTAN'S THROAT WAS RAW from screaming, his arms locked tight and aching from being held fast.

His brain couldn't seem to catch up with all that had happened. He'd just watched Maximian go up in flames and had thought that was truly awful—and it was, but Max had been a phoenix. Fire was his nature, his life and his death. There was no escaping it.

Veronyka was not a phoenix. And yet she'd walked willingly, gratefully, into that sweltering heat, the waves so hot that Tristan's skin felt scorched, and he was so beyond fear that his mind felt fractured, disassociated from his body.

The fire continued to blaze, high and strong, crackling and pulsing like some flaming heart. It was alive in a way that made Tristan want to rear back. He'd hated fire for most of his life, but he hated this fire most of all . . . because it had taken Veronyka.

Was life without magic truly worse than death?

Because that's what had happened, wasn't it? Veronyka had given the fight against Val and the strixes everything she had, including her magic. That was why Rex and Xephyra were inconsolable, why Tristan sensed something missing inside, some empty room in his mind that had once been full of . . . something. He'd called out for her, he'd begged and pleaded and received nothing in response. He'd never seen her look so hopeless—and that was when he knew.

She had given up everything.

She had given up him. She had given up Xephyra.

And however much that hurt him, it hurt Veronyka more.

Tristan stopped fighting.

Maybe this was a mercy. Maybe this was easier than living without the magic that had defined her life—for better or worse.

She had even lost Val . . . her life's most enduring and complicated relationship.

Maybe this was what she wanted.

Ronyn and Latham still held his arms, but their grip had slackened now that Tristan was no longer struggling against it. Ronyn's eyes were bright with unshed tears, and Latham's face was pale under the smears of ash and blood.

All around, people stood and watched the conflagration.

Watched Veronyka burn alive.

Tristan's throat hitched.

But there was something happening within the flames. They were shrinking—no, not shrinking, but changing, jumping, and warping around a shape that was becoming visible in the center.

Tristan's heart stopped. Was it—could it be?

Veronyka.

The fire blazed around her, on her—through her, her chest glowing with incandescent light. Flames licked across her arms, her clothing, and her hair—but nothing *burned*. When she lifted her gaze, her eyes shone molten, like embers in a hearth.

She was unearthly. Terrifying and magnificent.

All was silent as her image solidified, as the fire receded and she stepped, wholly unharmed, out of the flames.

Xephyra let out a triumphant shriek, and something inside Tristan blazed back into life. Rex took up Xephyra's call, and so did the other phoe-nixes, their song reverberating in Tristan's bones.

She was back. All of her.

She was back.

And in her arms where Val had been, there was a feather crown instead. Val's crown, surely, except the night-black feathers had gone sunlight shades of red and gold and brilliant purple. Veronyka stepped clear of the dying fire, nothing but a bed of burning coals behind her, yet the crown was alive with the same flames that had been crawling across her skin.

She looked down at it, then up at the gathered assembly. Then she lifted the crown and placed it on her head.

Again, the fire didn't touch her. It seemed as if it couldn't, as if they were one and the same.

Tristan lurched forward, the hands that had held him slack now against his skin.

Then he was on his knees, staring up at her. It seemed the right thing—the only thing—to do.

Her gaze settled on him, warm and loving and brown-eyed once again. But her chest . . . it still glowed, flickering slow and steady. Like a pulse.

Like a heart.

Veronyka Flameheart, he found himself thinking—stupid, dim-witted words, especially since he didn't know if she could even hear them—but she lit up like the rising sun, her smile brilliant and beautiful.

It has a nice ring to it, she said into his mind, and a wash of relief and happiness welled up inside him. He pressed a hand to his chest, recalling their vows of loyalty from what felt like ages ago, and Veronyka mirrored him, lowering onto one knee.

Tristan sensed more than saw the people around him following suit—one by one they dropped to their knees and pressed their hands to their chests, gazing at her.

At Veronyka Flameheart, the Fire-Crowned Queen.

I will die in a bed of ash and flame . . .
then I will be reborn again in just the same.

- CHAPTER 70 -
VERONYKA

WITH LIFE CAME DEATH—Val had taught her that. For every new phoenix, for every life saved, was one lost.

In Veronyka's case, there were two.

The pyre from which Veronyka had emerged had claimed two lives— Ignix, the world's first phoenix, and Avalkyra Ashfire, the Feather-Crowned Queen.

Veronyka stood vigil beside the ashes, wondering if the past ever really died, or if it lived on because *she* lived on. In her blood lived the legacy of all the Ashfire queens, and even the not-quite-queens like her mother and her sister-aunt.

When she'd stepped out of the flames and put on her crown, the people around her had taken to their knees and bowed their heads. Queen *and* apex once again. They had given her their loyalty, and she had given it back.

After they stood, friends and family had approached her with wary disbelief.

Tristan was there first, taking her hand in his and lifting it to his lips. His cheeks were damp, tear tracks streaking through the dirt, and he was almost reverent as he pressed her palm to his mouth, eyes closed, his breath shaky—like he feared she might disappear at any moment.

You scared me, he said through the bond.

I'm sorry, Veronyka said, but he shook his head, refusing the apology because there was no need, really. He knew her down to her bones, including the fact that she'd needed to do this. He was only grateful she'd returned.

Just don't do it again, he added, smiling against her skin.

Xephyra was next, and not nearly as gentle. She barreled through the crowd, all pointy wings and sharp beak, and butted Veronyka in the chest, hard—half admonishment, half panic. Like Tristan, it seemed she needed to touch Veronyka and *remain* touching, as proof that she was really here and not some figment of their imaginations. Rex remained close by Xephyra, though he ran his beak briefly through Veronyka's hair and nudged her once or twice before stepping aside.

Theryn approached next, openly sobbing. Then he drew her into the kind of hug that reached across time and space. He hugged her mother in that moment. She felt it, and for once she did not resent being the placeholder. Alexiya hovered nearby until Theryn yanked her arm and pulled her in as well.

As more people crowded forward—Riders and soldiers—Tristan released her hand. Not because he wanted to go, but because he was commander now and had things to do. Veronyka remembered that not everyone had been able to step out of their flames.

I'll take care of it, Tristan promised, just as he had with Morra. And he did.

It wasn't long until pyres dotted the countryside, just as phoenixes had dotted the battlefield—just as stars dotted the sky.

Clusters of people moved about, adding bodies to the blazes, or staring desolately as bone became ash, as life became death, as present became past.

Veronyka stayed by Val's pyre, clutching the phoenix-feather crown in her hands. Like the fire before her, it no longer burned. It was still and lifeless in her hands.

Her grip tightened as she clutched her last tether to Val, to the sister she had lost. Then she placed the crown onto the ashes and watched until it burned away.

Eventually she left, but she was not the only mourner paying tribute at those dead flames. Sparrow stood behind her, jaw set and face wet with tears. It was not her first pyre—not her first loss—but this time she had Elliot by her side and a familiar raven on her shoulder. She was okay.

They were all okay.

Or at least they would be, once Veronyka was through.

They gathered before the night was out, friends and family and Phoenix Riders, ready to see Veronyka off. She had business in the capital.

Tristan hesitated beside Rex, a question in his gaze. *Do you want me here to handle things?*

Veronyka shook her head. "I want you by my side," she said aloud. "Always."

He smiled, dimpled and brilliant, and Veronyka had no choice but to tug him down by the front of his tunic and cover his smile with a kiss.

His arms wrapped around her waist, lifting her clean off the ground, and sounds of surprise and laughter—even a few catcalls—broke the silence.

When at last they released each other, Tristan grinned down at her, cheeks flushed and eyes bright.

Veronyka didn't know if she would actually be queen—there was work left to do—but wherever she wound up, whatever she did, Tristan would always be her king.

Climbing into Xephyra's saddle again felt like coming home. Veronyka rested her head against her bondmate's neck, marveling at her bravery, her courage, her fiery heart.

I could not have done it without you, Veronyka told her. *And I would not want to.*

For once, it seemed, Xephyra was without words. She crooned softly in her throat, sending up a cloud of sparks, and Veronyka watched them soar into the sky.

☙ ☙ ☙

Dawn was breaking as the Phoenix Riders flew into Aura Nova, Veronyka at the head of the flock. They arranged themselves in a queensflight—an honor guard formation from the Reign of Queens, with banners flying and her best Riders ranged behind her. Fourteen total, including Tristan and his patrol members, Alexiya and Doriyan, Sev and Kade, and the rest of the flock trailing behind.

They made straight for the Nest.

As they flew over the battlefield, across the river with its hastily repaired bridge and the ranks and ranks of soldiers sprawled across the landscape, hundreds of necks craned toward the sky.

But no weapons lifted; no shouts rang out in fear or alarm.

They simply watched a piece of history come back to life, the world changed and made new. Some even waved or nodded their heads in greeting or respect.

Veronyka glanced at Tristan, surprised and humbled, and he laughed in delight.

Word had reached the Grand Council already of the battle and Veronyka's trial by fire, and as they landed in the courtyard out front—not a side door as they had before—the members were there to greet them. They bowed respectfully and moved aside, and there was Commander Cassian, or maybe he was just Cassian now, looking tired and weak and leaning heavily on a cane. Veronyka felt a pang for having ruined his finely carved phoenix-headed one.

Tristan rushed forward and embraced him. He had told Veronyka about Maximian's sacrifice, and Veronyka felt a rush of pity and compassion for the man. Xephyra sidled up to her, and Veronyka stroked her feathers.

As Tristan stepped aside, Cassian spotted Veronyka. He bowed—or tried to, given his physical state—but Veronyka stopped him with a hand on his arm. She met his cool brown eyes, soft and sad in a way she completely understood, and hugged him too. He seemed startled by this, but the rest of the Grand Council took note. The man was exiled no longer.

To Veronyka's surprise, Cassian had managed to get his hands on Lord Rolan's documents proving her birth. He said they had a rogue empire soldier to thank, and Veronyka whirled around to see Sev standing at the edge of the group. He shrugged nonchalantly, a baby phoenix in his breast pocket, and next to him, Kade winked.

Their footsteps echoed as they entered the vast room, which was filled to the brim with people—the Grand Council members, plus assistants and secretaries and people off the street, Veronyka suspected, until the guards started shoving civilians out the doors and slamming them shut.

Despite the commotion, Veronyka's gaze never left the high-backed chair that sat where the judge's podium had been during her last visit.

It was golden, intricate, and finely wrought, weaved in patterns of feathers and fire. The backrest was a spread-winged phoenix, and its eyes were inlaid with jewels.

She did not take it.

Instead, she stood atop the dais and waited.

The room—more than a hundred people—watched her, the silence broken by rustling fabric and scraping feet. There was evidence here and there of Sidra's attack—scorched walls and missing furniture, and a new judge stood next to her to start the proceedings. Veronyka cast a glance at Tristan, seated in the front of the crowd, and he beamed at her with pride and admiration.

There was a shifting above, and Veronyka stared up into the rafters, where all the Rider phoenixes perched, making the members of the council slightly uneasy. Xephyra was next to Rex, and their feelings matched Tristan's.

Veronyka was given the floor at last, and she addressed the waiting group.

"As I'm sure you've all heard, my name is Veronyka Ashfire—daughter of Pheronia Ashfire. I am here today after a hard-fought battle against a horde of creatures from legend, led by a rebel queen straight out of history." She paused, her throat tight. "Both were defeated, but we could not have done it alone. We did it together, and I would see the Phoenix

Riders and the Golden Empire on the same side forevermore."

Applause greeted her words. Some enthusiastic, some measured—but it died down quickly. Everyone, it seemed, was waiting for what would come next.

"As you know, thanks to the diligent research of Lord Rolan of Stel, I am not yet of age. Therefore, I am not yet able to be crowned queen. I will be eighteen on the anniversary of the Blood War next year."

Some council members glanced at one another—relieved, she thought, and already planning their next moves.

"Until then," Veronyka continued, "I wish to be formally recognized as heir to the throne and given all the responsibilities and privileges that come with it—including, unless I am mistaken, a seat on the council?"

The conversations that had been happening quickly died out, while other members sat straighter in their chairs, listening intently. The judge nodded in answer to her question, but Veronyka was well versed on her rights, thanks to Cassian and the hours they had spent poring over books inside his library at the Eyrie.

"I believe it is also within my rights to add and remove council members—with just cause, of course." She glanced at the judge, and once again, she nodded. The whispers and murmurs picked up, a note of anxiety in them that had not been there before. "And to call meetings and put forward motions; to suggest new laws and changes to existing ones?"

The judge didn't bother nodding this time, because it was clear Veronyka knew what she was about.

The council members were in a right state now. Some huffing and puffing and muttering loudly enough for her to hear, while others smiled and leaned back, enjoying the show. More than a few whispered into Cassian's ear, begging for insight, but he only shrugged mildly, giving her a grin.

"Wonderful," Veronyka said, finally taking the golden seat. "Let's begin."

It was a busy few weeks.

First she had to be officially recognized as an Ashfire heir, and the records had her listed with her two new epithets, Flameheart and the Fire-Crowned Queen.

Next, she reinstated Cassian as the governor of Ferro, and appointed him acting general. He knew how to deal with funds for the wounded, repairs to the bridge and the road—and other important cleanup and restoration efforts.

On Cassian's advice, Veronyka dismissed Lord Rolan's remaining supporters, finding among the papers that held her proof of identity all the evidence she would need to implicate them in his shady dealings and backdoor bargains. The fact that they were the same people who had sentenced Olanna to die made their dismissal—as well as the forthcoming criminal charges—all the more satisfying. There was also General Rast's trial, which was extremely well-attended. It appeared he had made more enemies than Veronyka realized, even beyond the families he'd blackmailed into supporting him for nearly two decades. The verdict was swift—life imprisonment—and the start of a long process of undoing the damage he'd done to his captive animages and their families.

After that she put forward the appropriate motions to abolish the magetax and the registry and see that every bondservant across the empire was freed. Those serving for violent crimes or because of involvement in the Blood War would undergo new trials. The rest would be given paid work and restitution for their years in bondage.

The council's Minister of Coin nearly had an apoplexy at that, but Veronyka was ready for his objections—and provided an estimation of the ex-General Rast's net worth, which had been accumulated through bribery and coercion and therefore stripped as a part of his guilty sentence. Rather than absorb the funds into the royal coffers—as she was within her rights to do—she offered them toward the animage effort instead and expressed her confidence that the council could find whatever additional money they might require.

Every law against phoenixes and Phoenix Riders was also struck down, making them full citizens of the empire once more. With the heir to the throne an animage Phoenix Rider, they didn't have much of a choice.

Given the attitudes of the Rushlean farmers and their Unnamed militia, Veronyka suggested that the citizens of Pyra should vote on whether or not they wished to rejoin the empire, under its new laws and with its new Pyraean Phoenix Rider heir.

It had been a close decision, but after announcing the motion and polling the inhabitants, the people of Pyra had decided to rejoin the empire. Veronyka knew there would be more work to do, first in rebuilding Pyra into the thriving province it had once been, but also in keeping an eye on any remaining members of the Unnamed who might try to revolt once again.

After many of the council's more toxic members had already been removed and their replacements—heavily vetted by Cassian—were voted in, including a new governor of Pyra, Veronyka created several additional positions to represent animages and their interests, including seats for Phoenix Riders.

This way, they could govern themselves and not be beholden to their king or queen—now or in the future. This meant that one of the seats belonged to Tristan as their new commander. It was up to him to appoint the others.

The council had expected many of her ordinances and handled them with varying levels of grace. There would be more to come, she was sure, but for now Veronyka felt like she could breathe.

She didn't know what the next year would bring, if she would ever truly feel ready to take the crown and ascend the throne. But after struggling with it for what seemed like her entire life, Veronyka knew who she was—even without Val—and she *wanted* this opportunity. She wanted to be the one to fix things. She trusted herself to do what was right, and with positive changes happening every day, she felt like the empire was in good hands.

By embracing who she was, inside and out, she could make the world a better, safer place. She could protect the people she cared about—either in the sky on her phoenix, or in the capital on her throne.

It is the way of the phoenix.

- CHAPTER 71 -
SEV

SEV WOKE EARLY INSIDE the apprentice barracks, luxuriating in his softly swaying hammock, nothing but the gentle sounds of sleep all around him.

He'd been dreaming about flying and came back to wakefulness with a smile on his lips—and a phoenix perched on his chest.

Felix croaked and Sev lurched, sending his bed swinging.

Mutters and curses broke out across the room, most of them resigned. Felix cocked his head, shameless at having disturbed their sleep. Again.

Ersken was going to kill him.

Felix was *supposed* to sleep inside the Eyrie with the other apprentice mounts, but he simply refused to follow the rules. No matter where Sev was or what he was doing—sitting late in the dining hall, laughing with Kade, Veronyka, and Tristan; doing his chores, like repairing armor and cleaning saddles; or even studying in the library and practicing his Pyraean language lessons—Felix found a way to him. The precocious phoenix even made an appearance when Sev was in the bathhouse once, resulting in several angry bathers, water everywhere, and Sev having to carry a sopping-wet—but extremely pleased with himself—Felix back down to Ersken while wearing nothing but a towel.

It had gotten so bad that Ersken had taken to *locking* Felix inside his office at night, but somehow, the enterprising phoenix had gotten free. Sev knew he should be mad, but every time he saw that smug face and those bright eyes, it was like the bond re-formed all over again.

Below him, Kade sighed. "He's better at locks than you are."

Sev poked his head over the edge of his bed, grinning. "Or he has better friends."

Sev dressed and left the barracks with Kade, Felix riding proudly on his shoulder. He spotted Sparrow leaving the next building over with a phoenix of her own in tow.

Felix chirruped a greeting, and Sparrow's phoenix, the resurrected Ignix, lifted her tiny head imperiously.

She, too, was supposed to remain inside the Eyrie each night, but thought herself above such rules. She always got out, and more often than not took Felix with her. While she rode on one of Sparrow's shoulders, a glossy black raven rode on the other.

Sparrow grinned, walking over to Sev and Kade and reaching out a hand for Felix. Together, the three of them made for the Eyrie.

"She's a bad influence on you, isn't she?" Sparrow lamented, stroking Felix's feathers.

Ignix croaked indignantly.

"It might be the other way around," Sev said fairly, and Felix cocked his head.

The training yard was bright with early-morning sun when Sev arrived, the sound of construction echoing over the stronghold as the final repairs to the phoenix statue atop the temple were completed. Sev spotted Ivan there among the workers, perched on his phoenix, shouting instructions as they hoisted the newly painted and polished statue back on its plinth.

That night they would light the beacon again and gather for food and drink and celebration.

Though he still wasn't very good at it, Sev practiced hard with blade and bow, Veronyka's father, Theryn—the new weapons master—a patient teacher. He had Alexiya help with spear lessons, and while they fought as much as they taught, disagreeing on pretty much everything from style and technique to weapon upkeep and maintenance, Sev rather enjoyed the show.

Kade was in more advanced combat lessons, but Sev didn't mind. He trained with Sparrow and Theo and Emma, and the many other new apprentices that had joined their flock—thanks to Veronyka's trick with the heartfire and the extra eggs Avalkyra had brought to the Eyrie—becoming fully entrenched in a life he'd never dared imagine for himself.

And now that the war was over, Sev considered what his future might be.

Maybe he'd be a courier like Rosalind or a builder like Ivan. There were other positions, too, that Veronyka and Tristan were working hard to prepare for, including mapmakers, tourist guides, and even explorers—Sparrow's whole face had shone with excitement and wonder when he'd told her about that one. There was even a position called recruiter, and Sev very much liked the idea of finding lost and lonely animages like himself and bringing them home.

At the end of the day, Kade was always waiting for him so they could walk to dinner together. The only time Sev could truly get Felix out of his hair was when Jinx offered the hatchling a ride on her back. The two disappeared into the Eyrie, streaking across the evening sky, their gold and violet feathers aflame in the setting sun.

Sev looked around, happy and safe and among friends. He belonged here, with the Phoenix Riders. This was his home. "I want this forever," he said quietly—it was still hard to wish sometimes, to dare to say his hopes out loud.

Kade smiled gently, amber eyes soft as he squeezed Sev's hand. "I think you've got it."

The weight of the world is easier to bear,
I think, with others by your side.

- CHAPTER 72 -
ELLIOT

ELLIOT STOOD ALONE AT the bottom of the Eyrie.

The sun was setting in the sky above, and twilight already blanketed the lower levels.

He was staring at the tunnel where Sparrow and Ignix had been buried—collapsed no more, the last of the debris cleared away. There was still some damage to be repaired, but the passage was reopen at last.

It had been a massive job, getting the Eyrie up and running again. With Beryk gone—Elliot swallowed thickly—the newly instated Commander Tristan had named Elliot as his successor. Both of them were out of their depth, but he and Tristan were fumbling through as best they could.

While Tristan reestablished patrols, assigned leaders, and welcomed new apprentices, Elliot organized the construction crews, hired additional stronghold guards, and inventoried what remained of their supplies. He found housing and servants, purchased food stores and weapons, and restocked the Eyrie for the winter ahead.

He missed Beryk acutely, his every daily task a reminder of the kind and patient mentor he had been, but he tried to honor the man's memory by putting all he'd learned from him into practice. To Elliot's immense surprise, his father even helped. He knew a thing or two about staffing and had connections in the empire for some of their harder-to-replenish items. Now that trade was open between Pyra and the other provinces, Elliot could expand his suppliers and keep the Eyrie well equipped.

William had already returned to his position in the empire, but he'd stayed with them for two weeks, spending as much time with his children as possible. Elliot still harbored some resentment toward him for what had happened to their family, but they were all here, alive and happy, and he found it harder and harder to hang on to the grudge. His father had made plans to visit for the winter solstice festival, and Elliot was actually looking forward to it.

"Come on, Elliot, we're gonna be late!"

He turned at the sound of the familiar voice. Sparrow was coming toward him, a huge smile on her face and a bird on each shoulder, like some kind of spear-wielding, phoenix-riding riverboat pirate.

Fife squawked his usual indifferent greeting, and Ignix gave him a close once-over. She might be newly reborn, but she'd lost none of her solemnity or self-importance since coming out of the flames.

Elliot recalled their hours-long vigil at the old phoenix's pyre.

There were dozens of people around them at first: mourning loved ones, paying respects, and some just soaking up a bit of living history. But eventually they dwindled until it was just the four of them: Sparrow, Elliot, Jax, and Fife.

His joints had ached and his eyes had itched with tiredness before he finally spoke. "Maybe we should—"

"A few more minutes."

"I think it's time we—"

"A few more minutes."

Elliot would have stayed with Sparrow however long she wanted—he'd promised, hadn't he?—but it was concern for her that made him want to leave in the first place. He didn't know how to tell her that not all phoenixes came back.

He didn't want to break her heart all over again.

But then out of nowhere she'd dropped to her knees, plunging her hands into the ashes and lifting up the tiny newborn firebird.

Holding the phoenix close to her face, she'd stared with eyes that couldn't see—but she *did* see. She saw and felt and wept with unreserved joy.

Elliot had knelt down beside her, watching with awe as she placed the hatchling on the ground and it pecked its way through the ashes. Then out of nowhere she'd turned and flung her arms around him.

It had been a very good end to a very bad day.

"Where's Riella?" Sparrow asked him now.

To his immense surprise, he didn't know.

He'd managed to let go in recent weeks, so busy with his work that he barely had time for meals, let alone following around his sister. He figured that was probably a good thing. He knew she was safe, that she had a life and friends here, and that was all that mattered.

"She's already gone up," said Ersken, moving toward the stairwell. "No doubt she's lookin' for the two of you. Best hurry. I doubt they'll delay much longer—even for a Lightbringer." His eyes twinkled.

After the battle, Veronyka had told Sparrow that she was, apparently, descended from Callysta Lightbringer. That was what Ignix had said, anyway, and so the two had done some investigating. They found an old Lightbringer family tree, noting a branch that deviated from the main family after Cordelia Lightbringer ran off with a stable boy. Veronyka had put in some requests for census records, and they hoped to use them to track down Sparrow's surviving relatives.

"That's *Lady* Lightbringer to you," Sparrow said, grinning, and Fife squawked.

"I'll call you Lady Lightbringer the day you call me Lord Ersken," he called back, and Sparrow laughed.

Jax fluttered over, still saddled from the day, and Elliot took Sparrow's hand.

She flushed, squeezing tightly, and Fife cocked his head, giving Elliot a threatening sort of look. He still bore scars on his ears from Fife's previous reprimands, and he reassured the bird that he would never hurt Sparrow again.

Never again.

Jax took them in wide, soaring arcs up to the stronghold, and Sparrow clung to Elliot's middle, her head resting against his back.

Riella was, indeed, waiting for them—surrounded by a cavalcade of animals, including some familiar characters, like Ruff the sheepdog and Carrot the cat. The courtyard was crowded with people standing along the stronghold walls or huddled together on barrels and crates or seated on the cold cobblestones.

Much to Jax's delight, Riella and the animals clambered on top of him, treating the phoenix like a ferry on a river crossing as they crawled across his saddle or dug their claws into his reins. Once everyone was settled, he carefully leapt into the air and found them the perfect spot on the roof of the administrative building, the very same roof where Elliot and Sparrow had spied on the commander's private meeting months previously.

Riella had come prepared, unfurling a thick blanket across the tiles for them to sit on. It was massive, and Elliot was about to point out its needlessly large size when another phoenix soared over the lip of the roof—Jinx, carrying Kade and Sev and Sev's new bondmate, Felix.

Everyone found a seat on the blanket, Riella cuddling with the animals while Sev leaned against Kade, who draped his arm across his back.

Riella glanced over at Elliot, nodding at them pointedly.

Yes, Elliot understood—clearly, his talk with Kade had been wholly unnecessary.

Next to him, Fife and Ignix jostled for position on Sparrow's narrow shoulders.

Fife was bigger than Ignix—for now—but the tables would turn before long. Still, he spread his wings wide, causing Ignix to squawk and lose her balance. Fife puffed out his chest smugly. "Don't get used to it," Sparrow warned, before reaching for her bondmate. "Come 'ere then, Iggy."

Ignix gave Sparrow a flat stare, and Elliot laughed. Ignix hated that nickname almost as much as Elliot hated being called Elly, and refused to respond to it, but Sparrow insisted she'd come around.

Before they could get resettled, Riella withdrew a bag of candied ginger and pitted dates. Every creature on the roof scuttled toward her, and even Sev held out his hand.

Sparrow was abruptly alone, and she shifted self-consciously. Her hands kept opening and closing—her spear was still tucked in Jax's saddle—and wind whipped across the rooftop, stirring her dirty-blond hair. Elliot took off his coat and draped it over her shoulders. She brightened at the touch, but when he moved back again, she seemed to deflate.

Jax, who had a beakful of ginger, rolled his eyes at Elliot so thoroughly his head lolled on his neck.

Mind your business, Elliot muttered, waving him off. He took a deep breath and slid closer to her. Another breath, another slide.

She sat up straighter, sensing him there, and then he screwed up his courage and lowered his arm around her shoulders, taking his cue from Kade. Sparrow leaned into him, a rare, soft smile on her face.

The crowd below quieted as Veronyka and Tristan mounted the ladder to the top of the temple. Their phoenixes were perched on the railings, and on Tristan's insistence, Veronyka held a torch to the statue and set the beacon ablaze.

The flames crackled and hissed, lighting the sky, and everyone cheered.

Starting with Rex and Xephyra, the other phoenixes in attendance—perched on rooftops or scattered across the courtyard—also burst into flame. Small and large, clustered together or perched in solitary brightness, they warmed the cold night and surrounded the Eyrie in a circle of light.

Elliot rested his cheek atop Sparrow's head and stared once more into the flames.

I will let go of the past and start this journey anew.

- CHAPTER 73 -

VERONYKA

VERONYKA AND TRISTAN STAYED out long after everyone else.

First they moved among their friends—and in Veronyka's case, family—sharing a drink and a laugh as they celebrated coming together and reclaiming the Eyrie.

It was truly a joy to have Agneta there, taking Morra's place in the kitchens, and her father to help with combat training. He'd initially been worried about abandoning Haven, but then Jonny had offered to take control of things and to help transform the small community into their first Arborian outpost. That, plus Agneta's *vehement* insistence that he come with her was all it took to convince him. There were others from Haven as well, including Gus, who helped Old Ana in the vegetable gardens when he wasn't following Agneta around like a puppy dog. Veronyka knew her grandmother enjoyed the attention and had even allowed Gus to *escort* her to the festivities this evening. She wore a Fire Blossom in her hair, gifted to her by Gus, who glowed proudly with her on his arm.

While Alexiya continued to bicker with both her mother and her brother with typical frequency, her relationship with Doriyan had reached a surprising cease-fire. He'd survived his run-in with Sidra on the battlefield, and despite the fact that she'd slit his throat and attempted to kill him—leaving a nasty scar—Doriyan had begged Veronyka to bring Sidra here for imprisonment.

It was true that the empire was not yet equipped to handle such a thing—especially when a phoenix was involved—and so she had agreed to give Sidra and Oxana a joint cell inside the Eyrie. Doriyan visited them daily, usually with Alexiya in tow, and Veronyka got the distinct impression her aunt was there to protect him. A bizarre thought, but her instincts were better than most—she was a shadowmage, after all.

While Veronyka and Xephyra were still technically the apex pair, the magic that bound their flock together was looser than before. Like Veronyka's crown, it was a mantle there for the taking when she was ready or when she needed it.

Despite the increased power of that group bond, Veronyka had lost a bondmate, which meant she'd lost some magic, too, even if Val had been a constant threat while alive. That was their relationship in a nutshell, giving and taking and loving and hating, and Veronyka didn't know if she'd ever fully understand what they'd had.

When the beacon had burned low, the phoenixes and their human counterparts slowly drifting off to bed, Veronyka found Tristan across the cobblestones.

He'd been with his patrol, laughing and talking with the kind of ease she rarely saw in him. The position of commander suited him, and he finally seemed confident in himself and his role at the Eyrie. Lysandro was no longer here, preferring to work with Cassian in Ferro after his bondmate died in the battle. Hestia was also there with the former commander, nursing him back to health and making sure he didn't work himself to the bone, as was his nature.

Ronyn chatted with his sister, who was visiting from Petratec, and Latham and Anders remained attached at the hip—as they had been since the end of the war. Anders's arm was in a sling, his shoulder still bandaged, and Latham was currently helping him eat. Anders beamed at the indulgent care he was receiving and planted an impulsive kiss on Latham's cheek.

Latham's face burned red, but he didn't move away or tell Anders off. In fact, Veronyka thought he was smiling underneath the flush.

Spotting her, Tristan reached for her hand, and their fingers knitted neatly together.

Without a word, they strolled out the gates and through the village. Tristan trailed his fingertips over the buildings and through the bushes at the edge of Ana's garden, as if savoring the feeling of home.

They wound up in the open field in front of the village. The grass was cold and crisp underfoot, but Rex and Xephyra—who had followed in the air—landed before them and warmed the ground beneath their feet like a pair of cats patting down their bed.

Veronyka and Tristan flopped onto the grass together, still hand in hand, and as Veronyka stared up at the stars, Tristan leaned over her, a flower in hand.

"What's this?" she asked, recognizing the Fire Blossom. "Gus give you an idea?"

"The man's got moves," Tristan said with a grin, tucking the flower behind her ear.

Next to them, Rex spat a crumpled Fire Blossom at Xephyra's feet. She cocked her head at it, nosing around the grass with her beak, before eating the flower whole.

Veronyka snorted, and Tristan groaned. Rex puffed out his chest in pleasure.

"So, how are you enjoying your new office, Commander Tristan?" Veronyka asked. The words felt strange in her mouth—and strange to Tristan's ears too, but she knew he liked them as well. She felt it.

He had recently taken over his father's office, which had acted as temporary storage while they'd cleaned out the rest of the building. It had been officially reinstated to its original purpose just this morning.

"Not at all, actually," he said, laughing. "I had a letter from my father waiting for me before I even sat down. You just *had* to make him outrank me, didn't you?"

Veronyka laughed. She had indeed named Cassian her new general, which made Tristan his subordinate. Again. "It's a temporary position."

"And so is yours, isn't it?" he asked softly. Meaning her time here, with him.

"No. Whatever happens, this will always be my home. And my home will always be with you."

"I'm not sure that's how it works," he said. "Your throne is inside the Nest in Aura Nova—the empire's capital."

"Haven't you heard?" she asked, propping herself up on her elbow so she could look down at him. "I'm rewriting the rules."

His arm snaked around her back, and he pulled her in for a kiss. "As a matter of fact, I have. You've been doing that since I met you."

"And I'll do it again. I'll find a way to be a Phoenix Rider and a queen. I'll find a way to be exactly who I want to be. I've sacrificed a lot," she said, "but I won't sacrifice who I am."

He stared up at her, his golden eyes thoughtful. He smiled. "I never thought you would."

Veronyka kissed him again, lingering, before lying back down.

"Do you miss her?" Tristan asked.

"Yes," Veronyka answered simply. "I just . . . I hope she's finally at peace."

He tilted his head to the side, nudging against hers. "I think she is," he said, staring up at the sky.

Life had not been peaceful for Avalkyra Ashfire. Veronyka had once thought she did not want peace, but now she thought that maybe Val just didn't know how to achieve it. Not while she lived, at any rate. Veronyka thought of those moments in the flames, when the stars had descended all around her.

She nodded. "Me too."

They sat in silence for a while, Rex and Xephyra nearby, the world asleep around them.

"Are you tired?" Tristan asked eventually. There was anticipation in his voice.

She sat up again, quirking an eyebrow at him. "Not even a little bit."

He stood, reaching out a hand. "Fancy a proper ride, side by side?" He spoke the words as if from memory—and that's when Veronyka realized they were.

He'd spoken them the night of their first flight together on their own phoenixes. Then, the words had promised an impossible dream—a life of sun and wind and the sky all around.

Now, Veronyka was living it.

She beamed at him, just as she had done before. "Yes."

Many say the tale of the three sisters—Axura and Nox and Xenith, or sun and moon and stars—is a sad one. But those people simply do not know how the story ends.

For what is day without night, or darkness without light?

And what is a sky without stars?

Even when they are apart, they are together—bound for eternity—for they are nothing without each other.

—"Sun and Moon and Stars," from *The Pyraean Epics*, Volume 2, circa 460 BE

TIME LINE

NOTABLE RULERS FROM THE REIGN OF QUEENS (BEFORE THE EMPIRE, BE)

First Era, before dates and events were meticulously recorded (c. 1000–701 BE)

1000 BE – 800 BE	Queen Nefyra[1], the First Rider Queen: Chosen by Axura to be the first animage and the First Rider Queen. Ignix, the first phoenix, was her bondmate.
775 BE – 725 BE	Queen Otiya, the Queen of Bones: Defeated a rival Rider family that tried to usurp the throne.

Second Era, the height of Pyraean culture (701–279 BE)

701 BE – 645 BE	Queen Aurelya, the Golden Queen: Began construction on the Golden City of Aura, from which she derives her name.

---

1   *Despite having died soon after her love Callysta, Nefyra is the only queen mentioned in any stories, legends, or histories from Pyra during this period. Because these accounts were verbal, it is likely there were errors in dating, or perhaps Nefyra's heirs were named for their mother and grandmother, suggesting that Nefyra II, Nefyra III, and even Nefyra IV were the likely queens mentioned in these accounts. There is also the possibility that the line between myth and history has been blurred here, and the songs and myths were intended to depict the First Rider Queen as having a divinely long reign.*

| 412 BE – 335 BE | Queen Liyana, the Enduring Queen. |
| 335 BE – 317 BE | Queen Lyra the Defender: Mustered the Red Horde, the first-ever gathering of the entirety of Pyra's Phoenix Riders. Successfully defended Pyra from the Lowland Invasion. |

Third Era, the decline of the queendom (279–1 BE)

| 9 BE – 37 AE | Queen Elysia the Peacemaker: Her reign in the queendom was most notable for the loss of the Everlasting Flame and the mass evacuation of Aura. After leaving Aura, Elysia founded the empire and married the Ferronese King Damian. |

AFTER THE EMPIRE (AE)

37 AE – 45 AE	Queen Ellody the Prosperous: Reign of Prosperity.
45 AE – 56 AE	King Justyn the Pious: Reign of Piety. Transformed Azurec's Eyrie from a training facility into a pilgrimage site. Built the Pilgrimage Road.
56 AE – 95 AE	Queen Malka the Wise: Reign of Wisdom.

TIME LINE

95 AE – 121 AE	King Worrid the Learned: Reign of Learning. Born deaf, he designed a specialty saddle to accommodate his condition. Set up the Morian Archives, making sure the empire's histories were recorded by the priests and acolytes of the god Mori.
121 AE – 135 AE	King Hellund[2] the Just: Reign of Justice.
135 AE – 147 AE	Queen Bellonya the Brave: Reign of Bravery. Lost her arm as a child, became the fiercest spear thrower in the empire's history.
147 AE – 165 AE	King Aryk the Unlikely[3]: The Unlikely Reign.
165 AE – 169 AE	Queen Regent Lania of Stel: Reign of the Regent.
169 AE – 170 AE	Avalkyra[4], the Feather-Crowned Queen. Pheronia[4], the Council's Queen.
169 AE – Present	Reign of the Council.

---

2 *After he married his bold Queen Genya the General in 125 AE, many began to refer to this period as the Reign of the General.*

3 *So called because Aryk was Bellonya's youngest brother, fourth in line for the throne, and only ascended because his older brother and both her daughters predeceased her.*

4 *Neither princess was officially crowned, but both were referred to as queens before their deaths in the Blood War.*

GLOSSARY

GODS

Axura[5]**:** Goddess of the sun and daylight, as well as life, symbolized by the phoenix

Nox[6]**:** Goddess of the moon and darkness, as well as death, symbolized by the strix

deathmaidens: Servants of Nox, who lure lost souls into the dark realms

Miseriya: Goddess of the poor and hopeless

Hael: God of health and healing

Teyke[7]**:** God of luck, a trickster, symbolized by the cat

Mori: God of knowledge and memory, symbolized by the owl

Anyanke: Goddess of fate, symbolized by the spider

Soth: The wicked south wind, likely originating from the now-extinct Lowland civilization

Nors: The fair north wind, of similar origin to Soth, and still prayed to by the people of Arboria North

Eo: An obscure goddess of unknown origin favored among traders and messengers

Xenith: An alleged third sister of the ancient Pyraean pantheon of Axura and Nox

---

5 *"Azurec" in the Trader's Tongue*

6 *"Noct" in the Trader's Tongue*

7 *Teyke's cat was given the name "Felix" in the* Scrolls of Luck, *discovered in Orro at a Temple to Teyke, and according to that text is considered a god himself*

NOTABLE PEOPLE

Callysta: Lover and second-in-command of Queen Nefyra. Callysta's and Queen Nefyra's phoenixes were also mates: Cirix, the first male phoenix, and Ignix, the first female phoenix.

Queen Genya the General: Married to King Hellund the Just. Exiline was her phoenix. Successfully defeated the brigands that terrorized her husband's reign.

The Five Brides: Queen Elysia and her four royal sisters (Anya, Rylia, Cara, Darya). They helped secure peace treaties during the founding of the empire through marriage alliances.

The First Riders: Fourteen female warriors chosen by Axura to fight against Nox's darkness.

King Rol of Rolland: Ancestor to Rolan of Stel and originally called Rol the Unruly, he earned fame—and the nickname Rol the Betrayer—for his famed assassination attempt against Ferronese King Damian.

Rolan of Stel: Governor of Ferro, responsible for the attack on Azurec's Eyrie

Councilor Halton of Stel: Rolan's father

Lania of Stel: Wife of King Aryk Ashfire, mother of Pheronia Ashfire, Queen Regent of the Golden Empire

General Rast: Leader of the Golden Empire's military and credited with enforcing the animage registry and magetax at the end of the Blood War.

FAMOUS BATTLES

Dark Days: The dawn of time, when Axura's phoenixes battled Nox's strixes, saving the world from endless night

Lowland Invasion: Attempted invasion of Pyrmont (then the entirety of the Pyraean Queendom) by an unnamed civilization living in modern Pyra's Foothills

GLOSSARY

Stellan Uprising: A series of lords who banded together in Stel, attempting to wrest several major cities from empire control, eventually defeated by Avalkyra Ashfire

Blood War: The conflict between opposing heirs and sisters Avalkyra and Pheronia Ashfire

Last Battle: Fought in Aura Nova, final conflict of the Blood War

COMMON TERMS

animage: A person who has animal magic

shadowmage: A person who has shadow magic

Red Horde: The first-ever gathering of the entirety of Pyra's Phoenix Riders, under Queen Lyra's reign

False Sisters/Shadow Twins: Siblings born mere moments apart by the same father and two different mothers

Mercies: Phoenix Riders that checked battlefields for survivors and resurrections

Shadowheart: Spymaster, position in ancient Pyra in service to the queen

magetax: Tax charged to animages for the use of their magic

magical registry: Record of known animages in the Golden Empire

bondservant: An animage working off a criminal debt to the empire

mageslave: A derogatory term for a bondservant

dark realms: The endless black abyss where lost souls wander for eternity

Soth's Fury: A series of caves near Azurec's Eyrie, named after the south wind and currently in use as a Phoenix Rider training course

Silverwood: A stretch of forest near the eastern Pyraean Foothills featuring taller, straighter trees likely brought to the region by settlers from Arboria North

Prosperity outpost: Originally built by Queen Lyra the Defender during the Lowland Invasion and updated and heavily expanded by Ellody during her Reign of Prosperity

GLOSSARY

Copper Hill: A once-thinking mining community on the outskirts of Ferro, now home to warehouses, processing facilities, and an abandoned outpost-turned-prison

Haven: A secret hideout for animages located in Arboria

horde: The technical term for any flock exceeding one hundred birds

wing widow: A derogatory term for a Rider whose mount has died

Shadow Blooms: A spiky black flower that grows only on the upper reaches of Pyrmont, also commonly called "Deathmaidens" after the servants of Nox

PYRAEAN TERMS

aeti: Yes, affirmative

apex: literal translation is "first" but it generally refers to the highest-ranking bondmates in a flock. They are often oldest and strongest, but that is not always the case

apexaeris: Apex Rider or Apex Master

Aura: City/place of gold, and the ancient capital of Pyra

Aurys: River of gold, which flows from Pyrmont's highest peaks down into the valley of the Golden Empire

benex: literal translation is "second" but it generally refers to a secondary bonded pair, linked to the apex pair

diyu ma: "Long time," an expression or greeting

duovol: A two-Rider flight pattern, called a "queenstrike" when a queen leads the charge

impyr: Term of endearment translating to "little fire," originating in a Pyraean song

maiora: Grandmother

mundi apex phoenix: The world's first phoenix

nyx: Victory

onbra: Dark or shadow

pyr: Fire or flame

Pyra: City/place of fire; also known as the Freelands, an emancipated province of the Golden Empire

pyraflora: Fire Blossom, a tree with red flowers symbolic of Pyra. Petals can be made into poison, and sap is used for fireproofing.

phoenixaeris (s); *phoenixaeres* (pl): Phoenix Rider or Phoenix Master

phoenixami: "Phoenix friend," usually meant to indicate apprentices or young, untested Riders, and carried with it the hint of derision or condescension

phoenovo: Phoenix egg

petravin: Rockwine, a distilled Pyraean liquor aged with a blend of local herbs and flowers, made only in the small village of Petratec

sapona: Soaptree, plant used to bathe with

Sekveia: The Second Road, an ancient route through the wilds of Pyrmont that supposedly leads to lost treasure

stellaflora: Pale white Star Flowers used to commemorate the dead

trivol: A three-Rider arrowhead flight pattern

vollancea: A spear or single file flight pattern

xe: Prefix meaning "sweet" or "dear"; can also mean "brother" or "sister," based on the gender of the name it's paired with.

xe xie: Generic term of endearment translating to "sweet" or "dear" (xe) "one" (xie)

FOREIGN LANGUAGE TERMS

sia: Yes, affirmative in dialect of Arboria North

verro: Yes, affirmative in Ferronese

ACKNOWLEDGMENTS

Thank you to my agent, Penny Moore, for picking me out of the slush and seeing my potential.

Thank you to my editor, Sarah McCabe, for making my dreams come true and loving this world and these characters as much as I do.

Thank you to my publishers at home and around the world, to my subrights agents, my publicists and cover designers, and everyone who has had a hand in bringing these books from my head and into my hands.

Thank you to OwlCrate for taking a chance on my series and giving me stunning special edition covers. Thank you to Fae Crate for the endless support and enthusiasm (and merch!), and Uppercase and Totally Booked Crate for giving the Crown of Feathers series its first boost.

Thank you to my friends and family for the endless support and encouragement, and thank you especially to my writer friends, who understand the ups and downs of this career better than anyone.

As always, thank you to the readers, bloggers, booktubers, bookstagrammers, reviewers, librarians, and booksellers for championing this series. I couldn't be more grateful.

Last but certainly not least, thank you to the First Riders Street Team! You turned my fan base from a fledgling flock into a horde, and so many of you went above and beyond for me and my books. Special thank-you to Holly H., Liza F., Megan J., Alex C., Brianna B., Haley R. B., Brittany P., Laura W., Eileidh M., Callum C. (Val's #1 fan), Erika D., Lili H., Sam G., Hailey B., Leslie B., Leah T., Ali K. B. T., Shahna C., Maddi C., and Kathy P.

RIVETED

BY *simon* teen ♥

BELIEVE IN YOUR SHELF

Visit RivetedLit.com &
connect with us on social to:

DISCOVER NEW YA READS

READ BOOKS FOR FREE

DISCUSS YOUR FAVORITES

SHARE YOUR IDEAS

ENTER SWEEPSTAKES FOR THE CHANCE TO WIN BOOKS

Follow @SimonTeen on

to stay up to date with all things Riveted!

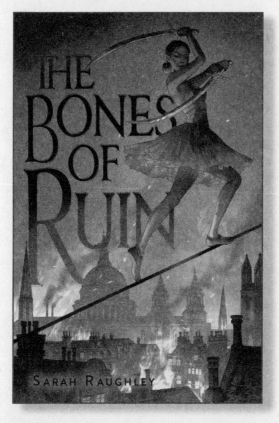

Monsters take many forms.